D0321604

of love & life

ISBN 978-0-276-44221-6

www.readersdigest.co.uk

The Reader's Digest Association Limited, 11 Westferry Circus, Canary Wharf, London E14 4HE

# of love & life

Three novels selected and condensed
by Reader's Digest

The Reader's Digest Association Limited, London

CONTENTS

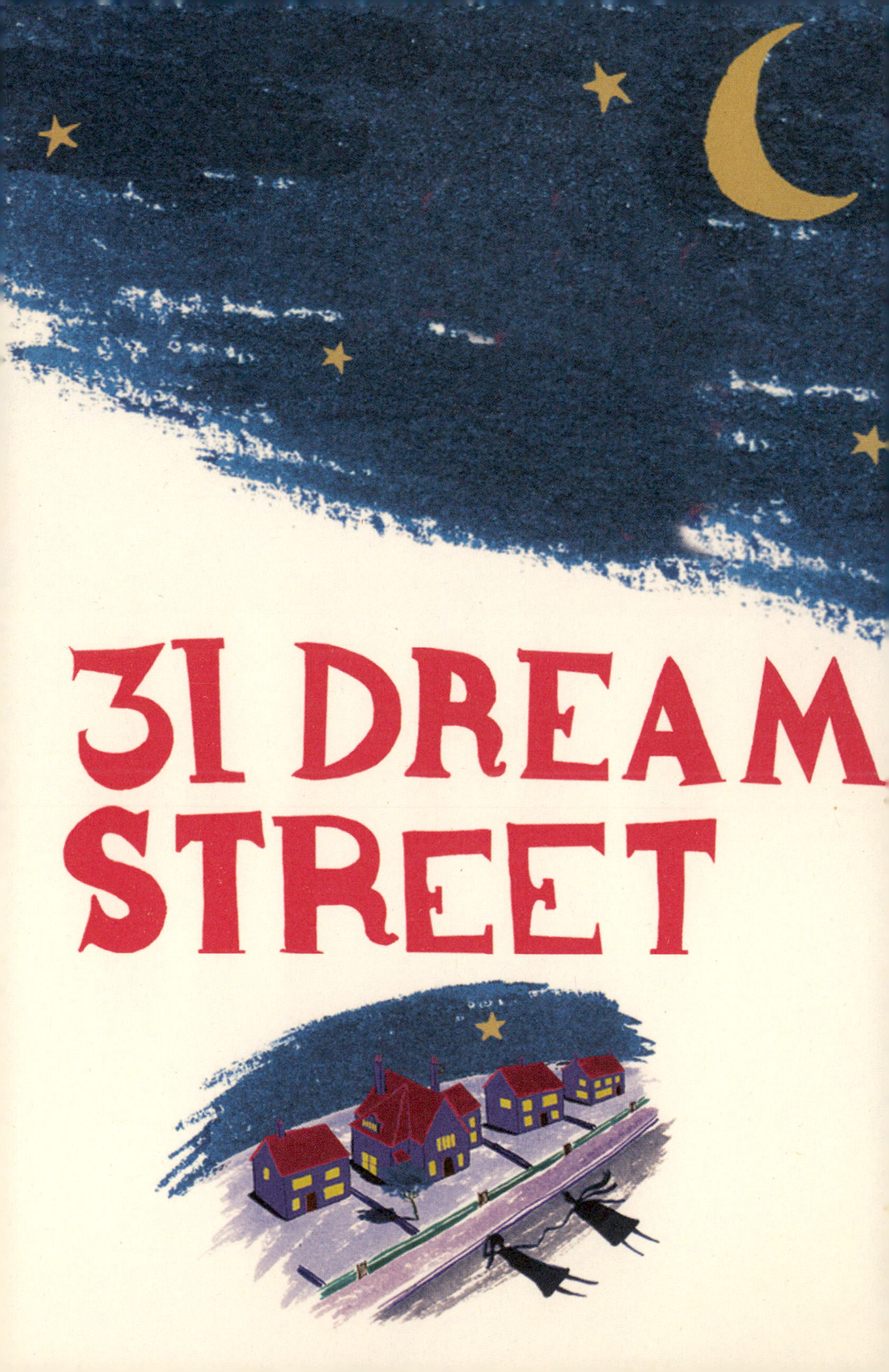
31 DREAM
STREET

Lisa
Jewell

The residents of 31 Silversmith Road, London N2, all had two things in common: they were down on their luck and desperate for a cheap place to stay. Now, in Toby Dobbs's rambling house they have found a safe haven—a refuge in which to take stock of their lives and start to dream again . . .

Prologue

LEAH PEERED THROUGH the gap between her curtains at the house across the street.

Detached from its neighbours by both its position and its appearance, 31 Silversmith Road was an eccentric building that stood alone. It rose three storeys and had been built 150 years earlier by a pair of retired silversmiths who'd chosen the location for its sweeping views towards the Hertfordshire countryside. To fully enjoy the view they'd commissioned an ornate wrought-iron verandah, which wrapped itself round the entire ground floor. Nowadays anyone sitting on the verandah could enjoy a view of nothing more inspiring than the terrace of characterless Victorian cottages opposite, and beyond that the upper floors of three brutal tower blocks, sprouting from the wilds of Enfield.

The silversmiths had chosen to decorate the exterior of their home with brightly coloured tiles picked up from their travels around the bazaars and flea markets of the world. On either side of the front door were richly coloured tiled panels depicting peacocks, which lent the house its unofficial local name of the Peacock House. In fact, when describing to people exactly where in East Finchley she lived, Leah would often say: 'You know, just opposite the Peacock House.'

As she watched, the front door opened, and the Girl with the Guitar emerged. She and Amitabh had nicknames for all the people in the Peacock House. As well as the Girl with the Guitar, there was Old Skinny Guy, Young Skinny Guy, the Teenager, the Air Hostess and Sybil (so-called because she changed her image so frequently and so dramatically that Leah and Amitabh were convinced she must have a multiple personality disorder). The Girl with the Guitar stopped at the bottom of the front steps and lit a cigarette. Then she pushed a strand of black hair behind her ear, slung her guitar case over her shoulder and headed left, towards the High Road.

Young Skinny Guy watched her, as he did every night, from his window on the second floor. His face was illuminated, as ever, by the light from his computer monitor, and his expression, as ever, was one of lovelorn resignation. He was a strange-looking fellow, not unattractive, but seemingly intent on making the worst of himself. His hair was an unrestrained mass of curls, and he had equally exuberant mutton-chop sideburns which sprouted from each side of his face like angel wings.

Leah had no idea who any of the people over the road were. She didn't know their names or their relationships. She had no idea who owned the house or what the set-up was. Was it divided into bedsits? Was it a house share? Or was it some kind of strange, interbred family? She'd lived opposite the Peacock House for nearly three years, yet she'd never had a conversation with anyone who lived there. Never even exchanged nods or smiles.

Leah was a curious person by nature. She liked to know what was what, who was who, how everything worked and fitted together. But she was also a Londoner who played by the rules regarding personal space and keeping yourself to yourself. So she sat and she watched and she wondered and she waited because she knew that one day, somehow, she'd find a way to answer all her questions.

Fifteen Years Earlier

August 1, 1990

Toby,

Jemma and I are leaving for Cape Town tomorrow morning. I'm sorry we'll miss your wedding next week, but I'm sure you understand.

I am enclosing a set of keys. I have bought you and Karen a house as a wedding gift. Peter got it at auction. I haven't seen it, but Peter assures me it was a good buy. In need of some TLC, but structurally sound. Which is just as well, as this house also represents your inheritance.

Property is the thing, Toby. You're on the ladder now. I can see big things happening with the London property market. Make the most of it.

Peter says there's one snag. A sitting tenant. I'm sure he'll be able to advise you on how to get him out. I've enclosed Peter's card, if you need him.

I wish you and Karen all the best for Saturday. Jemma and I will raise a glass of champagne to you both as the sun sets over Camps Bay.

Nothing much else to say except good luck, I suppose.

Best,

Reggie/Dad

September 2, 1990

Dear Toby,

This isn't working. Marriage isn't what I thought it would be. I expected more, not just you and me and a smelly old man rattling around inside a big, damp old house without a penny between us. I think I've realised that I don't love you enough to live in penury with you. I thought I did, but I don't.

You're a good man, Toby, but you're not enough for me. Please don't hate me.

Karen xx

A ROOM OF YOUR OWN?

Finchley-based poet, unexpectedly alone
in rambling Victorian mansion, has three big
bedrooms to fill. Shared kitchen and bathrooms.
Rent negotiable, but reasonable.
Preference given to artists and performers.
Please write to tell me why you should live here.

November 1990

Dear Lonely Poet,

My name is Ruby Lewis, I am sixteen years old and I'm a singer. My mum threw me out last week because her ugly husband kept hitting me. Which was my fault, apparently. I'm staying with this man at the moment, but I don't really like him. Anyway—I'd really like to come and live in your house because it sounds really cool and because I can't afford to pay proper rent. One day I'm going to be the most famous singer in the world and then I'll buy you a Lamborghini to pay you back.

Please let me live with you. You won't regret it.

Lots of love,

Ruby xxx

April 2002

Dear Sir,

My name is Joanne Fish and I am an actress. I am thirty-one years old, single and currently living in New Cross. I do not have much experience of sharing houses, but I was attracted to your advert because I am currently at an unexpected crossroads in my life. Your advert struck me like a neon sign on a long and circuitous journey. I realise you will have received a thousand responses to your advert and that the onus is on me to make myself appear more interesting and needful than the other nine hundred and ninety-nine, so I will try my best.

I have had an interesting life. I have lived abroad and in various corners of this country, including Luton (!) and the Isle of Man. I have had many jobs, from the sublime to the ridiculous. I once spent a summer sticking eyes on balls of fluff in a factory that produced promotional 'bugs'. I also once spent a summer helping a famous actress rehearse for a role while she was suffering from a mild case of amnesia.

I am currently researching a role for a film that is due to begin filming at the end of the year. It is a small role but pivotal and the director is very well known. Unfortunately the project is top secret so I can't divulge any more information than that. It does mean that I will not be earning a regular salary until filming commences (although I will take on occasional temporary work), so the possibility of being able to pay rent on an ad hoc, flexible basis could not have come at a more opportune moment.

I am also clean, tidy, reliable, polite and non-smoking.

I look forward to hearing from you.

Yours, in good faith,

Joanne Elizabeth Fish

February 2004

Dear Sir/Madam,

I have to admit I don't usually read 'Private Eye' but someone left it in the toilets at work so I thought I'd have a flick through and your advert caught my eye. Not for myself, you see, I'm a married man with three kids and a house in Hainault, but for my friend, Con.

Con works with me at Condé Nast. He's an assistant in the post room here, been working here for about a year now. He's a nice lad, a bit of a loner, but reliable to a fault. He's young, eighteen I think, and what's happened is that his mum's done a runner to Turkey and left him alone. His grandmother raised him and then after she died the mum came back and promised him the world, rented some luxury flat for the pair of them and then two months later she buggered off again. Poor kid couldn't afford the rent on his own so he moved out, about a week ago. Now I reckon he's sleeping rough. He gets the papers, looks at the ads for rooms but he can't afford anything decent, not on what he earns here. I've tried to persuade him to come home with me but he's too proud, and, if I'm honest, we haven't really got the room for him anyway.

I know your advert says you want creative people and Con's not exactly that, but he is young and just starting out and this could be the moment in his life which makes or breaks him. When I was his age I got in with a bad crowd, lots of popping pills, fighting, that kind of thing. Lucky for me I met Chrissie and fell in love. She showed me a better way to be, you know? She saved me.

Maybe you could save Con.

Hoping for your kindest and fullest consideration.

Yours faithfully,

Nigel Cadwallader

September 2004

Dear Toby,

It was lovely to meet you the other night. I just wanted to say thank you again, for what you've done for my Con. It fears me to think what might have happened to him if you hadn't taken him in and given him a room. You are a very good man.

The reason why I'm writing is that I'm in a bit of a bind. I won't go into too much detail, but suffice it to say that I need to find somewhere to live. Con said that he's happy for me to share his room, but he said I should write to you, as you like to do things properly. So, would it be OK if I shared with Con for a while? I'll pay you rent and it will only be for a few weeks, just until I get myself settled back in the country and get myself a job.

I really need to be near Con now, after what happened to him when I left the country. I feel so guilty and I've got so much to make up for. If you would allow me to spend some time with him in your beautiful house, I'd be forever in your debt.

Yours faithfully,

Melinda McNulty

Chapter 1

EARLY MORNINGS were the only time that Toby felt that his house belonged to him. Everyone was still sleeping. It was just him, in his pyjamas, sieving flour into a bowl, tap, tap, tap, against the palm of his hand.

Toby made bread every morning. It was a ritual, something that Karen had done every day when they were together. The first morning after she left he'd come downstairs and immediately started pounding dough, desperate to re-create the scent of his failed marriage. He didn't even eat it any more, just left it on a cooling tray every day for his tenants to enjoy.

Toby had slept badly and his usual sense of melancholy was now overlaid by a thick blanket of tiredness. It was three days into the New Year and life had already fallen back into place. He was still trapped in this mausoleum of a house, still surrounded by people he didn't know and didn't want to know. He was still married to a woman whom he hadn't seen since he was twenty-four. He was still an unpublished poet and he was still penniless.

A pile of bills sat on his desk upstairs, unopened and unpaid. Next to the pile of bills was a pile of rejection letters from publishers and literary agents. And next to that was a letter from a local estate agent informing him that there were people queuing down the street, apparently, to buy a house like his for unseemly amounts of money. While Toby was grateful to them for alerting him to this fact, it was really of no possible use to him. Toby's house was full of people who had no intention of leaving, and he had no intention of making them.

Toby finished making his dough and pressed it into a loaf tin, which he then slid into the Aga. He could hear the tinny drone of someone's radio alarm switching itself on upstairs and he headed quickly back towards his room, before he inadvertently crossed paths with anyone. He glanced at things as he passed through the house. A pair of Con's trainers sat under the coffee table in the TV room. Ruby's black lacy cardigan was hanging from the back of the armchair and Joanne's Clarins face powder sat in a little plastic pot on the coffee table next to Ruby's cereal bowl.

This was his world, had been for years. A world of other people's possessions, rhythms, dramas, smells and habits. His presence left no imprint on the dynamics of his home. It was as if he didn't exist. What would it be like to live alone? he wondered. To come home and find everything as he'd left it? To never have to take someone else's unwashed saucepan out of the kitchen sink to pour himself a glass of water? Never to be woken up by the sound of someone else's snoring or someone else's lovemaking? Would he feel more substantial? Would he feel more alive?

He climbed the two flights of stairs to his room, three at a time, and closed the door silently behind him.

Ruby watched Con leaving for work from her bedroom window. He was a lovely looking boy, clear skinned, well proportioned with startling indigo eyes. But Ruby didn't find him attractive. She didn't appreciate younger men. She liked older men, men who were a little creased, like secondhand books.

'What are you staring at out there?'

Ruby turned and smiled at the man in her bed. Paul Fox. Her slightly creased forty-five-year-old lover.

'Nothing,' she teased.

She sat on the edge of her bed. One of Paul's feet was poking from the bottom of the duvet. She picked up his big toe between her thumb and forefinger, put it between her front teeth and bit down on it, hard.

'Ow.' He pulled his leg back under the duvet. 'What was that for?'

'That,' she said, 'was for ignoring me last night.'

'What?' His brow furrowed.

'You *know* what. Eliza walked in and suddenly it was as if you didn't know me any more.'

'Oh, Christ. Ruby—she's my *girlfriend*.'

Ruby and Paul's relationship had always been an informal mix of occasional business and no-strings pleasure. He got her the odd support slot for one of his acts, they got together once or twice a week for sex or drinking or both, and he paid her what he jokingly referred to as a 'salary', a small monthly cheque, just to keep her ticking over. It was easy come, easy go, a bit of reciprocal fun that had worked for both of them for the past five years. Ruby didn't expect anything more from Paul. But at the same time she couldn't help feeling a bit gutted that six months ago Paul had fallen in love with a forty-two-year-old earth mother from Ladbroke Grove with two kids, her own business and a vineyard in Tuscany.

Ruby glanced at herself in the mirror. She had an image of herself that she carried round in her head. It was an image of a smoky brunette with black eyes and creamy skin and a look about her as if she'd just had sex or was thinking about having sex. Generally speaking the mirror reflected back exactly what she expected to see. Every now and then it didn't. This was one of those moments. Her hair was dull and dirty and she had a big spot on her chin. She wondered what Eliza looked like first thing in the morning and then realised that it didn't matter because Paul was in love with her and to him she would look beautiful no matter what.

There was a knock at the door.

'Ruby. It's me, Toby.'

She sighed and opened the door.

'Hi. Sorry, I was just, er—oh, hi, Paul.' He peered over her shoulder and threw Paul a stiff smile.

Paul put up a hand and cracked an equally stiff smile. He looked silly, arranged between Ruby's marabou-trimmed cushions and fake leopard-skin throws with his big hairy chest and his mop of greying hair. He looked, Ruby suddenly and overwhelmingly realised, like a silly handsome man having a silly adulterous affair. She gulped silently.

'Yes, I was just wondering about the rent. Just wondering if maybe you could give me a cheque today. It's just, there are some bills, and if I don't send a cheque by the end of the week, then, er, well, there'll be no hot water. Or heating. That's all.'

'Fine,' sighed Ruby, 'fine. I'll give you a cheque tonight.'

'Yes, well, you did say that last week, and you didn't. I haven't had any rent off you since the end of November, and even then it wasn't the full amount and—'

'Toby. I'll give you a cheque. Tonight. OK?'

'Right. OK. Good. See you. See you, Paul.'

'See you, Toby.'

Ruby closed the door, and turned and smiled at Paul. He peeled back the cover and smiled at her invitingly.

'Sorry, mate.' She flipped the duvet back over his naked body. 'I'm not in the mood.'

Paul threw her an injured look. 'Not even a quickie?'

'No. Not even a quickie.' She winked at him, softening the bluntness of her rejection. She wasn't in the mood for a scene. She knew there was a Big Conversation waiting to happen, but she didn't want to have it now. Right now she just wanted to have a shower. Right now she just wanted to feel clean.

Con pulled the glossy brochure out of the envelope and flicked through it, his eyes taking in the images a second at a time. Blue skies, palm trees, creamy beaches. But this wasn't a travel brochure. This was a brochure for the Right Path Flight School in Durban, South Africa. Con gazed at crop-haired men in icy white shirts and epaulettes, sitting in tiny cockpits lined with a thousand buttons and lights, knobs and levers, and felt a thrill of excitement. Then, before anyone could ask him what he was looking at, he slid the brochure back into the envelope and headed for the eighth floor.

The *Vogue* fashion department looked like a normal office. It had desks and computers and printers and wastepaper bins. It had phones ringing and fax machines chirruping. It looked like a normal office, but it absolutely wasn't.

Con partly relished the point in the day when he pushed his trolley through the *Vogue* fashion department and partly dreaded it. He liked looking at the girls, rail-thin, delicate as wisps of smoke with their serious clothes and their perfect skin. And he liked the way they talked, their husky Marlboro Light voices and the peculiar shapes they made out of ordinary words. They fascinated him. And they repulsed him. It annoyed him that they existed so separately to him. It wound him up that he could move through them with his trolley, invisible. They passed him their packages and parcels; they asked him stupid questions about costs and timings.

In his world, outside the gilded gates of the Condé Nast building, Con was a player. He met his friends in the pub on a Friday night and girls, *good-looking* girls, willed him to pay them attention. Here he was just a postboy.

One of these wraith-like girls approached him now, clutching a white Jiffy bag. She had fine blonde hair and pale waxy skin. She was wearing a suede waistcoat with a shaggy trim over a grey lace top. Her eyes were icy blue. Con had never seen her before.

'Erm,' she started, handing him the envelope, 'this has to go recorded. Will it get there by Friday?'

Con examined it. It was addressed to someone in south London. 'Yeah,' he said, 'should be OK.'

'Excellent,' she said. And then, miraculously, she smiled. Not one of the practised smiles that these well-brought-up girls usually served him with, but a proper burst of sunshine. 'Thank you,' she said. 'Sorry . . . what's your name?'

Con felt a flush of surprise. 'Connor,' he said. 'Con.'

'Con,' she repeated. 'I'm Daisy.'

Daisy, he thought. Perfect. That's what she looked like. A colourless, uncomplicated flower, tiny and well formed. 'That's nice,' he said.

'Thank you.' She smiled again. Her teeth were slightly crooked, but very white. 'My sisters are called Mimosa and Camellia. I must have been a very plain baby.'

Con laughed.

Daisy said, 'It's my first day today. I'm in charge of letters and things so you'll probably find me bugging you about stuff.'

Con shook his head. 'That's OK,' he said.

'Good,' she said. And then she went back to her desk.

Con dropped the white Jiffy bag onto his trolley and pushed it towards the doors at the far end. As he passed Daisy's desk she looked up, mouthed the word 'Bye' and waved at him. He waved back, his heart leaping around in his chest like a wild salmon.

As the door closed behind him and he found himself in the corridor outside, he breathed out and leaned against the wall. He had a curious feeling that something significant had just happened, that his life had reached a mini-roundabout, that suddenly he had options. And all because a beautiful girl called Daisy had smiled at him.

It had snowed the night before, and Silversmith Road was gleaming with ice, so when Leah left her house on Thursday morning and saw Old Skinny Guy lying face-down on the pavement, his arms and legs spread out as if he were making angels in the snow, her immediate assumption was that he'd slipped and fallen.

'Hello,' she called out, making her way tentatively across the slushy road. 'Hello. Are you OK?'

Old Skinny Guy failed to respond in any way. Leah leaned down and shouted into his ear. 'Are you OK? Do you need any help?' The man lay motionless and Leah began to suspect that there might be something seriously wrong.

'I'm going to get someone,' she shouted. 'I won't be long.'

She hurried towards the Peacock House, climbed up the steps and banged against the front door. A figure appeared through the stained glass of the door and then he was there, in front of her, Young Skinny Guy, all sideburns and hair and slightly panicky facial expressions.

'Yes?' he said.

'Er, the old man,' she began, 'he's there,' she pointed behind her. 'I think he might be dead.'

'Oh Jesus.' He peered at the prone figure on the pavement. 'Oh shit. Let me . . . God. I need shoes.' He glanced down at a pair of unfeasibly long and bony feet. 'Hang on. Just a sec. Hold on.' He turned to go, but then spun round again. 'Have you called an ambulance?'

'No.' Leah shook her head.

'Right. Maybe that's the thing to do. Right. Shoes. Back in a tick.'

She was on her mobile phone, in the middle of trying to explain what was wrong with the old man to a woman at the emergency services, when Young Skinny Guy lolloped back down the hallway wearing a pair of gumboots. He followed her down the front steps and out onto the pavement. 'I'm not sure if he's breathing or not,' Leah said to the woman at the other end. She glanced at the skinny guy who was crouched over the old man with his ear to his mouth. He shrugged.

'No,' continued Leah, 'we're not sure. He's very old.'

'Ninety-seven,' said the skinny guy, picking up the old man's wrist and feeling for a pulse.

'Jesus,' she said to the woman. 'He's ninety-seven.'

Gus Veldtman was pronounced dead half an hour later and taken away to Barnet General Hospital, where it would later be ascertained that he had died of a massive heart attack. Leah and the skinny guy stood together on the pavement and watched the ambulance pull away.

'Well,' said Leah, looking at her watch, 'I guess I'd better get on.'

'Off to work?'

'Yes.' She nodded. 'I run a shop, up on the Broadway.'

'Oh, really,' he said. 'What sort of shop?'

'It's a gift shop.' She smiled. 'A very *pink* gift shop.'

'I see.' He sighed. 'I see.'

'Is there anything else I can do?' she asked.

'No.' He ran the palm of his hand across his face. 'I'll call his relatives. They'll sort it out, I suppose.' He shrugged and tucked his hands into his pockets. 'But, thanks . . . sorry, what *is* your name?'

'Leah. Leah Pilgrim.'

'Leah.' He smiled. 'I'm Toby Dobbs, by the way.' He offered her a hand the size of a baseball mitt to shake.

'Toby,' she repeated, thinking that of all the possible names she'd ever considered for Young Skinny Guy, Toby was absolutely not one of them. 'Funny,' she said. 'I've been living across the road from you for nearly three years and I finally get to talk to you because someone dies.' She shrugged. 'That's London for you, I guess.'

Toby nodded his agreement.

'So, who was he? Gus? I thought maybe he was your grandfather.'

Toby laughed nervously. 'No. Gus wasn't my grandfather. Gus was my sitting tenant.'

'Ah,' she said. 'I see. So it's *your* house.'

'Yes.' He paused. 'It is.'

'And the other people who live here—they're . . .?'

'My non-sitting tenants.' Toby was starting to look somewhat strained by the conversation.

'I'm sorry,' said Leah. 'The last thing you need right now is me asking you questions. It's just—I'm such a nosy person and I've been wondering about your house for years. Wondering who you all were and how you all knew each other and . . . Well, anyway. I'll let you get on. And if there's anything you need, you know where I live. Please—just ask.'

Toby smiled. 'Thank you. I will. And, Leah?'

'Yes?'

'Thank you so much.'

'What for?'

'For being here. Thank you.'

Toby pushed open the door to Gus's bedroom. The room was papered with a terrible striped flock in burgundy and cream, and hung with ugly oil paintings lit by brass light fittings. The curtains were slightly flouncy in blue floral chintz and the carpet was a flattened rose-coloured shagpile. The double bed sagged in the middle like a hammock and was dressed in burgundy sheets and a thick layer of woolly blankets. The room smelt, not as you might expect, of oldness, or of loneliness, but of malted milk and elderly cat.

The malted milk could be explained by the fact that Gus ate a whole packet of the biscuits every day. The elderly cat couldn't really be explained at all.

Toby walked towards Gus's desk. It was positioned in the window and looked out over the back garden. Gus had a proper old-fashioned typewriter. He also had piles of books and paperwork and a collection of old tin snuffboxes in a glass box. There was a manuscript on the desk. It was obviously very old and was covered in faded pencil marks and ink amendments.

Gus's clothes hung in a burr-veneered 1920s wardrobe from heavy wire hangers. And there, at the bottom of the wardrobe, lay a red plastic tray filled with cat litter. A solitary cat poo poked out of the grey nuggets—it was fresh. On the other side of the wardrobe was a green saucer filled with brown pellets, a small bowl full of water and a huge bag of Science Diet.

'What are you doing?'

Toby jumped and clutched his heart. 'Shit.'

It was Ruby. She was eating a banana. 'Sorry. I thought you'd heard me come in.'

'Look at this,' he said, pointing inside the cupboard.

She peered in over his shoulder. '*What!*' She grimaced.

'I know. And it's fresh. Did you know he had a cat?'

She shrugged. 'News to me. Where is it?'

They both glanced around the room in unison. Ruby finished her banana and dropped the skin nonchalantly into Gus's wastepaper bin. Toby noted the action and filed it away as yet another reason why he should stop being in love with her. He now had about almost twenty reasons why he should stop being in love with Ruby Lewis.

She'd slept with more than fifty men.

She left her toenail clippings on the bathroom floor.

She always slammed the front door when she got in, even though Toby had asked her not to, politely, about a hundred and fifty times.

She swore too much.

She smoked too much.

She never gave anyone their telephone messages.

She rarely paid her rent.

She was the centre of her own universe.

She called him 'Tobes'.

She flirted with everyone, all the time.

She did only one wash a month and would then drape and festoon every radiator in the house with the entire contents of her wardrobe, leaving Toby in the position of having to stare at her knickers while he ate his dinner.

She thought literary classics were boring.

She thought Radio Four was boring.

She thought staying in was boring.

And she thought, more pertinently, that Toby was boring.

She told him all the time, 'God, Tobes, you're *sooo* boring,' whenever he tried to broach a subject that was in any way important or even slightly domestic in nature.

She laughed at his clothes and his hair and was awful, really, in so many ways. But, God, so beautiful and, God, so amazingly talented.

'Under the bed?' she suggested.

'What?' Toby snapped out of his reverie.

'Maybe that's where his cat lives.'

'Oh. Right. Yes.'

She fell suddenly to her hands and knees, and Toby glanced at her denim-clad behind as it swung from side to side like a searchlight.

'Oh my God. I don't believe it.'

'What?'

'*Hello*,' she whispered to something under the bed. '*Don't be shy. It's OK*.'

'What?' Toby stopped staring at her bottom and joined her on his hands and knees.

'Look.' She pointed into the corner. 'Over there.'

Toby blinked and a pair of eyes blinked back at him. 'Oh my God.'

They managed to coax the little creature out by shaking its food bowl and making lots of silly noises.

'That's the smallest cat I've ever seen in my life,' said Ruby, watching it crunch delicately on nuggets of Science Diet.

It looked like a slightly insane illustration of a cat. It had a gigantic head and a tiny body and stringy black fur. It looked like it might be even older than Gus.

'I can't believe he kept a cat in here all these years,' said Ruby. 'Why did he keep it secret?'

'Lord knows,' said Toby. 'Maybe the old landlord didn't allow animals in the house. Maybe he thought I'd make him get rid of it.'

Toby stood up and stretched his legs. 'What the hell are we going to do with it?'

'I don't want it,' said Ruby, recoiling slightly.

'Neither do I.'

'We'll have to get rid of it. Give it to a home. Or something.'

'Oh God.' Toby sighed as yet another job added itself to the list of Things He Had To Do Because Gus Had Died. He'd already spent an hour on the phone trying to track down Gus's great-niece. He'd then somehow found himself offering to host a 'small drinks party' after Gus's funeral the following week, which would be hideous, absolutely hideous. Next, he had to find a new tenant for Gus's room, which would probably necessitate redecoration. And now he had to do something about this odd little cat.

Toby glanced around the room again. 'I can't believe he's dead.'

'Me neither,' Ruby replied.

'Ninety-seven years,' sighed Toby. 'He's taken ninety-seven years of life to the grave with him. All those experiences, all those emotions. People he loved, places he's seen—gone.' He clicked his fingers and let his head drop into his chest. 'I wished I'd talked to him more. Wish I'd let him pass on his stories to me. I could have kept them for him.'

'Oh, stop being so maudlin, Tobes. He was a miserable old bastard. He didn't want to share his stories with anyone. I tell you what you need.' She stretched and yawned. 'A stiff drink.'

'But it's not even five o'clock.'

'Yes. But by the time I've made the drinks and brought them back it will be. Rum and Coke? Gin and tonic? Something stronger?'

Toby stared at Ruby, his face pulling itself automatically into an expression of disapproval. But he let it go. He couldn't be bothered playing the fusty old stick, not today. 'A glass of red wine would be lovely,' he said, letting a small smile soften his face.

'Good boy.' She beamed at him.

She left the room then and Toby watched her go. Ruby Lewis. The love of his life.

The little cat scurried back under the bed at the sound of a slamming door downstairs and Toby went to the window and stared out across the rooftops. The snow would be gone by tomorrow morning, taking the memories of a freezing January day with it. London snow was like life: here today, gone tomorrow. What was the point of it all?

Ruby returned, clutching a bottle of Cava and two long-stemmed glasses.

'I found this in the fridge,' she said. 'I think it's Melinda's.'

'Oh my God, she'll go mental.'

'Yes,' Ruby winked. 'I know. But it just seemed fitting.' She popped the cork and poured them a glass each. 'To Gus,' she said, holding her glass aloft. 'A funny old bastard, but he always left the seat down.'

'To Gus,' said Toby. 'And to the future.'

In bed that night, Leah lay awake for longer than usual. Her head was full of Gus and Toby and peacocks and cold pavements. How did a person end up living in a house full of strangers, without a wife, without a family? How did a person end up so totally alone? And if she were to die at ninety-seven, she mused, she wouldn't even have a great-niece to claim responsibility for her remains. Her brother, Dominic, was gay, so no nieces or nephews to have kids and keep her in relatives in her old age. It was all down to her.

She glanced across at Amitabh's slumbering form. As usual, he had kicked off the duvet and was lying flat on his back. Leah manoeuvred herself onto her elbow and looked at him properly. She stared at the line of his nose and the contours of his forehead. She touched his thick hair with the palm of her hand. And then she leaned over and brushed his lovely cheek with her lips.

'Jesus!' he jumped. 'What! What is it?'

'Nothing,' said Leah springing away from him. 'Nothing. I was just kissing you, that's all.'

'Why?'

'Because . . . I don't know. I just wanted to.'

'Jesus. It's nearly two. Why are you awake?'

She shrugged. 'I can't sleep. It's that man. Gus. I can't stop thinking about him.'

'Oh God.' Amitabh pulled the duvet back over himself.

'How do you do it?' she said. 'I mean, you must see it every day. Old people, dying, alone. Doesn't it, I don't know, doesn't it . . . *get to you*?' Amitabh was a nurse in a geriatric ward. He knew about these things.

'Oh, Leah. Not now. Please.'

'But is it better or worse if they're alone? Does it seem sadder if there are loads of relatives and grandkids and things, or is it worse if there's nobody there at all?'

'Let's have this conversation in the morning, shall we?'

'I don't want to end up all on my own,' she said.

'It's OK. You're a nice person. You won't be on your own.'

'Yes, but being nice isn't any guarantee that you'll get married and have kids and that all your friends won't die before you, is it?'

'It helps,' he said.

'Hmmmm.' Leah sank back into the bed and pulled the duvet over her chest. Within ten seconds Amitabh's breathing had grown heavy. Ten seconds later he was fast asleep. Leah looked at him again and suddenly knew what she had to do. It was obvious. She'd never felt more certain of anything in her life.

'Am. Amitabh.' She shook him gently by the shoulder. 'Am.'

'Oh God! What?' He turned over and stared at her accusingly.

'I love you.'

He raised an eyebrow at her.

'No. I mean, I really love you. And I want to be with you for ever. You know. Until I die. I want to marry you.'

'*What!*'

'I want to marry you.'

'Oh my God. You're being serious, aren't you?'

'Uh-huh.'

'Jesus.' His face softened. 'Leah. It's so late. I can't . . .'

'It's OK,' she said. 'You don't need to answer now. Think about it.'

'Is this to do with that old man? Are you having some kind of crisis?'

'No,' she said. 'Honestly. No. It's just made me think, that's all. About what's important. About what I want. And I want you. For ever.'

'Let's talk about it in the morning,' he said.

'Yes,' she said, 'let's.'

Wallace Beeton sat behind a desk the size of a dining table and turned paperwork with long, dry fingers. 'Mr Veldtman has left instructions that you be the sole beneficiary of his estate.'

'Estate?'

'Yes. Mr Veldtman has bequeathed you all his personal possessions which are, I assume, in your property?'

Toby thought sadly of the ugly prewar furniture and the snuffbox collection. 'Yes. That's right.'

'And guardianship of his cat.'

'Oh God. Really?'

'Yes. With the strict instruction that it must stay with you. Until it dies. Or you die.'

Toby gulped. 'And if I die?'

'Then it should be sent to live with Mr Veldtman's great-niece in Guernsey. Right. Next.' He pulled out another sheaf of paper and cleared his throat. 'Mr Veldtman has a, er . . . novel in print.'

'He does?'

'Yes. Published in Dutch in 1930. And reprinted twelve times since. Mr Veldtman has a royalty account with a firm of agents in The Hague. He has instructed that his literary estate be bequeathed to you and any payments be paid directly into your bank account.'

'Wow, really?'

'Yes. But to put that into perspective, Mr Veldtman's royalty payment for the past six months was five pounds and twenty-six pence.'

'Oh. OK. And, er, is that it?'

Wallace Beeton shrugged his shoulders. 'Yes.'

'Right. It's just that when I spoke to Gus's great-niece on the phone last week she intimated to me that Gus might have had some stocks and shares and such?'

'Really? Well, there's no evidence of that here'—he waved his long fingers over the paperwork piled on his desk—'perhaps he sold them. Or perhaps,' he said, with a twinkle in his eye, 'he kept it all underneath his mattress?'

Toby yanked up the corner of Gus's mattress and felt around underneath. He found nothing at the near side of the bed so he climbed onto the mattress and pulled back the further corners.

He saw something then, slotted into the back of the bedstead. It looked like a notebook, or possibly a diary. He leaned across the bed and pulled it out. It was a thick book, crammed with bits of paper.

Toby sat down and opened the book. It smelt of wet leaves and damp lino. On the front page, in predictably spidery handwriting, were the words 'Property of Augustus Veldtman'. Toby flicked through it to determine what kind of journal it was and soon realised that what he had in his hands was, basically, the inside of Gus Veldtman's head: lyrics, poetry, shopping lists, accounts, letters, thoughts, quotes, bills and scripts. There were lists of pills he'd taken, books he'd read, meals he'd eaten. There were bus tickets and doctor's prescriptions and postcards.

Most of the contents of the book were mundane and repetitive, but there was also much talk about a person called Boris.

'Boris continues to ignore me. He thinks this game will bring him my attentions, but he is wrong.'
'It is the fault of Boris. He is a selfish and ill-mannered individual. I hope he shall die before too long.'
'Boris and I enjoyed an hour of fresh air today in the garden. He sat on my feet and we admired the triumphant blue fists of hyacinth bursting through the chill February sod.'

It wasn't until Toby read the passage: *'Boris seems to have developed a digestive complaint. I have been compelled to replace his litter five times today,'* that he realised that Gus had been referring to his cat.

Toby pulled back the corner of the mattress and peered through the wooden slats. Boris looked up at him. 'Hello, Boris,' said Toby. 'Gus tells me you're selfish and ill-mannered.' The cat turned away and curled itself into a ball. 'And maybe he's right.'

And that was when he saw it. A black fabric bag wedged between the bed slats. Attached to it, by an elastic band, was an envelope addressed to him. He opened it and pulled out a letter, typewritten on thin, crackly paper:

My dear Toby,

Well, finally I am gone. I sincerely hope that my death didn't cause you too much inconvenience, that I didn't drag on with some incessant disease or terrible plague. If I did, then I apologise. I chose to be alone and, if that choice resulted in you being responsible for me in any way that you found tedious or bothersome, then I do apologise.

I have bequeathed to you my meagre possessions and my meagre cat. Do what you wish with the former, but please be kind to the latter. And of course there is my literary 'estate'—ha!—for what it is worth. Additionally, and more importantly, I have fulfilled the cliché of the elderly person who does not trust anyone else to look after their money and hoarded my life's savings underneath my mattress. I am not sure of the exact amount, but it is a substantial sum. I would like you to have it, but on one condition. And THIS IS VERY IMPORTANT. You are a good man, but misguided. These people in your house do not appreciate you or your generosity. They are holding you back. My greatest fear for you, Toby, is that you will end up like me, alone, misunderstood, unappreciated, and I fear this could happen all too easily. Please, Toby, use my money to make your life everything it could be. Sell your house; lose your shackles. The house is just bricks and mortar. Repair them, then repair your soul.

I do not believe in an afterlife so I will have to trust you to fulfil my instructions. But you are the most trustworthy man I have ever known, so I feel confident that you will do so.

God bless you.

Your friend,

Augustus Veldtman

Toby breathed in and out slowly, trying to calm his racing heart. And then he picked up the bag, pulled open the drawstrings and peered inside. He saw a flash of red and shut it again. Red—wasn't that the colour of a fifty-pound note?

He opened it again and pulled out a note. It *was* a fifty, crisp and glossy and mint. He pulled out another one. And another one. He poured the contents of the bag onto the bed. It was a sea of red. He clapped his hands across his mouth, so that he wouldn't scream or squeal or shriek. 'Calm down,' he soothed himself. 'Just—calm down.' He took a deep breath and began counting. Five minutes later he stopped.

£62,550.

Sixty-two thousand five hundred and fifty pounds.

Slowly and methodically he piled the notes back into the bag, stuffed the bag up his jumper and, with the stealth and light-footedness of an alley cat, he made his way back to his bedroom.

Amitabh didn't mess about when he got home from work the following night. No sooner had he unwrapped himself from his winter layers than he'd sat Leah down on the sofa, turned off the TV, picked up her hands and said, 'Leah, I love you. But I'm not going to marry you.'

She sighed. 'I knew it.'

'I'm really sorry.'

She dragged her hands through her hair and sighed again. She couldn't think of anything to say.

'It's just, I couldn't do that to my parents.'

'What?'

'It would kill them, completely.'

Leah stared at him in confusion. Amitabh's parents *loved* her. Amitabh's parents thought she was delightful.

Amitabh sighed. 'Look,' he said, 'I'm thirty now. It's all well and good mucking about in your twenties . . .'

'Mucking about?' Leah felt her stomach muscles knitting themselves into a knot.

'God, no, not mucking about. I didn't mean it like that. It's just, you and I. This . . .' He gestured around the room. 'This can never be . . . I can't marry you. Not now. Not ever. My parents can accept you as a girlfriend, but never as a wife.'

Leah could hear the words, but couldn't make sense of them. 'What?' she said. 'Because I'm white?'

'Yes, because you're white. Because you're Christian. Because you aren't professional. Because your brother's gay. Because you drink. Because you swear.'

'Oh my God.'

'I thought you knew this. I thought you accepted it.'

'No,' she said numbly. 'No, I didn't. I thought they liked me.'

'They *do* like you.'

'So why . . .?'

'It's the way things are, Leah. That's all.'

'So what if we didn't get married? Couldn't we just carry on the way we are?'

Amitabh stared at the ceiling and exhaled. 'It's not as simple as that. I'll have to marry *someone*.'

'Why?'

'To have a family. I have to have a family.'

'You don't need to be married to have a family.'

'Yes—' He stopped and sighed. 'I do.'

Leah gulped then as everything finally made sense. 'So are you saying that the past five years have just been . . . *a phase*?'

'No. Of course not. I just didn't think it through. I was young. I didn't think that you and I would last so long . . .'

Leah stared at him, at this *stranger* with whom she'd shared the past five years of her life. She'd read stories about interracial couples who'd found themselves in this position; she'd seen them on the *Kilroy* show and she'd felt so smug, thinking that that would never happen to her and Amitabh because his parents approved of them as a couple.

'Are we going to split up?'

He nodded. 'I think so,' he said.

Leah started to cry.

January 12, 2005

Toby,

It has been a long time. I'm sorry not to have been in touch but that's the way life goes. Jemma and I are divorcing. She is to stay in Cape Town with the boys (we have two sons, 12 and 9) and I am moving to Johannesburg. I have some business to attend to in London at the end of March and will be staying in my flat in Chelsea for a couple of weeks.

I would like to see you again. I am interested to see what became of you, and what became of the house I bought you all those years ago. Peter tells me the house should be worth more than half a million in the current market, in a finished state, so that should be sufficient to subsidise your 'poetry'! I've watched the book pages of *The Times* over the years, waiting for a mention of your name, but, alas, have seen nothing!

Anyway—I look forward to hearing a full report of your life. I haven't given up on the possibility that you might still have made me proud. I believe you will be forty soon, the age at which a man knows whether or not he will be able to call himself a success when the grim reaper comes to call.

I will be in touch, via Peter.

Best,

Reggie (Dad)

It was almost impossible for Toby to ascertain what all the disparate members of his household were up to at any given point of the day, so finding a moment when the house was empty so he could invite an estate agent in for a valuation was a challenge.

But a few days after his father's letter arrived he found himself unexpectedly in possession of the knowledge that Ruby was at rehearsals, Joanne and Con were at work and Melinda was ensconced in a salon in Crouch End having her highlights done. He got straight onto the phone to the estate agent who'd written to him about all the people who wanted to buy his house.

The agent who arrived at his house five minutes later was called Walter. He had a moustache. 'Well, I must say that this is a very exciting opportunity,' were his first words upon entering the house and shaking Toby's hand. 'It's not often that a property like this comes onto the market.' He wrote something in an A5 notebook. 'Oh, yes,' he said, gazing around the entrance hall. 'Oh, yes, yes, yes. Quite magnificent. So, you are the owner, Mr Dobbs?'

'Yes, that's right.'

'And you've owned the house for how long?'

'Fifteen years. Almost.' Toby gulped. The combination of Walter's suit, moustache and notebook made him feel like he was being interrogated by a detective from a 1970s TV drama.

Walter nodded approvingly.

'I must warn you,' said Toby, sensing that Walter was getting too excited, too soon, 'I haven't maintained the house particularly well. It's in need of a fair bit of TLC.'

'Ah, well, let's see it, then.'

Toby led him through the house. Due to the short notice, he hadn't had a chance to tidy or clean, and random items were strewn carelessly about the place: shoes, mugs, papers, hairbrushes, CDs, the combined detritus of five people's separate existences.

'It's a bit messy, I'm afraid. I live with quite a few people and they're all out.'

'Oh, so you don't live alone?'

'No. I live with some friends.'

'I see. No family, children?'

'No,' he said, 'just us grown-ups.' He laughed nervously.

Walter didn't say much as they moved round the house, just scratched notes into his notebook. Toby felt guilty as he opened the doors of his tenants' rooms for Walter to peruse. He never, under any circumstances, went into his tenants' rooms. He tried his hardest not to look at anything.

Ruby's room, predictably, was the messiest. The windows were hung with silky lace-trimmed shawls and dusty strings of fairy lights. Her bed was unmade and overloaded with cushions and discarded underwear. A full ashtray sat on her dressing table, surrounded by scruffy cosmetics and piles of jewellery. It looked like the bedroom of a student, of someone who'd just left home and didn't know how to look after themselves.

Con and Melinda's room was bare and minimal. Melinda's bed was made with a neat crisp duvet and two fat pillows; Con's mattress on the floor was unmade and messy.

'How many bathrooms do you have?' said Walter, heading towards Joanne's room.

'Two,' said Toby. 'One on each floor.'

'Good,' he said. 'Any en suite?'

'No. I'm afraid not.'

Toby pushed down on the handle to Joanne's door and realised with some surprise that it was locked. 'Ah,' he said, turning to face Walter. 'Erm, it seems it's locked.'

Walter nodded.

'Joanne—very private girl,' Toby offered, pointlessly.

Upstairs, Toby showed Walter his own overstuffed room and Gus's garishly decorated room, apologising for the smell of elderly cat and explaining that the cat's owner had recently passed away. By the time he led Walter into the back garden and noticed for the first time the pile of compost that had been sitting on the lawn since the end of last summer and the weeds sprouting forth from every conceivable—and inconceivable—crack and crevice and the old bicycle tyres, the rusty treadmill and the aged fridge, Toby was feeling thoroughly depressed. He couldn't imagine that Walter would be prepared to put his house on the market for £50, let alone £500,000.

He offered him a cup of tea and sat down with him at the kitchen table.

Well,' began Walter, 'it's a beautiful house. But, as you say, there are some maintenance issues. Not to mention some decorative issues and some lifestyle issues.'

'Lifestyle?'

'Yes. Because here's the bottom line. I could put this property on the market for you tomorrow, as it is, and probably, if we could find a buyer or, more likely, a developer prepared to put in the work, we would probably be looking at something in the region of seven hundred and fifty thousand pounds.'

Toby stopped breathing.

'*But.* If you were able to replace the kitchen, the bathrooms, do some basic work in the garden and, more importantly, *remove your house-mates* and give the place the feel of a *proper* family home, we could be asking for considerably more.'

'How much more?'

'Oh, I would say that this house, redecorated, modernised, made fit for a family to move straight into, I could put it on the market for around nine hundred thousand pounds. Maybe even a million.'

'*No?*' Toby blinked. 'Surely not that much?'

'Oh, yes, definitely. This house is unique, Mr Dobbs. There's nothing else like it in the area. People will pay a premium for unique.'

'So, if I were to put it onto the market now, what do you think would happen?'

'I would expect to sell it to a developer. Maybe to be developed into two or three apartments. Or to a family with a fondness for home improvements.'

'What would you do, if you were me?'

'Well, if I had the cash at my disposal, I would make the improvements myself. Most definitely.'

'You would?'

Walter nodded, emphatically. 'Without a doubt. But you'd need to get cracking on it. The market's precarious right now. Get your tenants out, get your builders in, get the house on the market. Maximise your profit.'

'Right,' said Toby, feeling a sense of unbridled panic galloping through his insides. 'Right. Then, that's what I'll do.'

Toby did something he'd never done before after Walter left. He made a list. Suddenly there was so much to consider, so much to do, and he thought that setting it down in writing might somehow make it easier to control.

Things To Do

1 Buy new sofas
2 Look at kitchens
3 Look at bathrooms
4 Get builder in to quote on works
5 Get plumber in to quote on works
6 Get decorator in to quote on works
7 Get tenants to move out
8 Sell house
9 Move to Cornwall (?)
10 Get divorced
11 Stop being in love with Ruby
12 Find someone proper to be in love with
13 **START LIVING**

Chapter 2

LEAH FOUND IT hard to believe that she'd ended up working somewhere called the Pink Hummingbird.

It was the most violently, unremittingly feminine shop in London. It had a sugar-pink façade and windows strung with feather-shaded fairy lights. It sold things that only girls would ever want to buy, such as gem-encrusted picture frames and writing paper scented with eau de toilette. The ceiling was dripping with bejewelled chandeliers and whitewashed bamboo birdcages. The walls were hung with Venetian glass mirrors and soft velvet hats in shades of plum and passion fruit. It sold underwear constructed from pure gossamer and presented in tissue-lined sateen boxes with rosebuds on the lid; cushions made from pastel-tinted Mongolian sheepskins; pens decorated with lilac glitter and wisps of marabou.

It was sugar-coated decadence on a sickly scale.

Leah wasn't really a pink sort of girl. Leah liked wearing chunky footwear and hard-wearing jeans. She wore the minimum of make-up and no perfume. Her only concession to femininity was her hair, which she wore long and wavy, and her fingernails which she kept manicured and shiny. She didn't really need make-up. She had one of those scrubbed land-girl kind of faces that looked better with just a touch of eyeliner and a pinch of the cheeks. Maybe that was why Ruth had offered her the job. Maybe she hadn't glanced down and seen the chunky-heeled boots. Maybe she hadn't noticed that Leah was wearing a T-shirt with a logo on it. Maybe she'd just taken in the cute face and the girlie hair and decided that Leah was a Pink Hummingbird in the making.

Whatever the reason, Leah had been managing Ruth's shop for five years now, ever since Ruth had relocated herself to LA and opened Pink Hummingbird II in Beverly Hills. Leah quite liked working here. It was a sweet-smelling antidote to the scruffiness of the rest of her life.

But if someone had told her ten years ago that one day she'd be thirty-five years old, unmarried, non-homeowning and managing a gift shop in Muswell Hill she'd have kicked them in the shin. Still, here she was selling overpriced gewgaws to girls and grannies and clinging—she could feel it as keenly as an oncoming train today—to the sheer rock face of an existential crisis, by the tips of her shiny fingernails.

The doorbell of the Pink Hummingbird sounded at three o'clock, just as Leah was about to tuck into a tortellini salad. She jammed the plastic tub under the cash desk and glanced at the door.

It was Toby.

He was wearing a cream cable-knit turtleneck jumper with narrow black jeans and a red scarf. On his head was a grey ribbed woollen hat. His shoes were enormous and shiny, but somehow he managed to pull the whole look off, even with his abundant and unfashionable side-burns. She smiled when she saw him; she couldn't help herself.

'Hello,' he said, peering at her from beneath the Chinese-print paper parasol she'd been hiding behind.

She peered back at him. 'Hello.'

'It's me,' he said, apologetically, 'Toby.'

She nodded and smiled. 'Yes, I know.'

'So,' he said, nervous eyes taking in the shop, 'this is where you work?'

'Yup. Uh-huh. This is my . . . pink and fluffy world.' She spread her hands outwards.

'It's nice,' he said. 'I hope you don't mind me turning up like this, unannounced. It's just, I'm not sure, really, but I just feel a bit strange that I haven't seen you since what happened the other day. And you mentioned that you worked in a pink gift shop and I was passing and assumed that this must be the pink gift shop you were talking about. So I thought I'd come in and say hello. And thank you. Again.'

'What for?'

'For being so cool, calm and collected in a crisis.'

'Ah, well. If nothing else, I am good in a crisis.'

'Yes, indeed you are.'

'So. Have you had the funeral yet?'

'Yes. On Tuesday.'

'How was it?'

'Oh, miserable,' he said, smiling. 'Horrible. It rained all day and his relatives were gruesome.'

'Oh dear,' Leah replied, smiling back.

'Yes, but lots of interesting things have happened since.'

'They have?'

'Yes. My life's been sort of turned upside down, really.'

'In what way?'

'Well . . .' Toby paused and licked his lips. 'Look,' he said, 'I hope you don't think I'm being strange, but I recall you saying that you considered yourself to be a curious person, about human beings, that is, and unfortunately curiosity is not one of my fortes, and I'm in a very strange quandary and I really need to, God, this will sound so American and so inane, but I really need to *share*. And I know we're strangers, but I don't really have anyone else whom I feel *comfortable* discussing these things with . . .'

'You want to talk to me?'

He nodded.

'About your problems?'

Well, yes.'

'Cool.' She smiled, sliding down from her stool. 'Let's go for a coffee.'

They went to the Ruby in the Dust. Toby ordered a cappuccino and Leah had a peppermint tea and a slice of cheesecake. She glanced up at Toby. He had a foam moustache and some chocolate powder dusted across his stubble. She resisted the temptation to wipe him down with her paper napkin and smiled at him.

'So,' said Toby, 'this is the thing. Gus has left me some money. Posthumously.'

'Well, obviously.'

'Yes. And now, in a weird twist of fate, my estranged father is coming back to London to see me and, frankly, I never thought I'd see him again, and I'm forty next year and I just feel as if this is my last chance to, you know, make a life for myself, because I've become stuck in a terrible, terrible rut, come to a kind of grinding halt, I suppose, and now I have both the incentive and the means to do something about it, to refurbish the house and put it up for sale. But there's a snag.'

'There is?'

'Yes, my tenants. I need them all to move out. So that I can renovate the house and sell it before my father comes back.'

'Which is when?'

'End of March. Ten weeks.'

'OK. So why can't you just evict them?'

'Because . . .' Toby paused, then sighed. 'Oh God, I know that's exactly what I should do, but for some reason I just can't bring myself to do it. For some reason I feel personally responsible for them all.'

'But why?'

'Because, well, because they're all so *lost*.'

'Lost?'

'Yes, all of them, to varying degrees. And the only reason they're living in my house is because they have absolutely nowhere else to be. No friends, no family, no safety net. And if I evict them, then what will happen to them? What will become of them all?'

'Well, yes, but surely that's not your problem, is it?'

'No, not technically, but I do feel a certain level of responsibility. It was me who invited them to live with me, after all. It was me who placed classified adverts, who selected them on the grounds that they were genuinely needy. It would be like kicking people out of a halfway house.'

'So what are you going to do?'

'Well, that's precisely it. The only way I would feel comfortable about asking them to move out is to ensure that they have somewhere else to go. The only way I could ask them to leave would be if I knew that they were all . . .'

'Happy?'

'*Yes*. Exactly. That they were all happy. And I don't really know anything about the people I live with, beyond what brand of breakfast cereal they eat. I don't like asking people questions. It makes me feel uncomfortable. But unless I can find out more about my tenants I don't stand a chance of satisfying their needs. And in your capacity as a naturally curious person, I wondered if you might be able to help me, or at least *advise* me on ways to *access* the inner workings of their minds.'

'You want me to teach you how to be nosy?'

'Well, yes, I suppose . . .'

'Well, it's easy. You just have to ask loads of questions.'

'Oh God. What sort of questions?'

'I don't know. Just ask them how they are. What they're up to. What their plans are.'

'Really?' He winced. 'But won't they think I'm being very interfering?'

'No, of course they won't. People *love* being asked about themselves.'

'Do they? I don't.'

'No, well, not everyone. But most people. And I could help, too, if you like.'

'You could?'

'Mm-hmm. I could get talking to them. Nose around. You know?'

Toby looked at her in awe. 'You'd do that for me?'

'Of course I would. I told you. I'm desperately nosy.'

She smiled then, as the idea caught her imagination. She'd spent three years watching these people across the road, three years wondering who they were, what they did and why they were there, and now she was being asked to find out. Officially.

'Well, if you were really happy to do that, then, wow, that would be amazing. And in fact, it's my birthday next week, my thirty-ninth, and I'd been thinking I might invite a few people to the pub and, maybe, if I did that you might like to come along, too. Give you a chance to . . .'

'Be nosy?'

'Yes.' He smiled. 'And your, er, boyfriend? Husband?'

Leah threw him a questioning look.

'The doctor. The Asian chap?'

'Oh, Amitabh. My ex-boyfriend. We split up.'

'Oh. Hell. Sorry. I er . . .'

'And he's a nurse, not a doctor. We split up last week. I suggested that we get married and he suddenly went all Indian on me. Said his parents would disown him. So, that's that.'

'I'm very sorry to hear that.'

'Yes, well.' Leah shrugged, holding back her tears so as not to embarrass him.

It fell silent then for a moment. Leah glanced up at Toby. He was staring wistfully out of the window. 'OK, now,' she said, smiling, '*that* was a perfect opportunity for you to practise being nosy. A curious person would want to know more about my breakup.'

Toby stared at her blankly.

'So—ask me some questions.'

'But you've just told me why you broke up. What else is there to ask?'

'Well, for example, you could ask me how long we'd been together.'

'Right. OK. So, how long had you been together?'

'Nearly three years.'

Toby nodded.

'And?'

'And what?'

'Ask me more questions. Ask me how we met.'

'So—how did you meet?'

'We met at his cousin's wedding. I was a colleague of the bride. I think she invited me only because someone else dropped out.'

Toby nodded awkwardly.

'Go on,' she said, encouragingly.

He cleared his throat. 'And, er, was he nice?'

'Yes,' she said, 'he was. Very nice. But obviously not as nice as I thought he was.'

'And what are your plans now?'

'Well, Am's moved into nurses' accommodation and I'll have to find somewhere else to live.'

'And, er, how do you feel about that?'

'I feel very annoyed, very sad and very nervous.' She paused then as her bottom lip trembled. She blinked away some tears and laughed. And then, she couldn't resist it, she picked up her napkin and brushed the chocolate off his chin. 'There, you see,' she said, forcing a brittle smile, 'it's easy, isn't it? Being nosy.'

'Yes, I suppose.'

'So—do you think you can do it? Do you think you can get to know your tenants?'

Toby nodded. 'Yes. I really think I can.'

Joanne was in the kitchen. She was wearing a pair of jeans, a red jersey polo neck, and very sensible flat leather shoes. Her hair was cut into a short layered bob and held back on one side by a glittery hair-slide that looked incongruously girlie against her prematurely middle-aged outfit. She looked shocked to see Toby in the kitchen and almost turned to leave, only stopping to acknowledge his presence when he said hello to her.

'How are you?' he ventured, cautiously.

'Fine, thanks,' she muttered, as she filled the kettle from the tap. He waited for her to ask him how he was, or at the very least to offer him a cup of tea, but she did neither. Instead she hummed gently under her breath and stared out of the window while the kettle boiled noisily.

'So, Joanne.' He paused, not quite sure how to continue, but knowing that he had to. 'How long have you been living here now?'

She spun round. 'What? God . . . I'm not sure.' She pursed her lips and stared up at the ceiling.

Toby waited, wondering whether she was working out how long she'd lived here or if she was just staring at a damp patch.

'Two years and eight months,' she said finally.

'Right.'

'And twenty days.'

'Right,' repeated Toby.

'I moved in on the 4th of May, 2002. It was sunny.'

'Was it?' he said, rubbing his chin, as if trying to remember the day.

'Yes. I moved from southeast London. They had a march. It was for marijuana. There were people dressed up as cannabis leaves walking down my road. I was glad to be leaving.'

Toby laughed, relieved that Joanne had injected some levity into the stilted conversation, but she just stared at him blankly. 'Why d'you ask?'

'I don't really know,' he said. 'I was just wondering.' The kitchen fell silent except for the sound of a teaspoon going round and round in Joanne's mug.

'And how are you finding it?'

'What?'

'The house. Living here. Are you happy?'

'It's fine. I have no complaints. Why?' Her eyes narrowed. 'Is there a problem you wish to discuss?'

'God, no, not at all. I just wanted to make sure that you were doing OK. That's all.'

'Right.' She nodded tersely and squeezed her tea bag against the side of her mug.

'And how's work?'

'Fine.' She dropped the tea bag into the pedal bin.

'Are you still, you know, still doing the old acting?' Toby had broken into a light sweat.

'No,' she said, dropping the teaspoon into the dishwasher basket.

'And the role? The one you were researching, did that, er . . .?'

'No. It fell through.'

'Oh dear. That's a shame. Anything else in the pipeline?'

'There is no pipeline.'

'Oh,' he said. 'Oh. OK. So what sort of work are you doing at the moment?'

Toby saw her chest cave in then expand again as she took in a deep breath. 'Look, Toby. I have to be honest. I'm not a morning person. I like to drink my tea and read my paper and not talk to anyone until I really have to. So if you don't mind . . .?'

Toby nodded. 'Of course,' he said, 'I understand.'

Part of him admired Joanne for being so forthright. Another part couldn't believe how rude she was. He glanced surreptitiously at her hands. She had a ring on the index finger of her left hand, plain gold with no stones. Round her neck was a silver chain with a ring and a locket hanging from it. And there, on the inside of her wrist, was the first hint that Toby had seen of the real Joanne. A tattoo. Joanne had a tattoo. On the inside of her wrist. Like a jailbird. Or a prisoner of war. Or a delinquent schoolgirl with a fountain pen. Joanne had a past. He was just going to have to find a way to get it out of her that didn't involve normal, everyday, polite conversation.

'**H**ello, Con,' Toby opened, coming upon him eating a Big Mac in the front room.

'Hiya.' Con glanced up and looked at Toby in surprise.

'Good day at work?'

Con shrugged. 'Nothing special.'

'So,' Toby said after a moment, 'do you think you'll stay at Condé Nast for much longer? Is there any promise of a . . . of any *career progression*, at all?'

Con laughed and wiped a fleck of ketchup off his chin. 'Er . . . no. Definitely not. Unless I want to be post-room manager. Which I don't.'

'But what about the publications? The magazines. Surely there must be possibilities there?'

He laughed again. 'Not for the likes of me there aren't. It's like one of those fucked-up dreams, that place. On one side you've got reality—that's us lot in the post room, the caterers, the cleaners—then on the other side you've got this whole other world, these posh people, my age, live in Chelsea, don't know what day of the week it is, kind of floating round, like, you know . . . *oblivious*. They're the ones that get the careers. We're just there to make sure they get their letters and their lunch.'

'Oh,' said Toby. 'I see. So, if you don't want to be the post-room manager and you don't think there are any other opportunities there, what's your game plan? What's next?'

'My PPL.'

'Your what?'

'My private pilot's licence.'

'You're going to learn to *fly*?'

'Yeah. Why not?'

'God, well, isn't that very expensive?'

'Can be.' He shrugged. 'But I've been looking into it. If I go to South Africa it's a third of what it would cost here. I've been saving since I started work, and I've calculated that I need only another eighteen months at Condé Nast to earn what I need. Then I'm off. Get my licence. Go to the Caribbean. Chartered flights. Island hopping. The good life. Oh, man . . .'

'Right, so, er . . .'

'I tell you what, if it hadn't been for Nigel writing to you and me getting this room, and the, you know, the great deal on the rent, there's no way I'd have been able to think about learning to fly. That was a good day that was, the day we met.'

He smiled at Toby: a lovely warm smile full of gratitude, and Toby sighed quietly. This was exactly what he'd wanted. This is what this house was for. It was for allowing people to follow their dreams. His main criterion for choosing housemates was that they should benefit in some positive, constructive way from having tiny outgoings. The only exception to this rule had been Ruby, whom he'd offered a room to on the grounds that he wanted to have sex with her. He'd offered Con a room because he felt sorry for him, because his mum had abandoned him, because he had no fixed abode and was about to lose his job and end up on the streets. And now, a year later, Con had a dream, too. He wanted to fly planes. And Toby should have been delighted. Instead he felt trapped.

Toby thought sadly about his wedge of magic money that had appeared out of thin air to make real the dreams he'd had in the wake of Gus's death. What was more important, wondered Toby, his own silly middle-aged need to prove himself to his father or a young man's future?

He sat for a moment, staring blankly at the television, listening to Con slurping his cola, letting his dreams slink away like naughty children. Then he slapped his hands against his thighs and got to his feet.

'I was thinking,' he said, 'that I might invest in a pair of new sofas. What do you think?'

Con looked at him in surprise, then at the aged blue sofas dressed with tatty ethnic cushions. 'Yeah. Why not? Go for it.'

'Cool.' Toby put his hands in his pockets. 'I'll go shopping tomorrow. Sales are on now. Good time to go.'

And for now, he mused, new sofas might just have to do.

Melinda McNulty was forty-five. She maintained her toned size-ten figure by going to the gym three times a week, attending two power-boxing classes a week, and doing Pilates on her bedroom floor in front of the TV. She ate Special K breakfast bars in the morning, then went off to Stansted Airport where she worked as a check-in girl for Monarch. Her cupboard in the kitchen was full of things such as Snack-a-Jacks and instant noodle soups. She drank Cava ('It's better than champagne') pretty much every day of the week, and went clubbing on Saturday nights with her friend Zoë, who was twenty-eight. She wore too much make-up, too much perfume and very tight velours track suits in bright colours that showed her muscled tummy.

When Toby saw her get back from work that night, smart and trim in her airline uniform, he deliberately sought her out. He found her ironing in the front room.

'Hello, m'Lord!' She had the penetrating and unripened voice of a fifteen-year-old girl. It was very disconcerting. 'How's it going?'

'Good,' he said. 'Excellent. How are you?'

'Yeah, I'm good, too. Just getting some ironing out of the way.'

Toby glanced down at the pile of clothes growing on the arm of the sofa. They appeared to be mainly Con's clothes. 'Do you want a cup of tea?' he offered.

'Ooh, yes.' She pursed her strawberry-pink lips into a crinkled ring. 'White, one sugar. Can I have the mug with the cats on it? You know, the big one?'

He didn't know, but searched the kitchen cupboards until he found it. When he came back, Melinda was sitting crosslegged on the sofa, examining a glossy, blood-coloured toenail. 'Ooh, thanks, Toby,' she said, stretching her heavily ringed hands towards the mug, 'just what the doctor ordered.'

Toby sat next to her and rested his tea on the coffee table.

'I hear you're getting rid of these,' said Melinda, stroking the fabric of the sofa.

'What?'

'The sofas. Con said you're thinking of buying new ones.'

'Yes,' he said, 'that is the plan. They've done their service, these ones.'

'They have,' she agreed. 'How's that weird cat?'

'Boris?'

'Is that what you're calling him?' She laughed.

'Yes.'

'Oh, I like that. He looks like a Boris. How's he getting on?'

'He's fine, as far as I can tell. Very low-maintenance. I'm not that keen on the whole litter tray thing, though. It's not very pleasant.'

Melinda turned to face him, one knee tucked up under her. Her hair was the wrong shade of blonde for her colouring, slightly yellow, as if it had been left out in the sun for too long. She didn't have any wrinkles at all until she smiled, and then she got a set of very dramatic crow's-feet that exploded from the corners of her eyes like fireworks. But she had beautiful eyes, a clear Caribbean turquoise, fringed with heavy black lashes. 'I know this sounds dreadful'—she leaned towards him, conspiratorially—'and don't take this the wrong way, but I much prefer it here now that Gus's gone.'

Toby glanced at her in horror.

'Not that I didn't like him. Don't get me wrong. But it was just a bit weird, wasn't it, having him around? But now he's gone it just feels *perfect* here. You know something, Toby, I *love* this house, I really do. Can't imagine living anywhere else now.' She glanced up towards the towering ceilings. 'I couldn't move back into some poky little purpose-built with paper walls now. I'm *ruined*.' She laughed.

Toby gulped. 'So you're happy, are you, sharing a room with Con?'

'Oh, it's lovely. You know, I was thinking I might ask you about Gus's room, now that he's gone. Thinking I might ask if I could move in there. But then I thought, do I really want to move out of Con's room? And I don't. Really don't. I love sharing with him. He's such a great boy. And being apart from him for so many years, I missed out on a lot. But now . . . we're *so* close,' she gushed. 'It's like we're best mates, you know? We're equals. It's lovely now. Everything's lovely.' She smiled and caressed her mug. 'What about you, Toby? You've been single for a while. Anyone special in your life?'

'Er, no,' he began. 'Not at the moment.'

'Ah,' she cooed sympathetically, squeezing his leg gently, 'that's a shame. How old are you now?'

'Thirty-nine,' he said, 'next week.'

'Yes. It's a funny age that. I remember my late thirties. You start panicking, thinking you're running out of time. You know, every birthday I look in the mirror and think, not yet, Mel, you're still looking good. Have to work at it, mind, but it's so worth it. Especially in my line of work. Looking good is so important.'

'You mean, being an air hostess?'

'Well, no, not an air hostess exactly. Ground staff now. Keeps me closer to home, closer to Con. But image is still mega-important. You're the first contact the customer has with the airline. And if you look crap, well, that's not going to make the customer feel very confident about their flight, is it?'

Toby nodded sagely, thinking that he would be more likely to base his confidence on the condition of the aircraft than on the eye shadow on the check-in girls.

'Well,' she got to her feet, 'you're a lovely fella. I'm sure someone'll come along when you're least expecting it. And you've got tons going for you.'

'I have?'

'Yes, you're lovely and tall. Girls like tall men. You've got this amazing house. And you're generous and caring. I mean, look at us all, all us waifs and strays. Where would we all be without you, Toby, eh? You took my Con off the streets. You've given me a chance to be with my boy. You've looked after poor Ruby since she was a kid. And what would have become of Gus if he hadn't had you to take care of him? You're a hero, Toby. And what woman doesn't want a hero?'

Toby picked up his mug and left the room, unable to think of one single thing to say in response.

Toby stood up, then sat down again, enjoying the sensation. He caressed her arms gently, then stood up again. She was so beautiful, a long, lean sliver of leather-clad perfection. He glanced across at her sister and sighed with pleasure.

They were the most beautiful sofas in the world.

They'd arrived half an hour ago, on a big white van with the word CONRAN on the side. Six thousand pounds' worth of midnight-blue calfskin and milk-coffee suede. He could have bought two whole bathroom suites for that, or a brand-new kitchen. He could have paid for someone to come in and redecorate the whole house. He could have recarpeted throughout and bought a new boiler. But then, he thought, glancing fondly at his new sofas, where was the wow factor in a cheap kitchen or a swath of new carpet? Where was the inspiration? These sofas were going to inform the rebirth of this house, set the benchmark for style and taste. These sofas were seminal.

Toby heard the front door go and footsteps behind him. He felt suddenly embarrassed, caught red-handed with expensive sofas. He tried but failed to arrange himself into some kind of natural position, and, when Ruby walked in two seconds later, he was perched on the edge of the coffee table.

'Oh,' he said, 'it's you.' He stood up.

'Oh. My. God.' She'd seen the sofas. 'Oh my God,' she said again, moving in for a closer look. '*What are these?*'

'New sofas.' He sniffed.

'Yes, I can see that, but, I mean—they're *beautiful*.' She caressed one tenderly and let her leather jacket fall to the floor.

Toby smiled grudgingly. 'Thank you.'

'I can't believe you bought these. They must have cost *a fortune*.'

'Well, yes, but they were in the sale.'

She sat down and ran her hands over the mocha suede. 'Well, Toby Dobbs, who would have guessed that you had such great taste?'

Toby felt a surge of pride rise slowly through him like a bubble in a spirit level.

'Where are they from?'

'Conran Shop,' he mumbled through his fingers.

'*Conran?* Jesus, Toby, did you *steal* them?'

'No, of course not. I paid for them. Cash.'

'But how the hell could you afford them?'

Toby sighed. He'd known he'd have to offer an explanation at some point. 'Gus. He left me some money. In his will.'

Ruby's eyes widened. 'No! How much?'

'A few thousand. Not that much. Not really enough to be buying sofas from the Conran Shop. But I just . . . I don't know . . .'

'You wanted them?'

'Yes, I wanted them.'

'Oh, Tobes.' Ruby rested a hand on his knee. 'That's OK. That's what normal people do all the time. It's called *extravagance*. Embrace it.'

Toby smiled. 'So,' he said, 'you like them, then?'

'I *love* them.'

'Good,' he said.

'But, really,' she said, 'how much did Gus leave you? Exactly?'

'I'm not telling you!' he said adamantly, folding his arms.

'Oh, Tobes. I can't believe you don't trust me. God, as if I'd steal your money.'

'I'm not saying you'd steal it.'

'Yeah, well, whatever. I'll find out somehow. You know me.'

Toby smirked. He'd lived with Ruby for fifteen years, but he wasn't entirely sure he did know her. He knew what she sounded like when she was having sex. He knew her moods and her patterns. But did he know *her*?

'So,' he said, 'what's happening with Paul Fox? He hasn't been around for a while.'

Ruby shrugged. 'We had a bit of a row last week.'

'Oh, right. What about?'

'Oh, you know, *Eliza*.'

'Well, really, I'm not sure what you expect. I mean, the man has a girlfriend, for God's sake.'

Ruby raised her eyebrows. 'Oh God, Tobes, don't start on me. I don't need you telling me what to do.'

'I'm not trying to tell you what to do, but I don't understand why you have to keep underselling yourself the entire time.'

'You mean you want me to settle down with a nice boy?'

Well, yes. Isn't that what you want?'

'No. Not even slightly.'

'But what's going to happen to you?'

'Happen?'

'Yes. Where will you go? What will you do?'

'I don't know what you mean.'

'I just mean . . .' He was about to say, you're thirty-one, you're single, you've got no career and I'm about to kick you out of the only home you've known since you were sixteen. He was about to say, you're free-falling and you've got no one to catch you. He was about to say, *I don't want you to end up like me*. But he didn't. Instead he smiled. 'I'm just worried about you, that's all.'

Well, don't be,' she said. 'I can look after myself.'

'Good,' he said. 'Good.'

Chapter 3

IN THE PAST WEEK Leah had seen a bathroom with mould growing on the carpet, a kitchen with a pet rat on the counter and a bedroom with no windows. She'd been told variously that she was allowed to watch television only until nine o'clock, that she would have to stay out on Friday nights and that she wasn't allowed to drink alcohol in the 'common parts'. If the flat was nice, then the flatmate was awful; if the flat was awful, then the flatmate was even worse.

Leah phoned Amitabh when she got home from a murky basement flat on Hornsey Lane. She phoned him partly because she was missing him and wanted to hear his voice, but mainly because she was so cross with him for putting her in this position in the first place.

'Hello, it's me.'

There was a split second of silence. 'Hello.'

'How are you?'

'Good,' he said, 'I'm good. How are you?'

'Shit. I'm shit. Actually.'

'Oh.' She could hear Amitabh sitting down, presumably on his bed. She could imagine him stroking his chin like he did when he was uncomfortable.

'Yes. This whole flat-hunting thing is a nightmare. I'm too old for flat shares. I'm too set in my ways. I can't live with anyone else.'

Amitabh sighed. 'I can't understand why you're not looking to buy.'

'Because,' she said crossly—they'd had this conversation a million times—'I have one hundred and two pounds in my bank account and last time I looked flats in London were going for a bit more than that.'

'Get a mortgage,' he said. 'They're doing one hundred per cent mortgages again now, you know. A hundred and ten per cent even.'

'Mmm,' she said, 'that's a good idea. Tie myself up for the rest of my life with the mortgage from hell that I will never be able to pay off *because I work in a shop*. And of course never actually *go out again* because I won't be able to afford to.'

Amitabh sighed once more.

'This is all your fault, you know. I mean, what were you *thinking*?'

'I wasn't thinking. I was just . . . *being*. You know.'

'No. I don't know. All those weddings we went to, didn't you ever stop to think about what was expected of you? Didn't you sometimes wonder what was going to happen to us? How it was all going to end?'

'No,' he said, 'I honestly never did. I suppose that it hadn't occurred to me that I was getting so old. That we were *both* getting so old. I suppose I just thought that we had for ever.'

'So,' she said, 'if that old man hadn't died and I hadn't proposed we'd just have carried on, would we, carried on indefinitely, until one day we'd suddenly have woken up and realised we were fifty?'

'Yes. No. I mean, I'd have realised sooner than that that it wasn't working, but the old man dying made it happen earlier.'

'Well, then, praise be to Gus for choosing his moment so well. Because it's bad enough being in this predicament at thirty-five. Imagine if I'd been forty? In fact, you know something? At this precise moment I'm feeling a lot of anger towards you . . . *a lot of anger.*'

'Oh God, Leah. I'm sorry.'

'Yeah, well, sorry's not going to help. Sorry's a load of bollocks frankly. *You're* a load of bollocks. A load of pathetic, selfish, fat—'

'Fat?'

'Yes, fat. And hairy. But that doesn't matter, because some poor woman will have to marry you because her mum and dad tell her to.'

There was a stunned silence, followed two seconds later by a roar of what Leah at first assumed was indignation, but quickly realised was laughter.

'Oh God, Leah. You're so funny. I miss you.'

Leah felt her adrenaline levels drop and her muscles relax, then she smiled. 'I miss you, too,' she said. 'Loads.'

It fell silent for a moment, then Leah looked at her watch. 'Shit,' she said, 'I've got to go.'

'Go where?'

'To the Clissold Arms. It's Toby's birthday.'

'Toby who?'

'You know, Toby, across the road. Young Skinny Guy. Except he's not that young. He's thirty-nine.'

'How come you're going to the pub with him?'

'He invited me. He wants me to meet his housemates.'

'What—you mean you're going to meet the Teenager? And, and the Air Hostess. And *Sybil*?'

Well,' she said, 'maybe. I'm not sure who's coming.'

'And the Girl with the Guitar?'

'I told you, Am, I don't know.'

'Oh God, that's not fair. I lived there for three years, then I move out and five seconds later you're getting in with the neighbours. Can I come?'

'No, Am, you can't. We don't go out together any more, remember?'

'But we're friends, aren't we? We can still see each other?'

'I don't know. Maybe. Look, I have to go. I'll speak to you soon, OK?'

'OK,' he sniffed. 'And, Leah?'

'Yes?'

'I love you.'

Leah got home from the Clissold Arms just after eleven. She slammed the door behind her and leaned against it, heavily, her body wilting with the relief of finally being home. The evening had been a resounding failure, a disaster in fact. Only Con and Ruby had turned up and they'd spent the entire night flirting outrageously with each other before disappearing back to the house at ten o'clock, presumably to have sex with each other. Toby had watched the whole mating ritual unfurl with undisguised anguish and Leah had tried desperately to keep a jolly stream of conversation going. She'd learned nothing about Toby's housemates, other than that they had the hots for each other, and all she'd learned about Toby was that he was obviously miserably in love with Ruby.

She sighed and gazed around the flat. She hated living here without Amitabh. She thought back to her conversation with him earlier that day, him saying that he loved her. And then she did something ludicrous. She picked up the phone and she called Amitabh's mother.

'Hello, Mrs Varshney. Malina. It's Leah.'

'Leah?'

'Hi, how are you?'

'Leah. It's very late. I'm in bed, you've just woken me up and I'm tired. Is everything all right?'

'Yes. No. It's just. Is it true what Amitabh says? Would you really not want to have me as a daughter-in-law?'

She heard Malina sighing loudly down the phone. 'Oh, Leah, Leah, Leah. What can I say to you?'

'Say it's not true. Say he was wrong. Say that you would be proud to have a girl like me as the wife of your youngest son.'

'And so I would,' she replied softly, 'so I would if I were someone else. If I were Mrs Smith and my parents were from Berkshire and I went to church every Sunday, then there is no other girl I would like better for my son to marry. But that isn't the case.'

'But what if I converted to Hinduism? I could do that.'

'It's not about *religion*, Leah. It's about family and lineage and caste and tradition. I can't do anything about it.'

'But, Malina, I love him so much.'

'I know you do, my sweet girl. But there is a fact here that has to be faced.'

'What's that?' She sniffed.

'The fact is that if my Amitabh loved you as much as you love him, then he would marry you and be damned. The fact is that my Amitabh hasn't finished looking yet.'

Con pulled open his wardrobe and leafed through his clothes. They all looked wrong this morning, for some reason. Too bright, too clean, too considered. His jeans were too new, too blue, too many fussy zips and buckles. Eventually he settled on his old Levi's, a white flannel shirt with a grey windowpane check, and his brown suede Pumas. It still wasn't right—the white of the shirt was too intense, the jeans had the beginning of a tear in the knee that looked a bit fake, even though it wasn't, and the Pumas were too new-looking—but it was a step towards the look he'd been going for.

Melinda watched him from her bed. 'How come you're wearing your old jeans?' she asked suspiciously.

'I dunno. Just fancied something a bit old school.'

'Is this about Ruby?'

'*Ruby*?' he scoffed.

'Yeah. Are you trying to impress her or something?'

'Why would I do that?'

'Er! Why d'you think?'

Con sighed and touched his hair in the mirror. 'No, Mum, I am not trying to impress Ruby. I told you, what happened—it was nothing. I'm not interested in Ruby.'

'Then why . . .?' She paused mid-sentence. 'Never mind, forget it. Men. You're all a mystery to me.'

Con, in all honesty, was feeling like a bit of a mystery to himself in the wake of Friday night. He'd fancied Ruby for ages, but not in a specific way, just in that general way of fancying fit women. He walked past her on the stairs, thought, she's fit, stopped thinking about her. He saw her walking up the road in tight jeans and dangerous boots, thought, she's fit, stopped thinking about her. That's how it was with Ruby. Just vague, general fancying. So the fact that he'd slept with her on Toby's birthday was inexplicable. It was partly her teasing about how he'd never had an older woman and a little voice in his head saying: got to have an older woman, tick a box, 100 things to do before you're thirty.

It had felt wrong the minute they made the decision and, by the time they left the pub, Con knew he was making a mistake, but it was too late then. He couldn't pull out; he'd have looked like an idiot. So he'd completely gone to town. He had to live with this woman after, see her every day. He had to give her the best he could offer otherwise he'd never be able to look her in the eye again. So he had.

He didn't know what happened next. He didn't want to go back there, he knew that much. Once was enough. She wasn't his type and he just wasn't really that into her. Judging by the way she was with her other blokes, that shouldn't be a problem, though.

'Is this shirt a bit spoddy?' he asked his mum.

'No.' She smiled. 'It's lovely. But what's the big deal? You're only going to work. Who's going to care what shirt you're wearing?'

'No one,' he said. 'No one.'

She was sitting at her desk in the window, with a shaft of sun cutting through her at a diagonal. She was wearing a cream chiffon shirt with roses on it, a cotton waistcoat with pockets, and a tiny denim skirt with a frayed hem. Her fine hair was rolled up at the back and her shoes were flat-bottomed and pointy. She looked like a little fairy, all pale and diaphanous.

She turned at the sound of his trolley and leapt to her feet. 'Oh God,' she said. 'Shit, sorry. Is it three o'clock already?'

Con nodded.

'Shit. I haven't got it all together.' She started scanning her desk with her hands, trying to lay them on all the relevant envelopes and bits of paper. 'I'm going to be a minute or two. Is that OK?'

This happened all the time. Dippy bloody teenagers, fresh from A levels, doing a bit of work experience before university, or graduates back from a year learning to scuba dive and smoke spliff on other continents. They didn't wear watches. They never knew what time it was. Everything was always a last-minute panic. Usually it really bugged him. But not in this case. In this case he was happy for Daisy to take as long as she liked, panicking prettily around him like a distracted butterfly.

'So,' she said, flicking through a pile of cream envelopes, 'how are you today?'

'I'm good,' he said. 'Very well indeed,' he added, somehow feeling a need to be a bit suave. His grandmother had always tried to get him to speak properly, to use proper manners. Then she'd sent him to the roughest comprehensive in Tottenham, where good manners and properly enunciated vowels didn't really count for much.

'How are you?'

'Mental,' she said, looping an elastic band round the envelopes and handing them to him. 'They're all off on a trip tomorrow, so of course everything has to be done, like, five minutes ago.'

She loaded up his trolley with squidgy packages and slippery bags of clothes as she talked. 'Are you going back down to the post room now?'

'Yes,' he said.

'I'll come down with you. They're waiting for something from Miu Miu and apparently if it doesn't get here in the next ten minutes then the entire population of the world is going to get a terrible disease and die—apparently. I might as well just sit in dispatch and wait for it.'

They stepped into the lift and stared at the doors, awkwardly, until Daisy broke the silence. 'So,' she said, 'where do you live?'

'Finchley,' he said.

'Finchley? Where's that? Is that north?'

'Yes. North of Hampstead. South of Barnet.'

'Is it nice there?'

'Yeah. It's OK. I live in a nice house, so it's good. What about you? Where do you live?'

'Wandsworth,' she said. 'Just off the common. Nice area. Crappy house.'

'Why? What's wrong with it?'

'Oh, it belongs to my sister's boyfriend and it's just tiny, you know, a little tiny weeny cottage with teeny tiny rooms. The kitchen is about as big as this lift. But I shouldn't complain. It's nice of them to let me live with them and at least I've got somewhere to live, you know.'

Con nodded and thought about telling her that he used to be homeless, slept on a piece of cardboard and got washed in a public toilet, but decided not to.

The lift flumped to the basement floor and the doors slid open. Daisy helped Con manoeuvre his trolley through the doors.

'So, who do you live with in your nice house? Friends? A girlfriend?'

Con felt a surge of excitement. It was the way she said it: 'A girlfriend?' She was fishing; she wanted to know if he was single. And suddenly he felt the possibility that this girl from another place, from a world of ponies and Caribbean family holidays, might actually want to be with him, a boy from Tottenham, who'd been brought up by his grandmother in a second-floor council flat.

'No,' he said encouragingly, 'no girlfriend. I live with my mum.'

'Oh, you're still at home?'

'No. I mean—she lives with me. In my place.'

'You share a place with your mum?'

'Yes. But not just my mum. Loads of us.'

'What? Like a commune?'

He smiled. 'Yeah,' he said, 'a bit. This poet bloke owns it and rents out rooms.'

'Wow—a poet.'

'Yeah. He's a bit strange, kind of like a recluse, but he's a good bloke.

And the house is massive. All sorts of people have lived there. Artists and singers and actors and stuff. It's a really cool place.'

The boys in the post room all glanced up curiously as Con walked in with Daisy, their eyes straying to her slender legs, but she seemed oblivious to their attentions. Usually, when people from 'upstairs' had cause to come 'downstairs', you could sense their need to assimilate themselves briefly in this alien environment. But Daisy wasn't bothered.

Con led her to the dispatch area to look for her parcel. 'Anything in from Miu Miu for Vogue fashion department?' he asked Nigel.

'Yeah,' said Nigel, grabbing a big plastic bag off a rail. 'Just in, two minutes ago.' He handed the bag to Con and smiled at Daisy. 'Hello,' he said, gormlessly. 'And who are you?'

'Hello.' She smiled back. 'I'm Daisy.'

'Hello, Daisy. I'm Nigel.'

'Do you like Miu Miu, Nigel?'

Nigel smiled. 'My favourite,' he said.

'They do nice shoes, too.'

'Oh, yes,' he agreed, 'lovely shoes. But not as nice as those Christian Louboutins. Now those are really nice shoes.'

Daisy laughed. Nigel laughed. And Con watched in wonder as they joked together, this lardy forty-something man from Hainault and an angel from the eighth floor. And he knew it then. Daisy was within his grasp. It was just a matter of time.

Toby's love for Ruby ebbed and flowed like the tide. When he'd first met her fifteen years ago he'd been consumed by lust for her. It had overwhelmed him to the point that he'd had to question the validity of every emotion he'd ever felt, even for Karen.

On her second night in his house, she'd brought home a monstrous man she claimed was an 'old friend' and made love to him so loudly and for so long that Toby had had to go downstairs to sleep on the sofa. And so began a succession of 'old friends' and 'great mates' and 'best buddies' all clambering in and out of Ruby's bedroom—some of them once and never again, some of them on a regular basis.

The fact of Ruby's sexual promiscuity had not stopped Toby falling in love with her. When it was just the two of them, watching TV, watching a band, having a drink, discussing music, when it was just Toby and Ruby, it was the best thing in the world. He learned to switch off when she was keeping male company, to immerse himself in something distracting, to turn up his music and sit it out like a forecasted downpour.

But then Ruby met Paul Fox.

Toby *hated* Paul Fox.

He hated him because he was wealthy and successful.

He hated him because he called everyone 'mate' in his stupid mockney accent, even though Toby knew he was an ex-public-school boy (it took one to know one).

He hated him because he'd once overheard him referring to him as Mr Rigsby.

He hated him because he was being unfaithful to his loyal girlfriend, even though he'd never met her.

But mainly he hated him because he'd somehow managed to persuade Ruby to sleep with him at least once a week for the past five years. Toby didn't think things could get much worse than Paul Fox.

But now they had.

Ruby had slept with Con.

This represented, as far as Toby was concerned, a dramatic slip in her standards and, as such, a seismic shift in the way he viewed her. It was time for her to go. And, more importantly, it was time for him to stop loving her. He just wished someone could show him how.

Ruby's handbag vibrated. She pulled out her phone and wiped some crumbs off the screen. It was Paul. This was the first time he'd called since the night they'd argued about Eliza and she wasn't sure she wanted to talk to him. She stared at the screen for a moment, then pressed the accept button.

'Hello,' she said.

'Hello,' he replied. He sounded businesslike, but friendly. 'Where are you?'

'In rehearsals with the boys.'

'Are you free this afternoon? For an hour or so?'

This usually meant that he wanted to come over for sex. 'Erm, I'm not sure. Why?'

'I need to see you. To talk to you. I can pick you up. How about tea at the Wolseley?'

Ruby laughed. 'Tea at the Wolseley?'

'Yes. I've got a meeting in Green Park at five, so you'll have to get yourself home. I'll pick you up at three.' He hung up without saying goodbye.

Ruby switched her phone off. Tea at the Wolseley? This was going to be very strange indeed.

The woman at the front desk appeared to know Paul. 'Of course,' she smiled, when he asked if they had a table available without a reservation.

They were led through the cavernous restaurant by a small girl in black and shown to a table at the back. Ruby looked around in awe. It was like a vast black-lacquered cathedral, held up by forty-foot pillars and hung with chandeliers the size of transit vans.

Paul had spent most of the journey here chatting to someone called Mike on his Bluetooth, so they hadn't had a chance to talk yet, but Ruby knew that something was wrong.

She ordered half a dozen oysters and a glass of champagne, figuring that she could eat sandwiches and cake at home any time she wanted. She glanced at Paul. 'So,' she began, 'what's up?'

'I've got something to tell you.'

'Right.'

'I've asked Eliza to marry me.'

Ruby winced and grabbed the edge of the table to steady herself. 'Excuse me?'

'I asked her to marry me. And she said yes.'

'Oh my God.' She laughed, though she wasn't amused. 'You've got to be kidding.'

'I'm not.'

'But, you've only known each other for six months.'

'Eight months, actually.'

'Eight months. Whatever. It's not very long.'

'No, it's not. But then I'm not very young. And neither is she.'

'Yes, but . . . getting married. That means—' And then it hit her, exactly what that meant. It meant no more her. 'What about us?'

'Well, that's the thing, Rubes. That's what I wanted to talk to you about.'

'Oh God.' Ruby let her head fall into her hands.

'There's no way that this can carry on.' He gestured at the two of them. 'No way. It's one thing messing around in a casual relationship. But, you know, we're talking engagement rings here. We're talking major commitment. And I can't have you in my life any more.'

Ruby laughed. 'Don't be ridiculous. Of course you can. You're my best mate.'

'No, Ruby, I'm not your best mate. You don't have a best mate.'

'What?' Ruby sat up straight.

'Well, you don't. I'm sorry. You have friends. And you have lovers. But you don't have a best mate.' He stopped and appraised her for a moment, as if he was about to say something harsh. 'But, anyway . . . anyway.' He sighed, and pulled his hands down his face. 'I didn't bring you here to give you a character assassination. I brought you here because I wanted to do this properly. Because you deserve it. So here . . .'

He pulled open his jacket and removed a box from his inside pocket. He passed it to Ruby.

'What is this?' she said.

'Open it,' he said, nodding at the box.

The box clicked open and something glittered at her. It was a tortoise-shell hair comb, one of those Spanish-style ones. It was decorated with tiny pink rubies set into the shape of flowers. Ruby gazed at it for a while not sure how to react. It was a beautiful gift, but what did it mean?

'Do you like it?'

'Yes,' she said, 'it's beautiful. But why have you given it to me?'

'To say thank you. To say goodbye.'

'Right.' She let the box snap shut and laid it gently on the table in front of her.

'Was it a mistake?'

'No,' she sighed. 'No. It's stunning. It'll be nice to have something to remind me of you. Of us.'

'Are you being facetious?'

'No,' she said, 'of course not. You don't owe me anything. This was always a, you know, an easy-come-easy-go thing. It's fine.' She stopped and caught her breath as a dreadful thought occurred to her. 'But, what about our arrangement?'

'Well,' he said, 'obviously that's going to have to stop.'

'Right,' she said, panic surging through her. 'So what am I going to do? How am I going to pay my rent?'

'Toby will let you off the rent, I'm sure.'

'Yes,' said Ruby, 'but what about everything else? What about food and clothes and . . . and . . . *life*?'

'You'll find a way,' he said. 'You'll get a job, sell a song. It's time for you to grow up, Ruby . . .'

'Christ,' she felt panic engulf her, 'what's going to happen to me? I'm overdrawn as it is. Fuck. Can't you, maybe, just lend me some money. Just to tide me over?'

'No, Ruby. I can't. This is it. This . . .' He gestured at the gift box. 'And this . . .' He gestured at her oysters which had just been placed in front of her. 'After this there's nothing. It has to be like this.'

'What—not even fifty quid?'

Paul sighed and pulled out his wallet. He pulled out a sheaf of twenty-pound notes and slid them across the table to Ruby. She covered them with her hand. It was more than fifty, probably about a hundred. She slipped them into her handbag without looking at them. 'Thank you,' she said, then she stared at her oysters, while she tried to corral her thoughts. Who was the first person to eat an oyster? she wondered. Who prised open that first shell and thought it would be interesting to put it in their mouth? She spooned some pink vinegar and shallots into the shell, picked it up between her thumb and forefinger, tipped it into her mouth and bit down on it, once, twice, swallowed it. She glanced at Paul. He was watching her wistfully over tented fingers. 'Aren't you worried about me?' she said softly. 'Aren't you scared I won't survive?'

'You'll be fine,' he said. 'I know you. You're a strong woman and you will be absolutely fine.'

Ruby smiled stiffly. Because if that was what he thought then he really didn't know her at all.

Con was in the kitchen, washing up a dinner plate. Toby smiled at him as he reached past him to grab a glass off the draining board. 'All right?' Con said.

'Yup,' he said, 'just getting some water.'

He was about to leave the kitchen and head back upstairs when Con turned round. 'Toby?' he said. 'Would you say that you were posh?'

Toby smiled. '*Me?*'

'Yeah. What are you? I mean you're obviously not working class, but are you posh or middle class, or what?'

'God,' he said, 'I don't know. I've never really thought about it.'

'It's just . . . it's funny, isn't it? Meeting people and they talk a certain way or look a certain way and you think you know what sort of background they've had, but then maybe you're wrong. I mean, there are people in stately homes who haven't got any money. And you—you own this huge house, but you haven't got a penny to your name. Are you still posh? Or does being poor make you common?'

Toby smiled and leaned against a chair. 'Well, I suppose I'm middle class in some ways. My father's a businessman. My mother was a model. I was brought up in a four-bedroom house in Dorset, nice but no land. But then I went to a pretty snazzy public school, hung out with some pretty posh people. And now, as you say, I'm penniless. I don't have a career, but I own a property.' He shrugged and smiled. 'I'd say I'm a bit of a mess, really.'

'But you see, compared to me, you're still posh. My mum's pretty much homeless. I don't know what my dad did. I was brought up on an estate, went to a comp. It's all about the inheritance, isn't it, what you get when they're gone? Whatever happens to you, you'll have this house, maybe some more off your dad when he goes. I'll get nothing. Well, unless my dad's actually really rich and suddenly remembers that he's got a son . . .'

He stopped and stared at Toby for a moment. Toby fiddled with the glass in his hand and waited for Con to continue. He wanted to talk about Ruby, it was blindingly obvious.

'I've met this girl,' he said eventually.

Toby nodded. Here it came.

'At work. And I'm trying to work out how posh she is.'

Toby blinked and tried not to show his surprise. 'Ah, I see. So, tell me what you know about her.'

'Well, she's about my age. She's a junior in the fashion department at *Vogue*, so she probably earns less than me. She's called Daisy and her sisters are called after flowers I've never heard of. She lives in Wandsworth with her sister and her boyfriend. He owns it. It's really small, apparently. And that's it. She talks posh and she looks posh. But she's comfortable around normal people, you know.'

'So, what's the problem? She sounds lovely.'

'I don't know,' he said. 'I think she's interested, but I don't want to blow it.'

'Well, what would you usually do if you liked someone?'

'I don't know.' Con shrugged. 'Just play it cool, I guess.'

'Right, so, that's exactly what you should do. Just because she's . . . *posh*, doesn't mean she's any different to other girls.'

'Yeah. Yeah. You're right. I should just be myself. Anyway, I'd better get on. See you later.' He sidled past Toby and into the living room.

Toby went back to his room, feeling slightly bemused but touched that Con had felt able to confide in him. The fact that Con was showing a serious interest in a girl gave Toby hope. Maybe Con was getting ready to move on. Maybe it wouldn't be so difficult to get him out of the house after all.

Toby smiled to himself as he sat at his computer and gazed across the street. The lights were off in Leah's front window. He wondered where she was. Maybe she was looking at another flat share. Or maybe she was on a date. He'd watched her coming and going from his bedroom for years without giving her a second thought. She had a boyfriend. Girls with boyfriends wore a kind of invisibility cloak. They didn't exist.

As he stared at her window he saw her. She was walking towards her front door. Her hair was in a ponytail and she was carrying two fat M&S carrier bags. She stopped outside her house and started feeling around in her handbag. Eventually she brought out a bunch of keys and headed to her front door. A light was activated by her presence and for a moment she was lit up like an actress on a stage. Her front door clicked open and she walked through it. And then, suddenly, she turned, as if someone had called her name, turned and looked straight up at Toby.

He almost ducked, but didn't. Instead he smiled at her and waved. She smiled, too. And she looked, for just one brief, fleeting and exhilarating second, like the most beautiful woman Toby had ever seen in his life. The thought brought a rush of simmering blood to his head. He gulped and turned his gaze back to his screen.

Ruby saw him coming home through her bedroom window. His hair was different—softer, less spiky, less manicured. It was the first time she'd seen him since Toby's birthday and her reaction took her by surprise. A jolt of excitement, a quiver of happiness. The boy she'd shared her home with for more than a year, the boy she'd seen as nothing more than a schoolboy with a job, had turned into a man.

She glanced at her reflection in the mirror. She looked fine. She'd thought about crying when she got back from the Wolseley, but changed her mind and decided to have a bath instead. She was glad now, as Ruby had a face that didn't recover very easily from the indignity of crying.

She smeared a little concealer underneath her eyes, then blobbed some translucent pink gloss onto her lips and went downstairs.

Con was in the kitchen, boiling the kettle. He jumped when he heard her come in behind him.

'Hello, stranger,' she said, pulling open the fridge.

'Hi,' he said, turning back towards the sink.

She pulled out a carton of mango and passion fruit juice and poured herself a glass. 'How are you?'

He nodded. 'I'm good. I'm fine. How are you?'

'Excellent,' she said. 'It's been a long day, but it's looking up now.' She smiled at him.

'Cup of tea?' he said.

'No, thanks.' She pulled out a chair and sat down. 'Can't believe I haven't seen you. It's weird.'

'What's weird?'

'You know—after what happened last week. I haven't been avoiding you, you know. I've just been busy.'

'Yeah,' he said, dropping a flattened tea bag into the bin, 'me, too.'

'Had a gig last night. Didn't get home till five.'

'God, you've got more energy than me. I can't do late nights any more.'

Ruby laughed. 'You're nineteen!'

'Yeah, I know. I'm a growing boy. I need my sleep.'

Ruby laughed again. She glanced at him. He looked as if he was about to leave the room. She stalled for time. 'I like your hair,' she said. 'Looks better without all that stuff on it.'

'You think?'

'Yeah, softer.' Ruby felt a wave of longing fall across her like a shadow. He was so new, so clean, so unformed. She wanted to touch him. 'What are you up to tonight?'

He shrugged. 'Waiting on a couple of calls. Probably heading out to meet some mates.'

'And if not . . . Any plan B?'

'No, not really. Probably just get a DVD and order some food in.'

'Is your mum in tonight?'

'No. She's meeting Zoë from work.'

'Right,' she said. 'So . . . maybe you should just knock your plans on the head. Maybe you should just . . . *stay in*.' She smiled as she said this and cocked her head to one side, but he didn't seem to be reading her.

'You reckon?' he said. 'Why's that?'

'Oh, I don't know. It's just, I'm in tonight. Your mum's out. Seems a shame not to, you know, make the most of it.'

'Oh,' he said, realisation finally dawning upon him. 'Oh, right. Yeah. I see what you're saying.'

'So,' she stood up and faced him. 'What do you reckon? I've got a DVD player in my room.'

'Christ. I mean'—he hooked his hand round the back of his neck—'I kind of promised my mates I'd see them tonight.'

'Oh,' she said, mentally untangling the past three minutes of conversation, trying to find the bit where he'd sounded ambivalent about going out. 'Sorry, it sounded as if you didn't have firm plans. It was just an option, that's all.'

'Yeah, yeah, I know.'

'It still is, if your mates blow you out.'

'Right. Thanks.'

Ruby touched his arm. She hadn't meant to, but she couldn't help herself. 'I'll be in my room,' she said, 'if you change your mind.' And then she moved her hand to his cheek. His skin felt like wax under her palm, cool and smooth and pliant. 'See you,' she said. She picked up her glass of juice and sauntered from the kitchen, feeling suddenly, horribly as if she was barking up the wrong tree.

Con pushed open the doors to the *Vogue* fashion department and tried to look cool, calm and collected.

Daisy was walking urgently towards him, a knitted bag slung diagonally across her chest, dressed in a grey coat and scarf.

'Oh, hi,' he said. 'Where're you going?'

She smiled at him, then grabbed his sleeve, pulling him out of the doorway and into the hall. 'I'm bunking off,' she whispered. 'I've just told them my aunt's dead.'

He raised his eyebrows at her.

'It's fine,' she said. 'I don't actually have an aunt, so I'm not hexing anyone. I just had to get out of there.'

Con had never skived off a day's work in his life and felt slightly shocked. 'So what are you going to do?'

'Haven't decided yet. Was thinking I might just go home.'

'Seems a waste,' he said.

'Hmmm.' She furrowed her eyebrows together. 'Maybe you're right. Maybe I should be more imaginative. I know what we should do.'

'We?'

'Yes. Let's go to Borough Market and buy loads of yummy food.'

'But I can't skive off.'

'Of course you can.'

'Well, what will I tell them?'

'Tell them your friend's really upset because her aunt's dead and you have to look after her.'

'What? No way. That's what girls do.'

'God, I don't know, then. Tell them you feel sick.'

Daisy rubbed some lip balm over his forehead and Con told his boss that he'd just thrown up. Five minutes later they scurried away together towards Oxford Circus, sniggering like the schoolchildren they'd only just ceased to be.

Borough Market was another world. Con had barely set foot in a supermarket in his life, let alone a food market. Con really wasn't a food person. He had very little interest in it beyond how cheap it was and how filling it was. It helped if it tasted good which was why he liked McDonald's. He knew it was crap, the stuff he put into his body, but he couldn't bring himself to care about it. Food was fuel, stomach lining, alcohol absorber—that was all.

But Daisy obviously thought differently.

She was dashing round this place, caressing jars of gooey brown onions and misshapen hunks of bread. She sniffed at wedges of pungent cheese and lumpy phalluses of cured meat.

'Do you like gravadlax?' she said at one point, pushing some hair out of her face with a fistful of carrier bags.

'Grava-what?'

'Gravadlax. It's salmon, cured with dill.'

'I don't know,' he said. 'What's it like?'

'It's a bit like smoked salmon,' she said, 'but not so salty.'

He shrugged. He'd heard of smoked salmon, but he'd never eaten it. 'I'm not really into fish,' he said.

Well,' she said decisively, handing over a five-pound note, 'then you'll like this. It's not really like fish. It's more like . . . *ham*.'

She bought huge cheese straws and slivers of rust-coloured salami, cylinders of chalky cheese and a box of large eggs the colour of clouds. Feeling guilty that Daisy was spending all her money on food that he probably wouldn't even like, Con slipped away to find a bottle of wine.

'What're you having it with?' said a man in a striped linen shirt.

'I don't know. There was some fish and some oysters and some olives and stuff.'

'Sounds good.' He smiled. 'How about a bottle of Pouilly-Fuissé?'

Con parted with a twenty-pound note with a gulp and took the tissue-wrapped bottle from the man. 'Make sure it's cold,' he said. 'But not too cold. OK?'

Daisy's house looked like a normal house, shrunk down. It had a door on the front, and two windows, and that was it. The front door opened directly into a tiny living room with a tiny sofa and an armchair in it. At the back was a kitchen built into a conservatory that gave onto a garden the size of a bus shelter. But it was all very smart, all very modern. Through the garden doors, Con could see a chrome patio heater and tropical plants in cobalt-blue pots.

'Nice house,' he said.

'Thank you,' she said. 'Small but perfectly formed.' She sounded slightly breathless and broke into a rattling cough.

'Are you OK?'

'What?' she said. 'Oh, the cough. It's nothing. Just a bit of a chesty thing.'

'Is that your sister?' He picked up a framed photo of a biscuity-blonde girl who looked like Daisy, but fatter.

'Yup, that's Mimi.' She dropped her carrier bags onto a small antique pine table in the kitchen and started unpacking them. 'And that's her boyfriend, James, sitting behind her.'

'They look nice,' he said, putting it back.

Daisy was now chopping lemons into quarters. The drizzle outside had turned into heavy rain and the glass of the built-on kitchen started to steam up. The table was starting to resemble one of the food stands at Borough Market. There was a silver tray piled high with crushed ice and murky oysters, dishes layered with meats and cheeses, and tumbling bunches of bloomy grapes. 'Have an olive,' said Daisy. 'They're delicious.' He peered into a bowl and considered what he saw. Olives, in his experience, were small, black, wrinkly and sat on top of pizzas. They were not dark green, the size of walnuts and swimming in khaki oil with red bits in. 'Nah,' he said, 'I'm not really into olives.'

She turned then and appraised him. 'Do you actually like *any* food?' she asked teasingly.

He shrugged. He'd been rumbled. 'I like some food. Just not . . .'

'Olives and fish?'

'Yeah.'

'But you like cheese?'

'Yeah, I don't mind cheese.' He smiled.

'And salami?'

'Yeah, I think so.'

'And bread?'

'I love bread.'

'What about bread with olives in it?'

'Hmmm . . .' He looked down. 'Maybe.'

She laughed. 'So—what do you eat, then? What's your favourite food?'

'McDonald's.'

'No!' Her eyes widened.

'Yeah. I love McDonald's. Really, really love it.'

'But apart from McDonald's. What else do you like?'

He looked up again. 'Curry, sometimes. Chinese. A good fry-up.'

'Oh God.' She placed her hands against her collarbones. 'This is fate! You've been sent to me for a reason. I have to re-educate your palate. Now, eat one of these olives immediately!' She slid it between his lips before he had a chance to protest and suddenly he found himself chewing on something with the texture of old prunes and the flavour of rancid dog food. He gagged on the thing, but kept chewing. His teeth hit something hard in the middle, like a bullet, but he kept chewing. Daisy stared at him expectantly. Eventually some other flavours started to break through—pepper, tuna, cheese, salt—and, by the time he finished chewing, he was on the cusp of enjoying it. He swallowed and beamed at Daisy triumphantly.

'Where's the stone?' said Daisy.

'What, the hard thing in the middle?'

'Yes, the hard thing in the middle.'

He shrugged. 'Swallowed it.'

She brought her hands to her mouth and stifled a laugh. 'You didn't?'

'Yeah,' he said. 'Wasn't I supposed to?'

'No. You're supposed to spit it out.'

'Oh shit. Is it bad for me?'

'No.' She shook her head, smiling. 'I don't think so. You might end up with an olive tree growing in there, though.' She pointed at his belly.

He glanced down, then up, and smiled. Well,' he said, 'I reckon if I can eat an olive stone and not notice, then I'll probably be all right with the rest of this stuff.' He gestured at the table. 'Bring it on.'

For the next two hours, Con did something he'd never done before. He dined. He feasted. He repasted. He lingered over his food. And even though not everything was to his liking (particularly the goat's cheese), he enjoyed the majority of it. But mainly what he enjoyed was sitting at a table, under opaque, steamy glass, drinking perfectly chilled white wine and listening to Daisy talk.

Everything about Daisy intoxicated him.

'Tell me something really interesting about yourself,' she said, pouring coffee from a cafetière into two white cups.

'Why?'

'Because there's something really mysterious about you and I want to know what it is.'

He nodded at her slowly. 'OK,' he said. 'Well, after my mum went off to Turkey last year, I lost the flat and had nowhere to live. So I slept on the street. In a shop doorway. For two weeks.'

'What—*you*?'

'Yes.'

'God, I just can't imagine that. You're so . . . *immaculate*.'

'Immaculate?'

'Yes, your hair and your clothes. Not a crease or a smudge. You smell of Persil. You look as if you've just stepped off the pages of a catalogue. I mean, how was it? Was it awful? Did you wash?'

'Yes, I washed.'

'Did you beg?'

He laughed again. 'No! I was still earning a salary! It was only for a fortnight.'

'God, though. How terrible.'

He shrugged again. 'So,' he said, 'what about you? Tell me something about yourself.'

'Hmmm,' she said. 'Are you sure you want to know? It's a total downer.'

'Yes,' he said, 'I want to know.'

'Well, there's this thing about me and I don't usually tell anyone about it, but I'm telling you because . . . I don't know. I've got this feeling about you . . .' She stopped for a second and glanced at him. 'There's this thing, this *condition*, with my lungs. They make too much of this mucousy stuff and I have to take all these pills and do all this massage so that my airways don't get blocked up. But I'm also more prone to infections and stuff. It basically turns you into a complete wuss, this condition. I once spent a week in hospital with a cold. All wired up. Life and death. Pathetic.'

Con stared at her for a moment, not knowing what to say.

'I told you it was a downer.'

'But you don't seem ill.'

'No. I don't feel ill. But then, I've had this all my life, so I don't really know what it's like to feel healthy.'

'What's it called, then, this condition?'

'It's called cystic fibrosis.'

'Oh, yeah, I've heard of that.'

'Well, who cares about a silly old condition anyway, frankly? Life is for living. And eating. And drinking. Talking of which,' she grinned, 'shall I open another bottle of wine?'

Con nodded and watched as she took a bottle from the fridge. Her smallness, her *translucence*, took on a new and unsettling significance in light of what she'd just told him. She wasn't a fairy or a nymph. She wasn't a Condé Nast flibbertigibbet. She was ill. Seriously ill.

Con took a deep breath and tried not to ask her if she was ever going to get better.

Ruby turned the last page of the *Barnet Times* and sighed. She just could not be arsed with applying for any of these stupid jobs. She did not want to be an office administrator for a charity. Nor did she want to be a sales assistant in a photography shop or a receptionist for a firm of accountants.

She wanted to be a singer/songwriter. That was all she'd ever wanted to be and while she'd had the security of Paul's monthly payments into her bank account she'd been able to fool herself that that was what she was. Now she was just unemployed and broke.

A Conran van had pulled up outside the house that afternoon and two blokes had started unloading things in boxes, things in bags. She watched them in amazement from her bedroom window, waiting for them to pull away before running downstairs. Toby was feverishly ripping parcel tape off packages in the hallway.

'What the fuck is all this stuff?'

'Just stuff,' he muttered. 'Things for the house.'

'Wow,' she said, picking up a leather wastepaper bin and examining the price tag with raised eyebrows. 'A ninety-five-pound bin.'

'It's quality. It'll last for ever.'

'And what's in that gigantic box?'

'Coffee table.'

'Ooh—let me see.'

'In a minute,' he said.

'This is like Christmas,' she said. 'Let me open something, will you?'

'No,' snapped Toby, pulling a clear Perspex globe out of a box.

'What is that?' She pointed at it, accusingly.

'What does it *look* like?'

'It's a plastic globe. But why?'

'Because . . . because . . . *I like it.* That's why.'

'Fair enough.' She sat back on her heels. 'So,' she started, 'this money from Gus. I thought we were talking a couple of grand, but look at all this stuff. What was it? Twenty? Thirty? A hundred?'

Toby tutted and glared at her. 'Ruby. Please. I've told you already. It's none of your business.'

'Well, actually, it is. It's my business because you're my friend. And it's my business because . . .' She drew in her breath and waited until she'd made eye contact with him. 'Because Paul just dumped me and he's stopped my allowance and I'm completely skint.'

'Paul? Paul Fox?'

'Yes. Paul Fox. He's marrying that old bat and doesn't think that married men should be subsidising young girls' lifestyles. Which is fair enough, I guess. And this money you've got . . . Gus's money . . . I'm just thinking that if there's enough for plastic globes and leather bins, there's probably enough for a loan?'

Ruby waited for Toby's face to soften. Toby had never let her down. Before she'd met Paul, he'd always let her off her rent, lent her a fiver here and there. And now he actually had some proper money, surely he'd spread a little her way?

He paused for a moment and Ruby watched as he chewed thoughtfully on the inside of his cheek. And then he turned to her and said, 'No.'

'What?'

'No. Sorry, Ruby, but no. You're thirty-one. Nearly thirty-two. You're a grown woman. It's time for you to, you know, look after yourself.'

'I'm not asking you to *look after* me,' she snapped. 'I'm asking you to lend me some money. Just until I get myself sorted out.'

'Yes, but that's the problem with you, Ruby. You won't sort yourself out. You'll never sort yourself out until you absolutely have to.'

'What does that mean?'

Toby sighed. 'I'm just saying that you've always had people round you to prop you up and maybe it would be good for you to, you know, take responsibility for yourself. Stand alone for a while.'

Ruby looked at him in amazement. 'Alone?'

'Yes.'

'Excuse me. Are you Toby Dobbs?'

'What?'

'You know, Mr Caring and Sharing, Mr My-Home-Is-Your-Home. Toby "No one should ever be alone" Dobbs?'

He tutted.

'What's happening to you, Toby? You used to be the most generous person I know.'

'Yes,' he muttered, 'well. Look where that's got me.'

Ruby sighed. She was wasting her time. 'Fine,' she said, 'whatever. I'll work something out.'

'Good.'

'Right.' She got halfway up the stairs, then remembered something. 'Tobes?'

'Yes?'

'I can't pay you any rent this month, you know?'

'That's fine.'

'Are you sure?'

'Yes. Just don't tell the others.' And then he turned to her and a small smile twitched the corner of his mouth and Ruby knew then that she still stood a good chance of persuading Toby to part with some of his money.

Chapter 4

A MAN CAME into the shop on Saturday morning. This was unusual in itself, unaccompanied as he was by a woman. Just a man. On his own.

He was a big man, about six foot one and broad across the back. He had very dark hair, thinning on top but thick elsewhere, probably about forty-five, maybe a well-preserved fifty. He was wearing a leather coat, jeans and slightly battered boat shoes. He was handsome, if you liked that kind of thing, which Leah didn't. He seemed to be taking a great interest in the furniture, particularly a small cream desk stencilled with faded amaryllis. He turned at her approach and smiled.

'How much is this desk?' he asked. He had an accent, very soft. She guessed at Italian.

'Three hundred and fifty pounds,' she said, smiling her best Pink Hummingbird smile. 'It has a matching stool'—she pointed behind her—'with an upholstered seat. And there's a range of filing boxes to complement it. Linen-covered,' she finished.

'Do you deliver?'

'Uh-huh.' She nodded. 'It's free within a three-mile radius.'

'How soon?'

'When would you like it?' she asked him.

'Immediately.'

'Monday morning?'

He beamed at her. 'This is exactly why I came here. Local shops. Personal service. Are you the owner?' he asked.

'No. I'm the manager.'

'Good,' he said, 'good. Maybe you could help me. I've just moved into the area, post-divorce, and I want to surprise my girls—I have two daughters, thirteen and fifteen years old. They'll be staying with me every other weekend and I want to give them bedrooms to die for. I want glitter, fluff, flowers, lights—all that stuff. Everything you can offer me. Do you offer a design service?'

'Well, no, but I am happy to make recommendations within a budget.'

'There is no budget.'

'Right, you mean . . .?'

'I mean, money is no object. In fact,' he lowered his voice, conspiratorially, 'I will give you five hundred pounds to choose the furniture. Choose the accessories. Come to my house. Arrange things. Five hundred pounds. Cash.'

Leah glanced around her to make sure that her assistant had not heard their conversation. Five hundred pounds. That meant that she could afford to stay in the flat for another month.

'OK,' she said. 'But I can only do furnishing. No decorating.'

'That's fine,' he said. 'The rooms are already decorated.'

'Great.' She beamed. 'What colour are they?'

'Pink.' He smiled at her.

'Perfect,' she said.

Leah stayed at work until ten o'clock that night. She ordered in a pizza and spent the night pretending to be the daughters of a wealthy Italian businessman. Jack had given her brief descriptions of his girls (Lottie: thirteen, clever, outgoing, into football and music; Lucie: fifteen, clever, shy, into reading and her boyfriend). 'They're no princesses, my girls, but I want their rooms to be fit for royalty,' Jack had said.

Leah picked out fluffy cushions, beanbags, mirrors, lamps and bedding. She ordered a pair of miniature chaises longues in bubblegum-pink velvet and two sleigh beds in cream and lilac. She ordered red Perspex bookshelves for Lucie, a huge disco glitter ball for Lottie's ceiling and enormous pastel-coloured sheepskin rugs for both of them.

The bill came to nearly £6,000. Leah gulped and hoped that Jack would approve. And then she folded her pizza box in half, disposed of it behind the shop, turned off all the lights and headed home.

Leah turned into Silversmith Road and glanced across at the Peacock House. The lights in Ruby's room and Con's room were switched off, but Toby was there, as ever, framed in his window, his face lit up by the glow of his computer screen. Leah felt a wave of warmth pass through her. He looked up from his monitor and saw Leah gazing up at him. She raised her hand to him and smiled. He waved back, then he stood up and indicated that she should wait there, that he was coming down. Eventually the front door opened and Toby appeared, dressed in a huge green sweater, black track-suit bottoms and lambskin slippers.

'Hello! Hello!' He pranced across the street in his furry slippers. Leah swallowed a smile.

'Hi!' she said.

'How are you?'

'I'm fine,' said Leah. 'You?'

'Yes, I'm fine, too. Look. I just wanted to say, I'm really sorry about the other night.'

'Oh, honestly, Toby, it's fine.'

'No, it's not. It must have been miserable for you. I have no idea what those two were thinking'—he indicated his house—'and I wasn't much fun myself. I just wanted to say, well, thank you for trying, I really appreciate it. But I've decided to give up the whole idea.'

'What?'

'Yes. I'm not going to sell the house. My father will just have to accept me the way I am.'

'But, Toby. I got the impression that this wasn't just about your father. I thought this was about *you*, about moving on, getting out of a rut.'

'Yes, well, it was. But, really, I've tried talking to those people and there's no way any of them are ready to leave yet. I mean, I can't even get a whole sentence out of Joanne. Con's saving up for flying lessons, which is just *amazing*, but it means that he really needs to stay in the house—and Melinda's not going anywhere without him. And as for Ruby—well, she's worse than ever, dumped by her boyfriend, sleeping with Con, begging me for handouts. She can't even afford to pay the rent. I've been trying to get quotes from builders, but they don't return my calls and, frankly, I'm starting to remember why I found myself in this rut in the first place. Because getting anything to change is just so unbelievably difficult.

'This is my rut.' He shrugged. 'I made it and now I have to lie in it. But thank you. Thank you for trying. You're a really nice person.' He smiled apologetically, then he turned and headed back towards his house.

Toby was listening to his crappy music. Con could hear it through his bedroom door. He didn't know what it was, but it wasn't modern.

He knocked firmly against the door, once, twice, three times, until Toby finally appeared. He was in a thigh-length stripy jumper and black drainpipe jeans, unwittingly fashionable.

'Hi, sorry to bother you.'

Toby smiled. 'No, not at all. I wasn't really doing anything, just, you know . . .' He trailed off, hooking his hand round the back of his neck.

'Can I ask you a favour?'

'Sure. D'you want to come in?'

'I need to borrow your computer.'

'Right, of course.'

'Except I don't know how to use them. Well, except the system at work. But I don't know how to use the Internet. Can you help me find something?'

'Of course, sure.'

Toby moved some paperwork, notepads and textbooks into one large pile, then pulled up a stool for Con to sit on.

'Is that all your poems and stuff?' asked Con.

Toby glanced at the pile. 'Well, sort of, I suppose. It's notes and ideas. I write my actual poetry straight onto my computer.'

'Right. And what sort of stuff do you write?'

Toby grimaced. 'Kind of . . . well, it's hard to say. It's all so different.'

'Yeah, but are they long poems, short poems? Do they rhyme?'

Toby smiled. 'No. They don't rhyme. And they're quite short. OK.' He placed his huge hand over the mouse and jiggled it. His computer came to life and he brought up Google. 'So, what is it you want to look up?'

'It's an illness. It's called cystic fibrosis.'

'Ah, right.'

He typed it in and hit a button. A big list came up on the screen. 'Now what was it that you wanted to know, exactly?'

'Well, shit, it's . . .' He ran a hand through his hair and stared at Toby. He may as well tell him. 'Remember that girl I was telling you about?'

'The girl at work? The posh one?'

'Yeah. Her. Well, I went to her place and she cooked for me and stuff. And then she told me that she's got this condition, this . . .'

'Cystic fibrosis.'

'Yeah. And it made sense because she's really little and delicate and her skin's kind of, you know, blue. And she's got this cough. But I didn't really want to ask her too much about it, you know? In case it made her feel like a freak. And I just want to know what it is. What it means. Like—is she really ill? Is she going to die? That kind of thing.'

'Fuck.' Toby sucked in his breath and ran a hand over his chin. 'Right, let's see what we can find.'

Con had known, even before Toby started clicking on his list and reading stuff out. He'd known it was bad. It had been obvious from the very first moment Daisy had mentioned it to him. She'd had that tone of voice, that tone of someone who knows they've drawn the short straw.

According to the Internet, Daisy's life was already difficult and uncomfortable. She needed daily physiotherapy to dislodge the mucus that built up in her lungs, she had to take drugs to help her body absorb nutrients, and drugs to help prevent lung infections. She needed to consume higher than average daily calories, but experienced poor weight gain and the chances of her carrying a child to full term were low.

She was also, apparently, quite likely to die in her thirties.

Con and Toby sat in a numb silence for a minute.

'God, Con, I'm really sorry,' Toby said.

'Yeah, it's bad, isn't it?'

'Quite bad, yes, but remember, medical breakthroughs happen every day. And she could last a lot longer than the average, even without a breakthrough.'

'No,' Con shook his head, 'it's bad. Whatever way you look at it. She can't have kids and even if she could she wouldn't be around to see them grow up. And you know, that must be why she lives with her sister. I bet her sister does all that chest shit for her every day. So she's, you know, reliant on other people, just to get out of the house in the mornings. Her life sucks.'

Toby sighed and touched Con's knee. 'Do you think *she* thinks her life sucks?'

Con shrugged. He thought about her enthusiasm for food, her love of her family, her passionate views about everything. She didn't *act* like someone who hated her life. She acted like someone who couldn't believe her luck. 'No,' he said, 'I don't think she does.'

'Well, then,' said Toby, 'best thing you can do is carry on as if you never saw any of this.' He indicated the screen. 'Best thing you can do is help her to enjoy her life.'

Toby gave Con a poem before he left. 'I wrote this on the morning of my mother's funeral,' he said. 'It might help you work out how you feel about Daisy.'

'I didn't know your mum was dead.'

'Yes, she died when I was thirteen. Breast cancer.'

'God, I'm sorry.'

'Yes, well . . .'

'It's funny, though. I've been living here for nearly a year and I never knew your mum was dead. You don't talk much really, do you?'

'No,' said Toby, 'no. I don't suppose I do.'

Con closed his bedroom door behind him, kicked off his trainers and sat down on his mattress, crosslegged. And then he read Toby's poem:

Young
I saw you yesterday.
You wore an old lady's nightdress, it wasn't yours.
You were young.
I saw you the day before.
You wanted to dance, but you couldn't get out of bed.
You were young.
Young. And beautiful.
Soon it will be winter.
I will be older. You will be young.
I'll look in the mirror, see a grey hair.
A boy will call to me in the street,
Hey! Old man!
Still, you will be young.
Young and beautiful.
For all your days.

Con folded up the poem, slid it onto his bedside table and cried for the first time since his grandmother's funeral.

Giacomo Caruso's house was the nicest house Leah had ever seen. It was an Arts and Crafts mansion on the best street in Muswell Hill, with a hallway the size of Leah's living room. All the rooms were wood panelled, the windows were stained glass, and outside, in the manicured garden, there was a swimming pool. With a pool bar.

Jack poured her a glass of iced water from the filtered-water dispenser in his huge stainless-steel fridge and let her wander round while the Pink Hummingbird delivery boys unloaded the van. Downstairs there were two living rooms, a billiards room, a study, a dining room and a luxury kitchen–diner built into a huge conservatory at the back.

Upstairs were four bedrooms and five bathrooms. Leah didn't like to ask what the fifth one was for. She complimented Jack on his impeccable taste. He brushed away the compliment by informing her that he'd bought the house fully furnished.

'So, what do you do?' she asked him, perching herself on a Perspex barstool in the kitchen.

'Textiles,' he said. 'I make fabric. Silk, organza, tulle, chiffon.'

'Lovely.'

'Yes. It is. But now I am retired. I still own the mills, but I don't have to look at them any more.'

'Are they in Italy, your mills?'

'Yes. Near the lakes. I still have a home there, but I use it now only for holidays.' He sighed. 'I love England. But I wouldn't choose to live here. I live here for my girls. And I live here because I cannot resist English women!'

Leah laughed.

'I came to London when I was twenty-one, I met a girl called Jenny, I fell in love. And that was it. My first wife was English—Elaine. Beautiful girl. Peaches and cream. The marriage lasted only a year, but by then I was addicted. And then there was Paula, my ex-wife, the girls' mother. Blonde hair, blue eyes, big bum. I love English bums. So, I am destined to be here for ever. For the love of my children and for my love of English bottoms!'

Leah laughed again, suddenly feeling conscious of her blonde hair, blue eyes and size fourteen jeans. 'How long have you been divorced?'

'A year. I've been living in a rented flat, in Hampstead, searching and searching every day for my perfect castle! I wanted something quintessentially English and this'—he gestured at his home—'is it. Now,' he sighed, 'I just need to find my queen.'

The boys finished unloading the van and Leah went upstairs, where she spent two hours arranging cushions, throws and picture frames, plugging in fairy lights and hanging mirrors. She dressed the sleigh beds with pastel polka-dot bedding and hung the windows with swaths of lilac dupion. It was starting to get dark when Jack came upstairs to see how she was getting on. The rooms looked beautiful, fairy lights twinkling in the dusk.

'Perfect.' He beamed. 'Absolutely perfect.' And then he started crying.

Leah looked at him with alarm.

'I'm sorry,' he said. 'I'm still very emotional. I didn't want it to be like this. I didn't want to live apart from my wife, my children. I didn't want to be a weekend father.' He sniffed, loudly. 'I wasn't meant to be alone. I'm not designed for it. But this'—he gestured at Lottie's room—'so beautiful. So perfect. She will love it. Both of them will. Thank you!' And then he threw his arms round her and squeezed her to him. 'Here,' he said, 'why don't you stay? I'll cook you dinner. What do you like to eat? Fish? I have some beautiful fresh tuna in the fridge. Tuna and capers? Or a salade niçoise?'

'Oh, I'd love to, I really would,' Leah lied. 'But I have to go back to the shop, cash up, lock up.'

'Ah, well. Maybe another time, then. But for now'—he pulled an envelope out of his back pocket and handed it to her—'for you.'

She smiled and took the envelope. It was satisfyingly plump. 'Thank you,' she said.

'And any time'—he led her to the front door—'you're passing, you have my card, phone me. If I'm in, come over. I'll cook for you.'

Con made sandwiches for Daisy on Wednesday morning, using slices of Toby's homemade bread. Toby let him use some of his stuff to make the sandwiches—a bag of lettuce and a packet of smoked salmon. He put some green leaves in called rocket, which looked more like weeds than salad, but Toby said it was really good stuff. And then he doused the whole lot in black pepper and fresh lemon juice. Toby helped him with the whole thing, wrapped them up for him in white paper napkins, put them in a plastic bag.

'Get some freshly squeezed orange juice, too,' he suggested as he handed over the sandwiches.

'What, the stuff with all the bits in?' Con grimaced.

'Well, yes, but you can get it without bits in it, too. It's called smooth.'

Con smiled and left for work.

Daisy and Con were having lunch on a bench in Green Park. It was eight degrees, but the sun was strong. Daisy took another bite of her sandwich and smiled. 'This is absolutely delicious. Did you really make it yourself?'

'Uh-huh.' He swallowed a mouthful and nodded.

'I am seriously impressed. Where did you get the bread from?'

'Toby made it.'

'Is this Toby the poet?'

'Yeah. He bakes a loaf of bread every day.'

'Really? That's so sweet! So, what's he like, this Toby? Is he broodingly handsome and mysterious?'

Con laughed. 'Er, no. Not really. He's kind of . . . he's very big. Tall. Big hands. Big feet. Big nose. And sort of scruffy. Mad hair, big sideburns. He's really shy, and really clever. I kind of like him.'

'And is he a successful poet?'

Con laughed again. 'Not that I know of.'

A pair of joggers ran past them, a man and a woman in matching Lycra suits. Con finished his sandwich and tucked his screwed-up paper napkin into the plastic bag. He glanced at Daisy's hands. Long fingers, a single ring in the shape of a daisy, blue veins, a smudge of butter. He reached over and took hold of one. She squeezed his hand back and smiled at him.

'I'm really touched,' she said, breaking the silence, 'that you went to all this trouble with the sandwiches.'

'It was nothing,' he said, rubbing the tip of his thumb back and forth across her fingernails. 'In fact,' he said, smiling. 'I'd go so far as to say that it was a pleasure.'

'You mean you enjoyed cooking something that didn't involve a kettle or a microwave.'

'Well, I wouldn't call it cooking, but it was, you know, fun. I liked it.'

'Well, then,' said Daisy, 'in that case, I present you with a challenge, Connor McNulty.'

'Oh, yeah?'

'Yeah. How about you invite me over for dinner at yours?'

'Dinner?'

'Yes. Dinner. With a starter, a main course and a pudding. And wine.'

'Are you serious?'

'Deadly.'

'But my house. It's full of . . . *weird* people.'

'I like weird people.' She smiled.

'And it's one thing knocking together a sandwich, but a whole meal . . . I might poison you.'

'You'll be fine. I've got faith in you.'

'You have?'

'Yeah. Definitely. You're one of those people, I reckon, one of those people who'd be good at anything they put their mind to.'

He shook his head and laughed. 'So how come I only got two GCSEs, then? And what am I doing working in a post room?'

'You're only nineteen. You were homeless, for God's sake. And your grandma died. Just you wait. One day you'll be flying that private jet across the Caribbean Sea. But, oooh, wait, no, you won't just be the pilot. You'll be the *owner.* There'll be a beautiful woman by your side drinking champagne and you'll fly over your sprawling beachside estate, and you'll think to yourself, I used to live in a house full of weirdoes in Finchley and spent my days wheeling bitchy women's letters round a big building. And you'll smile, and the beautiful girl will smile, and you'll remember me saying this to you. You really will.' She gripped his hand tightly in hers. 'Give yourself a chance. You're special, Con, really special. And your life's only just beginning.'

Con gulped. Only nineteen.

Daisy was only eighteen, but she was already two-thirds of the way through her life; halfway if she was lucky.

'You'll be that girl, though? The girl on the plane. That'll be you, right?'

She smiled. But she didn't reply.

'Joanne!' Leah cried. 'Hi!'

Joanne was wearing a black leather coat, black lacy-knit tights and black ankle boots with furry bobbles hanging off them. Her hair was black and held back with diamanté cherries. She was wearing red lipstick and black eyeliner, and looked like Juliette Binoche on a very bad day.

'I hope you don't mind me accosting you on the street like this, but I've been meaning to talk to you about something.'

Joanne narrowed her eyes at Leah. 'Sorry,' she said, 'but who are you and how do you know my name?'

Leah looked at her in surprise. Surely she must have noticed her at least once during the past two years? 'Er, I'm Leah? Toby's friend? I live there.' She pointed at her front door. 'Just over the road from you.'

'Oh,' said Joanne, 'I see.'

'And the reason I wanted to talk to you is, and I know this might sound a bit strange, but I've noticed that you take great care over your appearance . . . always wearing different clothes, different hair. I mean, I'm just lazy when it comes to clothes and make-up. Jeans, boots, bit of mascara—that's as far as I go. I haven't changed my image for years. And that's what I wanted to talk to you about. I run a gift shop in Muswell Hill, the Pink Hummingbird?'

'Oh, yes.' Joanne nodded. 'I know it.'

'Well, we're having a special open evening, on Friday night, to celebrate the launch of a new cosmetics range.' She pulled a piece of pink card out of her pocket and handed it over. 'It's all a hundred per cent organic, imported from California. We're going to be one of the first London stockists. The company are sending us over one of their make-up artists and they'll be doing free make-overs, free wine, snacks and stuff. I'm only allowed to invite a handful of guests and I just thought it seemed like the sort of thing you might enjoy?'

Joanne turned the card over and squinted at it. 'When did you say this was?'

'Friday night. Six thirty to nine.'

'Hmmm.' Joanne turned it over again. 'I don't know.'

Well,' Leah said, 'if you can't make it, please let me know. Numbers are tight and I'd like to pass your invitation on to someone else if you're not going to come.'

'No,' she said, slipping the card into her bag. 'I'll come.'

'Excellent.' Leah beamed. 'I'm really glad. It's going to be such a lovely evening. You'll love it.'

And then something remarkable happened—Joanne smiled. 'I look forward to it,' she said. 'Thank you for inviting me.'

Joanne was the first guest to arrive at the Pink Hummingbird on Friday night. She was wearing her black leather coat over a black jersey dress and bottle-green shoes with leather laces that crisscrossed up her ankles. Her hair looked as if she'd used crimpers on it and she was wearing bottle-green eye shadow. Leah removed her coat and put it in the stockroom. 'I'm so glad you came,' she said, handing her a glass of white wine. 'Did you come straight from work?'

Joanne nodded distractedly and gulped a mouthful of wine. Her eyes swivelled round the shop, taking in the detail—the lamps, the silk flowers, the mirrors.

'Where do you work?' asked Leah. 'In town?'

'Yes,' said Joanne. 'Where's the make-up?'

Leah started, shocked by her brusque manner. 'Erm, it's through there, in the back room. But they're not quite ready yet.'

Joanne glanced at her watch. 'I thought you said six thirty? It's six thirty-two.'

'Yes, I know. They won't be long. Just another minute or two. So, what do you do, Joanne?'

Joanne sighed. 'I'm an actress,' she said.

'Oh, wow! Really? Like a real proper actress?'

'Yes, well, I trained at the Central School of Speech and Drama.'

'Wow. So, have you been in anything I'd have heard of, like a movie?'

'No. I shouldn't think so. I mostly do stage work.'

'So is that what you're doing at the moment? In town?'

Joanne shook her head. 'No. I'm working on something else at the moment. There are some nice things in here.'

Leah was finding it hard to keep up with the abrupt conversational leaps Joanne kept making. 'Oh,' she said, 'yes. It's very feminine.'

'Yes,' said Joanne. 'I like those camisole tops.' She pointed at some rose-pink pointelle jersey underwear with silk ribbon trim.

'Lovely, aren't they? Come with matching knickers and trousers.'

'Mmmm.' Joanne smiled. 'Do you have any other clothes?'

'No. Not really. Just a bit of lingerie, some hats, some slippers.'

'Oh.' She looked mildly disappointed.

'You're really into clothes, aren't you?'

Joanne smiled again. 'Clothes, to me, are like paint to an artist or words to a writer.'

'I've noticed,' said Leah, choosing her words carefully, 'that you're quite experimental with clothes.'

'Yes,' said Joanne. 'I am.' She'd finished her wine. Leah poured her another glass. She could see Joanne was getting fidgety.

'Let me just see how they're getting on back there.'

Clarice and Maya from Santa Monica were set up and waiting, brushes at the ready. The doorbell rang. Leah let in a gaggle of Muswell Hill yummy mummies in designer jeans and Joseph Shearling coats, then went to find Joanne. She was admiring a pair of ivory silk slippers with pink embroidered butterflies on them. 'Cute,' she said, putting them down.

'Gorgeous, aren't they? Anyway—the make-up artists are ready at the back. Do you want to come through?'

Joanne seemed rapturously interested in every detail of the blînk organic cosmetic range. Leah watched as Clarice stripped Joanne's face of make-up, with pads of cotton wool and a liquid cleanser infused with green tea. She then gave Joanne's face a gentle massage with something called 'angel oil'. Devoid of make-up, Joanne looked young but tired.

Leah waited at the front of the shop for Joanne to emerge from her make-over.

'Wow,' said Leah. 'You look really beautiful.'

And she did. Without her own heavy-handed approach to make-up, she looked soft and pretty and warm. 'Are you happy with it?'

'Yes,' said Joanne. 'I am. Well, thank you for inviting me. I've had a very nice night.'

'Oh, you're not going already, are you?'

'Yes.'

'But what about those silk slippers? Did you want to get a pair of those? I can give you them at a discount. Twenty per cent off?'

Joanne turned to look at the slippers. 'Hmmm. How much are they?'

'Twenty pounds. Sixteen with the discount.'

'What about that jersey camisole?'

'Yup. That's thirty-nine pounds ninety-nine. I can let you have it for thirty-two pounds?'

'OK,' Joanne said, swinging her handbag round onto the cash desk. 'Do you take Switch?'

Leah sent her assistant to collect the slippers and the camisole, and hoped that she would be as slow as she usually was. 'So,' she said, to the side of Joanne's head, 'are you going home now? Back to Toby's?'

She turned to face her. 'Yes.'

'He's lovely, isn't he, Toby?'

She threw Leah a strange look. 'Yes,' she said, 'I suppose so.'

'And that house is amazing.'

'Yes. Rather poorly maintained, though.' She turned impatiently to see what the shop assistant was doing.

'What's it like living with all those people?'

'All which people?'

'The people? In Toby's house?'

Joanne shrugged. 'It's fine.'

'Really? It's just, I've just split up with my boyfriend and now I've got to move out of our flat and I've been looking at all these flat shares and the thought of having to share with people I don't know is just awful. How do you do it?'

'I ignore everyone. I pretend they're not there.'

Leah looked at her in amazement, then she laughed. And then, amazingly, so did Joanne. 'I know,' she said, 'it's not very nice. But if I actually acknowledged their existence I'd go insane.'

'So, will you be moving out soon?'

The assistant arrived with the slippers and went off to find the camisole top.

'No. Sadly not.'

'No lovely man in the background who you're secretly dying to move in with?'

'No.'

'Shame.'

'Not really.'

'Ah,' said Leah. 'Fair enough. I'm starting to feel a bit the same myself,' she said, taking the top from the assistant. 'I thought my future was in the bag, but suddenly I'm thirty-five and I've got to start again. It does make you feel a bit . . . *lost*. You know.'

Joanne pursed her lips. 'There are worse things,' she said, 'than splitting up with someone.'

'Oh,' said Leah, 'right, yes. I suppose there are.'

Leah took Joanne's card and swiped it through the terminal. 'Did you split up with someone? Is that how you ended up in Toby's house?'

'No.' She tapped her pin number into the terminal. 'Not really.'

'Not really?'

'Life is episodic. A certain passage of my life had come to a close. It was time to move on.'

'That's one way of looking at it, I suppose.'

'It's the *only* way of looking at it.' She gave the terminal back to Leah.

'But even if you believe that life is episodic, surely there's a continuity between chapters?'

'Not necessarily. I'm the heroine of my story. I can go where I like and never meet the same person twice.'

'Like a road movie.'

'Yes, I suppose—like a road movie.'

Leah placed Joanne's slippers and camisole in a carrier bag and handed it to her across the cash desk. 'Ah,' she said, 'but the whole deal with a road movie is that the protagonist is either running away from something or in search of something.'

'And who says I'm not?'

'Running away? Or looking for something?'

'Both.'

They were just reaching the kernel of the conversation and Leah had run out of excuses to keep Joanne in the shop. Her next question had to be a bull's-eye.

'And how far along the road are you?'

Joanne smiled. 'About halfway,' she said.

'Ah,' said Leah. 'The hardest place to be.'

'Indeed,' said Joanne. And then she turned and left, cutting a swath through the chattering womenfolk of Muswell Hill like a small but very sharp knife.

Toby and Con were in the kitchen together. Toby was stuffing hunks of Greek cheese into raw chicken breasts and Con was wrapping them up in filmy slivers of Parma ham. In the oven was a tray of miniature new potatoes and garlic cloves, slathered in olive oil and strewn with pine nuts and rosemary. Some tenderstem broccoli sat in a steamer basket on the work surface and in the fridge there was a pot of homemade tuna pâté, which they would have with some pumpkin-and-sunflower-seed bread rolls that Toby had baked specially this afternoon.

'Thanks,' Con said to Toby. 'Thanks for all of this.' And then, quite unexpectedly, he found himself giving Toby a hug. Not a bear hug, but a sort of clasp.

'You're welcome. It's nice to have an excuse, you know, to do some proper cooking. It never seems worth it just for me. Anyway—I hope you both have a great night. And you shouldn't be disturbed. I happen to know that Joanne's out tonight and I don't suppose Ruby will be around, not on a Friday.'

Toby went upstairs and Con checked the time. Seven twenty-five. He heard the front door go and jumped. And then he held his breath, hoping that whoever it was would just go about their business and not wonder why there was music coming from the dining room and the smell of baked rosemary coming from the kitchen.

Footsteps creaked across the hallway floor towards the kitchen, then they stopped. Slowly the door opened and there was Ruby. Con exhaled.

'What the . . .?' Ruby looked around the dimly lit room in wonderment. 'What the fuck is going on here?'

Con sighed. 'Just dinner,' he said.

'Who for?'

'For me,' he said, 'and a friend.'

'A friend, eh?' She smirked, sat down and pulled a packet of cigarettes from her handbag.

'No!' he said. 'Don't.'

'Don't what?'

'Don't smoke in here. In fact, don't smoke anywhere tonight.'

'Er . . . excuse me?'

'My friend. She's not very well. She's got a lung thing, condition. So please don't smoke.'

'Oh my God, have I walked into some parallel universe? Spooky old music, candlelight, ill girlfriends.'

'Just don't smoke, that's all. Please.'

Ruby nodded tersely, once, and put the cigarettes back in her bag. 'Just for you,' she said, 'just this once. So—who's the lucky girl?'

'She's no one,' said Con. 'Just a girl.' He watched the clock on the TV click from 7:29 to 7:30. 'Look, Ruby,' he said, 'I'm not being funny or anything, but she's going to be here in a minute and I kind of made out we'd have the house to ourselves tonight. So . . .'

'You want me to fuck off?'

'Yeah, well. Yeah.'

She sighed and stood up. 'Fair enough,' she said, 'but don't expect me to lock myself away in my room all night, OK?'

She picked up her bag and turned to leave the room.

'What's she got then, this girl? Asthma or something?'

'Yes,' Con said, nodding. 'She's got asthma.' Then the doorbell rang.

Ruby could hear them chatting through the gaps between her floorboards. She couldn't distinguish any words, just a symphonic series of bass rumbles, mid-tone gurgles and the occasional cymbal crash of laughter. As far as she could ascertain there hadn't been an awkward silence yet, and Con's 'friend' had been here for nearly two hours.

She headed downstairs, her third spurious visit to the kitchen of the evening. She'd caught only a fleeting glimpse of the girl as Con had ushered her through the front door and straight into the dining room. She was very small, thinner than Ruby, with that sort of very fine, very blonde hair that Ruby thought of as 'chalet girl' hair. She got a whiff of flowery perfume and a flash of silver ballet pump and crocheted shawl.

She poured herself a glass of water and picked at some leftover bread and pâté. Con and the girl were talking about someone called Nigel and laughing a lot. Ruby wanted to light up a cigarette and blow smoke through the keyhole, straight at the back of the girl's head.

The sound of a chair being scraped across the wooden floor next door disturbed her train of thought. 'No, leave those,' she heard Con saying.

'No, no, no,' said the girl. 'Let me. You've done everything.'

Before Ruby could think about whether to stay or leave, the girl was standing in front of her, carrying a pile of dirty plates.

'Oh,' she said, 'hello.'

'Hi.' Ruby took a second to consider her own appearance. She was in jeans and a grey T-shirt, hair moderately clean, face moderately made up, drinking a glass of water and minding her own business. She smiled. 'I'm Ruby,' she said.

'Oh, hi. Yes. Con's mentioned you.' She put down her pile of plates and offered Ruby her hand to shake. 'I'm Daisy.'

Daisy. Yes, she would be a Daisy.

She was pretty, in that undefined way that these sorts of girls often were. Small, straight nose, fine eyebrows, little chin. Pretty enough, thought Ruby, but not as good-looking as her. And she looked painfully young, younger, possibly, than Con himself.

'Nice to meet you,' she said, her eyes taking in the rest of her. Fitted cream blouse, grey woollen shorts to just below her knee, a strange necklace with leathery things hanging off it. Kind of a mess, but she carried it off. So,' she said, 'you work with Con?'

'Yes. I'm at *Vogue*.'

'Ah.' Ruby nodded. Of course. A fashion girl. 'And I believe he cooked for you. How was it?'

'Delicious,' Daisy said, smiling. She had slightly crooked teeth, but they suited her.

'Really?' Ruby grimaced. 'Are you sure?'

'Honestly! I promise. I'm so impressed with him. Considering when I first met him he wouldn't eat anything except McDonald's.'

'Oh, yes. His beloved McMeals.'

'I know! He's my project. I'm determined to get him to eat healthily.'

'Well, sounds like you're doing a pretty good job already.'

'Con tells me you're a singer?'

'Yes. That's right.'

'What sort of singer are you?'

'Oh, you know, kind of rocky, bluesy, soully. Depends what kind of mood I'm in, really.'

'That must be amazing. Getting up on stage and singing in front of all those people. How do you do it?'

'Vodka,' said Ruby, suddenly feeling the need to embellish her rock-chick credentials. 'Lots of it. I never go on stage sober.'

'God, I don't blame you.'

Daisy stooped to scrape some leftovers into the bin.

'So, Daisy. How old are you?'

'Nineteen,' she said, 'well, nearly. It's my birthday in February.'

'God. I can't imagine I was ever that young.'

'Well, surely you're not that much older than me?'

'I'm thirty-one,' she said, bracing herself for the customary blast of disbelief.

'No!' said Daisy, right on cue. 'I thought you were much younger.'

The door opened, then, and Con appeared. He looked at Daisy, then at Ruby. A coldness passed across his face. 'Oh,' he said, 'I didn't realise you were down here.'

'Just came down for a glass of water.'

'Right.'

'Me and Daisy have been chatting.'

'Right,' he said again.

'I hear your cooking skills are quite impressive?'

He shrugged. 'Well, yeah. Toby helped. But it was pretty good.'

'Wow. You'll have to cook something for me sometime.'

'Yeah. Right. Anyway, we're going back now.' He put a hand gently round Daisy's waist to guide her towards him. Ruby felt something bitter and acidic rise up in the back of her throat.

'Nice to meet you,' said Daisy.

'Yes,' said Ruby, 'likewise.'

The door began to close behind them. 'Have fun,' she called after them. But they didn't hear. Ruby listened at the door to see if they were talking about her, but the conversation passed seamlessly back to themselves, as if the encounter with Ruby had never happened. She saw Con's hand on Daisy's back like an imprint left on her retina by a flash of light. She heard them laughing together—Con's rough estuary snigger, Daisy's crystalline Chelsea chime.

She caught sight of her reflection in the blackened glass of the kitchen window and stopped for a moment. Who was she? What was happening to her? She had now been rejected twice in a fortnight, in both instances for someone diametrically different to her. It wasn't as if she wanted commitment; it wasn't as if she was making any demands beyond sex and a bit of a laugh. What was wrong with men today? What did they want with flat-chested asthmatic girls and forty-two-year-old divorcées with stretch marks?

Ruby poured herself a large glass of Melinda's vodka and took it to her bedroom, 'accidentally' spilling some on Daisy's shawl on the way.

Con stared at a spray of Daisy's hair that had fallen across her cheek. He'd been resisting the temptation to move it for the past ten minutes, concerned that he might wake her. She started to stir and Con quickly rearranged himself, to look a little less like he'd been staring at her while she slept.

She looked around the room as her eyes opened.

'Morning,' Con said.

She turned and smiled. 'Morning.' She pushed herself up onto her elbow and looked at him. 'God, you're handsome in the mornings.'

He blushed. 'Thanks,' he said. 'You look pretty good yourself.'

'I doubt it,' she said, pulling her hair away from her face. 'Mornings are not my best time of day. What time is it, anyway?'

He glanced at his radio alarm. 'Nine fifteen.'

'Oh God, I'd better get going.'

'Really?'

'Yeah. Chest stuff.' She tapped her collarbone and began to cough. 'Sorry,' she said, turning away from him. 'Mornings are worst. Mimi usually gets to work on me first thing. In fact, I'd better call her, let her know I'm on my way back.' She pulled her handbag towards her, coughed again as she pulled her mobile from her bag. Her breathing was becoming laboured and heavy.

She spoke to her sister. Con could hear the concern in Mimi's voice from the other end of the line. It was clear that Daisy didn't do this sort of thing very often. 'It's not that late!' protested Daisy. 'Yes. I'm leaving now. I don't know. The Tube. OK, then, a cab. Look, Meems, I'm really sorry, OK? I didn't realise you were going out today. I'll be there as soon as possible. I'll call you when I'm in a cab.' She switched off her phone and smiled apologetically. 'Not impressed,' she said.

'I could tell.'

'I don't blame her. It's a real bind for her, you know, having to do my physio every morning. It's not fun and it means she can't do anything spontaneous. She always has to think about me. I should have told her I wasn't coming home last night. That was selfish of me.'

'The physio,' he said, 'what your sister does for you? Is it difficult? I mean, could someone else do it for you?'

She shrugged. 'I suppose so. It's just lots of hitting me on the back, hitting me on the chest, moving me round in different positions.'

'Could *I* do it for you?'

Daisy turned and gazed at him.

'That way you wouldn't have to rush off. That way you could stay. If you wanted.' He gulped.

She smiled and brought the crown of his head to her lips. She kissed his head deeply. Con could hear the machinations of her broken lungs through her rib cage. 'You are so lovely, Connor McNulty. I knew you were, the first time I saw you. But it's not that simple. Mimi would have to show you what to do. And besides,' she said, 'it's a bit like going to the loo with the door open, isn't it? Not very romantic.'

Leah pulled open the Yellow Pages and flicked through it until she found the number for the Central School of Speech and Drama. She dialled the number and spoke to three different people before she was finally put through to someone who was able to help her.

'I'm looking for information,' she said, 'about an ex-alumnus. Her name is Joanne Fish.'

'What exactly did you want to know?'

'Well, I'm a casting assistant and we're thinking of calling her in for an audition, but we wanted a bit of background on her first. So, you know, anything really, anything you're allowed to tell me.'

'That would really depend on how much information she let us have, and whether she kept in touch. Hold on and I'll see if I can find her file,' she said.

Leah stared through the window while she waited, feeling her heart racing under her rib cage with the excitement of lying.

'Right,' said the woman on the other end of the line, 'I've got her file. Let's have a look. Aah, yes, well, she graduated in 1993.'

'What about marital status, family? Any information like that?'

'No, but her emergency contact is given as a man called Nicholas Sturgess.'

'Oh, great, do you have a telephone number for him?'

'Well, yes, but bear in mind this is out-of-date information. The number still has the old code.'

'Can I have it?'

'I don't see why not. The number is 081 334 9090.'

'Great, thank you. Anything else?'

'No,' said the woman. 'There's no record of any work after graduation, though that could be because she didn't stay in touch. But, ahm, she does seem to have given us some information about, well, I hope this doesn't have a negative impact on your casting decisions, but according to my records she got her first acting qualification at, er, Holloway.'

'Holloway?'

'Yes, Her Majesty's prison.'

'She was in prison?'

'Well, yes, it would appear so. She took a foundation course there, in acting. I assume that that must have been while she was incarcerated.'

'God, does it say what she was in for?'

'No. That's all it says. Gosh, how fascinating.'

'Yes,' said Leah, 'that really, really is. Thank you so much. You've been incredibly helpful.'

Chapter 5

DAMIAN RIDGELEY WAS a medium-sized man, about thirty years old, with hair the colour of Lucozade and a grey French Connection T-shirt on. He wore a ring on his wedding finger and a chain round his neck. He was standing on Toby's doorstep, but Toby had no idea why.

'Leah sent me,' he said.

'Leah?'

'Yes, you know, Leah. From over the road. She said you had a job for me.'

'She did?'

'Yes. Didn't she tell you?'

'Well, no. But then I haven't seen her for a few days.'

'Well,' he said, 'do you? Have a job?'

'Well, that depends, really. What sort of job are you qualified to do?'

'I'm a project manager. I renovate old houses.'

'And you're a friend of Leah's?'

'I'm her second cousin. Or her half-cousin. Or something like that.'

'Oh, I see. Right, well, then, why don't you come in?'

Damian perched himself on the edge of one of the Conran sofas a few moments later and sipped a cup of peppermint tea (Toby liked that he'd asked for peppermint tea).

'So,' he said. 'What do you think? Is it the sort of job you'd want to take on?'

Damian nodded, slowly. 'Yeah,' he said. 'Sure. There's no restructuring, no building work. I mean, essentially you're just looking for a face-lift, yeah?'

'Yeah.'

'Cool.' He pulled a notebook and an expensive-looking pen from the inside pocket of his denim jacket and made some notes. 'I've just had a cancellation, so I've got some guys at a loose end. I could get some people in next week. When are the bathrooms and kitchen coming?'

'Well, I haven't actually bought them yet.'

'Cool. No worries. We can crack on with the plumbing, the roof. Get on with the kitchen and stuff once you've chosen them. I can get you what you want at trade if you'd like.'

'You can?'

'Sure. You go shopping, tell me what you want and I'll get it for you. I can get you your white goods, too. Whatever it is you need, just let me know. I'll charge you for my time, but it'll still work out much cheaper.'

'That would be great. I seem to have got into a bit of a habit of overspending on things for the house, so it would great to save a bit of money.'

'Make up for the extra you'll be spending on me, then.' Damian smiled and Toby breathed a sigh of relief. Damian was obviously a true professional.

'Will you require a deposit? Something up front before you start?'

'I'll put a quote together, put it through your door later on today. If you approve, I'll let you have a schedule of works. Once the boys are in and we're all happy, I'll ask for twenty per cent of the invoice. Total payable at the end of the project. Simple. Easy. No room for complications. Just how I like it.'

Toby took Damian's hand at the door a few minutes later and shook it warmly. Then he went upstairs and slowly, deliberately and, he hoped, not prematurely, ran a line through items 4, 5 and 6 on his to-do list.

Toby saw Leah come back a few hours later. He gave her half an hour to make herself at home, get into her pyjamas, do whatever it was she usually did when she got in from work, then he headed downstairs.

He felt a sudden surge of nerves as he stepped across the road to Leah's house and stood outside her front door for a full five minutes, trying to work up the courage to ring on her doorbell, but she looked happy to see him when she came to the door. She was wearing faded jeans and a black cashmere sweater. Her hair was down and she was wearing glasses.

She took them off as she led him inside and placed them on top of an open paperback. He tried to see what book she was reading, but didn't recognise the name of the author.

'I'm so glad you came over,' she said, hooking a strand of blonde hair behind her ear. 'I've been meaning to come and see you, actually, but then I see you up there, in your window, and you always seem so *engrossed*. I hate the thought that I might accidentally disturb you in the middle of writing a poem and ruin the whole thing.'

'Oh, no, you must never worry about that. I am eminently disturbable, I can assure you.'

'Can I get you a coffee? A tea?'

'Tea would be great. Thank you.' He watched her move to the kitchen and fill the kettle. 'I saw Damian today.'

'You did? Excellent. I'm so glad. How did it go?'

'I think I'm in love.'

'He's brilliant, isn't he?'

'He is. And he's starting work next week.'

'Fantastic!'

'Thank you for organising that for me. I'm incredibly grateful.'

'Oh, I'm so relieved. I was really worried that you might think I was being a bit meddlesome.'

'Meddlesome? No, why would I think that?'

'Well, you said you'd changed your mind about selling the house.'

'Yes, but that was mainly because I couldn't stomach finding someone to do the work when everyone I came into contact with was a complete cowboy. But now I've met the venerable Damian . . .'

'You've changed your mind?'

'Well, yes, I suppose I have. Although the problem of extracting my deep-rooted tenants is still no closer to a resolution.'

'Ah, right. That's another thing I have to confess to having taken into my own hands.'

'It is?'

'Uh-huh. I invited Joanne to a party at the shop last week.'

'You did? My God—did she come?'

'Yes.'

'Well, that's quite remarkable. Did you manage to uncover any interesting facts about her?'

'I found out that she trained at the Central School of Speech and Drama. So I phoned them and asked questions about her and guess what?'

'What?'

'She's been in prison.'

'No way! What for?'

Leah shrugged. 'I don't know. But it was years ago, when she was young. And guess what else?'

'What?'

'I have a phone number for her next of kin. A man called Nicholas.'

'Wow! And who is he?'

'I don't know. I've tried calling but there's never a reply and there's no answering machine, so I'm just going to keep trying. But he's obviously someone significant. And that's not all.'

'It isn't?'

'No. I've found a man. For Melinda. A big, handsome Italian with a huge house in Muswell Hill who's sweet and lonely and loves English blondes. They're made for each other. We'll have to set them up on a blind date.'

'My God, Leah. You're a marvel.'

'I know!' She smiled.

'And you know something else?' he said as he took a mug of tea from her outstretched hand. 'I'm so glad it was you who found Gus on the pavement. I don't know you very well but it's obvious that you're a good person and not just a good person but a truly special person.'

'Oh, well . . .' Leah shrugged awkwardly.

'No, really. You're so confident and uncomplicated. And frankly, your boyfriend, that nurse chap, I mean, I'm not sure what he was thinking. I can only imagine he must have been threatened by your overall . . . *greatness*, and that's why he didn't want to marry you, but really, by any measure, you are entirely eligible and really very . . . *desirable*.'

He stopped. A police siren started up in the background. Leah laughed.

'Oh God. Did I just say desirable?'

Leah nodded.

'Oh, really . . . I didn't mean . . . . that sounds awful. I just meant, in the same way as a piece of antique glass or a certain outcome to a situation might be desirable, not that I desire you, sexually, though you are, sexually desirable, but that's not what I was trying to say. Oh God . . .'

'Oh, Toby.' Leah laughed. 'It's OK. I'm flattered.'

'You are?'

'Well, yes. I'm thirty-five, I've just been dumped, I'm not the slim thing I used to be. I feel a hugely long way away from desirable. So thank you. And I'm really glad that I found Gus on the pavement, too, because if I hadn't I'd have moved out of this flat without ever having had a conversation with you and that would have been very sad. Because you're great, too. So . . . there you go . . .' She trailed off and Toby noticed that she'd turned rather pink.

Well,' he said, 'thank you very much.' He grabbed his mug off the coffee table and took a big gulp, slightly too big it turned out as it hit the back of his throat and started trickling down the wrong way. He tried to redirect the tea down the right side of his throat, but the harder he tried to stop himself choking the more the choke built up until finally with eyes streaming and bulging and his mouth full of tea he could control it no longer. He tried to direct the regurgitated tea into his mug, but such was the force behind the explosion that he wasn't able to. Instead the tea sprayed all over Leah's coffee table.

Leah got to her feet. 'God, Toby are you all right?'

Toby couldn't reply; he was coughing too hard, the sort of harsh, painful hacking cough that feels as if you might actually die of it.

'Here, let me get you some water.' She ran into the kitchen and emerged with a glass of water and a roll of kitchen towel. She passed him the water and helped him tip it to his lips.

Toby finally stopped coughing and Leah looked at him with concern. 'Are you OK?'

He nodded, found his voice. 'I sprayed your glasses. And your book. I'm really, really sorry.'

'Well,' she said, smiling, 'that's the last time I give you a compliment.'

He grinned. 'It's been so long since anyone said anything nice to me that I actually almost die when someone does!'

Leah laughed and sat down. 'Well,' she said, 'how about we get together again, some time soon, and if you like I'll say some more nice things to you, just for the practice?'

'That would be great,' he said, 'but go easy on me. I'm a compliment novice.'

'Oh.' She smiled. 'I'll be gentle, I promise.'

Toby loved going to bed. It was the highlight of his day. He loved the sense that the day was done and now he could surrender himself to the vagaries and randomness of his other life—his dream life. Toby loved to dream. In his dreams the sun shone and he travelled the world. In his dreams he made lasting, intimate connections with strangers and with friends. In his dreams he always had on exactly the right clothes and said exactly the right thing.

When he came to bed that night, however, he wasn't ready for sleep. The friends of his nether world waited like shadows in the wings of his mind, but he didn't want to meet them yet. For now, he wanted to dwell in reality.

Because, for the first time in fifteen years, the reality of his day had been far, far better than anything his tired, confused brain could come up with. Because, for once, something good had happened to him.

He'd spent time with a woman. They'd had a cup of tea together and their conversation hadn't come close to drying up. They'd made an arrangement to meet for a walk across the Heath. And then they'd stood outside the woman's house and they'd both stopped and smiled and, even though they hadn't kissed, a current had passed between the two of them, an invisible crackle of something entirely possible, something that made the prospect of tomorrow thrilling and terrifying. And that was why Toby finally succumbed to sleep that night. Not to escape his present, but to hasten the arrival of his future.

Boris seemed, if anything, to be getting even thinner. His fur looked even stragglier and his eyes looked even bulgier. Toby was concerned that this was more than just a weird-looking cat, that this was a cat preparing to meet his maker, so he made an appointment for him at the nearest vet.

He was staring out of his bedroom window, pondering the logistics of getting a cat from Silversmith Road to the surgery, which was a ten-minute walk away, without a cat box, when it occurred to him.

Melinda's car.

He was staring right at it.

Before he'd given himself a chance to think of a dozen reasons why he shouldn't do it, Toby was knocking on Con and Melinda's bedroom door.

Melinda opened it. She was wearing a pink towelling dressing gown. Without her make-up, Toby noted, she looked much younger, much more approachable. She smiled when she saw him. 'Hello!'

'Hi, there!' Toby smiled back, wondering, not for the first time, how this pink, blonde, overly genial woman had ended up living in his home.

'This is a rare privilege.'

'It is?'

'A visit from the lord of the manor! *I am* honoured! What can I do for you, love?'

'Are you busy today?'

'No, not particularly.'

'It's just, I'm a bit worried about Boris. And I've made an appointment for him at the vet's later and I was wondering, if it's not too much hassle for you, if you'd mind taking us there? In your car?'

'What time?'

'One o'clock?'

She smiled. 'No worries. I'd love to. I'll see you downstairs at one.'

Melinda, now restored to her usual state of casual glamour, tapped her foot pedals gently and methodically, as if they were driving a church organ. And she talked. And she talked. And she talked.

Toby sat in the back with Boris on his lap in a cardboard box trying to find an opportunity to start the conversation he'd been hoping to engineer since he'd first set eyes on Melinda's car this morning. He waited until they approached a roundabout, as he'd noticed that she tended to stop talking for a moment when she was concentrating, then he said the first thing that came into his head.

'So, are you . . . *seeing* anyone at the moment, Melinda?'

'Why? Are you interested?'

'Good Lord, no. I mean. No, not at all. Not that I wouldn't . . . not that I don't . . . but no. I was just wondering.'

No,' she said, 'no. I'm young, free and single. And that's the way I like it.'

'It is?'

'Yes. Bloody men. I've had it up to here with them all. In my opinion, men are just liars and losers and idiots. Well, not you obviously, Toby.'

Toby drew in his breath, about to do something that was so out of character for him that he felt like his head might fall off. 'So,' he said, 'then you wouldn't be interested in meeting my friend Jack?'

She laughed. He couldn't blame her. 'Your friend Jack?'

'Yes. Well, not *my* friend, exactly. A friend's friend. She's been raving about him. Says he's amazing. Apparently.' He breathed out, feeling quite dizzy with embarrassment.

'Oh, yeah?' Her head turned from side to side as she approached a junction to turn right. 'Well, if he's that great, then why doesn't she want him for herself?'

He shrugged. 'I don't know,' he said. 'Maybe she doesn't fancy him.'

'Well, then, he's obviously a minger.'

'No, no, no. Not at all. Apparently he's very handsome. And very rich. I have to admit, I've never met this man, but he does sound like quite a catch.'

'Oh, bless you, Toby, and your way with words. Quite a catch, eh?'

'Well, apparently.'

Melinda pulled in to the car park behind the vet's and turned off the ignition. 'You want to fix me up with this rich old guy who your mate don't fancy?'

'Well, I wouldn't say he's old . . .'

'What sort of age is he, then?'

'I'm not sure. Your age, I think. Maybe a little older. And he's Italian.'

He felt her go still in the driver's seat, like a child hearing the distant tone of an ice-cream van. 'Italian?'

'Yes. Jack. Short for Giacomo.'

'*Giacomo*.' She let the name run across her tongue and over her lips. 'Is he dark?'

'I don't know. I could find out for you if you'd like.'

'And when you say rich, how rich exactly?'

'I don't know exactly, but he's got a four-bedroom house in Cranmore Gardens. With a swimming pool.'

'And he's not married?'

'No. Recently divorced. Two teenage daughters. Desperately lonely, according to my friend.'

'Nah,' she said, 'sounds too good to be true. Sounds dodgy.' She pulled her keys out of the ignition, slung her handbag over her shoulder and headed towards the vet's.

The vet was unable to find any medical reason for Boris's deteriorating condition. 'Boris is very old,' he said, sympathetically. 'Leave him be, see how he goes and, if he gets much worse, bring him in and we'll put him to sleep.'

'How long do you think he's got?' Melinda asked as if she were playing a bit part in a daytime soap.

'That's hard to say.' The vet patted Boris's head. 'Could be a few days, could be a few weeks.'

'So, basically, he's dying?' said Toby.

'Basically, yes.'

Melinda started to cry then, thick rivers of mascara running down her cheeks.

But Toby felt a curious sense of unburdening, of a loosening of the straps tying him into his rut. Boris was dying, but slowly, day by day, Toby was being reborn.

The sun came out that afternoon, just as Toby left the house. It matched his mood. He hadn't been for a walk across the Heath in a very long time. He hadn't, now he thought about it, been out on a Saturday afternoon for a very long time. Saturday afternoons were for other people, Toby felt, for people with children and people with partners and people who'd been in bed all morning because they'd been out all night. Saturday afternoons involved partaking in activities of which

Toby had no experience—playing sport, doing the weekly shop, seeing friends. People did things on Saturday afternoons that they couldn't do during the week because they were at work. Toby, being without gainful employment, had no need to venture out on a Saturday afternoon. But now Toby had a friend, and Toby had somewhere to go.

He met Leah outside the underground station and they walked down The Bishops Avenue together. Toby and Leah weren't the only people to decide that it was a nice afternoon for a walk around Kenwood. The grounds around the house were thronging with designer prams, big dogs, and toddlers in fleecy hats. The sky was a brilliant shade of blue and the sun was a blinding white orb behind the leafless trees.

They were ascending a small slope and Toby felt his lungs begin to strain against the amount of breathing he was having to do.

Leah stopped and turned to look at him. 'Are you OK?'

'Yes,' he said, holding his hand to his chest and squinting slightly. 'Just a bit . . . *breathless*.'

Leah smiled. 'Are you really that unfit?'

Toby nodded. 'Too much time . . . in front . . . of my . . . computer.'

'Oh, dear Lord, that's terrible. It's barely a slope. You should start exercising.'

'No, no, no.' Toby shook his head and they started walking again. 'I'm not that kind of person. I don't do gyms.'

'Swimming,' she said, 'try swimming. It's the best all-round exercise.'

'Oh, I don't know. I have a slight phobia of swimming baths. The smell of chlorine, the eerie echo, women in rubber hats. And I get claustrophobic in goggles.'

Leah laughed. 'Come with me,' she said. 'I go every week. And I don't wear a rubber hat.'

'You don't?'

'No. I promise.'

'Well, then, maybe I will. Though I must warn you, I don't have entirely the correct physique for swimming trunks.'

'And what exactly is the correct physique for swimming trunks?'

'Oh, you know, muscles, shoulders, buttocks—all that business.'

'Well, I've got muscles, shoulders and buttocks, so we should sort of balance each other out.'

Toby envisaged Leah in a damp swimsuit, her muscles, shoulders and buttocks shiny and wet. 'OK,' he said. 'Yes. Why not? Let's go swimming.'

'Good,' said Leah. 'It's a deal.'

They headed back to the main house and queued for tea and cake in the café. It was mild enough to sit outside, so they took their trays into the courtyard and found themselves a table.

'Did I tell you that Con's girl stayed the night?' said Toby, stirring the bag round his teapot.

'What, the posh one?'

'Yup. He cooked her dinner. Well, *we* cooked her dinner. Her coat was still in the hallway the next morning.'

'That's brilliant.'

'You know, I'm starting to feel rather fond of Con. There's more to him than I originally thought. In fact, I'm starting to feel more warmly disposed towards all my tenants. And, you know, in a strange way, I'm quite enjoying being . . .'

'Nosy?'

'Yes.' He smiled, and poured tea into his cup. 'Yes, being nosy. It's fun.'

'Well, I *am* having a good influence on you, aren't I?'

'Yes,' said Toby, 'I'd say you are.' He glanced up at Leah. Her cheeks were the colour of strawberry sauce. She looked divine. He stared at his hand for a while where it rested against his teacup. It wanted to move; it wanted to slide across the table top and lie on top of Leah's hand. Toby talked to his hand. 'Don't do it, hand. It'll spoil everything.' But the hand seemed intent on disobeying Toby's instructions. He watched as it moved across the table, slowly, disembodied from him, like something out of a zombie movie. It was halfway across the table when someone suddenly boomed in Toby's ear, 'Leah! Leah!' and it came scuttling back to him like a nervous cat.

There was a large man standing behind him, in a fur-lined parka and trendy jeans.

'Am!' said Leah. 'My God!'

'Hello,' said Amitabh.

'Am—you know Toby, from across the road?'

Amitabh smiled at Toby. He had a lovely face. 'Well, I don't *know* Toby, but I recognise you from through the window. Good to meet you.' They shook hands.

'Who are you here with?' said Leah.

'No one.' Amitabh shrugged. 'Just me. I was supposed to be studying this afternoon, but I couldn't face it. Thought I'd get some fresh air.'

'Right,' said Leah. 'So, just got here? Just leaving?'

'Just got here.' He pointed at a table behind them with his tea and cake on it. 'Mind if I . . .?' He pointed at their table.

'No,' said Leah. 'Why not?'

She grimaced at Toby while Amitabh went to get his food and mouthed a 'Sorry.'

Toby shrugged, trying to look as if he didn't care much one way or the other about Leah's ex-boyfriend crashing headlong into the nicest afternoon he'd had in fifteen years.

Amitabh put down his cheesecake and cappuccino, and sat next to Leah. 'You look good,' he said to Leah. 'You're wearing make-up.'

'Yeah, well, us single girls have to make an effort.'

He smiled. 'So—what have you two been up to?'

'Nothing much,' said Leah. 'Just walking. Just chatting.'

'I've got to say, mate, and don't take this the wrong way, but it's kind of unnerving seeing you like this.'

'Like . . .?'

'You know—*out*. I've only ever seen you through the window. Me and Lee—we thought you were agoraphobic, to be honest.'

'You did?'

'Am!'

Toby tried to look amused. He stared at Amitabh's mouth, at the way it moved when he talked. He was intense, robust, alive, full of chat. He could kind of see how he and Leah would have worked together. They were both youthful for their years, young in their style of dressing, with a fresh-faced, puppyish approach to the world. But he could also see why they'd split up. Leah was ready for phase two of her adulthood. Amitabh was stuck firmly in phase one.

Toby finished his tea and buttoned up his overcoat. 'Look,' he said. 'I think I'm going to head off, leave you two to catch up.'

'What? No,' said Leah, 'don't go.'

'No, really. I've got some stuff I need to get on with and you two haven't seen each other for a while. I'll see you soon, Leah. And nice to meet you, Amitabh.'

'Oh, Toby.' Leah got to her feet. 'I don't want you to go. What about going for a pint at the Spaniards?'

'Another day, maybe.' He smiled and gave her a perfunctory kiss on the cheek. 'See you soon.'

He walked away then, towards the entrance. For a moment, for an hour, Toby had felt like just another man, out on a Saturday afternoon, out with a friend, inhabiting a world he usually only viewed as a spectator. Until a large, jovial man in a parka had crashed into his moment of normality and reminded him that he really didn't belong out here at all.

By Monday evening Damian's men had removed one bathroom and fitted a new one. By Tuesday evening they'd removed and refitted the second bathroom. On Wednesday morning, Damian came round to check their work and pick up his deposit.

'Nice suites,' he said in the bathrooms. 'They look good.' He peered into a box of limestone tiles on the floor. 'These for the walls?'

'Yes. And the floors.'

'Lovely,' he said. 'Smart.'

'And what about decorating, Damian? I was thinking grey walls, white woodwork, occasional flashes of blue?'

'Occasional flashes of blue, eh?' Toby and Damian turned round at the sound of a female voice. It was Ruby. She was wearing a slash-necked T-shirt and a tiny sliver of faded denim that Toby assumed was a skirt.

'Oh,' said Toby, 'hello.'

'Hello, yourself. What's going on?'

'This is Damian. He's running this project.'

'Project?'

'Well, not project, but he's in charge of the works. The, you know, the bathrooms and kitchen.'

'Hello, Damian!' She threw Damian one of her smiles and flipped her pelvis out at an angle. She was so obvious, so shameless. Toby felt a flutter of embarrassment for her. She peered into the bathroom. 'I'm amazed you think we deserve such luxury, Tobes. Limestone tiles, power shower. It's wasted on us, really.'

Well,' said Damian, 'it's what the market wants.'

'Yes, but who cares what the market wants. We're not the market. We're just a bunch of scallies.'

Toby had stopped breathing. Damian looked confused. 'But the people who live here after you, they'll want to see a well-presented house, they'll want to see high-quality bathrooms.'

Ruby laughed. 'Nobody's going to live here after us! Toby would never sell this place.'

Damian glanced from Toby to Ruby and back again. 'Oh,' he said, 'right.'

She saw the confusion on his face. 'Did you think Toby was doing all this work so that he could sell the house?'

'Well,' he said, 'yeah. That was kind of the impression I'd got, but, obviously . . .'

'Toby—*are* you selling this place?'

'No,' he said, 'no way.'

'Are you sure?' she said. 'Because I couldn't stand it if you did.'

'No,' he said, 'I realise that. That's why I'm not selling it.'

'Good.' She smiled at him. 'Good.' Then she turned to smile at Damian. 'I've lived here since I was sixteen, you know. It's the only real home I've ever known.'

Damian nodded, uncertainly. Ruby went back to her room.

'Oh dear,' said Damian.

'Indeed,' said Toby.

Toby counted his money on Wednesday night. He'd given Damian £10,000 in cash that morning and felt that it was time to start being more organised with his money.

He had £32,650 left. Enough to pay for a kitchen, to pay Damian, to buy new curtains, new carpets, get a gardener in, then maybe still have some left over for a new PC and a widescreen telly. He entered the sums into a spreadsheet, and smiled. Everything was on track.

There was knock at the door and Toby quickly shut the drawer and flicked his computer screen. 'Hello?'

'It's Con. Can I come in?'

'Of course.'

Con walked in. 'Those bathrooms—' He gestured behind him with his thumb. 'They're amazing. Like something in a hotel.'

'Glad you approve.'

Con edged into the room and looked at Toby's screen. 'I'm not disturbing anything, am I?'

'No. Far from it. What can I do for you?'

'Right.' He sat on Toby's bed. 'It's a bit embarrassing, actually. But I was wondering if you'd be able to show me how to . . . do a poem.'

'Do a poem?'

'Yeah. I want to give something special to Daisy. And she's not the sort of girl who'd go for jeweller and that kind of thing. So I thought I might, you know, write something for her. Something nice.'

'A love poem?'

'Yeah. I kind of know what it is I want to say. I just need to know how to make it into a poem.'

Toby smiled. 'Right,' he said. 'Well, I can't necessarily show you *how* to do it, but I could certainly help you.' He pulled a notepad from his desk and a pen from his pen pot and passed them to Con. 'Write down some words, phrases. Just scribble them down.'

Con took the notepad from him and furrowed his brow. 'Do they have to be rhyming words?'

Toby smiled at him. 'No. Just *feeling* words.'

'Right,' he said, tapping the Biro against the page. 'OK.'

Toby pretended to be researching important things on the Internet, while Con scratched away with the Biro.

'I've finished,' he said, handing Toby the notebook.

Toby read out loud: '"changed my world" "precious" "different to anyone else" "real" "special" "I feel like I've found my way" "better than me" "an angel" "magic" "inspiring" "more than I ever thought I'd get".'

Con laughed nervously. 'This is a bit embarrassing,' he said.

'No, no. Not at all,' Toby said reassuringly. 'This is wonderful. Really.'

'Will I be able to make a poem out of it?'

'Yes,' he said, 'definitely. Now—what is this poem for? To tell her that you love her?'

'Yeah,' he said. 'I guess. I just want her to know how I feel about her. But I also want her to think I'm, you know, clever.'

'Clever.' Toby smiled. 'I see.'

'Well, *creative*. I think she probably knows I'm not clever.'

'OK, well, first of all we need to give it a title. Any ideas?'

'Yes,' said Con. 'Yeah. I know exactly what I want to call it. I want to call it: "My Sunshine Girl".'

Con left Toby's room two hours later, clutching his ode to Daisy close to his chest.

Toby sighed, feeling waves of happiness undulate through his body.

Con's poem hadn't been particularly brilliant or even particularly poetic, but it had been honest and true and sweet and raw. And it had moved Toby deeply. He gazed across the street now, to Leah's flat. She hadn't been in touch since their afternoon at Kenwood, but then, Toby hadn't really made himself available for contact. He'd kept his curtains drawn at night and himself to himself. But as he peered through his curtains, he felt a surge of positive energy ripple through him. If Con could walk so fearlessly into a love affair with someone so completely different to him, then why couldn't he? People didn't need to match to be together. Just because Leah was sporty, organised, tidy, fresh, easy-going and gregarious, there was no reason why she shouldn't want to spend time with someone lazy, messy, scruffy, neurotic and antisocial. She'd made it very clear that she found Toby's company enjoyable. It was she, after all, who had instigated their weekend meeting and it was she who had suggested swimming. The onus, therefore, was on Toby to accept her offer. The next move was his. By sitting in his room, thinking of reasons not to pursue his friendship with Leah, he was creating a self-fulfilling prophecy. By assuming that he was unlovable he was ensuring that he would remain unloved. By assuming that he was unwanted he was ensuring that he would remain alone.

He opened his wardrobe door and looked at his list of things to do, at points 11 and 12.

Stop being in love with Ruby.

Find someone proper to be in love with.

And that was when it hit him. He *had* stopped being in love with Ruby. He'd stopped days ago and he hadn't even noticed. After fifteen years of stultifying obsession and pointless devotion, he was free. And it was all thanks to Leah Pilgrim, his very own sunshine girl.

Leah craned her neck to the right to peer at her alarm clock. It said 8.30. She blinked. It couldn't be 8.30—she'd set the alarm for 7.45 a.m. But then—small doors in her mind started opening—she *hadn't* set it last night, had she, because last night she'd . . .

Her head swivelled to the left.

Amitabh.

In her bed.

She let her head drop back onto her pillow and sighed. They'd gone to the pub last night. He'd suggested it at Kenwood on Saturday afternoon. 'It seems a shame,' he'd said, 'not to be friends. I miss you.'

Given that she missed him, too, she'd agreed to meet up with him on Wednesday night. Ending up in bed with him hadn't been part of the plan. But after a few beers it was so easy just to slip back to the flat, order a curry from their favourite takeaway, open a bottle of their favourite wine, look at each other and realise that nothing had changed, that she was still Leah and he was still Amitabh and that neither of them had ever stopped loving each other, not really, and that it felt good to hold someone familiar and warm and it felt good to kiss someone you've known for so long and that sex is even better when you've been apart for a while and that what happened next wasn't really important because it was all about making each other feel better, just for a night. Just for old times' sake.

'Am.' She shoved his shoulder. 'Am. Wake up. It's eight thirty.'

'It's OK. I don't have to be at work until three,' he mumbled, his eyes still closed.

'Yes, well, I have to be at work in half an hour, so get moving.'

'Oh, Lee, let me sleep. I've still got my key. I can let myself out.'

Leah paused for a moment, considering the consequences of letting Amitabh stay here without her. 'OK. But don't make a mess.'

'I won't.'

'I'm going to have a shower. D'you want a cup of tea?'

'Mmmm, yes, please. I miss your tea.' And then he tucked his hands under his cheek and fell asleep with a very contented smile on his face.

Ruby was having breakfast with a fat man in a suit when Toby came down to collect the mail. They were sitting together at the dining-room table, Ruby in a dressing gown, on the man's lap, watching him eat toast.

She turned and smiled at Toby when he walked into the room.

'Morning, Tobes.'

'Morning, Ruby.'

'This is Tim.'

'Morning, Tim.'

'God, I have to say, this is very weird,' said Tim. 'This set-up. This house.'

'What's weird about it?' said Ruby.

'I don't know. All these people. It's strange. I mean—I just saw an air hostess. In the full get-up. What's that all about? Aren't you all a bit old to be flat-sharing?'

Toby shrugged and smiled. 'That's a very good question.'

Ruby pulled herself off Tim's lap and ruffled his hair. Her dressing gown gaped open slightly at the front and Toby got a view of her entire left breast. Toby had had many inadvertent views of Ruby's breasts over the years, which had served only to fuel his desire for her, but glancing at her breast now he felt curiously unmoved. He was unafflicted. He was free. And with that thought he pulled on his brand-new overcoat and headed across the road to Leah's flat.

Toby didn't notice Leah's receding figure as he crossed the road towards her flat. He didn't see her rushing towards Fortis Green, her hair uncombed, a slice of toast in her hand. He was aware that he may have missed her, that she may already be on her way to work, but he had a handwritten note ready to drop through her letterbox, as a contingency measure.

He examined the front of his T-shirt as he waited at Leah's door and was pleasantly surprised to find no stains of any description. If she hadn't answered the door by the time he'd counted to ten, he'd assume she was out and leave the note.

At the number eight a figure appeared in the hallway.

Toby prepared his face into an expression of warmth and good intentions. The door opened and Toby's face collapsed. It was him, the man, the nurse. It was Amitabh.

'Oh,' he said, 'I thought you'd be the postman.'

'No,' said Toby. 'Though I do have a letter. For Leah. Is she in?'

'Sorry, mate. You've just missed her. She left about two minutes ago.'

'Oh,' said Toby, 'bad timing. Never mind. Well, do you think maybe you could pass this on to her?' He passed the envelope to Amitabh.

'Sure. No problem. I'll make sure she gets it.'

Toby paused. 'So, are you, have you . . . moved back in?'

Amitabh scratched his head. 'No,' he said, 'not yet. But watch this space.' He smiled and he winked, and then he closed the door.

Toby stood for a while, staring at the stained glass of Leah's front door. What an idiot he was. What a complete and utter fool. Why hadn't he considered the possibility that Leah's unexpected encounter with her ex-lover on Saturday afternoon might have led to some form of reconciliation? Why hadn't he remembered how messy and unruly life could be, how unmanageable an emotion love was. He called himself a poet, yet he consistently proved himself to be completely out of touch with even the most basic tenets of human nature.

When Karen had left him fifteen years ago, he'd filled his house with people from all walks of life—people with stories to tell and journeys to share—but instead of learning from them he'd used them to insulate himself from the world. And now that he was finally unpeeling all the layers and revealing himself, it was very disappointing to see that he wasn't an eccentric struggling artist with a fondness for unusual people, that he was just plain old Toby Dobbs, the tallest boy at school, the disappointment to his father, the man whose own wife hadn't wanted to live with him for more than a month.

He sighed and he turned and he headed back to his house. He made himself a cup of tea and, instead of taking it to his room, he took it up to Gus's. He lay down on Gus's shaggy carpet and he stroked Gus's dying cat and he wondered, really and truly, what *was* the point of it all.

'Daisy's not in today,' said a girl whose vowels were so twisted with poshness that Con could barely understand a word she was saying.

'Oh,' he said, 'right. Do you know what's wrong with her?'

'No idea,' she said. 'I didn't ask.'

Con felt an icy sense of dread. He took the lift back down to the post room and pulled his mobile phone out of his pocket. She didn't answer her mobile, so he took a deep breath and called her home number. Again, there was no reply. He tried both numbers every ten minutes until finally, at half past two, someone answered her mobile. It was a man's voice, impatient and gruff.

'Hello. Is that Daisy's phone?'

'Yes. Who is this?'

'It's Con. I'm a friend of Daisy's from work. Who's this?'

'I'm Daisy's father.'

'Oh.' Con stopped slouching against the wall and brought himself up straight. 'Hello. Is Daisy all right?'

'Well—we're all at the hospital right now . . .'

'The hospital. Shit. I mean, God. Is it serious? Is she OK?'

Daisy's father sighed. 'Well, we're waiting for some X-rays. It looks like another pneumothorax.'

'What . . . what's that?'

'It means she's got air around her lungs.'

'Shit. Sorry. Will she be OK?'

'Look. I'm terribly sorry, but I have to go now. Maybe you should come to see her.'

'Would that be OK?'

'Of course. She's at St Mary's. Bring her something nice to eat. The food here is terrible.'

Con followed the signs to Daisy's ward, clutching a bag of sandwiches and a bunch of roses. Her bed was at the furthest end of the small ward, underneath a window. Mimi sat at one side of her bed; a small woman with silver hair sat at the other side.

He edged towards the bed nervously. He was about to be confronted by both Daisy's illness and her family. He felt overwhelmed.

The small woman turned as Con approached and smiled. She had a dimple and crooked teeth. 'Connor!' she cried, getting immediately to her feet to greet him. 'I'm Helen, Daisy's mother.'

'Hello,' he said, accepting a coffee-scented kiss to his cheek.

'Daisy,' she said, touching her knee, 'look who's here. It's Connor.'

Daisy was held up by a thick wedge of pillows and had a tube coming out of her chest, attached to a jar of water. She was clutching an oxygen mask in her right hand. It was attached to a tank. Her skin was very blue and her hair was lying in lank strands on her pillow. She smiled wanly at him. 'Sexy, huh?' she said.

He rested the roses on the bed and smiled at her. 'You look lovely,' he said. 'A bit pale . . .'

'You mean a bit blue,' she croaked. 'Not to mention a bit tubey and a bit ill.'

'Here.' Daisy's mother moved her plastic chair towards him. 'Sit down, Connor. I think I might stretch my legs. Meems—are you coming?'

'Yes,' said Mimi, getting to her feet. 'I could do with a wander. See you in a minute.'

Con waited until the two women had left the ward, then he kissed Daisy on the lips. 'I brought you some sandwiches,' he said, showing her the bag.

'Ooh, yum. What have we got today?'

'Tuna and capers.'

'Ooh, lovely. I love capers.'

He unwrapped the sandwiches for her and passed her a square.

'So,' he said, 'what's this pneumo . . . pneumo . . .?'

'Pneumothorax. It's air around the lungs. It's horrible. I've had it before, but not this badly. I've got to lie here with this thing sticking into my ribs for at least three days . . .'

'And then what—then you can come home?'

'Then I can come home.'

'So it's not, you know, not something that might . . .'

'No. It's not going to kill me. Just ruin my social life for a few days.'

'Oh,' said Con, 'oh, that's good, then, that's . . . oh . . . God . . .' And then Con felt all the pent-up anxiety he'd been carrying round all day suddenly leave his body in an enormous *whoosh* of emotion and he started to cry. 'Oh God,' he sniffed, 'I'm really sorry. I just thought . . . when your dad said you were in the hospital I just panicked. And then he wouldn't tell me if you were going to be OK and I just thought that you were going to . . . and I couldn't handle it if anything happened.'

Con pressed the heels of his hands into his eye sockets, trying to stem the flow of tears. Daisy passed him a paper tissue from a box on her trolley. 'I'm sorry,' he said, 'I'm being pathetic. You must think I'm psycho.'

'Of course I don't,' said Daisy, clutching his fisted-up hands with hers. 'I think it's really sweet.'

'Oh God,' he laughed, and wiped his face with the tissue, 'that's even worse.'

'I can't believe you were that worried about me.'

'Of course! I mean, I know we've only known each other a few weeks, but you're really important to me. You're, you know, special.' He gulped.

Daisy squeezed his hand. 'You're very special to me, too.'

'I am?'

'Of course you are. You're up there, you know, up there with my mother and my father, my sisters, my best friend. You really matter to me. You . . .' She stopped and tried to catch her breath. 'Sorry,' she said, a moment later. 'I should stop talking for a while . . . it's . . . hard . . .'

'No. Don't talk. You don't have to say anything. Look—here. I've got you something else.' He pulled the poem from his jacket pocket and handed it to her.

She looked, unfolded it and started to read. Con watched her intently as she read, trying to gauge her reaction. She folded up the poem, rested it on her lap and smiled.

'Con?' she said.

'Yes?'

'I love you, too.'

Mimi and Helen came back a few minutes later with plastic cups of coffee. Then Daisy's father returned and shook Con warmly by the hand. They were a noisy family, talkative and open and full of booming laughter. They wanted to know all about Con and didn't seem at all fazed or desperate about Daisy's situation or about the fact that she was dating someone like him. They weren't like anyone Con had ever met before.

There was talk of Daisy spending a week at home recuperating. 'And of course,' said Helen, touching Con's knee with her birdlike hand, 'you must come to stay, for as long as you like.'

'Yes,' said Daisy's father. 'We've already got one fellow in the house.'

Con looked at him questioningly.

'Camellia's at home at the moment and of course her fellow couldn't bear to be separated from her for a minute, so he's staying at the house. Nice chap. He's a bassoonist, plays with the LPO. You'd like him . . .'

Con left the hospital at eight o'clock that night, letting the cold night air swallow him up. His breathing was hard and fast, his heart full of the euphoria of escape. He'd just seen reality, the very basic truth of Daisy and him, of what they were doing and where they were going. And he couldn't handle any of it. He couldn't handle her close-knit family, their talk of 'the house', of bassoon-playing boyfriends and invitations to stay. He couldn't handle their unquestioning acceptance of him, because he knew it was borne out of nothing more than middle-class politesse. But more than anything, he couldn't handle the fact that the first woman he'd ever loved was going to keep getting ill and that one day she was going to die and that there was absolutely nothing he could do about it.

Toby spent the whole of Thursday looking out of the window. He saw Amitabh leaving Leah's flat at two o'clock. He saw the builders passing in and out of the house, taking stuff out of their van, putting stuff back in their van, throwing things onto the skip, sitting on the wall eating sandwiches. He saw the sun start to fall and the moon start to rise and he saw Melinda park her car and climb the front steps. He saw Ruby going out with her guitar. And, at eight o'clock, he saw Leah come home. He watched her open her front door, lean down to pick up some letters, then disappear. He saw her switch on her lights, draw her curtains. He wondered what she'd think of his jauntily worded little message, expressing his desire to join her at the Crouch End swimming baths one day this week (if he promised not to try out his butterfly stroke). He wondered if Amitabh would be coming back tonight.

He was about to go downstairs, to get himself something to eat, when he saw something else through his window. He saw Joanne, looking flustered and panicky in dungarees and a leather flying jacket. She was walking very fast and kept looking behind her. Toby saw a man, following behind. He was tall and slim with fine shoulder-length hair. He was shouting to her. He saw Joanne turn to the man and shout something back. And then he saw Joanne start to run towards the house. He heard her footsteps up the front stairs and he saw the man chase after her. He heard the front door slam shut and he heard the man's fist beating against the door. He got to his feet and ran down the stairs, two at a time. Joanne was standing breathlessly at the foot of the stairs.

'Jesus, Joanne. What's going on? Are you OK?'

'I'm fine,' she said, pushing past him to get up the stairs.

'But who's that man at the door? Why is he following you?'

The man beat at the door again.

'I don't know,' she said. 'He's no one.'

'My God. Shall I call the police?'

'No,' she said, 'don't do anything. He's just mad, that's all. He'll go in a minute.'

Toby glanced around the empty hallway. The man was still banging on the door. 'Go away,' he shouted through the door. 'Go away. I'm calling the police.'

'I want to see Joanne.'

'Well, she doesn't want to see you. You're scaring her.'

'I just want to talk to her.'

'I told you. Whoever you are, she doesn't want to talk to you.'

'Please,' said the man, 'please. Just let me see her. I have to see her.'

The man's voice had softened now and it sounded to Toby as if he might even be about to cry.

'Who are you? What do you want?'

'My name's Nick,' he said. 'I'm Joanne's husband.'

Chapter 6

THE THIRD WEEK of February dawned clear-skied and sunny, and a few degrees warmer than it had been.

Things were progressing. The house was growing up. The bathrooms were tiled and the lights were fitted. Toby had taken one look at the finished bathrooms and immediately gone out and spent £300 on fat bath towels in shades of taupe and chocolate. There were tilers on the roof and a plumber had replaced the water tank and all the radiators.

The decorators were starting next week and Toby had been staring at colour cards for days on end, trying to decide between a hundred different shades of beige and grey. He had a box of carpet swatches under his desk (Sisal or seagrass? Or should he just strip the floorboards?). Two young men called Liam and Guy were currently replacing the kitchen, so the fridge was in the hallway and everyone was using a two-ring electric hob in the dining room. The place was a mess, but it was being transformed.

By the time Toby's father arrived at the end of March, the house would be complete and on the market. But it would still be full of people.

Ruby was still sleeping with Tim and surviving on handouts and the occasional poorly paid gig. The wheels appeared to have come off Con's fledgling love affair with the posh girl from *Vogue*. Melinda was revelling in the luxurious transformation of the house and more determined than ever to stay. And Joanne had disappeared. Literally. She'd left for work the morning after her 'husband' had followed her home and had not been seen since. She'd put an envelope under Toby's door containing a cheque for the next month's rent and a note suggesting that she'd gone on holiday.

And Leah—Leah was cohabiting once more with her nurse.

She never did respond to Toby's note about the swimming baths and their paths hadn't crossed since. She was, once more, simply the woman across the road with the nurse boyfriend. And without Leah, Toby was lost. The list taped onto the inside of his wardrobe remained untouched, paused at number 7, like a freeze-framed video. So he sat, in his room, in his window, pretending to write poems and waiting for something to happen again. Toby was back at square one.

Leah felt all wrong. Amitabh had moved back in and she really didn't know why. It had been nice at first having him there, but two weeks on and the novelty had already worn off and Leah was left with a big list of questions: Where are we going? Are you going to go against your family and marry me? Do you love me? Do I love you? *Is this what I want?* What exactly did she want? She was thirty-five. Surely she should know by now?

She pondered her situation during a quiet morning in the shop. They'd just had a big delivery of alphabet cookie cutters and she was unpacking them in the stockroom. She fiddled with them on the floor, arranging them absent-mindedly into words. LEAH. AMITABH. And then, weirdly, TOBY. She scuffed them together, hurriedly, into a puddle of letters, and took them upstairs. She was alone in the shop. Her assistant wasn't due in until eleven. She looked around the shop and sighed. What was she doing here? Why was she arranging cookie cutters on shelves? Something was wrong. Something was missing.

I am thinking bout u, my ruby-chews I am thinking that I luv u! I need u. can't breathe without u. c u tonight. T xxxx

Ruby smiled tightly and switched off her phone. She was in a launderette on the High Road, watching her underwear swirl slowly back and forth inside a gigantic tumble drier. The tumble drier at home was out of commission while the kitchen was being replaced and she'd been forced to bring her washing here. Not that she minded. She liked launderettes.

She opened her in-box and read Tim's message again. She should reply, but she didn't know what to say. She'd never told a man that she loved him before, even when she had. Once those words were uttered, everything changed. She would lose her power; he would expect more of her. But worse than that, Tim Kennedy would probably leave his wife.

Ruby had slept with married men before; she'd heard all the clichés about problematic marriages and unempathetic wives. A dozen men had told her how unhappy they were at home. But Tim was different. He really was unhappy. And he really would leave his wife. He'd leave her tonight. All Ruby needed to do was say the word. Tim Kennedy was in love, like no one had ever been in love with her before. He sent her text messages twenty times a day. He sent her flowers; he bought her jewellery. He'd offered her his heart on a cushion.

He adored her. And Ruby had to admit, she quite liked it. It had been a long time since anyone had felt so strongly about her and it couldn't have come at a better time. But she didn't love him. She didn't even particularly like him. But right now, with Toby probably selling the house, Con ignoring her and Paul abandoning her, Tim was all she had left, and Ruby needed him, more than she could bear to think.

She pressed reply and started to type: thinking I might love you too. See you tonight xxx

'It's time,' said Melinda, peering over Toby's shoulder at the cat, which was curled up against the wall, body expanding and contracting like a set of poorly maintained bagpipes.

Toby nodded his agreement. 'Shall we go?'

Toby picked up the cat, wrapped him in an old bath towel and took him down to the car.

They sat next to each other in silence in the waiting room at the vet's. Toby tickled the top of Boris's head absent-mindedly with his index finger. Melinda flicked through a flimsy gossip magazine.

'Boris Veldtman?'

Toby looked up. The receptionist smiled at them. 'You can go through now.'

'Ah, yes,' said the vet, peering at Boris, 'yes. He's very close to the end now. Very close and experiencing a fairly high level of discomfort. It's up to you, but most people tend towards ending things sooner rather than later.'

Toby and Melinda exchanged a look. Melinda nodded.

'OK,' said Toby, 'let's do it.'

The vet nodded sombrely. A nurse brought through a hypodermic syringe and Toby and Melinda patted Boris's bony back while the injection was administered.

Toby and Melinda watched the cat, rapt. His breathing continued long and heavy, up and down, for a few minutes, until finally it started to slow. Melinda grabbed Toby's hand and squeezed it hard. He squeezed her hand back. A minute later, Boris stopped breathing. Toby turned to the vet. 'Is he . . .?'

The vet put his stethoscope to Boris's rib cage. He nodded. 'Yes,' he said, 'he's gone. Would you like me to leave you alone for a moment, just to say goodbye?'

'Yes,' said Toby, 'if that's OK?'

The vet and the nurse left the room and Toby and Melinda stood over Boris, stroking his warm, lifeless body and squeezing each other's hands. Melinda sniffed. Toby glanced at her. There were tears rolling down her heavily made-up cheeks. 'Poor old Boris,' she said. 'It's so sad.'

'I know,' soothed Toby, 'I know.'

'But at least they're together now. Him and Gus. Up there,' she said, casting her eyes upwards.

'Come on,' said Toby, 'let's go home.'

'But what about Boris? What shall we do with Boris?'

'I don't know,' said Toby. 'I assume that they sort of deal with that.'

'Oh, no,' she cried, 'we can't leave him here. We need to give him a proper burial. A proper farewell. A proper farewell. See him on his way. And then we have to have a wake.'

'We do?'

'Of course,' she said. 'It's the decent thing to do.'

Leah had just noticed with some pleasure that it was nearly five o'clock and it still wasn't dark. It was the same realisation that she had every single year at around this time and it was always a good moment. It meant she'd broken the back of winter, that the long hard slog of it was over. She opened her handbag, searching around for a packet of mints. Her hand passed over a note. She pulled it out and opened it up. It was Toby's note about swimming:

Dearest Leah,

Today I did three press-ups. I feel I am now ready to tackle swimming. If I promise not to attempt my butterfly stroke, would you permit me to join you next time you visit the baths?

Yours, with affection, Toby x

She smiled and refolded the note. It was about the fortieth time she'd read it and every time it had made her smile. She loved his old-fashioned turn of phrase and the fact that he signed the note with a kiss. The doorbell tinkled and she glanced up. It was Jack. She had the curious sensation of two good moments blending into one another and doubling in size. She smiled widely.

'Jack! Hello!'

'Good afternoon, Leah. You look very happy.'

'Oh, don't be fooled. It's just a momentary lapse.'

Jack pulled a concerned face. 'You aren't happy?'

She smiled. 'I'm fine. How are you?'

'Excellent. I've been on a diet and I've lost nearly half a stone.'

She eyed him up and down. He looked exactly the same. 'Well done!' she said. 'You look great.'

'Thank you. And you, Leah, are looking more scrumptious than ever.'

'Scrumptious?'

'Yes. Like a delicious pudding. Something rich and creamy, with whipped cream on top. *Scrumptious!*'

'Right.' She laughed uncertainly. 'I'm not sure how to take that, but thank you, anyway.'

'A compliment!' He smiled. 'Take it as a compliment. But I did not come here today to give you compliments. I came to invite you to dinner.'

'Oh!'

'Yes. I have a professional kitchen, a spectacular dining hall and no one to cook for. I have been waiting and waiting for you to knock on my door, but you never came. And now my wife has taken my girls away for a whole week! So—here I am, all alone in my big house. Imploring you to join me for dinner. Bring your special friend, if you like?'

'My special friend?'

'Yes, I assume a woman as beautiful as you must have a boyfriend?'

'Yes. I do, actually.'

'Ah.' Jack sighed.

'But, if it's OK, I'd love to bring my friend Toby. And maybe another friend of mine. A woman?'

'A woman! Yes. Please. A woman, for Jack. You are so kind, lovely Leah. So kind.'

Leah smiled.

'Is she pretty, this woman? In fact, no, no, don't tell me. Let it be a surprise. I will see you and Toby and your woman at eight o'clock, on Saturday. Come hungry. I will cook enough for a dozen.'

The sun had gone for the day and the windows of the dining room were black mirrors. Toby had buried Boris in the garden and he and Melinda had been drinking now for two hours.

'You're a funny old sod, Toby, you know that?'

Toby shrugged. 'Am I?'

'Yes. I've never met anyone like you before.' Melinda poured a shot of tequila into her glass. They'd already drunk two bottles of Cava.

'Oh,' said Toby. 'Is that a good thing or a bad thing?'

'Good, of course. You're a good person. But it's taken me a while to realise that.'

'Oh, has it?' Toby picked up the bottle of tequila.

'Yeah. I thought you were a bit stand-offish when I first moved in. You kept yourself to yourself, didn't stop for a chat. But the past few weeks, you seem to have come out of yourself a bit. And you're lovely. Really lovely. You've got so much going for you, you really have. But you don't half make life difficult for yourself.'

'What do you mean?' Toby poured some tequila into his glass.

'I mean—you should get out more, make more of yourself. You know, you're not a bad-looking fella. Got a bit of a schnozz on you, but you've got a lovely face. Beautiful brown eyes. And yet . . .'

'And yet what?'

'Well, your hair, those . . . *things* growing out of your cheeks, the way you dress. You're not doing yourself any favours.'

Toby blinked.

'You know what would suit you, Toby? A shaved head. You know, like Justin Timberlake. A pair of clippers. Number one. The whole lot—off.'

'My head is rather a strange shape. I'm not exactly sure that would be the best look for—'

'And you should probably take the time for a trip to a dental hygienist.'

'Oh my God—are you suggesting that I have halitosis?'

'*No.* You just need a serious image overhaul. I mean—what's with all the secondhand clothes?'

'What's wrong with secondhand clothes?'

'Well, *other people* have worn them.' She shuddered delicately and got to her feet. 'There's enough good cheap clothes out there. You don't need to buy other people's castoffs.'

'But I've bought a couple of things, lately. I mean—a jacket, some shoes, a coat.'

'Yes. I saw. And very nice they are, too. But you need to start from scratch, Toby, love. I'll come shopping with you, if you like. Steer you in the right direction.'

'That's very sweet of you,' he said, 'really. But I've pretty much spent all my money now, on the house.'

'Ah, well. The offer's there, if you need it. It's lovely of you, you know, making the house so nice for us all. I would never have had you down as having such good taste.'

'Yes, well.' He smiled. 'I surprised myself.'

She held her glass aloft. 'A toast,' she said, 'to you. For all your kindness. God bless you, Toby, for looking after me and my boy. God knows where we'd be without you. Cheers.'

They banged their glasses together and downed the drinks.

'Toby—can I ask you a personal question?'

'Er, OK.'

'When was the last time you had sex?'

'God, er, um, well, it must have been . . . fifteen years ago?'

'No! Oh, well that makes me feel better!'

'Why—when was the last time you, er . . .?'

'Last summer. In Turkey. Just before I moved back here. I should have been married by now. Then he hit me.'

'Ooh.' Toby recoiled.

'Yes. I know. Managed to get to forty-four years of age without a man ever laying a finger on me and then, *bam*. I was out of there faster than you could say one-way ticket to Luton Airport. No man hits Melinda McNulty.' She shook her head defiantly. 'Never been so happy to see English soil. Nearly kissed the tarmac when we hit the runway. And then to find that my beautiful boy was living in this gorgeous house in such a nice part of London. Kind of killed my travel bug off for good.'

'So, Melinda, you know, I've always wondered and I've never really wanted to ask before, but why . . . why did you leave Con? Why didn't you bring him up?'

'Ah, yes.' Melinda took a sip of tequila. 'I've asked myself that question so many times, and I think what it all boiled down to was *confidence*, you know? I was twenty-six, but a *young* twenty-six. Con's father didn't want to know. And I tried, I really did try, but I just felt like I was so *crap* at it. And then my mum would walk in and Con's little face would light up and he'd stop crying and I just thought: You know what, what am I doing here with this baby who hates me? He's not happy; I'm not happy. And I knew my mum would do a better job of bringing him up than I would. So I got this rep job based in Spain. I came home every couple of weeks at first, to see Con, but in the end I couldn't handle it—the coming and going, the emotional stress of it all. And they had such a unit, Con and my mum. They were such a little team. I felt kind of sidelined. So, in the end, I just stopped. Just tried to forget about him . . .' She sniffed and dabbed her eyes with a piece of kitchen roll. 'Not that I ever did. You can't forget your own child, can you? Not when you're a mother.'

'So, when did you see him next? After the last time?'

'At mum's funeral. Oh God, that was dreadful. Seeing Con, for the first time, this big lad, so handsome, so sad, so good. And everyone looking at me, pointing, that's her, that's the one who ran away to Spain.' She shuddered. 'Worst day of my life. But then'—a small smile lit her face—'after that, once my mum was buried, when it was just me and Con sitting in the pub . . . you know what? It was perfect. He didn't judge me. He just comforted me, you know, because my mum was dead. He blew me away, just totally blew me away.'

'So, why did you leave again? Why did you go to Turkey?'

She shrugged and sighed. 'I don't know. We'd just got this flat together, me and Con, a really fancy place in Leyton. I really wanted to show Con that I was serious about us, about our relationship. I was stupid, really. I thought that we were going to have this *amazing* experience, that we were going to go out together all the time, get to know each other, just kind of lose ourselves in each other, really. And then when I realised that he had his own life, his own friends, that he wasn't going to make me the centre of his world, I got the hump, I suppose. And did what I always did. Ran away. It didn't occur to me that he'd be kicked out of that flat. I just thought he'd be fine. So when I came back and found out that he'd been living rough—I've never felt so awful in my life, just thinking of my poor beautiful boy, in a doorway, nowhere to call home. I keep myself awake at night a lot over that, I can tell you. And I will never, ever leave him again, that's for sure.'

'Well, yes, I can see how you feel, but surely at some point a mother has to let their child . . . *do their own thing.*'

'Well, if Con wants to get rid of me, he'll have to ask. Otherwise, I'm stuck like glue. Me and men—we're done. There's only one man in my life now, and that's Con.'

They downed the rest of their tequilas and sat in contemplative silence for a while. And then the doorbell rang.

Toby pulled himself heavily to his feet. He was horribly drunk. He banged his toe against the corner of the stairs and couldn't remember which way to turn the handle to open the front door. It took him a minute or two to place the man standing on his doorstep with a suitcase and bleeding nose. He knew he looked familiar, but he needed more information to identify him.

'Hello, Toby,' said the man.

'Hello, er . . .'

'Tim. Remember? Ruby's friend. Is she here?'

'God. I don't know. I've been . . . I haven't really been paying attention. She might be.' He stood at the foot of the stairs. 'RUBY! RUBY!'

She appeared on the landing, looking annoyed. 'What?'

'Your friend's here.'

'What friend?' Ruby made her way down the stairs.

'Er . . .' Toby sighed. He'd forgotten already. 'Sorry, what's your name again?'

'Tim,' hissed the man, dabbing some blood from his nose.

'TIM!'

'What?' cried Ruby. 'Oh God, Tim! What happened to your nose?'

'Sophie hit me.'

'She *hit* you? Jesus. Why?'

'Because I told her about you.'

'Oh, fuck. Tim.'

'And I've left her. Look.' He pointed at his silver Samsonite. 'I've left her, Ruby. I'm free.'

As Leah approached her front door that night, a taxi stopped in the road and a man got out. He hauled a large suitcase out behind him, wheeled it along the pavement, then dragged it up the steps of the Peacock House. Leah stood and waited for someone to come to the door of the house. It was Toby. He looked flushed and a bit unsteady. Eventually, Toby held open the door and the man walked in. And then the door closed again.

Leah stared at the house. Her skin was crawling with curiosity. She'd completely lost touch with the comings and goings in the Peacock House since Amitabh had moved back into the flat. But now she had the perfect reason to catch up. Jack's invitation.

She crossed the road and knocked on the door. Toby opened it. It was clear, now that she was in close proximity to him, that he was extremely drunk.

'Oh my goodness,' he said. 'Leah. How totally lovely to see you.'

'It's been a while.'

'I know. It has. Entirely my fault.'

'No. Mine. I'm sorry. I've been meaning to come over for days now . . .'

'Well.' Toby smiled. 'You're here now. And you find me somewhat drunk, I'm afraid. Melinda and I have been having a wake.'

'Oh, no. Who for?'

'For Boris. Little Borissy Boris. No longer with us, sadly. But happily, too. If you believe in angels. Do you believe in angel cats, Leah?'

Leah smiled. Toby was funny when he was drunk. 'No,' she said, 'I don't.'

Toby leaned against the doorframe and smiled at Leah. She smiled back at him. 'Do you think I should shave off all my hair?' he said, rubbing his hands over his unruly mass of curls.

Leah laughed. 'What?'

'Melinda reckons my hair's in a state. Said I should shave it all off, like some pop-star fellow. What do you think, Leah?'

'No.' She shook her head and laughed again. 'You've got the wrong-shaped head for shaved hair.'

'That's exactly what I said. You're very observant, Leah. It's remarkable, what you pick up about people. I wish I was more like you.'

Leah shrugged and smiled. 'You're more observant than you think.'

'I think not. For example, if I were more observant, I might have guessed that you and your ex-boyfriend would be reunited. And if I were really observant I'd have predicted that Ruby's new boyfriend would arrive on my doorstep on a Monday night, having left his wife. But I am not. I see nothing. I hear nothing. I sit alone, disconnected. An island . . .'

'No man is an island, Toby.'

'Well, then I am a headland and you, Leah, are the causeway.'

He smiled weakly at her. 'Oh God,' he groaned, letting his head fall onto his fist. 'Listen to me. Just listen to me. What a drunken, pretentious idiot. And I am absolutely sure you didn't come here to listen to my pitiful blatherings. What can I do for you, lovely, lovely Leah? Would you like to come in?'

She turned to glance at her flat, at the lit-up windows and the signs of life. 'No,' she said. 'No. I'd better get back.'

'Yes, yes, yes. Of course, of course.' Toby nodded emphatically.

'But I just wanted to let you know, Jack came into the shop today, Italian Jack?'

'Oh, yes?'

'And guess what? He's invited me over for dinner on Saturday night. And he said I could bring whoever I wanted. So? Are you free?'

'What? Me?'

'Yes. You and Melinda.'

'Oh my God. You mean, this is it? The big set-up?'

'Yes,' said Leah. 'That's exactly what I mean.'

'Oh God. How exciting. I mean, yes, I'm free. And I'm sure Melinda will be. Melinda!' he called over his shoulder.

'Yes?'

'Are you free for dinner on Saturday night?'

'Depends. Who's asking?'

'Me. I'm asking.'

'Then, yes.'

Toby smiled. 'Excellent,' he said. 'So, who'll be there?'

'You, me, Jack and Melinda.'

'And what about Am . . . Ama . . .?'

'No. Not Amitabh. He'd hate it.'

'Well, that's wonderful. Just great.'

'And also—isn't it about time we went for that swim?'

'Oh, so you did get my note, then?'

'Yes. Amitabh gave it to me. I've just been, you know . . .?'

'Yes, I do know. I know, I know, I know. I am *knowing*.'

'So, shall we go?'

'Go where, lovely Leah?'

'Shall we go swimming. This week, maybe?'

'Yes. We shall. Definitely. When would you like to go?'

'Thursday afternoon? It's my day off.'

'Thursday afternoon, it is. I will invest in some new trunks. And maybe a St Tropez Spray Tan.'

'I'm going out on Saturday night,' she said to Amitabh a few moments later. 'With Toby.'

'What—him over the road?'

'Yes.'

He threw her a look.

'Why?' she said, defensively. 'What's wrong with that?'

'There's nothing *wrong* with it,' he said. 'It's just a bit weird, that's all.'

'Weird?'

'Yeah. Weird. I mean—he's strange. He's not the usual sort of person you'd be friends with.'

'He's not strange at all. He's completely charming, as a matter of fact.'

'OK, OK. There's no need to be so defensive. I'm just not sure about him, that's all. Do you think maybe he fancies you?'

Leah spilled farfalle into a pan of boiling water and sighed. 'No, of course he doesn't. He's in love with that dark-haired girl, Ruby.'

'How the hell do you know that? Did he tell you?'

'No. It's just . . . *obvious.*'

Leah stirred a fork through the pasta and pulled a jar of pesto sauce out of the fridge. She was finding this conversation very annoying. She was finding Amitabh very annoying. Where Toby was like an old Victorian bureau, full of tiny drawers and cubbyholes and secret compartments, Amitabh was more of a blanket box.

'Where's he taking you, then, the old charmer?'

'We're going for dinner,' she said.

'Very nice,' said Amitabh, plugging his earphones into his hi-fi, 'very nice indeed.'

Leah forked some pesto out of the jar and into a bowl and ground her teeth together, very gently.

Ruby opened her eyes. Her gaze alighted upon a large silver suitcase.

She took a deep breath and turned her head to the left. Tim was lying facing her, staring at her. She jumped.

'Sorry,' he said, pulling her hair away from her eyes. 'Sorry. I just . . . it's so amazing, waking up with you.' He kissed her shoulder. 'Everything will be fine, Ruby-chews, you'll see. I'll make sure everything is fine.'

He got out of bed and started to dress himself. Ruby rolled onto her back. 'Where are you going?' she said.

'To the office. I can't take any time off. But—on Saturday, you and I are going flat-hunting.'

'We are?'

'Yes. Where do you fancy? I've always fancied living in Clerkenwell. How about that? A warehouse apartment. Or what about Soho? A nice little penthouse in the middle of town?'

'What—you're going to buy me a flat?'

'No. Not buy. Rent. For now.'

'But I can't afford to pay the rent here, let alone in the West End.'

'Don't be silly,' he said, smiling at her, indulgently. 'You don't have to pay anything. That's what I'm here for. I tell you what'—he looped a Thomas Pink tie round his neck and folded his shirt collar down over it—'you think about it. Make a list of places you'd like to live. We'll talk about it tonight.'

'OK,' said Ruby, whose mood had improved rapidly at the thought of quirky little one-bedroom flats above sex shops in Soho, 'let's.'

Con opened the yellow carton and pulled out his Big Mac. He considered it for a moment before he brought it to his mouth, stared at the tongue of sludge-coloured meat, the road accident of relish, the damp lettuce, the smear of glistening mayonnaise. He closed it and put it back in the carton.

He was sitting in the break room at work, surrounded by men and newspapers, half-eaten sandwiches and plastic cups. He picked up the paper carton of French fries and ate them rhythmically, robotically, while he flicked through the *Evening Standard.*

'Connor McNulty, I don't believe it! I turn my back for five minutes and you're back on the McDonald's!'

Con looked up. So did everyone else in the break room. It was Daisy. She was wearing brown leather shorts with a cream blouse and grey waistcoat. Her hair was in a thin plait and she was clutching a big paper bag from the deli round the corner.

'Daisy,' he said. 'You're back. I didn't realise.'

'Yes.' She put the paper bag down on the table and took the seat next to him. 'It was my first day back yesterday, actually.'

'How are you? You look . . . *great.*'

'Yes.' She nodded. 'I feel pretty good. It was great to have some time at home. Some good old-fashioned parental TLC. How are you?'

'Yeah. I'm good.'

'Good.' She smiled, and pulled the paper bag towards her. 'Well, I've got us panini. Tuna and cheese, or ham and cheese. Which do you fancy? If you've got any room after all those *McDonald's chips*, that is.'

Con took the tuna panini and grinned. 'Our kitchen's being replaced,' he said. 'Nowhere to make sandwiches.'

'That's no excuse.' Daisy licked some grease off her thumb. 'That's what delis are for.'

'You know what, though?' He pointed at his Big Mac. 'I couldn't eat it. I just looked at, I mean *really* looked at it. And that was that. Had to shut the lid on it.'

'Hoorah!' she cried. 'You are cured! My work here is done.'

Con smiled and bit into his panini.

'So,' she said, carefully. 'I missed you.'

Con glanced at her. He tried to think of something to say that wasn't reciprocal, but wasn't heartless either. He couldn't.

'I'd kind of thought you might visit. Or phone,' she said.

'Yeah,' he said, staring at his sandwich. 'I just . . . it was . . .'

'It's OK,' she said. 'I wasn't expecting you to explain yourself. I mean, I know, illness can be scary. Especially at our age. I know it's not something everyone can deal with. But, a phone call might have been nice.'

'Yeah,' he said. 'You're right. I'm sorry.'

'Mimi said you might have been a bit freaked out by our parents. All that stuff about coming to stay at the house.'

'Nah,' he shook his head. 'Your parents are cool.'

'Then why?' she said.

'Why what?'

'Why'—her eyes filled with tears—'why haven't I heard anything from you for nearly two weeks?'

He stared at her, desperately trying to find an explanation that wouldn't make her cry even more. 'Oh, Daisy . . .'

'Is it me? Is it actually nothing to do with me being ill or my family? Is it actually just that you're not interested?' A tear fell from her eye and landed on her cheek. 'Because if that's the case then I'd like to know.'

'No,' he said, 'of course not.'

'Then what is it? Because, really, it's just not entirely normal, is it, to write someone a poem, tell them that you love them, then leave them in hospital, seriously ill, and not get in touch again?'

Con glanced at the other blokes in the room, out of the corner of his eye. They were all watching, listening. He shrugged. 'Everything's cool,' he said.

'Is it?'

'Yeah . . . I'm just. It's just . . . not . . . *God.*'

'No. It's fine.' Daisy dropped her panini onto the table top and stood up. 'Really. It's absolutely fine. Don't bother trying to explain. It'll only make things worse.' She gripped the straps of her handbag with one chalky-white hand, stared at Con for a moment, and then left.

The room fell silent. Con listened to his heart throbbing under his rib cage. He let his sandwich fall out of his hand.

'Jesus, Con,' said someone, at the back of the room. 'You bastard.'

Con exhaled, feeling embarrassment, guilt and sadness.

Melinda came to Toby's room on Tuesday evening. She was holding a box. 'Now,' she said, sailing past him and towards his bed. 'Don't freak out, but I've come to sort you out.'

'Sort me out what?'

She opened the box and pulled out a black contraption with a cord coming out of it. She looked around the skirting boards to locate an electricity socket, then she plugged the contraption in. 'Now,' she said, wheeling his office chair away from his PC and towards his bed, 'come over here.' She patted the seat. 'Sit down.'

'Er, Melinda, what . . .?'

'Trust me, Toby. This is for your own good. Now—sit—down.'

He followed her instructions. He assumed that the vibrating black thing was some kind of massage device, and prepared himself for a pleasant sensation between his shoulder blades. Instead Melinda started rubbing it against the left side of his face and, he had to admit, it wasn't an entirely unpleasant feeling.

'Is that nice?' she said.

'Well, it's not awful, but . . .' He stopped when his gaze fell upon the floor. Tiny tumbleweeds of his hair lay on the carpet. He slapped his hand against his cheek, where for nearly half his life there had been hair. He felt skin, soft and smooth. 'Oh my God! Melinda! No!'

He got to his feet and felt the contraption skidding through his hair.

'Shit, Toby, will you sit still?'

'Oh God.' He grabbed the side of his head and felt a channel of baldness. 'What have you done? *What have you done?*' He raced to the mirror and gazed at his reflection. He had one sideburn and a section of hair missing. He looked like he had a terrible, terrible illness.

'I can't believe you've shaved my sideburn off!'

'Well, what did you think I was going to do with a pair of clippers?'

'I didn't know they were clippers.'

'What on earth did you think they were?'

'I don't know . . . some kind of massage device. I thought you were going to give me a massage.'

Melinda slapped her hands over her mouth and let out a snort of laughter. 'Oh shit,' she said. 'Toby. I'm sorry. I thought everyone knew what clippers look like.'

'Yes, well, apparently not.' Toby looked at himself in the mirror again. He looked away, in horror. 'Oh, Melinda. What are we going to do?'

Toby glanced at the time on his PC. It was 11:23 a.m. And it was Thursday. He sighed and pulled his boots reluctantly from underneath his bed. He wound a scarf round his neck and picked up an old mug.

He paused before he left his room, and glanced at himself in the mirror. He still couldn't countenance the more or less hairless man who stared back at him. They'd been forced to take the whole lot off, until he was left with a smattering of stubble. The sideburns, of course, were beyond rescuing. Melinda had taken the second one off and Toby had watched it fall to the floor in tufts with a sad, heartbroken gulp.

Seeing so much of his face alarmed him. He stroked his cheeks continually, feeling for stuff that used to be there. His scalp was bizarre, pink and unaired, like a testicle. He wore hats pretty much all the time now. Melinda had insisted that he looked gorgeous, 'like that bloke in *Doctor Who*'. But to his eyes he just looked bald—and slightly alarming. He bared his teeth at his reflection, and gulped.

In half an hour he would be at the dentist. He'd phoned to book an appointment with the hygienist and they'd somehow, by some kind of dental stealth, booked him in for a standard appointment, too. He hadn't been to the dentist in years. They would, he knew it, insist on pulling out half his teeth and then on drilling holes in the rest of them.

He took his boots and his mug downstairs. He put the mug on the black granite work surface of his new kitchen and pulled on his boots. The kitchen fitters had finished last night and it was, of course, the most beautiful kitchen Toby had ever seen. It had aubergine-coloured cabinets and a six-ring hob and a breakfast bar and an American fridge with a water dispenser. The kitchen floors had been stripped and stained to look like American walnut and there were a dozen twinkling halogen lights hanging from tracks on the ceiling.

Melinda's food boxes were piled up by the back door, waiting to be unpacked tonight. Sticking out of the top was her tequila. Before he'd had a chance to question what he was doing, Toby had removed the cap and swallowed three large slugs. He didn't trust anaesthetics.

It was 3.20 p.m. Leah had arranged to meet Toby outside Park Road Baths in Crouch End at three o'clock. She glanced up and down the road once more before giving up and making her way inside.

The pool was quiet. She liked coming here on her day off. She padded barefoot to the end of the pool and slid into the water. It was lukewarm, viscous, immediately calming. She ploughed up and down the bath, feeling the tension leave her shoulder blades, her neck, her hips. After four lengths, she stopped and hugged the edge of the pool. And that was when she saw him.

She wasn't sure it was him at first, the tall, thin man in the tiny schoolboy Speedos that clung film-like to every lump and bump of his genitals. He had no hair and a very strange lopsided face. But as he approached and began to smile, she knew without a doubt. It was Toby.

'Oh my God,' she said. 'Toby. You look so . . . what happened to . . .'

'I'm a monster,' he said. 'Melinda attacked me with a pair of clippers, then a man called Mr Shiyarayagan pulled out one of my teeth.' He opened his mouth to show her the gap. 'And now I am virtually naked in a public place for the first time since my school days.'

The left side of his face was slightly swollen and palsied with anaesthetic. His voice was muffled. 'And I'm sorry I'm so late. It all took so long at the dentist's. I saw the hygienist, too, who felt that my teeth needed nearly an hour's worth of her attention.' He shook his head, disbelievingly. 'It's been a very strange week.'

'Well,' said Leah, 'you may as well continue the theme. Jump in!'

'Oh God.' Toby peered at the water. 'This is just so . . . I haven't been in a pool for so long. I mean, maybe I can't even swim any more?'

'Of course you can. Come on—I'll meet you at the shallow end.'

Toby was looking a little bit wobbly. He stood on the side of the pool contemplating the water, swaying slightly.

'Are you OK?'

'Yes,' he said distractedly. 'I am. It's just the air in here. Doesn't it make *you* feel light-headed?'

'No,' laughed Leah.

'You're probably used to it. It must be the chlorine. Or something. I have to say, I'm feeling really a bit odd.' He took a step closer to the edge and closed his eyes. He swayed unsteadily to the left, then he swayed unsteadily to the right. Then his entire being, all six foot something of it, swayed forwards, poker straight and headfirst into the shallow end of the pool.

'*Toby!*' Leah watched in horror as a thin plume of red ribboned its way up to the surface of the water. Toby's body lay motionless on the bottom of the pool. The lifeguard blew a whistle and people started running towards them. Leah hooked her arms under Toby's armpits and brought him to the surface. 'Oh shit, Toby. Are you OK?'

His eyes were closed and he had a large gash above his right eye. An elderly man appeared at Leah's side and helped her to pull Toby from the pool. Leah scrambled out of the water and pushed her way to him through a cluster of people. 'It's OK,' she said, pushing past the lifeguard. 'I'm a qualified first-aider.' Toby was unconscious and bleeding profusely. She tipped his head backwards and pinched his nose. Then she pulled his lips apart and brought her mouth down over his, to apply the kiss of life. Someone had pressed a towel to his forehead and someone else was calling an ambulance. Leah pushed her hands against Toby's chest, then blew into his mouth again.

Finally, as she took her mouth away from his for the fourth time, Toby coughed. Leah rocked back onto her heels and exhaled heavily. There was an audible sigh of relief from the crowd of onlookers.

Toby coughed again and this time a fountain of chlorinated water left his mouth. He opened his eyes and looked straight at Leah. Then he looked around at the sea of faces. Then he sat up. 'Leah,' he croaked, looking at her in awe. 'Did I just drown?'

'Yes.' She nodded.

'But you saved me?'

She nodded again.

He touched his fingertips to his temple. 'Am I bleeding?'

'Uh-huh. There's an ambulance coming.'

'Oh God, what's going on, Leah? What's happening to me?'

'It's fine,' she soothed. 'You'll be fine. Do you think you can stand up?'

'Yes,' he said. 'No. I don't know. Do you think I should try?'

'Yes.' She smiled and helped him to his feet.

He took the bloodied towel from the man who'd been holding it against his head. 'Thank you,' he said. 'Thank you, everybody.'

He clung on to Leah as they moved towards the changing room, his bare skin against hers. She pulled him towards her by the waist and was struck by the feel of his flesh under her hands. It felt so hard, so vital, compared to Amitabh's softly upholstered body. It was oddly gratifying, almost *thrilling* to see Toby unwrapped, stripped bare of his hair, his clothes, his dignity. It made him real, not just another character in her own personal soap opera, but a *man*.

Someone retrieved Toby's clothes from the changing rooms and now the two of them were sitting together in reception, waiting for the ambulance.

'You'll need stitches in that,' said Leah, peering underneath the bloodstained towel.

'Ah, well,' said Toby wryly, 'that just caps off my week, I suppose.'

'I'm really sorry,' said Leah. 'I feel so guilty.'

'Oh, no.' He looked at her in concern. 'You mustn't feel guilty.'

'Well, I do. It was my idea for you to come swimming. And now you're injured. You could have *died* in there, Toby.'

'No,' he said, 'it's entirely my fault. I had tequila for breakfast . . .'

'You didn't?'

'Yes. I'm ashamed to admit that I did. Not because I have a drink problem, although from my recent appearances you'll probably find that hard to believe. And then God knows what they gave me at the dentist. Gas and air and drugs and . . .' He shuddered. 'I was a fool to come. But I've just been looking forward so much to seeing you . . .'

'Really?'

'Yes, it's all that's got me through the week. The light at the end of the tunnel.'

'Oh, no. And look how it ended up.'

He smiled at her. 'It's ended up fine,' he said. 'I have a scar to add character to my face. And I've been kissed by a beautiful woman. Not that I can really remember much about it.'

Leah smiled, feeling strangely delighted by his description of her as a beautiful woman. 'It was very nice,' she said. 'You're a very good kisser.'

'Even when I'm comatose?'

'Absolutely.'

'Well, that's good to know,' he said, 'for the next time I'm kissing somebody in an unconscious state. And I'm so grateful to you for not letting that man save my life.'

'The lifeguard?'

'Yes. I would have been horrified if I'd come to, with his hairy chops all over me.'

Leah laughed. 'That's why I didn't let him. I knew you'd be appalled.'

He smiled at her and Leah was suddenly struck by how incredibly different he looked without his hair and sideburns.

'You know something,' she said, 'I was wrong. You've got a very nice-shaped head. In fact, I prefer you without your hair.'

'You do?'

'Yes,' she said. 'You used to look like Tom Baker. Now you look like Christopher Ecclestone.'

'Oh,' he said. 'That's what Melinda said. Is that a good thing, then?'

'Yes,' she said. 'It is. It's a very good thing indeed.'

The ambulance pulled up outside the baths and Leah got into the back with Toby.

'You know you don't have to come with me, don't you?'

'Yes,' she said. 'I know. But I want to.'

'Good,' said Toby. He took hold of her hand. 'Good.'

They were still holding hands when the ambulance pulled up outside A & E ten minutes later.

Chapter 7

TOBY NOW RESEMBLED a Gorbals hard nut on a Sunday morning. They'd closed his gashed forehead with eight stitches and his eye had swollen up and taken on the coloration of the late stages of a Caribbean sunset. People kept their distance from him when he walked down the street, even in his brand-new agnès b jacket and suede desert boots. He was a towering skinhead with a black eye, stitches and a missing tooth. Everyone he came into contact with recoiled at the sight of him. In some ways it freaked him out; in other ways it liberated him.

And maybe that was why he suddenly found himself able to take the reins, to take control of his house. He had until next week to break the news to his housemates that he was selling the house and that they had to move out. After that he had three weeks to redecorate their rooms (regardless of whether or not they were still in them) and finish off the house. He couldn't afford to mess around any more.

He headed for Con and Melinda's room first. The old Toby would have felt impolite knocking on his tenants' doors in the middle of the evening. The new Toby didn't give a shit.

Con opened the door to him. Melinda wasn't in the room.

'Hello, Con. D'you mind if I come in?'

'No. Sure.' Toby glanced around the room, quickly making mental notes for his decorating scheme. 'Do you mind if I . . .?' He pointed at the edge of the carpet and fell to his knees. 'I just need to see if you've got floorboards under here.' He pulled back the green patterned carpet and peered underneath. 'Um-hmm.' He nodded to himself and pushed the carpet back down onto the tracks. 'Very good.'

Con looked at him. 'What are you doing that for?'

'Oh, just thinking about taking up all the carpets, you know, stripping all the floorboards. Just wanted to check yours were sound.'

Con nodded and sat on his mum's bed.

Toby passed his palm over the velvety crown of his head and smiled. 'So, Con. How are things? I feel we haven't spoken for a while. All going well with Daisy?'

Con shrugged and fiddled with Melinda's hairbrush.

'Ah, dear, that seems a bit . . . unpromising. Is it not working out?'

'Yeah, well, the whole thing was a joke, really.'

'Oh,' said Toby, 'why's that?'

'I dunno. Her family, you know—they were just so . . .'

'Condescending? Arrogant? Unwelcoming?'

'No. None of that. They were really nice to me when I met them, but it seemed a bit . . .'

'Fake?'

'Yes. Well, no. It just didn't make any sense, that's all. They've got this beautiful girl, they've sent her to the best schools, looked after her, watched her going in and out of hospital since she was a kid. I mean, surely they'd want the best for her?'

'Well, yes, but I don't see your point.'

'Well, it's obvious, isn't it? Why would they want someone like me hanging around their girl?'

Toby sighed. 'Have you talked to Daisy about this?'

Con shook his head, pulled a hair out of Melinda's hairbrush and twisted it round his little finger. 'We're not really talking any more.'

'You mean, it's over?'

He shrugged. 'Yeah. I guess so.'

'But, Con, that's ridiculous. You're in love with this girl. You've cooked for her, written her poetry. This girl was all set to change your life.'

'Yes!' Con slapped the hairbrush against his thigh. 'Yes! Exactly. She was all set to change my life. And I didn't want her to. I like my life. I've got plans. Things I want to do.'

'You can do those things with Daisy, surely?'

'What—go off and live in the Caribbean? And what happens next time she gets a lung infection, or a chest infection? What happens then, when we're a plane ride away from the nearest decent hospital? What do you think Mummy and Daddy dearest will think about that? No, man—it's just too . . . I can't do it. I can't.'

'Well, couldn't you tailor your plans a bit? Maybe you could, I don't know, island-hop in the Channel. Guernsey, Jersey, Sark, the Scillies. Or around the Med, the Greek islands?'

'No,' said Con, 'no. I had a plan. Eighteen months at Condé Nast. Get my licence in South Africa. Head to the Caribbean. I'm sorry, Toby, I know you were really into the whole me and Daisy thing, and I really appreciate everything you did. But it's just not going to happen. OK?'

Toby sighed. 'Well,' he said. 'I think that's a shame, I really do. Real love, it doesn't just pop up when it's convenient, you know? Real love is a pain in the arse. You have to make compromises for it.'

'Yeah, well. I've made enough compromises in my life already.'

'What sort of compromises?'

'Looking after my gran. Working in a shitty job. Sharing a room with my mum.'

'I thought you *liked* sharing with your mum?'

'No. Of course I don't.'

'Then why don't you tell her it's time to move on?'

'No way! I can't kick my own mum out.'

'Why not? She's done it to you.'

'Yeah, but that's different.'

'Why is it different?'

'I don't know. It just is.'

Toby sighed. This called for drastic measures. 'Look,' he said, 'how much does it cost to get your pilot's licence?'

Con sniffed. 'About twelve grand.'

'And how much have you saved up?'

'About five.'

'Right, so you need another seven grand. And you reckon you can save that up in eighteen months?'

'Yeah. If I'm good. If I keep away from the clothes shops, you know.'

'I think that would be pushing it. I think it'll take you more like two years, on your salary. So here's a deal. I lend you the seven grand, you go off and get your licence, pay me back when you get a job. But there are two things I need you to do in return . . .'

Toby's next stop was Joanne's room.

He'd barely seen her since the night the man claiming to be her husband had turned up out of the blue. She'd disappeared for a fortnight and returned three days ago, her hair cut short and bleached white. Nobody, of course, had asked her where she'd been. Curiosity was futile; everyone in the house knew that.

Toby had a plan. It was a simple plan, and one he only now felt able to put into action. His plan was to play her at her own game. He would be as brusque, rigid and inhuman as Joanne, and it needed a man with a skinhead and a black eye to pull it off. Toby breathed in and patted her door with his knuckles.

'Yes?'

'Joanne. It's Toby. Could I have a quick word, please?'

It took a full minute for Joanne to come to her door and when she did she opened it an inch, revealing just a slice of her face to Toby.

'Yes?' she said again.

'Could I come in?'

Her eyes flashed at him in alarm. 'No,' she said. 'I'd prefer it if you didn't.'

'Right,' said Toby. 'Well, then would you mind coming to my room?'

Joanne narrowed her eyes at Toby. 'OK,' she said. 'Give me a moment.'

She was wearing pyjamas when she sidled through the door of Toby's bedroom a minute later. 'What happened to your face?' she asked.

'I fell into the shallow end of a swimming pool, headfirst.'

'And is that why you've got no hair?'

'No,' he said, 'that was Melinda. She decided I had too much hair and took matters into her own hands.'

Joanne nodded and inched a bit nearer. 'It looks better,' she said. 'You did have too much hair before.'

'Oh,' said Toby. 'Right. Anyway. The reason I wanted to see you was to talk to you about what happened here last month.'

'I don't understand.'

'Nick. Your husband.'

'I told you. I don't have a husband. He was just some lunatic—a druggie, probably.'

'Well, how did he know your name?'

She shrugged. 'I have no idea.'

'And if you don't know him, then why did you disappear for two weeks?'

'I told you. I was on holiday. Have we finished now?'

'No. We haven't. Here.' He passed her a can of lager. She took it silently and opened it. 'You wrote to me three years ago. You told me that you were an actress at an interesting crossroads in your life. You told me you'd be acting in a film and that you wanted a room here to give you the freedom to research your role before filming started. That was 2002. It is now 2005 and all I have seen you do is go to work and return home most days with some shopping bag or other. Which leads me to conclude that you have a lot of expendable cash. Which makes me wonder what you're doing here?'

Joanne flushed. It was the first time Toby had ever seen any colour pass through her face.

'Well,' she said, 'you don't know anything about me . . .'

'Indeed I don't. And that's what I'm concerned about. All I know is that you have lots of money, lots of clothes, an attitude problem and a very unhappy ex-husband called Nick. Now, if I knew more about you I might be able to muster up some sympathy for you, but, as it is, I'm finding it harder and harder to feel anything for you at all.'

'I'm not asking you to feel anything for me.'

'No. You're not. But you are asking me to live with you, when you could afford to live pretty much anywhere.'

'I don't have to live here.'

'Then why do you?'

'Because . . .' She paused. 'Because this is where I live.'

'But you don't even like it here.'

'Who said that I don't like it here?'

'My friend Leah. It seems you told her that you found it hard living with us, that you dealt with us by pretending we weren't here.'

'Oh, for God's sake.'

'But it's true?'

'Well, yes, to a certain extent. Sharing a house with people is difficult.'

'Which brings me back to my original question. Why do you live here, when you could afford not to?'

'I don't know.'

'Right, well, I think I know the answer. I think you live here because it means that you don't exist because your signature isn't on anything. I think you live here because you're hiding from something or running from something. And I think that something is Nick. Your husband.'

Toby paused, waiting for Joanne to deny once more that Nick was her husband. But she didn't. Instead she let her head drop dramatically onto her hands. 'He's not my husband,' she said, softly.

'Then who is he?'

'He's my fiancé. Was. He was.'

'Right.' He paused again.

'Did he come back again? While I was away?'

Toby nodded.

'What did he say?'

'Nothing. But he asked me to give you this.'

She looked up at him. Toby reached behind him into his drawer and pulled out a letter. He passed it to her.

She held the envelope in her hands for a moment, running it across her fingertips, staring at the handwriting on the front.

'Would you mind,' she said, 'if I opened it here?'

Toby gulped. 'No. Of course not.'

'Good.' Her hands were trembling slightly as she opened the envelope. She slid the paper out slowly and unfolded it. Her bottom lip was caught under her top teeth as she read.

After a moment, she refolded the letter, and slid it back into the envelope.

'Well,' he said, 'is it what you expected?'

'Mm-hmm,' she said, nodding.

'Are you OK, Joanne?'

'Yes.' She stood up. 'I think so. I . . .'

Toby waited for her to continue. Her lips were moving strangely, trying to form words and control tears at the same time.

'I think, if it's OK with you, that I might, erm, go back to my room now.'

'Yes,' said Toby. 'Of course. Will you be all right?'

'Yes,' she said, 'and thank you for the beer. And the talk. It's been good. I need to go now, and think. Bye.' She threw him a tight smile and left the room, the letter clutched tightly in her fist.

Toby sighed.

Two down, two to go.

Melinda got back from work at five o'clock on Saturday afternoon. Con followed her into the kitchen. 'Cup of tea?'

'Oh, yes, please.' She pulled off her shoes and rubbed her feet. 'What a bloody day. I was going to go to the gym, but I really don't think I can face it.'

'Good,' said Con. 'Stay here. We'll have a nice chat.'

Her face softened and she smiled.

'So,' he said, dropping a tea bag into a mug, 'how's everything?'

'Blimey.' She laughed.

'No. Really. How are you? How's your life?'

'I'm fine, thank you, Connor. How are you?'

'Don't take the piss, Mum.'

'Sorry, love. I'm sorry.' She reorganised her face and considered his question. 'I'm pretty good, actually,' she said.

'Yeah?'

'Yes. It's nice just to be *here*. You know, in one place. Not on the move. And it's so nice hanging around with you.'

Con smiled tightly. 'Even though you have to share a room with me?'

'I *love* sharing a room with you, Con.' She paused and glanced at him. 'Are you trying to tell me something?'

'No.' Con shook his head and filled the kettle from the tap. 'No. It's just, I was talking to Toby last night and he said he'd invited you out for dinner tonight at some bloke's house.'

'Yeah. Can you believe it? He told me about this bloke weeks ago, said he thought I'd like him. Next thing I know he's set us up on a blind date.'

'I think you should go.'

'What? No way.'

'But why not? He sounds great.'

'I don't care how great he sounds. The last thing I need in my life right now is a bloke.'

'What's wrong with blokes?'

'It's not the blokes that are wrong. It's me. I forget what's important. Like you.'

Con flicked on the kettle. 'Mum,' he said, 'I'm nineteen. I'll be twenty in July. I don't need you by my side to know that you care.'

'I know you don't, but . . .'

'You know I don't hold it against you, don't you, that you weren't around? You know it's not a big deal to me?'

'Well, you say that, Con, and I've always appreciated that you haven't made me feel bad about what happened, but, really, how can you not hate me? I mean, I was your mother and I abandoned you.'

'You didn't abandon me, Mum. It's not like you left me outside an orphanage, is it? You left me with a truly great woman.'

'Is that really how you feel?'

'Yeah. Definitely. Don't get me wrong, I'm not saying you wouldn't have been a great mum, but Gran was the right person to bring me up. And leaving me with her—you did the right thing, Mum. Totally.'

Con had wanted to say that to his mum for so long, since that very first time he'd seen her at Gran's funeral. There were no 'mistakes' in life—just a series of random decisions that led to a series of random outcomes, good and bad. How could he blame his mother for doing something that had caused him no harm? For making a decision that had hurt her more than it had hurt him?

Melinda looked up at him. Her eyes were brimming with tears. 'Do you really mean that?' she whispered.

'Yes,' he said. 'Totally.'

'Oh, Con.' She got to her feet and embraced him. 'That means so much to me, to hear you say that. So much. I've hated myself for so long, for being so weak.'

'Well, stop it.' He squeezed her back, his nose buried in her shoulder. She smelt of Gucci Rush and Fairy fabric conditioner. She smelt like his mum. 'I love you, Mum.'

'I love you, too, Con.'

'But you know we can't live like this any more?'

'Well, no, obviously we can't. I mean, that would just be . . .'

'I'm going to South Africa.'

'Yes,' she said, 'I know you are.'

'No,' he turned his back to her and pulled the tea bag out of her mug. 'I mean I'm going soon. Next month.'

'What? But how can you . . .'

'Toby's lending me the money.'

'Toby?'

'Yes, look. I think Toby's up to something.'

'Why, what did he say?'

'He didn't say anything. It was just . . . I don't know, something in the air. And why would he be doing all this work to the house just for our benefit? I think he's going to sell the house. I think it's time to move on.'

'Oh God, but *where*? Maybe I could come to South Africa with you?'

Con laughed. 'No, Mum! South Africa's about me. It's about finding myself. It's time for you to find yourself now.'

'I'm a bit old for finding myself, aren't I?'

'Well, you know what I mean. I mean—you hate your job. You could go back to air hostessing.'

'I'm too old for that, too. I'm too old for all those jobs I used to love, repping and stuff. Let's face it, I'm too old for adventures. I'll be fifty before I know it.'

'Well, then, how about settling down with a nice man?'

'Oh, I see. You mean, *Toby's* nice man?'

'Well, yeah. Why not? Come on, it's a Saturday night, you can have a few drinks, something nice to eat. And the worst thing that can happen is that you don't fancy the bloke. You'll have had a nice night out with Toby and it won't cost you a penny. Go on.'

Melinda looked at him suspiciously. 'Are you trying to get rid of me?'

'Yes,' he said, 'I am. But only because I love you. Only because I want you to be happy.'

Melinda smiled. 'All right, then, I'll go.'

Con beamed. 'Excellent!' he said. Then he kissed his mother on the cheek and took the stairs two at a time to Toby's room to tell him that he'd completed the first half of their bargain.

Melinda had pulled out all the stops for her blind date at Jack's house. She was wearing a turquoise satin dress with sequins round the neckline and contrasting green satin stilettos. Her hair was swept back and held in place with a bejewelled comb and she was clutching a tiny gem-encrusted handbag. Toby met her at the bottom of the stairs and gasped. 'Wow, Melinda, you look quite superb.'

She beamed at him. 'You don't look too bad yourself.'

'Why, thank you.' Toby smiled and glanced down at his new black trousers and black stripy shirt, bought that morning in a sale at a menswear boutique on the Broadway.

'I'm really glad you changed your mind,' he said.

'Yes,' she said, 'well. Me and Con had a good chat about stuff earlier.'

'Oh, you did?' Toby feigned surprise.

'Yes. He's not a kid any more. He's got his life. It's time I got mine.'

Toby smiled. 'Good,' he said, 'very good.'

The doorbell rang and Toby spun round. He could see Leah's outline through the stained glass. He bounded to the door to let her in.

She was wearing a purple silk shalwar kameez and jeans. Her hair was down and wavy with a small diamanté clip holding it back at one side. It was the most feminine Toby had seen her. 'You look lovely,' he said, holding the door open for her. 'That top is stunning.'

'Thank you,' she said. 'I haven't got any proper evening clothes, but I've got piles of these things. Amitabh's mum was always bringing them back for me from Mumbai.'

'Well, I must say, they really suit you.'

'Thank you,' she said again. 'And you look amazing.' She stroked the sleeve of Toby's shirt. 'New outfit?'

'Yes.'

'Well done.' She smiled at Melinda. 'You look beautiful,' she said.

'Thank you very much. So do you.'

The three of them stood for a moment in the hallway, beaming at each other.

Well, then,' said Toby. 'Shall we go?'

The chemistry between Melinda and Jack was instantaneous.

'Oh, but, Leah, you have brought me a goddess!' said Jack, holding Melinda's outstretched hand in both of his and gazing at her in awe and wonder.

Whether Melinda's reaction to Jack was influenced in any way by the guided tour of his house that he insisted on giving her within moments of her stepping through the front door was impossible to gauge.

Jack and Melinda returned, both looking smiley and delighted.

'Isn't this place *gorgeous*?' said Melinda, smoothing her skirt and seating herself on the edge of the sofa.

Jack's smile broadened and he offered everyone Bloody Marys.

'So, Toby.' Jack passed him his glass, replete with celery stick and crushed black peppercorns. 'What have you done to yourself? A sporting injury?'

'Oh, my eye? I fell into a swimming pool.'

'He was drunk,' chipped in Leah.

'Well, only a little bit. It was the drugs, really . . .'

'The *drugs*?' Jack raised an alarmed eyebrow.

'Not those sort of drugs. Dentists' drugs. I had a tooth removed. I shouldn't have gone swimming.'

'It was my fault,' said Leah. 'We went for a walk in Kenwood and he nearly passed out walking up a slope and I was so horrified by how unfit he was that I made him come swimming with me—'

'Even though I haven't swum since I was sixteen—'

'And to prove it he wore his school trunks—'

'Yes. It's true. They still have my name label in the back.'

'I am impressed that they still fit you,' said Jack, patting his own girth. 'I would be happy to get my school trunks onto one thigh these days.'

'Don't put yourself down,' said Melinda. 'You've got a lovely physique.'

'For an old man, you mean?' Jack smiled. 'I work out,' he said, 'at the gym, three times a week.'

'Oh, really, which gym are you at?'

'Esporta,' he said.

'Oh, yes,' said Melinda, 'I know the one. Very smart. I'm at the Manor on Fortis Road. Plus I do Pilates twice a week and kick boxing on a Wednesday.'

'Yes,' said Jack, his eyes skimming appreciatively up and down her body. 'It is clear that you look after yourself. But, not too well, I hope.'

'What do you mean?' She giggled.

'Well, it's not good for a woman to exercise away all her . . . softness. It's not good for a woman to feel like a man.'

Melinda laughed and Jack smiled. 'And now, I must go and stir something.'

'Need a hand?' said Melinda.

'That would be lovely.'

Toby waited until they'd left the room, then nudged Leah gently with his elbow. 'You are so good at this,' he whispered.

'What?'

'You really do know people. I mean, Jack and Melinda—genius.'

Leah smiled and rubbed her fingernails against her collarbone. 'I can't deny I have a certain knack.'

'He's got a maid in there!' said Melinda, bursting back into the living room. 'Some little Asian girl—wearing an *apron*!'

'Oh my God,' said Leah. 'That's dreadful.'

'Why is that dreadful?' asked Melinda. 'I'm sure he pays her well. And you can't expect a man like Jack to look after a big house like this all by himself.'

Leah shrugged. 'So,' she said, 'what do you think?'

'What do I think? I think he's gorgeous. Totally. And such a nice man. So funny. And that accent . . .'

'Look,' said Leah. 'We need a secret code. A special thing that you say when you want to get rid of us.'

'Yes,' said Toby, 'we'd hate to outstay our welcome.'

'I'm not that sort of girl,' Melinda said primly, 'but if I say ai carumba, then scarper.'

Over the course of the next three hours Jack and his Filipino maid, Marietta, served up five courses of superb Italian food. Platters of aged Parma ham and cornichons, truffle and wild mushroom soup, sea bass with lemon and parsley, and Amaretto-soaked pears with cloves and vanilla cream. He poured bottle after bottle of expensive wine into huge glasses and served them homemade almond biscotti with tiny cups of coffee from a proper Gaggia espresso machine. Then, once they'd finally started to digest the first four courses, Jack brought out a cheese board and a bottle of pudding wine the colour of early-morning pee.

'Ai carumba,' said Melinda, caressing her distended belly. 'I've never been so stuffed in my life.'

Toby and Leah folded their napkins, made their excuses, collected their coats and left.

'**W**ell,' said Toby, pulling on a knitted hat outside Jack's house. 'I think we can safely call that a success.'

They smiled at each other.

'Walk me home?' said Leah.

'Yes,' said Toby, 'why not? Although it is, of course, a little out of my way.'

They headed towards the Broadway. The pubs had just closed and the streets were full of drunk people looking for cabs. Toby instinctively brought his arm round Leah's waist to protect her. He didn't even realise he'd done it until they turned into Silversmith Road and it was still there. 'So,' he said, 'swimming again on Thursday?'

She laughed. 'Only if you're sure you can face it.'

'Absolutely,' he said. 'What doesn't kill me makes me stronger.'

'Great,' she said. 'It's a date. But you might want to buy yourself some new trunks.'

'Oh dear. Were they terribly embarrassing?'

'Well. They weren't the best look.'

'New trunks it is, then,' he said. 'And if you're free, afterwards, I'd like to take you for a drink. Just to say thank you. For saving my life.'

'I didn't save your life!'

'Yes, Leah, you really did. And in so many ways.' He sighed and looked at her. He couldn't believe that he had to deposit her at a house that she shared with another man. 'So—what's going to happen with you and your nurse? Is he going to marry you now?'

Leah shrugged. 'I don't suppose so. But then, I never really wanted to marry him in the first place. I just wanted some sort of confirmation, I suppose, that my life was going somewhere. That I wasn't going to end up like Gus.'

Toby nodded. 'So is it—going somewhere?'

'No,' she sniffed, 'not really.' She laughed wryly.

'Then why . . .?'

'Why did I take him back?'

'Well, yes.'

'Because he asked. And because . . . because I was lonely.'

'Oh, Leah.' Toby stopped and turned her towards him. 'How could a girl like you ever be *lonely*? Someone as vital and good and clever as you.'

'Well, if I'm so clever, then why have I let this man back in my life when I know that any day now his mother will present him with some twenty-year-old from Mumbai with eyes like coals and he'll be gone in a flash.'

'So, if that's the case, then why has he moved back in?'

'Because it's better than living at the nurses' home. Because I'm a nice girl. Because he can't cope with the reality of what's expected of him.

Basically because he's in some sort of state of arrested development.'

'So, you're back at square one?'

'Totally. All I know is that as long as Amitabh's living with me I don't have to hand in notice on the flat, therefore I don't have to look at any more shitty flat shares and I can pretend that I'm still a grown-up.'

'Can't you find somewhere on your own?'

She shook her head. 'Can't afford it.'

'Leah—this is crazy.'

'I know. I know it is.' She sighed and lowered her eyes.

'Just tell him to go!'

'I can't.'

'You can! I'll lend you some money.'

'Oh, Toby, I can't. I . . .'

'Yes. You can. I've got no mortgage on my house, you know? Once I sell it I'll have hundreds of thousands of pounds.'

'Yes, but you'll need that, to buy a new house, start your new life.'

'I'll need some of it, but not all of it.'

'No way, Toby. Absolutely not. You've spent the past fifteen years subsidising other people. It's time to let go, let people take responsibility for themselves. But thank you. Thank you for offering. You are a very generous man.'

Toby smiled wanly. 'To a fault, it seems.'

She squeezed his hand and smiled. 'Yes, well, maybe.'

Toby squeezed her hand back and then, because it seemed like it wouldn't be entirely the wrong thing to do, because she wasn't in love with her nurse, because she was lonely and lost just like him, he reached out with his other hand and stroked her cheek. Her skin was cold and smooth under his palm. She lowered her eyes briefly, then smiled. 'You've got cold hands,' she said.

'And you've got cold cheeks.'

'Time to go home,' she said.

'Yes,' he said, 'let's go home.'

He draped his arm across her shoulders and they walked down Silversmith Road in a warm and companionable silence.

Con completed the second half of his bargain with Toby on Monday. At lunchtime, instead of hiding in the break room as he'd been doing every day since Daisy had been back at work, he went upstairs to the fashion department.

She was sitting on the edge of another girl's desk, looking at some photographs. She glanced at him as he walked in, then glanced away again, muttering something to the girl.

'Daisy,' he started.

She looked up at him again, in surprise. 'Yes?'

'Are you busy?'

Daisy looked at the girl, then back at Con. She shrugged. 'No,' she said, 'not really.'

'Fancy lunch?' He held a plastic bag aloft. 'I made the bread myself.'

Daisy sighed, frowned, looked at the bag, looked at him. 'OK,' she said. 'Give me a minute.'

They took the sandwiches into Hanover Square and sat awkwardly side by side on a bench. Con passed a sandwich to Daisy. She took it silently.

'Crab and cucumber,' said Con. 'Homemade bread and organic butter.'

She handled the sandwich sadly. 'I'm leaving,' she said after a moment.

'What?'

'*Vogue*. I'm leaving *Vogue*. Leaving London.'

'Why? It's not because of . . .?'

'No. It's not because of you. Though what happened, it didn't really help. No, it's just not working out. I hate my job. I hate London. And it's not fair on Mimi, having to look after me. So I'm going home.'

'When?'

'I'm working out my notice. Three weeks, then I'll be gone.'

Con stared at his sandwich. He didn't know what to say. 'What will you do?' he said eventually.

Daisy shrugged. 'I don't know. I've got a friend who owns a restaurant in the village. I could see if he's got anything for me there. Maybe waitressing. I don't know. All I know is that I gave it my best shot.'

'That's fair enough, I guess.'

'Yes,' she said. 'It's the right thing. I feel happier already.'

'I'll miss you,' he said.

'Will you?'

'Of course I will. Look, Daisy. I'm sorry,' he said. 'I don't really know what happened.'

'It's OK,' she said. 'It's done. You don't need to say anything else.'

'No, but I do.' He turned to face her. 'Look, you were right. I freaked out, at the hospital. Seeing you like that, thinking you might be, you know, *dying* and your family, they're so different to mine. You know, bassoon players with the Philharmonic whatever. I left that hospital feeling like I'd been on another *planet*.'

'So, why didn't you just say? I would have understood.'

'I don't know.' He shook his head. 'We were in the break room, all those blokes in there. And I didn't know myself what I wanted to do. But then, seeing you, every day when I collected the post, up there—' He pointed at her floor of the Condé Nast building. 'We were like strangers. And I realised that I have to give this a chance. Because, you know, love's not always *convenient*, *is* it? Sometimes it's just a pain in the arse. But if you don't try, then you don't know. And I want to try. And I want to know. Because otherwise I'll spend the rest of my life wondering what happened to the first girl I ever cared about, what happened to you. And that would tear me up, totally.'

It was silent for a moment. Con put his untouched sandwich back in the bag.

Daisy sighed. 'I don't really understand. What exactly are you saying?'

'I'm saying that I love you and that I'm sorry for what I did and that I want to be with you.'

'Oh, Con. It's too late now. I'm moving away. It's all too late.'

'No,' he said, 'it's not. Toby's offered to pay for my flying lessons. I've spoken to a couple of schools in South Africa that have got places, where I could start next month. But if you say that you'll forgive me, if you say that you'll let me into your life, let me look after you, I'll wave goodbye to South Africa. There are flying schools in this country. They're more expensive, but Toby's said he'll lend me the money. I could be anywhere. Anywhere that you are.'

Daisy sighed again. 'But I'll still be ill. My parents will still be my parents. My sister's boyfriend will still be a bassoonist.'

'Yeah, I know all that. But I won't be *me*. I won't be a postboy who shares a room with his mum in a jumped-up squat. I'll be a trainee pilot. I'll have my own place. I'll be, you know, *going somewhere*. Being someone. I'll be good enough for you.'

'But, Con,' she said, 'that's the whole stupid bloody point. You already were.'

'No.' He shook his head. 'I wasn't. I really wasn't. But meeting you and knowing you, you make me want to be everything. I want to look after you. I want to make you proud.'

Daisy smiled then, and picked up his hand. 'There's a flying school two miles up the road from my parents' place,' she said.

'Really?'

'Yeah. I'll pick you up a brochure, if you like.'

'Cool.'

Con nodded and smiled. Then they both picked up their sandwiches and ate them in silence, their hands firmly grasped together on the bench between them.

Toby put a bowl of tortilla chips on the coffee table and glanced at the time. It was just before eight, two minutes until the house meeting was supposed to start. Ruby was the first to appear.

She collapsed on the sofa and scooped up a handful of tortilla chips. 'So—this is all very mysterious. *House meeting*. Hmmm . . .' She put her index finger to her lip and adopted a sarcastic tone. '*I wonder what it could possibly be about?*'

Footsteps on the staircase behind them heralded the arrival of Melinda and Con. They both sat down on the other sofa and Con helped himself to a handful of chips.

The last person to arrive was Joanne, fresh from work and clutching a Jane Norman carrier bag.

Toby stood up. He glanced around the room. Four pairs of eyes gazed back at him. This was it, the moment he never thought would come, the scenario he'd never been able to envisage. 'Thanks for coming,' he began. 'I know you've all got busy lives.'

Ruby snorted, like a teenage girl in the back row of the classroom.

'Anyway, the reason I've brought you all together tonight is because I have an important announcement to make, one that will impact on all of you. As you know, my father bought me this house fifteen years ago, as a place for me to live with my wife. As you also know, my wife left me three weeks later and I haven't seen her since. Since then I have used this house as a place for people to stay for a while, when life isn't on their side, a place for people to work out their dreams and hopes, and hopefully find a way to move on. I would probably have gone on using the house for those aims indefinitely, but for two events that occurred within two days of each other. I received a letter from my father, announcing that he was coming back to the country and wanted to see how I was doing. But just before that, Gus, my sitting tenant, died and I discovered a letter from him under his bed, telling me that he had left me a sum of money, with specific instructions that I use it to refurbish this house. And to, er . . . well—to get on with my life. Because Gus felt, as I now feel, that I've got rather stuck in a rut, rather *lost* my way. So I will be putting the house on the market as soon as the renovations are complete. And, I'm afraid, I will have to now give you all four weeks' notice, as of today.'

Toby stopped and lifted his gaze from a stain on the carpet.

'Ooh,' said Ruby, her hand against her chest, 'what a *shock*.'

The other three just stared at him blankly.

'Well,' said Con, eventually. 'I think that's cool. I do.'

'Yes,' said Melinda, 'good on you, Toby. You deserve it.'

Toby looked at Joanne. Her face was blank. She placed her hands on her kneecaps, then rose slowly to her feet. Then she left the room, her footsteps silent and unfathomable.

'Joanne, it's Toby.'

The door opened and Joanne's face appeared. She'd been crying.

'What?' she said.

'I want to talk to you.'

'What about?'

'About what happened just now. About moving out.'

'It's fine,' she said.

'Well, no, it's clearly not fine.'

'It is,' she said, starting to close the door.

Toby stuck his foot in the gap and waved a bottle of white wine at her. 'Here,' he said, 'share it with me. Let's have a drink and a talk.'

'I really don't want to talk. It's your house. You can do what you want with it. It just would have been nice if you'd given us all a bit more notice. Evidently you've known about this plan of yours for a while. Since Gus died. I don't understand why you're only telling us now.'

Toby smiled. 'Well,' he said, 'perhaps if you let me in, I could explain.'

She shook her head. 'It's a tip in here. Let's go to your room.'

Joanne looked like a small, rather unwell child with her white-blonde hair, her red eyes and pinched nose.

Toby handed her a glass of wine and she took it gratefully.

'I understand,' he said, 'that it might seem strange that I've only just given you all notice, but there's a reason why I didn't tell you sooner.'

She nodded wanly and sipped her wine.

'I felt as if you were all my responsibility and that therefore I couldn't just kick you out without ensuring that you were all ready to go. So I've been trying to get to know you all a bit better. Which I've found rather hard. But I've also found it strangely exhilarating at times, the journey over the past few weeks, the things I've learned about the people with whom I live. I really feel as if I've made an impression, as if they've moved on in some way. But you, Joanne, I don't know. You're . . . *impossible*.'

A small wry smile cracked her deadpan face. 'Yes,' she said, 'I know.'

'I haven't a clue who you are, where you're from, what you want, why you're here. So I'm resigned to having to let you go out into the world as I found you. A mystery. An enigma. A lost soul . . .'

'I am not lost.'

'Oh, Joanne. Of course you are. You're nearly middle-aged, yet you have no profession, no home, no friends. You change your image with the frequency of an immature teenage girl, you spend all your money on clothes and cosmetics, and yet you never go anywhere. And then this man arrives, this sad man with tears in his eyes, a man you used to love, who still, it seems, loves you. He leaves you a letter that makes you cry, yet you ignore it. You carry on as if it never happened. I mean, Joanne, what is it that you left behind when you came here? What could be so bad that living with strangers is preferable? Why have you allowed yourself to become a peculiar, unlovable *freak* when clearly you have known love in your life, when clearly you have known more?'

Joanne gulped and rolled her wineglass between her hands, disconsolately. 'Is that what I am?' she asked, her eyes brimming with tears. 'A freak?'

Toby nodded. 'Yes.'

She sighed and let her head fall onto her chest. 'I just, I don't know what else to be. I can't remember how to be *me* any more.'

'You?' said Toby. 'What was you?'

'Me was . . .' She sniffed. 'Me was someone who'd lost their way in life, then found it again. Me was in love. Me was happy. Me was . . .' She paused, stared into her wineglass then looked up at Toby, her eyes luminescent with sorrow, 'a *mother*.'

Joanne Fish was born in Ipswich in 1971. Her parents split up when she was five years old and she moved with her mother to Norwich. Her mother died in a car crash when Joanne was ten and she moved to London to live with her father and his girlfriend in Lewisham. Her father was an actor, an alcoholic, always out of work and spending his dole money in the pub. His girlfriend was called Drew. She was twenty-one and a drug user. Joanne's father left the two of them alone most nights when he went to the pub. Joanne would watch Drew in fascination, fixing up her drugs. She'd been living with her father and Drew for nearly two years before the inevitable happened and Drew offered to let her try it for herself. Joanne had just turned twelve.

Drew moved out when Joanne was thirteen and took her drugs with her. That was when Joanne started stealing to feed her habit. She was expelled from school and put into care.

Between her fourteenth birthday and her eighteenth birthday she spent a total of eighteen months in juvenile detention centres and she was given her first proper prison sentence a week after her eighteenth birthday—three years for aggravated burglary. It was at Holloway that she finally found something she loved to do. Acting. Her teacher was a tall, thin man called Nicholas Sturgess, ten years her senior. He proposed to her the day she was released and she moved straight into his house, a three-bedroom terrace in New Cross.

She got a place at the Central School of Speech and Drama, completed a BA in Acting in Film and graduated when she was twenty-five. Her father died of liver failure two years later and Joanne nursed him until the end. Shortly afterwards, she and Nick started talking about having a family. They tried for three years without success, then embarked on a course of fertility treatment. Joanne's years of drug abuse had damaged her reproductive organs, but finally, six months after starting treatment, Joanne fell pregnant and she delivered an eight-pound baby girl on New Year's Day. They called her Maisie and took her home. Joanne had never felt so happy in her life. For once she had everything a person was supposed to have. A career. A home. A lover. A family. Maisie was a good baby, but Joanne was tired. Very tired. The labour had taken her through two nights without sleep and she still hadn't recovered. So Joanne slept when Maisie slept, either next to her on the double bed or on the sofa while she fed.

One Thursday afternoon, when Maisie was three weeks old, Joanne put her to her breast, her small soft body resting on a pillow on her lap. She switched on the television and adjusted Maisie's head slightly, angling her nipple back into her baby's warm mouth. And then she fell asleep.

When she woke up, Maisie was still and cool on the pillow. She put her hand to her cheek, gently, not wanting to wake her. Her skin felt icy. She looked blue. Joanne picked her up, and held her to her chest. Maisie flopped from side to side. She patted her back. She laid her back on the pillow and stared at her. What had been only a faint sense of discomfort had grown into a sickening certainty. Her baby wasn't breathing. She rested the pillow on the sofa and got to her knees on the floor.

She opened Maisie's mouth and tipped back her head. She breathed into the sweet milk-scented cave of her mouth, once, twice, three times. She put her ear to her baby's tiny rib cage and listened for her heartbeat. She couldn't hear it. A sob caught in her throat and she choked. She opened her mouth to scream, but no sound came.

She called the ambulance. She told them what had happened; she told them where she lived. She put down the phone, then she rested her cheek on her dead baby's stomach until they came and took her baby away.

Nick met her at the hospital. Asphyxiation. Her baby had been suffocated to death, by her. She'd crushed her against the pillow, with the weight of her tiredness and the depth of her sleep.

They buried her the following week, just the two of them. Joanne couldn't deal with anyone else. She couldn't deal with anything. Nick said, 'It's not your fault, it's my fault. I should have taken more paternity leave. I should have been there for you both. I knew how tired you were.' Nick said, 'We will get over this. We will.' Nick said, 'I love you, Joanne. I love you. Please, don't cut me out.'

And then, five months after Maisie's death, sitting in the waiting room at the doctor's surgery, hoping to be prescribed antidepressants strong enough to block out all the pain, Joanne saw Toby's advert in *Private Eye*. She picked up her pills from the chemist, she went home and she composed a letter full of lies. When Toby wrote back and offered her the room, she packed a suitcase and left. She left Nick a note that said: 'Don't try to find me.'

She settled into Toby's house and started temping. Every week a different company, a different role. And Joanne loved the freedom that the anonymity of temping gave her. She could be anyone she wanted. She made up stories. I live in Chelsea. My husband's an art dealer. I live in Chiswick with my sister—she's a hairdresser. She took each job as if it were a role in a film. She planned her costumes, researched her part, learned her lines.

Then, one day, she'd been walking home from the underground station and a tall, fair man had grabbed her elbow. It was Nick. 'I thought you were dead,' he said. 'I thought you were dead.' She packed a bag and she checked herself into a small hotel in Bloomsbury. She stayed there for two weeks, until she ran out of money, then she came back to Toby's house. Toby had changed. His hair was cut brutally short. He had a black eye. He made her talk to him. It was the first time she'd talked to anyone, as herself, as Joanne Fish, in more than two years. It was very strange. Toby gave her a note from Nick. It said, 'Please, Joanne, come home. I haven't moved on and I can't until you're back where you belong. Nothing in this world makes any sense without you. I love you.'

She didn't know what to do, what to think. She'd put Nick in a box when she moved into Toby's house and she'd imagined that he'd have done the same with her. She thought about him occasionally, imagined him with a new wife, a new baby, getting on with his life. And who could blame him? She couldn't imagine why he'd ever have wanted to be with someone like her in the first place, someone whose arms were scarred by years of drug abuse. She'd failed as an actress. She'd failed as a mother. She'd failed as a human being. But for some reason he still wanted her in his life.

She kept the note close to her at all times. She absorbed its meaning word by word, day by day. And every time she read it, she let a little bit more of her old self trickle back into her soul. And then Toby called a meeting, told her something she'd never thought possible. He was selling the house, kicking her out. He talked to her in his room, told her she was turning into a freak. She'd suspected as much, but to hear it put so frankly, so directly, was like having a bucket of iced water poured over her head. She went to bed at midnight that night, full of wine and thoughts and feelings. She glanced around her room, at the shadowy lumps of unworn clothes and the ghostly images of her dead mother and father in the frame next to her bed. She picked up the picture and peeled off the back cover. Then she pulled out a picture of Maisie and held it to her heart, hot, steady tears flowing down her cheeks.

Ruby started packing on Tuesday. Tim had signed a contract on a two-bedroom penthouse flat off Carnaby Street and they were moving in on Saturday.

She looked around the room, taking in all the detail, the cornicing, the layers of dust, the tendrils of old cobweb, the cheap furniture buried under layers of her possessions. She'd been here, in this room, since she was sixteen. She'd written countless songs, practised countless chords, slept with countless men. She eaten her supper up here, she'd cried up here, she'd got drunk with her friends. This *was* her home. It had never really occurred to her that she'd leave. She'd never imagined that Gus would die, that Toby would change, that she'd be packing away the contents of her room and leaving here for ever.

There was a gentle knock on the door. She sighed.

'Yes?'

'Ruby, it's me. Can I come in?'

'Sure.'

The door opened and Toby walked in. He was wearing a really quite nice grey crew-necked sweater with really quite nice jeans. With his short hair and his clean-shaven face he looked strangely, almost unnervingly good. Ruby didn't like it. Toby wasn't supposed to look good. He was supposed to look like Toby. This house wasn't supposed to have sexy bathrooms and a designer kitchen. And Ruby—well, Ruby wasn't supposed to be moving into a flat with a nice but fundamentally dull banker called Tim. She was supposed to be unconventional. She was supposed to live on the edge. But right now her options had dried up. Right now Tim was all she had.

'I brought you a cup of tea,' said Toby, handing her a steaming mug.

'Oh,' she said, 'thank you.'

'So,' he said, 'how's it going?'

She shrugged. 'Only just started,' she said. 'It's tempting just to throw it all away. Start afresh.'

'Well, then, why don't you?'

'No,' she said. 'I can't. If I throw this lot away, I might just evaporate.' She tried for a smile, but didn't quite make it. Toby threw her a concerned frown.

'Are you sure about this?' he said. 'About moving in with Tim?'

She nodded defensively.

'Because you don't have to move out right now, you know. You've got a couple of weeks.'

'A couple of weeks?' she said. 'Oh, well, why didn't you say? That's *plenty* of time for me to get a job and earn enough money to put down a deposit on a flat and sort my entire life out, isn't it?'

'Ruby, I've been trying to encourage you for weeks now, ever since you and Paul split up. I've been saying to you that you must take responsibility, grow up. You could have gone out and found a job, but instead you went out and did what you always do—found a man.'

'Yeah, well, it's all right for you. Your rich *daddy* bought you a big house and now you're cashing in. You'll be fine. But what have I got? Nothing. Nothing but a nice body and a good voice. And if I can't earn a living from my voice, then I have to fall back on the only other thing I'm any good at.'

'No, Ruby. You're wrong. You don't know what you're capable of because you've never tried. You came to this house as a talented singer/songwriter with a penchant for booze and seedy men. And nothing's changed. You haven't changed. Because you're too scared to see what else you can do in life.'

'I'm not scared,' she said. 'I'm not scared of anything. You're the one who's sat in his room for fifteen years, wasting your life. I've been out there. I've been living. It's not my fault things haven't worked out.'

Toby sighed. 'No. It's not. It's not your fault. It's my fault.'

She looked at him questioningly.

'I made life too easy for you. I should have been tougher. I should have seen what was happening and done something to stop it.'

'What was happening? Christ—you make it sound as if I'm some kind of failure.'

'No.' He shook his head sadly. 'I don't think you're a failure. I think you're incredible. I just wish you believed that, too.'

Toby crossed the room, and kissed the top of her head, before turning and leaving, closing the door silently behind him. Ruby sat for a moment, thoughts going round her head like a cyclone. Then she picked up a book and hurled it at the back of the door.

On Thursday morning, Ruby and Tim filled a hire van with Ruby's accumulated clutter. Tim bought a magnum of Bollinger, which he left in the fridge as a thank you to the house, and they left. Nobody saw them off. As the van pulled away from the house, Ruby glanced up towards Toby's window and saw him there, a pensive figure, staring sadly down into the road.

Ruby swallowed the lump in her throat and concentrated instead on the road ahead, on her new life, on the man by her side, on the future.

Toby met Leah outside Park Road Baths on Thursday afternoon. In his carrier bag he had a brand-new pair of trunks, purchased that very morning from his favourite menswear shop. They were black with a grey stripe down the sides and made of a very unembarrassing cotton fabric that didn't cling to anything at all. Leah looked windswept and dishevelled when she arrived, but she was smiling widely and greeted Toby with a kiss on the cheek.

'Nasty day,' said Toby, following her towards the entrance.

'Vile,' she said, smiling at him over her shoulder. 'Perfect day for a swim.'

Leah was already in the pool when Toby emerged from the changing rooms, clutching his towel to his chest.

'Just be careful,' she teased. 'No stunt dives this time.'

He put the towel down on the side of the pool and carefully picked his way to the shallow end. He lowered himself onto his bottom and let himself slide into the pool. Leah swam to him and got to her feet. Water cascaded off her body. She was wearing a black swimming costume that gleamed in the fluorescent light. Toby tried not to let his gaze wander too freely around her impressive form . . . but it was impossible. She looked so good that he wanted to throw her over his shoulder in the manner of a caveman and make love to her in the undergrowth. He gulped and tried to turn his attention to the matter of getting his whole body under the water and afloat.

He started off on his back, having some vague recollection that that was easier than swimming on your front. Leah smiled encouragingly at him. 'Are you OK?' she mouthed. He nodded, causing water to flood over his brow and into his mouth. He flung himself over onto his front and choked. He really wasn't designed for this. If the optimum aerodynamic design for swimming was, say, the dolphin, then Toby was more of a newborn giraffe. Leah, on the other hand, was sleek and solid and built for the water. She smiled as she swam back towards him. 'Why don't you just splash around in the shallow end for a while, wait until you've got your fins back.'

'My fins?'

'Yes, everybody's got fins. They're invisible. You just have to work out how to operate them.'

'Right.' Toby nodded, unconvinced, and flipped himself over onto his back again. He floated there for a while, listening to the gurgle of underwater movements, the muted echoes of shouting children, and considered his next move. Because he hadn't come to the swimming baths today with Leah to *swim*. Today he was going to take another big step towards his future. Today he was going to do something utterly amazing, but potentially devastating.

Toby had a lot of news to fill Leah in on in the pub over the road. She listened rapt as he told her all about Con and Daisy getting back together and Ruby moving out with Tim. She was moved to tears when he told her Joanne's story and delighted when she heard that Jack had invited Melinda out for dinner.

'So it's nearly all come together?' she said.

'Yes.' He nodded. 'Just got to get the house finished and I'll be ready to move on.'

'To Cornwall?'

'Yes,' he said, 'or maybe Devon. Look.' He pulled open his carrier bag and took out a sheaf of papers: 'I printed these off today, for you to see.' He handed her the papers and watched her while she flicked through them. They were properties he'd found on the Internet. Fishermen's cottages and Georgian town houses and windswept bungalows and barn conversions. Each one represented a dream of some kind or another, a suggestion of a lifestyle, of an existence.

'What do you think?' he said.

'I think,' she said, 'that living in London is the biggest rip-off known to man. I mean, look at this one—' She pulled out the details for a double-fronted cottage facing the sea in a fishing village in Devon. 'That's probably what my flat's worth. A piddling little one-bedroom flat in Finchley? Or a gorgeous three-bedroom cottage *facing the sea*?' She shook her head. 'These are amazing. Completely. I could happily live in any one of them.'

'You could?' he said, his heart starting to race lightly.

'God, yes. Oh, wow, look at this one. Look at the garden. And that kitchen. And it's even got a shop . . .'

'Do you like that one, then?'

'It's amazing. Imagine living there, running your own little shop. How lovely would that be?'

'I think it would be the loveliest thing imaginable,' he said. 'Completely perfect.'

'So, wow, which one are you going to buy?'

'I'm going to buy,' he said, 'the one that you like the best.'

'No,' she laughed, 'it's your dream. You have to decide.'

Toby glanced down at his beer, then back up at Leah. Her hair was still damp from the swimming pool. Her face was clear of make-up. She was so vital, so healthy, so alive. He could imagine her throwing sticks for dogs on beaches, cycling up a hill to get the papers, going for a bracing dip in the sea in the middle of winter. She was a country girl trapped in an urban existence. She would thrive in the country. She would blossom. And so would he.

Toby took Leah's hand in his and breathed in deeply. 'I think you should come with me,' he said.

'What?' She smiled. 'To look at places with you, you mean?'

He breathed out. For a moment he said nothing. He knew exactly what he'd intended to say, what he *wanted* to say. He wanted to say, 'No, come with me and *live with me*. I need you in my life.'

But as he listened to the words in his head, another voice started whispering in his ear, saying, 'This is mad. I mean, why would you leave everything behind to come and live with me? You didn't even *know* me two months ago. And you've got a boyfriend and a job and I'm just some weird bloke who lives over the road. You know, some bloke who's still married to some woman who's probably dead, for all I know. Some bloke who's managed to be in love with a selfish, silly, horrible cow for fifteen years even though he knew it was pathetic, some bloke who *claims* to be a poet though he's written nothing worth even *looking* at for years. For some reason I'd got it into my head that you and I had some kind of future together, that you and I made sense. I thought I was going to make this wild, random, *utterly insane* suggestion and that you would actually give it serious consideration.'

'Ha!' he said, loudly and unexpectedly.

'What?' said Leah.

'Nothing,' said Toby. 'Just, er, I was going to say, but, now, I don't know. And, I just . . . *shit*.' He punched the table. 'I'm such an idiot.' He pulled on his overcoat and began stuffing the property details back into his carrier bag. Leah gazed at him. 'I'm sorry,' he said, 'I have to go. I have to, er . . .'

'Toby,' she said. 'What's the matter? Don't go.'

'Sorry,' he said, 'I have to. Goodbye.'

Leah and Amitabh waited outside the station at Ascot for his father to collect them. Malina had invited them over for lunch.

A gigantic Mercedes SUV swooped to a halt in front of them and Hari got out. He greeted his son with a firm hug and Leah with kisses on either cheek. Leah sat in the back as they headed through the countryside towards their cul-de-sac of executive new-build houses.

Malina was her usual charming self and met them at the door with squeezes and kisses. She brought them beer and asked Leah a million questions about her health and her family and her life. She stood over the hob in their immaculate kitchen, stirring big pans of fragrant-smelling curries and basmati rice.

They had lunch round the dining table, surrounded by framed photographs of Amitabh and his sisters and his brother, in their graduation gowns. Above the fireplace was a family portrait, Hari, Malina and their four children, posed together in a studio in bland early 1990s clothes with too-long hair.

Leah helped herself to another serving of spinach and lentils, and tore off a strip of roti. Amitabh was sweating slightly, rivulets running down his temples, which he mopped up at intervals with a linen napkin.

'Are you OK?' Leah asked, nudging him gently.

'Yeah,' he said, 'I'm fine. I'm just feeling a bit . . . it's nothing.'

Amitabh didn't speak again for the duration of the meal, just grunted in response to questions and shovelled food into his mouth. He was fidgety and distracted, as if he were planning to do a runner.

'What on earth is the matter with you?' Malina finally snapped as she cleared away pudding bowls. 'Are you ill or something?'

'No, I'm not ill. I need to . . . God, I need to do *this*.'

He launched himself from his chair and suddenly he was on his knees, on the floor, at Leah's feet. He grabbed her hands with his sweaty ones and he gazed into her eyes. 'Leah,' he said, 'two weeks ago Mum and Dad offered me a bride. I saw her picture; she is very pretty. And I spoke to her on the phone. She's really nice. A trainee barrister, twenty-six years old. And . . . and I thought about it. I really did. I wanted to want it. I wanted to do the right thing. But all I could think about was how happy we are and how much I love you. And then it hit me, like a bullet, in the head. I can't live without you. I tried it and it was horrible. And I want you to know how serious I am about you, about us. So . . .'

He put his hand into the back pocket of his trousers and pulled out a small velvet-covered box. With clumsy, sweaty fingers he snapped it open and presented it to her. It was an engagement ring. 'Leah, I love you. Will you marry me, please, and be my wife?'

Leah stared at the ring, then at Amitabh. His brown eyes were moist with emotion. The ring was lovely—a plain silver band with a round-cut diamond in it. She watched as he pulled the ring out of its crevasse and started guiding it towards the third finger of her left hand. Then she looked up and saw Hari and Malina and pulled her hand away. 'But,' she said, 'but what about your parents?'

Amitabh looked at them. 'I'm really sorry, Mum, Dad,' he said. 'I know you wanted different things for me, but I'm nearly thirty-one and I'm too old to compromise, too old to do what I'm told. And that girl, she was great. You chose well for me and I appreciate that, but she's not . . . *she's not my Leah*.'

Leah caught her breath and stared at Hari and Malina. Hari was nodding, inscrutably; Malina was crying. Nobody said anything.

'Well,' said Amitabh, finally taking hold of Leah's hands again, 'will you? Will you marry me?'

Leah closed her eyes tightly. When she opened them again, Amitabh was still staring at her. 'I don't know,' she sighed eventually. 'I really don't know.'

'But—I thought this was what you wanted.'

'It was,' she said. 'It's just. It's a bit unexpected. I need time to think. I need . . .'

'Give the girl time to think,' said Malina, stroking her son's shoulder.

'Yes,' agreed Hari. 'This is a big question you have just asked her. Let her breathe.'

'Yes,' said Malina, 'let her breathe.'

Leah smiled wanly and hooped her arms round Amitabh's downcast shoulders. She pressed her face into his thick hair and breathed in his smell, her favourite smell in the world. 'I'll go home,' she whispered. 'You stay here.'

His head nodded faintly underneath her lips. She kissed his crown, then his cheeks, and then Hari drove her back to the station.

Chapter 8

All the structural work had been completed now. The windows had been reglazed, the kitchen and bathrooms were done, the front path had been relaid, the plumber had been, the electrician had been and the plasterers had been. All that was left now was the fun stuff. Painting, carpets, gardening, curtains.

Toby decided that some retail therapy was needed. He'd been in his bedroom pretty much continuously since Thursday evening, nursing the open sores of his self-orchestrated humiliation. He couldn't bear even to peer through his curtains in case he saw her or, worse still, in case she saw him. But it was Monday morning now. She would be at work. The streets were safe. He pulled open the bottom drawer of his desk to get out some cash and gasped.

The drawer was empty.

Over the course of the next ten minutes he searched every single corner of his room, every drawer, box, tray, corner, nook and cranny.

He upturned everything, looked on top of everything, behind everything, underneath everything. It couldn't be. It was impossible. Inconceivable. The fact of the nonexistence of £30,000 could be explained away by only one possibility. Someone he lived with had taken it. He sat on the edge of his ransacked bed and tried to make sense of things. It couldn't be Con. He'd already promised to lend him all the money he needed. There was no reason for him to steal from him. Equally he was sure it couldn't be Melinda. She just wasn't the type. That just left Joanne, a convicted burglar, an ex-drug addict about to be made homeless, or Ruby, a penniless, self-centred musician who'd left the house on Thursday morning without a forwarding address. It could be either of them. '*Shit*,' he hissed at himself, '*shit, shit, SHIT*.'

Leah had her lunch at a café across the road on Monday afternoon. She ordered a bagel and a fizzy water and breathed a sigh of relief. She had so much stuff swirling around inside her head that it was good to be alone. She rested her head on her hands and glanced around the café. Immediately she saw three couples, surrounding her on three sides, seemingly planted by fate to help her consider her situation. On her left sat an Asian couple; young, smart, trendy, sharing a newspaper over two cappuccinos. On her right was a mixed couple: him, Asian; her, white and pregnant. In front of her sat a white couple, with a small baby in a sling. Every possible permutation of her destiny surrounded her. Mixed marriage, arranged marriage, pregnancy, parenthood. And then she saw herself, reflected in a mirror on the other side of the café, a person, no longer a girl, sitting alone with a huge decision to make and no one to help her make it.

Two months ago she'd been ready to settle down, but now, oddly, she wasn't. Her time away from Amitabh had given her space to see that there might be other things in store for her.

She lifted her handbag onto her lap and pulled out a piece of paper. It was the details of the cottage in Devon, the one with the vacant shop at the front that Toby had given her to look at on Thursday. She sighed, imagining herself there, in that snug, simple place. She thought about what she might sell, from that tiny bow-fronted shop. Cakes? Underwear? Hardware? Records? And then, unexpectedly and magically, she imagined Toby there, too, standing with her at the shop counter, his big hands unpacking boxes, smiling shyly at a customer.

She folded the particulars into four, slipped them back into her handbag and headed back for work, feeling only marginally less confused.

Within two minutes of his phone call to Damian explaining his unfortunate situation, three men in overalls had switched off their radio, collapsed their ladders, loaded their van and left. Toby watched them from his window, reversing their van out of its parking space, disappearing up the road, going somewhere to paint walls for someone who could actually afford to pay them. Half an hour later Damian arrived, looking very serious.

'This is bad,' he said.

Toby nodded and handed him a cup of Japanese green tea.

'I know,' said Toby, 'it is truly the epitome of bad. I had thirty thousand pounds and someone has taken it and I have absolutely no way of getting it back. You're not going to take me to court, are you?'

Damian took a sip of his tea and smacked his lips together. He pondered the question. 'No,' he said, eventually. 'No. You're a friend of Leah's. You're a good bloke. But my men need to be paid and we need to work something out.' He got to his feet and started pacing the room. Toby watched him anxiously.

'I tell you what,' he said, 'how about this? I've got a development going on in Mill Hill. I need to furnish it. And this stuff,' he gestured around the room, 'would look the part.'

'What? My furniture?' Toby asked in horror.

'Yeah. These sofas, the coffee table, any other stuff you've got. Conran, you said it was?'

'Yes, but . . .'

'How much would you say it was all worth?'

'Christ. I don't know. Six grand for the sofas, three for the coffee table.'

'Cool. Nine grand. OK, so I'll take this lot and then I'll take the rest when you've sold the house.'

'What, really?'

'Yeah. I like keeping things uncomplicated, you know?'

Toby nodded. He shook Damian's hand, firmly and gratefully, at the door five minutes later.

'I'll let you know about picking up the stuff,' said Damian. 'Probably be early next week, I'd have thought.'

'Excellent,' said Toby, attempting to make the prospect of having no furniture sound like a real treat. 'And the men? They'll be here tomorrow morning, will they?'

Damian gave him a quizzical look. 'The men?'

'Yes. Your men. To finish the job.'

A slow smile of understanding dawned across Damian's face. 'Oh, I see. No,' he said, 'they won't be coming back. I've pulled the job.'

'You have?'

'Sorry, mate. No choice in the matter. But, look, good luck, yeah? And I'll be in touch.'

Toby watched Damian walk down the street, climb into his battered old Land Rover and drive away. Then he turned round and headed inside. The house was a shell. There were approximately sixty walls, fifteen doors, twenty radiators and eighteen window frames to paint, six flights of stairs to carpet and two and a half thousand square feet of floorboards to strip and stain. In two weeks. With one paintbrush, one ladder and one pair of hands.

He had only one option. He had to put it on the market as it was, unfinished, half baked. He had no choice.

Leah watched Toby materialise, foot by foot, as he descended the stairs. She felt a surge of pleasure and smiled.

He led her into the kitchen and she gasped. 'Oh my God. What an absolutely amazing kitchen. Must have cost a fortune.'

'Not as much as you might think. Damian got it for me at trade.'

'Ah,' she said, smiling. 'Good old Damian.'

'Yes,' said Toby, 'indeed. And luckily for me he is good old Damian. Otherwise I'd be on my way to court by now.'

Leah threw him a questioning look.

'Someone's stolen Gus's money. My money. All of it. Every last penny.'

'No!' Leah slapped a hand over her mouth. 'Who?'

He shrugged. 'I don't know,' he said. 'I thought it might be Joanne, but I confronted her and she would have to be an extraordinarily good liar to have pulled off such a convincing denial. And then I thought maybe it was Ruby, that she'd taken it before she left. But then I remembered that I'd seen the money after she moved out. And besides, why would she need to steal my money when she's got Tim to pay for everything? So now I've got no idea. There was no sign of forced entry and nothing else has gone missing.'

'Could it have been one of the builders, perhaps?'

'No.' He shook his head. 'No. The money was still there on Saturday and I realised it had gone on Monday morning before I'd been out of my room. It has to have been someone in the house. But I can't think who.'

'What are you going to do?'

'Nothing,' he said. 'Damian's taking my furniture in lieu of a third of what I owe him and he's taking the rest when I've sold the house. And in the meantime I'm left, stranded, in this bare shell of a house, without a penny to my name.'

'Aren't you going to finish it?'

'No,' he said, 'I'll have to put it on the market as it is, half finished. I shouldn't imagine it will affect the value . . .'

'No, but that's not the point, is it? It's about the house. About knowing that you did it justice. You can't just leave it like this. Where's your closure?'

'My closure?'

'Yes. This house has been your best friend for the past fifteen years. You can't just abandon it, half done. You need a proper ending.'

'I agree. I do. But how? I can't afford to pay anyone and it's too big a job to take on by myself.'

'Well, then, ask the others.'

'No. They've all got full-time jobs. I can't expect them to take time off work.'

'So, do it over the weekend. You could have a painting party. Invite everyone you know, give them a paintbrush, a beer and some pizza. The place'll be done by Monday morning.'

'I'm afraid I don't know quite enough people to pull that one off.'

'Oh, surely you must. What about all the people who've lived here over the years. You must have stayed in touch with some of them?'

'No,' said Toby, 'not really. I'm not really a staying-in-touch kind of person.'

'But you must know where they are?'

'Well, most people left forwarding addresses, yes.'

'And phone numbers?'

'In some cases.'

'Well, then, phone them up! Tell them you're in trouble. Remind them how you helped them out when they were in trouble. Tell them that they owe you.'

Toby shook his head. 'No. I can't. I hate the phone as it is. The thought of phoning all those people, all the how are yous and the catching up and the . . . the . . . *chatting*. It just . . . urgh, no. I'm sorry.'

'Right, then, I'll do it. Give me your address book and I'll do it.'

'Really?'

'Yes. Really. I want to see this house finished every bit as much as you do. Tell me who to call, and I'll call them. I'll enjoy it. It'll take my mind off . . . things.'

'Things? What sort of things?'

Leah paused, wondering whether or not to tell Toby about Amitabh's proposal. She shook her head and smiled. 'Nothing,' she said, 'nothing. Just, you know, work and stuff. Here,' she said, reaching into her handbag for the cottage details, 'I brought this back. You left it at the pub, the other day when you, er . . .'

'Stormed out inexplicably?'

'Yes,' she said, smiling. 'When you stormed out inexplicably.'

'Hmmm.' He rubbed his chin and smiled ruefully. 'Yes. I'm very sorry about that. And I'm afraid I can't really offer you a particularly satisfying explanation for it. I was just, er, feeling a bit *overwhelmed*.' He took the paper from her hand and gazed at it for a while. 'This is the one that you liked, isn't it?'

'Mm-hmm.' She nodded. 'I've become a bit obsessed by it, actually. Thought I'd better give it back to you before I did something stupid like *buy* it.' She flashed her eyes at him and laughed.

'That wouldn't be stupid,' said Toby.

'Well, yes,' she said. 'It would, actually. I haven't got any money, for a start. Let alone the two hundred and twenty-five other reasons I could give you for not moving to the country.'

'Like what?'

'Oh,' she said, 'like not having a job and not being able to get a decent curry and not being near my parents and Amitabh . . .' She paused.

Toby nodded. 'Yes. I see.'

It fell silent for a moment. Then Toby sighed. 'Ah, well'—he folded the paper back into four—'maybe I'll buy it and then you can come and visit.'

She smiled. 'Good plan,' she said. 'And I would like to stay in touch, you know. Once you've gone. It would be a shame not to.'

'I agree.' He nodded. 'Whole-heartedly. Utterly. Whatever happens. Let's stay in touch.'

'Yes,' said Leah. 'Let's.'

Joanne bought herself a glass of red wine and took it to a table by the fire. She glanced at her watch. It was nearly eight o'clock. She took a sip of wine and waited, her heart beating quickly under her sweater. Getting dressed for this meeting had been strange. She'd forgotten what sort of clothes she liked to wear when she was just being herself. She'd settled on jeans and a cashmere sweater with ankle boots and a nice belt. Her hair was still very blonde, but she'd styled it softly onto her face and put on subtle make-up in shades of brown and pink. She wanted to look nice for him, like the girl he remembered, not the peculiar person she'd become.

At exactly eight o'clock the door opened and Nick walked in.

Joanne gulped. He still looked the same. The fine, shoulder-length hair, the slight physique under a sensible jacket and scuffed old boots. He smiled at her, shyly, and headed towards her. They greeted each other with barely there kisses and gently squeezed arms.

'How are you?' she said.

'I'm fine,' he said. 'You look nice. I like your hair.'

'You do? I'm going to dye it back. It's just, you know, temporary.'

He smiled and nodded. 'So,' he said, 'I'll just get myself a drink. Are you all right?' He pointed at her wineglass.

'Mm-hmm,' she said, nodding.

She watched him at the bar, remembering the shape of him. He came back with a pint of something and put it on the table.

'So, you got my note, then?' he said.

'Yes. Toby—that's my landlord—he gave it to me a couple of weeks ago. I've been, er . . .'

'Thinking about it?'

'Yes.' She smiled tightly. 'And we've been busy at the house. Decorating it. Toby's selling it and someone stole all his money and he couldn't afford to pay the, you know, painters and decorators, so we did it ourselves. I've been sanding floors. Look, I've got blisters . . .' She showed him the palms of her hands.

He winced.

'Yes, so. It's been a busy few days, so, er . . .'

'No, that's fine. I wasn't expecting you to reply immediately. I mean, it's been three years.'

'It has.'

'Yeah. I thought you were dead. Thought you might have thrown yourself off a bridge. God, I've thought and thought and thought. I just never thought you might be merely getting on with stuff.'

She smiled tightly. 'I wouldn't call it getting on with stuff.'

'You wouldn't? What would you call it?'

'Existing. I've been existing. I've been pretending and acting and fooling myself and everyone else around me. I've been . . .' Her voice caught. 'I've been the unhappiest girl in the whole wide world.'

She started to cry then, aching, primal tears that came from the deepest wells of her being. Nick moved his chair nearer to hers and held her in his arms. 'It's OK, Jo,' he soothed, stroking her hair and kissing her juddering shoulders. 'It's OK. I'm here now. I'm here.'

Joanne sobbed and let Nick soothe her, his familiar hands on her hair, his warm breath on her skin, the only man she'd ever loved.

'Come home,' he said. 'Please, come home.'

She buried her face in Nick's chest, breathing in his smell, the smell of Saturday nights curled up on the sofa watching DVDs, of climbing into bed at night, the smell of her life before Maisie had died and taken everything good with her.

'Yes,' she said. 'Yes. I want to come home.'

Leah's painting party turned into a painting week. A dozen people turned up at various points throughout the following ten days, bearing brushes, ladders and floor sanders; curtains, carpets and plants. It was bizarre, emotional, nostalgic and moving. Ex-tenants who Toby hadn't seen in more than ten years arrived at the front door, sometimes with wives and husbands and children in tow. Leah herself came over every evening after work, sometimes alone, sometimes with Amitabh. Con and Daisy did the garden. Melinda risked her vinyl-tipped nails to help and even brought Jack along one night to finish painting her room. And Joanne—Joanne was a revelation, forgoing a week's temping to work full-time on the house, sanding all the downstairs floors.

Toby had never spent so much time out of his bedroom and found the entire experience utterly exhilarating. Catching up with old friends, meeting new people, the constant hum and chatter of lively conversation, loud music, ring pulls snapped on cans of lager, sanders buzzing, lawn mowers growling, nails being knocked into walls, curtains being hung. The house felt thrilling and alive, a triumph of teamwork born of goodwill and humanity.

And then, finally, one Thursday afternoon, when everyone else had gone, Leah and Toby slid to the floor in the living room, opened a can of lager each, looked around and declared the house complete.

'It's beautiful,' said Leah.

'It is, isn't it?' said Toby. 'Wonderful.'

'You clever man.'

'Clever?' He looked at her and shook his head. 'Not a bit of it. This is all down to you, all of it. I couldn't have done any of this without you.'

'Oh,' she said, 'I'm sure you'd have found a way.'

'No,' he said, 'I wouldn't. I'm fundamentally useless.'

She laughed. 'So, what now?'

Well,' he said, 'Joanne's moving out tomorrow, back to New Cross. Back to Nick. Con's going to stay with Daisy at her folks' place. Melinda's going to stay with Jack.'

'And your dad?'

'He's due on Monday. I haven't heard from him, but . . .' He shrugged. He felt strangely numb about the prospect. Not excited; not nervous—just slightly sceptical. He couldn't remember enough detail about his father to be able to truly imagine what it would be like for him to be there, in front of him.

'What time's he coming?'

'Afternoon,' said Toby. 'Teatime. About four.'

'Are you going to bake a cake?'

'Of course.' Toby smiled. 'If I can't show him a wife or grandchildren or a reasonable income, the least I can do is make him a bloody good cake.'

Leah smiled. 'You could show him a girlfriend.'

He looked at her and frowned. 'And how exactly would I do that?'

'I'll be her.'

'Sorry?'

'I'll come along and pretend to be your girlfriend.'

'Oh God, Leah, but that's lying. I'm terrible at lying.'

'But, really, when you think about it, it's not that much of a leap from the truth. I am a girl. I am your friend. And we do have . . . well, we have a bond. Don't we?'

Toby gulped. 'Well, yes,' he said. 'I think we do.'

'And we are affectionate. I mean, we've held hands, we've hugged. I've kissed you. Sort of . . .' She laughed.

He gulped again. 'That's true,' he said.

'So, really, it wouldn't take much to convince your father that I was your girlfriend. We could just—be ourselves.'

Toby shrugged and nodded and tried to look nonchalant. 'Yes, well,' he said. 'When you put it like that.'

'You don't even have to say I'm your girlfriend. You could just leave it to your father to *assume*, based on our . . . *chemistry*.'

He nodded again and swallowed some lager. 'Good plan,' he said. 'Really good plan.'

'That is, of course, if you don't mind your father thinking that I'm your girlfriend.'

'Why would I mind my father thinking that you're my girlfriend?'

'I don't know. Maybe I'm not your . . . type?'

'My *type*? Good grief, Leah. Any sane man would be proud to present you as a girlfriend. You're the archetypal girl next door.'

'Or girl over the road, in this case.'

Toby smiled. 'Well, yes. Indeed.'

'So, is that a plan, then? I'll come over, Monday afternoon, give you a few kisses and cuddles? Charm your father. Eat some cake?'

'That sounds like a *glorious* plan.'

'Well, hello!' Daisy's father strode across the driveway. 'Welcome to Beens Acres!' He shook Con by the hand and took his small case from him. 'Is this all you've got?'

Con nodded. 'Yeah,' he said. 'I travel light.'

He looked up at the house. It wasn't as big as it had been in his head, probably about the same size as Toby's house, except surrounded on all four sides by fields.

'This is really good of you,' he said to Daisy's dad as they climbed the steps to the front door.

'Oh, it's nothing at all,' he said. 'All the girls have their boys to stay at some point. We call this the Beens Hostelry for Lovesick Boys.'

Con smiled. 'It's only temporary,' he said, 'just until I get accommodation sorted out.'

'Yes, yes, of course. Spend as long as you like.'

There was a very big dog in the hallway. Its tail beat loudly against the tiled floor and its ears flattened against its head with repressed excitement. 'This is Rory,' said Mr Beens. 'There's a small one somewhere, too, called, variously, depending upon who you ask, Smarties, Arthur or Bongo. You'll meet him soon, I'm sure.'

The hallway was large and cluttered, full of books and lamps and piles of outdoor clothing. Through a door to the left, Con could see a big dusty sitting room.

Daisy appeared at the doorway. She beamed and ran towards him. 'You're here,' she said, wrapping her arms around him.

'I am,' he said.

'I didn't hear your cab.'

'No,' he said. 'I walked from the station.'

'Oh, no! Why didn't you phone? We could have picked you up.'

'No,' he said. 'Honestly. It was fine. I've never been to the country before. I wanted to see it.'

'Never been to the country?' said Mr Beens, incredulously.

'No,' he said. 'Never.'

'Well,' said Mr Beens, 'a double welcome to you, then, from us, *and* from the country.'

Daisy looped her arms round Con and kissed him on the cheek. 'Come on. Let me show you round.'

Con followed her through the house and the dog followed them, stopping every time they stopped and sitting down patiently, as if it was the first time he'd seen the house, too. The place was a weird mix of tasteful antiques and random garish pieces of furniture from the 1960s and 1970s. It was a house that didn't care too much what anyone thought of it, a house that was comfortable in its own skin and Con could sense immediately that he would be fine here. It was a house fit for anyone, rich or poor, young or old.

'And this,' said Daisy, opening a door on the attic floor, 'is your room.'

It was a large room, with a low sloping ceiling and a Velux window in the roof. A tiny dormer window looked out over the driveway and the main road. The bed was a single, clothed in a bright duvet and a fat pillow. There was a small pine wardrobe at the other end of the room and a Victorian washbasin and jug on a wrought-metal stand, with a lilac hand towel. 'Is this OK?' said Daisy.

Con looked around. 'It's perfect,' he said. 'Really perfect.'

'Good.' She smiled. 'You do know, though, don't you, that they wouldn't have the slightest problem with you being in my room?'

'I know,' he said, 'but it just doesn't feel right. It feels . . . *disrespectful*.'

'Oh, Con. You're so old-fashioned.'

'I know,' he said. 'I'm a gent. And I want to give your parents something,' he said. 'Some money. For letting me stay.'

'No way,' said Daisy. 'Dad would be insulted.'

'He would?'

'Yes. He doesn't consider this house to be *his* house. As far as he's concerned it's *our* house. Us girls. He wouldn't dream of taking money from you.'

'Well, then, let me buy them something. A gift.'

'No,' she said. 'Don't do anything. Just relax. Just be yourself. My parents don't expect fancy presents and best behaviour. They just expect good company. Oh—and maybe a hand in the kitchen. I've told them all about your culinary prowess.'

'Oh God, you haven't, have you?'

'Of course. They're dying to try your home-baked bread.'

'Oh shit.'

'What?'

'I don't know if I can make bread on my own, without Toby there to tell me what to do.'

'Of course you can. We'll do it together. You and me.' She took his hand.

'You and me?'

She nodded and smiled. 'Come on,' she said. 'Let's get started.'

Ruby peeled the foil wrapper off the meal in front of her and peered cautiously underneath it. A sliver of grey chicken breast with something brown and lumpy buried inside it, a smattering of tiny peas, a cluster of oily potatoes, all coated in a viscous tan-coloured sauce.

'Pretty gross, huh?' The man next to her pointed at her tray and smiled.

'Mmm,' she said, nodding, 'not really what I fancy.' She'd been aware of the man sitting next to her since she'd first taken her seat on the plane three hours ago.

'Troy,' he said, offering her his hand to shake.

'Ruby,' she said.

'So, what takes you to New York, Ruby? Vacation?'

'Yeah,' she said, 'kind of.'

'I'm not from New York, myself. I live in Pittsburgh. I'll be getting a connecting flight.'

She nodded and smiled and smoothed cream cheese onto a cracker.

'So, Ruby, what do you do?'

'I'm a singer,' she said. 'A singer/songwriter.'

'Wow.' He regarded her with admiration. 'What sort of singer? Are you famous? Should I have heard of you?'

She laughed. 'No,' she said, 'not unless you've been hanging out in dingy clubs in north London.'

'Ah, no,' he conceded. 'Not quite my scene.'

'No, I didn't think it would be.'

'But you're good, huh? A good singer.'

'I'm bloody brilliant,' she said.

He laughed again. 'I bet you are,' he said. 'Waiting for your big break?'

'Waiting and waiting and waiting. This is my last-ditch attempt.'

'Oh, right. New York or bust?'

'Yeah,' she said. 'That kind of thing.'

'Well, hey, look, in the meantime, I should give you my card. My sister's getting married next month, been looking for a singer.

Something unusual, something a bit . . . *edgy*, you know. If your luck doesn't come up, give me a ring.'

Ruby shook her head. 'No,' she said, 'not my thing. But thanks for the offer.'

'Well, I tell you what, my sister knows some big people up at Sony, up at Geffen. Might be a good opportunity to meet some people, make an impression.'

Ruby turned and smiled at Troy. 'Now that,' she said, 'sounds very interesting.' She took the card from between his fingers and slipped it into her handbag. And then she let Troy F. Shultzberg buy her a bottle of champagne.

31 SILVERSMITH ROAD, N2
£995,000

Five double bedrooms, two bathrooms, three receptions, kitchen/diner, 45ft south-facing garden

A beautiful and unique residence on this ever-popular road just off the High Street. No. 31 is a fully detached double-fronted villa full of period features and brimming with character. Subject to a recent sympathetic refurbishment, this extraordinary house would make an ideal family home and an early viewing is recommended.

Toby had grown used to waking up alone in his big, empty house. He celebrated his aloneness by tuning the radio to Radio Three and letting classical music flood every room in the house. His kitchen was as clean and uncluttered as it had been before he went to bed the previous night and the five hooks in the hallway bore only his own jacket, coat and scarf. He'd taken to having a paper delivered daily, now he knew that nobody would get to it before him. He performed a strange but very enjoyable dance as he prepared his breakfast in his pyjamas.

He considered his plans for the day ahead. He would walk down to the High Road and buy some fresh flowers for the house. Then he would go to Budgens and pick up the ingredients for his cake. Somewhere in his dusty collection of memories of his father he had an inkling of a fondness for fig rolls (or was it Garibaldis?), so he would pick up a pack or two of those.

When he got home, he'd put some real coffee on to brew and bake a loaf of bread, not because he wanted either coffee or bread, but because he had two more viewings that morning and he wanted the house to smell delicious. He'd done six viewings over the weekend and the house had been on the market for only three days. He enjoyed showing people round. He was so proud of it that he wanted as many people as possible to see his beautiful house before it was sold and locked up against the world again.

After the viewings he'd make his cake (he didn't want to mess up the kitchen beforehand) and while it was in the oven he'd have a bath and a shave, then he'd put on some clean clothes and some new shoes, and go downstairs to await the arrival of his father.

'**D**oes that include service?' Reggie eyed the waiter through slanted eyes.

'No, sir,' said the waiter. 'It doesn't.'

Reggie sighed and pulled a handful of coins out of his pocket, which he dropped onto the tray disdainfully.

He glanced at his watch. Three thirty. He looked out of the window at the street outside. It was raining. Of course it was raining. This was London. Admittedly March wasn't the best time of year to be here, but, still, he remembered now exactly why he'd left in the first place. Bad coffee, overpriced food, never-ending rain.

It occurred to him that he'd arranged to see his son this afternoon. Well, *he* hadn't arranged it; Peter had arranged it. He pulled a piece of paper out of his wallet and looked at it.

31 Silversmith Road, London N2. Where the hell was London N2? And how was he going to get there? He sighed and put the paper back in his wallet. He thought of his big peculiar son, his mass of unkempt hair. Was it really worth trekking all the way out to some godforsaken part of north London to find out that they still had nothing in common, that he still didn't like him very much?

But then, he'd like to see the house he'd bought him all those years ago. And he'd like to see Karen and any children they may have had together. His grandchildren. He had no other plans for this afternoon. Sod it, he thought. He'd go.

He allowed a man by the front desk to fold him into his overcoat, then he unfurled his umbrella and left the restaurant. He waited a while on the corner of Dover Street and Bond Street for a cab to appear. When one failed to materialise he began to walk, feeling the legs of his trousers soaking up the rain with every step. He zigzagged through the streets of Mayfair, his eyes scanning the street constantly for that welcoming amber glow. Finally he saw a cab, just dropping off a fare.

'London N2,' he said breathlessly.

'Sorry, mate,' said the driver. 'I'm on a call. Pre-booked.'

'*Shit*,' hissed Reggie, under his breath. 'Where are you going, then?'

'South Ken.'

Reggie thought briefly of his son, waiting for him on the other side of London. And then he thought of his warm flat in Chelsea, where he would be alone, required to talk to no one, to do nothing.

'Fuck it,' he said. 'Take me there. Take me to South Ken.'

'**O**h God, Toby,' said Leah, stroking his back. 'I'm really sorry. I can't believe he didn't come.'

Toby stared though the window at the street outside. He'd watched dusk come and go and now it was dark. There'd been no phone call, no word from his father or from Peter. He and Leah were sitting side by side at the dining table. The chocolate cake sat in front of them, a forty-five-degree wedge missing. A plate of Garibaldis and fig rolls sat untouched next to a brand-new white china teapot. Toby tried to feel sad about this poignant arrangement of objects, tried to be hurt by the non-appearance of his father. But he couldn't.

'You know what?' he said. 'I don't care that he didn't come. I really don't. This isn't about him any more. And I'm not sure it ever was. This'—he indicated the house—'this is about me. About . . . I don't know, about *growing up*, I suppose.' He laughed wryly and wiped some icing off the edge of the cake plate with his fingertip.

'Are you suggesting that you weren't a grown-up before?'

'No. I was a nearly forty-year-old teenager. Wearing the same clothes, writing the same crappy poems, in love with the same woman . . .'

'Ruby?'

'Yes, Ruby. How did you know?'

'Blatantly obvious.'

He raised his eyebrows and sighed. 'Well. There you go. Wearing my schoolboy crush on my sleeve like an adolescent. I made a list, you know, after Gus left me his money, after my father wrote to me. A list of things I needed to do. It started off with buying new sofas and it ended with this.' He cast his arm round the room. 'I've achieved nearly everything I set out to achieve.'

'You should feel very pleased with yourself.'

'I do,' he said. 'Now I just need to finalise the divorce, move to

Cornwall and marry someone, and my list will be done and dusted.'

'Marry someone?' She smiled. 'You put that on your list?'

'Well, not marry someone, necessarily. Just, you know, meet someone. Someone special. God, that sounds so naff.'

'No, it doesn't. It sounds absolutely right. Everyone should have someone special.'

Toby nodded and a silence followed. 'What about you and Amitabh? You seem to be getting on well.'

'Do we?'

'Yes. Well, from what I can see.'

She laughed. 'Well, that's funny because we're not at all.'

'Oh dear. Why's that?'

'Because,' she said, sighing, 'because he asked me to marry him . . .'

Toby turned to gaze at her in amazement. 'Oh my God. *Really*?'

'Uh-huh. A couple of weeks ago. And I still haven't given him an answer.'

'You haven't?'

'No. I just keep changing my mind. I don't know what to do.'

'But you told me you didn't want to marry him.'

'I know. I know I did. But it's all about options, isn't it? It's all about where I go next. And really and truly, where do I go next? If there was a sign somewhere, something to guide me on to the next turn in the road, then . . .'

'Then you'd turn him down?'

She nodded and smiled ruefully.

'Oh, Leah . . .'

'I know,' she said. 'I know. Pathetic, isn't it? I'm sure life wasn't supposed to be like this. I'm sure the idea was that you met someone and you knew, that it was one thing or another, that it was black or it was white. But life—it's so stupidly *grey* half the time, isn't it?'

'Oh, but, Leah. It doesn't have to be. I mean, look at me. My life was as grey as it gets. And then, well, *you* came along. And made everything technicolour.'

Leah laughed. 'I did? How?'

'Just by being you. By being so alive and fresh. By seeing beyond my strange demeanour and finding a perfectly nice, normal bloke underneath there whom I never knew existed. And when I say that I owe all of this to you, I'm not just talking about the house, my tenants, all of this. I'm talking about this man, sitting next to you, who goes out to shops and chats with old friends, and solves problems for people and buys his underwear from Marks and Spencer's. I owe this man to you. Completely. You've transformed me, Leah, and I can't bear to think that having made my world kaleidoscopic that you'd compromise your own right to a proper, satisfying ending.' He turned his chair to face her properly. 'I've spent my entire life letting the world wash over me. But not any more. It's my turn now. And I want you to know without a scintilla of uncertainty that I could be happy with you for ever. I want you to know—' He stopped, blinked, looked at Leah. 'That I am completely in love with you . . .'

She stared back at him, speechless.

'Does that surprise you?' he said.

She nodded mutely.

'I've been wanting to tell you for ages. That was why I ran out of that pub the other day. Because I was about to tell you, then I lost my nerve. Completely. But now I've realised. I've only got one stab at this. I'll be off soon and we won't be neighbours any more and you'll get married to someone who you're not sure about and it'll all be way too late.'

'Toby, I . . .'

'Leah. It's fine. You don't have to say anything. I only want you to know this. Not to act on it. I want you to be armed with the knowledge that someone else loved you. That you had options, even if it was only me. I know that someone like you would never love someone like me.'

'Why not?'

'I don't know. Because I'm me, because I'm . . .'

'Tall, dark and handsome? Clever, charming and funny?'

Toby frowned. 'Come on, now,' he said. 'Don't be facetious.'

'Who's being facetious? I'm being completely and utterly sincere. You and me. We fit.' And then, to prove her point, she turned her chair towards Toby's, brought Toby's face towards hers with her hands, and said, 'I'm going to kiss you now. Is that OK?'

Toby nodded, and when her lips met his he felt everything suddenly fall into place and make perfect sense for the first time in his whole ridiculous life.

'I can't believe you just did that,' he said.

'Neither can I,' laughed Leah.

'That was lovely,' said Toby.

'It was, wasn't it?'

'Can I take it that you're not going to marry Amitabh?'

'Of course I'm not going to marry bloody Amitabh.'

'Well, then,' said Toby, 'in that case, I think you should kiss me again.'

Chapter 9

DIDCOT WALSH
312 High Road London N2 1AG

April 2, 2005

Dear Toby,

I am writing to confirm the offer received this morning for the asking price of £995,000. The buyer is chain-free and hoping to exchange within six weeks. Hopefully it should be a smooth process. I don't foresee any problems. I will be in touch shortly.

Yours faithfully,
Walter Didcot

'Oh, hello, this is a message for Toby Dobbs. It's Susan here from Tixall's in Penzance. Just to let you know that I've spoken to the owners of Chyandour House and they've accepted your offer of £289,000. They've also agreed to take it off the market for a week, pending the sale of your own property. Hope this is OK and I'll speak to you soon . . .'

In the	BARNET County Court,	
between	TOBY BERTRAND DOBBS	the Petitioner
and	KAREN JANE DOBBS	the Respondent

referring to the decree made in this cause on the

4th day of MARCH 2005 whereby it was decreed that the marriage solemnised on the

7th day of AUGUST 1990

at LAMBETH REGISTER OFFICE, THE TOWN HALL, BRIXTON HILL SW2 1RW between

TOBY BERTRAND DOBBS	the Petitioner
and	
KAREN JANE DOBBS	the Respondent

be dissolved unless sufficient cause be shown to the court within (six) weeks from the making thereof why the said decree should not be made absolute, and no such cause having been shown, it is hereby certified that the said decree was on the 22nd day of APRIL 2005 made final and absolute and that the said marriage was thereby dissolved.

June 2, 2005

Dear Toby,

Wow! Thanks! I've just got my balance and the money's gone in! Couldn't believe all those zeros! Thanks a lot, mate. It's the most decent thing anyone's ever done for me and I won't let you down.

Sorry I haven't been in touch much. I've been really busy. Flight school starts next week and I've been looking for somewhere to live. I'll be sharing with some other guys, students from the school. The flat's not that great (I miss number 31), but it'll be fine for a year or so. I'll be glad to move out of Daisy's place, too. It was really nice and everything, but I don't like to freeload.

Things are going great with Daisy. She's on really good form and you can tell just by looking at her that the country air is better for her than being in London. She's waitressing at her mate's restaurant in the village. I've been helping out there, too, washing dishes and stuff, just to tide me over. She's thinking about doing a cookery course, setting up a catering thing. I reckon she'll be brilliant. And cooking's something you can do anywhere, isn't it? Anywhere in the world.

Her mum taught me how to do her physio. It's really easy, actually. And she's doing so well at the moment that it doesn't even take that long. I won't be able to do it any more when I move out, but at least I know how to do it now, if we ever end up living together. As for how I feel about her illness, I'm doing what you said, just having fun with her. I'm a strong bloke. Whatever happens in the future, I can take it. Well, I'll have to . . .

I quite like it out here, in the sticks. I miss my mates, of course, and my mum, but I don't really miss London. How are you, anyway? Have you moved yet? Maybe you're in the country, too. Weird, eh?!

Anyway, I just wanted to say thanks a lot for the money. And for everything. I'll write again when I'm settled at the school. And watch your post. You'll be getting an unexpected invitation any day now!

All the best,

Con

June 5, 2005

Dearest Toby,

Well, here I am in Kathmandu! Nick's taken a year's sabbatical from work and we're going to travel the world. We started in Islamabad, came down India through New Delhi and then up the hills to Nepal. Next stop Malaysia. Having an amazing time. I'll send you postcards whenever I can. Hope you're happy. I am!

Love, Jo xxxx

Dear Toby

Melinda and Jack are engaged!

Please come and help us celebrate at

41 Cranmore Gardens, London, N10 5TY

on Saturday, June 23, 2005

Toby watched the removal van pull out of Silversmith Road and headed back inside. The house was completely empty now. Not a stick of furniture; not a picture or a plant. The sun streamed through the front windows, highlighting the house's natural beauty. He wandered for a while, from room to room, just as he'd done the very first time he'd seen the place. This was exactly how he'd wanted the house to look that day, all those years ago. Leah had been right to persuade him to finish the job. Leaving would have been much harder if he hadn't.

He took the stairs towards the upper floors, as he'd done a thousand times before. The thud of his footsteps reminded him of Gus's slow rhythmic steps, up and down the stairs, day in, day out. He peered into Joanne's room, Ruby's room, Con's room. And then he took the next flight of stairs and went into his own room. There was a roll of packing tape on the floor and an empty box. And there, where his wardrobe had been, was a piece of paper. He picked it up and looked at it.

Things To Do

~~1~~ ~~Buy new sofas~~
~~2~~ ~~Look at kitchens~~
~~3~~ ~~Look at bathrooms~~
~~4~~ ~~Get builder in to quote on works~~
~~5~~ ~~Get plumber in to quote on works~~
~~6~~ ~~Get decorator in to quote on works~~
~~7~~ ~~Get tenants to move out~~
~~8~~ ~~Sell house~~
~~9~~ ~~Move to Cornwall (?)~~
~~10~~ ~~Get divorced~~
~~11~~ ~~Stop being in love with Ruby~~
~~12~~ ~~Find someone proper to be in love with~~
13 **START LIVING**

He smiled and pulled a pen out of his jacket pocket and with a flourish of intent and satisfaction he drew a thick black line through the last two words.

Toby pulled on his oven gloves, opened the Aga and lifted out the loaf tin. He tipped the loaf onto a cooling tray and opened the kitchen window. It was 8.30 a.m. and the sun was already high in the sky.

The cantankerous screech of seagulls circling overhead was as familiar now to Toby as the sound of the waves hitting the shingle beach across the road. He'd been here, at Chyandour House, for three months, and the sounds of his new life thrilled him to the core.

The kettle reached its climax and clicked itself off. He filled the teapot and tapped the bread. Still too hot to slice. He pulled two mugs off the hooks that hung from the dresser and put them on a tray. Then he carried them through to the breakfast room, where he arranged them on the pine table he'd found in a junk shop for thirty-five pounds.

He poured out two mugs of tea and turned on the radio.

Leah peered through the tiny dormer window, to the beach across the road. The boats were out already, with their crab pots. Solitary anglers lined the shore, casting for the whiting that were back for the autumn.

Leah had only been here for three months, but already she knew about the seasonal variations of aquatic life around the headland, about the tidal patterns, about the likelihood of a good catch, or a bad one. She also knew about the problems with the new headmistress at the primary school, that Mrs Wendle had been taken to the hospice on Friday night and that the beer served at the Plough up the road was watered down. It wasn't difficult to pick up local knowledge. All you had to do was keep your ears open as you walked around the village. All you had to do was talk to people.

She headed downstairs, bowing to avoid the low ceiling halfway down and stooping to collect some mail from the doormat.

Toby smiled at her as she walked towards him. 'Tea?' he said.

'Lovely,' she said.

She leaned down and kissed him on the lips, then dropped the mail on the table in front of him.

'Oh, look.' She pulled a newspaper from the bottom of the pile. 'The paper's here.'

'Oh, fantastic. Let's have a look.'

Leah leafed through the pages. 'Look!' she announced. 'There it is!'

Sea-Bay Auction Services

Leave it with us—we'll sell it for you!

12 Bayview Parade
The Seafront
Portscatho
(right next to Prowse the Grocer)

Want to find a home for your old heirlooms, clutter and bric-a-brac?
Haven't got the time or the inclination to sell it yourself? We'll take all the hassle out of it for you. Just bring us your unwanted possessions and we'll market them for you on e-bay. If we don't sell it, you don't pay us a penny.

WHAT HAVE YOU GOT TO LOSE?!

** GRAND OPENING TODAY – SATURDAY AUGUST 13th**

Bring this flier and claim a free cup of tea and a slice of cake. We look forward to seeing you!

Toby Dobbs & Leah Pilgrim

'It looks great, doesn't it?'

Toby nodded. And then he stopped smiling and stared at an envelope on top of the pile. The writing looked strangely familiar. It had an American stamp on it and had been addressed to Silversmith Road and redirected. Slowly he sliced the envelope open with a knife and pulled out a handwritten letter, three sheets long.

Dear Toby,

What can I say? Sorry doesn't really seem sufficient. I can't really explain why I did what I did. I was scared, I suppose, and angry. I realised immediately that I'd made a mistake moving in with Tim and I freaked out. I came back to the house. I was going to ask if I could stay for a few days, but you were out. And then I saw that cash in your room and something took me over. I felt like you'd let me down, abandoned me when I needed you most. So I took the lot and went straight to the airport and bought a one-way ticket to the States.

It's been a real trip. I stayed at the Chelsea at first. That was a blast. Then I found a room in a flat on the Lower East Side. I played at someone's wedding a few weeks later, mainly cover versions, but I threw in a couple of my new songs. And what do you know—someone liked them and bought them off me for $5,000! Some girl band is going to use them. Apparently they're really famous, but I've never heard of them.

I tried to persuade the guy to let me record them, but guess what he said? He said, 'Beautiful girl, the world does not need another chick with an attitude and a guitar.' Pah! That kind of took the shine off selling my songs. I went into a bit of a decline after that. I know, I know—I never appreciate what I've got. It's never enough, is it?

I started drinking quite heavily. Got through a lot of your cash that way. Pissed off my flatmates. And it was when they threatened to kick me out that I realised I needed to take control of my life. So I joined AA.

Yeah, yeah—I can hear you laughing from here! I know, it's hard to imagine. But it's been great. I'm on the 12-Step Program (only one 'm'!) and part of that is that I have to redress any imbalances in my life, undo wrongdoings, make amends and apologise. I've written to Tim and his wife, to say sorry for fucking them around. And now here's my apology to you.

Toby, you are one of the greatest people I've ever known. It's taken being away from you for me to be able to see that. You took me in when I had nobody else and you took care of me and all I ever did was belittle you and take advantage. You're a better person than I could ever hope to be and I am so sorry to have broken your trust and let you down. You didn't deserve it. I really hope you managed to sell the house and that you have moved on and found happiness. No one deserves a happy ending more than you. I hope you can find it in your heart to forgive me, but if you don't that's fine.

As for me, well, there's no happy ending in sight just yet. I've written some more songs, but they didn't go for them. To pay the rent I'm working as a waitress in some trendy Vietnamese place in Greenwich Village. I haven't had a drink for five weeks and that, for now, is enough. I'll get there in the end, I know I will. When I do, I'll let you know. And maybe one day I'll be able to buy you that Lamborghini!

With love and respect,

Ruby xxx

Toby passed the letter to Leah and sighed. He felt something in his heart loosen, untwist itself. Ruby was alive. Ruby was safe. Tonight, for the first time since she'd moved out of his house, Toby could fall asleep without wondering, without worrying. After nearly sixteen years, the last residual traces of Ruby had finally been expunged from the soft, sticky corners of his consciousness.

'That's good, isn't it?' said Leah, passing the letter back to him a moment later. 'Good news?'

Toby smiled. 'Very good news indeed.'

'So,' said Leah, 'are you ready to go to work?'

Toby nodded, and together they headed towards the front of the cottage, towards their shop.

Lisa Jewell

Profile

Born: 19th July 1968, Middlesex Hospital, London.

Family: daughter, Amelie, and husband, Jascha.

Previous novels: *Ralph's Party, Thirtynothing, One-Hit Wonder, A Friend of the Family, Vince and Joy.*

Website: www.lisa-jewell.co.uk

The story of Lisa Jewell's publishing success is as close to a real-life fairy story as you can get. 'I was a secretary on holiday in 1996 when my life changed for ever. I'd just been made redundant three weeks earlier, from my job as a director's PA, and was with a group of friends in a villa on Gozo, drinking, eating and sunbathing my sorrows away. Late one night, my friend Yasmin and I were sitting out by the pool chatting drunkenly about the meaning of life, etc. She asked me what I was planning to do when I got back to London. I told her I would enlist with some temping agencies and see where that led me. She asked what I *really* wanted to do. I told her that in a dream-world I would like to write a book, but that I couldn't possibly because I didn't have the time, the money or the experience. Yasmin, a positive kind of girl from Australia, didn't see it that way. She told me I had enough redundancy money to put off working for a month, I had a boyfriend with a computer and I had the desire. What was stopping me? She made me a bet that night—she would take me out for dinner to my favourite restaurant if I spent the next month writing the first three chapters of a book. Never one to renege on a bet, particularly one involving food, I set about it the day after we got home.'

Lisa quickly wrote three chapters and sent them off to ten agents. Back came nine rejections, but the tenth asked to see more of the novel. She was thrilled but also worried that she wouldn't be able to finish it, since she was now working full-time. Jascha (then her boyfriend and now her husband) asked her to move in with him so that she could afford to work part-time and finish her novel. The book, *Ralph's Party*, was published to critical acclaim and soon became a best seller.

'So 2007 looks like a year for change . . . Some of the changes are scary, some of them are thrilling, but ultimately I cannot wait.'

31 Dream Street is Lisa's sixth novel and she is busy working on the next one. 'I have been struggling through book number seven, slowly, painfully, but, I think, surely,' Lisa writes in her diary, which can be found on her website. 'I have a hundred pages now, which have been examined by Judith, my agent, and found to be acceptable. So I just have to finish it. My contractual deadline is September, but I have had to impose a fresh deadline on myself because next summer I will mostly be having a new baby! Yes, I am four months pregnant, with daughter number two. She is due on the 18th May and I would very much like to have a clean slate and spend the summer enjoying her and not struggling to finish a book. Whether or not I will meet the deadline is anyone's guess, but that's what I'm aiming for, so the next few weeks will be pretty hard-going.

'So 2007 looks like a year for change. We're hoping to extend our flat into the flat upstairs which would be incredibly exciting. Amelie starts nursery, my first hardback, *31 Dream Street*, is being published, I'm having another baby and finishing another book. Some of the changes are scary, some of them are thrilling, but ultimately I cannot wait.'

Taken from Lisa Jewell's official website at www.lisa-jewell.co.uk

KATY GARDNER

HIDDEN

'Eighteen, nineteen, twenty!

Coming! Ready or not!'

Poppy loves to play hide-and-seek, and as Mel searches the house for her daughter, she is confident that she will find her in one of her usual hiding places. But, forty-five minutes later, Poppy is nowhere to be found. Mel's concern turns to panic, then to fear, and finally to the dreadful realisation that her daughter has disappeared . . .

PROLOGUE

29 NOVEMBER, 2003

TAKING A BREATH and straightening his back, Dave Gosforth paused at the threshold of the flat, his large hands twitching at his side. Despite the contraction of his diaphragm, his stomach pressed uncomfortably against his paper suit. Breathing in a second time, he mentally sucked the spare inches in. He had been planning an hour in the gym, but mercifully had been waylaid by the call. Now, as he tugged at his zip, the new fitness regime that only yesterday he had solemnly pledged to follow was banished into a section of his mind marked 'later'.

He stepped into the hall, surveying the scene. Behind him the front door was hanging slightly ajar: no sign of forced entry here. Moving slowly down the hall he took in the scuffed walls and unopened bills, left in a heap by the mat. To the left was the living room: he'd leave that till last. On the right was the kitchen. Pausing by the plywood door, he registered the crater in the middle: a violent kick probably, or a body, falling hard. Stepping past, he looked carefully around the room.

The place was a right mess. The table was overturned, the floor scattered with crockery, and a wooden stool smashed in half. Between the sink and the capsized table the lino was scratched with skid marks: a woman's heels, dragging backwards, perhaps. Blood was smeared across the wall, sprayed over the freshly kicked-in door, and congealing in pools on the floor.

For the few moments that he looked carefully around the room, Dave allowed himself the small thrill he experienced each time he had a new case. He liked to be the first on the scene, even before the pathologists or photographers had arrived, when everything was still fresh. You could learn a lot, simply by standing still and looking. Take this kitchen, facing onto a concrete walkway in a mean 1970s block of flats on the outskirts of Margate. The strip lighting was on, so the attack must have taken place last night, or in the dim of the winter morning. The broken bowl and splattered cereal implied it was during breakfast. The pathologists would confirm the exact time of the woman's death, but by the look of the scummy coffee by the sink, it was about twelve hours ago. She'd most likely been alone: there was no evidence of a second mug or cereal bowl.

From the kitchen a trail of blood led across a stretch of beige carpet towards the squalid living room. On the wall opposite the kitchen door, older stains had been joined by a reddish handprint.

Entering the living room, Dave looked calmly around. The woman's body was slumped over the sagging settee, her head resting on her arms. Were it not for the browning puddle that had gathered underneath her waxy cheek, she might have been having a nap. He gazed at the pale face: the closed, heavily made-up eyes, the half-open mouth, bright pink with lipstick. More blood soaked into the torn foam where she was lying; her black baby-doll dressing gown was virtually shredded, the skin beneath sliced with gashes. It wasn't nice to look at, but his primary emotion was neither shock nor disgust, merely dispassionate interest.

A minute later he was outside on the walkway with the beat bobby who'd found her.

'Got a name?'

'Jacqui Jenning. Been here about a year.'

'Got a boyfriend?'

'Not that we know of. From what the lady next door is saying, she had a bit of a reputation.'

'Right . . .'

'"Dirty little tart" were her precise words.'

'You've got this lady here, have you?'

'John's talking to her. She called at six ten, said she was coming back from work and saw the mess through the kitchen window. Didn't hear anything this morning, though.'

'OK. We'll need a door-to-door on the whole estate. There's been a hell of a fight. Someone must have noticed something.'

Downstairs, the scene-of-crime lads had arrived. As he heard their boots clumping up the concrete steps, Dave pulled his shoulders back a fraction, gathering his thoughts.

'All righty,' he muttered to himself. 'Let's get going.'

He didn't get away for another four hours. He'd managed to call Karen and warn her he'd be late, so she'd put his dinner on low and told Harvey not to wait up. By the time he'd driven across Margate and returned to Herne Bay, it was nearly midnight. He parked the car in the driveway and sat in the dark for a moment, staring at his lit-up house. Like wiping mud from one's shoes, he needed a moment to sluice off the details of the evening before going inside. He took a pride in not letting his work get to him, but all the same it was unpleasant stuff: a prostitute getting her skull poked in by what looked like a chisel.

Levering his heavy frame from the driver's seat, Dave stepped onto the drive with relief.

Forty miles away in the depths of South London a woman lay skewiff across her bed, her small daughter's arm thrown over her back. A well-thumbed edition of *Horrid Henry* was abandoned beside the pillow; more books littered the floor. The woman had not meant to fall asleep so early and would wake a few hours later, dry mouthed and stiff in her daytime clothes. For now, however, her mouth twitched with a fleeting smile. Another day finally finished, she was alone with her dreams.

As the couple slept, the lights of passing cars threw patterns against the wall. Outside, the city thrummed, a low roar that neither mother nor daughter noticed. They still had almost a month left: over twenty-nine uneventful days before the woman would visit Peckham to value a flat, fall in love with a stranger, and their lives would become inextricably linked to the fate of poor dead Jacqui Jenning.

1

26 FEBRUARY, 2005

IT'S FIVE PAST FOUR on the last Saturday in February, and we're playing hide-and-seek. It's Poppy's favourite game, always has been. At fifteen months old she'd stand in the middle of the living room with her chubby fists bunched over her eyes, imagining herself invisible. Later, she learned to crouch behind the door, but when I stepped into the room she'd jump out, giggling. She never let *me* hide, that wasn't the point. What she liked was the delicious anticipation of being caught: that terrifying joy of being swooped upon by giant adult hands that tickled and squeezed. She'd make me find her, over and over again, like a video clip being endlessly replayed.

These days it's more sophisticated. First, I have to hide, but no longer am I allowed to simply hover behind the door. Now it has to be *hard*. '*Mummy!*' Pops'll shout in irritation if I make it too easy. 'I am *not* six, OK?' Fact is, she's only just turned seven, but six has become a distant and despised land, filled with pink teddies and frilly frocks.

So I have to hide somewhere challenging enough for her to feel she's being taken seriously, yet not so obscure that she'll never find me. After my three turns, it's her go. Currently I'm on hide number two. I have Jo strapped to my chest in one of those complicated strappy slings. As Poppy counts I lope softly out of the kitchen and into the corridor, my hands clutching the back of the sling so Jo, who is bunched up and gently snoring, doesn't get jiggled.

In the corridor I pause, deciding where to go. We've been living in the building for nearly eight months, yet still I feel like an interloper. Behind me is the prefab kitchen, tacked to the side of the house. We're planning to demolish this as soon as the build's complete, but for now Si's set up a temporary sink with plumbing for a washing machine and I'm cooking on a camper gas stove. Then there's this odd dark corridor where I'm currently standing, with its concrete floor and damp patches. This connects the kitchen with the main building, opening out onto the open-plan living area on the ground floor. We've done the most work here: wooden flooring, mostly fitted, new windows on each side so you can see out to the river and fields, and Si's state-of-the-art lighting. It's an investment, Si keeps saying; it'll be *fine*.

In the middle of the room there's a sunken den, with our three-piece suite and the TV, and in the background is the enormous picture window that Si fitted before Christmas. A door on the far wall leads to a newly plumbed toilet. At the back of the room are two sets of steps on either side that rise to the gallery at the top. The new wooden stairs are on the right, near the kitchen, and the old metal steps are on the left. On the first floor six rooms, once used for storing hops, lead off the gallery. We've cleared three so far: our bedroom and Poppy's room have been decorated, the third is Si's painting room, and the bathroom has just been fitted. Past these rooms, on the far side of the gallery, are metal steps leading to a huge loft storeroom at the top. The plan is to fit a spiral staircase and make this a suite of rooms for B&B guests, with en-suite bathrooms and panoramic views over the estuary.

In the kitchen Poppy's reached fifteen. I make for the curtains. It's a bit obvious, but I can't face climbing all those steps with Jo in his sling. I'll wrap myself up tight, cocooned in the thick white calico, and pray she doesn't spot my trainers. Here she comes. By the time she calls 'Ready or not!' she's already halfway down the corridor.

'I'm going to get you, Mummy!' she cries, her feet scampering over the wooden boards in the living room. 'I know where you are!'

Rather than continue towards the curtains, she goes clattering up the metal steps. Jo's wriggling, so I lean over, trying to loosen the sling. Upstairs, I can hear the slam of our bedroom door. I'm starting to fret about Poppy climbing the rickety metal steps to the large storeroom in the loft. I've forbidden her to go up there: the steps are treacherously steep and on the other side of the padlocked door the floor is unfinished. Worst of all, on the far side of the loft the door to the winchhouse opens onto a small platform onto which sacks of wheat or hops used to be raised from the barges below. The rusted winch is still there, projecting over a sixty-foot drop into the mud.

Until a short while ago I could hear Si banging about but now everything is quiet. At my bosom the wriggling is growing more determined. I place my hand on the fluffy head that's protruding from the sling, but it's too late. Like a cat spoiling for a fight, Jo starts to yowl. Now Poppy's running along the gallery, her feet thudding above me. She stops for a moment, listening, then hurtles down the stairs, a four-foot vortex of triumphant fury, blonde plaits flapping, skinny legs skidding to a halt in front of the curtain, which she rips back like she's proving a point.

'*Mum!* Why do you always have to let Jo spoil it?'

'He's a little baby,' I say, frowning at her as I step from the curtains. 'I can't stop him from crying.'

'You can. You just let him do that so you don't have to play with me.'

'I'm *trying*!' I say pleadingly.

I squat down, releasing Jo from his corduroy bondage and unhooking my maternity bra. Two seconds later he's latched on. Poppy stands over us, glowering. What she wants, she keeps telling me, is to go back to it being just her and me, in our London flat. She doesn't need a daddy or a brother, she says. All she needs is me.

'Why don't I skip my last go and you hide?' I say.

'It's still your turn.'

'It'll work much better this way round. Then you can have your tea and we'll go to Pat's.'

'I don't want to go to Pat's!'

I suck at my teeth, wanting to scream.

'Come on, Pops,' I say. 'Go and hide and Jo and I will count to twenty, then we'll come and find you.'

'Jo can't count,' she says, then turns on her heel and strops off.

I count slowly, hoping that Jo will have finished his sucking by the time I get to twenty. As I'm calling out the numbers, I hear a door somewhere open and close. If Poppy was still angry she'd have slammed it, but this is quiet and deliberate, so the game must still be on. At nineteen, I push my little finger into Jo's mouth and gently pull him off my boob. Tying the straps back around my middle, I haul myself up.

'Coming!' I call. 'Ready or not!'

It's then that I hear the car, the distant growl of an engine starting up on the lane. Si must have gone out. I'm partly relieved but a bit panicked too. All day I've been waiting for this, and now I need to move quickly. I have to finish the game as quickly as I can, then put the rucksack into my car and leave.

'OK, missus!' I shout. 'Where are you?'

The click of the door seemed to have come from behind me, but whether this means that she's upstairs or in the kitchen, I'm unsure: the building is so large and, as usual, I was distracted by Jo. Checking the downstairs toilet, I haul myself up the steps. Recently Poppy's taken to scooting from one room to the next as I search, making the game last longer. Rocking the sling from side to side to get Jo back to sleep, I push open my bedroom door. All I can see is the silhouette of a rucksack and crumpled pyjamas. Bending unsteadily, I check that Poppy isn't hiding under the bed. She's not in the wardrobe, either. I close the door, moving down the gallery.

She's not in her bedroom. For a moment I imagine that the rippled mound of her duvet contains her body, but when I pull it back there's just her discarded nightie and Cookie, her blue panda.

I pace on down the gallery. Any minute now, Si could reappear.

'Come on, Poppy,' I call. 'I give up!'

There's no answer. Leaning over the wooden railing I peruse the huge living room. Not a trace. I hurry back along the gallery, pushing open the doors and glancing quickly inside all the rooms: there's no one there. When I reach the metal steps that lead to the door at the top, I grab hold of the railings and start to pull myself up, then stop with relief. The padlock is still hanging from the bolt on the door.

I return down the steps and take the wooden stairs leading from the gallery, still calling Poppy's name. I have been hunting for her for over ten minutes and am teetering on the cusp that divides irritation from unease. The ground floor is too open-plan for effective hiding, so even though I prod the curtains, I've guessed she isn't here. I walk through to the kitchen, but she isn't under the table or behind the back door. She isn't hiding under the coats that are bundled on the floor, nor is she squatting in the cubbyhole where I keep the dustpan and brush.

'Poppy!' I call again. My voice has taken on a different timbre: higher and more fretful. 'Come on, sweetheart! We need to go!'

The building remains silent. I run back into the living room, then freeze, holding my breath so I'll catch the smallest sound. But there's nothing, just Jo's snuffling and the brush of a branch on a window.

'Poppy!' I yell once more. 'I give up!'

There is no reply. My emotions are now tipping from irritation to something darker: a gathering panic. Where the hell *is* she?

'Poppy!'

Biting my lip, I climb back upstairs. There is no cause for alarm, I tell myself. This is the game. Poppy hides, I seek. Yet as I scuttle along the gallery again, an unformed dread is curling deep inside me. Nearly twenty-five minutes have passed since I heard a door closing. I crash back downstairs and stand by the picture window, trying to remain calm. Behind me the house buzzes with my daughter's absence.

Poppy must be outside. I gaze through the glass at the building site that constitutes our garden: mud, breeze blocks resting against the side wall, tarpaulin covering the abandoned foundations. Apart from my Fiat, the drive is empty. As I thought, Si has taken the car and gone. There is nothing for Poppy out here. The weather's bitter; more flecks of snow drift in the air. It's inconceivable that Poppy would have gone outside in her thin T-shirt and ra-ra skirt. All the same, I open the door.

'Poppy!' I shout at the grey afternoon. '*Poppy!*'

Could she have run along the path beside the creek? In a short while it will be dark. My daughter is not an adventurer, she will surely get lost among the labyrinth of paths that weave through the marsh and the desolate landscape of decaying boats and mud flats; she could slip, fall into the salty water. I start to move outside, but Jo flinches at the cold, screwing up his little face in disgust. Grabbing my puffa jacket and zipping it round him, I place my hands over his warm head. In a moment I will find her and this biting panic will be rendered ridiculous: the groundless fears of an over-protective mother.

'Poppy! Where *are* you?'

Clambering round the tarpaulin, I reach the fence that rings the property. The boat yard stretches behind the warehouse. Across the yard and to the right a muddy lane leads past the Perkins's cottage, followed by a row of garages and Trish's place. At the front of the building, a small path twists through clumps of reeds to the riverside. Beyond that, the marsh sprawls towards the dulling sky. Stumbling towards the creek, I scan the arching horizon, fear cresting in my chest.

'Poppy!'

The land is so flat that had she gone along the path I would surely be able to glimpse her small figure. But all I can see is a man with a dog walking fast towards me, his shoulders hunched at the cold.

'Have you seen a little girl?' I call. The question makes Poppy's disappearance real, another step towards all-encompassing panic.

'No, love.'

He's in his sixties, buttoned up in a thick raincoat and wearing a hat. His labrador trots happily behind him.

'We were playing hide-and-seek,' I say, trailing off as the man stops by the fence.

'Bit cold for that, isn't it?'

'I can't find her anywhere. I was worried she'd gone off by the river.'

'There aren't any little girlies down there, love. There's just gulls and crabs and lots of mud.' He chuckles and moves on.

He's right. Poppy may barricade herself into her room in a sulk, but she hates solitude and I know she would never go to the river alone.

I jog back to the kitchen, hoping that I will find her sitting at the table smirking at me in triumph, but the place is exactly as I left it. I gaze numbly at the scene, longing for her with a physical force that clogs my throat. According to the kitchen clock, it's ten to five. That means that over forty minutes have passed since I called 'Ready or not!' Poppy has gone. My beloved daughter has gone. This simple statement is so terrifying that my legs buckle.

Jo is beginning to squirm, but I ignore him. Running down the corridor, I hurry to the bottom of the steps that lead to our bedrooms.

'Poppy!'

I am praying for noise: a shuffling of feet or even a sob, but none comes. I heard the car, I keep remembering, the movement of tyres on the gravel drive. I am too panicked to let the thought take form.

One faint hope remains. Grabbing my phone from the sofa, I press in Trish's number. Her mobile rings twice, then she picks up.

'Hi, Mel! What are you up to? Are you OK?'

'It's Poppy, Trish. I can't find her . . .' My voice is high and shaky, almost out of control. 'We were playing hide-and-seek . . . she's not come over to you, has she?'

'I'm not at home. I'm just coming back from Tesco's.'

'Oh God, Trish . . . Si's gone too!'

Now I've said it, there's no going back. We're no longer playing, no longer edging around the hole that has opened at our feet. Poppy has gone. *And Si's car is no longer in the yard.*

'Hold tight, honey,' Trish says. 'I'll come over as soon as I can.'

But I cannot bear to stay here, waiting. I have to take action. This time I run to the back door, throwing it open. I stumble across the boat yard, turn into the muddy lane and walk to the first cottage on the right. Only a few days ago Bob Perkins hailed us with the news that he and Janice had adopted a baby hedgehog they'd found wandering in the reeds. Perhaps Poppy is with them, I think wildly, feeding it warm milk as she munches on a scone. Yet even as I bang on the door of their neat cottage, I know that I will not find her inside.

As the door opens, my instincts are confirmed. Bob peers out from behind half-moon specs, a copy of *The Times* folded under his arm. 'Hello, Melanie. Anything the matter?'

'I've lost Poppy. I thought she might be with you . . .'

He frowns. Janice is hovering behind him suspiciously.

'We haven't seen her.' Something tight-lipped and closed comes into his expression, like he's already made up his mind. In my panic I had forgotten the events of the last forty-eight hours: the things my neighbours have seen and the conclusions they must have drawn.

I nod frantically, barely aware of what I'm saying. 'I have to get back, perhaps she's there . . . I mean, I have to call the police . . .'

Then I am back in the muddy lane, my arms wrapped round Jo.

Inside the warehouse once more, my fingers tremble as they pick up the phone and punch in 999. As I wait for my call to be answered, I picture Detective Chief Inspector's Dave Gosforth's face, then push it from my mind. There's no connection . . . there can't be.

'Hello, caller. What service do you require?'

'Police,' I whisper.

Trish arrives first. I have put Jo in his baby bouncer and have just finished ringing the parents of Poppy's few friends as she strides through the back door. The response of the two mothers I have spoken to is identical: surprised concern, underlain by a thinly disguised stratum of disapproval. Only careless mothers lose their children, their shocked voices imply; this is not something that could happen to *them*. Gulping back my hysteria, I replace the receiver and turn to find Trish closing the door behind her.

The moment I see her face the terror that's been bulking inside me dissolves, impossible to repress. Trish is holding out her arms and I fall into them, the hard bundle of her baby pressing into my tummy.

'Trish, Poppy's gone!' I sob when eventually I let go of her. 'We were playing hide-and-seek and she vanished!'

She steps back, regarding me with her kind brown eyes. We've only been friends for a couple of months, yet as I clutch her hand and gaze into her pretty face she's my only ballast in this sudden tidal wave.

'Tell me what happened.'

We sit together at the cluttered table. In his baby bouncer on the floor, Jo burbles happily. As I talk I knead at my wedding ring, 'We were playing hide-and-seek, and I was looking for her. I mean, I heard her going upstairs . . . And a door closed . . . Then I went up to look and she was gone . . .'

'What about Si?'

'He came back this morning! He's been upstairs all day, working on the top floor . . . Then later I heard this door close behind me and the car drive off . . .'

'And this was before Poppy hid?'

I shake my head. 'I don't know!'

'Have you called him? I mean, perhaps there was a mix-up and he thought he was meant to be taking her out or something . . .'

She trails off, watching me thoughtfully. She is so pregnant that she has had to push the chair back from the table and sit astride it, her hands folded over her woolly jumper like an obese diner reclining after a large meal.

'The police have taken his mobile . . .' I can't continue, for my teeth have started to chatter, like a joke-shop skeleton.

'You're freezing. Put this over you.' Pulling the jumper she's wearing over her head, she slips it over my shoulders. She's right. I'm still wearing my puffa, but shock has turned me to ice.

'I'll make some tea,' she says, rising.

A few minutes later the police arrive. First the lights of their car sweep up the lane, then I hear the smack of a car door, followed by their boots crunching on the drive. Trish lets them in as I huddle under her maternity jumper. I am shaking uncontrollably.

There are two of them: a young man, with a smooth, inexpressive face, and a woman, who's blonde and pretty, with light blue eyes that scan the untidy kitchen impassively. The policeman offers me a limp hand and tells me his name is Police Constable Johnson.

'We've received a report of a child missing from this address,' he says, turning to Trish. 'Are you the mother?'

'That's *me*.'

I stand, not caring when my trembling legs bump the kitchen table. PC Johnson has pulled his notebook from the front pocket of his jacket.

'And your name is . . . ?'

'Melanie Stenning.'

He jots it down, not making the connection.

'What's the age of the child?'

'She's seven. Her name's Poppy.'

'Can you give me a description?'

'She's got blonde hair, tied back in plaits, and blue eyes, and . . .' I trail off. How can I describe my child with the bland words that he is waiting to jot down? She is gorgeous, dazzling, an explosion of light.

'What was she wearing?' PC Johnson says, in a tone edging towards boredom.

'A denim ra-ra skirt and a pink top with love hearts over it, white trainers . . .'

'We'll need a photo, if you've got one.'

'We think her stepdad's taken her,' Trish interjects. 'Mel heard his car leaving just after she'd gone.'

'I'm not sure,' I mutter. 'I don't know why he'd . . .'

'Hold on a minute, ladies. Let's take it one thing at a time.'

I bite my lip. I do not want to take it one thing at a time. I want the police to be out in the freezing evening with a fleet of cars, whizzing down every road in the whole damn country, searching for my child.

'And where did you last see your daughter, Melanie?'

'Here, in the house. We were playing hide-and-seek.'

'And I take it you've thoroughly searched the premises?'

'Of course I have. She's not here.'

'Do you know what time it was when you last saw her?' he continues patiently.

'About four? We started playing at about a quarter to. I hid and then it was her turn, then I heard a door close . . .'

'The door to . . . ?'

'I assumed it was somewhere upstairs, or maybe the kitchen, but it could have been anywhere . . . I mean, I wasn't really listening.'

He peers in the direction of the corridor. 'And there's a possibility that your husband may have taken her out?'

I stare at the unswept floor. I do not want to start crying, not now.

Trish moves closer, taking my hand and squeezing it. 'We're worried he's not going to bring her back.'

'Or perhaps she's wandered off somewhere . . .' I add weakly.

'Does your husband have a mobile?'

'No.' I stare at him obstinately, refusing to explain why.

'And do you know where he might have gone?'

I shake my head. London? His mother's house, with its echoing rooms and mouldy carpets? Anything seems possible, for over the last months Si's normal habits and patterns have become unrecognisable.

'I have no idea.'

'Can you describe the vehicle?'

'It's an old white Volvo Estate. I don't know the registration. He borrowed it from his friend this morning.'

'Can you tell us how to contact this friend? We'll need the registration number.'

'His name's Ollie Dubow. Si was working with him. His mobile number's pinned up over there.' I point to a cork board on the far wall.

'Righty ho,' says PC Johnson, nodding. 'I'm going to get these vehicle details and give them to our control unit, then we'll have a scoot round the property to make sure she's not still hiding from us, shall we?'

I shrug impatiently. Jo has started to complain. Squatting by the bouncy chair I unclick the harness and pull him out, burying my face in his warm body. I can't believe that Si would take Poppy, but, however much I will it not to be so, she has gone. For the first time the reality of what has happened crashes into me. I start to sob, rocking Jo backwards and forwards as if it were him who needed comforting.

When I look up, the policewoman is standing by the door, talking into her radio. PC Johnson and Trish have disappeared. From the top of the lane I can hear the high-pitched whoop of a siren and see the blue lights of back-up cars outside.

'You're married to Simon Stenning, Melanie, is that right?' the policewoman asks kindly as she clicks the radio back into her belt. I nod, wiping my cheeks with my sleeve and not meeting her eyes. Jo wants to feed, so I have absent-mindedly given him my little finger to suck.

'He's Poppy's father?'

'Her stepfather,' I mutter. 'And we were just about to leave.'

2

SIX MONTHS AGO I would no more have considered leaving Si than throwing away a winning lottery ticket. My life had been unexpectedly and joyously transformed by this diffident, surprising man. He was hardly my type: an unshaven forty-year-old painter who no longer painted; a dreamer, with wrists so thin that when I placed my fingers round them I could feel the bone beneath. I went for blunt, bullish types who were good at sports and drove too fast. None of them had ever made me happy, but they were my default mode.

We met on 28 December, 2003. Objectively that's only a short time ago, but to me it feels like for ever: a distant life that's fading fast. It was the tail end of a miserable holiday, the dog days between Christmas and New Year's Eve. I was back at work, returning to London from Pat's with relief rather than regret. It had been the worst Christmas that I could recall, probably because I had finally relented to Pat's pressure and taken Poppy to her house in Buckinghamshire. She had tried so hard to do it 'properly'. She had filled the sitting room with an enormous Norwegian tree garlanded with ornate gold baubles and glass animals that she must have acquired specially, for they had never appeared during my childhood. Around the tree were placed not so much gifts as strategic statements: a set of saucepans and a recipe book for me; a doll and pram for Poppy, the sort of traditional toy that in Pat's fantasy her young granddaughter would adore. Every meal was planned with military precision, every day filled with outings in which Poppy and myself were paraded triumphantly in front of Pat's friends. I had forgotten her neediness and her pretensions. Now, visiting for the first time in three years, I remembered why I had left.

I behaved badly. I drank too much and snapped surly remonstrations when I should have been biting my lip. Pat was lonely and unhappy: retired and widowed at sixty-five, wishing she had more to show for her life. She had wanted a family, but back in the late 1960s IVF was a sci-fi dream. So she had ended up with me: another woman's reject, who despite all their entreaties to work harder and take more care had deliberately flunked her A levels, squandered three years on the rave scene, then bunked off to Goa.

When Pat and Michael's natural daughter would have got a well-deserved 2:1 in a sensible subject like accountancy or law, I was doing drugs in India. When she would have been painstakingly building her career, just as her civil servant father and school teacher mother had done, I was working in a bar and partying in Oz. When their natural daughter would have married a sensible young chap and then, a year or so later, produced a grandchild, I was getting knocked up by a bartender and bringing up my baby in Australia. In the neat trajectory of their well-trimmed life, I suppose I was their only real failure.

I drove back to London fast, my music cranked up loud as Poppy dozed in the back. OK, so I was a useless daughter and a useless mother. I had wanted freedom from my adoptive parents and the dull aspirations they represented, but somehow had become ensnared in dreary responsibility. In Oz I would have been on the beach, drinking stubbies as Poppy played in the surf. As my windscreen wipers sloshed the pouring rain, I couldn't remember why I'd ever returned. Yet the truth was that by the time Poppy was two, her father had left and I had been drifting, taking one meaningless job after the other to pay the rent, and moving from one disastrous relationship to the next. So I had chosen to come back to Britain, not so much to return home, as to escape the person I was becoming.

The next morning, the office had an air of mournful neglect. I opened the windows at the sour stench of dog-ends and removed a clutch of empty bottles to the small kitchenette where we made our coffee and, despite strict instructions from head office, smoked our fags. After that I had a stab at rearranging the plastic Christmas tree, which had been knocked over during the last, tipsy day at work, scattering its load of Christmas cards on the acrylic flooring. The usual rush of vendors and buyers would start in the New Year, but Don had insisted we remain open over these in-between days. 'Never miss a deal,' he'd lectured on my first day. 'Remember, the more we sell, the more we earn!'

I had nodded earnestly at this injunction, but in reality didn't give a monkey's. I was bored with the estate agency: the greediness of my clients and colleagues, the endless half-truths and promises that were required to close a sale. It was just another job, and today was just another day. Poppy was playing at her friend Jessie's and I was in the kind of mood where I wasn't much bothered what happened.

A Simon Stenning had left a message on my voicemail. He sounded harried, as if he was rushing somewhere: 'Hi. I want to shift my flat in Queen's Road pronto. If you could call me back, I'd be grateful.' He'd left a number and the address of his place, which I dutifully noted down as I listened impassively to the handful of remaining messages.

I called Simon Stenning at noon, hoping that he wouldn't be in and that, with the rest of my calls answered, I would be free to lock up the office and go home. Annoyingly, he picked up immediately. He couldn't afford to wait, he announced; was there any chance I could come round today? By two that afternoon I was ringing the bell to an ornate Victorian villa that backed onto Nunhead Cemetery.

The man who opened the door was not what I'd expected. His posh voice and polite impatience had conjured up an out-of-hours businessman, with a gleaming Jag and designer jeans. In contrast, the caller was a scruffy mess: his baggy jeans splattered with paint, holes at the elbows of his jumper and dark hair that curled over his shoulders. I immediately warmed to his appearance of frayed gentility. I liked the way he took my hand as I introduced myself as Mel Middleton, shaking it heartily as he peered a little short-sightedly into my eyes.

'You're not what I was imagining,' he said, letting me into the communal hall. 'The woman from Bonhams was wearing stilettos and this headset phone thing. Quite terrifying.'

I glanced down at my jeans, laughing. 'Sorry to have forgotten the power suit. I wasn't expecting any appointments today. My boss would kill me.'

'Well, we'd better not tell him, had we?'

He led me upstairs to the first floor and pushed open the door to his flat. 'Bonhams valued it at three ten. I wanted a second opinion.'

I smiled. 'I'll just have a wander around, if that's OK?'

'Sure.'

I edged round the bicycle that blocked the small hall, and walked into the front room, sizing up the large bay windows and high ceiling. The boards were bare—a fashionable plus—but the walls were dingy and scuffed and the furniture shabby. Even worse for a potential sale, the room was crammed with large canvasses.

'You're an artist?'

'Was.' He folded his arms. 'The muse abandoned me.'

'At least you had a muse. Some of us spend our entire lives not knowing what to do with ourselves.'

It was too personal a comment for the situation and hardly likely to elicit his business, but Si pulled a face that I interpreted as an empathetic grimace. As I turned away his fingers brushed my arm.

'May I see the other rooms?'

He led me into the bedroom, which was covered in discarded clothes and yet more canvasses. I glanced at the women's clothes heaped in one corner; a lacy skirt, high-heeled boots, a scramble of underwear.

'I'll get this stuff cleared out by the end of the week,' he said, gesturing vaguely at the pile. He seemed suddenly upset and I grimaced sympathetically. Almost half of our sales came from the demise of love: homes that were once so hopefully woven together left fraying and ripped when one half of the partnership walks out.

Moving on down the corridor, we entered the kitchen.

'My *God*!'

I was facing a large painting hanging lopsidedly from the wall. I gawped wordlessly, struggling to think of something complimentary to add, yet as I took in the angular nude facing me, my mind stalled. She was very thin, her clavicles and pelvic bones sticking out alarmingly as she flopped backwards, untidy curls tumbling down her back. Her expression was both angry and somehow imploring. I stared at the image, swallowing hard. On one side of the picture the artist had deliberately smudged her face with a dark smear, making her seem disfigured, as if she had been knocked about.

'It's all right, you don't have to say anything,' Si muttered behind me. Striding to the wall, he grabbed the edge of the canvas and yanked at it hard until, unbalancing from its hook, it shuddered to the floor.

Embarrassed, I glanced hastily around the room, trying to summon up a light-hearted comment. 'This room's a good size.'

He ignored me. 'So, what do you think?' he asked abruptly. Something in his face had shifted since our earlier banter, his mouth becoming more set, his forehead creased. 'Speed is the main issue here. I want to release my capital as quickly as possible.'

'I wouldn't want to put it on the market at more than two ninety,' I said quickly.

It was both a relief and a disappointment to be back in the safe territory of conveyancy. He nodded, his face relaxing.

'OK,' he said briskly. 'Well, thanks a lot for coming over. It's always good to get a second opinion.'

We started to move back down the corridor, our business finished. I felt like a fool. Five minutes earlier I had imagined that we were flirting, but now, a boring task completed, I was being summarily dismissed.

More policemen have arrived. They are going to concentrate on tracing the vehicle that Si was driving, I am informed as I slump numbly in his patched-up armchair. They've looked round the building, inspected the yard, and for now are assuming that Si has taken Poppy in his car. Outside, it's dark. While there was still ebbing light there was hope: Poppy had wandered off somewhere, the game was still on. But now it is night. On the floor beside me Jo is leaning over in his bouncy chair, chuckling as he attempts to grab his toes. As Trish bends down and tickles him under the arms, a heavy-set man who was introduced a few minutes earlier as a 'police search advisor' squats beside the armchair.

'We need to have some of Poppy's property, for forensic evidence,' he says gently. 'If you have a hairbrush, perhaps, or some of her clothing?'

I stare at him with alarm. 'Forensic evidence?'

'It's nothing to be alarmed about at this stage, Melanie. It's just so that we can extract her DNA. We're trying to get the full picture.'

This is hardly reassuring. 'I just want her back,' I whisper feebly.

'That's what we all want. And to help us arrive at a positive outcome we need to get as much evidence as possible. My officers are going to conduct a search of the areas surrounding your property and—'

'You're wasting your time. She's not anywhere around here. She's been taken by her stepfather!' Trish snaps from behind me. I glance round, glad of her support. She is holding Jo against her shoulder. Reaching down, she gives my arm a little squeeze. 'OK, hon?'

'Just about.'

The police officer straightens up, looking offended. 'I can only reassure you that we're vigorously pursuing all lines of enquiry.'

'You need to find Si's car,' says Trish, giving him a withering look.

As I stepped outside Si's building I remembered that Natalie had taken the girls to the flicks. The film was due to end at 4.30, so I had an hour to kill before picking Poppy up. I turned from Vestry Road into Peckham High Street, where the Christmas lights were already on: a dismal show of illuminated Disney characters stretched over the road. It was the first day of the sales, and the shop windows were plastered with posters announcing the bargains to be had inside. I trudged wearily past, glancing despondently at the offerings. My reflection stared back: a slimmish thirty-something woman wearing overly tight jeans and ankle boots, with curly brown hair that needed cutting and a startled expression on her drawn face. My gleaming Australian skin had faded to an unhealthy pallor a winter or so earlier, so now I was as pasty as the other south Londoners who jostled beside me.

I turned into a small bistro, offering soup and a crusty baguette for £2.50. To be honest I was not much interested in the food. What I wanted was a large glass of wine, succour against the dreary day. Plonking myself down at a table by the window, I stared through the misty glass at the pedestrians and thundering traffic. I had just about had enough of London. I had come here to provide Poppy with at least some stability, but I was thinking of moving on: perhaps taking up my friend Josie's offer and joining her in Bali for a month or two.

'Hello again.'

I glanced up with a start. Si was standing over my table.

'Hi!'

Blood swamped my cheeks, a stupid schoolgirl's blush. Plucking the menu from the table, I pretended to busy myself in the choices. He must have left his flat a few minutes after I had and followed me down the road. Had he seen me mooning at myself in the shop windows?

'I'm not stalking you, promise,' he said. 'Well . . .' He paused, staring directly into my eyes. 'Actually, I am. I wanted to apologise for being so rude,' he continued. 'All I can say is that I don't usually go around attacking canvasses like that. It's just that I've had a heavy day or two.'

'I wouldn't worry,' I said reassuringly. 'We see all kinds of interesting behaviour in this job. People can get incredibly stressed about moving.'

'But I do worry.'

If I was a different person I would have asked him outright what had happened between him and the nude. He would have sat down and shared my wine and perhaps, in the unexpected intimacy that sometimes occurs between strangers, he would have told me everything. But I was never so confident or brave.

'Is this place nice?' I said hastily. 'I skipped breakfast, so I'm starving.'

'Tut, tut.'

'I also really fancied a drink . . .'

'That sounds more up my street.'

I chuckled, surprised at how much I welcomed his company. Away from the grey light of his hall he looked healthier, almost handsome, in a faded, rumpled kind of way.

'I'm going to do a detox for New Year. Or that's what I'm telling myself.' I paused, aware that once again I was drivelling. Si was looking at me wistfully, his long fingers clutching the top of the chair opposite.

Sod it, I thought. To hell with Don's *Code of Conduct for Conveyancing*.

'Why don't you stay and have a drink?' I asked.

I didn't get to Nat's until after six. She had fed Poppy and Jessie pizza and ice cream, and by the time I arrived they were curled on the sofa in a contented haze, watching a *Blue Peter* Christmas special.

'You look well,' Nat said meaningfully. 'Your eyes are all sparkly.'

I gave a little yelp of laughter, already too excited to keep it to myself. 'I've just met a *man!*' I whispered. 'Nat, he's *really nice*.'

'And you're pissed.'

'I am so not!'

She laughed. In the two years that Poppy and Jessie had been in the same class we had fallen into an easy routine of reciprocal school pick-ups and sleepovers. I had Jessie on Mondays and Nat took the girls to ballet on Thursdays. At weekends Jessie often stayed the night with us so that Nat could have her boyfriend over. We were the sole members of the Single Mothers of Buckingham Road Club: non-judgmental support guaranteed. I leaned over and inspected my face in her hall mirror. It was true that I was a trifle bleary.

'What *are* you like, Mel? You go off to work and end up scoring!'

I stuck out my tongue at her. 'You're a fine one to talk.'

When Poppy and I got home the answering machine was flashing promisingly in the dark. I ran Poppy a bath, squatting by the tub with my hand trailing in the water as we played I-Spy, then pulled her out into a warm towel and sat her on my lap as I brushed her teeth. 'Wrap me up like a sausage!' she'd cry, and I'd roll the towel around her, so that only a tufty patch of hair appeared at the top. Then I'd tickle her toes until she screamed. After that we'd cuddle up together under my duvet and read stories. Then I'd let her snuggle down and go to sleep in my bed. Pat had disapproved, of course. By her age she should be sleeping alone, she'd lectured me during our Christmas visit. I was making a rod for my own back.

After Poppy had gone to sleep I opened a beer and, sitting on the edge of the sofa, pressed 'replay' on the answering machine. I wanted to savour the message. It had been a long time since I'd felt so excited. It was like a chink of sun appearing through thick packed cloud.

'Miss Middleton?' Si's voice sounded even more upper class than I remembered. I pictured him sitting opposite me in the café, his tall frame cramped by the narrow chair, the curl of dark hair on his arms. As he'd inspected the menu he'd placed a pair of wire-framed specs on the end of his nose: a boyish intellectual. I shouldn't let myself feel like this, I told myself; I hardly knew the guy.

'It's me, your untidy vendor from this afternoon. I was wondering if we might arrange a meeting to discuss my sale in more detail. Perhaps some time tomorrow?' He paused. 'I think we may have the potential for a promising deal.'

I told Don that I had an appointment to view the flat of a Mr Stenning, and met Si outside Nunhead Cemetery. It was an unconventional setting for a first date, overlooked as it was by Victorian angels and ivy-covered cherubs. We pushed through thick brambles to find forgotten family mausoleums and, in the middle of the cemetery, a derelict chapel. He came here when he needed to think, Si explained as we wandered inside. If I had been alone I would have found the place frightening, but, with Si beside me, could sense its tenuous beauty.

'I once spent a whole summer here painting the angels,' he murmured as he stood gazing up through the jagged roof to the grey sky.

'Wow. I'd love to see them.'

'You can't. They're gone.'

He kicked at the mossy stones, turning abruptly back to the path. My careless words must have hit upon a sore memory. When I caught up with him he was leaning against a large stone cross, smiling again, the angels apparently forgotten.

'So, what do you think of my urban wilderness.'

I blinked, sensing that a great deal rested on my reply. 'I love it.'

He licked his lips thoughtfully. 'But?'

'But let's not come here in the dark, OK?'

'Oh, don't be such a wimp! Come on, I'm going to take you to my favourite picnic spot.'

Stretching out his arm, he grasped my hand in his and we wandered down the weedy paths. He'd first broken into the cemetery one summer night about fifteen years ago, he told me. He was a student at the time, studying art at Camberwell. That particular evening he'd feasted on a handful of magic mushrooms that he'd picked in Brockwell Park. He couldn't recall how he'd got to Nunhead, only that he had scaled a wall and landed among the graves. Lying spreadeagled against a stone cross, he'd imagined himself taking to the air, his greatcoat spread wide as he flew over south London, towards the river. He had crept back to his digs in the dawn mist, chilled and bemused.

'And you've had a thing about graveyards ever since?'

'You could say that, yes.'

We had arrived at a tombstone, our breath billowing in the winter air. Reaching into his knapsack, Si produced a block of chocolate and a small flask of brandy. 'Tell me more about you,' he said, passing me the flask as we huddled together. 'I know you've got a daughter called Poppy'—I nodded at him, pleased he had remembered her name—'and you work as an estate agent and you used to live in Australia, and you've never had a muse, right? But what's your life *like*?'

It may have been an odd way of phrasing the question, but his interest delighted me. 'Mostly it's just dull routine. I work, pick up Poppy from school, look after her, watch TV and go to bed. If I'm lucky I'll get pissed with one of my mates every couple of weeks. It's not exactly how I thought I'd end up spending my life.' I stopped, regretting the bitterness in my voice.

'So what happened?'

I took a swig of the brandy, enjoying the sensation of warmth spreading down my gullet. Where should I start? Should it be with my childhood, with Pat and Michael and their bruised disappointment at my inability to conform? Or my squandered youth, bumming around the world? The truth was that I'd never felt that I fitted in: certainly not in the various provincial towns where I'd been brought up. Throughout my childhood I had experienced the intangible sense of being a visitor in a place where I did not belong. With my dark hair and olive complexion I *looked* so different from my sandy-haired parents, perhaps that was partly why. But I was also unable to apply myself to the activities that would have brought them pleasure: academic success, an interest in clothing and cookery, a nice hobby like horse riding or gymnastics. I stubbornly rejected everything they yearned for me to do.

Moving to the other side of the world hadn't made me happy either. I was floating without direction, a rudderless boat on glassy waters, aware that, apart from being a mum to Poppy, my life was taking place at the margins of something I was unable to grasp. And now, as I perched next to Si on the freezing tombstone, explaining how this had happened seemed like a gargantuan task.

'I guess I messed everything up,' I said flatly. 'I let myself drift. I should have gone to university and everything, but I ended up a single mum, working in a pointless job.'

'You make it sound as if that's the end of the story,' he said, breaking off a large chunk of the chocolate and popping it into his mouth. 'It could be just the beginning, couldn't it?'

I shrugged, not sure how to respond. 'What about you?' I asked. 'What's it like being a painter?'

'I'm not a painter, not any more.'

'You're . . .'

'A "property developer".' He chuckled, presumably at the pomposity of the label. 'I'm planning to use the money from the flat to do up some place in Kent. I'm going to make a heap of money, then retire to Spain and spend my dotage growing olives. What do you think?'

'Fantastic!'

'It's not just a daydream. I'm really going to make it happen. Just watch me.'

I bit my lip at the notion, so casually mentioned, that I might be around to see him realise his plans. 'I'm sure you will,' I said, suddenly too shy to look into his face. 'It sounds wonderful.'

I did not ask about the woman who had been living in his flat.

After I had collected Poppy from school that afternoon, Si came to tea. As I opened the door to him he greeted me with a gentlemanly kiss, planted on my cheek, then presented me with a packet of Jaffa Cakes and, from the inside pocket of his battered suede jacket, a small sheet of paper covered by a pencil sketch of an angel. As he pressed it shyly into my hand, it seemed loaded with meaning. I leaned the picture self-consciously against the phone.

I was anxious about Poppy: either Si would be put off by the reality of a child in my life or she would take against him. Since my return to London I had not been in the habit of starting relationships with men, far less bringing them home.

As Si stepped inside the flat, looking around and nodding at me in apparent approval, my heart tightened with terror. What the hell was I doing, inviting a stranger here? The date was only meant to involve a cup of tea and a biscuit, but already I felt as if we had crossed an invisible line. In the next room I could hear Poppy's footsteps, tramping towards the door. A second later, she flung it open.

'Who are *you*?'

'I'm Simon. Who are you?'

'Poppy.'

'Hello, Poppy. Do you prefer to shake hands or to bow?' Simon held out his hand expectantly.

She stared at him in silence, her eyebrows furrowing. 'What's bowing?'

'This.'

Whipping off his beanie, he bent his body into a deep, courtly bow.

Poppy giggled. 'That makes you look silly.'

'I know, but it's obligatory in the presence of a princess.'

'You're weird.'

But I could tell she was pleased from the way her sparkling eyes followed him along the hall. We trailed into the living room, a small procession led by this tall stranger who already felt so familiar. Then there was me: an awkward flummox of maternal anxiety. Finally came Poppy, who had folded her arms over her chest and was frowning.

'This place is boring,' she announced. 'Do you want to see my room?'

As Poppy led Si down the hall into her room, I bustled round the kitchen, arranging the cupcakes Poppy and I had made and brewing tea. From down the corridor I could hear laughter. Eventually Poppy and Si arrived in the kitchen, still bantering, and we squeezed round the table, drinking tea and gobbling the cakes. Si had a way of teasing Poppy that I had seldom seen in an adult, least of all a man with no children of his own: as if she and he were equals in comedy combat. I watched them together, smiling at my daughter's pleasure.

Eventually, well past seven, Poppy began to rub her eyes and yawn, her body drooping onto the table. Gathering her into my arms, I carried her to the bathroom, where I wiped her face with a flannel and gently brushed her teeth. Then I popped her into bed, kissing her on the cheek as she rolled over. For a moment I stayed by her pillow, my cheek pressed against hers. Making her happy and keeping her safe were all that mattered. All the same, my legs were trembling as I walked back towards the kitchen.

The first time we made love was at Si's flat, about a week after the visit to Nunhead Cemetery. It was one of those crisp winter days of bright blue skies and zero temperatures that make one unaccustomedly clear-headed. I told Don that I was going to measure up Mr Stenning's flat for the property details that we would shortly be emailing to our clients, making sure that he noticed me placing the digital camera and dictaphone into my bag.

Si must have been waiting for me, for the downstairs door buzzed open before I had even pressed my finger to the bell. I trotted up the stairs, my heart banging. Above me, he was standing on the landing.

'Hi.'

'Hello there.' He held out his hand, staring. I had taken more trouble with my appearance than usual: my usually unruly hair was piled on top of my head, and, rather than my sensible boots and trousers, after much deliberation I had decided on a tight velvet skirt and heels.

'You look fantastically beautiful.' The teasing in his voice had gone.

'Can I come in?'

As he stepped aside I entered a transformed flat. The piled-up canvasses and heaped clothes were gone, the wooden floors were swept; in the grate in the sitting room a fire was blazing.

'You've been busy!'

'I've got a buyer.'

I jerked round, my heart fluttering in my mouth. 'Oh!'

'With Bonhams, I'm afraid. And they're paying the asking price.'

I pulled a face at him, feigning disappointment. 'Well, I'd better go then, hadn't I?'

'Not so fast, Ms Middleton . . .'

He pulled me into his arms and my lips found his. As we crumpled ungracefully onto the floor in a tangle of limbs and already discarded clothes, I kissed him greedily, my hands in his thick hair. I wanted to feel his skin against mine, to press him into me, give myself up, feel the world fall away as he became mine.

3

'MEL?'

I look up with a start. Detective Chief Inspector Dave Gosforth is standing before me, his arms folded, his face faintly puzzled. I'd hoped I would never lay eyes on his ugly mug again, with its piggy eyes and red-tipped nose.

'It's me again, I'm afraid.'

I shrug. I do not trust myself to speak.

'I'm going to be taking over the search for Poppy,' he says slowly. I still do not respond. 'My colleagues tell me that you heard someone leave the house just before you started to look for her, is that right?'

'I heard a door close, and then a little bit later a car driving away . . .'

'And when you looked, the car that Simon had borrowed from his friend was no longer in the drive?'

'No, it wasn't.'

He pauses meaningfully and my stomach lurches.

'There's been a sighting,' he says. 'We've been talking to someone who was working in the yard. Apparently he saw a white Volvo Estate driving fast towards the lane at about quarter past four. The witness also clearly remembers seeing a little girl who answers to Poppy's description in the passenger seat. I'm afraid we now have to assume that Simon's taken her.'

I turn and stare into his expressionless face. 'But I don't know why he would . . .'

'There are lots of reasons . . .' His hand is hovering over my arm as if he is considering giving it a reassuring squeeze. 'People in distress often do silly things.'

I jerk my arm away from his pudgy fingers. 'What about the river? She could have fallen into it . . . And the houses along the road, have you asked if anyone's seen her?' Yet even as I speak I know how obvious it must seem.

'For the time being we're scaling down our activities in the immediate vicinity,' he says carefully, fingering the radio which has started to crackle at his belt. 'I'm calling a halt to the search of your property and we're putting our resources into tracing Simon's vehicle. We've put out a national alert for the car; a newsflash is going out in the next hour; all the seaports and airports have been alerted. There's every reason to believe that we'll quickly locate the car and get Poppy back to you.'

'But he wouldn't . . .' It's too late. Tears are sliding down my face, running in rivulets down my nose and over my dry lips.

I was not used to having a regular relationship. There had to be a catch: either Si would have a change of heart and disappear from my life with a puff of emotional smoke, or what had grown so vigorously between us would flower too soon, followed by a sudden and fatal withering of interest. The truth is that I had no idea what to expect. I was thirty-five, but inexperienced in matters of the heart.

Yet rather than my usual trajectory of fleeting desire followed by a brief and usually disappointing fling, we seemed to be travelling in the opposite direction: our pleasure increasing with each week that passed. We slipped into a comfortable routine. Most evenings Si turned up at teatime, just as he had done the afternoon he'd presented me with his angel. As I put Poppy to bed he'd cook, then we'd open a bottle of wine, gobble up whatever vegetarian feast he had concocted and fall into bed like lustful teenagers. He spent every weekend with us too, his quiet, humorous presence so unobtrusive that it was hard to recall what life had been like before. Overnight, almost, we had become a family.

Poppy treated Si as if he had always been around. After only a few weeks he was virtually living with us, but I don't think she ever felt displaced. Rather, he had an ability to fade into the background whenever it was 'her' time. He'd brought his battered guitar over by then, as well as a box of books and a rucksack stuffed with clothes. As I ran Poppy's bath he'd sprawl in the living room, strumming. She loved watching him play; increasingly she'd eschew my proffered bedtime book for the glamour of sitting at his feet and gazing lovingly up at him.

I was so happy in those early days that it scared me. On the rare occasions that Si failed to appear I slipped into a gloomy mistrust that darkened what had previously seemed to be composed entirely of light. *This* was the true pattern of my life, I fretted: fleeting attachments, leading to nothing. Si must have discovered my true character and scarpered. What self-respecting man would want to be lumbered with a drifter with no obvious talents, a six-year-old daughter and a grotty rented flat?

That he had once moved in more elevated circles was obvious from his accent, the occasional, glancing references to the house where he had been born and the public school where he had been sent at thirteen. He always insisted that we were alike, and when together I would agree. Yet, when apart, doubts seeped into my thoughts like pollution into a river. He was in a different league, I'd decide. I was used to blunt, non-reflective men, who never expressed their emotions or wanted to 'talk'. I was also used to coming home and finding they had gone. I had never put much effort into these relationships and was rarely surprised or upset at their disappearance: they felt fleeting and inconsequential, like brief sunny days that could only end.

If those affairs had been day trips to places where I did not wish to stay, I now felt as if I was exploring an exciting new country. But I was unprepared for such a journey, perhaps that was the problem. I had departed without a map, or indeed any obvious way home.

It was early April, the season of daffodils. Si and I were striding down a series of steep-banked country lanes, knapsacks on our backs, the warm sun on our faces. So much for winter gloom, the flowers seemed to declare: spring has arrived! In the trees, birds called excitedly. Yet despite the idyllic morning, I felt oddly downcast. We had started the walk hand in hand, but a mile back had broken apart, falling into a steady silence that could be interpreted in various ways: demonstrating either how relaxed we now were or, as I was increasingly convinced, that something was wrong.

It was our first weekend away from Poppy, and I was jangling with nerves. To take so much time for ourselves seemed too big a leap. Displaced from our normal setting, Si and I would discover each other to be strangers. Since we had left London he had been behaving strangely, too. Despite constantly reassuring myself that everything was normal, I kept turning to find him watching me.

As we reached the bottom of the hill he started to talk about the property he had seen the day before. It was a warehouse on the outskirts of a small town on the Kent coast, and pretty much derelict.

'It's breathtaking, Mel, everything I wanted. I'm sure this is the one.'

I walked quietly beside him. When he reached out his hand I seized it tightly. I felt as if I were watching the scene from afar.

'It's even got planning permission attached,' he went on. 'Apparently they had a buyer last year who went ahead and got the plans drawn up but couldn't get his finances together.'

'Oh.'

'I still can't believe the price they've got it on for. I can't decide whether to just whack in the asking price or try to get them down a bit.'

'Try it and see.'

We had reached a corner where the lane branched left onto a dirt track that was surrounded by water meadows.

'So,' Si said, suddenly swinging me round to face him. 'Why so glum, dear chum? What's up?'

I glanced away from his inquisitive eyes.

'Nothing.'

'Yes, there is. You haven't stopped sighing since we got out of the car.'

I eyed him reluctantly. 'I suppose I'm just thinking about how if you're going to be buying this warehouse and doing it up there won't be much point in you staying in London.'

For a moment he stared at me, then he started to laugh. 'Oh, you stupid woman!' Grabbing my waist, he pushed me through the open gate and up against the stone wall that bounded the meadows. I tottered backwards, the rough stones grazing my skin.

'Ow!'

'Come here, you daft bat. I thought it was obvious!' He was pulling up my T-shirt now and rummaging with my jeans, yanking them down.

'Si! Someone will see!' Peering over his shoulder, I gazed around the field. The cattle at the other end glanced back disinterestedly.

'So what? Let's give the cows a thrill . . .'

Pulling him towards me, I helped him out, not minding when my backside knocked against the mossy wall, or even when we slid down together, into the long wet grass.

Afterwards we lay panting and laughing. The back of my jeans was soaking and Si's knees were stained green.

Sitting up, his face was suddenly serious. 'What on earth makes you think I'm going to leave?' he asked quietly. 'Why can't you trust me?'

His face was puzzled but not unkind. As I looked into it I knew that I would never voice the true reason: I could never trust him because, no matter what he said, I was convinced he couldn't love me.

'I don't know . . .'

Taking my hand, he kneaded it gently between his calloused palms. 'I was actually thinking about how we could all go down to Kent together. You and me and Poppy.'

For a moment I thought I must have misheard. I sucked on my lip. 'But where would we live?'

'In the warehouse! After we've made it a bit more habitable. You keep saying how much you hate your job and loathe living in London. We both need to start afresh, so let's go for it. Please, Mel, let's at least give it a try.'

'I'm not sure,' I said weakly. 'I'm crap at long-term relationships. You don't know what I'm really like.'

Leaning towards me, he pulled me against his muddy jacket. I could smell wet wool and the furl of tobacco in his pocket. 'What are you talking about, you silly woman? Of course I know what you're like.'

'Do you?'

'Yes, I do! Look, you've got to stop defining yourself by what happened in the past. Let's move on from all that and start again. A double escape act.' He hugged me, kissing my forehead. 'This will be a new start for both of us.'

'And you think that's possible do you?'

'Mel, please, just trust me.'

He pulled back, staring intensely into my face. If you had asked me about love three months earlier I would have given a bitter laugh. Not for me, Sunshine, I'd have retorted, save that for the movies. But now, as I regarded Si's searching eyes, I could sense the hope unfurling.

'OK,' I said, blinking back tears. 'You're on.'

I gave notice on my flat and announced to Don that I was intending to leave the agency. He took the news with a sage smile.

'Thought something was up,' he said, giving my shoulder an avuncular pat. 'What with all the sexy dressing. Shame though, you've made some good sales.'

I grinned, taken aback by the praise. I had never thought that I was good at anything, but now it seemed that anything was possible.

Poppy received the news with a satisfied nod. 'Does that mean Si can be my new dad?' she said after I'd finished telling her how we were going to move to Kent. The question took me aback. I had not considered that Poppy might see Si as a potential father.

'Well, your dad lives in Australia,' I said carefully.

'But he's not real.'

'Of course he is.'

She scowled. 'Not like Si's real,' she said plaintively. 'You have to make him be my daddy, Mum.'

'It's not quite as simple as that.'

She peered at me crossly. Then her face suddenly cleared, as if she had made up her mind. 'Of course it is!' she laughed.

The only dissenting voice was Nat's. Perhaps it was my fault for assuming that she would be as thrilled as me that the membership of the Single Mothers of Buckingham Road Club was to be halved. I told her my news in a babble of tactless glee, forgetting that only a month earlier she had been dumped by Ned, her on-off boyfriend.

'That's great,' she said flatly, after I had finished raving about the warehouse and how Si and I were going to wipe our slates clean and start our lives over. 'And have you actually seen this warehouse place?'

'No, but Si says it's amazing.' We were sitting in her canary-yellow kitchen, drinking red wine, while Jessie and Poppy rampaged upstairs. Nat sipped from her glass, not commenting, and I charged on. 'It's such a departure for me, Nat. I mean, all my life I've just muddled along, not getting anything out of men, and now, suddenly, this wonderful guy appears out of the blue and my whole life is transformed!'

'And you think you know him well enough to go and live in the sticks with him, do you?'

I glanced up, surprised by the sharpness of her tone. 'Yeah, I reckon I do,' I replied. 'I mean, we *really* connect with each other.'

She shrugged. 'So how much do you know about him?'

'Well, like how he used to be a painter, and how he's got into building and . . .'

I stopped. It was true that there were gaps in my knowledge. After the incident with the painting, Si had never mentioned the woman who had shared his flat, for instance, and I had never probed. He did not want to discuss the past, he told me. Our relationship was about the present and the future, not what had gone before.

'It's just that if it were me I'd want to know everything about him, for Jessie's sake,' Nat said sulkily. 'Like, for example, where does he stay when he's not at your place?'

I was growing increasingly irritated. 'In his flat.'

'I thought you said he'd sold it?'

'Well, he has. Or he's about to. God, Nat, I don't know! Does it matter? I can't go over there anyway, can I? With Poppy at home?'

She pulled a face.

'What's that expression meant to mean?'

'Just that you should be careful. He sounds a bit too good to be true.'

For a moment I considered the unkind things I might say back: that Nat was so negative and untrusting it was little wonder she could never keep a man, for example, or that if she wanted to meet someone new she should stop moping around and stuffing her face with chocolate. But instead I managed a tight smile.

'But he is true, Nat,' I said quietly. 'He loves me and I love him. I've spent thirty-five years alone, and I'm not going to turn down the chance of changing that just because he hasn't told me the name of his mother's second cousin.' Standing up, I pushed back my chair. 'Poppy!' I shouted up the narrow stairs. 'Get your shoes! It's time to go!'

We parted by Nat's bright pink front door, with its rainbow streamers and Free Tibet stickers.

'See you later then,' I said casually, pretending to busy myself with Poppy's coat so that I wouldn't have to kiss her goodbye. 'Take care.'

'Yeah.' She shrugged glumly. 'You too.'

'I'll give you a ring.'

But as Poppy and I clomped down the tenement steps, I knew that I was lying.

My house has become a 'crime scene', which can only be touched by police wearing white gloves, the disorder of Poppy's discarded toys and clothes 'evidence', to be recorded in their notebooks and hauled away in plastic bags. I told them I was going to the toilet, but I have escaped to the living room, away from the beeping of their phones and endless questions. And now I am finally coming apart. I stagger around the room calling out her name, as if the hide-and-seek was still on.

But it's not a game. Tears are pouring down my face, my body overtaken by vast, shuddering sobs. I feel as if I have been turned inside out, my heart and innards dragging on the police-trampled floor where my daughter once played.

'Mel . . .'

Glancing up, I see a woman standing in the door. She is wearing a homely sort of trouser suit, the kind that a middle-aged middle manager might acquire in Marks & Spencer, and has short greying hair, cut into a nondescript bob. She was introduced to me five minutes ago as Sandra somebody or other, a 'family liaison officer'.

'Shall we go and sit down?'

'No!' I scream. 'I don't want to sit down! I want you to stop pissing around and find my daughter!'

Unfazed, she walks across the wooden floorboards towards me. I sink to the sofa, weeping; my outburst has shocked me into silence.

'If you want to be left alone, that's fine,' she says placidly as she sits down beside me. 'But we can't let you lose it like this. You've got your little one to take care of, for a start. Do you want me to get your GP to come over and give you something to help calm you down?'

I shake my head. My face is slimy with tears, my sleeve soaked. Sandra expertly places a wad of tissues into my clenched hands.

'It would help if we could carry on talking,' she continues. 'There's still an awful lot of things we need to find out. For Poppy's sake.'

I nod. I feel exhausted, my chest aching from crying. 'OK.'

'Tell me about your relationship with Simon, then. You'd only recently got married?'

'Last summer.'

'And things were going well?'

I stare at her: such a bland question that leads to such complicated answers.

'Not with all you lot coming round and hassling him,' I mutter. Sandra gives me a disappointed look, as if I were a recalcitrant pupil, unable to muster the correct answer. 'And the building was a bloody mess,' I add.

'You and he were doing it yourselves, is that right?'

'Pretty much. We had builders to start with but we ran out of money.'

'Right . . .' She is nodding vigorously, soaking it all in.

'But you know all this already. Si told DCI Gosforth and his lackeys about it yesterday or whenever the hell it was.'

'Mel . . .' She takes my limp hand, holding it between her warm palms. 'I know this is a terrible time for you, but you must understand that I'm not the enemy, I'm trying to help.'

I am unable to respond. I can feel the approach of another swell of tears. Pulling my cold fingers away from Sandra's grasp, I stuff them between my thighs.

'Let's talk some more about Simon,' she says, sitting up a little straighter. 'How did he get on with Poppy? Were they close?'

I look up, glowering at her. 'What do you mean, "Were they close"?'

'I mean, what kind of stepdad did he make? I'm trying to build up a picture of their relationship, that's all . . .'

'He was lovely to her.'

'And they spent a lot of time together?'

'Look,' I snap. 'If you're hoping to find out that he was some kind of paedophile then you're barking up the wrong tree. Sometimes they spent time together, sometimes they didn't.'

Sandra chooses to ignore my tone. 'What kinds of things did they do together?' she asks chattily, as if we were old friends having a gossip.

'Oh, I don't know. He was teaching her to juggle. Or he'd play the guitar and she'd sing. He hasn't seen her so much lately. He's been away.'

'Did he ever lose his temper with her?'

'Why would he do that? If anything it was me . . .'

I stop, looking quickly away. I cannot bear to think of all the times in the past few months that I have shouted at Poppy.

'He was violent towards you?' she asks eagerly.

'No, of course he wasn't! I mean it was *me* that got angry with Poppy.'

'So Simon didn't ever lose his temper with either of you?'

For a while I am silent. How will she respond if I tell her the truth? Everything I say will be taken as evidence of his guilt. She will cluck sympathetically and make little notes in her pad, and I will know for sure that my nightmares have come true.

'No,' I say. 'He never lost his temper.'

She knows that I'm lying. She smiles at me blandly, shifting position as she thinks of another tack.

'So, apart from you,' she says, 'who are his main social circle? The people he likes to hang out with?'

'I don't know,' I mumble. 'He doesn't really have that many friends. We've only been here since the summer and he's been away in London or wherever for most of that time.'

'But what about old friends? His work colleagues?'

I shrug again. Six months ago I felt as if I had known Si for ever, but where once my vision was clear, now it has blurred into something I no longer recognise. 'There was his mate Ollie, who he was working for in London. It's his car that Si's been using.'

Sandra gives a small nod. 'Yes, we're talking to him. Now what about Simon's family?'

Oh God. I gaze at the floor, trying to summon the energy. 'His mother lives near Tunbridge Wells, but I'd be amazed if Si was with her,' I say quietly. 'They don't exactly get on.'

4

WE DROVE DOWN to visit Alicia one stormy Sunday in late April, a few weeks after the scene in the cow field. The evening before, Si had mentioned that he had some business to complete with his mother and dropped it casually into the conversation.

'I thought I'd go and see my mother tomorrow,' he said as he sat at the table in my flat, watching me cook. I busied myself with an onion, avoiding his gaze. I knew I shouldn't pressurise him, that I should relax and let our relationship take its course. Yet ever since we had agreed that Poppy and I would join him in Kent I yearned for more: some evidence that the relationship was to become permanent. Taking me to meet his mother was one such sign; not taking me would signal the opposite. The silence stretched between us. I *had* to stop being so needy, I resolved.

'I'll take Poppy swimming then,' I muttered, tipping the chopped onion into my wok.

'Or you could come with me . . .'

Repressing a broad grin that threatened to engulf my face, I shrugged, as if I didn't much care one way or the other. 'OK, then.'

Later, as I lay beside him in bed, I allowed myself to slip into an idle fantasy in which Alicia was my mother-in-law. We would be the best of friends, I imagined, swapping recipes and homely stories about Si. Perhaps she would take an interest in Poppy and we would spend school holidays staying in what I imagined to be her country mansion.

We set out early the next morning. I had arranged for Poppy to go to a friend's, had gone through numerous changes of outfits, and had spent ten quid on a bouquet of stiff, plastic-wrapped roses from Asda. Si chucked them into the back of the car without comment. He had told me very little about his mother, except that she had been divorced from his now-dead father and lived alone.

For the first part of the drive he seemed normal, chatting about when we might move in to the warehouse, but as we left the motorway his mood changed. He hunched over the steering wheel, his face strained. Every question I asked was answered by a non-communicative grunt. It was the first time I had seen him like this and I spent the rest of the journey staring out of the window at the waterlogged fields, my fingernails digging into my palms.

'We're just going to stay an hour or so, OK?' he announced as we skidded to a halt at the end of the long gravel drive.

The house was an ugly slab of Victoriana, with Gothic turrets and large, dirty windows. The place had a semi-derelict, neglected feel to it: the curtains of the ground-floor windows were drawn and the windows at the top were obscured by ivy. I trudged across the drive behind Si, my heart sinking. When he reached the front door, he took a deep breath, then lifted the knocker and banged it hard. Slipping my arm round him, I leaned against him for a moment. 'Don't get stressy,' I whispered, imitating Poppy. 'I'm used to dodgy families, OK?'

For a brief second he smiled. 'You don't know what she's like,' he muttered, then his face clouded again as the door swung open.

A tall, gaunt woman stood before us. She could have been any age from fifty-five to seventy: her face was unlined, but her wispy hair white. She had swept this into an untidy bun that was coming down on one side. Like Si, she was very thin. Her handsome face was so similar to his that for a bizarre moment it seemed almost as if I were greeting him. My handshake was, however, met with a limp show of fingers.

'Hi!' I gushed. 'It's so lovely to meet you! I'm Mel.'

Alicia took a step back, arching her eyebrows in obvious surprise. Clearly, Si had not told her about me.

'You're over an hour late,' she eventually said, addressing Si, who merely shrugged and walked past her into the hall.

Still determined, I handed her the roses. She held them loosely, hardly glancing at them. 'I'm afraid all they smell of is plastic.' I gave her a resolute smile. 'It's hard to get nice things in our bit of London.'

She nodded, looking me up and down. I had eventually opted for my red leather jacket and a long wool dress. Underneath were stacky black boots that I now regretted. I willed her to look away from my clothes and meet my eyes. It was obvious that Si had not told her about me.

'You're older and less pretty than Rosa,' she said. 'Let's hope this time Simon behaves a bit better.'

For a moment I was unsure that I had heard her correctly. As the words finally made connection with my brain, I could feel my face turn scarlet. 'I'm sure he will,' I murmured.

She gave a fleeting smile, then stepped aside. Behind her, Si had disappeared into the dark house. 'I haven't had time to tidy everything up for you, so you'll just have to take me as you find me,' she snapped. 'Come on, then, in here!'

Like an obedient spaniel I trotted across the large hall, with its muddy flagstones, dog baskets and fusty portraits of ancestors. On the far side, a grand staircase swept upwards. Past this a door opened onto a drawing room, where Si was now standing at the window.

The room was as dirty and worn as the hall. The walls were grey and the furniture sagged. A chaise longue covered in faded yellow silk was pushed under the window. The Persian rug that covered the floorboards was, in places, almost worn through; the arms of the sofa by the grand fireplace spilled ancient straw innards. I gazed around, registering the unhappy decay. The place smelt of wood smoke and dogs.

'Like sherry, do you?' Alicia asked, shoving a smeared glass into my hand. Turning her back on me, she addressed Si. 'What about you?'

He ignored her. 'What have you done to the yew?' he muttered.

'Bloody thing's been dead for years. Had to have it chopped down.'

He did not comment, just raised his eyebrows and turned back to the window. I stared at his back, feeling stranded. It was as if, on entering the house, he had morphed into a male version of his mother.

'It's a beautiful house,' I offered, knowing instantly how gauche I sounded.

'It's a heap,' Alicia replied morosely, pouring a large tumbler of sherry. 'It's falling down around my ears and I can't afford to get it fixed.'

'Si's good at building—'

At this, Si swung round, shooting me a look of such ferocity that I stopped mid-sentence, sucking miserably on my lips.

'He never comes near the place,' Alicia said sourly. She gulped some sherry. 'When he does bother to turn up, it's because he wants money.'

'Ma . . .'

She turned on him, her expression oddly collapsed. 'Anyway, this time you've had a wasted journey. Rosa was here yesterday. I gave everything to her.'

'You *what*?' Simon's expression was grim.

'She came down yesterday morning. Took the box off with her with all the papers. She said you could sign them in London.'

For a moment I thought that Si was about to hit his mother. He took a step towards her, his fists clenched. 'How could you be so stupid?'

'What on *earth* do you mean?'

'You know exactly what's going on!'

'I most certainly do not! I don't know anything. You never bother to tell me.' From the way she obstinately turned back to the sherry, I could see that whatever it was Alicia had done was deliberate.

'For *fuck*'s sake!'

I had heard enough. Si's behaviour was making me clammy with horror, a sudden swirl of nausea causing the room to tip towards me. Placing my glass carefully on a once-elegant Georgian card table, I looked around for my jacket, which minutes earlier I had placed nervously on the arm of the sofa. Retrieving it, I clasped it in my arms.

'I'm going,' I said quietly. Then I turned away and walked back towards the front door.

Si caught up with me halfway along the drive. I had heard the crunch of the car's wheels, but did not glance up until he had drawn alongside me, pushing the opened passenger door into my path. For a moment I considered ignoring him. Everything I had dreaded was confirmed. Si was still involved with the woman who had been living with him in Peckham, the spiky nude with her tumbling black hair. All this time I had been constructing fantasies about our future, but to him I was just a temporary diversion from his *real* relationship, this *Rosa*, a woman so trenchantly inserted into his life that she could appear at his mother's doorstep and bear away his business papers without question.

'Mel, sweetheart, please get in the car—'

'Piss off.'

'Babe, I'm sorry. My mother's not noted for her tact. I should never have dragged you down here.'

I glanced at him furiously. 'It's nothing to do with your mother,' I hissed. 'It's you.'

'Please, Mel. You shouldn't have seen me behave like that. It's just—'

'It's just what? You've clearly got another woman on the go.' I could no longer bear to look at him. What was it that Alicia had said? *You're older and less pretty*. The humiliation rose inside me in a hot wave of mortification. I started to jog on down the drive. It was just as Nat had warned. Si was just toying with me, perhaps so he could have somewhere to stay in London. Or maybe it was just the sex: a change of body type, something to break the routine. I was *so* stupid! Behind me I could hear the car door slam and the sound of footsteps on the gravel.

'Mel, please!'

He caught up with me and tugged me backwards, so that I was forced to turn and look into his pale face. He had *tears* in his eyes, I saw with shock. And, as he gripped my elbow, his hand was shaking.

'It's not how it seems.'

I shook his hand away. 'How is it, then?'

'I was living with this woman Rosa before I met you, but it's over.'

'So why's she coming down here and taking papers away?'

'Because she's a bitch. She's trying to prevent me from selling my flat. She doesn't want me to move on.'

It was exactly what I yearned to hear. I folded my arms. I was still feigning anger, but the hot fury that had propelled me out of the house and down the drive was receding.

'Look,' Si continued. 'It was very intense with her at first, but now I'm with you I can see that I never really loved her. It started off just as a sex thing but it got too heavy too quickly, and she wouldn't let go. I finished it at Christmas and now she's trying to make trouble.'

'So why didn't you tell me about it before?'

'Because I wanted to put it behind me.'

'You're not lying to me, are you?'

'Of course not.'

I stared into his distraught face. When I eventually spoke, my voice was faint. 'I really couldn't take it if you were still sleeping with her, Si. I've been messed around too many times by too many arseholes. And I've got Poppy to protect, too. I've got to be one hundred per cent sure that I can trust you.'

'You *can*, I promise. I'm not sleeping with her. All I'm doing is trying to get rid of her.'

I glared at him, searching for lies. Anger was making me unusually assertive. 'If I find out that she's still in the picture, then that's it. I'm off.'

'Mel, please, I promise you.' He stood back, gazing imploringly into my face. '*You're* the one I choose, OK? Rosa's in the past. Finito.'

He steered me back towards the car. We climbed in and he switched on the ignition. I felt numbed, like I'd taken a hefty dose of painkillers.

When we reached the road, Si put his foot down hard, speeding down the winding lanes. I stared out of the window at the blurring banks of cowslips and primroses.

'You weren't very nice to your mum,' I said eventually.

His face hardened. 'She deserves it. Look, the day's been a complete cock-up. Let's try to forget about it.'

Or did things happen in a different order? I stare at Sandra, the family liaison officer, and realise how frayed my memory has become. I remember marching out of Alicia's house and shouting at Si on the drive, but wasn't this after a more prolonged visit, involving a walk around the grounds of her house? Or was that the second time I visited, when Si wasn't there? I gaze at Sandra's kind, round face until it blurs, but the past has been torn apart so violently that I cannot sew it back together. All that is left is this jumble of disconnected threads that I am sorting so desperately through.

It was not the sherry nor even Si's behaviour that made me feel nauseous that day. The next morning I could not finish my morning coffee. Even more strangely, alcohol was suddenly tasteless, like sipping meths. The weeks slipped past, and I no longer wondered at my symptoms. By the time I did the test I was nine weeks pregnant.

Three weeks later I was lying naked on the crumpled sheets, my damp body pressed into Si's side. He had just returned from Kent and, after a short and friendly tussle on my bed, was lolling on his back, his arms behind his head. As usual he was talking about the warehouse. The deal was almost sealed and he'd found a surveyor. Like a small boy with a new toy, he was obsessively enthused.

'We'll strip everything back to the basics, expose the beams, knock through at the top,' he was saying enthusiastically. 'The roof's a bloody mess though. I'll have to get someone to look at it.'

I rolled away from him, lying on one side as I pushed my finger through the soft hairs on his chest. I had already attempted several times to tell him about the blue line that had appeared on the pregnancy testing kit, but I always shied away. It was too much too soon. We had discussed living together, but not having a baby. And for some reason the recollection of our unhappy visit to his mother had become entangled with how I feared he might react.

'How's your tummy, anyway?' he said, running his palm over my belly. I stared down. My stomach was still flat.

'It's not really my stomach that's the problem,' I said.

'I thought you said you were feeling sick?'

I looked past Si's untroubled face to my small bedroom, with the photos of Poppy in various stages of infancy. When I had told Pete about Poppy's conception, his face had contorted with disgust.

'I *am* feeling sick, all the time.'

'Shouldn't you go to the doctor?'

I did not reply. My hand dropped quietly off Si's chest. All I had to do was say the words and everything would change.

'No, not yet.'

My heart had started to beat very hard.

'What do you mean, "not yet"?'

'Can't you tell?'

Now he was quiet, too. I could feel the sudden tension in his body. 'Tell what?'

My palms were sticky. 'I think I might be pregnant.'

His silence was a deep, dark hole into which I was falling. For what seemed like many long minutes we lay next to each other on the bed, neither of us looking at the other or speaking. Then he took his hand off my belly and folded his arms.

My nerves were making me breathless. 'Well?'

'Well what?' He was sitting up now and reaching for his sweater. I watched him getting dressed in numbed disbelief. The scene was tipping into everything that I'd dreaded.

'Well, what do you think? Why aren't you saying anything?'

'I don't know what to say. Have you done a test?'

'Yes.'

'And it was positive?'

'Yes.'

'Right.'

I had thought that he was different from the others, but now it seemed that I was wrong. He stood up, reaching for his jeans. The bedside clock told me that it was already nearly two. In half an hour I would be collecting Poppy from school and he would be gone.

'I hoped you'd be pleased,' I said quietly.

He turned, finally looking straight at me. His face seemed sorrowful. 'If you really are pregnant then I guess I am pleased,' he said. 'I'm sorry, I'm not quite in the "having babies" frame of mind at the moment. And I thought you were on the pill.'

'I think I must have forgotten to take it . . .'

He did not reply. Grabbing his mobile from the bedside table, he slipped it into his back pocket, then bent to tie up his trainers.

'Where are you going?'

'I've got a meeting with some finance people. I'll give you a ring.' Straightening up, he brushed his cold mouth against my cheek, then turned away.

'When are you coming back?' My voice had faded to a hoarse whisper. My foolish fantasies of building a new life with Si were collapsing.

'It's going to be difficult over the next couple of weeks, hon. I've got to really get going on nailing this deal and getting it all sorted.'

'Are you walking out on me?'

He turned round. His face seemed already to have closed up. 'Of course I'm not. It's just going to be a bit busy for a while, that's all.'

Then he was gone.

I cried for the rest of the day: jagged bouts of sobbing, interspersed with periods of barely controlled calm when I fetched Poppy, sat with her over tea and put her to bed. I cried when she was finally asleep, throwing myself on the bed and giving in: great shuddering gasps of grief that made my ribs ache, like I'd been beaten up. It felt so familiar, yet at the same time I was reeling with shock. Si had seemed so sincere and had given me so many assurances that I still could not truly believe his reaction. Could I have completely misjudged his character?

The next day I awoke to a headache and a state of dull despondency. I was too proud to call Si, and switched off both my answering machine and my mobile phone so as not to hear his resounding silence. Despite all his promises, he had turned tail and fled. He would almost certainly be back with the nude. Right now, as I shuffled round the kitchen attempting to make breakfast, he was probably enjoying the feel of her.

Another week passed and still Si did not make contact. By now Poppy had started to ask after him. She chirped on about the dress she planned to wear at our wedding and I could not bring myself to blurt out the truth, which was that Si had disappeared from our lives as swiftly as he had taken them over. The crying was finished now, overtaken by a thick pain, lodged somewhere in my chest. When Nat approached me in the playground I found myself taking her arm and strolling home with her as if we had never quarrelled. Ned had tried to return, she said, snorting derisively. The floozie had dumped him and he'd come round in tears, begging for forgiveness. She told him to sod off, she finished, chuckling with triumph. Men: who needed 'em?

She did not ask about Si.

Then, late one Friday night in June, as I slumped in front of the TV, the doorbell rang. It was three weeks after Si had walked out and I had convinced myself that I would never see him again, yet as I stumbled blearily into the hall, my heart was crashing at my ribs.

'Who is it?'

'Me.'

I flung open the door. Si was standing in front of me smiling sheepishly. The sight of him made my insides swoop with joy.

'Can I come in?'

I shrugged and stepped aside. I wanted to appear haughty and indifferent, but it was impossible to keep up the pretence. He followed me into the kitchen, watching as I put on the kettle. My hands were shaking so crazily that I could barely operate the switch.

'Mel, darling . . .'

I glanced round. He was slouched against the cupboards, looking pleadingly across the narrow kitchen. He looked like a scruffy dog begging for chocolate. 'I'm so sorry,' he said slowly. 'I've behaved like a total shit. I love you. I want us to be together for ever. It's not that I don't want a baby, it's just that it was so unexpected. It freaked me out.'

A tug of anger pulled inside me. 'Have you been with her?'

'With who?' His voice was ominously quiet.

'That *woman*.'

He flinched. 'Like I told you, it's *over*! This isn't about her, I promise. I've finished it for good. She's never going to get in the way again.'

I folded my arms. 'What is it about, then?'

'It's just about me, being in a mess and getting scared.'

'And how do you think I felt when you disappeared like that?'

'I'm sorry. I've behaved appallingly and I know there's no excuse.' He paused, perhaps expecting me to question him further. When I didn't, he said, 'Look, I want you to have this.' He fumbled in his pocket, finally producing a small black box, which he now handed to me.

I pulled at the gold catch on the box. Inside was a plain gold band with a single ruby set in the middle.

'Let's put everything behind us,' Si whispered. 'Marry me, Mel. It'll be a brand-new start.'

I allowed myself to smile. I wanted to cry, and scream with laughter, and collapse into his arms, and dance hysterically around the room, all at the same time.

'And you've really finished with this Rosa woman? You haven't been with her, have you?'

'Like I told you before, it's history. One hundred per cent.'

Stepping decisively across the kitchen, he pulled me into his arms. From the shuddering of his shoulders, I gathered that he was crying. When I finally pulled away, his eyes were red.

'So will you marry me?' he whispered. 'Please say you will.'

I gazed back at him, my stupid heart still bashing at my ribs. Of course I was going to marry him. It felt like my last stab at happiness in a life that so far had yielded only disappointment. Why should I choose to remain alone?

'OK then.'

'Thank God!'

He was gripping me so hard that my tummy was getting squashed. I pushed him gently away.

'What about the baby?'

For a moment he seemed confused. Or perhaps he was trying to work out how to respond. Then, falling to his knees, he placed the side of his face against my bump.

'I can't wait to meet him,' he breathed.

I couldn't stop myself. I was grinning so widely it felt as if my face might split. 'Or her,' I said, punching him lightly on the shoulders.

I give my head a little shake, looking round the room in confusion. Stripped of our rumbustious domestic disorder—Poppy's gymnastics on the sofa, her figure skating on the wooden floor, Jo's nappies and clothes strewn around—it has become a place I only vaguely recognise. How could we have believed we might make this place our home?

I don't know how long I have been sitting here, my chilled hands held inside Sandra's. I blink at her, as if surfacing from a dream.

'Where's Jo?' I say, jumping up. 'I need my baby!'

'It's OK, love. He's fine. Your friend's put him down in his cot.' Her proficient hands are now round my shoulders, pulling me back down.

'But where's *Poppy*?' I wail.

'We're doing everything that we possibly can to get her back, Mel. There's just been a newsflash on the evening news and it's gone out on the radio, too. Every force in the country has been alerted. The whole nation is looking for the car.'

I ogle her, trying to force meaning into the words. How can it be that Si has suddenly become Britain's Most Wanted Man? He loved Poppy. Despite everything that's happened, why would he want to hurt *her*? Nothing makes any sense. All I know is that I yearn for my daughter with a physical force that makes me gasp. She has been plucked from me, spirited away by a monster.

'He didn't take her,' I whisper. 'Si wouldn't do that. He'd never put Poppy in danger.'

Sandra does not reply. She sits beside me, nodding and holding my hands as if she were my best friend, but her mind is made up. I am, in her view, a wife in denial.

'Poppy was having these nightmares!' I blurt. 'She said there was someone in the warehouse!'

'Uhuh . . .'

'There were letters, too! It had nothing to do with Si!'

'What letters, Melanie?'

'I don't know. We thought they were from a friend, but she wouldn't let us see them. And she kept saying there was a ghost wandering about upstairs . . .' I am crying again, my cheeks slick with tears. 'We kept telling her there wasn't anyone there.'

I accept the wad of tissues Sandra is proffering, squeezing out more hot tears. Poppy, sitting up in bed, screaming herself hoarse; my bleary reassurances, half asleep, not really concentrating; Poppy appearing in our bedroom, crying in a way I had rarely seen: deep sobs, her whole body shaking. There was a bad person standing on the gallery, she whispered. They were going to come back and get her.

'A lot of children have nightmares,' Sandra says quietly. 'Perhaps she was worrying about school?'

I slump against the sofa, too exhausted to continue. Sandra is right. I am clutching at straws. I have to face the facts. I have not forgotten them, though I wish I could. This is not the first time that my home has been filled with police, you see. Only yesterday Dave Gosforth was here in a different guise, his white-suited men carrying away our belongings in carefully recorded plastic bags, as he leaned against his car, regarding me without sympathy. He'd done this a hundred times before, his bored eyes proclaimed.

Yes, I have to face facts. Less than thirty-six hours ago, I watched through the window as DCI Gosforth steered Si towards his car. Such an odd couple: the inspector, with his expensive leather jacket and neatly ironed jeans, and the suspect, with his long hair and fraying clothes. Si slipped into the back of the unmarked car without even glancing back to see if I was watching. It was as if in the course of that devastating exchange in the kitchen all life had been bleached away, turning him from human being into ghost.

And now they're here again, with their careful questions and forensic procedures. Yet what no one has yet said out loud is that only yesterday morning, 25th February, my husband, Simon Stenning, was arrested on suspicion of murder.

Dave Gosforth leaned against the breeze-block wall of the Stennings' kitchen, cupping his hands against the wind. Christ, it was freezing. Blinking away the fragments of ice that were blowing into his face, he huddled over his lighter, willing it into life. Finally, after three or four tries, he produced a shivering flame. Sucking on the cigarette, he breathed out, relaxing a fraction as he stared grumpily across the marsh. The last hour had been one of frenetic activity, in which they had done everything in their power to trace the car Simon Stenning was driving. The vehicle's registration had been circulated to every force in the country. All over Britain patrol cars were cruising, ready to spot him. The airports were on alert, too, although it was unlikely he'd be heading abroad. They'd confiscated Stenning's passport with the pile of personal effects that they'd taken from his house yesterday.

Yet Dave was as close to panic as he had ever been in twenty years of service. The moment the call had come that afternoon, summoning him back to the warehouse, he'd been tight with anxiety. The stupid prat had taken the little girl! This was not something he had anticipated. Now he needed a minute or two alone, so he could think it through.

It was a dramatic turn of events, that was for sure. If he'd so much as considered that Stenning would play a trick like this, he'd have applied to the magistrate and held him for another forty-eight hours. By then the forensic results would have been in and, if luck was on their side, they could have charged him. The bloke was obviously as guilty as sin regarding the unsolved murder of the Margate prostitute, Jacqui Jenning, back in November 2003. Dave had been edging towards that way of thinking when they'd arrested Stenning the day before. Now he was 99.9 per cent certain. And the stupid pillock had panicked and done a runner, taking the kid with him.

The wind was making his cigarette burn down fast. He took another drag, then flicked the stub towards the creek in disgust. His wife Karen would have his guts for garters if she smelt the tobacco on him, so perhaps it was just as well that he wouldn't be going home soon. He'd been trying to give up for months. Patches, hypnotism, aversion therapy, he had tried them all, but a week ago he had caved in and snapped open a new packet. Karen still hadn't guessed. It was bad, bad, bad.

Reaching for his mobile, he punched in his home number, picturing the phone ringing in their comfy living room, with its new wool carpet and nice bright prints. Karen would be watching TV, perhaps nibbling on some chocs. She was always moaning about her weight, but to him she was perfect: voluptuous, as he put it, nice and curvy; not like the scrawny woman on the other side of the breeze-block wall whose life Simon Stenning was in the process of wrecking. He appreciated that Mel Stenning was attractive, but she was too brittle.

'Hello?'

'It's me.'

'Hi, honey!'

'I'm going to be late.'

'Aw!'

If Karen minded about his unpredictable absences, she never showed it. That was what being married to a copper was like, she'd say if he started to apologise for yet another cancelled outing or ruined dinner. He was her big hero, going out and catching all those baddies; she wouldn't change a thing. Now, just hearing her voice was making him feel better, like warm hands spread over an aching back.

'Things have taken a bit of a turn for the worse, love. I don't know when I'm going to get home.'

'OK, lovey. You take care of yourself.'

'I'll ring you later.'

Slipping the mobile into his pocket, Dave Gosforth turned back to the warehouse. Shuddering, he stepped back into the kitchen.

5

HIGH SUMMER, and life seemed perfect. Si had returned, his sudden disappearance a blip that we did not allude to. I forced myself to forget about Rosa: Si had made his promise and I had chosen to believe him. Now, as London wilted under the smoggy July heat, I luxuriated in his presence. I had spent so long alone that I had forgotten what it was to have the regular comfort of another person's body. Seven months into our relationship and still it thrilled me to see him lolling on my pillows. I would never take him for granted or succumb to boredom, I was sure, for the old Mel was fading away, her droopy defeatism defeated by joy.

Si radiated happiness. He was away in Kent for much of the time, but when he returned his cheerful energy gusted warmly through the flat. He would wander from room to room, singing loud and excruciatingly bad renditions of 1980s pop songs and joshing with Poppy. He could not wait to be a father, he declared. He delighted in the baby's growth, resting his hand proprietorially over my stomach.

We talked about the future, not the past. He knew a little about my childhood, but showed scant interest in learning more. We had visited Pat for lunch shortly after I had agreed to marry him, and perhaps that said it all. Over soup, roast ham and apple crumble she had subjected him to a rigorous interview about his schooling, his training in fine art and his subsequent career prospects. He refused to play the game, dodging her questions with foggy vagueness.

On the subject of his own background he would rarely be drawn. Sometimes he'd recount anecdotes about his student days at Camberwell but made no reference to friends or lovers. If there had been girlfriends, they were edited out. He'd lived alone in a caravan for a year in the Scottish Highlands, painting, and had had a long spell hitch-hiking across Europe. He didn't seem to require the company of others.

As the months went by I learned that if I enquired about his childhood, his face would harden and he'd change the subject. Questions involving the recent past elicited a similar response. The only thing that mattered was our future. Then he'd start discussing the warehouse, or how once in Spain we might keep goats. It was a strange experience, like swimming in tropical waters and hitting unexpected eddies of cold.

At other times his silence was more comfortable, a shared peace that I had learned not to interrupt. We often sat together in the evenings, his arm round my shoulders, saying very little. By now I had grown used to his quietness. He had a stillness to him, I told myself. The new, calm centre to my life.

In August 2004 we were married in a shabby south London registry office, with Poppy as my bridesmaid and a small gaggle of friends and Pat to witness the event. It was a muggy London morning, the heat spread thick under the polluted skies, covering us with a layer of slime. I wore a cream silk dress that stuck sweatily to my protruding belly, and white irises in my hair that after only a short while inside the sweltering

Marriage Suite drooped with exhaustion. We repeated the vows, signed the book, and emerged onto the municipal steps, breathing in the marginally fresher air with relief. Jessie and Nat threw a handful of confetti at us, Ollie kissed me on the cheek and Pat took us to lunch at an Italian restaurant in Streatham. I was unsure of her views on my changed circumstances. From the corner of my eye I noticed her gazing at me with the same expression she had once assumed when I was a rebellious teenager, yet when I looked at her directly she smiled brightly back.

Whatever Pat, or indeed Nat, thought of our hurried wedding was immaterial. I was groggy with pleasure. I sat squeezed against Si's side throughout the meal, the baby fluttering inside me like a trapped butterfly. Watching Si do a balancing trick with Poppy's breadsticks, I felt a swirl of exhilaration at my good fortune. I was married. My daughter had a father, and would soon have a baby brother. My fairy godmother had waved her magic wand.

After the meal Poppy went to stay at Pat's, and Si and I blew three hundred quid on a room at the Ritz. The expense did not matter, Si insisted, for he was currently flush. There had been some kind of business deal involving Ollie about which he remained vague, and I did not press for details.

The opulence of our room was overwhelming: heavy velvet drapes, a vast bathtub with a Jacuzzi, and a bed only slightly smaller than my living room. We sat on its brocade edge, giggling like school children. Si had already opened the complimentary champagne, glugging at the bottle as he inspected the contents of the fridge. I sipped at my glass, knowing I wouldn't finish it; the bubbles gave me indigestion. Leaning over, Si removed my satin pumps. Brushing the back of his hand against my cheek, he pulled the irises from my hair.

'Your face is all sprinkled with flower dust,' he muttered. I sagged against him, lifting up my arms like a child as he pulled the dress over my head. When he placed his head between my breasts I buried my hands in his thick hair, bending down to kiss his rough face.

'I love you.'

I had said it to Poppy, but never to a man. The words sounded strange: too intimate and innocent for such a swanky setting, with the roar of Piccadilly outside and muffled footsteps in the corridor beyond.

'I love you too, babe.'

Tears clogged my throat. I stared down at Si's head, my hands exploring the smooth skin underneath the back of his shirt. I had known him for less than a year, but his body felt like familiar territory; home, almost, the place where I finally belonged.

'This is the way it's always going to be,' Si continued huskily. 'You and me and Poppy and the baby, for ever and ever.'

We were moving to the warehouse a week after the wedding. I had not seen it since June, on a dull, damp day that had filled me with gloom.

'You have to remember that what we're looking at is potential,' Simon had kept repeating that day, as he'd parked the car on a verge in the road. 'It's in a bit of a state at the moment.'

We were on the edge of the town, the creek that led through the marshes to the River Swale a little way ahead. We got out of the car and walked along a muddy lane that led past a row of garages and cottages to a boat yard. The building loomed at us through the misty drizzle. Beyond the yard was a large Victorian warehouse that had once serviced barges and coasters from London and Rotterdam. Following Si past deserted boats and beached yachts, I trudged towards the three-storey slab of industrial real estate, my spirits rapidly deflating.

The interior of the building was derelict. There was no running water, no electricity and virtually no roof. We clambered over the rubble, gazing at the echoing expanse.

'So? What do you think?' Si spread out his arms, grinning.

I stared around the place, trying not to shudder. 'It's going to be a challenge.'

'Yeah, but imagine what it'll be like when it's fixed up. Properties like this sell for a small fortune, especially so close to London.'

I nodded, trying to appear cheerful. In the rafters above, a rowdy flock of starlings swooped and squawked like affronted revellers whose party had been crashed, and the movement of the birds and musty stink of the building had me heaving.

'You both go ahead,' I gasped. Si's surveyor had arrived for a meeting. 'I think I'll wait outside.'

I spent the remaining hour squatting on the banks of the river, staring across the muddy water at the flat fields and leaden sky as Si discussed plans with the surveyor. It did not matter about the state of the building, I told myself. Like Si said, I should see it as an opportunity.

Six weeks later, Si assured me that there had been radical changes. The building was connected with electricity and water, and an ad hoc room had been built onto the back where we planned to cook until the kitchen was fitted in the main building. The rest of the summer was to be spent in a mobile home in the back yard. By Christmas, Si promised, the place would be habitable.

We therefore spent the days immediately after our night at the Ritz packing up our possessions. Si had sold his furniture along with his flat, and during my few years living in London I had accumulated remarkably few possessions. Besides the beds, my futon and some tables and chairs, all I had were a few boxes of kitchen equipment, several suitcases of clothes and another carton or so of books. Poppy's contribution was more considerable. She had four boxes of toys, a large bag of dressing-up clothes, a bike, and Bertie, her hamster. When removal day arrived, we spent the morning cramming all of this into Si's newly purchased van. By midday we were ready to go. Si sat at the wheel of the van with Poppy beside him, Bertie's cage on her lap. I squashed into my beaten-up Fiat, filled to bursting with suitcases and bags. We would travel in convoy.

Poppy and I had said goodbye to Nat and Jessie the day before, with hearty assurances that we would stay in touch.

There was no send-off party, no wistful farewells from neighbours. Poppy and I had said goodbye to Nat and Jessie the day before, with hearty assurances that we would stay in touch.

'You take care of yourself, yeah?' Nat had whispered as we parted. Her plump fingers, with their psychedelic glass rings, clutched my arm.

I flashed her a cheery smile. 'Of course I will!' Why did she always have to be so cautious?

As my car pulled away from the kerb of the tatty, busy street where Poppy and I had lived for the last two years, all I felt was a rush of excitement. The roads were surprisingly quiet and in under an hour we had turned off the A2 and were progressing through Sittingbourne towards the coast, past acres of orchard and vineyards, towards the marshland that was to become our home.

Steering the car down the pretty Georgian road that led through the town, I followed the van's bumping backside. Turning off into the lane, we drove past the cottages and garages and suddenly there it was: the place where our dreams were centred. In the hot sunlight the warehouse appeared transformed, rising majestically on the other side of the boat yard, the winch that still hung above the creek on the far side glowing in the sunlight, a gang of seagulls yabbering cheerfully on the roof. As I gazed up at it, the place seemed like an escape route to a new life, full of welcome and possibility.

We passed the boats and drew up in the drive. Ahead of me, Si was lifting Poppy from the van.

'Welcome to your new home, darling.'

She peered doubtfully around. 'Are we going to live on a boat?'

'No, you silly sausage, we're going to live there!' Si pointed at the warehouse, grinning.

Poppy frowned. 'What, in a factory?'

'Sort of. But it's going to be a lovely house, too.'

'Are there chocolate-making machines inside?'

Si laughed, stretching. A great deal had happened since I had last been here: trucks and diggers were parked in the front yard, the roof had been mended and the temporary breeze-block kitchen completed. A skip filled with rubble had appeared, and scaffolding supported the riverside wall. Parked behind the warehouse was our mobile home, which Si had spent the last few days preparing. Around us, boat masts clinked in the breeze like wind chimes.

'Come on, Pops,' I said, holding out my hand. 'Let's go and explore.'

'What about Bertie?'

'He'll be all right in the van. We can find a nice place for his cage.'

We followed Si into the warehouse. Here, too, much had changed: the rubble had been cleared away, the walls partly plastered and the space for a picture window that Si had designed knocked through. Gaping wide and covered with blue plastic sheeting, it looked like a badly dressed wound. Beside me, Poppy groped for my arm.

'Is this where I'm going to sleep?'

'No, darling. Soon we're going to make you a lovely bedroom upstairs.'

'Will there be ghosts?'

I squatted beside her, holding her soft hands in mine. Over the last few weeks I had been too preoccupied to prepare her properly for the move, I thought with a jab of reproach.

'No, my most gorgeous and wonderful girl, there won't be ghosts. It's going to be a lovely house, with masses of room for your toys and all our stuff. You're going to have the prettiest bedroom you can imagine. We'll paint it your favourite colour and Si will do a mural for you, of animals or fairies. Would you like that?'

She stared solemnly back. It was indeed hard to imagine.

'And then right at the top,' I continued, 'we're going to make rooms for guests to come and stay, so we can make pots and pots of money. Right now Si's fixing it all up for us, so until then we're going to live in a sweet little house in the garden. Won't that be fun?'

'Are we going to be living in a shed?'

'No, my love, it's called a mobile home. Shall we go and see it?'

She did not respond. Pulling her hand from mine, she gazed at the raw bricks and gently flapping sheets. In retrospect I should have seen the darkness reflected in her eyes. I should have swept her into my arms and hurried away from this godforsaken building, out into the bright sunlight, then back, past the swaying boats, down the lane towards the town. Instead, I walked across the floor and inspected the new wooden staircase that led to the upstairs rooms.

Later, I strolled with Poppy along the edge of the creek, the path snaking along the muddy banks towards the mouth of the river where the brown water swirled out towards the Isle of Sheppey.

The sky stretched above us, already fading into the deep indigo of an August evening. From the fields, I could hear the cry of larks; above the water a flock of swallows darted and dipped. Back at the warehouse Si was cooking Poppy's tea. When she'd finished eating we would take her to the Portakabin and pop her under the dribbling shower. Then I would settle her in the boxy room where we had unpacked her toys and placed Bertie's cage in a corner. Since those first shaky minutes inside the warehouse, her mood had lifted. She had loved the mobile home, with its fold-out beds and secret cupboards, and was now running ahead, her hand trailing through the long grasses that swayed across the path. Suddenly she halted, swinging round to face me.

'Mummy?'

'Yes?'

'When are we going home?'

I stopped. 'This is our home now, darling.'

'But what about my *school?*'

'You're going to be starting a new school, here in Kent. Do you want to walk there tomorrow and have a peek through the railings?'

Her face dropped. 'No.'

'I bet there'll be some nice girls. And you're going to be in Year Two!'

But she wasn't listening: she was scampering ahead, her skinny legs bashing the reeds as she skipped away towards the place where the curlews dipped and swaggered in the glistening mud.

August passed swiftly, a succession of seemingly identical hot, dry days interspersed with dramatic downpours during which we huddled in the mobile home, laughing as bullets of rain ricocheted off the metal roof. A few hours later the puddles would be reduced to cracked craters, the water instantly absorbed by the parched earth.

Poppy and I slipped into a seamless routine in which very little happened or got done, each day as empty and aimless as the last. Around us was frenzied activity, with Si rising at dawn to attack the roof beams with his sander, and the builders arriving a few hours later, obliterating the early-morning peace. They were working on the roof as well, swarming over the rafters like ants as their backs turned scarlet in the sun. I grew accustomed to their presence: the chipped mugs bunched in the sink, the din of their radios and mobiles and the constant crashing of their tools. By four they roared off in their vans, allowing the cry of curlews to fill the sudden silence.

Yet while I am able to remember these details, I can barely recall how Poppy and I spent our time. We had picnics on the bank of the creek, and played hide and seek among the boats. Sometimes we whiled away the afternoons with felt tips and stickers in the cool of the breeze-block kitchen, or Poppy would play alone in the long grass that had survived the onslaught of the builders' trucks, while I dozed in the sun. Like a picture chalked on a well-trodden pavement, very few details remain.

By the end of the month, the air had assumed a soft haziness, the horizon smudged by the dust of distant harvests, the evenings dipping more quickly into dusk. In less than a week, Poppy would start her new school. For a final holiday treat she was staying with Jessie and Nat for the weekend, so Si and I were alone. The warehouse was quiet, the builders having knocked off for the weekend. Unaccustomed to the silence, we wandered through the dim shadows of the ground floor, then up the new wooden staircase that led to the gallery with its six storage rooms. We climbed on up the steep metal steps, the light drawing us upwards to the loft. One day there would be stunning blonde wood flooring and whitewashed walls. Today, however, the rotting wooden boards gave way to alarming gaps.

As we emerged from the gloom of the gallery below, it felt as if we had entered another world: golden sun splashed onto our upturned faces. The works to the roof finally completed, four large skylights now opened onto the blue sky. We stood in silence, staring out of the windows at the view of the glistening creek below us, snaking across the marshes. Beyond came a flat stretch of fields, and, in the distance, the industrial cranes and cooling towers of Sheppey. Above us, the vast sky, with its wisps of herringbone cloud, left me breathless.

'Do you love me?'

'What?' I turned to look at Si. Perhaps it was the play of light on his face, but today he looked older than his forty years, his skin more lined, his brow indented with deep creases.

'Do you love me?' he asked intently. 'I mean, *really* love me?' His pale face peered into mine with what seemed like trepidation, as if he had seen some unexpected shadow cross my eyes.

'Of course I do! Why are you asking me that?'

He shook his head. 'I need to know if I can be honest with you. I mean, really share things.'

'What kind of things?'

'Things that happened in the past . . . with previous relationships.'

I frowned, momentarily irritated by his unexpected intensity. I did not want to talk about previous relationships, especially not Rosa. I thought that was what we'd agreed: the past was gone; what mattered was the future. Now, just when I was content to do as he wanted, living only for the present, he had decided to dredge everything up.

'Of course you can,' I said vaguely. 'You know that.'

'I mean, supposing there's stuff that's happened to one of us that the other should know about? We could, you know, wipe the slate clean . . .'

Placing my hand on his back, I ran my fingers over the bumps of his spine. 'There isn't anything to tell you,' I said softly. 'Like I told you, I've been involved with some twats. It doesn't make any difference to how I feel about you.'

'But maybe you've made mistakes . . .'

I felt chilly. Why the hell was he cross-questioning me like this?

'I still don't see what difference it makes.'

'I just want us to be honest with each other. I mean, about mistakes we've made.'

'OK, then,' I said, taking a breath. 'I've probably made more mistakes than you've had hot dinners. I got knocked up by a useless plonker in Australia who I thought was deep because he never said anything. Since then, what few pathetic flings I've had have been a disaster. They were all just dope-heads who sold me a pack of lies and screwed around. You're completely different and that's why I love you in a way I could never, ever, have loved them. OK?'

Si peered morosely across the room. Something was wrong: it was in his eyes, in the way he had just turned his back on me, and in this sudden coldness that made me shudder with apprehension. I clutched my arms round my belly, trying to pretend that nothing was happening. In the end, I could bear it no longer.

'I've never loved anyone before you,' I whispered, placing a tentative hand on his slim, strong forearm. 'We don't have to wipe the slate clean. There isn't anything to say.'

When eventually he replied his voice was so low that I barely heard it. 'But what if *I'd* done something terrible? Would you still love me?'

God, what a fool I was. If I could, I'd go clattering up those metal steps again, throw the door open and scream at myself, standing in the sunshine in all my glorious, pregnant naivety, my hands clutched over my eyes and ears like two of the little monkeys. 'Listen to him!' I'd yell. 'Ask him what he means!'

But if Si had something to tell me, I was desperate not to hear.

'What could you do?' I said lightly. 'You promised you'd never betray me and I trust you. What more do we need to say?'

Dave Gosforth wiped his hands on his shorts and glanced round his newly tidied garden in satisfaction. Beside him lay a large pile of grass clippings: Karen had been nagging at him to cut the lawn for weeks, and finally he had relented. After that there was Harvey's bike to mend and some trellises to be put up on the back wall. None of these activities were his idea of how to spend such a glorious day. It was sweltering. They should be at the beach, or at a nice open-air pool, not stuck at home with Karen's mum about to arrive for Sunday dinner.

Next door were having a barbie. Trails of smoke were drifting over the fence; a little way down the garden he could hear the fizz of opening lagers. If he got a chance he'd pop over and join Barry and Maureen after dinner, he thought. Meanwhile, back in his own garden, his mother-in-law would be spreading her hefty legs over the sun lounger which he would have been commissioned to place in exactly the right shady spot.

As Dave pushed the lawn mower back into the shed, he registered the depressingly familiar signs of her arrival: the faint plink of the doorbell, then a flicker of movement through the sliding living-room doors. Karen's patience with her mother was saintly. They'd moved her here to Herne Bay a year ago so that she could be closer to them, and as far as Dave was concerned she'd been a pain in the bum ever since.

'She's my mum, love,' Karen would say if he objected to her by-now-obligatory appearance at their house for Sunday dinner. 'I can't have her spending all weekend alone, can I?'

'Harvey, go inside and say hello to your grandma.'

His son ignored him. Dave stood by the shed, vacillating between irritation and comradeship. Bony-kneed in his Man U kit, the boy had been kicking a ball against the back wall for the past hour.

'I said, go inside and say hello!'

Striding across the grass, Dave picked up the ball, frowning in mock anger at the eight-year-old. 'I'm sure she'll want to hear all about your match on Thursday. You know how much Grandma loves football.'

'Aw, Dad!'

'Come on now, Harv. It's time to go inside and face the music.'

Putting his heavy hands on the boy's shoulders, he led him inside.

The meal was as dreary as he'd anticipated. As his mother-in-law droned on, Dave downed two and then three glasses of wine, deliberately ignoring the disapproving glint in Karen's eye. It was all right for Harvey, who could bolt down his food then slip off his seat and back into the garden, but Dave had to sit politely through two long courses.

There was no denying it: he was in a filthy mood. Most weeks, he'd approach Monday with purpose and energy, yet today he did not anticipate the start of the working week with an ounce of relish. The previous week had gone unusually badly. First there'd been a critical article in the *Kent Enquirer*, a two-page spread of local unsolved crimes which hinted strongly at police incompetence, and which put Jacqui Jenning's case at the centre. Then he'd had a less than enthusiastic chat with his superintendent about his chances for promotion. And, finally, on the Friday, there'd been an angry visit from Jacqui Jenning's mother.

Mrs Audrey Jenning wasn't the kind of mum you'd expect for what the law still referred to as a 'common prostitute'. Instead, she was a respectable lady in her fifties, who, sitting primly on the edge of the seat he'd offered, virtually spat blood at him.

She simply couldn't understand why the police still hadn't caught her daughter's murderer, she'd snarled. They'd surely got enough evidence from her flat, they'd held the body for the post mortem for months, they must have had enough time. Was it that they didn't really bother about working girls? Perhaps they assumed that their families didn't care? Jacqueline hadn't always been living in that way, that was one thing she wanted him to know. The woman's shaking hands had produced a photo from her handbag: a pretty teenager, smiling for the camera. She'd been a lovely girl, good at everything. She had got ten GCSEs. She should have gone to university. It was those blasted drugs.

By the time Mrs Jenning had finished, Dave had wanted to bang his head on the table. Instead he had had to act professionally, reciting each avenue they'd explored, outlining the number of hours, days and weeks they'd spent on door-to-door enquiries, checking every tiny lead, and eventually explaining that some crimes were simply never solved, no matter how hard the police worked.

As Karen ushered her mother into the garden, Dave cleared the table. He should try to stop brooding about Jacqui Jenning, he told himself as he slotted the greasy plates into the dishwasher. It wasn't his fault they'd not found a single significant lead. In his experience, homicides involving prostitutes were particularly difficult to crack, and this had been one of those cases that had refused to fall into place.

He was pretty sure that the perpetrator had been a client. Jacqui had been known to trawl for custom in the Starlite night club. A bouncer remembered seeing her leave at about two in the morning on the day of her murder. She'd been with a tallish, white man; CCTV film showed a drunken couple meandering across the shopping precinct at 2.23 a.m., heading towards the taxi rank, but the cameras had caught only blurred images. None of the local minicab drivers remembered giving them a lift. But somewhere, the lunatic who'd punctured her skin with over thirty stab wounds, then gouged out a sizeable part of her brain, was strutting around enjoying his freedom.

The case was still officially open, yet after nearly nine months of enquiries, Dave had serious doubts they'd ever find Jacqui's killer and he couldn't help but see it as a personal failure. They had plenty of forensic material from her flat, but none of it helped. The bloodstains matched only Jacqui's DNA; frustratingly, too, all but one of the prints they'd found belonged to her. The only real lead they had was some semen stains on the sheets of her dishevelled bed. But, short of demanding that every man in the country donate a sample, this led nowhere. The national DNA computer base produced nothing.

Dave didn't feel particularly sympathetic: most prostitutes led chaotic and violent lives which, if they were unlucky, ended abruptly. It was a shame that young girls had to get involved with drugs and the sex trade, but he couldn't take on the world's problems. No, what angered him was that it should be so easy for someone to commit murder then melt back into their normal life. He was neither a political nor a religious man, but what he believed was that justice should be done.

He wandered outside, hearing the whine of his mother-in-law's voice, which was like an irritating insect that one wanted to swat. He had to stop thinking about the Jacqui Jenning case. They would continue to follow every new lead; the enquiry would remain open. Yet the likelihood was that her murderer would never be caught.

6

AUTUMN. CLOUDS ROLLED OVER the flats, bringing estuary mists, northern winds and driving rain that the sun was no longer able to vanquish. The grasses that edged the creek-side path stiffened and died; the blackberries turned sour. The swallows that in late August had perched in chirping rows on the telegraph wires were gone too; the colour drained from the landscape as it would from old clothes that had been washed too often. Grey, brown, dark green. In the wings, winter waited.

Poppy started school. I took her in the first week of September, holding her hand tight as we edged through the throng of children and mums. They were a different lot than the London crowd: women in four-wheel drives with the comfortable appearance of the Home Counties. For the first time since we left London, I missed Nat.

'I don't want to go.'

Poppy whimpered it so quietly that, had it not been for the fierce manner in which she now gripped my arm, I might not have noticed.

'Come on, sweetie. It's going to be fine. You're going to meet lots of new friends.'

'But they aren't my friends.'

Squatting down, I pulled her into my arms. Around us, a group of little girls who would surely be in Poppy's class were calling excitedly to each other. Blonde plaits, sparkly silver anoraks and pink leggings: a gaggle of girlie girls, types that in London Jessie and Poppy had despised.

'But they will be once you've got to know them. Come on, Pops. You've got to be brave.'

She pulled away, standing angrily before me in the alien playground, my lovely tomboy, with her jeans and trainers.

'I don't want to be brave!'

'Come on, love. Look, there's your teacher . . .' With considerable effort, I straightened up. The bending had made my womb tighten into a fake contraction, a gentle squeezing that in two months would turn to ferocious labour. 'She's waving at you.'

Miss Graves, a pretty young woman that Si and I had met briefly in

June, was smiling at us reassuringly. 'Hello, Poppy! Are you going to come inside with me?'

She had no choice but to nod. Slowly, reluctantly, she released my hand and followed her teacher across the playground and into the school building. Head drooping, shoulders bunched, she looked so small and lost that I couldn't bear to watch. Turning quickly away, I pushed swiftly past the milling mums and out of the gate.

Back at the warehouse, there was nothing for me to do. The floor was being fitted downstairs, and upstairs the bedrooms were being replastered. Si was still sanding on the top floor. We wanted to have at least part of the building habitable by the time the baby arrived. Regarding the naked gaps where the kitchen was to be fitted, the raw brickwork and trailing cables, I wondered if it would ever happen.

Meanwhile, I got to know our neighbours. Bob Perkins introduced himself to me in the boat yard after Ronnie, his labrador, jumped up with such enthusiasm that, like an unbalanced skittle, I was nearly knocked over. I'd already noticed him walking the dog along the riverside path: a retired chap who was now telling me eagerly how he and his wife had been living in their cottage for nineteen years.

'Doing up the warehouse, are you?'

I winced apologetically. 'Yes. Sorry about the noise.'

He shrugged. 'It's about time somebody tried to do something with the place. It's a white elephant, been left to rot for years.'

I gave him a bright, determined smile. 'We're hoping to open as a B and B when it's finished. It's such a pretty spot.'

He looked around doubtfully. In front of the warehouse a large dredger was rusting into the water. Further down the creek an old barge lay sunken and forgotten, its roof peppered with holes. The working yard, where boats were repaired and docked for the winter, was behind us. This was the graveyard: where the corpses of abandoned boats were left to decay in the mud, a place of maritime ghosts.

'I suppose you might get some people that were interested . . .'

Other characters slowly came into focus: Richard, the owner of the boat yard, who accepted a beer when Si showed him round; Janice, Bob's wife, whose manner was faintly disapproving—perhaps it was the noise of our builders, or the churned-up lane—and another lady, who walked her dog by the creek now nodded hello.

I would never have admitted it to Si or Poppy, but as I meandered around I missed Don and his sales team, and Nat and the hurly-burly of London like a limb that had been ripped off at the joint.

Poppy continued to trail to school reluctantly, gripping at me as we entered the playground and glancing back forlornly as Miss Graves led her inside. Each afternoon I longed for her to come skipping from her classroom like the other girls, waving their paintings and books like trophies in happy, girlie gangs, off to Brownies, or back to someone's house for tea. In contrast, Poppy was always alone. I had given up asking who she played with, for my question was invariably answered with a scowl.

While Poppy remained unattached to their children, I had no entrée to the groups of mums who waited so companionably in the playground. As I hovered on the edge they clustered together in cliques, ignoring me. It was reminiscent of being nine once more and back at my own primary school, where, on the instructions of a plump girl called Josephine, I was summarily blanked. For the other girls, friendship seemed to occur naturally. Yet for me it was constantly elusive.

Back at the warehouse the build was going badly. The team that Si had employed had done a good job of tearing out the decrepit interior and mending the roof, but now that the riverside wall was about to be rendered, a malevolent rot had been discovered in the brickwork that the surveyor had overlooked. The whole lot would have to come down, Si muttered gloomily. It would add another fifteen or twenty grand to the bill. Pipes were a problem, too. The plumber, who over the summer had connected the waterworks for the new kitchen, had messed up and the whole job would have to be redone, even though the kitchen units had been ordered and the flooring chosen.

Even worse, the builders suddenly disappeared. Si took it hard and refused to discuss the details. Withdrawing to the top of the warehouse, he spent long afternoons bashing at the rotten plaster with a pickaxe, reappearing grim-faced and fatigued. Until the far wall was rendered and replastered, we could progress no further.

I wanted to help him, but in my encumbered state there was little I could do. The baby weighed me down and I slumped around, contributing nothing. For weeks I had been unable to sleep, the fold-out beds of the mobile home proving both too narrow and too hard. As the baby punched and squirmed, I lay awake, listening to the wind rattling at the roof and dreading the exhaustion of the approaching day.

Then, some time in October, Poppy made a friend.

'Mummy!' she shouted happily as she met me at the gate. 'Can Megan come back and play?'

She was beaming up at me excitedly as she hopped from foot to foot.

Next to her stood one of the girls from her class, a sharp-faced child with pigtails.

'What, now?'

'Yes! Oh, please say yes! Please, please, please, please!'

'OK, if Megan's mum agrees.'

'Yes!' Poppy cried in triumph, punching the air.

'Which one's your mum, Megan?' I asked, turning to Poppy's new friend.

The girl pointed to a woman standing in the centre of a gaggle of mothers. I had noticed her before: a heavy-set woman who drove one of the showiest of the bull-barred trucks. On the first day of term I had attempted a smile as we had passed by the netball hoops, but she had gazed past me as if I wasn't there. Steeling myself, I grasped Poppy's hand and we walked across the tarmac towards her.

'Hello,' I said, smiling broadly. 'I'm Mel, Poppy's mum. We were wondering if Megan would like to come back for tea.'

The woman blinked back at me politely. 'Unfortunately Megan has ballet,' she said.

Beside me, I could sense Poppy deflate. '*Please*, Mum,' she hissed, tugging on my sleeve.

It was clearly of utmost importance that I nail this date.

'What about tomorrow?' I persisted brightly. 'We can bring her home, if it's a problem.'

Megan's mother gave me a tight smile. 'Tomorrow shouldn't be a problem,' she said. 'Isn't that nice, Megan?'

But Megan had run off and was giggling with the other girls.

I had strict instructions from Poppy concerning preparations for the tea. I was to supply Jammie Dodgers, crisps, peanut butter sandwiches and chocolate milkshakes. I should tidy up the mobile home beforehand, and not ask Megan embarrassing questions. On no account was Si to appear with his guitar. Her vehemence on this last point surprised me. Just a few months earlier his performances had been the high point of our evenings. Now, with new friends, a warbling stepfather with unravelling sweaters and sawdust in his hair, was obviously not cool

After I met them at the school gates the girls ran ahead as I waddled behind. Then, arms around each other's shoulders, they walked down the lane and through the boat yard, yabbering secrets. I watched them with relief. Clearly, I should not have been so impatient. Poppy was perfectly able to forge new friendships without my interventions.

Yet by the time the girls sat down for tea, the atmosphere had shifted. Unlike the happy chatter I had anticipated, they guzzled their food in silence, then disappeared solemnly into Poppy's small room. Closing the door firmly behind them, they did not reappear for another hour. I left them alone, listening hopefully for the sounds of laughter.

When finally the door opened, my hopes capsized. Poppy appeared first, slamming it behind her, her face pink with anger. 'Please can Megan go home now? I don't want to play with her any more.'

Megan appeared behind her, smirking. As I glanced at her face it occurred to me that her eyes had a vindictive, almost gloating glint.

'Oh, come on, girls! Megan's only been here a short while. Why don't we show Megan the river, Pops?'

'I don't want to go to the horrid river.'

'Actually, nor do I, Mrs Stenning.'

They remained intransigent. Whatever fragile bonds had existed before tea had been snapped apart as definitely as a broken twig. Folding her arms, Megan sat stiffly on the sofa as Poppy stomped back to her room. Ten minutes later Megan's mother arrived in her four-by-four.

'Never mind!' She flashed me an icy smile, glancing curiously at the mess strewn around the yard. A tremor of shock registered on her face. We were clearly trailer trash; Poppy's friendship with her daughter was not a relationship to be encouraged. 'Girls will be girls!'

Two minutes later they had disappeared, roaring back up the lane.

When I pushed open the door to Poppy's room I found her lying on the bed, the covers pulled over her head. Hair bobbles, star-shaped clips and baby pots of nail varnish were scattered across the floor, rejected birthday presents that had previously been shoved at the back of her drawers and only brought out for Megan's entertainment.

'What went wrong?' I asked gently.

'Nothing!' her muffled voice wailed. 'Go *away* Mummy! I *hate* you!'

My stomach felt as if it were filled with rocks. I sat down heavily on her bed, fiddling with the edge of her cover. 'Why do you hate me?'

'Because it's all your fault!'

'Why's it all my fault? I was trying to make things nice for you.'

She sat up, her tearful face contorted with misery. 'Because it was you who made me come here! I never wanted to live in this horrible place! Megan said it was *weird*! She said only losers live in caravans!'

'But this isn't how it's always going to be, sweetheart,' I said, trying to remain calm. 'We're going to make the warehouse really nice and then we're going to move in there.'

But Poppy merely stared back at me, blank-faced. 'Why can't we live like a normal family?'

'But we do live like a normal family!'

'No, we don't! Why are you lying to me? Megan said that if your mum's husband isn't your real dad that makes your mum all slutty!'

My mouth dropped open. How did seven-year-old girls learn to belittle people like this? 'That is total, utter nonsense.'

Poppy jerked away from my outstretched hand, pulling her cover back over her head. 'Go away! I really do hate you, Mummy!'

I trailed out to the kitchen and started to clear away the tea, sniffing disconsolately. How could I have a second child when I was such a failure with the first? It was yet another example of my foolishness. Everyone else made it appear so easy, but, however hard I tried, I remained a learner, who kept endlessly failing her test.

As Si worked with increasing fervour on the building, I sank ever deeper into lethargy. He couldn't afford to pause for long lunches or laze with me in the occasional late autumn sunshine, and he'd snap if I attempted to entice him away. I knew he was right: in order to keep our debts at bay we had to get the building ready for paying guests.

When he was not crashing around in the rafters, he was in London. There was 'business' to see to, he retorted in response to my questions. I knew better than to question him more closely. From the outset he had resisted my attempts to probe his affairs. 'Don't worry about it, babe,' he'd say, his expression impenetrable. 'Everything's fine.'

This was not how I had imagined our new life. I had not expected to spend most evenings in our mobile home alone as he zoomed off in his van for endless 'meetings' with architects and contractors. He was busy, I kept telling myself, that was why we no longer talked; when the build was finished our intimacy would return. And I was so heavily pregnant, too. 'After the baby comes' and 'after the build is finished' became my mantras, but sometimes I feared that our relationship was already over.

I had other worries, too. My due date approached with merciless speed. What only a few months earlier I had thought of in abstract terms was now vividly real. Poppy's birth had been a forty-eight-hour ordeal in which I had been convinced I was going to die. That my body would undergo this event for a second time both terrified and dumbfounded me. It simply could not be that the squirming lump which now inhabited my tummy would, in a month or so, fight its way out. The more I brooded, the more impossible it seemed.

I lay on the bed, prodding what I imagined to be the baby's bottom.

'Are you OK?'

I looked up with a start. Si was standing in the door of our bedroom, squinting at me in the late-morning light.

'I'm just having a rest.'

He wandered into the room, absent-mindedly setting down the hammer that he had been holding in his battered hands on the pillow as he sat down. Laying his hand tenderly on my naked belly, he leaned over and kissed it.

'So what's the matter?' He took my hand and nuzzled at my knuckles. 'Are you worrying about the birth again?'

I stared into his dusty face. Now that he was beside me, peering into my face with such gentle concern, my fears were melting away.

'I'm just being stupid.'

Si stroked my hair. 'It's not stupid to be scared, hon.'

I didn't reply. The truth was that until the birth there was little he could do to reassure me.

'I'm just feeling bad for Poppy,' I said eventually. 'I mean, how am I going to cope when there's two of them?' I rolled off the bed and eased my feet into some slippers.

'You'll cope fine. And it'll be great for Poppy to have a little brother.'

I glanced up at him. 'Why were you looking for me, anyway?'

'I've just had a call from Ol.'

'Oh?'

'He's having a bit of trouble on this conversion job. I'm going to go up to London for a couple of days to help him out.'

I stiffened. Turning away from Si, I walked towards the window and stared down at the muddy river. Outside it was spitting with rain.

'OK.' I had tried to keep the complaint from my voice, but the phrase sounded tight and forced.

'It won't be for more than a day or so. And I can't get anything more done on the loft until the oak's delivered.'

I shrugged, willing myself to turn round and smile. 'Really, it's not a problem, Si. Poppy and I will be *fine*.'

But after he had gone I went back to bed. He was lying, I thought darkly. He had had enough of me and was seizing any excuse to get away. Perhaps there was another woman involved. I had promised to trust him, but now tiny doubts began to bite into me. It would explain so much: the frequent outings, his new disinterest in sex. I was such a bad-tempered blob, why would he ever want to stay?

Forty-eight hours later I leaned against the front door as Si jumped out of his van onto the forecourt. I was both yearning to see him and dreading the signs of infidelity, in my increasingly paranoid state, I was sure I'd find plastered over his face.

'Hi, honey!' Leaping over a puddle, he landed neatly at my feet, gathering me into his arms into a great squashy hug. 'I've missed you.'

I did not return his embrace, just stood with my arms hanging loosely by my sides. Si pulled back, scrutinising my face.

'Are you feeling better?'

'Better in what way?'

He frowned. 'OK, let's start again. Are you feeling more *cheerful*?'

'I'm doing my best.'

I sounded bad-tempered and resentful, the kind of woman that any man in his right mind would wish to escape from. Was it hormones that were making me so suspicious? For a moment my mind cleared: I was pregnant, happily married to a caring man who had simply gone to London to do some work. Then I remembered Rosa, and the studied nonchalance with which Si had told me he was leaving, and my paranoia pushed my good sense aside.

'You haven't been with some other woman, have you?' I blurted. Slowly, almost wearily, Si shook his head. I was sure that I saw something dark pass over his eyes. 'Honestly, Mel, of course I haven't.'

Then, surely too hastily, he brushed past me and into the warehouse.

And now it all fits sickeningly together, like the handcuffs that DCI Gosforth clicked with such bored competence round Si's wrists. *Supposing I did something terrible?* he'd asked and, fool that I was, I assumed he was talking hypothetically. But even then, when I was pregnant with Jo, it now seems that I was correct and he *was* still seeing Rosa. Yet why would he take Poppy? Something is missing in the story that the police have down so pat. It *cannot* be true; Si would never put Poppy in danger, whatever mess he was in.

But the facts remain. I was playing hide-and-seek with Poppy, and I heard a door close behind me. A few minutes later, Si drove away. I continued to search for Poppy, but she had vanished. The police must be right. They're the professionals, experts in the unravelling of personal tragedy. Poppy has gone, and Si has taken her.

I am sitting on the sofa, rocking. When I open my eyes, I see that Sandra has positioned herself at the other end of the sunken cushions. There she sits, quietly watching. I cannot recall how long I have been here, or when she joined me. Outside the night has taken over.

'There's some news, Mel,' Sandra says quietly.

I stare at her, my stomach plummeting. For a second or so something blocks my throat. From the way she is looking at me, I know it's bad.

'What kind of news?'

'There's been another sighting of the car—a member of the public in response to the newsflash. He remembers spotting a vehicle which sounds similar to the car Simon was driving. It was about four thirty, on the Sittingbourne road.'

I swallow, feeling the weight of this news sink into me. 'What does that mean?'

'We're not sure yet, but it's an important lead. The reason the man remembers the car so clearly is that it overtook a slower vehicle and our witness had to swerve into the verge to avoid a collision.'

'Right.'

Sandra pauses. I am clutching my hands together.

'The man also noticed a little girl sitting in the passenger seat.'

'You mean he saw Poppy?'

'That's what we're assuming, yes.'

In the background, there's a hubbub of voices and the beep of a mobile phone. Upstairs, Jo has started to cry. I can hear Trish soothing him in her sing-song voice. After a second or so, the wailing stops.

'I just don't understand why he'd take her . . .' I feel nauseous, sweat prickling my skin. All I can think is that it must be some kind of ghastly mistake. Si's a careful driver, a loving stepdad. This *can't* be him.

'We're afraid he might be planning something silly.'

'Something silly?'

Sandra bites her lip. 'We're very gravely concerned for Poppy's safety. What I can tell you at this stage is . . .'

I do not hear the rest. Jumping up, I dash to the toilet.

There are arms around me, soft bodies to lean against. I am being propelled across the living room and seated back on the sofa. Someone has draped a duvet round my shoulders; Trish is fussing around with a coffee table and a steaming mug. I still can't hold the drink, for I am shaking uncontrollably, like I did after my waters broke with Jo.

'Have some of the tea, sweetheart,' Trish is saying. 'It'll help warm you up.' She's handing me the mug, but I push it away.

'I want Jo,' I whisper. 'Bring me Jo.'

He's placed in my arms, his arms stretching upwards, his eyelashes fluttering against his pearly skin. I clasp his bundled body, my trembling fingers automatically pulling up my jumper. Now, as I bring his head towards my nipple, I feel a little better.

'Is there anything else I can get you?' Trish says, leaning over and touching me lightly on the hand. I take in her concerned face and the swell of her own baby, stretching her woollen dress.

'I'm fine,' I say. 'You should get a sit-down, too.'

'The police are doing their best . . .' She stops, glancing with a hopeless shrug across the room, presumably in the direction of the various officers that remain in the building.

'Yes,' I say. 'I know.'

'Do you want me to sit with you?'

'Actually, would you mind if you left me alone for a little?' I give her hand a squeeze, showing it's nothing personal.

'Cool. If you need me, I'll be in the kitchen.'

I nod, watching her sway gracefully across the cluttered room. Perhaps she's going to talk to Sandra, or DCI Gosforth will bombard her with questions about our family life. They won't find anything out, not by talking to her, or to any of the neighbours. Jo slurps and smacks his lips, oblivious to his sister's plight. As I watch him I know what I have to do. I have to stop panicking and start focusing. It's no good weeping and being so passive: I'm the one who has the answers.

What I have to do is remember everything that happened.

7

JO ARRIVED at the end of November 2004. To my shock my waters broke in the shower, just before I went to bed. Si heaped towels round my shoulders and I rested for a while on the puddled floor, worrying about Poppy. This was not meant to happen until December, when Pat had agreed to come and look after her. What were we going to do now?

Then came the contractions, erasing all thought. How can the human brain recall that level of pain? I don't remember how it felt, just that the only possible position was standing, my arms draped round the sink, my bottom waving in the air. There is no dignity in childbirth. Jo arrived just after the midwife had come clumping up the stairs.

Despite my fears, I was still alive and the baby was perfect. He didn't cry, just lay in my arms blinking. Ten tiny fingers and ten tiny toes, long skinny legs: our little son. Si was ecstatic, bounding around like an over-excited puppy as he made tea for the midwife, tried unsuccessfully to locate a bottle of champagne and helped to tidy up. When he cradled Jo in his arms, his face was softer than I'd ever seen.

'I can't believe it,' he whispered, his eyes filling with tears.

How could I have doubted him? In the days that followed, the formless anxieties that had beset me over the last months of my pregnancy vanished without trace. It must have been my hormones that made me so paranoid, I decided. It was ridiculous to imagine that Si was anything but the most devoted of partners. The man I had fallen for in London was back. Here he was, making me lunch as I fed Jo, or sweeping him away to change his nappy. Gone was the tight-lipped silence of the autumn. He had never been happier, he declared one morning as he covered my face with kisses. Having me and Jo and Poppy was like a dream come true.

Work on the warehouse ground to a halt, but Si no longer seemed to care. The plumbing had been sorted out and the builders would reappear in a couple of weeks to install the new kitchen, he insisted. Until then, there was little he could do. We had moved from the mobile home into the warehouse a few weeks earlier, and welcomed the change. The building was unusually quiet, filled only with the sounds of Jo's crying or the clatter of our footsteps on the wooden floors. If previously the boat yard had resonated with the screech of drills or crash of hammers, now all that could be heard were the yowl of the wind and the constant chink of nylon ropes against masts, like cowbells. Winter was here, turning the marshland wild.

Si returned to his painting. He set up his materials in one of the bedrooms-to-be along the gallery, transforming it into a makeshift studio and working late into the night, while Jo and I dozed in front of the TV. It was because he was finally at peace that he could paint again, he muttered, shyly producing a landscape of the creek, with the gas towers of Sheppey rising in the distance. A week later he completed a series of charcoal sketches of me lying on the sofa with Jo. They were so good that I tried to persuade him to take them to a local gallery. Predictably, he refused. He wasn't ready, he said; he needed more time to recover. Distracted by a fretful baby, I did not ask what he meant.

In December, everything suddenly changed. He had received a call from Ollie, Si announced one blustery afternoon as the wind screeched across the marsh. He was having a work crisis, there was some kind of deadline. We were in the bathroom at the time, Si hovering by the door as I bent over the changing mat, arranging Jo's nappy. To be honest I was barely listening. I glanced vaguely in Si's direction. 'Oh dear . . .'

Now he was telling me in detail about a contractor having let them down; something to do with deliveries of tiles and a restaurant that had to be open by Christmas. He would have to go up to London and give Ol a hand, he concluded. Wrapping Jo in his nappy, I picked him up. All I registered was that Si was being unusually verbose. It was another side of our freshly invigorated intimacy; now that everything was finally working out so well, he was starting to relax and let me in.

He went to bed early and left for London before I had woken up. When he returned the next afternoon—4 p.m. on a dull winter's day—it was almost dark. I noticed the headlights of his van moving down the lane and hurried to the front door to greet him, happy that he was back so early. Yet as he climbed from the van, I felt myself grow cold.

Si looked terrible. His face was pallid and his shoulders stooped. In the twenty-four hours since I had seen him he seemed to have aged about ten years.

'What's the matter, Si? Are you ill?'

'I'm fine.' He did not even glance at me, but as he slammed the van door I saw with a shock that his lower lip was swollen and bloody, as if he had been punched.

'What happened to your lip?'

'Oh, that.' He put his fingers to his mouth, wincing. 'I was hammering in this skirting board and my hand slipped. Smacked myself with the bloody hammer.' He gave me a ghostly smile.

'Have you put some antiseptic on it? Shall I get some?' I attempted to put my arms round him, but he pushed me gently away.

'Nah, it doesn't need it.'

He moved away from me into the cavernous ground floor of the warehouse, refusing to meet my eyes.

'Has something happened?'

He wasn't listening. He peered vaguely in my direction, shaking his head as if he had barely heard the question. Wandering around the room, he fiddled with some cables in the kitchen area, picked up a loose floorboard that still had to be fitted, and leaned it against a wall, then slipped away from me and went upstairs. The last time I had seen him like this, when he had failed to meet my eyes or answer my questions, was just after I had told him I was pregnant. I felt as chilled as the winter air that blasted through the open door.

Jo developed colic. The early peaceful weeks of his life became a distant country, only dimly remembered. Now, my days were dominated by his crying. I spent my evenings jigging him on my shoulder as he bawled. I rarely finished a meal, for every time I attempted to eat he'd start screaming again. In the afternoons I took him on brisk walks, my speed increasing with the level of yowls that emanated from the buggy. If I was lucky, he would sleep for a few hours after I picked Poppy up from school, then the evening ordeal would begin.

I bordered on hysteria. Poppy had never been like this. She had fed and slept, occasionally rousing to stare dreamily around. I was nauseous with exhaustion, my head ached continually, my senses muffled as if I had been wrapped in cotton wool. As the warehouse descended further into chaos, my relationship with Si comprised grunted exchanges. He tried to help, but every time he took Jo from my arms the level of screaming increased. Accepting defeat, he returned upstairs.

Poppy was left largely to her own devices. It sounds callous, but I had little choice. After school, she'd watch TV. If we were lucky, Jo would sleep during her tea and bath. After that I barely had the energy to read her a story, far less sit by her bed chatting like we used to. At weekends, she tended to play by herself or was occasionally invited out by one of the few girls she had finally befriended in her class. Si sometimes took her swimming, or we'd go for muddy walks, Jo strapped round my chest as we tramped across the marsh.

It was after we'd returned from one of these walks that Poppy received the first letter. It was lying on the doormat, and when she saw it her face lit up.

'Ooh look, Poppy!' I cried as we pushed open the front door. 'I think you've got a Christmas card!'

Grabbing the envelope, she started to rip it apart.

'Who's it from?' Putting his hand on her shoulder, Si peered down at the scrap of paper she was holding tightly between her fingers. 'Is it from somebody at school?'

'None of your business!' Scrumpling the note into a ball, she ran across the ground floor and up the stairs. A few seconds later we heard the slam of her door.

Si and I exchanged glances.

'What was that all about?'

'Search me.'

Jo cried for the next two hours, only calming as I paced the floor. So by the time I managed to ascend the stairs to talk to Poppy, Si had fed and bathed her and she was asleep.

We hunkered into something roughly resembling a routine as Jo became marginally calmer. Now that he could hold his head upright, I was able to pop him into his bouncy chair, where he watched with interest as I scurried around the room, trying to tidy. Yet despite this gradual improvement, I felt exhausted. He was growing hungrier, and had taken to waking me three or four times a night to feed. I began to make up the occasional bottle of milk formula for him.

Befuddled with fatigue, I kept losing things and forgetting appointments. When Sally Travis, the mother of one of Poppy's few friends at school, bounded up to me in the playground, all set to whisk Poppy off to a play date with Lily, I stared at her blankly, my memory of the arrangement deleted. As I was feeding Jo a few evenings later, I remembered that I was due to attend the school's parents' evening in ten minutes' time. Arriving in a red-cheeked flurry twenty minutes later, I found the school gates locked, the classrooms in darkness. It had been the week *before*, I now recalled. Even worse, the week after Jo's birth I had lost my house keys, dropped, presumably from the handle of the pram, where I'd taken to slinging them.

Now my bag disappeared, too. It was the first week of January, just over a year since I had valued Si's flat. We'd had a quiet, happy Christmas, just the four of us, with a roasted goose, some good red wine and a huge trifle. Despite our perilous finances, we'd scraped together enough money to give Poppy a bike and Jo a Happy Tot Touch and Play centre. For Si, I had bought oil paints and brushes. In return he presented me with a silver charm bracelet, something so beautiful that, as I pulled away the soft tissue paper, I was unable to speak. Despite his silences and general air of distraction, he still loved me. Everything was going to be all right.

Outside, the weather was quiet and grey, the soft winter light that fell across the marshes during the mornings dipping quickly to dusk in the afternoons. We went for walks, built fires in the new wood burner, played Mousetrap with Poppy, and it finally felt as if we were a family.

Then, one morning, when reaching for my credit cards at the end of the supermarket shop, I realised that the leather satchel in which

I carried my purse, Jo's nappies, toys, and my mobile had disappeared.

I began to search frantically through the carrier bags, scrabbling past tin cans, toilet rolls and cartons of juice, but finding no satchel. On the other side of the checkout, the rotund cashier folded her arms, watching unsympathetically as I trotted out the little dance of panic, peering underneath the trolley, then down the queue of impatient customers that bulged behind me. Could I have left the bloody thing in the car?

'Sorry,' I croaked. 'I can't find my bag.'

The woman at the till sniffed. 'Do you want to leave your groceries here and come back for them later?'

I nodded mutely. In his sling, Jo had started to whinge.

'Poppy!' I shouted. She had squirmed her way past the queue of trolleys and was milling hopefully in the sweets and snacks aisle. 'We have to go home and get some money!'

I drove home in a fury. How could I have trailed round the supermarket for over an hour and not noticed that my satchel was missing? It was the last straw. I would have to replace my mobile, get new house keys cut and cancel my credit cards. I had also lost about thirty pounds in cash. Perhaps the satchel had been stolen. More likely, I had simply allowed it to fall off the trolley. My incompetence made me bash my hands so hard against the steering wheel that I bruised my knuckles.

Back at the warehouse, Si was loading the van. As my Fiat bumped down the muddy lane, I could see his long figure bent over the heavy plastic cases that stored his tools. There was something melancholic in his stance, I noticed. Drawing up beside him, I lowered my window.

'I've lost my bloody bag.'

He stared at me uncomprehendingly. 'Oh God,' he said vaguely.

'Can you come back to Tesco and pay for the shopping?'

He stood on the drive, blinking at me. It was a freezing January morning, in which flecks of ice drifted half-heartedly around the boats, yet he was only wearing a T-shirt. I stared at his goose-pimpled skin.

'I don't have any cards,' he said.

'What do you mean you don't have any cards?'

'I think I must have left them at Ol's . . . when I was there the other week,' he finished lamely. He looked mutely down at his work boots.

It was true that our Christmas purchases had been made from my own account: money I had saved from my estate agency job. At the time I had hardly noticed; now that we were married, what difference could it make? But how could Si have been so absent-minded as to leave them at Ol's and only now seem to notice?

'But that was *ages* ago!'

'I know, I . . .' He trailed off, his gaze flicking away from my face. 'I've got some cash.' Reaching into his pocket, he produced a wad of notes, presumably payment for one of his jobs. 'Have this. It'll tide you over . . .'

I glanced at his face in sudden trepidation. Why was he talking about 'you' rather than 'we'? And why was he packing up the van?

'Where are you going?'

'London.'

'You're going to work for Ollie again?'

He stared at me sullenly. 'Kind of,' he muttered, kicking at the dirt. 'I've taken on a job.'

'And in the meantime, what am I supposed to do about money?'

'That little lot should last you a while.' He nodded at the roll of notes. 'By the time it's run out the bank will have sent you a replacement card. We'll just have to get overdrawn for a bit.'

'Mummy!' Poppy trilled behind me. 'When are we getting out?'

Leaning back, I unclicked her seatbelt.

'Go inside and watch TV.'

Grinning at Si, she skipped past him and into the warehouse. Jo, thankfully, had dozed off.

'What kind of job is it?' I had a sick feeling in my stomach.

'It's a mate of Ol's. He's taken on a big refurbishment in Kennington. They need some carpentry doing.' He paused, obviously choosing his words carefully. 'It's going to take a couple of months.'

I stared at my hands, still clutched round the steering wheel. 'A couple of months?'

'We need the money, Mel. I can't afford not to take this up. I'll come home at weekends.'

Everything he said made sense. We could not continue with the building until we had more cash. He was an experienced carpenter. He had worked wonders on the loft. If anything, this was a lucky break. Yet inside my head a voice hissed that he was lying.

'So you're going now . . . Where are you going to stay?'

His eyes went foggy. 'I'm just going for the night, to dump my tools in Ol's lock-up and size the place up. I'll be back tomorrow afternoon.'

I slumped in my seat. Why was he only telling me about this now, when he was about to go? 'Fine. I'd better move the car round then.'

'Mel?' He was squatting by the car window now, pushing his face close to mine. I could smell coffee on his breath. 'I love you, babe, OK?'

Blinking back my tears, I pushed the car into reverse.

8

THAT NIGHT, POPPY had her first nightmare. I woke with a jolt to the sound of screaming, staring in confusion around the darkened room. The noise was terrible: not the familiar low-pitched wailing of a half-asleep child, but sharp bursts of yelling, as if she was being cornered by a monster. Next to me, Jo was fast asleep. *Poppy!* Leaping out of bed, I pattered down the gallery to her room.

'Poppy! What is it?'

Peering around her room, I tried to make out her shape in the dull orange glow of her night light. At the sound of my voice the screaming had slowed into a low animal moan. As my eyes grew accustomed to the dark, I saw that she was cowering in the far corner of her bed.

'Darling, what's happened?' Stumbling across the room, I took her in my arms. She clung to me, wiping her tears on my T-shirt.

'There was a person outside my room! They were walking past. I saw them going down the stairs.'

'It was a nightmare—'

'No, it wasn't! They were out there, I saw them!'

She pointed to the gallery, in the direction of Si's studio, the steps to the top floor and the metal stairs that led to the ground floor. Could she have spotted a burglar? The image of an intruder creeping around downstairs was too horrible to countenance.

Stepping out of her room, I listened for sounds from the room below, my heart pattering in my mouth. But there was nothing, just the whisper of wind and the tapping of boat masts outside.

'There's no one there, promise.'

Walking back across Poppy's bedroom, I flicked on the light. The contents of the room were revealed: her chest of drawers, covered with drawings and felt-tip pens; her clothes, heaped over the small wooden rocking chair that Pat had given her for her sixth birthday; a muddle of toys, pushed into a plastic crate.

'Who would want to burgle us? All they'd get is a sack of rubble. You dreamt it.'

'They must have run away.' Tears were still spilling down her cheeks. Standing up on the bed, she put out her arms to be picked up, the way she did when she was a toddler. 'Poppy go in bed with Mummy.'

The muscles in my face tightened. We had been having this fight ever since Jo's birth. At nights she had started clamouring to come into bed with me, alternately using her baby voice or shrieking angrily that I no longer loved her.

'Honey,' I said, trying to keep the tension from my voice. 'There isn't room. Jo's in there. I don't want him to get squashed.'

'Poppy go with Mummy!'

I swayed blearily by the door, prevaricating. I wasn't strong enough for the fight that was brewing. Relenting, I padded across the floor and let her cling to me for a while, her strong legs crossed determinedly around my back.

'Poppy sleep with Mummy!'

But I had made up my mind. 'Stop talking like a baby,' I said tersely, putting her down. 'You're seven years old, not two. Go back to sleep.'

'Poppy wants *Mummy!*' she yelled.

I did not stay to hear the rest. Closing her door firmly behind me, I hurried back to my own bed, made so huge by Si's absence, and the tiny figure of Jo, stretched out on his back. After a while Poppy stopped yelling. I, however, was hopelessly awake. I turned onto my back, then rolled onto my side, arranging and rearranging the pillow. Poppy was jealous of Jo, uprooted from her life in London, and had so many changes to adapt to. Yet I was unable to provide the time or comfort that she required. I should pay her more attention, I decided miserably. Of *course* she was going to be traumatised. The combination of guilt and exhaustion made me weepy.

Outside, a bird started to chirrup as the light began to seep under the curtains. I turned onto my back, cursing. If I were more attentive, I would have carried Poppy back to our bed, evicting Jo to the empty cot that waited on the other side of our room. I had sentimentally assumed that she would adore her baby brother, yet all he had done so far was to displace her from my affections. As a second horribly merry bird joined the first, I replayed the scene in my mind. I had experienced similar nightmares as a child, imagining bogeymen under the bed, their skeletal hands shooting out and grabbing my ankles. A bad person had been standing at the top of the stairs, Poppy had cried. And then, when I arrived, she had regressed four or five years. It was such an obvious cry for attention. Yet, once again, I had refused to listen.

I am outside. Rain is driving into me, covering my dark hair with a fine sheen. I tip my head at the wind. I want to be cold. I want my clothes to be soaked, the freezing water beating on my skin. How can I sit inside in the warmth, sipping tea, when my daughter is lost? I want to be punished for everything that I failed to see and everything I failed to do.

Splashing past Sandra's maroon saloon, I make it to the edge of the boat yard, gazing past the rocking masts to the black emptiness that stretches beyond. Is Poppy out there? I start to stumble towards the path. As the racing clouds unveil the moon, my surroundings are illuminated: banks of mud glistening in silver light, then endless marsh.

'Mel, what are you *doing*?'

I feel hands on my shoulders, pulling me back. Turning, I see Trish's face looming over me.

'I have to look in the marsh . . .'

'Poppy isn't going to be out there, hon.'

'Where the hell *is* she then?'

'Si's got her.'

My legs give way. I flop against the bulk of Trish's body, dragging at her shoulders. I am making a strange keening sound.

'But why would he take her?'

She shrugs disgustedly. 'He's lost the plot, I suppose.'

'Do *you* think he murdered those women?'

She starts to lead me back to the warehouse. Right now, I would give anything to be in her position: expecting her first child, safe and unentangled. That I once pitied her seems ludicrous.

'I think most men are capable of anything.'

I stop, staring into her face. I feel hollowed out, as if everything I once believed has been scooped from inside me. A good man, family life, stability: that was all I wanted. I thought it was built with bricks, but my house was made of straw; one puff from the wolf and it has collapsed around me.

Placing her arm across my shoulders, Trish leads me inside the kitchen. The police have gone, leaving their mugs by the sink. From the living room I can hear Sandra talking on her mobile.

'I should have listened to Poppy,' I moan, sinking into the chair that Trish has placed proficiently behind me. 'I never listened. She was getting those letters. And the nightmares . . . maybe it's connected?'

Trish gazes back at me. Her eyes are bloodshot and she looks tired. She should be tucked up in her cottage resting, not becoming ensnared in my crisis. Yet the prospect of dealing with the police alone fills me with terror; she is my sole support, the only friend I have left.

'There was never anyone prowling around the warehouse,' she says quietly. 'It was just . . .'

I am not listening. My mind can't settle on anything long enough to carry out a normal conversation.

'What's the time?' I say, jerking upright.

'Eight fifteen.'

'Oh Jesus,' I wail. 'She's been gone for nearly four hours!'

As she pauses by the table, Trish takes a sudden breath. She is about to say something, I am sure. At the very least, she must be thinking what a fool I've been. She *told* me to leave Si, but I ignored her. Yet, whatever she was going to say, the moment passes and her face softens.

'Shall I make another cup of tea?' she asks.

I was growing accustomed to Si's absence. In an odd way I was calmer without him. There were no signs of disenchantment to brood over, no impatient exchanges or incomplete explanations that I might interpret as lies. He rang every night, texted that he loved me and returned at weekends tired, but with another roll of cash. Not wanting to provoke an argument, I did not mention the strange loss of his credit cards.

Jo was more settled, too. At seven weeks old, he had clicked into a predictable routine of naps, feeding and happy sessions spent kicking his legs under his play centre. I had not spent an entire evening jiggling a screaming baby for weeks, I realised. The image of our new life flickered on the horizon, like the mirage of water along a desert road.

Then, one morning, as I was slapping magnolia paint onto the plaster in the new bathroom, I heard a crash downstairs. It was loud enough to make me start. Placing my paintbrush back in the tray, I walked cautiously to the top of the stairs.

'Hello?'

I felt like a fool, calling out to the empty building. Perhaps it was a dog or fox, investigating our bins. Walking gingerly down the stairs, I stepped across the half-laid floor. Through the high windows I could see the motionless sails of the boats that were beached in the yard. I waited for perhaps five or six seconds, breathing quietly as I tried to discern the direction from which the sound had come. Then I heard a noise that turned me cold: the soft click of the latch.

Spinning round, I scurried towards the back door. Was there someone in the house? A builder, perhaps, returned without warning? Or *Si*? I had not heard a vehicle, but perhaps he had parked in the lane.

'Si? Is that you?'

Flinging open the back door, I ran round the side of the building. In the distance I could see a man pottering around a yacht. I must have imagined the noise, I told myself as I walked back through the door. All the same, my hands were trembling.

That night I took no chances. Rather than confront another of Poppy's nightmares, I tucked her directly into my bed. It was not that I believed in the ghost that she still swore she had seen on the gallery and who she now claimed had 'climbed into her dreams', the bed-sharing was simply for a treat. Nor was I being overly twitchy if, for the third time that evening, I checked that the doors and the windows of the warehouse were locked. When Si came home he could chortle at my precautions. But he didn't know how it felt to be a woman, alone.

Like the riverine sludge that flowed down the creek, one week ran into the next. During the days I decorated the bedrooms or tucked Jo into his pram for long, meandering expeditions to the shops. After school Poppy watched TV as I cooked her tea. Had she not been so changed, it would have been like the old days in London. But in small, barely perceptible ways, she was a different child. She had become quiet, sullen almost. She no longer wanted to cuddle, nor did she skip into school, singing. Instead, she trailed behind me, tutting crossly if I tried to take her hand. Perhaps it was that she was growing up, already at seven moving intangibly out of my reach. Or maybe, like me, she was adjusting to this new, isolated life.

'She's had a lot going on,' Sally Travis concluded one afternoon as she perched on the sofa, waiting for Lily and Poppy to appear from upstairs. 'I'm sure it's just a phase.'

I sipped my tea, wishing I had not brought the subject up. Lily was the youngest of four and Sally radiated maternal confidence, taking any upset from her kids with a wry shrug of her shoulders. As I glanced at her contented face, I suddenly wished I could be like her. What, after all, did I have to show for my so-called unconventionality? I had wasted most of my adult life avoiding what she represented, yet all I had encountered were loneliness and uncertainty.

'I know she needs more attention,' I said. 'But it's really hard to give it with Jo around . . .'

'And didn't you say she was having nightmares?'

'It's really awful. She's waking me almost every night.'

For a moment I imagined telling Sally everything: how Poppy's nightmares left me jangling with half-formed fears, the odd sounds I now imagined emanating from the uninhabited parts of the warehouse. She was nodding sympathetically, but as she sighed and ran her manicured hands through her middle-aged bob, I knew that I would never be able to confide in her.

'Oh dear,' she said, as if Poppy's behaviour was a run-of-the-mill irritation, one of those annoying little blips that all mothers must endure. 'Is there something up at school, do you think?'

'I don't know. It all seems fine. She never really talks about it.'

'Is she part of Megan's crowd?'

I looked up sharply. 'She was for about a week, but not any more.'

'Ah . . .'

She seemed on the brink of saying more, but must have decided against it, for she gave herself a little shake, placing down her mug. 'I ought to be getting along. I've got to pick up Harry from football.'

Ten minutes later, Poppy and I stood by the front door, watching the Range Rover reverse down the drive.

'Do you like Lily, then?' I asked, brushing my fingers against her golden hair.

'Mmm.'

'It's great that you're making some friends at school.'

It was the wrong thing to say, in this new relationship where I had to choose my words carefully. She jerked angrily away. 'Mummy! Why do you always have to keep going on about friends?'

It was during this period that I met Trish. We'd caught sight of each other several times before we actually spoke, in the shopping precinct or passing with a slight smile in the boat yard. I was not in the habit of eyeing up strangers, but in Trish I had instantly recognised a potential pal. It was partly the way she was dressed, her long parka, cropped hair and cowboy boots signalling a boho chic that was unlikely to have originated in provincial Kent. She was pregnant, I clocked, as she smilingly made way for Jo's buggy one morning by the creek. I suspected that she was alone, too. Perhaps it was that she seemed to be as keenly aware of my presence as I was of hers, unlikely behaviour for someone enjoying cosy coupledom. I could sense her eyes on me as I wandered along the cobbled street that led past Woolies and Boots; when we passed for the third time in as many days, by the side of the river, she gave me a shy nod. I decided that she must be the person who had moved into the empty cottage at the end of the lane. Only that week I had noticed blinds at the windows and discarded packing cases in the front garden.

Jo enabled us to finally introduce ourselves. He'd been whingeing all morning, and now, as we made our way up the lane, Trish appeared from her front door.

'Someone's not happy!' She grinned at me cheerfully. Reaching the pram, she peered inside. 'Poor little thing. Is he hungry?'

'He's got a cold.'

'Ah . . .'

Jo had quietened, and was concentrating on Trish's face.

'Isn't he beautiful?' she whispered.

'I don't know. Is he?' A minute earlier I had been tight with irritation, now I was gooey with maternal pride.

Straightening up, she threw back her head, showing off her long neck as she laughed. 'Of course he is. Just look at those eyes! How old?'

'Nine weeks.'

'And is it easy? Or just back-breaking? You have to tell me! I mean, how do you begin to manage with it all?'

She didn't have a wedding ring, but in her nose she wore a tiny diamond. Her easy smile and breathless questions made me want to grip her arm and tell her everything.

'Oh God. I don't know what to say!'

'You've got a little girl too, haven't you? I've seen you taking her to school. How do you cope with *two* of them? I just can't imagine it. I can barely look after myself, let alone someone else!' She laughed again, but panic flashed in her eyes. She was about eight months pregnant, I calculated, glancing surreptitiously at her belly.

'I just muddle along, I suppose.'

For a moment she was silent, then, 'I'm Trish, by the way,' she said, shooting out her hand. 'Sorry, you must think I'm mad, accosting you on the street like this.'

'Mel. I live in the boat yard, in that wreck of a warehouse. Have you just moved in?' I nodded at the cottage.

'Two weeks ago, from London. It was kind of a lifestyle decision. You know, for the baby . . .' She grimaced.

'Have you met Bob and Janice yet?'

'Yeah. Janice baked me a cake. Isn't that sweet?'

The mewing was growing in intensity. Placing my fingers around the pram handle, I gave it a little shake.

'I have to get him home and feed him. Do you want to come and have a coffee? If you don't mind the place being a bit of a state . . .'

She laughed again. From the faint glow of her cheeks I could tell that she was pleased.

Trish stayed the whole morning, putting her feet up on Poppy's sticky, jam-smeared stool as I pottered around the kitchen.

'It's a bit of a tip, I'm afraid,' I said, watching her glance around the room. 'What with the building work and everything, there doesn't seem much point in cleaning it up. We're hoping to move out of this room and into our new kitchen by the end of spring.'

She shrugged. I had the impression that she hardly noticed the domestic squalor, let alone passed judgment. 'That's a great angel,' she said, nodding at the sketch that Si had given me in London. I'd had it framed and it now hung above the sink, an icon of our new life.

'Yeah, my husband drew it for me. We had our first date in Nunhead Cemetery and there were all these stone angels there. He's an artist . . .'

'How romantic.'

I handed her a mug of tea, registering the irony in her voice. Why should she care about my love affairs?

'Tell me about *you*,' I said hastily. 'Why have you moved down here?'

She was an out-of-work actress, she said, surviving off the odd advert. She'd done a couple of police serials last year, and had made a minor appearance on *EastEnders*. I eyed her as she sipped at the tea. I did indeed vaguely recognise her. She'd moved down to Kent to escape the pollution, she continued. And of course property prices down here were so much cheaper. Having the baby was obviously going to make an acting career difficult, so she was considering a change of direction. Maybe she'd write a novel. And yes, she was single, her boyfriend having dumped her when she refused to terminate the pregnancy.

'What an arsehole, eh?' she finished. 'But then I just thought, sod it, I'll show him. And since we had that particular discussion I've discovered that he was also screwing some other tart on the side . . .' She paused, her lips quivering wickedly. 'So I'm pondering my revenge.'

'Good for you. You mean like cutting up his suits?'

'That kind of thing, yeah.' She laughed wickedly.

As I mushed up a banana for Jo's lunch, I found myself telling her about Pete. Or rather, I gave an edited account, centring on his various infidelities, refusal to pay the bills and inability to look after Poppy.

'To tell the truth, I'd pretty much given up on men before I met Jo's dad,' I continued in a gush. 'But now everything's changed. I've never been so happy in my life. It just goes to show, sometimes Prince Charming really can come along, even if he is a bit frayed at the edges!'

'In what way is he frayed?' she asked, smirking humorously.

'Well, he's been around a bit, I suppose. And he can be a bit absent-minded. He's a painter, so he has a tendency to disappear upstairs and not come down again until midnight. But I'd rather he was doing that than off with someone else!'

If I was being insensitive, Trish did not appear to notice. 'What kinds of pictures does he paint?' she asked, still smiling.

'Oh, landscapes and stuff. As a matter of fact I'm not actually allowed to see what he's working on at the moment. He's incredibly secretive.'

I stopped, embarrassed by how much I'd revealed. I had, after all, only just met the woman. I had been tactless, I realised, boasting about how perfect my life was when she was alone.

'So,' I said quickly. 'Do you know if you're having a boy or a girl?'

9

SOUTHEAST ENGLAND was stuck under high pressure, bringing still grey days in which nothing seemed to change. It was the drabbest month. How can one feel joyous when the sky is the colour of puddles and everything is covered by mud? In the few patches of grass that remained in our back yard, snowdrops were appearing, but the memory of how the creek could glisten in the sun like a string of diamonds, or the call of the summer swifts, was too distant to grasp. Inside the warehouse the ground floor was still only partially laid. The kitchen remained unfitted and the top floor was uninhabitable.

Poppy still woke at night, only sleeping through when I allowed her into my bed. There were more letters, too. They usually appeared on the mat at weekends, but she always got to them before me, bearing the envelopes silently to her room. One morning, when she was at school, I finally gave in to my curiosity and searched her room. I found no sign of them: not under her bed, or at the back of her drawers, or folded beneath her mattress. Yet I was sure she was keeping secrets, turning away from me, closing up like the petals of a flower denied light.

It was around this time that I received an odd phone call. I was in the bedroom dozing with Jo when the shrill bleep of the phone dragged me into bleary wakefulness. Grabbing the receiver, I hauled myself up.

'Hello?' It was a man's voice, brusque and slightly slurred, as if its owner had been drinking. 'Stenning there?'

'No, he's not,' I snapped, already affronted. 'Who's calling?'

The caller chuckled unpleasantly. 'Don't worry who I am, darling. Coming in later, is he?'

I sniffed huffily, on the brink of retorting that Si's movements were none of his damn business. 'He's away at the moment,' I said stiffly. 'Can I take a message?'

More sleazy laughter. I pictured a fat, pink man, with hairy arms and tattoos; a builder, no doubt.

'Sure can, love. Tell him Boz called and that I'm getting a teeny bit fed up.' Then he rang off.

I punched in Si's mobile phone number and he answered immediately. 'Hello.'

'It's me. Where are you?'

'On site. I'm just measuring up these banisters . . .'

'A man phoned you.'

'Uhuh . . .'

'Called Boz. He was very rude.'

Silence. I could feel the tension ratcheting up my responses.

'He said he was getting fed up. Who the hell is he?'

A longer silence.

'Aren't you going to answer?' My voice was small and whiney.

'He isn't anyone. Look, I'm right in the middle of something. I'll call you back, OK?'

For the second time that afternoon, my line went dead.

Later that evening, Poppy appeared by my side as I was bobbing Jo in the baby bath in our half-finished bathroom. Her face was dreamy, her finger trailing slowly along the untiled wall. She had changed from her school clothes into a floaty white ballet dress and gold-spangled sandals taken from her dressing-up bag. For a while she just stood beside me, gazing down at my sudsdy arms as I squeezed water from the sponge on to Jo's tummy. It was a new game, and he loved it, throwing back his arms and giggling in delight as the water splashed his skin.

'Look at Joey,' I murmured. 'He likes being tickled.'

She wasn't listening. She leaned against me. 'Mummy?' she said. 'Is there still a ghost in this house?'

I stopped squeezing the sponge, my hands hanging motionless above the bath. 'Of course not, sweetheart!' I said brightly. 'Why do you ask?'

'There's this big fat person creeping along the gallery. I saw them coming out of that room where Si paints all his pictures.'

'What?' Throwing down the sponge, I stared at her in horror. 'Are you telling fibs, Poppy?'

'No!'

Grabbing Jo from his bath, I wrapped his streaming body in a towel, then bundled him onto the changing mat, fastening his nappy with an angry tug. I should not be reacting with such irritation. If I were a good mother I would be asking her calmly for details, trying to discover why she was making up such stories. But I was too tired for empathy, my nerves rubbed raw.

'I don't believe you! How can there be someone wandering around upstairs? How on earth would they have got inside the building?'

I was shouting at her now. Bending her head, she started to snivel. 'I'm just telling you what I saw. Why do you always tell me off?'

'Oh Jesus, this is all I need!' Picking up Jo, I marched out of the room. 'Come on then, show me this ghost!'

There was no one wandering around the gallery. There couldn't be. I had taken care to lock all the doors to the building when we returned from school. As we reached the steps that led to the loft, we stopped, gazing up. As usual, the door was fastened with a large metal padlock.

'You haven't been playing up there, have you?'

'It's locked!'

'You know how dangerous it is—'

'*I haven't been up there!* Why do you always think I'm doing bad things?' She was howling now, her reddened face scrunched with misery. Softening, I put my free hand on her shoulder and gave it a rub. If I had not been holding Jo, I would have pulled her into my arms.

'All right, honey. I shouldn't have been cross. It's just that the idea of you going up there gives me the willies. Now, let's put Jo on your bed. You can look after him while I have a look round.' Moving into her room, I placed Jo on her duvet, bolstering his body with pillows. 'You can watch him for me. Just stay there, OK?'

She nodded silently, placing her hand gently on his tummy. Leaning over him, she started to croon a lullaby in his ear. As I reached the door, she stopped singing. 'It's a bad person,' she said. 'They want to hurt us.'

Ignoring this, I stalked back along the gallery and down the stairs. It was dark down here; the only source of light was the glimmer of the soundless TV; deserted by viewers in the centre of the den. Walking towards it, I squatted down and switched it off. Straightening up, I stood motionless, listening. The building was silent, an unnatural hush, as if someone were holding their breath. Around me, dim shapes loomed: the bulk of the sofa; a heap of something on the floor; the hulk of unpacked boxes, behind which the man might be hiding.

No. I was not going to feel afraid. This tale of an intruder was merely one of Poppy's stories, a ruse to grab my attention. Striding purposefully across the room, I flicked on the light, glancing around the littered space in relief. The shapes on the floor had been formed by a large pile of cuddly toys; the boxes revealed no lurking figures. Trotting down the corridor, I glanced quickly around the kitchen. The door was locked; the windows closed. There was no one here.

Returning to the living room, I climbed the stairs to the gallery.

'Pops!' I called. 'Are you and Jo OK?'

Taking her lack of response as affirmation, I moved along the gallery to the metal steps that led to the locked door at the top. There would be nothing up there, I was sure. All the same, as I started to climb, my pulse jumped skittishly.

The padlock was the sort that was released by a security number rather than a key. Twisting the components into the correct code, I pulled it apart and pushed up the hatch door, which swung back with a crash against the wall. We hadn't rewired up here yet, so there was no light. For a short while I stood on the threshold of the room, gazing into its dark interior as the roof beams and lumpy walls came into focus. Through the windows the cloudy evening sky dimly radiated. As I stepped on to the broken floorboards I tried to make out the skulking shapes. A pile of dustsheets; Si's work bench, which he used for sawing; an old CD player, splattered with paint.

'Is anyone there?' My breath puffed white in the frigid air.

The question was ludicrous. How could there be anyone hiding up here? Glancing over at the winch-house door, I turned sharply away. In August I had stood in the hot sun in this very spot, my head resting on Si's shoulder. Now everything had changed. Si was gone, and the building that had once promised us a happy future remained unfinished, its echoing rooms empty and dark. I stepped back through the doorway and clicked the padlock back into place.

Back on the gallery, I opened the doors of the empty rooms and peered inside: just rubble, broken boards and crumbling walls. Moving on, I turned to the last room, which Si had been using as a studio. I had not been in here for almost a month. Stepping inside, I gazed around: the usual muddle of paints and rags was strewn about, an easel leaning against the paintings of the marsh. In the corner was a stack of the charcoal sketches of me, asleep with Jo.

But it was not these that attracted my attention. Directly opposite the door, leaning against the window, was a huge canvas that I had not yet seen. In the gloom, I could make out a vast painting of a nude. She had the same angular bones and jutting hips as the woman I had seen in Si's London kitchen. At her sharp breasts was what must have been a tiny infant, but looked more like a wound: an indistinguishable scrawl of reds and pinks. The woman's head was turned away, her features blurred. The background was splattered with what appeared to be splotches of blood.

The picture exuded a violence that made the heat rise in my cheeks. Was this what Si really felt about me and Jo? No wonder he had not wished me to see his latest work. Turning away, I walked from the room, slamming the door behind me. Now, as I paused outside on the gallery, I heard a sudden thump.

'Poppy?'

From her bedroom came the sound of Jo shrieking vigorously.

'What the hell's going on?'

Bursting into the room, I saw Jo wriggling on the floor, his face puce.

'What the hell have you done to him?'

Scooping him up, I cradled his rigid body. There were no obvious bumps, just a red mark on the side of his cheek where presumably he had hit the floor. As I turned furiously towards Poppy, crouched in the corner of her room, she jumped up, placing her hands over her ears.

'I don't want to hear your shouting! He just fell off!'

'You were meant to be watching him!'

'I couldn't, could I? The ghost was outside, running away!'

I had finally had enough. Yanking her up by her sleeve, I pulled her to her feet, then grabbed her wrist, my fingers digging into her skin. *'Will you stop lying?'*

'I'M NOT LYING!'

We stood in the middle of the room, eyeballing each other. I wanted to shake out a confession, but suddenly she crumpled into a flouncy heap of ballerina dress. 'You just don't love me any more!'

'Oh, honey, I do!'

And now I was sobbing too, holding Jo with one arm and Poppy with the other; a soggy bundle of need and regret.

When Si finally called, I was asleep. Surfacing from uneasy dreams, I reached groggily for the phone. 'Hello?'

'It's me.'

From the hubbub of voices in the background, he was obviously in a bar. Glancing at my clock, I saw that it was nearly eleven. I pictured him huddled in some south London pub with Ollie and the lads.

'I'm asleep. Why didn't you call back earlier?'

He paused, catching the accusation in my tone. 'Sorry, but I've had a hard day.'

I was spark awake now, my anger rekindling into bright, shooting flame. If he thought that measuring and cutting up bits of wood was hard he should try a day alone with Jo and Poppy in a semi-derelict warehouse booby-trapped with power saws, broken floorboards and suspected prowlers.

'Well, so have I,' I retorted. 'Jo fell off the bed and Poppy thought she saw someone wandering along the gallery again.'

'But there wasn't anyone there?'

'Of course there wasn't. She's just making things up to get attention.'

'Well, that's all right then, isn't it?'

I did not reply. In the background I could hear the chink of glasses and a sudden burst of laughter. Four or five seconds passed in silence. As I shivered in the dark I could focus only on how deserted I felt.

'And who the hell is Boz?' I demanded angrily. 'It's not very nice, you know, answering the phone to some crook who's after your husband.'

'He's not a crook,' Si said evenly. 'He's a tiler. He's fed up because we're behind on the job.'

'So why's he ringing me in Kent?'

'Because he's a prize prat.'

Another long pause. 'When are you coming home?' I mumbled. 'I miss you so much.'

'I know, babe. I miss you too.' He sounded defeated. 'But we've got to work flat out to meet the deadline.' He paused. 'Ol's talking about doing a big push over the weekend.'

I stared across the dim room. I did not feel I could bear for Si to be away a single night longer.

'Fine.'

'Don't guilt-trip me, Mel—'

'I'm not guilt-tripping you, I'm just tired. I'm sorry if I've been grumpy but I need to go back to sleep. Good night.'

Without waiting for his reply, I switched off the phone.

A few days later, Trish dropped by to pick up a bag of Jo's newborn baby clothes. Since that first morning in our kitchen, when we had talked with such intensity about men and life, we met up most days.

Now, as she rummaged through the bag, I was trying to explain why I felt so angry with Si.

'I mean, I know he has to work. It's just that I'm so fed up with dealing with everything alone.'

I stopped. She had pulled out a tiny blue Babygro and was holding it adoringly to the light.

'Oh, sorry, I should shut up about dealing with things alone.'

Trish shook her head, laughing. 'Don't *worry*! I'm completely fine with being a single mother. Saves a lot of hassle, if you ask me.'

'I can't exactly imagine you being single for long.' Despite the dark rings around her almond-shaped eyes, she was looking beautiful.

'But I will be! I'm finished with men. Don't look at me like that, Mel! It's the way I want it.'

'Really?'

'Well, take you, for example. I know you love Si, but does he *really* make you happy? I mean, from the outside it seems like all you do is fret and get upset because he's not here.'

I bit my lip. Was this really the impression I had given?

'You're worried that he's playing away, right?' she continued. I stared into her concerned face. I had been skirting around the idea for weeks, but she was right. The real reason why I did not like Si working in London was that I was unable to quell my paranoia about Rosa's continued presence in his life.

'That's how I was always feeling, too,' Trish continued. 'It drives you mad, doesn't it? Eats into you so you can't stop thinking about it.'

'It's not quite as bad as that . . .'

'No?' She eyed me sceptically.

'I mean, Si wouldn't do anything to jeopardise what we've got.'

She gave a low chuckle. 'Yeah, well . . .'

'He really loves me,' I said, feeling the colour rising in my cheeks. 'I know he does. Once he finishes this job and we've got the money side of things sorted, it's going to be fine.'

'I really hope it will, for your sake,' Trish said sadly. 'It's just that, in my experience, when men start suddenly having to be away all the time, it means trouble. I guess I'm a bit biased.' She shrugged, smiling kindly. 'But maybe your bloke's different,' she added lightly.

'He *is* different! I mean, I know all you've heard so far is me whingeing on about things, but wait until you meet him. Si's lovely. And he really adores Jo and Poppy.'

She nodded, but said nothing.

'Ooh look,' I said brightly, turning towards the window with a fake cheer that would surely fool no one. 'It's gone all misty!'

From the plate-glass windows I could discern the tips of the boat masts protruding through the murk, but the creek and surrounding marshes had vanished.

Later that day, swaddling Jo in blankets, I tramped up the muddy lane to collect Poppy from school, returning half an hour later with my damp hair flopping over my forehead and Poppy dragging behind. As we plodded past the boats, I noticed a large silver van appearing through the mist. It was parked behind my car, an unusual spot for someone merely visiting the yard. I was not expecting a visitor, and as we approached my skin prickled with unease.

Gripping the handle of the buggy, I passed the van's tail lights, noticing that the engine was running. It must be someone with work in the boat yard, or perhaps it was a delivery of kitchen fittings. Yet as I glanced through the windscreen, what I saw made my guts contract.

Slumped inside the van was a thick-set man, his large hands clutching the wheel, his eyes staring ahead. He was either completely bald, or he had shaved his head, skinhead style. As he registered my presence he turned and stared at me, his gaze moving slowly up and down my body and then towards Poppy, who had caught up and now silently placed her hand in mine. For a ghastly second or so, he grinned, then reversed the van down the drive and disappeared into the mist.

Poppy tugged at my hand. 'What was that man doing, Mummy?'

'I don't know. Perhaps he was lost.'

'He looked really horrible.'

'Well, he's gone now.'

I spent the rest of the afternoon watching kids' TV with Poppy. Then I cooked her some tea and ran her bath. I fed Jo until his eyes rolled back in his head and he went limp with sleep, read Pops a story and tucked her into my bed.

It was dark now, the fog impenetrable. I sat in the kitchen, supping a glass of wine and trying to forget about the man in the silver van.

I drained a second glass of Merlot, my senses sufficiently numbed. In a short while I would stumble up the stairs and crawl into bed. Then finally I could blank out. The van driver must have been taking a break, I told myself. Perhaps he had turned in the wrong direction at the bottom of the lane and was trying to get his bearings.

Standing up, I began to clear the clutter, lifting plates to the sink in a half-drunken muddle. When I heard a crash from the yard outside, I gasped, almost dropping the pan that I was about to dunk in the water. Now the handle of the kitchen door was being rattled and turned, and through the frosted glass I could see a figure, pressed up against the door. I stood frozen by the sink, my heart stalling.

It was Si. Dropping his bag on the floor, he pulled off his wire specs and blinked at me tiredly. He had lost weight since last week, his threadbare clothes hanging off his thin frame, his long hair hanging lankly over his face.

'You gave me a start!' I bounded across the kitchen, my arms out to hug him. 'I thought you were a burglar,' I whispered as I buried my face in his overcoat. 'Why didn't you ring and tell me you were coming?'

His hand hovered over my hair. Then, suddenly, he pulled it away. 'It was a snap decision,' he said flatly. 'There's an unexpected delay on the flooring, so there isn't anything to do.'

I glanced up at him, about to ask more, but he seemed terribly tired, standing lifelessly in the middle of the breeze-block kitchen as I clasped my arms round his waist.

'But it's great to see you,' I said, slipping my arms inside his coat. Yet, rather than pulling me closer, Si shuddered slightly and broke away.

'It was a pig of journey,' he muttered. 'Thick fog all the way down.'

'Oh, poor you. Come and sit down. I'll get you something to eat.'

I was propelling him across the floor, willing him to take off the coat and let me cook for him, like in the early days of our relationship when he would sit at the table, doodling and regaling funny stories as we shared a bottle of wine. Yet as Si stood on the opposite side of the table, not sitting down, but gazing unhappily at the mound of mail that had accumulated there, the disjunction between how we used to be and how we now were made these simple aspirations appear impossible.

'More bloody bills . . .'

Money and the warehouse were subjects hemmed in with difficulty. Moving to his side and stroking his arm, I tried to divert his attention.

'Have you eaten, honey?'

He didn't reply, but gazed in a befuddled way across the kitchen.

'Si . . . are you all right?'

For a moment, as he looked around him, I thought he was on the verge of saying something, but then his mobile started to bleep. As he pulled the phone from his pocket, I noticed that both his hands were shaking. He pressed it to his ear and then walked rapidly out of the kitchen, taking care to kick the door shut behind him.

I picked up a glass and poured myself some more wine, then sat down at the table. Why was he always so secretive? We were meant to be partners. Ten, fifteen minutes passed. Si was clearly not going to return to the kitchen. Chucking the remains of the wine into the sink, I wandered groggily through the door and down the dark corridor into the warehouse.

The ground floor was in darkness. Fumbling up the stairs, I began to make my way along the gallery. Perhaps I would find Si soaking in the bath, his mood more relaxed and expansive. I was determined that we should not end the day so estranged.

He was not in the bathroom, but lying on the bed.

'Poppy was here,' he said as I pushed open the door. 'I've put her back in her bed.'

'She keeps having her nightmares so I've been letting her sleep here.'

Sitting down, I tentatively stroked his hand. It remained limp, his fingers not returning my touch. 'Who was on the phone?'

His eyes flicked away, fixing on a point somewhere above my head.

'Just someone about the build.'

'What's the matter?'

He winced in irritation. 'Nothing. I've got a headache, that's all.'

'Something's happened, hasn't it? Tell me what it is.'

Sighing, he finally turned to look at me. 'For God's sake, Mel, stop going on at me. It's just more crap about money, OK?'

My mouth was dry. I swallowed, trying to remain calm. 'You've lost so much weight,' I said, placing my head on his chest. 'Ol's been working you too hard.'

Sliding my hand over his stomach, I pushed my fingers downwards. 'It's been too long,' I whispered. 'Come and give me a kiss.'

As I lifted my face upwards, his mouth found mine. He kissed me hard and I began to relax, leaning against him as my body started to melt. Everything was going to be all right, after all. Like he said, it was just something boring to do with money. Sex was all that was required to pump the intimacy back into our marriage. We had not made love for so long; that was why things were so strained.

Then suddenly Si sat up, pushing me away. 'No, Mel, I can't . . .'

Falling back against the pillows, I gawped at him in mortification. 'Why the hell not?'

'I'm knackered,' he said shortly. 'And I've got a splitting headache.'

My cheeks were on fire. 'You don't love me any more,' I whispered.

It was the wrong thing to say, but I had drunk nearly a bottle of wine and his sudden refusal had unravelled my good sense. In the summer he would have pulled me into his arms, telling me to stop talking nonsense. But the summer was long past and everything had changed.

'For God's sake, don't start on that,' he said wearily. Swinging his legs over the edge of the bed, he stood up. 'I'm sorry, babe. I've got flu coming on or something. I feel like shit.'

'Where are you going?'

'If it's OK with you, I'm going to sleep on the sofa. I really need to get a good night's sleep and what with Jo and Poppy coming in . . .'

He stopped, his hand resting lamely on the handle. His eyes were sad, as if he was grieving about something he could not share. As I took in his dishevelled appearance, which once I had found so charming, I felt as if a boulder of grief were lodged in my chest. He was a stranger, really. I had believed we were close, but it turned out that the threads that connected us were as tenuous as gossamer.

'OK,' I said. 'Good night.'

When I woke, the fog was gone. I lay for a while on my back, listening to Jo's even breathing as the weak winter sun fell in patches across the bed. It was seven in the morning and Jo's last feed had been at midnight. For the first time since November I had slept for seven glorious hours without interruption. Now, as I rose on to my elbows and gazed at his plump face, I felt unaccustomedly well rested. Poppy had not woken either. My head was clear, like a smeared mirror that had been polished. It was a new day, the sun was finally shining, and I was filled with purpose.

Swinging my feet energetically onto the floor, I walked across the room and pulled up the blinds to the north-facing window, gazing out at the creek. A milky mist furled softly over the water, lapping mildly at the boats, then dissolving as it rose into hazy pink sunlight. Further away the marshes had been transformed into fairyland: the swirling white vapours twisting around the silhouetted trees before giving way to the sun. Pushing open the window, I breathed in the cold air. From now on, everything would improve. Jo was going to sleep through the night, Poppy's nightmares would cease, and whatever schism had taken place in my marriage would be healed.

Turning from the view, I wandered towards the small, west-facing porthole on the far side of the room which looked out across the drive and towards the boat yard. I thought I had heard the sound of a car's engine, moving down the lane. Now, as I wiped my hand across the grimy glass, I heard the distinct clunk of a car door being shut. I peered down at the drive, my heart jolting. Si's van had gone, I saw. In its place was a police car, its uniformed inhabitant at that very moment stepping round the puddles and approaching the front door.

'Good morning!'

The police officer gave me a perfunctory smile, cupping his identification badge in his palm. I glanced at it unseeingly, then up at his smooth-cheeked, youthful face. His uniformed presence, here on my doorstep, with his thick boots and the businesslike truncheon that hung from his belt, was causing my pulse to skitter with alarm.

'Am I speaking to Mrs Stenning?'

'Yes?'

Si was dead. He'd decided to go back to London and had crashed the van on the icy motorway. It was like a scene in the soap operas I'd taken to watching. This was the bit where the policeman asked if he might step inside. Then, as he imparted his news, I would collapse against the wall moaning with grief, one hand clamped over my mouth.

'Is your husband by any chance at home?'

My first reaction was relief, hot viscous stuff that pumped into my arteries, making me light-headed. 'I don't know,' I said faintly. 'His van isn't here. I'll go and have a look.'

Turning, I glanced around the living room. A folded duvet was heaped on the end of the sofa, but there was no sign of Si's clothes. Despite the story about the undelivered flooring, he must have risen early and returned to London without bothering to tell me. Feeling the disappointment fur my mouth, I hurried across the living room and down the corridor, hastily surveying the empty kitchen. After what had happened last night, his sudden departure smarted like a slap.

'He's already left,' I announced, returning to the front door. Upstairs I could hear Poppy's feet pattering along the gallery. In a minute or so she would be scampering down the staircase. Once she was in the living room she'd turn on the TV and jump onto the sofa, waiting for me to produce breakfast. It was our morning routine, as fixed and predictable as Monday following Sunday.

'Could you tell me where he is?'

'Up in London, working on a renovation.'

I scrutinised the policeman's bland, business-like expression. Now that my initial panic had subsided, a new emotion was developing: curiosity, mixed with blurry unease. 'Is it something urgent?'

He ignored the question. 'Do you have a number where we can contact him? Or the address where he's working?'

'Not exactly the address. It's just some building site where they're refurbishing this house . . .' I trailed off, embarrassed at my ignorance. 'You can always call him on his mobile.'

He nodded. 'Yes, we'll try that later. In the meantime, may I come inside for a moment? It won't take long.'

'Sure.' I stepped aside. What the hell was going on?

The policeman stepped into the untidy lobby. 'Do you have any idea who these people are?' He had produced a hard-backed copy of a photograph from his pocket.

I stared at the picture, my insides clenching. It showed a grinning couple relaxing on a boat deck. Behind them the sea was turquoise. The man was facing the camera, his arm flung over the woman's shoulders. I couldn't make out her features, but it was clear that she was beautiful. Her head was turned towards her lover, her eyes gazing at him. It must have been windy, for tumbling black curls flicked across her cheeks and into the corners of her laughing mouth.

It was Si and the woman whose nude portrait I had seen hanging in his London kitchen. My husband in another, happier life: his body less hunched and thin, his skin tanned and hair bleached from the sun. A good-looking man, clutching a beautiful girl who adored him. *Rosa*. The image winded me; everything I had longed that my marriage should be had been turned into a mockery by the couple's confident joy. What was it that his mother had said? *You're not as young and pretty as Rosa*. Thrusting the picture back into the policeman's hands, I folded my arms defensively.

'It's my husband. He looks a lot younger so it must have been taken a while ago. The woman's his ex-girlfriend.'

The policeman licked his lips. 'Does the name Rosa Montague mean anything to you?'

'Yes. That's her.'

'We're conducting a missing person's investigation,' he continued blandly. 'Ms Montague has been missing since before Christmas. We found this photograph by her bedside. We were curious about the identity of her friend.'

'She used to live with my husband in London,' I muttered. 'When I met him the relationship was over.'

'And that was when?'

'The Christmas before last. He'd finished with her some time before that though.'

'So you met him in December 2003?'

I nodded.

'Right.' Taking out his notepad, the policeman scribbled something down. 'Thank you. That's helpful.'

He was almost turning towards the door, almost bringing the interview to a close. Just because Si's ex-girlfriend kept a photograph of him, it meant nothing. So, she had disappeared. This did not mean that Si was involved. There was nothing whatsoever to worry about. But the policeman's boot was still on the step.

'There's just one other thing . . . We found your husband's credit cards in Rosa Montague's property,' he added casually. 'Were you aware that they were missing?'

My face swamped crimson. I spread my hands over my cheeks, trying to hide my confusion. Si had said he'd left the cards at Ol's in London! I took a deep breath, trying to steady myself.

'He lost them . . .' My heart was beating so fiercely the policeman must surely hear. 'I think he must have had them replaced by now.'

'I see . . .'

The officer gazed thoughtfully at me, perhaps hoping for further revelations. Was he aware of the devastation that his question had caused? Even if I had more to say, I would not have been able to speak.

'Here's a card with the number of the enquiry room,' he said chattily, pushing the pad back into his pocket. 'If you could get your husband to contact us when he comes in, I'd be grateful.'

'What about his mobile phone number?'

'We've already got that number. Thank you for your time.'

I gazed after him. He was turning now, about to step through the door. Did they really have enquiry rooms for every person that went missing? And how had they got hold of Si's mobile number?

'Try not to worry, Mrs Stenning,' he said, smiling. 'All we want to do at this stage is to eliminate your husband from our enquiries.'

Nodding at me, he walked across the drive and opened the door to his car. I closed the front door, my mind stalling. I could hear the car starting up, then the crunch of gravel under its wheels. For a moment, before I girdled in my panic and returned to Poppy and Jo and the preparations for their breakfast, I sagged against the closed door. All the time I thought Si was with Ollie, he was with *her*!

10

DAVE GOSFORTH TUTTED as he pushed the car into second. He had not been expecting such a remote or muddy track. The cottage was in the middle of thick woodland. He could see its crooked chimney rising from the trees like the witch's house in *Hansel and Gretel*. Inwardly cursing Clive Jenkins, the detective inspector whose call had interrupted a cosy morning with his paperwork, Dave changed gear again. As he'd said on the phone to Clive, this had better be something interesting.

After five minutes of navigating round the potholes, the car finally reached the bottom of the dell. Now Dave could see the property in its entirety: a small wooden-fronted house surrounded by the weedy remains of what might once have been a pretty cottage garden. The place had, however, been left to rack and ruin, and the grasses of what might once have been a pretty lawn were invaded by thistles and sycamore saplings. Pulling up on the verge, Dave climbed from his car.

The place looked like a slum. If he had a cottage like this, he'd turn it into a little palace. Then he'd set to work in the garden. His old dad had kept an allotment, so he'd learned all he'd need to know about vegetables from him. There'd be plenty of flowers, too: busy Lizzies and geraniums, maybe a rose bed or two, not these wild grasses. Banishing the fantasy, he stepped past the rotting gate and walked up the path.

The front door was open, and he could hear voices coming from inside. Striding into the narrow hall, Dave peered around. In contrast to the neglected appearance of the outside, the inside of the cottage was surprisingly well kept. He took in a neat front parlour, filled with china knick-knacks and classy antique furniture. It was probably the home of an elderly person, most likely a woman. The kitchen was a relic from the 1960s, or even earlier, but despite the aged feeling of the room, and the smell of damp, it was spotless. There were even two laundered tea towels, their corners folded back fancily, arranged symmetrically on the work surface. It was an odd touch.

'Dave!'

Turning from the kitchen door, he saw Clive Jenkins approaching from the bottom of the narrow stairs. The two men shook hands. They'd worked on a firearms case in Ramsgate a year back. The memory of a satisfactory result produced a pleasant glowing sensation in Dave, which spilled into a wide smile for his more junior colleague.

'What have we got, then?'

'A young woman who's gone missing. The lady who owns this place, Mrs Montague, rang us on Monday. She was concerned about her niece, who's been living here.'

'Right . . .'

'Apparently the niece hasn't been in contact since Christmas. The aunt's tried to call her, but she doesn't pick up the phone. It was the aunt's birthday last week and the niece had promised to come and see her in London, but she didn't show up. The old lady's getting on a bit and can't come down here herself, so she calls us.'

'And you come down here and have a look around . . .'

'. . . and what we find is that the place is all shut up, as you can see. Everything's clean and tidy, letters on the mat date from December, there's no food left rotting, no obvious evidence of a sudden disappearance. There's some personal effects that we've been checking out, including a man's credit cards that we found in her kitchen drawer, but to be honest we're not too concerned. Looks like you said. The young lady's just gone away . . .'

'. . . and forgotten to tell her aunt.' Dave folded his arms. It was as he'd suspected: a wild-goose chase.

'Exactly. But wait a sec before you start bawling me out. This morning we found something rather more interesting . . .'

Gesturing towards the front room, Jenkins led Dave across the hall, ducking through the small door frame then standing aside.

'Have a look in here, sir. See if you can spot it.'

Dave peered round the small room. It was decorated with the frayed gentility of the English upper-middle classes: a worn but valuable Persian carpet; china figurines that could have featured on *Antiques Road Show*; paintings in gilded frames that looked like originals. He walked across to the windows.

'The curtain on the left of the window has had a little wash,' Dave said slowly. 'But the one on the right hasn't. It's darker.'

'Yup. There's more, too.' Clive had joined him.

Dave peered at the wall next to the curtains. 'Yeah, I see it. The wall on this side's been repainted. It's a different shade . . . someone's been doing a spot of decorating.' Now that he was close up he could clearly see an area of at least thirty tiny brown spots that had been missed by the paintbrush. 'Forensics are going to have fun with this.'

'There're also some areas on the carpet where someone's had a go with a scrubbing brush,' the younger man said.

Glancing down, Dave took in the lighter patches on the carpet where it had been cleaned. 'Very interesting.' Dave nodded at Clive Jenkins in approval. 'What do we know about the missing woman?'

'She's called Rosa Montague. Lived here for about a year. There's a photo we can use. Had a boyfriend who was away a lot. The aunt hasn't met him, but we've got his details off his credit cards. I got the impression that the niece has a private income.'

'Have you contacted the boyfriend?'

'My lads are on it today.'

'Any other family or friends?'

Before Jenkins could answer, there was a sharp cry from the garden. Glancing through the leaded panes of the sitting-room window, Dave saw a uniformed officer, running across the garden.

'Over here!' he was shouting.

How does it feel when the surface on which you're treading gives way? Until those dreadful five minutes with the policeman on my doorstep, I still believed the ground beneath me to be solid. Now, unable to get a foothold, I tumbled into a strange territory that I did not recognise. Suddenly everything I thought was real was gone; a joke almost.

Si was still involved with his ex-girlfriend. Or rather, his former ex-girlfriend. *Rosa*. She had long dark hair and a model's body, and her elegant hands were draped round his shoulders as if this was their natural resting place. He had promised that the relationship was over, yet he was still visiting her, their intimacy sufficiently intact for her to keep his photo displayed. Now, as I brooded over every twist and turn of my marriage, Rosa's slanting shadow fell across my view. Nat had been right, damn her. This woman was the reason why he had taken such fright at the news of my pregnancy; it was to *her* place that he had scarpered. What had caused his sudden reappearance? A temporary lover's tiff? The thought of his hands on her body, and hers on his, made my stomach turn. As I pushed Jo back from the school, I had to clutch at the buggy handles to stop myself from keeling over.

Back home, I gave in to despair, curling foetally on the sofa and snivelling as Jo chewed on his teething ring. I felt such a fool. All the time that I had been immersed in my cosy fantasy of family life, Si had remained involved with Rosa. Conceivably, he had only married me out of pity. Whatever the reason, he did not love me enough to relinquish the stunning Rosa, in whose house he had only a few short months ago left his credit cards and whose calls he was still receiving.

Dragging myself off the sofa to change Jo's nappy, I realised that for a few short months I had been wandering in a world where I did not belong. I had crashed through the thin skein that had temporarily separated me from reality: single parenthood, a thickening, ageing body, and a life set apart.

Or was I over-dramatising? As the morning wore on, I convinced myself that things were not so bad. Perhaps Si had business affairs with this Rosa that needed sorting out. The papers, for instance, that she had taken from his mother: he would have needed to retrieve them. *That* was why he had been back in her house. It was a one-off, not worth mentioning. If, many weeks later, she had disappeared, leaving Si's photo by her bed, it had nothing to do with him. As the policeman had said, they merely wanted to eliminate Si from their enquiries. As he had insisted, I should trust him.

But just as I was starting to believe this benign version of events, I recalled the other phrase that the policeman had used. *At this stage*.

I made myself some lunch, then summoned the courage to call Si on his mobile. It was not rational, but I believed that his response would decide everything.

He picked up almost immediately.

'Hi!'

I could not speak. I had not expected such warmth in his voice, and tears clogged my throat. In the background I could hear the unmistakable crash of hammers.

'What's up?'

'I . . . I didn't know where you'd gone.'

'I'm sorry, babe. I was going to call you, but we've been rushed off our feet. Ol texted me last night to say that the flooring guys had fast-tracked the order and were delivering first thing this morning. If—'

'The police have been here,' I wailed. 'They want to talk to you.'

There was a long silence. Finally, Si said, 'Hang on, I'm going outside.' When he next came on the line his voice was muffled, as if he was cupping his hand over his mouth.

'What do you mean, the police want to talk to me?'

'A policeman was here this morning. They've found your credit cards.'

I pressed the receiver hard against my ear, willing him to produce an obvious explanation, some miraculous truth that would absolve him.

'My credit cards?' Si finally echoed. He sounded scared.

'Yes. They found them in your girlfriend's house.'

Another long pause. My heart was plummeting at his failure to deny that Rosa Montague was his girlfriend. Then: 'So why do they want to talk to me?'

'Why do *you* think?'

'I have absolutely no idea.'

'They said she's gone missing.'

He was silent. Perhaps he was working out what to say.

'Are they coming back?' he asked eventually.

'I don't know. There's a number for you to ring.'

If only I could see his face, then I would know the truth.

'You're still seeing her, aren't you?'

'No!'

'So how come your cards were at her cottage?'

'I had to go and see her to get the deeds of the flat back. I left them there. She's been playing these games with me—'

'But that was ages ago!'

'I know, but I had to go and sort some other things out with her. I swear this isn't how it looks, Mel.'

'Isn't it?' Squeezing my eyes shut, I blinked away more tears.

'Mel?'

'What?' From the kitchen came the sound of Jo crying.

'You do believe me, don't you?'

I glanced down the corridor, now distracted by wails that were rising to a sharp crescendo. 'What did you say?'

'You do believe me?'

'I have to go,' I muttered. 'We'll talk later.'

Putting down the phone, I hurried towards Jo.

I was supposed to be meeting Trish later that afternoon, but I told her I was coming down with flu. Fifteen minutes later she was standing at the front door, her hands on her hips in a parody of bossiness.

'Come on, give me that baby! You're going to have a couple of hours' kip before Poppy gets back.'

'Are you sure?'

'Of course I'm sure! I wouldn't offer if I wasn't, would I? Anyway, I need the practice.'

'You're an angel . . .'

As soon as they had gone I started to rummage through the papers piled on the kitchen table. I had over three unencumbered hours in which to search the house. I trawled through shopping receipts, builders' invoices and letters from the bank, unsure what I was looking for. Upstairs I went through Si's clothes. I found nothing. If he had been deceiving me, surely I would discover the traces of his infidelity?

In his studio I deliberately ignored the canvas of the woman with the baby-like wound and progressed to a pile of papers, shoved into a corner. On top was a catalogue for sliding windows, lying above a plan of the garden we had hoped to build. I studied the yellowing diagram sorrowfully. Would the garden ever be grown? As I stared at the faded paper, it seemed unlikely.

Finally, languishing under more catalogues for garden furniture and a chart of paint colours, was a statement from Si's bank. It was for December to January of this year. I pulled it from the envelope, my pulse romping. To start with, there was all the usual stuff: Unwins, for a crate of 'winter warmer' wines; supermarket bills; a jewellery firm in London that I assumed had supplied my bracelet. Then, suddenly, from 15 December, I no longer recognised the creditors. There was a petrol bill from a garage in Hayward's Heath, followed, after a long interval, by a bill for £80 from a hairdresser in South Molton Street, followed by £325 from a boutique in Bond Street on 29 December. After that was a list of cash withdrawals, until the statement stopped abruptly at the end of January.

I stared at the blurring figures, trying to remember when I had lost my bag at Tesco's. It was the first week of January, I was sure. That meant that when I was struggling to pay for my groceries, someone else—Rosa Montague presumably—was spending Si's money on her appearance. Was this his Christmas treat to her, to make up for his absence? Furiously, I crushed the statement into a tight ball and flung it across the room. Later I would retrieve it, smooth out the creases and fold it into my back pocket.

That evening, as I tidied away supper, I found Poppy's big blue eyes trained on me, as if she was trying to work something out.

'What's the matter, Mummy?'

I had made a supreme effort to disguise my distress, washing my face and tidying my hair. 'Nothing's the matter!' I brightly replied. 'Why should there be?'

'It's just that you look all cryie.'

I frowned, pretending to be perplexed. 'Well, I'm not.'

'Why are your eyes so red then?'

'I'm tired, that's all.'

Wandering across the room to where she was sitting at the table, surrounded by her crayons, I put my arm round her shoulders and kissed the top of her head, inhaling the sweet smell of her hair.

'What are you drawing?'

'It's just a picture of that ghost that I saw by the stairs.'

I stared at the paper, first turning cold, then very hot. As I had been clearing up, Poppy had produced a picture of the warehouse. She had made it very tall and narrow, with lots of boxy little windows facing out. Standing in front of the building were three stick people of descending sizes, holding hands. It was not these who attracted my attention, however; it was what she had drawn at the top. In the pointed roof she had depicted the dormer windows as a large rectangle. In the middle, staring out, was a purple face: a large head, with round eyes, a stick nose, and a big O for its mouth.

'Who's that?'

'It's the ghost.'

I did not know what to say. I cleared my throat. 'And who are those people at the bottom?' I asked eventually.

'That's you and me and Jo.'

'What about Si?'

She started to slide off her seat, grabbing my hand as she pulled me away. 'He doesn't live here any more.'

The children were asleep and I was painting the downstairs cloakroom. The physical activity was surprisingly therapeutic. With every swipe of the roller I was obliterating the ugly, scuffed surface of the wall and turning it into a vibrant canary yellow that defied melancholy. If only I could wipe out the events of the last twenty-four hours so easily. I dabbed at the ceiling, the paint sprinkling my hair, then moved on to an adjacent wall. I was feeling increasingly fatalistic. When Si appeared I would listen to whatever he had to say. Then I would know one way or the other whether he had betrayed me.

When I heard the sound of the van pulling up in the drive, I placed the roller back in the tray, wiped my hands and pulled off my overall. Then I walked into the living room, where I stood waiting for him.

The door swung open. The weather had turned windy, and the wooden handle crashed loudly against the lobby wall. Dropping his bag by Jo's buggy, Si strode into the living room. Unlike the evening before, when he had hardly seemed to register my presence, his eyes were fixed on my face. Placing his arms round my waist, he pulled me hard towards him. I stood motionlessly in his grip, my hands hanging by my sides. So much had changed since the evening before, and now I could hardly bear for him to touch me. Finally he gave up, releasing me as he took a step backwards, staring intently into my face. Again, he looked exhausted, his face sagging, his forehead riven by deep creases.

'I know what you're thinking,' he said.

'Do you?'

'The police showed you that photograph . . . they rang me about it this afternoon. Apparently you provided an identification.'

I nodded. 'I wasn't going to lie, was I?'

'Look, Mel.' He grabbed at my arm imploringly. 'I can imagine how this appears, but you've got to believe what I've always told you. Rosa and I are finished.'

I shook his fingers angrily from my wrist. 'Oh yeah? Then why do you keep popping in to see her?'

I glared at him. His grim expression seemed to confirm all my fears. Trish was right: he had been 'playing away', and now, when confronted with the evidence of his infidelity, was not even going to deny it. It felt as if, after weeks drifting in the doldrums, the wind had unexpectedly picked up and we were whizzing towards the end of our journey.

'What were you doing at her cottage?' I whispered.

If only he would look me in the eyes. 'It's like I said, there was some business stuff to sort out. I'd hoped I'd seen the last of her, but she managed to get our number off Ol and was hassling me about various things so I had to go over there.'

'It all sounds a bit odd to me.'

'Well, that's because *she's* odd.'

'So why didn't you tell me you were going to see her?'

'Because it was too complicated.'

It was a lame excuse. 'For God's sake, stop fobbing me off! In what way was it too complicated?'

He shook his head, his face paling with rage. *'It doesn't matter!'*

I remained silent, shocked by his vehemence.

'Look,' he said more gently. 'If I could have just walked away and never laid eyes on Rosa again, I would have been overjoyed. But things were more than a bit messy. The only thing that really matters is that it's *you* I love. I promise you, Mel . . .'

He was lying. Pulling the bank statement from my jeans pocket, I handed it over. 'If you wanted to get rid of her so much, why did you let her keep using your cards?'

He unfolded the paper. For a couple of moments he made a show of glancing down the list of withdrawals, yet the speed with which he did this indicated that he was already familiar with the statement.

'I don't know what you're talking about,' he murmured.

I could bear it no longer. With a roar of fury I hurled myself at him, my fists pummelling his chest, my feet ineffectively kicking his shins.

'You're lying, you shit! You promised me you'd never, ever do that!'

He was so much stronger than me. Grabbing my arms, he pinioned them behind my back, forcing me to stagger backwards on to the dusty floorboards. Suddenly he was on top of me, his fingers were in my hair, his lips moving over my face as he covered it with kisses.

'Why can't you just believe me?' he whispered.

Closing my eyes, I began to kiss him back. For that short moment, everything fell away. *This* was the sum of things, the driving force; nothing else mattered. Extracting my twisted arm from the floor, I brought my fingers to his face.

'I love you!' he groaned. 'Please, you've got to trust me, Mel . . .'

My fingers hovered around his bent head. With one small movement, I might change everything. I could stroke his hair, whispering my absolution, or pull his face up, so that my kisses exonerated him. Yet as I lay beneath him I was overcome by revulsion. He was deceiving me. And apparently I was expected to lie back and play the role of the trusting little wife.

Pushing him off with a furious shove, I rolled over, effectively shielding myself from his touch. From the floor above, I could hear a wail.

'Jo's crying,' I said, standing up. 'He needs his feed.'

Should I have foreseen the direction in which we were heading? If I were a different woman, less needy perhaps, with a tighter grasp upon reality, would I have already packed my bags, strapped my children into the back of the car and departed? As I pick over these last terrible days, I'm searching for clues, but everything is muddied by my conflicting emotions. The evening that Si came back from London and pushed me on to the floorboards, I still wanted to love him. He was the father of my baby, the man I believed had transformed my life. Was it really so foolhardy?

Trish has brought me a piece of toast. She has placed the plate on the arm of the sofa, giving my shoulder a sympathetic squeeze before tiptoeing back towards the kitchen. I'm grateful for her sensitivity. I do not want to talk to her, or to anyone. I need to sit quietly by myself, concentrating. Something is bothering me, a buzzing at the back of my mind that refuses to hush. There's so much other noise that I can't hear it properly: every time I try to concentrate I picture Poppy, flopped in the front seat of the Volvo as Si careers towards disaster, or the expression on her face when she pulled back the curtains and found me hiding there with Jo. But if I force my mind to focus, recalling every detail of the last few days, I realise that what I'm hearing is a distant bell, ringing in some forgotten corner. At first the sound was so faint and I was so panicked that I hardly noticed. But with every hour that Poppy's gone it's growing louder: the clanging of an alarm in a place we haven't thought of yet, somewhere completely unexpected.

11

DAVE GOSFORTH HAD a good feeling about Simon Stenning, a very good feeling. He was, as he had informed his superintendent the day before, 'an important lead'. Not only were his fingerprints all over Rosa Montague's house, but the joker's grinning photo was by her bed. To top it off they had found his credit cards in the kitchen drawer. Dave's hunch was that Rosa was Stenning's kept woman, a nice bit on the side that his current wife knew nothing about. Rosa was almost certainly dead, and in cases where women suddenly disappeared it was more than often their boyfriends or husbands who had killed them. She definitely hadn't planned to go away. Her clothes were hanging in her wardrobe, and her passport, plus a pile of other personal effects, remained in her aunt's bureau. More important, Rosa's medical records had confirmed that the blood round the window was her blood.

But it was not this alone that had excited Dave, it was what they'd found in her garden. It was one of those God-given gifts, one of the finest breakthroughs of his career. A week earlier the Jacqui Jenning case was as dead as a dodo, but now they were back in business. He took in the bustling investigation room with satisfaction. The scene of crime photos, which for fifteen long months had been furling around the edges on the board, no longer depressed him. They were going to crack this one, and when they did, it was going to be big.

'Clive! Come and join me.' Dave gestured to the chair opposite. 'All ready for our little trip?'

As he sat down, Clive Jenkins nodded at him good humouredly. 'All ready and willing. You sure you want to come?'

'Yeah, it'll be interesting to have a little look at what we've got.'

'Apparently the warehouse is a wreck.' Clive was already on his feet, glancing at his watch. 'Lips sealed over Jacqui, right?'

'Of course. We're going to go in there, keep it nice and simple. See how he reacts.'

Pulling on their coats, the two men walked across the busy investigation room.

The morning after Si's return the police were back. I had dropped Poppy off at school and caught sight of their car as I turned into the lane. As I wheeled Jo into the yard, I saw that Si was opening the door to two men. The leather coat of the first and dun-coloured puffa jacket of the second, worn over chinos, told me all I needed to know: they were plain-clothed policemen, returned to interrogate Si. They stepped quickly inside, the door slamming behind them.

Overnight the wind had worked itself into a fury, the boat sails flapping frantically as they rocked from side to side, the water on the creek ruffled into sudden splashing squalls. Ahead of me the warehouse loomed into a bruised, stormy sky. I shuddered, pulling my coat tighter. I had woken with a dull ache in the pit of my stomach. Now, as I hurried through the boat yard, the pain sharpened, making me weak with dread.

I entered the building through the kitchen door, closing it quietly behind me. Pulling Jo from the buggy, I crept along the corridor, holding his body tight against my chest to muffle his crooning. Through the connecting door, I could hear the men talking.

'What if I refuse?' Si was saying. 'You can't force me.'

The high-pitched, panicky timbre of his voice caused my throat to contract. I swallowed hard, straining to hear what was said in reply. One of the policemen must have been standing on the far side of the room, for with the clatter of the wind around the building I could only hear a dim trace of his words. Then, very clearly, what I now know to be Dave Gosforth's voice said, 'It's up to you, Simon. We can either do it here, nice and relaxed without any fuss, or we can bring you in and do it at the station.'

Si said something in reply, but I was unable to catch what. Now I could hear footsteps clumping across the wooden floor. Summoning up my courage, I pushed open the door. Si was sprawled on the sofa. Squatting next to him was the man in the puffa jacket. In his plastic-bagged hand he held a swab, which he was pushing into Si's mouth.

As he did this, the man in the leather jacket was sidling up to the coffee table and examining the photograph of Poppy holding a newborn Jo, which I had framed and placed there. At the approach of my footsteps he spun round.

'Mrs Stenning?' He stretched out his large paw. For a second I allowed his fingers to brush against mine, then I pulled my hand away. His cheeks had the raw, slightly bloodied appearance of a recent shave, and the end of his sharp nose glistened with moisture. His eyes were rimmed red, as if he had a bad cold.

'Detective Chief Inspector David Gosforth, Kent CID. And this is?'

'Jo.' I clutched his warm head a little more tightly to my bosom, not wanting this odious man, with his dripping nose, to infect my son. 'What are you doing?'

'Your husband has very kindly agreed to give us a DNA sample.'

There was clearly nothing kind about it. Inspector Puffa Jacket had finished now, and was placing the swab into a plastic bag. Si remained seated, staring morosely at the floor.

'What for?'

'Your husband is, as we say, "helping us with our enquiries",' Gosforth said. 'We've just been having a little chat about Rosa Montague, this young lady who's gone missing.'

'What about her? He's not with her any more. He's married to me.'

To my amazement, Gosforth chuckled nastily. 'I'm sure he is,' he said. Giving me a wink, he padded across the room towards the front door, his lackey following behind.

"We'll be in touch. Don't worry, we'll show ourselves out!' he called over his shoulder. As we heard the door slam, Si sagged forwards, his head dropping into his hands.

'Are you going to tell me what's going on?'

When he looked up, his face was lifeless. For a moment he seemed to be on the verge of saying something. Then, suddenly, he stood up.

'I'm sorry, hon, I . . .' His voice broke, his pink eyes glazing. If he had stayed like that for just a second longer I would have gone to him and put my arms round his shoulders and perhaps everything would have changed. But he turned hastily away. 'I'm going upstairs,' he said.

Five minutes later I had strapped Jo into his baby seat and driven my Fiat to the top of the lane, where the car was out of view of the warehouse. Once I'd parked, my shaking fingers punched Alicia Stenning's number into my mobile. Suddenly there was a click and Alicia's voice came on the line.

'Hello?' She sounded older and more frail than I remembered.

'Alicia?'

'Yes?'

'It's Mel . . . Simon's wife?'

A long pause. For a terrible moment I feared that we had forgotten to tell her about the wedding. Then I recalled the note she had sent, written in spidery italics on an old-fashioned card with her address embossed at the top: *To Simon and his new wife, from Alicia*. If there was supposed to be a present attached, we never discovered it.

'Yes?' she said again. 'What do you want?'

'I need to see you, if it's at all possible. Simon's in trouble,' I said. 'I can't talk about it over the phone.'

'I don't know. I . . .' Her voice quavered with uncertainty.

'Please?'

'When do you want to come?'

'Now?'

'All right,' she said at last. 'But for goodness sake, don't drag me into another of Simon's messes.'

An hour later I drew up in front of the house. She must have been watching out for the car, for as I pulled on the brake the front door opened and she stepped onto the gravel drive, regarding us silently as I pulled Jo from his seat. This morning she was dressed in slacks and a black polo neck that revealed her figure as surprisingly youthful. Her long white hair was untied, the wind causing it to whip round her face. Yet whilst my eyes were on her, she was not looking at me but at Jo. This was the first time she had seen her grandson, I realised with shame. We hurried across the drive, the wind buffeting us.

'This is Jo,' I said, holding him out. 'I'm sorry it's taken me so long to bring him over.'

For a few seconds she gazed at him, her face softening. Then suddenly she frowned. 'For God's sake, girl, come in out of the weather,' she barked. 'You'll give the poor child pneumonia if you keep waving him around like that.'

We stepped into the hall, where she plucked Jo out of my arms, holding him up and examining him as if he were a pedigree puppy.

'Just like his father,' she said. 'It takes me back.'

'He's a bit of a pickle sometimes,' I mumbled.

'Well, that's the same too, then!'

Marching across the hall and into the drawing room, she competently propped Jo's small body between two large velvet cushions on the sofa, then sat beside him, clasping his tiny fingers in her hand.

'He's a bit clingy at the moment . . .' I started.

'Oh, what nonsense! We're not having that, are we, young man? Not with your grandmama? Look, you can play with these keys.'

Scooping up the car keys that I had placed on the card table next to the sofa, she dropped them in his lap. I held my breath. For a moment Jo simply stared at them, undecided. Then his fingers reached down and brought them slowly to his dribbly mouth. I breathed out in relief.

'So why have you come?' Alicia said, turning to me. 'I gather this isn't merely a social call.'

The rebuke in her voice made me flush. 'No. I'm sorry to have just landed on you like this. I really have been meaning to come over. But Si's been away, you see, working on this refurbishment . . .'

'He's not trying to be a great artist any more, then?'

'We need the money.'

She raised her eyebrows, glancing towards the empty grate with what appeared to be anger. What had happened to cause such alienation between mother and son? I stared down at my knuckles, wishing we could be friends.

'The thing is,' I mumbled. 'I mean, the reason why I came over . . . I wanted to know about Rosa,' I blurted.

To my surprise she winced. 'What do you want to know?'

I should get it over and done with. Steeling myself, I managed to look into her watery blue eyes. 'The papers she took from your house. What were they about?'

'They were the deeds to her flat.'

'To *her* flat?' I swallowed. 'So Simon didn't own the flat?'

'I can't explain the exact ins and outs of it,' she said. 'They fought a lot, I'm afraid, and poor Rosa used to come to me for advice. She told me the flat belonged to her, so I can only assume that it did. I was keeping the papers safe for her,' she said, frowning. 'Since my son never tells me anything I've only heard Rosa's side of the story.'

I felt as if I were shrivelling up. 'I see.'

'Of course her family were terribly well-to-do. According to her that was always a big draw for Simon.'

'I can't imagine him thinking like that,' I murmured.

She ignored my comment. 'I was so thrilled when he first brought her home. She was such a lovely girl. She had a knack of really making one feel appreciated. She used to send me little presents, things she'd seen that she thought I'd like. Nobody had ever done anything like that for me before, so obviously I was very taken with her. But then Simon started behaving badly and upsetting her and one day she called and told me that it was over between them.' She gave her head a little shake.

'What happened?' My voice was so faint that for a moment I assumed she hadn't heard. She stared in my direction for a while, looking me over disdainfully. No wonder she despised me. Compared with Rosa's brilliant plumage, I was as common and plain as a suburban sparrow.

'Well, she left him. Why would a lovely girl like her put up with that kind of treatment?'

I stared back at Alicia, my face fixed. *Rosa had left Si!* All this time I had assumed that *he* had finished the relationship. I realised that this changed everything.

'What kind of treatment?'

'I'm afraid he hit her, dear. He was very jealous, apparently. Poor Rosa used to put up here when it got very bad. She needed someone to stand up for her.' She stopped, regarding me thoughtfully. 'You ought to be careful of him. He can be very changeable.'

I blinked at her, remembering Si's sudden anger at my questions, the way his mood would unexpectedly shift, like the darkening of the sky. 'I don't . . .'

'So what's this trouble he's in?' she said abruptly. 'Run out of money again?'

'It's nothing really,' I said, standing. I had been considering telling her about Rosa's disappearance, but now it seemed impossible. Plucking Jo from his nest of cushions I pushed my face into his belly for a moment. I had to get out of the house, before she saw me cry.

'Look, I'm sorry, I need to go. I've just noticed the time.'

'But you've only just arrived!' Alicia was on her feet, too. Placing her hand on my arm, she halted my progress. 'What's going on?'

'I don't know—'

'What don't you know? Why won't you let me help you?'

What would happen if I told her the truth? For a moment I imagined confiding everything: Rosa's mysterious disappearance, the visits of the police, Si's 'lost' credit cards. Could I also share my gnawing fear that my short marriage was doomed?

'Well?'

She folded her arms, waiting. Stepping away from her, I stared through the large bay windows at the tossing trees beyond the lawns.

'It's just that we've run a bit short of money,' I said, trying to sound breezy. 'I think the mortgage on the flat was a bit complicated, so we're trying to work it out, that's all.'

'What was complicated about it? The flat belonged to Rosa.'

With the utmost effort, I managed a tight smile. 'Oh, I don't know. Perhaps Si and I have had a miscommunication.' I started to move across the floor towards the hall. 'I'm sorry, I really do have to go,' I burbled. 'I'm meant to be picking my daughter Poppy up early from school. There's tons of roadworks on the motorway, so . . .'

She followed me wordlessly across the hall, tugging open the front door. As I stepped into the gale, Alicia gripped my arm.

'You can go in a minute,' she said. 'But first there's something I want to show you.'

Hooking her fingers round my elbow, she led me down the side of the house, past old garages and neglected herb beds, to the back. The grounds were far larger than had been apparent from the drawing-room windows. Bracing ourselves against the blustering wind, we stood on the mossy lawns, regarding the elegant box hedge that swirled in a semicircle round the grass, the rose gardens and, at the bottom of the slope, the ornamental pond. Tall firs that divided the garden from the ploughed fields beyond.

'You see over there?' Alicia gestured to a wooded area to the east of the lawns. Following her finger, I focused on a giant oak that billowed blowsily in the gusty air. In its branches were the remains of what looked like a tree house, the derelict structure rocking violently.

'Simon made it with his father when he was eleven,' she said. 'He did a lot of it himself. He was always very talented with his hands.'

'It's certainly lasted a long time . . .' I murmured.

'He used to spend all his time in it,' she went on, ignoring me. 'In the summer he put up a camp bed and slept out here. He never wanted to play with other boys. He just wanted to build things, and draw. His father was an artist too, you see . . .'

'I didn't know that.'

She laughed bitterly. 'No, Simon never mentions poor Leo if he can help it.'

I did not know what to say. Like so many areas of his life, any tentative questions that I put to Si on the subject of his family led to his face closing as firmly as a security shutter. I stared at the tree, trying to imagine Si up there, aged eleven. He'd have been a dreamer, planning inventions and contraptions as he camped up in the trees.

'Never made any money out of it, of course,' Alicia went on. 'If it hadn't been for my family we'd have been out on the street.'

'That must have been difficult.'

She glanced round at me, one eyebrow arched. 'In the end the stupid bugger hanged himself,' she added, deadpan.

I stared at her in shock, but her face remained unchanged. *Si's father had committed suicide!* 'In the woods over there,' she said evenly. 'Si found him.'

I gasped, my hand fluttering over my mouth in horror. 'Oh my God!'

Alicia did not respond. I stared into the dense trees, trying to imagine what Si must have suffered. The thought of how little he had shared with me clogged my throat.

'How old was he?'

'Twelve or thirteen. He never forgave me. Said it was my fault.'

'But that's terrible!' Involuntarily, I had gripped her arm. Glancing down at my hand, she allowed her fingers to brush against mine. 'Yes, I suppose it is,' she said softly. 'I daresay we mishandled the whole thing. Simon was sent away to school after the funeral, and not a great deal more was said. It was only when he was older that the difficulties started.'

I nodded, still clutching her arm. 'I'm sure it's not your fault.'

For a moment a flimsy intimacy had existed between us. At this clumsy comment, however, Alicia stepped backwards, grabbing at the tendrils of hair that flapped round her face. 'Of course it's my fault.'

Turning, she tramped back over the grass towards the house. Shifting Jo higher on to my hip, I followed her miserably. Despite the veneer of intimacy that marriage and shared parenthood had brought, I was beginning to learn how little I knew about Si. As I joined his mother on the drive she was gazing up at the tossing trees. She had wanted to explain her son to me, but my reaction had been thoughtlessly mundane.

'I should get going,' I said quietly. 'Thanks so much for—'

She shook her head. 'I've been a terrible mother, Melanie,' she said. 'When Simon was a teenager, I pretty much left him to his own devices.

I simply wasn't able to show him I loved him. That's why he hates me. I only wish I could start again.' A dark flush had risen on her cheeks. 'You're a good girl, I can tell that. Love him as much as you can.'

I nodded slowly. 'I'm trying.' My voice was wobbling perilously.

Putting out her hand, she placed it around Jo's soft cheek. 'Will you bring this little one to see me again?'

'I'd love to.' Leaning towards her, I kissed her cheek. We were oddly alike, I thought as, pulling away, I gazed back at her face.

For a second or so her fingers squeezed mine. 'He used to be such a good boy,' she whispered.

I kissed her again, awkwardly, but not without feeling. Then I walked with Jo to my car.

'Bye!' I yelled over the wind. Alicia stood on the drive, watching me but not responding. By the time I had fastened Jo into the baby seat and succeeded in shutting the car doors, she had gone.

I drove home fast, swerving round fallen branches and splashing through the grey puddles that pooled in the country roads. What Alicia had told me explained a great deal about Si's moodiness and reticence to talk about his past. Yet rather than dwell on this, my thoughts returned to Rosa. Relentlessly, I churned over what Alicia had said. If she was correct and Rosa had finished with Si, then he had chosen me on the rebound from a love that he had lost. She had evicted him from *her* flat, not the other way round. Perhaps he only took up with me because he needed a place to stay. And when he returned to me in the spring with his proposal of marriage, it was because she had rejected him once more. He had said she was a bitch, but he was obviously still seeing her: he had left his credit cards in her cottage and had done nothing to stop her from using them.

Pushing into top gear, I accelerated along a stretch of open road. The car skittered along the road like a marble. So, Rosa had finished with Si. So, she was missing. Surely it did not have to mean that Si was involved? His mother had said he could be violent, but he had never hurt me, had he? Then, recalling the way he had pushed me onto the floor, my chest tightened. The police had taken a sample of his DNA. What stains had they found in Rosa's house that they wanted to match?

Jabbing at the radio, I switched to a local station, trying to concentrate on the anodyne tone of the presenter. There was to be a phone-in concerning the provision of local care homes for the elderly. Taut with impatience, I jabbed at the button and caught the tail end of the local news. We were coming to the outskirts of the town; as I approached the traffic lights, I changed down to third gear.

'Some breaking news, just in,' the newsreader announced perkily. 'Kent police have confirmed that the weapon they believe may have killed murder victim Jacqui Jenning has been discovered in the garden of missing local woman Rosa Montague.'

I nearly hit the car in front of me. With a shriek I rammed my foot on the brake, narrowly missing its tail lights.

'Police are reported to be gravely concerned about Ms Montague, who has not been seen since Christmas,' the newsreader went on. 'Police checks at her home near Canterbury have revealed bloodstains in the property, which has apparently been empty since the end of December. Today, in an unexpected twist to the case, a chisel that was discovered in her garden is believed to match the weapon used to murder Jacqui Jenning, whose body was discovered fifteen months ago in a property in Margate.'

The lights turned green. The newsreader moved to traffic congestion on the M25, but I was no longer listening. *A chisel that was discovered*. The vehicle behind me was sounding its horn, but my car didn't budge. All I could register were those words, tangling up in my head until they no longer made sense. Despite all his guff about trust and truth, Si had lied to me. He had been seeing Rosa. And now a chisel, believed to be the same weapon that had murdered some other poor woman, had been discovered in Rosa's garden.

'Get a move on, ya stupid cow!'

I jerked the car forwards, my teeth chattering with shock. What kind of injuries would a chisel cause? For a moment the road ahead blurred. 'Calm down,' I whispered. 'Just calm down.' The chisel was nothing to do with Si. There was no hard evidence against him.

I reached the top of the lane. As the car splashed through the puddles, I passed Trish's place, then the garages, and finally Bob and Janice's little cottage, where I waved overly cheerfully at Janice, who was standing in the doorway. She did not wave back.

Outside the warehouse, Si's van was in the drive. Parking the Fiat, I slipped from the driver's seat onto the mud, taking care not to wake Jo, who was lolling in the back. Glancing up to check that I was not being observed from a window, I tiptoed to the back of the van, praying that the doors would not be locked. They swung open, flapping on their hinges, and I climbed inside.

The contents of the van was in a mess. I burrowed past heaped dust covers, a stepladder, mugs and discarded music magazines. Any minute now Si would wander outside and I would have to explain what I was doing. Delving more deeply into the back, I finally saw what I was searching for. I pulled the toolbox into the light and opened it up.

Everything was there: the tray for nails, bolts and nuts springing out first, covering up a second layer filled with tacks and screws. The next tray was piled with screwdrivers of various sizes. I had seen Si use them a hundred times or more, but had never before examined them. Now I pulled out the familiar tools with their scuffed yellow handles. These were innocent domestic implements, used for assembling flat-pack furniture, not for murdering women.

But when I reached the bottom of the box I felt myself grow cold. Nestling among a collection of small yellow-handled spanners was a new chisel with a smart red handle. I yanked it out, feeling dizzy. It even had the price tag attached.

'What are you doing?'

Twirling round, I found Si standing behind me.

'Hi!' My voice was high and hysterical. Dropping the chisel back in the box, I jumped clumsily from the van, banging my knee.

'I need to wake up Jo. He's been asleep for ages,' I cried.

But as I scurried towards my car, Si stopped me, his hand on my arm. 'What were you doing in the van?'

'Looking for a screwdriver . . . the wing mirror's coming loose.'

It was blatantly untrue. He stared at me, as if through a fog. His grey face was drawn, his eyes bloodshot. Raising his eyebrows, he walked over to the van and gently closed the back doors.

'Where've you been?'

'Just for a drive.' Opening the back door of my Fiat, I unstrapped Jo and heaved him out. When I turned round, Si was gazing at me. As my eyes caught his, he looked away, biting his lip. I could tell that he knew I was lying. He knew about the chisel, too, I was sure.

'Let me have him for a bit,' he said. 'It's ages since I've had a cuddle.'

I gripped Jo more tightly. 'I need to change him,' I mumbled.

'I'll do it. You go and pick up Pops.'

'It's OK. There's plenty of time.' Pushing past him, I hurried inside.

'**M**ummy, what's the matter with Si?'

'Nothing, honey. He's just busy.'

'Why doesn't he come and sing to me any more?'

'I'm sure he will later, once all this building is over.'

'Can I come in your bed tonight?'

I paused, regarding Poppy's eager face. With her body wedged next to mine, Si could not touch me. And if I was asleep before he came upstairs, we could delay the inevitable exchange that I was so desperate to avoid.

'All right, then. In fact I'm so pooped I think I'll come to bed with you now.'

'Yes!'

She punched the air in triumph, having just scored a rare and unexpected treat. After tucking Jo into his sleeping-bag, I quickly brushed my teeth and slipped into bed beside her.

'Mummy?'

'Uhuh?'

'That ghost isn't coming in the house any more . . .'

'Good!'

Enveloping her body in my arms, I kissed her silky hair. She was getting so big, her long bony legs knocking into mine.

Sighing, she rested her head on the pillow. 'I love you, Mummy.'

'I love you, too.'

Her eyes closed. Within seconds her breathing thickened, becoming slow and rhythmic. I lay beside her, my brain refusing to work properly, sticking on specific details, then sliding off in another direction. I recalled Alicia standing in the doorway of her house and the terrible things she had told me. And now Si was linked to this poor woman whose name I had never even heard before. How did the pathologists know she'd been murdered by the chisel? Were there marks on her skull, or was it from DNA or some other forensic clue? As Poppy sighed and flopped over, I recalled the scene in the drive. Si *knew* what I was looking for inside his van. Over and over the images churned. It was like being caught in a blizzard, with no idea of where to turn.

I don't know how long I lay next to Poppy, staring into the dark. By the time I heard Si's footsteps approaching the door, I had started to plan our escape. We would go to Pat's, I decided. I could not stay another night in the same house with this stranger, whose presence now made my heart dip with fear. His mother had said I should try to love him, but after everything I now knew, it no longer seemed possible.

He was in the bedroom now, padding round the bed and lifting the covers. I held my breath as he climbed inside.

'Mel?'

I lay rigidly under the covers, willing him into silence.

'Are you awake?'

Rolling over, I pulled the pillow over my head. 'Mmph . . .'

'I'm not involved with Rosa Montague going missing, you know that, don't you?' His voice was thin and faltering, as if close to tears. 'Mel?'

I did not reply.

We were woken the next morning at dawn. Downstairs someone was banging at the door. We both knew who it was.

Jumping up, Si threw on his clothes. His face was grey and, as he fumbled with the buttons of his shirt, his hands trembled. In the bed Poppy curled up tighter, gathering the covers around her.

'Who is it, Mummy?'

'No one. Go back to sleep.'

I hurried after Si, arriving at the top of the stairs just as he opened the door. As the policemen spoke to him he glanced back at me, his eyes panicked. The night before I had hated and feared him, but now my heart turned over with pity.

On the ground floor the two men were stepping inside: Dave Gosforth, with his leather jacket and brogues, and the younger man, this time wearing jeans. I could not hear what they were saying, but their faces were grave. I did not like their posture, either: it was too stiff and tense for another routine visit. Clattering down the steps, I arrived by Si's side just in time to hear Gosforth say, '. . . you do not have to say anything, but it may harm your defence if you do not mention when questioned something which you later rely on in court. Anything you do say may be given in evidence.'

'You're arresting him!'

Gosforth turned to me, nodding, as he slipped a pair of handcuffs expertly over Si's wrists. 'I'm afraid we are, Mrs Stenning. We also have a warrant to search these premises.'

'But he hasn't done anything!'

I could hold it back no longer. I pawed uselessly at Si's arms. 'You didn't kill that woman, did you?'

He bit his lip, not looking at me. Gosforth was now propelling him towards the door.

I fell back against the wall, watching aghast as Si was led out of the warehouse and into the back of Gosforth's blue saloon. There was a police van parked beside it, I noticed with shock. As Gosforth reversed his car round the builders' rubble, a second group of uniformed officers were making their way towards me. One of them started to introduce himself, explaining politely about the search warrant and the need to impound Si's van, but I hardly heard. All I could focus on was Si, disappearing up the lane in the back of the unmarked car. Not once had he looked back at me. Instead, he was staring straight ahead, his face set, as if all along this was what he had been expecting.

12

SI WAS ARRESTED on suspicion of the murder of Jacqui Jenning and the abduction of Rosa Montague. The police had had a breakthrough in the case, but the search team refused to tell me what it was. They trudged inside, not making eye contact as they swarmed through the building. The search of the premises would take all day, I was told. They would be grateful if I could provide a statement, too, so would I come straight back after dropping Poppy at school? They planned to take me to a police 'suite' where they'd be taking the statement.

I bundled Poppy and Jo outside, feeling sick. In the yard Si's van was being loaded onto a truck. I hurried up the lane, picturing his toolbox and the brand-new chisel.

Poppy ran into school without a word. As we'd hurried up the lane, I'd told her that a lady had gone missing and the police were trying to find out where she had gone. She nodded soberly, her eyes wide.

'Those policemen won't find that lady,' she suddenly announced as we reached the top of the lane.

'What do you mean, honey?'

''Cos she's in heaven. Si's turned her into an angel.'

I spun round, goggling at her. 'What?'

'He painted a picture of her. She was wearing a white frilly dress and had wings. I saw him burning her up. He said he didn't want to look at her any more.'

'Poppy!' Grabbing her by her wrist, I yanked her backwards. 'Which picture are you talking about?'

'I'm not telling you, Mummy!' Poppy hissed. 'Stop pinching, you're hurting me!' Wrenching her arm away, she glared at me. 'I *hate* you!'

We walked the rest of the way to school in silence.

After dropping Poppy off, I trailed back along the dreary streets, my head down as Jo's buggy bumped over the paving slabs. All the way to school I had reined myself in, but now I gave in to great hiccuping sobs. How could the man I had loved, who had fathered my precious baby, stand accused of *murder*?

When I got back to the warehouse, a car was waiting for me. I stood in the drive, watching in dismay as Si's plastic-bagged clothes were loaded into the police van. In the half-hour that I had been gone, the place had been ripped away from our tentative ownership. Plank by plank, the police were dismembering our life.

I was driven to Sittingbourne, where, in a quiet cul-de-sac, I was shown into a Barrett-like home. It was a special suite, where they conducted the more sensitive interviews, the plain-clothed policewoman who appeared from the back of the house pleasantly informed me. They couldn't haul a breastfeeding mum and her little baby off to the police station, could they? They would be recording the interview, she went on; among other devices the room into which I was shown was equipped with a video camera.

I was given a cup of muddy-coloured tea, but couldn't drink it. I breastfed Jo to sleep, trying not to weep at his innocence. Then the video was turned on and I was interviewed.

I sat in the comfy chair facing my interrogator, too horrified to process what was happening. Had my husband ever talked about his relationship with Rosa Montague? the policewoman asked, smiling politely. No, I mumbled, he never told me anything. Was I aware that he had been seeing her in December? Perhaps there was some reason why he had visited her cottage before Christmas? Would I know what it was? They were particularly interested in his movements during December. Could I account for them? Perhaps there were unexplained absences? I gazed back at her, unable to think clearly. Did Simon ever borrow my car? the woman asked. Could I explain why he'd apparently scrubbed the passenger seat of his van? At this information I clutched at Jo. In my experience Simon never cleaned *anything*.

And then there was the building work. What exactly were we doing to the warehouse? Stumblingly, I started to explain our plans, aware only of the woman's sceptical expression. Was she correct in thinking that a new floor had been laid in the living room? Did Simon do this work alone? Where else had floorboards been put down? Could I explain exactly what work had been completed since December? My mind felt overloaded, as if a fuse might blow. There had been no substantial new work on the warehouse since Jo's birth in November, I replied in a monotone. Si was sanding down the beams in the loft and painting it. Most of the living-room floor had been laid in September. The only digging that had taken place had been for drains and carried out by the builders, I couldn't recall when, and the plumbing had been redone.

The questions went on for hours, circling round Si's whereabouts and the building, returning again and again to the same topics, like a prowling cat about to pounce. Then suddenly the interview was over. If I could wait for a short while, they'd prepare a statement for me to read over and sign. After that I was free to go. It was 12 p.m., the middle of what I thought must be the worst day in my life. What I know now, of course, is that it was only the beginning.

The police car dropped me at the top of the lane. They'd be searching the premises until at least six or seven that evening, the policewoman told me. If I could spend the rest of the day with a friend it would be helpful. Helpful or not, it was inconceivable that I return to the warehouse while the police remained inside. Barging through Trish's gate, I hammered at her door. As she opened it, I virtually fell into her arms.

'Thank God you're in!'

'What on earth's going on, Mel? The police are everywhere.'

'I have to talk to you.'

Taking Jo from my arms, Trish led me past the sitting room, which she told me she was in the middle of decorating, and into her cosy kitchen. I slumped by the Aga while Trish clicked on the kettle. It was the first time I had been inside the cottage, for we had got into the habit of meeting at the warehouse. I gazed around, soothed by the warmth and brightness of the room. On the whitewashed table was an artful arrangement of pebbles and driftwood; on the wall she had hung an old-fashioned railway clock; underneath it the butler's sink gleamed.

'God, Trish,' I burst out, as she handed me my mug. 'Everything's in such a mess!'

'Tell me.' Squatting down, she brushed her fingers against my cheek.

'Si's been arrested. They think he's killed this woman . . .'

'Jesus!' Shock registered on her face and she placed an arm round my shoulders. 'How horrendous!'

For a while I flopped against her, unable to continue. Then, very slowly, I told her everything. I had trusted Si, I blubbed; I had truly believed that he loved me. But from the very beginning he had been lying. He had lied about Rosa, lied about the flat and lied about his credit cards. And now the police were trawling through the warehouse while Si was being interrogated by the police over the murder of one woman and the abduction of another.

'It's not exactly your average marital breakdown, is it?' I finished.

Trish's eyebrows were raised in amazement. 'Not exactly, no.'

'I know I ought to just grab the kids and leave him, but a bit of me still wants to believe that he hasn't got anything to do with these murders. I mean, suppose he didn't do it? One minute I'm thinking about that chisel and what it must have done to that poor woman in Margate and I'm terrified of him. Then the next minute I remember how much I loved him and I can't believe this is happening to us . . .'

'But it *is* . . .'

'Like, back in the spring he told me Rosa was this clingy bitch he couldn't shake off.'

Trish frowned, almost wincing.

'Are you OK?'

'Yeah, it's just another Braxton Hicks.' She put her hand on her belly, waiting for the tightening to pass. 'Sorry, hon, I'm still listening.'

'I mean, I really believed him,' I continued. 'It made sense. He'd had this horrendous relationship, he said, but he'd finished it. Yet now it's like everything's been turned upside down, what with his mother saying that *Rosa* ended it and he was devastated. So why does he keep telling me he can't stand the sight of her?'

'Maybe he's angry that she dumped him.'

'You mean enough to bump her off?'

In his buggy Jo had started to grumble. Rising, I pulled him from his harness, then flopped down again with him on my lap. 'I believed everything he said!' I wailed. 'He told me I was the only woman he'd ever loved! But now it turns out he was still seeing this Rosa woman.'

Trish looked at me sadly. Standing, she started to clear away the mugs. 'I think you should leave him,' she said flatly. 'I mean, what about the kids? Supposing you're putting them in danger?'

'Si would never hurt the kids!'

The expression on her face told me what she thought.

I spent the rest of the afternoon at Trish's cottage, leaving only to fetch Poppy from school. We did not return to the warehouse until after six. As we walked through the boat yard, I could see the police loading various bagged items into their vehicle. Eventually, I was given a form to sign, releasing the items for further investigation, then they were gone.

Inside the building, everything that remained had been tidied into neat piles and no longer seemed to be ours. I hated it here, I decided as I kicked at the loosened planks on the ground floor. However hard we tried to wrench it into our possession, the building would always remain an industrial warehouse: cold, draughty and damp. The place was malevolent, full of ghosts. It was being here that had ruined us.

Later that night I started to pack clothes into a rucksack. It was Saturday tomorrow, and I planned to leave for Pat's first thing. When the phone rang I ignored it, sure it was Si.

Dave Gosforth was pleased. They had the murder weapon, with traces of Jacqui Jenning's DNA smeared over it. They had Rosa Montague's blood on the walls of her cottage. And, most promisingly of all, they had a very interesting DNA match to the semen stain found on Jacqui Jenning's sheets. It had been a particularly sweet moment when the result of that little test had come in; no wonder Stenning had been so jittery about having his mouth swabbed.

They still didn't have enough evidence for a conviction, but Dave had high hopes that by the end of the week they'd be charging him with double murder. It was true that so far their evidence was wholly circumstantial. Even if Stenning was the man who had left the Starlite night club with Jacqui fifteen months earlier, it didn't prove that he'd killed her. And, disappointingly, the search of his property had failed to yield a body. But in a day or so they'd get the results of the DNA tests on the passenger seat of his van. Dave would put money on a direct match with Rosa Montague's DNA.

There was also the hope that Stenning would cave in and confess. At the moment he was saying nothing, asserting total innocence, but after twelve hours of their questioning Dave was confident he'd start to crack. They'd grill him for another hour or so, then they'd give him a little break and then start again.

I slept fitfully, waking every hour or so from uneasy dreams in which men forced their way into the building or chased me through claggy mud. In the bed beside me Poppy kicked like a donkey, while her baby brother yowled at intervals for a feed. I was exhausted. When morning came, I would get up and make Jo a bottle of milk.

By dawn I finally collapsed into deep slumber, waking with a start to find that it was nearly ten. Sitting up, I looked round the room in bemusement. They had snuggled in my bed all night, but now Poppy and Jo had vanished.

Pulling on my clothes, I stumbled out onto the gallery. What I heard had me running to the banisters. Beneath me, on the floor below, Si was lounging on the sofa with Poppy curled up beside him. Jo was balanced on his knees. He was squealing with laughter, his arms thrown back in ecstasy as Si tickled his tummy.

Poppy was beaming. 'Do it to me!' she pleaded. 'It's my turn now!'

I walked slowly downstairs. The scene was identical to so many others in which I had watched Si play with the kids: an unremarkably happy picture of family life. Now it was part of another world, like finding the ghosts of long-dead relatives sitting round one's table.

'Hi,' Si said turning round and smiling at me as I reached the bottom of the stairs. ' I didn't want to wake you. I've given Poppy her breakfast.'

I walked slowly across the floor towards him. His drawn face was anxious, and his left eye was twitching slightly.

'Mummy! Si says that as soon as he finishes making those rooms at the top, we're going to Spain!' Leaping from the sofa, Poppy skidded over the floorboards and into my legs. Reaching down, I fingered her hair. I could not take my eyes from Si.

'They let you out, then,' I murmured.

'They released me without charge. They don't have any real evidence.' He attempted to smile.

'How did you get back here?'

He blinked at me. 'I got Ol to come down. He's lent me one of his bangers. I dropped him at the station on the way back.'

'That's kind of him.'

'He's a very old friend.'

We fell silent, simultaneously glancing away from each other. We were like ill-matched partners on a blind date, struggling hopelessly for conversation.

'Have you done Jo's nappy?'

'Yup.'

'And he's had his bottle?'

'That too.'

'And now everything's going to be fine and dandy, is it?'

'So long as we think positive.'

His eye went into spasm. Reaching up to his father's face with his chubby arms, Jo pushed his tiny fingers inside his mouth.

'Watch out, sausage, or I'll bite you! Grr!'

Jo pealed with laughter. Placing him gently on the playmat, Si walked towards me, holding out his hands.

'But first we need to talk.'

I put a video on for Poppy and we filed into the kitchen, where I prepared some coffee. When it was ready I handed Si his mug and sat down at the table.

'I didn't do it, Mel,' he said quietly. 'I swear to you. But there is some stuff I have to tell you about.' He took a breath, as if steadying himself. 'I spent the night with Jacqui Jenning the night before she was killed,' he said quietly. 'The police have matched my DNA to stains they found on her sheets. That's why they arrested me yesterday. I was the last person to see her alive, so it's not surprising they wanted to talk to me. But I didn't kill her. And I'm not in the habit of picking up women in crummy night clubs, either. It was an idiotic thing to do, but I'd just finished with Rosa and I was very drunk and very angry.'

He stopped, placing his trembling fingers round his mug. 'I have no idea what's happened to Rosa,' he said. 'The last time I saw her was before Christmas. Like I told you, I had to go and see her to sort out some stuff. As far as I was concerned I was never going to see her again.'

I stared at my coffee. The milk had curdled slightly and now rose to the surface in greasy blobs. 'So what was all this stuff you had to sort out with her?' I said coldly. 'You've never explained to me what it was.'

'Oh God . . .' He ran a hand through his greasy hair. 'It doesn't really matter, does it, babe? It's all in the past.'

'Were you still sleeping with her?'

'No!'

'Then what the hell was it?'

Pressing his eyes shut, he rubbed at them with his thumbs. 'She was blackmailing me,' he said. 'Ol stupidly gave her our number and she started ringing up and saying she was going to come over here and give me even more grief. So I went to see her. She promised that all she wanted was to see me one last time, then she'd let me go.'

I folded my arms. I felt as if I were a child and he, the adult, was fobbing me off with fairy stories. 'What was she blackmailing you about?'

'I don't want to have to go into all that.'

'Just tell me the truth.'

'OK. If you insist.' Pushing back his chair, he stared into my face. 'I slept with her in May,' he said. 'I was confused about you being pregnant, so I went back to her for those few weeks that we were apart. It was completely stupid and I should have told you the truth at the time, but I was terrified of losing you. I'm really, really sorry.'

I gazed back at his exhausted face. 'So that evening, when you asked me to marry you and promised you hadn't seen Rosa, you were lying?'

'I was desperate not to lose you. Please, babe, say you'll forgive me.'

I shook my head in irritation. Perhaps he had expected a scene. But now that my fears were partly confirmed, all I felt was the cold certainty that I no longer loved him. 'Why did you lie about your flat?'

He frowned. 'What do you mean?'

'Your mother says the flat belonged to Rosa, not you.'

His expression suddenly changed. 'What the hell has my mother got to do with it?'

'I went to see her. That was what she told me.'

He glanced over at me in surprise. 'You did *what*?'

'I went to see her the day before yesterday. She told me that Rosa had owned the flat, not you.'

'She's *lying*!'

Without warning his hand crashed onto the table, spilling my coffee on to Poppy's school bag. I stared at the steaming puddle, hardly daring to breathe.

'So why should I believe you and not her?' I whispered. 'Seems like all you ever do is tell me a big fat pile of lies.'

Grabbing my hand, he gave it a violent squeeze. 'I'm not lying to you! Rosa manipulates my mother, Mel, like she manipulates everyone else.'

'You've never stopped being in love with her,' I said.

'Still in love? Jesus! If only you knew!'

'If only I knew what?'

'How much I detest her! Honestly, Mel, I can't stand the sight of her! We were "in lurve" for about two or three months, but ever since then I've been trying to escape from her. She's obsessive. It's like she's smothering me, moving into my flat, taking over my things, even bringing my bloody mother into it!'

I no longer cared about his lies. At that moment, all I was sure about was that our marriage was over. Glancing into his agonised face, I pulled my hand quickly away, rising to my feet. I could not bear to be with him a moment longer.

'Mel! Rosa's disappearance has nothing to do with me! Trust me!'

'You ask me to trust you, but you've never been honest with me, not once,' I said, my voice rising. 'From the very beginning you've been lying. You lied about Rosa, and you lied about your flat. Even if you wanted to tell the truth, I don't think you'd know where to start.'

He opened his mouth, then closed it. His face had assumed the hard, shut-in expression that had become so familiar. No longer caring how he reacted, I charged on. 'Well, I'm sick of your lies!' I spat. 'How can we build a proper marriage when you're always so secretive? I mean, why didn't you tell me about your father killing himself?'

Folding his arms he stared into space, his eyes blank. 'It's not something I find particularly pleasant to discuss.'

'Particularly pleasant? Jesus! I was such an idiot to . . .'

We both knew what I had been about to say. As I attempted to brush past him and move towards the door, he jumped to his feet and stood before me, blocking my exit. 'Where are you going?'

'I need to get Jo.'

'No, you don't, he's fine! Why won't you look at me?'

Slowly I turned my head towards him. For a terrible moment our eyes met. He looked crazed: the kind of person one might cross the road to avoid passing. Yet once I had loved him, but now he was a stranger, whose fantasies I no longer believed.

'You don't love me any more, do you?' His voice was soft, his fists bunched. I moved backwards, bumping into the cooker behind.

'I don't know how I feel about anything any more . . .'

'Please, Mel, don't say that. You and the kids mean everything to me!'

Now his hand was on my shoulder, as if he were about to push me to the floor. I had to get away. As soon as I could, I had to get the children and our bags into the car and accelerate up the lane and away from the warehouse and from him as fast as possible. It was exactly as Trish had warned: he was dangerous. He must not guess that I planned to leave.

'I do love you,' I whispered. 'I promise.'

The muscles in his face relaxed and he breathed out. 'I couldn't bear it if you didn't,' he said quietly. 'You're the only person left.'

Forcing myself to smile, I edged away from his taut body. 'I'm just feeling a bit upset,' I muttered. 'And I need the loo. I'll be back in a sec. Why don't you have a nice hot bath? We can talk about this more later.'

He nodded, finally moving aside. 'Yeah, that's a good idea.'

I took the stairs two at a time, crashing into the bedroom. Grabbing my half-packed rucksack from the floor, I flung it under the bed. Now I could hear Si's footsteps following me up the stairs. For a moment I froze, but, rather than enter the bedroom, I heard his footsteps stop by the bathroom. The door clicked open and then shut. After a second or so, the pipes began to gurgle.

I retrieved the rucksack and dumped it on the bed. Then I began to gather up the few things that I still had to pack: underwear and a change of clothes for Poppy and me, a handful of Babygros for Jo. Emboldened by the slooshing of water next door, I pushed the clothes inside the rucksack, hastily zipping it up. My purse was in my bag by the front door. The kids' coats were heaped in the lobby. Forcing myself to move more slowly, I strolled to the bathroom and stuck my head round the door.

Si was immersed in steaming water, his eyes closed. He was going bald, I noticed. The patch of scalp that showed through his thinning hair made my heart dip with unexpected pity.

'All right, love?'

He gave a start, his eyes opening. 'Yeah . . .'

'You look like you're settling in for the morning . . .'

'I'll be a while . . .' he said vaguely.

Nodding, I closed the door firmly behind me. Then, diving back into the bedroom, I yanked the rucksack from the bed, hauling it onto my back as I leapt down the stairs.

In the living room Poppy was still watching her video. Next to her, Jo had nodded off.

'Quick!' I hissed. 'Get your coat!'

Poppy's face crumpled with bemusement. 'Where are we going?'

'Out!' I bundled Jo into my arms.

'But I don't want to go out . . .'

'We have to. Get your coat, Pops! And can you get Jo's too?'

'No.'

I felt as if I might burst. 'Poppy, *please!*'

She must have registered the desperation in my voice, for she started to trail across the living room towards the lobby.

'Hurry up! Please, darling . . .'

I picked up my coat from a pile on the floor and put it on, then, pressing Jo to my shoulder with one hand and balancing the rucksack and my bag on the other arm, I nudged open the front door with my elbow. Upstairs I could already hear water draining from the bath.

'Come on!' I trilled. 'Everyone into the car . . .'

But outside the door, my words faded into the thin winter air. Parked haphazardly by the gate, the white Volvo that Si had borrowed was blocking my Fiat in. Even as Poppy pushed past me and skipped over the icy mud towards the passenger seat, I knew that whatever pretext I dreamt up, I could never ask Si to move Ollie's car.

'Poppy!' I yelled. 'Run into the kitchen and get Si's car keys from his coat!'

She swerved round, about to head back past me into the house, but as she did, I heard the creak of the stairs. Struggling to free myself from the rucksack, I dropped it onto the floor and covered it with my jacket.

'Forget it, honey!' I hissed. 'We'll go out later!'

Turning, I glimpsed Si's legs descending the stairs. For a moment he paused, presumably as he searched the room for us.

'Mel!' he called. 'Where are you?'

'Just here, by the front door. We thought we'd go out for a walk.'

He had reached us now. Linking his hands round my waist so that I was captured in his grip, he started to nuzzle the top of Jo's head.

'Hello, my gorgeous boy,' he crooned. 'How I love you!'

'We were just wondering if it was going to snow,' I muttered. 'The drive's pretty icy.'

'Yeah, it's foul out there. You'd be mad to go for a walk.'

Reaching for the door with his fingertips, he slammed it shut.

That's it. There's nothing more to tell. Shuddering, I look up, taking in the dark, deserted room. The police have gone, emptying the building of their bustling presence. The crackle of radios and stomping of boots on the stairs now seem like a dream. A short while ago Trish was here, I seem to remember. She must have retreated to the kitchen with Sandra, for down the corridor I can hear female voices.

Outside a few flakes of ice have stuck to the windows. When I stand and press my face to the freezing glass I see that it is snowing. I feel very calm. Around me, everything has receded. There's just me and what I remember. And now, as I place my hand flat against the pane, I know that only I can get Poppy back. What I have to do is focus.

After a while Si wandered upstairs and we could hear the rhythmic crash of hammering. The only other disturbance was the phone, which rang once. It was Alicia, sounding tearful.

'I've just heard the news,' she said. 'About poor Rosa. The police don't think that Simon's involved, do they?'

I gripped the phone with sticky palms. I did not want to lie. 'They've been questioning him . . . I don't know what they're going to do.'

Down the line I could hear her laboured breathing. 'He wouldn't do something like that, would he, Melanie?'

'I don't know . . .'

'Oh God . . .' She started to cry.

I held the phone to my ear, listening to her sniffs. 'You can talk to him yourself,' I said gently. 'He's here.'

'I'd prefer not to. He'll just get irritated with me.'

I did not contradict her.

'Will you let me know if anything else happens?'

'Of course I will.'

She rang off and I put the phone down.

Upstairs the noise continued, a furious banging that seemed to reach into the core of my body. I had no idea what Si was doing; all he had told me was that he had some jobs to finish in the storerooms along the gallery. I tried to ignore the racket, concentrating instead on the masquerade that everything was normal: getting the kids their lunch, changing Jo's nappies, playing hide-and-seek.

Now I see that I should have moved Ollie's Volvo the moment Si went upstairs. If I had, we would be with Pat, and Poppy would be safe. But I was afraid that on hearing the engine Si would look out and see what I was doing. Fool that I was, I waited until he must have emerged during the game of hide-and-seek and I heard him drive away. By then, of course, it was too late.

There is no time for regret; blaming myself will not bring my daughter back. As I turn away from the windowpane and shuffle slowly towards the stairs, I remain certain that Si would never harm Poppy. There is also that other thing, which has been bothering me ever since the police arrived this afternoon, the distant alarm. But, as before, I am unable to grasp it.

I start to climb the stairs, my mind whirring.

Si was upstairs, banging around. Some time, either just before or at the beginning of the game of hide-and-seek, the noise stopped. I hid and then it was Poppy's turn. I was counting up to twenty, concentrating on feeding Jo. Poppy ran off, and a little while later I heard a door open and close.

I had assumed that Si was working in the gallery storerooms because that was where he said he was going to be, but could I have overlooked the most obvious explanation of all? Might he have been not on the gallery, but in the loft storeroom? Supposing Poppy crept up the steps to the loft while he was working, hid in some cubbyhole, and then was mistakenly locked in by him? Despite all his talk of love and trust, he's clearly done a runner. Meanwhile Poppy might be stuck in the loft space, the musty Victorian walls blanking out her cries.

Reaching the top of the stairs, I hurry along the gallery to the steep metal steps that lead to the top floor. In their haste to find the car that Si's driving, the police haven't yet searched up here; the door remains fastened by the padlock. Now, as I clamber up the steps, my heart bangs furiously. When I get to the top my shaking fingers twist the lock into the correct alignment until it springs open. There's something dark and sticky smeared over it, and on the wall too. Pulling the padlock off the door and wiping my hands on my jeans, I step inside the room.

'Poppy? Are you here?' I step over the threshold, wincing at the cold.

Now that my eyes have grown accustomed to the gloom I can make out my surroundings: Si's work bench pushed to the wall and, spreading from the far side, an area of planks hammered into neat lines: the floor he must have been fitting. Through the dormer windows the clouds pull back to reveal the full moon. I take another step forwards. In the eerie light that has illuminated the loft, I can see almost everything.

Stepping carefully round the unfinished floor, I move into the centre of the room. There is an odd smell: wood dust, the heavy, earthy stench of damp, and something else which makes the hairs on the back of my arms bristle. It is so powerful that I can almost taste it: a metallic, heavy odour. My gaze settles on the abandoned winch-house and I freeze. The door is open and something—a pile of rags from the decorating, perhaps—seems to have been stuffed onto the platform where the goods were once unloaded from the barges below. As if to conceal it, a plywood board barricades the opening. As I whisper Poppy's name, I am filled with molten terror.

Grabbing the plywood, I toss it roughly aside, revealing a crumpled dustsheet. In places the fabric is soaked brown. Something lies underneath it: the shape is horribly bulky, stretching across the entire length of the platform. Squatting beside it, I start to pull at the material.

My first emotion is relief. Crazily, I almost laugh. This giant dummy, squished into the wooden hole, is not my daughter. It's too big and not wearing her clothes. Instead, it's a joke that someone is playing: a scarecrow, dressed in Si's clothes. Extending my hand, I pull at the chilly head, turning it to face me.

For two or three seconds I do not move. I gaze at the face, paralysed. Why is Si lying here, when he is meant to have taken Poppy? His chalky face stares back, a trail of black blood trickling from his nose. The top of his head appears to have caved in, the bald patch I noticed in the bathroom this morning replaced by a sticky mass of bloodied hair.

Is it me who's making this keening sound? I must have jerked back some distance from the dustsheets, for I find that I am curled against the wall on the far side of the loft. For some reason I am holding a clump of hair in my glacial fingers.

Other people have joined me up here. I can hear their footsteps, crashing over the boards. Someone gasps and shrieks Si's name.

There's too much noise and commotion. I push away the hands that come for me. Left on my own, I hug my knees, curling into a little ball. I'm so cold that I've gone numb. Is this how it feels to freeze to death? I can hear the singing of sirens and crunch of car doors outside. Blue lights flash across the darkened space, smothering the moon.

The room is filling with police. People barge around with their cameras and white suits like it's a fancy-dress party. Someone's fixed up a lamp; its white beam is flashing in my face, blinding me. If they had forgotten that I was here, now they've remembered. A woman I dimly recognise is walking to my corner, pulling me to my feet.

'Come on, Mel, love. We need to get you downstairs.'

I am being supported back down the steps, my lifeless legs dragging behind. I stumble on the bottom step, banging my shin, but don't much register the pain. *Si is dead, his head bashed in.* Someone is heaping blankets over my shoulders, I don't know who. All I can think of is Si's face, gazing expressionlessly. As I hunch over the table where I have been seated, a single phrase is repeating in my mind, over and over like a dirge. *Who has taken Poppy?*

13

I NEED TO PEE. I've been ignoring it for hours, but the urge is increasingly overwhelming. I rise unsteadily to my feet. Staring round the kitchen, I muster the energy to move.

'Let me come with you, Mel.'

It's the woman who helped me down the steps from the loft. As I glance at her tired face I remember that her name is Sandra and she's an 'FLO', whatever that means. All the time that I was slumped in the kitchen she was with me. I think she may have been holding my hand.

'I need the loo,' I mumble.

She guides me along the corridor to the toilet. When I have finished, she is standing outside, waiting. She trails behind me as I make for the living room. Can't she see that I need to be alone?

'Why are you following me?'

'I have to stay with you for the time being, I'm afraid.'

I gaze at her, trying to grasp her meaning. 'You mean I'm a *suspect*?' The concept is so ludicrous that I splutter with dismal laughter.

Sandra stares back, her face apologetic. 'I wouldn't put it like that.'

My legs can no longer hold me up and I sink to my knees. 'I didn't kill him!' I cry. 'Why would I kill him?'

'No one's saying that you did, love.' Bending over, she hooks her hands under my armpits and hauls me up. 'Let's get you comfortable.'

Some time later DCI Dave Gosforth joins us in the sitting room. He's too big for our squashy sofa and balances precariously on the edge. 'We need to ask you some questions, Melanie,' he says. 'Is that OK?'

'Uhuh.'

He folds and unfolds his arms. Si is dead and Poppy stolen. I feel as if a hole's been blasted through me. Beside that, nothing much computes. Sandra is still holding my limp hand, her eyes imploring.

'Can you tell us again what exactly happened this afternoon?'

'It was like I said. Poppy went upstairs to hide. I was downstairs with Jo, counting. I thought Si was in the room along the gallery that he used for painting. He was putting in some floorboards or something; there was a hell of a noise. Then it all went quiet and I heard a door. After a minute or so I heard a car in the drive . . .' My voice snags on a shard of pain. Swallowing hard, I manage to finish. 'I heard someone get in the car and drive it away.'

'But you didn't physically see Simon?'

'No.'

'And this was what time?'

'Four fifteen or so. I don't know exactly.'

I glance away. It's amazing that my mouth is still able to form words.

'Would you have kept the back door locked, or was it open?'

'It's always locked.'

'What about the front door?'

'It's a Chubb lock. You couldn't get in without a key.'

Dave Gosforth shifts a little closer. 'Is there anyone else who has access to your home? Neighbours perhaps? Or friends?'

'Bob and Janice Perkins have a key, in case we get locked out.'

'And they live . . . ?'

'Appledown Cottage. Just up the lane.' I turn hastily to Sandra. I've just remembered something. 'I lost my bag! It had my keys in it!'

'When was that?' Gosforth leans even closer.

'In January. I was in Tesco's. I had it on the handle of the pram.'

'Did you report it to the police and change the locks?' Sandra puts in.

'No. I cancelled all my cards, but I didn't think of that.'

'But the bag would have had your address in it, wouldn't it, Mel?'

I stare at Sandra's gently reproachful face. Now that she's saying it, I realise how stupid I've been.

'I don't know . . .' I shake my head. 'I mean, I suppose I just assumed that whoever had got the bag had taken the cash then chucked it away.'

Gosforth and Sandra exchange a glance. There's a pause, as if they're about to change tack, but I interrupt them.

'Where's Jo?' I ask querulously.

'It's OK, Mel.' Sandra pats my arm. 'Trish has taken him back to her place. She was planning to give him a bottle. I'm sure he's fine.'

I goggle at her, unable to respond. On the other side of me, Gosforth gives a little cough. 'We'll need to come back to these keys,' he says. 'In the meantime, can you tell me if there was anyone who may have had a grudge against your husband? Did he have any enemies?'

Instinctively I shake my head, but my heart jumps. What was the name of the guy that called? Biz or Baz or something. *Tell him I'm getting a teeny bit fed up*. The phrase had stuck in my mind for weeks.

'There was a man who phoned . . . called Boz? He gave me the creeps. He wanted Si, and when I told him he was out he was really rude. He said to tell him he was getting fed up.'

'OK.' The way Gosforth nods indicates that this information does not surprise him. He's clearly heard of this Boz character before.

'And then a few days later there was this silver transit van.' I shudder, remembering the man's expression.

'Go on.'

'I don't know if it was connected. The van was parked right behind my car one day when we came home from school.'

'Can you remember what he looked like?'

'Bald, overweight. He had horrible teeth.'

'We'll arrange a photofit,' says Gosforth.

There is a long silence in which they seem to be waiting for me to remember something else.

'OK, Mel,' Gosforth says carefully. 'I'm going to show you a transcription of some of the messages we found in the in-box on Simon's mobile. We were wondering if you could throw any light on them.'

Delving into the folder that he's laid on the coffee table, he produces a printed sheet, which he hands to me.

30/11/04 Meet at Bull 9PM. Need 2CU.
5/12/04 Were RU. Reply on return.
02/01/05 911645123. B.
28/01/05 UR dead.

'I don't understand,' I say faintly. 'What does that number mean?'

'We think it's a bank account. It's possible that Simon owed money. You're in quite a mess financially, aren't you?'

'Are we?' My voice is small and pathetic. The truth is I have no idea about our finances. 'But Si was working in London . . . he was earning four hundred quid a week.'

'I'm afraid he wasn't paying your mortgage, Mel,' Gosforth says.

I cannot stand the pitying way they are looking at me. I stare again at the messages. *UR dead.* Would Si have borrowed money from a thug who'd send messages like this? Yet it's true that ever since Christmas we've been floundering in debt, and he had never explained how or why. I'd assumed that the proceeds from the sale of his flat in south London had provided the deposit on the warehouse, but if, as Alicia insisted, it belonged to Rosa and he never actually sold it, then he must have raised the money some other way.

Suddenly I conjure up his face as he pulled the irises from my hair on our wedding night. What had Si said in our room at the Ritz? He was currently flush because of some kind of business deal involving Ollie . . . Now I could see that even our wedding night rested on these fault lines that have ruptured everything.

'Do you know what Simon was doing in Calais on the 15th of January?' Gosforth asks suddenly.

'No . . .' I press my fingers against my eyelids. Si went to London immediately after New Year's Day, returning only for Sundays until mid-February. 'I thought he was in London that week, on the build . . .'

'He may have been for some of the time, but not all of it. We can trace his movements from the calls he made from his mobile. He was in France again on the 6th of this month. Any idea what he was up to?'

I shake my head, aghast at how much the police have found out, and how little I know.

'Have you heard of a pub called the Bull?'

'No.'

'And you never met Boz? You just spoke to him the once?'

'Yes, I think so. Si said he was a tiler.'

'And apart from this silver van you never saw anyone else hanging around? I know it's hard after what's happened this evening, Mel, but try to concentrate hard. Even the tiniest little thing may be significant. Was there anyone else who seemed to take an interest in Poppy?'

Her name jolts me back to the present. Poppy! I start to stand, thinking that I must *do* something. Somebody has taken Poppy!

'I have to get her . . .'

Sandra's hand is immediately on my arm. 'That's not going to help, Mel. We need you to concentrate on answering the questions. It's very important you remember everything. We still have the sighting of Poppy in what we're pretty certain is Simon's car, remember?'

'Are you saying it was this Boz bloke? That he killed Si and took Poppy because Si owed him money?'

'We're not saying anything.'

'But why would he have killed that Jacqui woman?'

'Like Dave said, Mel, we can't make any assumptions. What's happened today may not even be connected with Jacqui Jenning.'

'You mean you still think that Si killed her?'

Sandra does not answer, just glances again at Gosforth.

'What we need,' he says slowly, 'is for you to tell us anything you can think of that may be relevant.'

I stare at him. I have just remembered Poppy's ghost.

I buck up and out of the sofa, jerking away from Sandra and Gosforth like a frightened rabbit. Poppy said there was a ghost creeping along the gallery. And then later she saw him in Si's studio. Yet rather than listening to her, I ticked her off, assuming she was lying. As I recall how impatiently I searched the warehouse that evening, returning in a fury to find Jo squirming on the floor, I want to crash my head against the wall, to punish myself until I'm senseless.

I never once listened to Poppy, or took her side. Even when she screamed in the night that she'd seen an intruder I didn't believe her. As I stumble towards the kitchen, the details of her night terrors return with horrible clarity. Every night her screams would yank me upright, my heart pounding. It was the fat ghost she'd seen by the stairs, she'd cried. He had crawled into her head and she couldn't get him out. Along with her increasingly difficult behaviour in the day, I had tucked the nightmares under the heading 'Jealousy of Jo', never bothering to probe further. Yet supposing that the figure she had seen in the gallery that night was real?

Lurching towards the kitchen table, I start to search desperately through the heaped bills and old newspapers. When I locate Poppy's picture I clutch it with trembling fingers, tears pouring down my face. Our warehouse, crayoned brown, with a pointy roof and lots of little square windows. Two stick figures: Poppy and her mother and next to them is a little blob: the baby brother. The stepfather is not depicted. And there, at the top of the building, gawping down with googly eyes, is Poppy's ghost. Could this have been Boz or one of his accomplices?

'Mel?' Sandra is standing beside me.

'Look!' I cry, waving the picture in her face. 'Poppy drew it the other day . . . she said there was a ghost in the house. She saw it on the stairs.'

She takes the picture from my hands. 'But you never saw anything?'

'I didn't believe her. I mean, I checked the house, but there was no one there.' I stop, remembering my impatient search of the building, ending in the discovery of Si's latest, horrible painting. There couldn't be anyone inside the building, I had concluded, because there was no sign of a break-in. Never did I consider that the intruder might have had a *key*. 'I thought she was making it up, to get attention.'

My breath is coming too fast; I can barely speak. I want Sandra to place her plump arm round my back, to coo that there is no ghost, no Boz, no people who wished Si harm. But she stands silently beside me as she looks down at the picture, her lips puckered unhappily.

'Perhaps this Boz person came back to kill Si, and Poppy got in the way,' I whisper. As I reel backwards, a uniformed officer steps into the kitchen, a sheaf of lined papers in his hands.

'We've just found these,' he says quietly, handing the papers to Sandra.

Returning Poppy's drawing carefully to the table, Sandra scrutinises them, her face unreadable. When she has finished, she hands them over. 'Any idea about these?'

They are letters, written in a tight, curling script that crawls untidily over the lines. *Dear Poppy*, the first letter reads. *Where watching you. Why dont you say anything. We keep waiting and waiting.*

It is unsigned. The second is even worse. I scan the few lines, feeling nauseous: *Dont try to get away. We will get you were ever you are. If you tell your mum I will break your neck.*

'We found them in the little girl's bedroom,' the officer is saying. 'They were down the back of the chest of drawers.'

'Someone was sending her letters,' I whisper feebly. 'She wouldn't let me see them. I should have insisted she showed them to me.'

Sandra gently pulls the papers from my hand. 'It's not your fault, Mel.'

'Yes, it is! From the beginning she was scared of this place, but I never bloody listened . . . how can you say it's not my fault?'

'Mel, calm down . . .'

But it's too late. I stand quivering with horror on the cement floor. Poppy tried to tell me she was being persecuted, but I never listened. All that time, when I had eyes only for Jo, there *was* a ghost. He was sending her letters, too, enacting his revenge on Si by hurting his family. I look round the ugly kitchen: my doomed attempts to cheer it up by taping Poppy's pictures on the walls. I hate this place.

Lumbering across the room, I push past the policeman and make for the door. I need to get away from this warehouse, sodden as it is with the secrets that Si was hiding from us. As the door bursts open I gulp at the freezing air, the cold smashing into me like a fist. Stumbling outside, I gaze around the yard in shock.

The world has turned white. In the hours since I climbed the steps to the loft a heavy snow has fallen, crusting the police cars that wait in the drive with a thick white topping. The boat yard and its outbuildings are blanketed; there is even a stack of perilously balanced ice on top of each boat mast, testimony to the glacially still air.

I am wearing only a sweatshirt and jeans with thin baseball boots on my feet, but I hardly feel the cold. I start to plough through the virgin snow, the compacted ice creaking beneath my weight. I stagger a little, bashing into the side of a police car and causing a wedge of snow to slump from the windscreen. Behind me, somebody is crunching through the snow.

'Mel! Come back in, love!' Sandra is tugging at my shoulders, so that I slither backwards. 'You'll catch your death,' she mutters.

'I don't bloody care! I have to find Poppy!'

'We're doing everything we can—'

'Leave me alone!' I scream, pushing her away. But it's no good. Other hands have grasped me; despite my kicking and squirming I am firmly escorted back into the building, where I start to howl, tears spurting as I crumple on the floor, all dignity departed.

Since I refuse to stay in the warehouse, it's been arranged that Trish will take me in. The doctor has visited, leaving behind a white plastic pot which rattles with Temazepam. I've promised to take two. Sandra has tucked them into my overnight bag, together with the nightie she's retrieved from under my pillow, my wash things, a packet of nappies for Jo and a clutch of clothes.

Despite the short distance up the lane to Trish's cottage, it's decided that I should travel there in Dave Gosforth's car. It takes him a while to scrape the snow off the windscreen, but finally, wheels slithering, we move off: me in the front with Gosforth, and Sandra in the back, my overnight bag on her lap. We glide through a transformed world, the track that leads up the lane soft and white, the trees sparkling. It is nearly one in the morning, and no one's around. At the top of the gleaming lane the shining windows of Trish's cottage seem like a cheerful galleon floating in still waters. When the car pulls up outside her gate, we climb out into two or three inches of snow. As we shuffle slowly through her front garden, our footfalls are muffled.

Trish comes to the door, extending a hand as she helps me inside.

'My poor darling,' she murmurs as we step over the threshold of the tiny flagstoned hall.

'Is Jo OK?'

'Sound asleep in baby's cot upstairs.'

We step into the snug kitchen. As before, everything is shining and clean: the floor scrubbed, the stripped wood table cleared, the washing machine humming with activity. Placing my bag on the floor, Sandra hovers, explaining the dose of tranquillisers I'm supposed to take, and that the pills are in my bag. She puts a card with her mobile phone number on the mantelpiece, and tells Trish what time she'll be back in the morning. Gosforth remains by the door, scowling at something. Does he really believe that I'm a suspect?

'If you could persuade Mel to get some sleep, it would be great,' I hear Sandra whisper. 'It's so kind of you to take her in.'

'It's the least I could do.'

I remain standing woodenly. Perhaps it is simply the passage of time, but rather than feeling better at having left the warehouse I feel considerably worse: the dread that's been building inside me somehow thickening. If only I could stop thinking of Si's staring white face.

'You can have the spare room,' Trish says. 'I've made up the bed.'

I nod, allowing her to usher me up the narrow stairs and into a small bedroom. It's decorated with Trish's usual panache, the floorboards painted white, the brass bed covered with a large patchwork quilt. Like the rest of the house, the room is spotless. Where is all the clutter?

I sit wordlessly on the bed, which sags at my weight.

'There's a towel by the washbasin,' Trish is saying.

'Where's Jo?'

'He's next door.' She pauses by the door. 'Do you want to talk?'

I shake my head. What I very badly want is to be left alone. But perhaps Trish feels duty-bound to keep watch over me, for she does not move, just leans against the door.

'I can't imagine how you must be feeling,' she says, her hand slowly circling her belly. She's changed into tracksuit trousers and a red jumper.

I shrug. I am willing her to turn and clump back down the stairs. I need silence, so I can trace this prickling thought to its origin. Rosa went missing at Christmas, the police said, just after Si went to see her. They found her blood in her house, and the chisel that killed the prostitute and most likely belonged to Si was buried in her garden. And then there was the passenger seat of his van, which he had so assiduously cleaned. All the evidence points to him, yet now he's dead and something else is forming in my mind. It's so close that it's almost solid.

'I just need to switch off for a while,' I mumble.

'I've got those pills in the kitchen,' she says eagerly. 'I'll go and get them.'

As I hear her go downstairs, I stand and walk onto the cramped landing, my fingers trailing over the rose-coloured walls. Pushing open the adjacent door, I step inside. The cot stands in the centre of the small room, bright moonlight pouring onto the floor. For a moment I take in the mural of animals that Trish has painted on the walls. Moving closer to the cot, I grip the wooden bars with my fingers. Jo is lying on his back, his arms stretched over his head in blissful repose. The sight of his perfectly snubbed nose, long lashes and Cupid's lips brings tears to my eyes. I reach over the bars and stroke his cheek. If only he would wake then I would have an excuse to scoop him up.

'I've got them.'

Trish's voice makes me jump. I had no idea she was standing behind me. As I turn, she holds out a glass of water and two small yellow pills.

'You are going to take them, aren't you?'

'Sure.'

Popping the pills into my mouth, I take a sip of the water.

'Night then, my poor darling. Let's just pray that by the time you wake up there'll be some good news.'

I nod, giving her a little smile that is supposed to signal that she does not need to worry, and brush past. Once inside the spare room, I push the door closed, then spit the bitter-tasting pills into my hand.

Every nerve of my body tingles, like I've received an electric shock.

14

DAVE GOSFORTH COULDN'T RELAX. He knew that there was currently nothing more for him to do: the scene-of-crime lads were at the warehouse, sifting through every shred of forensic evidence; the Met had arrested Barry 'Boz' Uckfield in a pub in Kennington, and DI Clive Jenkins had gone up there to interview him. Every police force in the country was searching for the missing car. He needed to get some kip so he could be fresh for the next day, but sleep eluded him.

He lay on his back, gazing up at the moulded ceiling tiles of the Travelodge in the Sittingbourne road. It wasn't the Saturday night he'd been expecting. Karen had been planning a special dinner for their tenth wedding anniversary. She'd been cooking most of the morning. But as soon as he'd got the call telling him that the little girl had gone missing, he'd told her the dinner would have to wait. Now he didn't know when he'd next be home.

The bed was too narrow for his wide frame, and he turned over, huffing. He felt like a pillock, truth be told. For days they'd been edging towards charging Stenning with the murder of Jacqui Jenning and Rosa Montague, but now their prime suspect was dead. Stenning had left his calling card on Jacqui Jenning's sheets the night before she was murdered and was missing a chisel that matched the one covered in Jacqui's DNA that was discovered in Rosa's garden. Even more promising were the stains on the passenger seat of his van. The DNA results had still to come in, but the fabric had been cleaned with bleach in an attempt to remove what Dave was sure would turn out to be Rosa's blood.

Stenning had been shifty in interviews about both his whereabouts and his relationship with Rosa Montague. He'd admitted that he'd been in her bedroom, but said that he had last visited her to retrieve some papers and that they'd had an argument. He had then told them a cock-and-bull story about how there'd been a fight, during which Rosa had deliberately plunged a knife into her arm. He'd driven her to hospital in Canterbury and had left her outside A & E—an event the hospital denied all knowledge of. Rosa was deeply disturbed, he'd told them. All he'd wanted to do was to get away from her.

The guy hid it well, but Dave had sensed a repressed violence in Stenning, like there was a little chink of normality missing. He felt sorry for the wife. She clearly didn't have a clue.

Despite the circumstantial evidence, however, they still didn't have a sufficient case for the CPS. There was no direct link to Jacqui Jenning's murder, either. Sure, there was the semen, but the one handprint they'd finally recovered from her kitchen wall didn't match Stenning's. Their only hope was the chisel. Whoever had buried the tool in the garden of Rosa Montague's cottage had done a bad job of wiping off the blood, and within twenty-four hours they had had a DNA match with Jacqui. It was almost certainly part of the set that Stenning still kept in his toolbox, with the same yellow plastic handle as the rest of his tools.

But now he was dead. Far worse, the little girl was still missing. The thought that he might have made a serious error of judgment made Dave's heart plunge. Sighing, he turned over again. Stenning's death was definitely murder. Puddles of blood lay all over the floor of that loft. Whoever had killed him must have got a good soaking.

But the worse thing was the child. They'd gone all out to find Stenning's borrowed Volvo, assuming he'd taken her, when all the time he'd been lying murdered upstairs. Bloody fools! Why the hell hadn't they searched the property properly, like they were trained to? Only now, when the girl had been missing for over twelve hours, were they scrambling around trying to trace Stenning's dodgy business contacts.

With a little moan, Dave Gosforth rolled over onto his back. If it wasn't Stenning who had taken the girl, who the bloody hell was it? The letters they'd found under the child's mattress, and messages on Stenning's mobile, implied that Barry 'Boz' Uckfield might be their man. He'd done five years for fraud in the eighties, eighteen months for money laundering in the nineties, and had only just escaped a sentence for GBH. He was currently operating as a property developer on the south coast, and yesterday Dave's team had discovered that he'd lent five hundred grand to Stenning back in the summer. They suspected that Stenning's trips to France were connected to this, possibly with a view to working on more of Uckfield's unscrupulous developments. Since then they'd fallen out, and now Uckfield was getting nasty about the money he was owed. But according to Clive Jenkins, who he'd spoken to only twenty minutes earlier, all Uckfield would admit to were the loan and mobile messages.

There was something else. It had been bugging him ever since he deposited Mel Stenning at her friend's house and drove out of town. It was something to do with Rosa Montague's place in the woods, but what? Shivering under the thin stretch of duvet, he concentrated hard. Rosa's blood was sprinkled around her house, yet in contrast to the chaos of Stenning's warehouse the place was as spruce as a holiday let.

Dave lay as stiffly as a pole, vortexed by thought. He had just remembered what he had seen in Rosa Montague's kitchen.

For what feels like hours, I lie motionless on top of the bed. Only a few yards away Trish and Jo are asleep, but I am wide awake. Eventually I sit up, swinging my feet to the floor. I am going to creep downstairs to the kitchen. There I am going to retrieve Sandra's card from the mantlepiece where, a few hours earlier, I saw her rest it. When I've got the number, I'm going to retrieve the mobile she slipped into my bag and call her. I'm going to tell her that Rosa Montague may have gone missing before Christmas, but she wasn't dead. Instead, she was alive and well and spending Si's money in South Molton Street.

When I reach the bottom of the stairs, I pause. The kitchen is to my right, the sitting room that Trish has been painting to my left. Through the half-open kitchen door the green light of the washing machine winks encouragingly. I push the door open, wincing at its squeak. Stepping into the room, I gaze through the dim light at the clock on the wall, which shows it is five past three. Almost eleven hours have passed since I last saw Poppy. On the far side of the room, on the mantlepiece, Sandra's card is visible in the slanting moonlight. Tiptoeing across, I reach up and retrieve it, peering around the room for my bag.

It's gone. It's not on the floor where Sandra put it as she ushered me into the kitchen. Nor has it been tidied under the table, or balanced on a chair. Returning to the hall, I pause for a moment by the sitting-room door. Somewhere inside the room I will either find my bag, or Trish's phone. All I need to do then is call Sandra. Gently lifting the latch with my fingers so that it unhooks soundlessly, I step over the threshold.

I glance around the room in surprise. I was expecting to see furniture covered in dustsheets, a semi-decorated room that reeked of fresh paint, but there is no sign of Trish's handiwork. Why would she lie to me about painting the room? Something is very wrong. Despite the cold, my hands are clammy. As I peer more intently around the room, my eyes fix upon the wall above the fireplace, and what I see makes me jerk backwards, gasping.

It's a painting of an angel. Not the demure figure by the chapel that Si sketched for me, but one of the more ostentatious statues at the entrance to the cemetery: stone arms reaching towards heaven, enormous feathered wings stretched wide. Expressionless eyes gaze from the canvas. Like the painting of the nude that hung in Si's kitchen, half of the face is deliberately obscured, this time by clinging ivy.

In the two or three seconds that I face the painting, I understand everything. I stand motionless. This cannot possibly be a coincidence.

'Mel?'

At the sound of my name I spin round. Trish is looking at me quizzically, Jo bundled in her arms.

'What's the matter?' she asks with a smile.

'I couldn't sleep . . .'

She takes a step towards me, her face crumpled with false concern. 'Didn't the pills work?'

I slowly shake my head. My hands are so slimy that I have to wipe them on the side of my jeans. 'Can I have Jo?' I whisper.

She does not move, just clutches him tighter. 'What's the matter?'

'You're Rosa, aren't you?'

She pretends to frown. 'I don't know what you mean . . .'

'You're Rosa . . .'

She smirks, and my sudden hatred of her lashes me like a whip. How could I have been taken in so easily? She's cut her hair and dyed it blonde, and the baby has added two or three stone to her previously slim frame, but the dark eyes and thin lips, currently curling into a cruel smile, belong to the girl on the boat. *Rosa*. I gawp at her in horror, fragmented memories hurtling through my mind. That first morning in my kitchen, she'd said her boyfriend had dumped her, gone off with some tart. She was plotting her revenge, she'd added.

'What do you mean?' she says, pulling her face into a little frown.

'You followed us here, didn't you? You found out where we lived.'

She smiles glassily back at me. I swear she is holding Jo more tightly. And now, finally, the detail that since this afternoon has been scratching at the back of my mind breaks loose. It was when she pretended to comfort me, out in the yard. 'There was never anyone prowling around the warehouse,' she'd said. But I am sure I never told her about what Poppy said she had seen.

'You broke into the building and spied on us,' I say slowly.

I am staring at her bump now, making the calculations. He'd slept with her in late May, Si had confessed. But he never had the courage to tell me that she was having his baby.

'I don't understand what you're going on about—'

'How did you know about the prowler?'

'Poppy told me,' she says with a laugh, as if aghast at the implications. 'Or you did. I don't remember.'

She's widening her eyes, still protesting innocence, but her face has turned a fetching shade of pink. I stand before her, my hands clenched. All the time I thought she was my friend, she was my enemy: revelling in my problems as she waited for her moment of triumph.

'It was you who stole my bag, wasn't it?'

'Listen, love,' she says slowly. 'Do you want me to get you some more of the Temazepam? You seem ever so het up.'

'I'm not het up. I just want you to give me Jo.'

I step towards her, but she dodges to the left, deftly avoiding my outstretched hands. As her eyes alight on the angel she gives a little comedy shriek, like she's just discovered something embarrassing. 'Oops! Looks like you've seen my angel.'

'Looks like I have.'

She doesn't miss a beat, just turns, grinning in a way that tells me she's grown bored of pretending. 'She's a bit more impressive than your tatty little sketch, isn't she?'

'What do you want?' I whisper.

'Just to get my revenge.'

She's still smiling: the cold grin of a psychopath. I stare into her pale face, my heart plunging as I recall Si's painting of the woman with the baby. It was of *her*. Poppy saw the 'fat person' up there the evening after I'd told 'Trish' he was painting again. She must have been overcome by curiosity, desperate to see what he was working on.

'You bitch!'

I lunge at her, but she hops out of my way. And she still has Jo. He's been woken by my shouting and is starting to cry.

'Fair's fair, hon!' Rosa coos. 'If you go around stealing other girls' men, you can't be too upset if they pay you back!'

'I didn't steal Si off you . . .'

'Nah, I know you didn't. It was me he was always passionate about.'

Barging past me, she moves down the hall, Jo's screams muffled in her shoulder. For perhaps two seconds I am unable to move. I am thinking about her washing machine, still only halfway through its cycle at three in the morning.

'You killed him, didn't you?' I breathe, but she is already at the front door, pulling her parka over her shoulders, one arm now circling my wriggling baby. She must have changed out of her bloodied clothes before coming to my assistance this afternoon, but forgotten to put them in the wash. Perhaps she bumped into Poppy on her way out of the warehouse and, being literally caught red-handed, bundled her into Ollie's Volvo, where, knowing Si, he'd probably left the keys in the ignition. When she answered my call forty minutes later she wasn't in Tesco's, as she claimed, but here, probably, hiding the car in one of the garages and erasing all evidence of what she'd done.

For one final moment she turns back to face me. Her face is transformed: drained of colour. 'The blood made such a horrid mess,' she says mournfully. 'But I had to do it, for the sake of our relationship. I mean, he was going around telling you all these lies. He told you he'd never loved me, didn't he? I couldn't have him saying things like that.'

Then, before I have time to react, she has opened the front door and is hurrying outside into the blasting cold.

'Where's Poppy?' I scream. 'What have you done with her?'

The door slams behind her and I hear a key turn in the lock.

With a moan of recognition, Dave sat up. Of course! Now that he had made the connection, it was so bloody obvious! Reaching for his mobile, he leapt out of bed.

They must have finished interviewing Uckfield, for Clive answered the phone immediately.

'Yup?'

Grabbing his trousers from the bedside chair, Dave started to pull them on, wedging the phone between shoulder and jowls. 'Do you remember the tea towels in Rosa Montague's cottage?'

'Not really, no.'

'They were folded up all fancily.'

Now it was Jenkins's turn to play the role of tired cynic. He'd been questioning Uckfield for most of the night, after all. 'Bloody hell, Dave! You're calling me at three thirty in the morning to discuss tea towels?'

'Yeah, I am actually. I've just remembered. That friend of Mel Stenning, where she's staying the night? In her kitchen they're folded exactly the same way.'

'And?'

'It's obvious, isn't it? I've never seen anything like those towels in my life. She *has* to be Rosa Montague . . . that's why the place was left so neat and tidy. Stenning never killed her. She packed up her aunt's cottage and followed him and his new wife to their nice new house . . .'

Down the line, Jenkins was very quiet. Dave continued to grapple with his trousers.

'You're saying this is Rosa Montague, all along? And she killed Stenning?'

'Could be . . .'

He'd made it into the boxy bathroom now, and was groping for the shirt that he'd hung on the radiator.

'What about Jacqui Jenning?'

'Maybe she killed her too. She could have taken that chisel from Simon Stenning's toolbox. Remember where we found it?' When Jenkins did not reply, he added, 'Did you get anything on Uckfield?'

'Not a twinkle. He's been at a football match all afternoon and—'

'Call the guys over in Faversham,' Dave interrupted him. 'Get them to go to the friend's house. Mel Stenning and her little boy aren't safe.'

I have to get out. I ram my body into the front door, but all I succeed in doing is bashing my shoulder. I hardly notice the smarting pain. I run into the kitchen and rattle the back door. Like the front door, it's locked and there's no key. Screaming with fury I kick it so hard that the wood splinters, but still the door doesn't budge.

Spinning round, I run back across the kitchen. As my eye falls on her tea towels, folded into a psychotically precise fan next to the washing-up, I strike them to the floor with a scream.

I fling open the door of the sitting room, searching frantically for the phone. It's on a table next to the sofa. Grabbing it, I press the 'on' button and wait for the dial tone, but the line's dead. Either she's deliberately cut me off, or it's the snow. Throwing down the phone, I dart towards the small bay windows, already knowing they'll be locked.

'Bitch!'

On the floor by the door is a heavy metal doorstop in the shape of a lion. Scooping it up, I move back to the window, then hurl it at the windows. The glass shatters on impact and cold air gusts in. Using the lion to knock out the jagged glass that remains, I haul myself through the window, landing with a soft thud in deep snow. Now that the blizzard has cleared, the moon has reappeared, illuminating everything.

It is so cold that my cheeks ache; my breath surrounds me in clouds. Tramping round the side of the cottage, I reach the front. Rosa's footsteps, left a few minutes earlier, lead across the garden. When I reach the gate I pause. From the look of the sagging line on the other side of the lane, it was the weather and not Rosa that cut the phone.

Yet while I cannot call for help, the snow gives me the clues I need. Rather than progressing up the lane, the tracks move along a small alley that cuts between Rosa's cottage and the garages. Stumbling along it, I follow her footsteps to where they join a small path which feeds into the riverside track about quarter of a mile north of the warehouse. This was her favourite walk, Trish once told me. I start to jog down the path, praying that she has not harmed my children.

In the distance I can see the grey line of water and a low huddle of boats. I run faster, the fresh snow crunching beneath my baseball boots. I have no plan, just the leaden certainty that somewhere in the derelict boats that I am fast approaching I will find Poppy and Jo.

When I reach the water's edge I stop for a moment, peering around. Lying low in the water are two abandoned vessels, one broken and rotten-looking, the second an old-fashioned fishing boat, its hulk green with slime. Its wooden cabin is lit up by what looks like a lantern, revealing the silhouette of a hunched adult figure, bent over something.

As I reach the water's edge I leap over the jetty, landing with a crash on the deck. 'What have you done with my kids?' I scream.

There is no response, just the soft splash of water as a clod of snow drops from the side of the boat. Diving towards the cabin, I shake the handle of the rusty door, banging hard against the wood with my fist. I can smell petrol in the air, a thick chemical fug.

The night remains silent.

'Fuck you!' I roar, throwing the entire weight of my body against the door. I am so desperate to get inside that, if I could, I would claw the boat apart with my nails. With a click the metal door swings open.

Rosa stands before me. For a second I barely recognise her. She has turned from pregnant beauty to bedraggled lunatic, her eyes darting from my face to the marshland behind. I want to lunge at her, to tear her to pieces, but something stops me.

'What have you done to Jo and Poppy?' I say evenly. The smell of petrol is overpowering.

She ignores the question; perhaps she doesn't hear it, for her eyes have a strange, disconnected expression. 'Is Si coming?' she whispers. 'I need Si to come and get me.'

She is holding something in her hands. Glancing down, I see the glint of Si's old lighter; one he claimed to have lost.

'He's not coming,' I say. 'It's just me.' From behind her, I have just noticed a flicker of movement.

Rosa peers dimly at my face. 'You've ruined everything,' she says softly. 'I was having his baby. He adored me. It was going to be so perfect. Just him and me and our child. We were soul mates.'

I swallow hard. 'You're deluding yourself. He said you were unbalanced. He was desperate to get rid of you—'

'Don't you dare say that . . .'

Suddenly her face contorts and her grip on the lighter loosens, her fingers beginning to unfurl. She seems to be having trouble controlling her breathing. 'I have to get rid of everything . . .'

I have just glimpsed Jo, lying in what looks like an old dog basket on the cabin floor. I want to push Rosa roughly aside and grab him, but I do not like the way her thumb keeps fiddling with the lighter.

As she moves further into the cabin, I have to stop myself from screeching out loud. Crouching in the shadows next to Jo's basket, her pale face turned in my direction, is Poppy. Her hair is wet and the blanket that she has wrapped round her shoulders stained with something dark. As I stare, I suddenly understand why the place reeks of petrol. All that Rosa has to do now is to make one flicking gesture with her thumb, and . . .

Swiping at her hand, I barge into her, trying to knock her sideways, but despite her condition she's surprisingly agile. Hopping to one side, she spins away from me. Roaring at the top of my voice, I leap onto her back, my fingers scratching her face. I have to get the lighter. She gasps, falling to her knees, and now I am punching her, my past, present and future reduced to the sum of my actions: fist against flesh, wanting to pummel her into oblivion.

But she disengages herself from my grasp and starts to squirm across the floor, moving ever closer to Poppy and Jo. Flicking at the lighter, she's stretching her arm in their direction . . .

What happens next is so sudden that I am barely able to take it in. As Rosa lurches towards Jo's basket, Poppy leaps from her corner. In the second that she flies through the air towards Rosa, she has the appearance of a tiger, her eyes wild. As I grab Rosa, dragging her backwards, Poppy's teeth sink into her outstretched wrist. Shrieking with pain, Rosa releases the lighter. With one sweep of her arm, Poppy sends it skittering across the cabin.

'Get out of here!' I yell, gesturing wildly at the metal door. Round-eyed with shock, Poppy scoots across the floor, the cabin door crashing behind her. Diving across the floor, I scoop Jo into my arms.

As I swing round, I see Rosa hunched over, her hands clutching her knees. She is making a low, animal sound. A pool of liquid is at her feet.

'Oh God, help me, please. I'm going to die.'

For a moment I stare at her. Her bloodied face is clenched with pain, sweat beading her forehead.

'You're not going to die,' I hear myself say coldly. 'You're in labour.'

As she starts to rock to and fro with pain, I turn and hurry towards the cabin door. Bursting through it, I clatter onto the deck, where Poppy is huddled against a snowy coil of rope.

'Mummy!'

Throwing my free arm round Poppy, I pull her towards me. Even if there were time to speak, I would not be able to. Hauling her onto my hip, I clamber with her and Jo to the icy riverbank. I do not know where I have acquired the strength to carry them like this, but I am jogging over the wooden walkway, moving as fast from Rosa's screams as is humanly possible. Now that I have them back, I never want to let my children go. It is only when Poppy pushes her wet face against mine and kisses me that I realise I am crying.

We do not get far. The children are too heavy, and after a few feet more, my legs buckle. As we sink into the snow, I hold Poppy and Jo tightly against me, small fingers clasped around my arms, legs gripping my waist. I have to try to keep them warm, so I pull them as closely as I can against my body, my hands cradling their heads. In those few moments of clarity, before the police torches catch us in their beam and we are surrounded by people and lights, I know that this is all that matters: to be with my children, to love and care for them. Burying my face in her oily hair, I hug Poppy like I'm never going to let her go.

EPILOGUE

JUNE 2006

THE WAY DAVE GOSFORTH saw it, the world was divided into two categories of people. First were the vast majority: those who were basically good, the ones who were the victims and not the perpetrators of crimes. Sometimes they got into a mess, but basically they were well-behaved, law-abiding citizens, trying to do their best. Then there were the others: baddies, as his son Harvey put it. It was a small but significant minority. Motivated by greed, unable to empathise with the people they hurt and never able to accept responsibility, they were the troublemakers, whose unpleasant activities he had dedicated his career to fighting. After twenty years in the game, if there was one thing he'd learned it was that good people, no matter how far they were pushed, did not turn into murderers.

Simon Stenning was not a baddy. During the first stages of their investigation he and Clive Jenkins had suspected he might be, but now it was clear that he was simply a poor sod who, having got into a bit of a mess, was unable to extricate himself without wading ever deeper into the mire. His real mistake was to get involved with Rosa Montague. He lied to his wife, too, which never helped. Oh, yes, and there was the little matter of impregnating Rosa while involved with Mel. To that extent, it was his own bloody fault.

Rosa Montague, on the other hand, was as evil as they come. She'd killed Jacqui Jenning in a jealous fury after Stenning had picked her up from the Starlite Club. It was all Simon's fault, she told the police when the doctors finally allowed them to interview her. He'd been so cruel to her, even threatening to end their relationship. So when he'd gone storming out of her flat she'd followed him. Watching him leave the club with that little slut on his arm was just too much. It was HER he loved, not that tart. They were soul mates. Surely it was only natural that she'd chosen to defend the relationship?

She had returned to her flat, pulled a chisel from Simon's toolbox, and then returned to wait outside Jacqui's flat. When she finally saw her boyfriend leave, she marched into the flat and bludgeoned her rival to death, adding the chisel wounds to the head for extra effect. Her hand-print matched the one they'd found in the hall, and, surprise, surprise, she'd left her prints all over the chisel.

Dave's team had to cobble the rest of the story together, for, after admitting to Jacqui's murder, Rosa refused to make any further comment. Yet Dave was satisfied that their version of events held tight. Based on what both Mel and Stenning's friend Ollie Dubow had told them, they built up a picture of Rosa Montague as a manipulative obsessive, who refused to accept that her relationship with Stenning was over. She was an expert in getting people to do what she wanted, Dubow had stated in his testimony. She had even managed to prise Simon and Mel's new address out of him, calling him late at night and begging for it. She was pregnant, she'd sobbed, she had to see Simon. So he gave her the number and she called, summoning Stenning to her cottage in the woods. There'd been a terrible scene. According to Dubow, Simon had informed Rosa that since he'd last seen her he'd got married and had a son; even if Rosa's baby was his, he wouldn't be returning. Rosa had punched him in the face, then made a show of cutting her arm, as a result of which Simon had driven her to the hospital in Canterbury in his van, dropping her at the entrance to A & E.

He'd have to tell Mel the truth, he'd confided to Ollie, but was dreading her response and was terrified of losing her. As for the credit cards, Dave and Clive decided that Simon must have left them there deliberately, perhaps in the hope that with the use of his money Rosa would leave him alone. After the scene with Simon she never sought treatment at the hospital in Canterbury, but must have returned immediately to the cottage. Then she'd cleaned up the mess and, after her shopping spree in London, departed for Kent.

Folding his arms, Dave took a step back from the front door, looking up at the large, dark house. There was money here, however dilapidated the place had become. They should pull that ivy away from the top windows, he was thinking, and give the place a lick of paint.

From behind the door he could hear laughter, then the sound of a woman's voice. With a click, the door opened.

Mel Stenning stood before him. She had lost weight since the year before and had her hair cropped short so that it clung in feathery wisps around her face. Unlike the grimy jeans and jumpers of the winter, or the formal trouser suits she had worn during the trial, she was dressed in a long cotton skirt and a black vest, showing off her Mediterranean skin. The haunted expression that had clouded her pretty features in the days that immediately followed the murder had lifted. Now, as she saw him standing on the step, she even smiled.

'Hello.'

'How are you doing, Mel? Is this a good time?'

'As good as any.'

She stepped back to let him in. Appearing silently at her side, Poppy slipped her hand into her mother's.

'Alicia's out with Jo. She's taken him to a toddler group in the village, can you imagine?'

He smiled, taking in the grand hall and wide, curving staircase. Sandra, who had remained in close touch with Mel, had told him all about how Mel and her children had moved in with their grandmother. The old girl was a little batty, she'd said, but the arrangement was surprisingly successful.

She led him into a huge room, filled with what, to his eyes, looked like a load of posh junk, but was probably worth a bundle.

'Poppy, why don't you go and have a play in the tree house? You can take Ginger up there.'

The little girl nodded and skipped out of the room.

'I've bought her a rabbit,' Mel said. 'She takes him everywhere.'

'How's she coping?'

Mel gave a faint shrug, her smile fixed. 'Getting better.'

They sat down. Despite his experience of meetings with bereaved relatives, Dave felt unaccustomedly nervous. Mel Stenning seemed so alone, perhaps that was it. He'd never admit it, but a tiny part of him felt responsible for what had happened. After all, if he had got to the truth earlier, Simon might still be alive.

'She was being bullied at school,' Mel was saying. 'That's what all those letters were about. A horrible little cow called Megan was sending them.'

He nodded. Sandra had mentioned this, too. 'Yes, I heard.'

'Apparently they thought it was hilarious to tease her about having a stepdad. It makes me feel terrible, that I didn't pick up on it.'

'These things happen, I suppose.'

'Only when parents aren't paying attention. I can't believe it was going on for so long and I never knew about it.'

'I'm sure it wasn't your fault.'

There was a long, awkward silence.

'So,' Dave said at last, squeezing his palms with his thumbs. 'I hope you don't mind me dropping in on you like this. It's a courtesy call, really, just to touch base with you after the trial. We're obviously pleased with the outcome.'

She nodded, her eyes fixed on his. 'She's not going to get out, is she?'

'She'll be in prison for the rest of her life.'

'What about the baby?'

'That was partly what I wanted to tell you. He's been adopted by a family in Chelmsford. Rosa won't see him again.'

Mel frowned, picking at the silky threads of the high-backed chair where she was seated. There wasn't a great deal else that Dave could tell her. She had attended the entire trial, sitting quietly at the back of the courtroom, her hands folded in her lap as she listened intently to the proceedings. When the jury had returned a verdict of guilty of the first-degree murder of Jacqui Jenning and Simon Stenning, and of the abduction of Poppy and Jo Stenning, she had nodded with satisfaction, then risen to her feet and left the courtroom. By the time Dave had battled through the media scrum, she was gone.

'How about you?' he asked. 'How are you feeling? You must have found the trial very difficult . . .'

She shook her head, as if it was irrelevant. 'All I can think is that I should have had the guts to trust Si,' she whispered. 'I thought he was lying to me.'

'It's hardly surprising, given what happened.'

'We promised we'd trust each other, but from the beginning I'd convinced myself that he couldn't ever love me.'

'Come on now, you mustn't blame yourself.'

'Why not?' Glancing hastily away from him, she wiped her eyes with the back of her hand. Since that terrible night when she had discovered her husband's body, it was the first time he had seen her cry. 'I'm not very good at relationships, you see. I always mess everything up . . .'

'I'm sure that's not true . . .' He was about to make the little speech he sometimes gave to victims about bad things happening to good people, but she interrupted him.

'The thing is, Dave, I've never had any real direction in my life. Before I met Si I was just drifting. That's why I married him, I suppose. I thought he could save me, make everything meaningful.'

Dave nodded, not sure what to say. Mel had risen to her feet and moved towards the large bay window from where, in the gardens outside, she could see Poppy running over the grass.

'Si thought that all he had to do was wave a magic wand and everything that had happened in the past would disappear. It was all bollocks, though, wasn't it? Imagining that all it would take to solve my problems was to meet some new person and be swept off my feet.'

Dave nodded. 'I suppose it's what a lot of people believe.'

'No, they don't.' She turned to face him, her eyes flashing. 'They might say they do, but most people are too busy getting on with their lives to waste them on stupid fantasies. Life isn't about waiting around for someone to save you. It was up to me to make things work, not some knight in shining armour.'

She was glaring at him almost accusingly. Glancing away from her fierce eyes, Dave scrutinised his shoes. He was accustomed to people's outpourings: the grief or anger or fear that flooded from them when seated in his interview room. Yet this encounter was different.

'I don't think I ever really knew how to love Si,' Mel said quietly. 'I thought I did, but if I'd really loved him I'd have trusted him, wouldn't

I? I wouldn't have been so afraid of hearing what he needed to tell me.'

'Oh, come on now . . .'

She was not interested in his reassurances. Her eyes flicked away from his, her face clouding with thoughts that she was not prepared to share.

'Mummy!' Poppy was yelling from the garden. 'Ginger's eating some dandelions!'

At the sound of her daughter's voice, Mel's face, which had seemed for a moment to be unbearably hard, softened. 'The point is, I'm not going to drift any more,' she said, almost smiling. 'The kids are all that matter now. That's why I'm going to stay here with Alicia and try to build some kind of normal life for them . . . OK, honey! I'm coming!'

Standing, she started to move across the battered drawing room, towards the garden doors.

It was after three. He decided not to go back to the station and his paperwork, but to slip off early. The morning had been humid and cloudy, but now the sky had cleared to brilliant blue. When he reached the dual carriageway he opened the car windows and pressed his foot down, enjoying the feel of warm air rushing at him, the bright summer light burning into his face. During his brief discussion with Mel he had felt gloomy and oppressed. Now that he was outside, however, the heaviness lifted off him, like mist evaporating. He was not a drifter, had never struggled for meaning. In his view you didn't need a degree in philosophy to work out the root of happiness: steady work, accomplishable goals, the love of a wife and children. How difficult was that?

He was approaching Herne Bay. In the distance he could see the flashing strip of sea, the glint of car bonnets parked by the beach. He drove a couple of miles through the centre of town, then turned into a suburban road. Around the corner, past the postbox: acres of neat, 1960s houses, with their tidy front gardens and manageable lawns. Past kids' bikes and gleaming saloons, shimmering in the sun. In less than a minute he'd be home.

He slowed down, clicking his indicator. Some of his neighbours had climbing frames and slides for their children, others had tubs of cheerful flowers by the front step. Finally he turned into the drive, noting the colourful front gardens with pleasure. Geraniums, delphiniums, peonies: the kinds of flowers you knew where you were with.

Katy Gardner

The bleak, windswept setting in Kent that provides the background for much of the action in *Hidden*, is a real place that has lingered in Katy Gardner's mind for several years. 'I lived in a small town in north Kent in the 1990s. It was a strange place in an oddly cut-off part of the country. Like my central character, Mel, I used to walk along a small river that led through a boat yard, snaking through the surrounding mudflats until eventually spilling into the Thames Estuary. Boats rotted in the mud and there was never anyone around. It always seemed to be windy, too: the cry of herring gulls drowned by the frantic clicking of masts and flapping of sails. One building in particular attracted my attention: a huge, derelict Victorian warehouse. It's been renovated now, just as Mel and her husband are trying to do during the course of the novel, but back then it seemed filled with ghosts. I'd always wanted to write about it, and when I was planning *Hidden*, this seemed like the natural setting for the story.'

Katy admits that she tends to tuck away all her experiences of people and places and hoard them for possible inclusion in a plot. 'When I'm at the "ideas" rather than the writing stage of a book, I'm like a magpie, swooping on anything that sparkles.' So how does she settle on a storyline? 'What one hopes for are eureka! moments, when a fully formed plot falls into one's lap. But in my experience, the process of putting the fragments of disparate ideas together into a story is far more laborious and, at times, frustrating. Maybe this is particularly the case with thrillers, where a carefully planned plot is vital. One might have a scary opening, but without a satisfying ending, and some great twists and turns, it isn't a contender.

'Somebody once said that story ideas are like buses. It's not so much that you wait for hours and three pull up at the same time, but rather that they have a tendency to arrive without their destinations clearly displayed on the front. The bus may initially head for the open road, but before you know it, you'll be dumped back at the depot!'

Katy says that her starting points are usually grounded in actual incidents. An important scene in *Losing Gemma*, her first novel, revolves around a central character becoming lost in the jungle. It was inspired, in part, by Katy's own experiences of backpacking, as well as a story she was told about a man who was forced to survive in the jungle for twenty-four hours after he failed to rendezvous with a tourist bus. Her second book, *The Mermaid's Purse*, concerned student–teacher relationships. 'I'm a university lecturer, and while I've never been stalked, I have a friend who was drawn into a disturbing series of incidents with a student. Lecturers are exposed to large numbers of students, some of whom, inevitably, suffer personal crises during their courses.'

> *'When I'm at the "ideas" rather than the writing stage of a book, I'm like a magpie, swooping on anything that sparkles.'*

As a lecturer in social anthropology at the University of Sussex, Katy is naturally drawn to writing about relationships, and her latest novel, *Hidden*, is no exception. 'My books tend to be preoccupied with apparently normal relationships that turn nasty, plus I've always had a somewhat macabre fascination with true-life crime stories. Forensic information, gleaned from the newspaper or the TV can add vivid detail to a scene. In *Hidden*, the police have a breakthrough when they find minute blood splatters on a recently painted wall, and this was part of a real case that I'd read about.

'It's in the news stories, too, that one hears about the personality disorders that contribute to murders. People with these disorders are hard to spot and can blend so seamlessly into the fabric of normal life that it's often unclear where the danger lies. Such a character lies at the heart of *Hidden*.'

While her thrillers may take her readers into the bleak world of dysfunctional people and distressing situations, Katy Gardner would appear to have her own life rooted in a very secure place. 'I live at the bottom of the Sussex Downs, which will always be my favourite place, whatever the season, and the beach at Ovington, near Brighton, is great place in the summer holidays. There are enough rock pools to keep my kids happily occupied for hours.'

Taken from www.penguin.co.uk

The Two Mrs Robinsons

Donna Hay

Anna lives with Oliver Robinson and their three-year-old son Charlie. Anna and Oliver met when she worked as a waitress at Oliver's restaurant.

Eve lives with her two teenage children, Matt and Georgia, and is separated from Oliver Robinson. It is Eve who helped Oliver build up his restaurant business.

Two very different women in love with the same man.

But two into one just won't go.

DECEMBER

EVE ROBINSON REMEMBERED how Christmas used to be. Before dawn, she and Oliver would be sitting in bed amid a sea of wrapping paper as Matt and Georgia opened their presents, squealing with excitement. Later, there would be a crisp, cold walk by the river before coming home to a crackling fire and the smell of roast turkey filling the air.

Five years later, it was all different. Oliver was off playing happy families with his girlfriend, Georgia was locked in her bedroom with her new MP3 player, and Matt was sleeping off his hangover after stumbling home at dawn and drunkenly felling the Christmas tree.

It was hardly the stuff Bing Crosby was dreaming of.

'Looks like it's just you and me,' she sighed to Benson the labrador. At least she still had some presents to open. Matt had given her a set of oven gloves and a novelty tea towel in a BHS carrier bag, while Georgia had splashed out on a jar of antiwrinkle cream.

'The woman in the shop said it's better than Botox,' she'd said.

'Lovely.' Eve thought about the hair colourant Georgia had bought her for her birthday, one that guaranteed to get rid of grey, and wondered if her daughter was trying to tell her something.

She wondered what Oliver's girlfriend Anna might be unwrapping at this very moment. She was sure it wasn't a novelty tea towel. Oliver had always been brilliant at giving presents.

The phone rang. For a fraction of a second before she picked it up, Eve thought it might be her mother. Vanessa was spending a month among the yurt makers of Kyrgyzstan, but surely it wasn't too much to hope she'd remembered her only child at Christmas?

But it was her friend Jan. 'Just calling to wish you a Happy Christmas,' she shouted, against a din of shrieking children. Although they were the same age, Jan had put off having babies until she'd established herself in her teaching career. Listening to the chaos on the other end of the line now, Eve was pleased her children had arrived unplanned in her early twenties while she still had the energy to cope.

'Happy Christmas to you, too. Sounds like Armageddon there. So what did Santa bring you? Did Pete buy you nipple clamps again?'

'Funnily enough, no. It was Chanel No. 5 this year.'

'Wow, I'm impressed.'

'Don't be, I bought it for myself. And wrapped it. I even wrote out my own gift tag. Why are men so crap at buying presents?'

'Oliver wasn't.' She heard Jan's sigh, but ignored it. They both knew what she was going to say next. 'I wonder what he's got Anna. A Barbie annual, I expect. That's the kind of thing she'd want at her age.'

'Eve!' Jan laughed, trying to be stern. 'Stop it. I'm in a difficult position here.' She and Peter had been friends of Eve and Oliver's since university, and they were trying to stay friends with them both.

'No, seriously, what did he get her?'

'I don't know.'

'Liar. It's underwear, isn't it? Something dead sexy.' Anna probably wore underwear like dental floss, unlike the M&S economy packs Eve always ended up buying. No wonder Oliver had dumped her.

'I told you, I don't know. And I wouldn't tell you anyway. TASHA! Stop that right now! Hang on a minute.' Eve listened to Jan dishing out some stern words on the other end of the line. 'Now, what were we saying?'

'We were talking about what Britney Spears got for Christmas. If you won't tell me I'll just have to ask her myself when I see her tonight.'

There was an uncomfortable silence. 'You're not going to Oliver's party?'

'Why not? We always go. Matt and Georgia like to see their dad on Christmas Day, especially as it's his birthday as well.'

'But you're not supposed to go to your ex's parties when you're divorced.'

'We're not divorced,' Eve reminded her tartly.

'I don't care, it's still all wrong. You get on better than me and Peter, and we're married.'

Eve smiled. 'Surely it's better for the children if we can all be civilised about it?'

'You're not very civilised to Anna. Don't you remember what it was like last year? You spent the whole evening giving each other evil death stares.'

'Look, I can't help it if she's not grown up enough to accept that Oliver and I are still friends, can I?'

'So you're not just going to this party to wind her up?'

'The thought hadn't crossed my mind,' Eve said piously.

Jan laughed. 'Right. And those are real reindeer tracks on my patio.'

'**I**s that new?' Georgia Robinson stood in the bedroom doorway, watching her mother struggle with the zip on her dress.

'As a matter of fact, it is.' With a giant sucked-in breath, she managed to wrench the zip up the last two inches.

'Where did you buy it?' She caught her mother's evasive look. 'Oh God, you got it from Top Shop, didn't you? You're nearly forty, for heaven's sake. Why can't you start acting your age?'

Her mother pulled a face at her. 'It's not that bad, is it?'

Georgia studied her carefully. She hated to admit it, but it looked quite good. The deep red swirly print suited her honey gold hair, and the soft jersey fabric hid all her flabby bits.

It was what it meant that troubled Georgia. There was only one reason why she'd want to wear a dress like that. Dad. Georgia despaired of her mum ever getting over him. She did this big thing about them being good friends, but it was obvious she was still mad about him.

She almost wished they didn't get on so well. Why couldn't she be more like Stacey's mum next door? Stacey had told her that she'd once tried to run her ex-husband over in her Fiat Punto. Exes always hated each other. Life got too confusing otherwise.

Her mum had no trouble hating Anna, which was a shame because Georgia liked her. It wasn't Anna's fault her parents had split up. It was a bit embarrassing, her dad having a girlfriend only six years older than her brother. But Anna was cool, and funny, and she made Dad happy. Although Georgia could never tell her mum that.

She'd tried to talk to Matt about the Mum situation, but all he did was shrug and say, 'It's no big deal.' He said that about everything except his stupid A levels and his crappy band. But Georgia knew better. Her mum could be annoying, but she loved her and she worried about her ending up lonely and bitter. If only Eve could find a man.

She closed the door on her mum and went back to her own room to get changed. Who listened to her, anyway? She was only fifteen years old, she wasn't supposed to know anything.

Oliver's restaurant was in Fossgate, the road that led down from bustling, touristy Coppergate to the humped bridge over the River Foss. Once the area had been part of the dark underbelly of York, home to the penniless Irish immigrants who flooded there during the famine. It still had an edgy feel about it; it's quirkiness was one of the things Oliver loved about it, and the reason why he'd first bought the failing restaurant fifteen years ago. That and the fact that it was cheap because the area was so down-at-heel. It had smartened up a bit since then.

Walking into Oliver's felt like coming home to Eve. The place had hardly changed since they first opened the doors. The atmosphere was cosy French bistro, with red checked tablecloths, and candles in wax-encrusted wine bottles. It was bittersweet for her, coming back here. Everything had a memory imprinted on it, from the polished floorboards they'd sanded for hours to the old lamps hanging from the blackened beams, which they'd picked up in a flea market on one of their shoestring holidays to France when Matt was a baby. The whole place was like a photo album of their lives together.

The place was already crowded with guests. Eve waved at Jan, who was talking to Frankie the chef, helped herself to a glass of wine from the bar and gave one to Georgia. 'Make it last,' she warned. 'It's the only one you're getting.'

'You don't say that to *him*.' Georgia shot a filthy look at Matt, who was checking his texts, his shaggy dark hair falling into his eyes.

'He's old enough to know better.'

'Is that why he threw up in the flowerbed last night?'

'Just the one,' Eve restated firmly. She scanned the crowd. 'I can't see your dad.'

'You know Oliver. He loves to make an entrance,' said a voice behind her. 'He's probably waiting for everyone else to arrive.'

Eve turned, coming face to shoulder with Adam, Oliver's cousin. He had a new woman with him, a cool brunette. 'Are you saying my estranged husband is an attention-seeker?' she said, mock stern.

'Oliver doesn't have to seek attention. He only has to stand there and it comes his way. It's the rest of us poor mortals who have to jump up and down to get noticed.'

Eve smiled. There was no way Adam would have wanted to be noticed. He was just about the shiest person she knew. He and Oliver could have been brothers, both tall and dark with warm grey eyes. But while Oliver held himself confidently upright, Adam seemed apologetic about his height, his shoulders permanently stooped.

'I'd notice you,' said the woman with him.

'You say that now, but you haven't met my cousin. I'm telling you, it was no accident he was born on Christmas Day.'

'Take no notice of him. He adores Oliver really.' Eve held out her hand. 'I'm Eve Robinson.'

'Imogen Walsh.' The woman's eyes widened. 'So you're Oliver's ex? Wow, I'm surprised you're here. When I split up with a man, all I ever want to do is take a pair of scissors to his suits.'

'I'll take that as a warning,' Adam said solemnly.

Imogen smiled up at him and stroked his chest. 'Oh no, I'm not letting you go for a while,' she purred.

How did he do it, Eve wondered. He was so quiet and self-effacing, and yet he always seemed to have a new woman in tow.

She knew that underneath that shy exterior lurked a sharp sense of humour and a warm, caring heart, but it had taken a long time for her to find that out. She'd been seeing Oliver for months before Adam even looked her in the eye. She felt slightly sorry for Imogen. She thought she had him now, but Adam's only real passion was for his work. He'd inherited the family's market-garden business when Oliver's father died seven years before. Since then he'd worked hard and turned it into a thriving concern, taking on more land, opening a farm shop and breaking into the organic market.

Maybe that was why he couldn't hang on to a woman for long, she thought. No one wanted to come second to a sack of potatoes.

'Here's Oliver now,' he said.

Eve had her back to the door, but she didn't need to be told he'd walked into the room. She could feel the tell-tale prickle on the nape of her neck, just as she'd felt it that night he'd strolled into the Students' Union bar more than twenty years ago.

'Is that his girlfriend?' Imogen whispered. 'She's very—'

'Young?' Eve finished for her.

She looked at Anna, running through the usual envious inventory of her youthful features. Twenty-four years old, skinny and sexy in a short black shift dress which showed off her schoolgirl slender legs. Shiny, spiky hair framed her elfin face, making her big chocolate brown eyes look even more huge and doe-like. Eve felt her bulges oozing over her control pants just looking at her. Anna was everything she wasn't. Not just thin and young and pretty, but cool and confident with it.

'Eve?' She hadn't realised she was gawping until Adam spoke. She grabbed the nearest empty wine bottle.

'Oops, looks like we're running low. I'll just go and get another couple of bottles from the kitchen.' It was a relief to escape and to be able to lose her fixed smile for a minute or two. Everyone was right, she shouldn't have come.

She was just making a fool of herself. She wished she could have had more pride and kept her distance but she couldn't resist it, like probing an aching tooth.

How many people had guessed she still had a massive, hopeless crush on her almost-ex-husband? Everyone, probably. They were all watching her, feeling sorry for her, not believing for a moment all her talk of staying friends for the sake of the children. At least Oliver had no idea. She would have died of shame if he'd found out.

She was coming out of the store room with an armful of bottles when he walked into the kitchen. Seeing him standing in the doorway. Eve felt the familiar, treacherous tug of attraction.

'Adam said you were in here.' He came towards her, arms outstretched, and for a panicky moment Eve thought he was going to hug her, until he said, 'Here, let me take those for you.'

She handed the bottles over, keeping a Rioja in her hand. 'Happy birthday, by the way.'

'Thanks.' He grimaced. 'Just think, next year it'll be the big Four-O.'

'I don't want to think about it, thanks very much. Georgia will probably have me wearing a burka by then.'

'You'll still look gorgeous.'

She fiddled with the label on the bottle to hide her confusion. 'We were beginning to think you weren't coming tonight.'

'We had a bit of a domestic crisis. Charlie was poorly this afternoon. Throwing up all over the place.'

'Over-excitement, I expect.'

'That's what I tried to tell Anna, but she wouldn't listen. She was convinced he had meningitis at least.'

Eve bit back the caustic comment. 'It's only natural for a mother to worry. How is he now?'

'Absolutely fine, just like I said he would be. Anna's mum's looking after him.' He nodded towards the bottle. 'Are you going to open that?'

'Shouldn't we go back to the party?'

'Let's have a quiet drink and catch up first.'

'I don't think Anna would like that, do you?'

'Why not?' He looked genuinely puzzled. That was Oliver, oblivious to everything. Including the effect he had on other people.

'I just don't think she'd appreciate us being alone together.'

'Anna's fine about it. Anyway, you're family. Just because we're not together any more doesn't mean I've stopped caring about you.'

She wished he wouldn't look at her like that, stirring up all those feelings she'd tried so hard to stop having for the past five years.

She turned away, found a corkscrew and started to open the bottle, then yelped with pain as the corkscrew slipped. 'Bugger!'

'Let me see.' He took her hand and inspected it. 'It's bleeding quite a bit. We'd better run it under the tap.'

Eve watched the water running over their hands. 'Well? What's the verdict? Will I be able to play the piano after this?'

'I expect so.'

'That's good news. I couldn't play before.'

Oliver grinned. 'Maybe this'll teach you not to mess around with sharp objects.'

'Says the man who almost took his fingers off in an onion-chopping contest.'

'That just goes to show I know what I'm talking about, doesn't it?'

They were still laughing when Anna walked in. 'Sorry to interrupt,' she said. 'But everyone's wondering where you are.'

Oliver let go of her hand. 'Sorry, Eve had an accident. I had to apply some first aid.'

Anna glared at Eve. 'I'll tell them you're on your way, shall I?' She slammed back through the doors.

'And you still think she's fine about us?' Eve said.

Eve was looking so good, Anna thought enviously, with her thick blonde hair and curvy body under that red dress. She felt like a wreck. She hadn't had time to shower or wash her hair, and her old black dress showed up all the shadows under her eyes. And she was worried she might still smell of sick from where Charlie had thrown up over her just before they left the house.

She looked around the room. How did she end up here? Twenty-four years old, with a three-year-old son and a crippling mortgage. Not to mention a couple of teenage stepchildren and a new group of fortysomething friends who, no matter how hard she tried, felt as if they didn't really belong to her. Talk about growing up fast.

She went to the bar to top up her drink and found Georgia crouched by the dishwasher, sneakily helping herself to a Bacardi Breezer. She jumped and nearly dropped the bottle when she saw Anna.

'Don't worry, I won't tell anyone. Actually, I wouldn't mind one of those myself.'

Georgia handed her a pink bottle. She was very pretty, with her flawless skin, long shiny dark hair and her father's grey eyes fringed with thick lashes. 'I didn't think grown-ups liked that kind of thing,' she said.

'I'm not feeling very grown-up tonight.' What she felt like doing was getting steaming drunk, telling Oliver's wretched ex-wife what she really thought of her, then heading off to the nearest club.

She popped the cap on her drink and sat down next to Georgia.

Georgia's mobile bleeped, announcing a text message. She pounced on it.

'Anything interesting?' Anna asked.

'Just my friend Stacey. She's having a party.'

'Shame you couldn't go.'

'Mum wouldn't let me. She doesn't approve of Stacey's family.'

Georgia abandoned her drink and went outside to call Stacey for a private update. Anna slumped against the dishwasher, sipped her pink drink and called her mum.

'How's Charlie?' she asked brightly.

'He's fine. He's watching TV with your nana. I take it you're not having a very good time?'

'Not really.' Anna's merry façade crumbled. 'Everyone's ignoring me, and I've just caught Oliver in a clinch with Eve.'

'What?'

'Well, not actually a clinch. But too close for my liking, anyway.'

'And what did you do?'

'What could I do? Start a fight?' She heard the sound of the TV playing in the background and ached with loneliness. 'I hate it here. Can I come home?' Anna peeped over the bar. Oliver was playing the genial host as usual, filling everyone's glasses, laughing and joking with his friends. Eve wasn't far behind, as if she was attached to him by an invisible thread. 'Nobody would notice if I left.'

'Oliver would notice.'

'I doubt it.'

'Oh, love. Just stay and give it another try. It's only for an hour or two.' Her mother sighed. 'If you leave now it'll be like admitting defeat.'

Eve was standing behind Oliver now, her hand resting lightly on his shoulder. He didn't look as if he was fighting her off.

'I'll try,' she promised. 'But don't blame me if I end up tipping a glass of wine over someone.'

'There you are.' Oliver greeted her with a kiss on the cheek. 'I thought you'd run out on me.'

'I called my mum to check on Charlie. He's fine.'

'You see? I told you he'd be OK.' He put his arm around her. 'Come and have another drink. Everyone's been asking where you are.'

She did her best to fit in with Oliver's friends. They all tried to be nice to her too, but it seemed as if every conversation ended with a joke or a story about the Good Old Days, when Oliver and Eve were still married. 'I'm really sorry,' Oliver said as they queued up for food later. 'I don't want you to feel left out.' He looked troubled.

'You can't help it. You and Eve had a history together, I can't change that, and neither can you.' That was what her head told her, anyway. Her heart still fretted that if Oliver kept being reminded what a great person his ex was, he might decide he wanted her back.

Of course, Fate conspired to make sure the only empty seats were on Eve's table. They'd hardly sat down before she ambushed Oliver, talking about a bill he'd promised to sort out. Anna gritted her teeth to stop herself asking why Eve couldn't pay her own damn bills and watched Matt messing around with his mobile across the table.

'Expecting a call?' she said.

He looked up, his eyes just visible through his mane of dark curls. He was tall and angular, a gawky collection of arms and legs and hair. 'Just checking my bids on eBay.'

'What are you after?'

'A drum kit.'

'Excuse me?' Eve looked up. 'You're not having a drum kit.'

'Apparently not,' he shrugged. 'I've just been outbid.'

Anna tried again, asking Matt about his university plans. Soon they were chatting about the colleges he'd applied to. All the time she was aware of Eve listening in.

'You should ask Anna for some tips,' Eve said. 'She's sure to be an expert. After all, it wasn't that long ago she was there herself.'

Be nice, Anna told herself, gripping her fork until her knuckles turned white. 'What course are you thinking of taking?'

'Forensic science.'

'Sounds impressive,' Oliver said. 'How did a pair of ignoramuses like us end up with such brainy children?'

'Speak for yourself. I'll have you know I worked hard at university. Unlike some people,' Eve said.

And then they were off again, tripping down Memory Lane hand in hand, laughing about all the things they got up to when they were students. Matt and Georgia joined in. They were so like a proper, happy family it made Anna's heart ache. She put down her napkin. 'I'm going to get some more food.'

Oliver caught up with her at the buffet table. 'I'm sorry,' he said.

'I'm amazed you ever split up with her, if your life was that wonderful.'

He looked hurt. 'You know it wasn't. OK, we were happy. Once. But that was a long time ago. Don't you see, the only reason we get on so well now is because we're not together?'

'Maybe you should tell her that?' Anna glanced back at Eve, who was watching them. 'She wants you back.'

He laughed. 'For heaven's sake! We're just friends.'

'I don't think your ex sees it like that. Why do you think she hangs around all the time? She's waiting for you to get tired of me. It's not as if you're actually committed to me or anything, is it?'

'I live with you. We have a son together. What more commitment could there be?'

You could marry me, she thought. But she didn't dare say it.

'We're just trying to be mature about our break-up for the sake of the kids,' Oliver said. 'Would you rather we were at each other's throats?'

She was tempted to say yes, but deep down Anna knew she didn't mean it. 'Of course not,' she mumbled.

'I love you, but I love her too. We had twenty years together, she's the mother of my children. She'll always be important to me. I know I can't expect you to understand what it's like, being so young—'

Anna's head snapped up. 'So I'm not expected to understand, is that it? I'm not mature and grown-up like you and Eve. Well, I don't think there's anything particularly mature about hanging around someone like a lovesick teenager. If anyone needs to grow up, it's your bloody ex!'

She thrust her plate into Oliver's hands, already heading for the door.

Her mum didn't seem surprised to find Anna shivering on her doorstep half an hour later. 'I had a feeling you'd turn up,' she said, pulling her dressing gown around her. 'Have you walked all this way?'

'I couldn't find a taxi. And I left my bag at the restaurant.' As flounce-outs go, it hadn't exactly been well-planned. She hadn't even remembered her coat. And it had started to snow.

'Come in before you die of hypothermia,' her mum said.

Keith, her partner, was in the sitting room, watching the TV with a glass of beer in his hand. He took one look at Anna standing in the doorway, dripping and bedraggled, and put down his glass. 'I'll—um—make myself scarce, shall I?'

'No, you watch the end of the film. We'll go in the kitchen.'

Her mum's kitchen was modern but warm and homely. She fussed around Anna finding her a pair of jeans and a jumper to wear, and drying her hair with a warm towel. Then she busied herself putting on the kettle. Anna had never known her mother sit still for longer than five minutes. When she wasn't working part-time as a teaching assistant at the local primary school, she was looking after her grandchildren, doing her elderly mother's shopping or catching up with coursework for her social-studies degree.

But then, Jackie had always worked hard. When Anna's father died leaving his wife with three children, she'd worked double shifts at the chocolate factory to make ends meet while going back to college to improve her skills. Anna admired her mum more than any other woman.

Jackie put down the bright yellow teapot in the middle of the table. 'So,' she said. 'Tell me all about it.'

She sat and listened as Anna poured out her troubles.

'For what it's worth, I don't think you've got anything to worry about,' Jackie said. 'Oliver obviously adores you and little Charlie.'

'So why won't he marry me?'

'Have you asked him?'

'I'm too scared.' Never in a million years did she imagine she would be that desperate to get married. At school, Anna had had bigger plans than that. She was going to be a hotshot lawyer, defending the underdog. And then she met Oliver.

She'd first met him when she'd worked as a waitress in his restaurant during the university holidays. She'd liked him immediately, but there was never anything more to it than friendship. He was happily married, or so she thought. But by the time she went back to work there the following summer, Oliver and Eve had split up. Although he insisted it was his idea, being away from his family was obviously destroying him.

He needed a shoulder to cry on, and she was there. He told her about the break-up, explained how he and Eve wanted different things out of life. He was a free spirit, she craved security. He wanted adventure, she wanted cosy domesticity. Realising how unhappy they were making each other, he'd walked away.

Anna confided in him, too, about her on–off relationship. She'd been seeing Danny Lynch, a solicitor in a law firm near her college. But he was ambitious, and had his sights set firmly on a future that didn't include her. Anna also suspected he didn't go short of female company while she was at home during the holidays.

At first it was just friendship between her and Oliver. But as time went on Anna began to realise she was falling in love. She and Oliver had the same quirky sense of humour, the same enthusiasm. They would talk for hours, sharing their wild dreams about going around the world in a camper van. Anna loved Oliver's gentleness and optimism.

Her mother was concerned about the age gap at first, but once she saw how much Oliver adored her daughter, she changed her mind. Eve was a different story. She was furious. Anna couldn't imagine why she was reacting so badly—after all, it wasn't as if she'd stolen Oliver from her, but the separation became ugly and it tore Oliver apart.

Then, just to make life even more complicated, she found out she was pregnant. She was in her last year at college, she had her whole life ahead of her, and her career to think about. She was sure Oliver wouldn't want a baby, especially with all the hassle he was getting from Eve. It took her ages to pluck up the courage to tell him. Like a coward, she did it on the phone from uni.

'So what do you want to do?' he'd asked.

'I suppose the sensible thing would be not to go ahead.'

Silence. 'And is that what you want?'

'Like I said, it's the only sensible option.'

He didn't argue, although she wanted him to. So with a heavy heart, Anna booked an appointment at the clinic.

But while she was sitting in the waiting room, she realised she couldn't do it. It was her child and she was going to have it.

As she came out of the clinic into the sunshine, she was almost run down by Oliver's dark green MG screeching to a halt in front of her.

He got out and slammed the door. 'Have you . . . has it happened?'

She shook her head. 'I couldn't.'

'Thank God for that.'

'I'm not doing it to trap you or anything,' she went on in a rush. 'I've been thinking about it, and . . . what did you say?'

'Anna, I haven't been able to sleep since you told me.'

'So why didn't you say anything?'

'Because I didn't want to put any pressure on you. You sounded so determined.'

'I thought it was what you wanted?'

'Let's face it, having a baby is the last thing either of us should be considering. It'll change everything for both of us.'

She frowned. 'Are you trying to talk me out of it? Because if you are, you're doing a damn good job.'

'No, but I need you to understand what you're doing.'

She looked at him ruefully. 'I suppose this means we'll have to cancel the round-the-world trip?'

'Oh, I don't know,' he grinned. 'You can get a cot in a camper van, can't you?'

And that was how it had been. Even when Charlie was born, they hadn't lost their sense of adventure. Anna knew Oliver was a free spirit, and she was careful not to try to tie him down, knowing that was where Eve had made her big mistake. But after five years, all she really wanted was some status in his life. It infuriated her to see Eve still wearing her wedding ring, as if she was the permanent fixture in Oliver's life and Anna was the passing fling.

'So why don't you think he'd want to marry you?' her mother asked.

'He doesn't think he's any good at it. He blames himself for the break-up with Eve. I sometimes wonder if he doesn't want to marry me because he wants to keep his options open.' There it was. Her worst fear, out in the open. 'It makes sense, doesn't it?' she went on. 'I mean, he and Eve were great together. Everyone says so. She's a brilliant mother, a fantastic cook and basically everything I'm not.'

'Don't put yourself down.'

'Mum, I bought our Christmas dinner from Marks and Spencer. I send Charlie to nursery with a sandwich from the petrol station.'

'But Oliver doesn't want a domestic goddess, does he? He wants you.'

Anna pulled a face. 'Let's face it, Eve's the one for him. They might have got back together if I hadn't come along and got pregnant.'

'Or he might still be living on his own?' Jackie said.

'I know Eve would take him back in a second,' Anna said. 'Maybe he's just waiting for the right time.'

'If you feel like that, maybe you should say something?'

'What can I say? I'm frightened to talk to him about it in case I give him the chance he's looking for.'

They were interrupted by Keith. 'There's someone to see you,' he said. Oliver stood behind him in the doorway, looking sheepish. His face was ruddy with cold, and melting snowflakes glistened in his dark hair.

'What are you doing here?' Anna asked.

'I came to find you.'

'You walked out on your own party?'

'There didn't seem much point in being there without you. I thought you might be needing these.' He handed over her coat and bag. 'Can I walk you home?'

The snow had settled quickly, laying a thick, muffling blanket over the deserted streets of the Cliffmead estate. Theirs were the only footprints in the perfect, crisp whiteness as they crunched up the street. They'd just crossed the main road when they spotted the huddled figure in the bus shelter. 'Jesus,' Oliver muttered. 'Poor sod. Imagine being out on a night like this.' Anna stayed at a cautious distance while Oliver went over to the man and shook him awake. The figure stirred, mumbled something and went back to sleep.

'At least he's alive,' Oliver said. 'Stinks of drink, though.'

Please don't say you want to take him home, Anna prayed silently. It wouldn't be the first time. She really didn't want another drunk sleeping it off in the spare room. The last one had left with her handbag and the CD player.

Oliver shrugged off his coat and laid it carefully over the man. 'There,' he said. 'That'll be a nice surprise for him when he wakes up.'

Anna looked sidelong at him. Thick, feathery flakes of snow settled on his hair and shoulders. He could hardly speak he was shivering so much, but he was still smiling. He'd just given his coat to a stranger on a freezing night. How could she bear to lose him for the sake of a ring on her finger?

JANUARY

'DON'T YOU THINK it's time we got a divorce?'

Eve went on unpacking her shopping from the supermarket carrier bags. 'What's brought this on?' she managed to say finally.

Oliver sat at the table. 'We can't let things drag on forever. It's not fair on you or Anna. I don't suppose it's come as a surprise to you,' he said. 'We knew it was bound to happen one day, didn't we?'

'Of course.' Except she didn't know. She'd allowed herself the shred of hope that he was clinging on to their marriage because it meant as much to him as it did to her. Now he'd slashed all those hopes. This was even more final than the day he walked out. It was all she could do to stop herself howling.

She wedged a roll of bin bags behind the bleach at the back of the cupboard. 'I suppose this means you're planning to get married?' She managed to get the words out without choking.

'I don't know. Probably.' He laughed. 'She might not have me.'

'Oh, she'll have you all right.'

Something in her tone must have given her away, because Oliver came and squatted down beside her, his gaze level with hers. 'You are OK about this, aren't you, Evie?'

'Would it make any difference if I wasn't?'

He looked troubled. 'It won't change anything. I'll still be here for you and the children. Nothing will ever change that.'

Didn't he understand this changed everything? It wasn't just the end of all her hopes; once Anna was Oliver's wife, she'd make damn sure there was no place in his life for her. She said, 'We'll see. Now go home, before Anna thinks you've been kidnapped.'

At times like this, she wished she had a mother she could phone for sympathy and advice. But Eve knew she'd be wasting her time calling Vanessa. Vanessa had never been convinced by her marriage to Oliver in the first place. 'Marriage is so outdated, so vulgar. I never brought you up to be so conventional.' Exactly, Eve wanted to say. It was because of her upbringing that she longed for marriage, no matter how vulgar it might be.

Vanessa Gifford was notorious even before Eve edged her way into her life. She was a sociologist, who'd written several academic books on world cultures. But mostly she was remembered for her explosive theories on sex and relationships. She believed in free love, which she practised enthusiastically on her commune in the Cotswolds. She was brilliant and fearlessly outspoken; TV shows and magazines always called on her when they wanted an outrageous opinion, and Vanessa didn't disappoint.

Vanessa freely admitted her daughter was an experiment. Eve never knew her father; her mother couldn't decide whether he was a Harvard psychology professor or a Hackney barman called Jon. She couldn't see why it was so important to Eve anyway.

Eve didn't mind growing up on the commune when she was small. It was only when she was sent to boarding school that it became really excruciating. But Eve could have put up with the teasing and torment. She could have tolerated her mother's communal living and even her occasional experiments with lesbianism, because she was still her mother and she loved her. What really hurt was The Book.

She was fifteen years old when her mother published *The Motherhood Myth*. Eve didn't even bother to read it, until one of the girls found an interview with Vanessa in the *Sunday Times*.

By Vanessa Gifford's standards, it was hardly shocking. There was no sex, no cranky ideas. Just the calm, statement that she had never loved her daughter. Maternal feelings were all in the mind, she said. She cared no more for her own child than she did for anyone else's.

Eve had cried for two days after she read it. It was like an atom bomb dropped in the middle of her life, blowing her whole world apart. Eventually she pulled herself together like the sensible girl she was, but there was a hole in her life that she couldn't fill. She didn't realise what it was until she went to university, and met Oliver. She had no idea what made him ask her out. Maybe with his typical kindness he realised she needed rescuing.

Being with him, Eve finally realised what had been missing from her life: someone who cared about her feelings more than their own. It was a heady sensation, to love and be loved in return.

They married soon after leaving university, and despite her mother's dire predictions, they were blissfully happy. Eve was carried along by Oliver's dreams of owning his own restaurant. She'd never had any ambitions of her own, apart from having a normal, loving family. But Oliver's dreams were big enough for both of them. They lived in a tiny flat, she taught at a local school while Oliver worked as a trainee chef in a restaurant, and they both saved like mad.

Luckily for Oliver, the owner took a shine to him and taught him all about the restaurant business. Then, when he decided to retire, he gave Oliver the chance of buying the place. It should have been their dream come true. But Eve had just found out she was pregnant. While Oliver wanted to buy the restaurant, she was determined they should have a proper home for their new baby. In the end, she won. But it was a hollow victory. Eve could see how disappointed Oliver was. So when, three years later, the restaurant came back on the market, she encouraged him to remortgage their home, even though by then she was pregnant with Georgia.

The early years were a real struggle. Eve worked during the day while Oliver took care of the children at the restaurant. Then, in the evening she'd take over. They were busy, exhausted and broke, but Eve had never been happier.

But as the years went by, it started to unravel. The restaurant was doing well, and Eve wanted to relax and enjoy the fruits of their labours. But Oliver wanted to expand the business. Eve couldn't understand why he wasn't satisfied with what they had. But Oliver craved adventure, excitement. He wanted to take risks, but Eve was scared of playing Russian roulette with her family's future.

She sensed he was growing restless, and panicked. She tried to hold on to him, but like sand, the tighter she held on, the faster he seemed to slip through her fingers.

In the end, she knew what was coming, even before he told her he was leaving. Just a break, he'd said, to decide what they both wanted.

In some ways it was a relief. Things had got so tense between them, he'd lost sight of all the good things in their marriage. She comforted herself that once he was away it would give him a chance to realise what he was missing and come home.

But then Anna came along and changed everything.

She was chopping onions when Matt and Georgia came home. She listened to them clattering around in the hall, bickering as usual.

Matt came into the kitchen first. He went straight to the fridge. 'We'll be eating supper in half an hour,' Eve warned as he emerged with a plastic wrapped cheese in one hand and a jar of Branston pickle in the other. 'I hope you'll be hungry.'

'I'm always hungry.'

'Fat pig,' Georgia came in, frantically texting.

'Airhead.'

'Braindead.'

'Be quiet, you two.' Eve massaged her temples.

Matt put the food down on the table and peered at her. 'Are you all right, Mum?'

'I'm fine.' She chopped the onions into a mush, her knife moving up and down rapidly. 'Your father came round to see me earlier.'

'Oh yeah?'

'We're getting a divorce.'

Georgia went on texting. Matt stopped buttering his sandwich and looked at her.

'You're all right about that, are you?'

'Of course she's all right,' Georgia said, before Eve could reply. 'It's not like they're ever going to get back together, are they?' She pressed the 'send' button on her phone. 'I'm going upstairs.'

Matt shrugged. 'She's all heart, my sister,' he said.

FEBRUARY

'AND THEN I GOT HOME and found she'd cleaned me out. She even took my railway memorabilia collection, and I know for a fact she hates trains.' The man looked at Anna across the desk. 'What do you think I should do?'

'I've got some information on mediation here—'

'Not about *her*. I don't care if I never see her again. But that railway memorabilia was unique.'

Anna gathered together some information on divorce and property and the man went away, still grumbling.

'Now there's someone who's got his priorities sorted out,' Elliott, the advice-centre manager, said as he flicked through that morning's post.

'I didn't like to tell him she's probably got rid of the whole lot on eBay by now.'

'I don't blame her if she has.' Barbara the receptionist looked up from the Sudoku puzzle in that morning's *Daily Mail*. 'Nasty little man. Did you see his shoes? My Bernard always says you can tell a lot from a man by looking at his shoes. And he should know, he was in the army.'

'Panzer division, presumably,' Elliott muttered to Anna.

'I hardly think it's our place to judge our clients,' Neil, ever the peacemaker, put in.

'And his eyebrows met in the middle,' Barbara went on, ignoring him. 'You can never trust a man whose eyebrows meet. That's a fact.'

Anna smiled. 'So let's get this straight. According to your theories, we can't trust anyone under twenty five or foreign, anyone who has ginger hair, body odour, more than three children, an IQ of less than 150, defective eyebrows or scruffy shoes?'

'You forgot the squint,' Elliott pointed out.

'Visual impairment, please,' Neil winced.

'Sounds like most of our clients.'

'You said it,' Barbara sniffed.

Sometimes Anna wondered why Barbara worked in a community advice centre. It was like Bluebeard becoming a marriage-guidance counsellor. Anna was convinced it was only a matter of time before she put on gloves to hand over the leaflets.

Neil, the other adviser, couldn't have been more different. He was a vegan, rode a battered old bike, and lived in fear of being politically incorrect or accidentally wearing leather shoes. His heart was in the right place, unlike Barbara, who didn't have one.

'Here's one for you.' Elliott handed Anna an envelope. 'Looks like a Valentine's card. Does Oliver know you have a secret admirer?'

'Hardly.' She ripped it open. 'It's an invitation to a debt-management workshop. Very romantic, I'm sure.'

'Personally, I think Valentine's Day is nothing more than another chance for big business to exploit the hapless consumer,' Neil said.

'You old romantic,' Anna teased him. 'I suppose that's what you told your girlfriend when you didn't get her a card?'

'I prefer the term "partner". And Ruth feels the same as me.'

'If you ask me, you're taking your life in your hands, not buying her anything,' Elliott said. 'Especially with her being pregnant and her hormones all over the place. She's probably planning to kill you.'

'I doubt that. Ruth's a Buddhist, like me.'

Elliott turned to Anna. 'So have you and Oliver got anything special planned for Valentine's night?'

'We *were* planning to go out to dinner.'

'Sounds ominous. What happened?'

'His ex, of course.' With her usual impeccable timing, Eve had called the previous night to announce that her boiler had broken. And of course, Oliver was the only person in the world who could fix it.

'Tell her to call a plumber. That's what everyone else does,' Anna had pleaded. 'She only has to say the word and you come running. She's not your responsibility any more.'

'No, but Matt and Georgia are still my kids.'

'They won't fall apart if you fix their boiler a day later.'

He thought for a moment. 'You're right,' he said.

'I am?' Anna replied, dazed.

'I'll call her and tell her she'll have to wait.'

Anna experienced a brief flare of triumph before the guilt flooded in. 'You'd better go,' she sighed. 'We'll both feel terrible if you don't.'

He kissed her. 'You're wonderful, do you know that?'

'One nil to Eve, then,' Elliott said when she told him.

'As usual. Anyway, how about you? Have you got a treat planned for a special lady?'

'Two, actually. I'm taking Becky and Jessica to the pictures.' He finished sorting the post and tucked his letters under his arm. 'I'm going to make a few calls. I'll be in my office if anyone needs me.'

He was barely out of earshot when Barbara said, 'Isn't that terrible? To be a widower at his age. He can't be more than—what? Thirty-five? It must be so hard for him. How long has his wife been gone?'

'About five years, I think,' Anna said.

'And to be left with two little kiddies at that age. It's heartbreaking, it really is.' Barbara shook her head pityingly.

Anna watched Elliott through the glass wall that separated his office from the rest of the centre. He reminded her of a young, absent-minded professor, with his Clark Kent glasses and curly light brown hair.

Anna hadn't known him when his wife was alive, and he rarely talked about her. But he doted on his two young daughters.

'Oh, look.' Barbara nodded towards the door. A delivery man staggered in under the weight of a huge bouquet.

Barbara glanced at the delivery note and handed them over to Anna. 'Someone loves you,' she commented.

'They do, don't they?' Anna could feel herself blushing as she read the card. How had Oliver dictated that to the florist?

'He should have sent a potted plant,' Neil said. 'It's so much better for the environment.'

Since Oliver wasn't due home until later and her mum was looking after Charlie for the evening, Anna arranged to go for a run after work with her friends Rachel and Meg.

Rachel was already limbering up on the river path beside Museum Gardens. It was five o'clock and already growing dark. The yellow lights along the path twinkled on the still black water.

Anna shivered in her track-suit top. 'No sign of Meg yet?'

'You know what she's like.' Rachel did an elegant stretch. She was tall and toned, her dark hair pulled back in a swinging ponytail. 'Can never drag herself away from those demanding brats—ah, here she comes now.' She nodded to where Meg was puffing towards them.

'Sorry I'm late,' she panted. 'Philippa needed me to check her spellings, and I had to pick Corey up from a play date. Then that cow from the PTA rang just as I was leaving. She wants me to bake a cake for the coffee morning on Friday.'

'Bitch. I hope you said no?' Rachel said. Meg looked shamefaced. 'God, you're such a doormat.'

'You don't know what she's like,' Meg wailed, struggling to capture her curly red hair in a rubber band. She was the opposite to Rachel in every way, small and plump with a round, harassed face.

Rachel glanced at her watch. 'Shall we go? I'm meeting Mark for a drink.'

'On Valentine's Day?' Anna and Meg looked at each other. 'Does this mean you and he are—?'

'No, it bloody doesn't! Not as far as I'm concerned, anyway.'

Rachel was a recruitment consultant, a successful divorcee in her thirties, with a designer wardrobe, a sporty BMW and a converted wharf flat. She and her husband Mark had split up shortly after their son was born. Anna and Meg had the feeling he wanted to get back with her, but Rachel was having none of it.

They'd all met at playgroup. Charlie was a year old and Anna was still feeling shell-shocked by motherhood, wondering how she'd ended up in a draughty church hall with a load of toddlers when she should have been downing tequila shots in the Students' Union bar, when she'd found herself next to Rachel in the Singalong Circle.

Rachel wasn't like all the other mums, in their jeans and fleeces and no make-up. She wore a tailored Hobbs suit and kept interrupting the songs to take calls from Japan on her mobile. Halfway through an action-filled rendition of *The Wheels on the Bus*, she'd turned to Anna and drawled, 'Stuff this. I don't know about you but I could murder a Martini.'

In the car park later they'd met Meg. Inside, she'd seemed like one of the most frighteningly competent of the mums. But outside they'd found her weeping behind the wheel of her Vauxhall Zafira while her three small children watched her with bug-eyed dismay and her baby howled in sympathy. 'Sorry,' she'd sniffed, wiping her nose on her sleeve. 'I think my Prozac must have worn off.'

Later, over a drink, they'd made friends. Now they met up regularly to run together.

'So what did Dave get you for Valentine's Day?' Anna asked, as they jogged over the railway bridge. 'Not more underwear?' Comfortably upholstered Meg had been understandably upset last year when her husband bought her a size ten thong.

'Dave's working in Dublin. He called to wish me a Happy Valentine's Day though,' she said, briskly cheerful.

'Big of him.' Rachel muttered. She and Anna agreed Dave was a smug, irritating git.

Anna's phone rang and she stopped to answer it, bending double to catch her breath. It was Eve. 'Have you seen Oliver?' she demanded.

'Hello, Eve. How lovely to hear from you,' Anna pulled a face at the others. 'No. I thought he was coming round to see you?'

'So did I, but he hasn't turned up. And I can't reach him on his mobile. Are you sure you don't know where he is?'

Yes, I've got him locked up so you can't get your hands on him. 'No idea. Sorry. Maybe he's changed his mind?'

'I doubt it. Oliver wouldn't let me down. I'll try him on his mobile again,' she said, and hung up.

'Or better still, call a plumber,' Anna muttered.

'She's got a nerve,' Rachel said.

'Tell me about it.' She wasn't too troubled as she sprinted after the others. Knowing Oliver, he was probably still at the restaurant. Hours could slip by when he was distracted by work.

They did a lap over Lendal Bridge, then Anna and Meg said goodbye to Rachel as she headed home back along the river path.

'Want a lift?' Meg said. Anna got in, pushing aside broken toys. 'I know, it's a nightmare. I'll be more organised one day.'

Anna retrieved a piece of Duplo from under her backside. 'I'm surprised you're still sane with four kids.'

'I don't think I am.' Meg gave a slightly manic laugh. 'No wonder Dave's away so much. The only time he gets any peace and quiet is when he's staying in a hotel. He hates living out of suitcases, but he has to do it for us. He works so hard,' she sighed.

I know, all that room service must be soul-destroying, Anna thought, remembering her lovely Oliver and feeling incredibly lucky.

They headed up towards Clifton Green. As they approached Rosslea Street, Meg jammed on the brakes to give way to a police car. 'Ooh look,' she said as they followed it down the street. 'Which of your neighbours has been naughty, I wonder?'

To Anna, it just looked as if Oliver was asleep. All he had was a tiny bruise on his head, and yet there were all those machines. Tubes and wires, and the whooshing sound of the ventilator breathing for him, the doctors had explained. That much she had managed to take in.

She held his hand, hating that his fingers lay so cool and lifeless, as if he'd already gone. That was the way the doctors were talking, preparing her for the worst. Extensive head injuries, they said. They couldn't operate because there was too much bleeding around his brain. They needed to carry out tests to assess his chances.

The nurse came in and Anna reluctantly let go of Oliver's hand and went out to where her mum was waiting in the corridor.

Jackie looked up sharply. 'How is he?'

'No change. Where's Meg?'

'She wanted to wait but I sent her home.'

'Thank God Meg had been there to drive her to the hospital and call her mum. Anna was shaking so much she could never have got there.

'I called Eve,' her mother said, 'I thought she should know.'

Anna couldn't even summon up a niggle of irritation. 'You're right. She should be here.' Then she remembered something else, and panicked. 'Who's looking after Charlie?'

'I've left him with Keith.'

She took a big, gulping breath. 'How am I going to tell him about this?'

'We'll cross that bridge when we come to it.'

Jackie didn't say 'if'. She knew too. They all knew Oliver wasn't going to make it, but no one wanted to say it out loud.

The doors at the end of the corridor burst open and in came Eve, followed by Georgia and Matt. Georgia was already crying, Matt was biting his lip. Trying to be a man. 'I want to see him,' Eve said.

It was strange, Anna thought. The very worst moment of her life and she was sharing it with Eve. Neither of them spoke as they sat either side of his bed, holding his hands. The children were waiting outside.

'Your mum said he had a heart attack?' Eve said at last.

Anna nodded. Those last moments of Oliver's life had been running through her head like a never-ending reel of film. She imagined him speeding along the ring road in his beloved MG, singing tunelessly to one of the Smiths CDs he loved to play at top volume. And then—

She squeezed her eyes tight shut, trying to block out the picture. Was it all over too quickly for him to react, or had he known what was happening? She wanted to believe that he'd been spared the pain and the panic, but she didn't know for sure. She saw the look on Eve's face and realised she was thinking the same thing.

'He's too young to die like this,' Eve said.

'He's not going to die,' Anna insisted. 'He'll pull through this.'

Eve said nothing. She looked down at Oliver's sleeping face, biting her lip.

She looked so pathetic, Anna wanted to yell at her. How could she give up on him? Why wasn't she willing him to live?

The doctor came in. 'Mrs Robinson?' he said to Anna.

'I'm Mrs Robinson,' Eve said.

He looked from one to the other in confusion. 'I don't understand. I thought—'

'We're not married.' Anna stared at the floor.

The doctor turned to Eve. 'In that case, could I have a few words in private?'

Anna opened her mouth to argue, but Eve got there first. 'I think Anna should hear whatever you've got to say.'

The doctor's grave face said it all. 'It's not good news, I'm afraid. The results of the tests show that brain-stem death has already occurred.' He paused. 'I know this is difficult for you, but you might want to think about making a decision to switch off the ventilator.'

'No,' Anna said straight away. 'No way.'

Eve ignored her. 'So you're sure there's absolutely no chance he could survive this?' she asked the doctor.

He shook his head. 'The tests are conclusive.' He looked from one to the other, Eve's face pale but composed, Anna's set with furious determination. 'I'll leave you alone to discuss this.'

He'd barely left the room before Anna started. 'We can't switch off that machine. You read about cases like this all the time. People coming back from comas after years and years—'

'This isn't a coma,' Eve said. 'You heard what the doctor said. It's only the machine keeping him alive.'

Then let it keep him alive a bit longer, Anna wanted to yell. She wasn't ready to face a world without Oliver in it. Not unless they could switch off a machine and stop her heart beating too. 'I don't want to let him go,' she whispered.

'You think I do?' Their eyes met across the bed. 'He's already gone.'

The machine whooshed, monitors beeped, filling the silence.

'So I'll tell the doctor, shall I?' said Eve.

Half an hour later it was just the two of them. The children came in to say goodbye to their father and then went outside to wait. Anna had sent her mum home. She and Eve sat across the bed, holding Oliver's hands. 'Are you ready?' the doctor asked.

Eve looked at her. 'Anna?'

'I—I'm OK,' she stammered, but her heart was crashing against her ribs. Across the bed, Eve's face was a blur. All she could see was her wedding ring glinting as she laid her hand across Oliver's. The sound of the machine seemed to fill the room. In a moment it would stop.

'Anna?' Eve's voice came from a million miles away.

She stumbled to her feet. 'I can't do it,' she said. 'I'm sorry.'

Outside, the bright lights hurt her eyes. Matt and Georgia were sitting further down the corridor. Matt had his arm wrapped around his sobbing sister. He sat up when he saw Anna. 'Where's Mum?'

'Still in there.' Suddenly Anna felt incredibly foolish. Why had she run away? Why couldn't she stay and see it through like Eve? She would never forgive herself.

Matt's voice was gruff. 'Is he—is it over?'

'Not yet.' She sat down beside them, put her arm around Georgia and reached for Matt's hand.

A few minutes later the door opened and Eve came out. She looked dazed. 'Mum!' Georgia shook Anna off to run to her mother. Matt followed. Eve gathered them into her arms, hugging them fiercely.

Anna watched them, feeling very alone. She wished she hadn't sent her mother home. She needed someone to hold her.

But the only arms she wanted around her were gone for ever.

She left them holding on to each other and crept away.

The children didn't ask what it had been like, and Eve knew she would never tell them. But the pain of those final moments would stay with her like a piece of ice in her heart.

'Mum?' Georgia's face was anxious, looking up at her. Eve hadn't realised she'd been holding her daughter so tightly, crushing her.

'Sorry.' She let her go and looked around. 'Where's Anna?'

'She was here a minute ago. She must have left,' Matt said.

Eve felt a twinge of concern for her, but in a way she was glad Anna had gone, and she'd been able to spend those last few minutes alone with Oliver. To have him to herself. It seemed right somehow.

As they were leaving, a nurse called her to one side.

'There's never a good time to do this,' she said, handing her a plastic bag. 'They're your husband's personal effects.'

Eve snatched her hand away. 'Anna should have them.'

'I was told to give them to you,' the nurse said. She walked away, leaving Eve staring at the bag. Keys, watch, phone, that battered old wallet she'd bought him years ago. There was something else in the bag. A small, velvet covered box. She had a strange feeling what was going to be inside before she'd even opened it. The ring was exquisite, white gold with a discreet diamond glittering at its heart. There could only ever be one reason a man gave a woman a ring like that. He was going to propose to Anna. It was Valentine's Day, after all.

She had a sudden picture of the moment he'd proposed to her, at the graduation ball. Being broke, all he could afford was a cheap cubic zirconia ring from a discount jewellers. Eve looked down at Anna's ring, fresh tears pricking her eyes, imagining Oliver's excitement as he planned when to give it to her. He always did love surprises.

'What's that?' She snapped the box shut as Matt came up.

'Your father's things.' She stuffed it back into the bag.

'What are you going to do with them?'

'Give them to Anna, if I can find her.'

But when they got to the car park, there was no sign of her.

Eve couldn't help feeling relieved. They'd both been through enough, without having to handle something like that as well.

It should have been miserable on the day of Oliver's funeral. But after a week of heavy grey clouds the February sun perversely decided to shine on the church, sending brilliant jewel-coloured beams of light through the stained-glass windows on to the assembled mourners.

The church overflowed with Oliver's friends. Eve was overwhelmed to realise how many lives he'd touched over the years.

There was a stir as Anna and her family entered the church. Eve glanced across the aisle at her as she took her seat. She looked even more childlike in her sombre black coat, her dark eyes huge and fearful in her pale face.

At least she had her family to support her. Eve envied her that. Her own mother had done her best to be sympathetic, but told Eve she couldn't be at the funeral because she would be in the States, drawing political attention to the plight of the South American Wanga people.

'You'll be fine,' Vanessa said breezily. 'After what he put you through, you hardly owe him your grief.'

So why do I still feel it? Eve thought as she put down the phone. She was in a strange position. She was Oliver's widow and yet she wasn't expected to mourn him.

Thank God for Adam. He'd been so brilliant over the past week, organising the funeral and everything that went with it, helping her and Anna over the awkwardness of who should do what.

Finally everyone was settled, and the service began. Once again, she silently thanked Adam for doing such a good job. He'd managed to get the tone of the sombre occasion just right, with Oliver's favourite songs instead of hymns, and his friends sharing their memories.

Then it was her turn. She'd decided to read Christina Rossetti's poem, *Remember*. But when she reached the lectern and looked out over the sea of expectant faces, her stomach began to flutter.

'Remember me when I am gone away, Gone far away into the silent land.' Her voice quavered, remembering how she'd gripped on to him so tightly in the hospital. She couldn't hold him back from that silent land, no matter how much she'd wanted to.

'Remember me when no more day by day, You tell me of our future that you plann'd.' She suddenly had a picture of the two of them, newly married, in bed in their dingy little rented flat on a freezing December day. It was the middle of the afternoon but they couldn't afford to turn on the heating so they huddled under the duvet for warmth. She lay in his arms, listening to him as he mapped out their future. That was the afternoon Matt was conceived, she'd been sure.

She saw the faces looking at her and realised she'd stopped reading. How long had she been standing there, tears running down her face? She looked at the page, but the words were a blur. She caught sight of Georgia's anguished face, but she couldn't move.

There was someone at her side. She looked round and there was Anna. She took the book out of Eve's hands and began reading from where she'd left off, her voice calm and clear. Then she touched Eve's arm gently, and guided her down the steps and back to her seat.

Afterwards, everyone headed back to the restaurant. Frankie the chef, still in his black suit, was carrying trays of food to the table.

'It all looks wonderful,' Eve said as she folded napkins.

'Do you think so?' Frankie ran his hand over his smooth, cropped head. He looked ill at ease out of his chef's whites. He was in his early forties, heavy set and attractive in an *EastEnders* hard man kind of way.

'You've done Oliver proud.'

'I wanted to get it right for him.' His voice was gruff with emotion. 'He was a good mate. I owe him more than I can ever repay.'

Eve felt a twinge of guilt. When Frankie first approached them about a job, she'd taken one look at his broken nose and prison record and said no. But typically, Oliver had insisted on giving him a chance.

'Let's just see what he can do,' he'd said. And he'd been proved right. Frankie was fiercely loyal to Oliver.

He stepped back to check the arrangement on the table. 'I just wanted you to know you don't have to worry about the restaurant. I can keep things ticking over for as long as you want. I don't suppose you know what's going to happen to this place now?'

'To be honest, I hadn't really thought about it.'

'No, I daresay you haven't. Anyway, if there's anything you need, you only have to ask.'

'That's really kind of you, Frankie.'

'Like I said, I owe it to Oliver.'

People began to drift up to the table, looking for something to eat. Eve left Frankie organising them and headed off to find a quiet table.

Adam stood over her. 'Do you mind if I join you? Or would you rather be on your own?'

'No, it's fine.' She pulled out a chair. 'Have you seen Anna?'

'I don't think she's here. Why?'

'I had something for her.' She still had the ring in her bag. She couldn't decide when would be the best time to give it to her.

'I don't think she could handle all this,' Adam said.

'She seemed very calm in the church. Much better than me, anyway.' Eve grimaced at the memory. 'I wanted to get it right for Oliver.'

'Oliver would have understood. It all got too much for you.'

They were silent for a moment, lost in their thoughts. Then Eve said, 'Imogen didn't come, then?'

'I didn't invite her. I didn't think it was a fun date.'

'So you're still together?'

'Don't sound so surprised about it.' His eyes twinkled.

'Sorry.' Another silence. 'Thank you for organising all this,' Eve said.

'It's no problem. I wonder what will happen to this place now?'

'Frankie was just saying the same thing. He said he'd keep running it for as long as I wanted. As if it's got anything to do with me.'

Adam looked thoughtful. 'It might have. Do you know if Oliver left a will? You're still his next of kin, remember. Do you want me to have a word with his solicitor?'

'Would you? That would be really kind.' She didn't like to tell him. She didn't care what happened to Oliver's restaurant, or his money.

'I suppose this means we won't be getting any sandwiches?' Nana said as they huddled in the back of Keith's Ford Mondeo.

Keith caught Anna's eye in the rearview mirror. 'She'd go anywhere for a free sausage roll, your nana.'

Anna smiled wearily back.

Keeping herself together for the funeral had exhausted her. There was no way she wanted to face everyone afterwards.

They turned off the main road and entered the sprawl of wide streets that formed the Cliffmead estate. Her sister-in-law Debbie was looking after Charlie with her own two toddlers at Jackie's house. They were all cuddled up on the sofa, watching a *Balamory* DVD.

'I'll put the kettle on,' her mother said, heading for the kitchen.

'Good idea.' Nana pulled off her hat. 'I'm spitting feathers.'

'Not for me,' Anna said. 'I'm going to pack. I'm going home.'

Jackie followed her to the foot of the stairs. 'You don't have to do that. You can stay here as long as you like.'

'I know. But I need to go back sometime.'

They'd all been so good to her, but Anna could feel herself struggling under the weight of their concern. Their kindness was beginning to feel oppressive.

'Are you sure you're ready to be on your own?'

'I won't know until I try, will I?'

Keith insisted on driving her home. It was the first time she and Charlie had been back in the house since the night Oliver died. As she put her key in the door she dreaded what she would find when she walked in. But everything was so heartbreakingly normal. She felt that if she called out Oliver's name he'd appear in the kitchen doorway.

'Where's Daddy?' Charlie asked.

Anna steeled herself. 'Don't you remember, sweetheart? We talked about this, Daddy died.'

Charlie frowned. 'He's not coming home?' She shook her head. Charlie considered it for a moment. 'Can I watch a DVD?' he asked.

Anna smiled. 'Good idea.' Once she'd found his favourite DVD and put it on, she set about unpacking and sorting out something to eat.

She walked around the house cautiously, bracing herself before she opened each door. Everywhere she looked there seemed to be a new memory to face, another little stab of pain and loneliness.

The phone rang, making her jump.

It was her mother. 'Just checking everything's all right.'

'Mum, I've only been out of your sight for ten minutes. And if you can manage on your own with three kids, I reckon I can cope with just me and Charlie.'

'I never said you couldn't cope,' Jackie said. 'As long as you know there's no shame in asking for help.'

A few more minutes of reassuring her mother she wasn't going to go into meltdown, and Anna put the phone down. She gave Charlie his tea—she couldn't face anything herself—and they cuddled up on the sofa watching DVDs until he finally dropped off to sleep, his dark head resting on her chest. Anna carried him upstairs. She hesitated outside her bedroom door. She was tempted to put Charlie to sleep in her bed, so she wouldn't feel so alone. But in the end she took him to his bedroom, with its star-patterned curtains and model aeroplanes hanging over the bed.

'I want to say good night to Daddy,' he mumbled sleepily.

She felt a stab of pain. 'Daddy's gone, sweetheart.'

'Will he be home later?'

Dear God, would she have to go through this every time? 'No.'

'I remember,' he yawned. Then turned over and went to sleep.

She went back downstairs, opened a bottle of wine and watched TV until the bottle was empty. She couldn't put it off any longer. She had to go to bed. She kept to her own side, out of habit, but as she reached over to switch off the bedside lamp, she caught the smell of Oliver's aftershave lingering on his pillow. Anna lay holding it to her stomach, her body curved around it, breathing in the faint scent of him as she lay there longing for sleep.

MARCH

Mum was going out to walk the dog again. Georgia had a nervy feeling in the pit of her stomach as she watched her clip on Benson's lead.

'Where are you going?' she asked.

'I'd like some time on my own. I need to clear my head.'

Georgia thought she'd done a bit too much head-clearing in the two weeks since Dad's funeral. Poor Benson was nearly exhausted from the new exercise regime. She followed her mother to the door. 'What's for supper?'

'That's a good point.' She stopped, distracted. 'I forgot to take anything out of the freezer. I'll have to bring back a takeaway.'

'Again? I'm sick of takeaways.'

'Then maybe you should cook,' her mother snapped. 'You know how the oven works, don't you?'

Georgia flinched. 'No need to bite my head off.'

'Sorry. I've got a headache. I'll feel better when I've had a walk.'

I doubt it, Georgia thought as the front door closed. Her mum had been walking for days now and she still hadn't got any better. Meanwhile, the house was falling apart. The washing basket overflowed and no one bothered to sort out the recycling. Georgia had been late home twice in the past week, both times on a school night, and her mum hadn't said a word. She was beginning to wonder if she even cared.

She hauled her dirty clothes down to the kitchen and opened the washing machine. A load of damp, musty smelling stuff fell out. How long had that been there? Georgia piled it back in with her own things. She was studying the various knobs and dials, wondering which one to push, when Matt came in. 'Do you know how this thing works?' she called over her shoulder.

'No idea. Where's Mum?'

'Out, as usual. Don't you think she's acting a bit weird?'

'In what way?'

'Look around. Even you must have noticed this place is a mess.'

He gazed around. 'It looks OK to me.'

Of course he wouldn't care if he lived in a pigsty; he *was* a pig.

She twiddled a few knobs experimentally and the washing machine gushed into life. 'It's not just the housework. I hear her walking about all night. And she's started smoking again.'

'She's hardly going to be running around singing, is she?'

'No, but . . . she's not helping us, is she? She should be taking care of us, not the other way round.' Now Dad was gone, she needed to know she could rely on her mum to keep her safe. 'I don't know why she's so upset. He wasn't even her husband any more, but he was our dad.'

Matt stared at her. 'You really are a selfish little bitch, aren't you?'

'It's all right for you, you're going to university soon,' Georgia fired back. 'I'll be the one stuck here looking after her.' She picked up her bag and slung it over her shoulder.

'Where are you going?'

'Out. Seeing as I'm such a selfish bitch, *you* can look after Mum when she comes back.' If she comes back. That was something else that haunted her, the fear that one day her mum might go out on one of her walks and just keep walking.

She went next door to call for her friend Stacey. The back door was open as usual, and her mum was in the kitchen, frying eggs and chips.

'Stacey's upstairs doing her homework.' She caught Georgia's longing gaze at the frying pan. 'Do you want some?'

'Oh no, I couldn't—'

'Go on, there's plenty. Grab a plate.'

'So what do you want to do tonight?' Georgia said, when she and Stacey had finished their tea and watched *Hollyoaks*.

'I've got English coursework to do.'

Georgia felt guilty. Stacey went to the local comp and worked far harder than she did at her private school.

'We could just go down to Jackson's and buy some sweets? Then you could get on with your work while I watch TV?' she suggested, desperate not to go home.

A group of teenage boys on bikes were messing about outside the shop. Stacey slowed down. 'Oh bloody hell,' she muttered.

'Do you know them?'

'They go to my school. That one in the white hoodie is Andy Taylor, he's the worst.' She took Georgia's arm. 'Just walk past, OK?'

They tried, but the boys wheeled their bikes into a barricade, blocking their way. 'Who's your friend?' Andy called out to Stacey.

'None of your business.' Stacey went to move past him but he reversed his bike across her path. She sighed loudly. 'Moron.'

Andy turned to Georgia. 'What's your name?'

'Georgia.'

'Ooh, Georgia.' He mimicked her accent. 'You're dead posh, you.' His mates fell about laughing.

'Come on.' Stacey pulled at her arm.

They spent ages choosing sweets but when they came out the boys were still waiting. 'Take no notice, they'll soon get bored,' Stacey whispered as they followed them up the street. But Georgia was quite enjoying the attention. Going to a private all-girls school she never met any boys. She couldn't resist sneaking glances back at them. 'You shouldn't encourage them,' Stacey grumbled.

'I'm not.' But a moment later Andy pedalled up alongside her. Steering his bike with one hand he pulled a packet of cigarettes out of his pocket with the other and offered it to her.

She shook her head. 'No thanks, I don't smoke. I don't see the point in paying a fortune for something that will kill me.'

'All right, love, I don't need a lecture. Anyway, who said I spent anything?'

'You stole them?'

'No, it was my birthday and the nice shopkeeper gave them to me.' He winked at Georgia. 'See you,' he said, and then he was off, his gang following. Georgia stared after him.

'Moron,' Stacey muttered.

'He wasn't bad.'

Stacey stared at her, appalled. 'Don't tell me you fancied him?'

Georgia shrugged. She wished she hadn't said anything as all the way home Stacey gave her a lecture on all the trouble Andy had been in, from fighting to smoking dope and stealing from the other kids.

'Your mum would go insane if you went near him,' Stacey finished.

Georgia thought about her mother, so preoccupied with her own problems. 'She probably wouldn't even notice,' she said wistfully.

The churchyard was coming to life after the long winter. Yellow and purple crocuses dotted the grass and frothy white blossom was bursting out on the trees lining the path. It was all wrong, Eve thought, that everywhere she looked the world seemed to be springing up with new life when Oliver wasn't there to see it.

Maybe it wasn't right for her to come here every day. But nothing felt right at the moment. She could just about get through the day if she didn't have to think. But as soon as someone asked her to function, even if it was only Georgia asking what was for supper, she could feel the pressure building up inside her head. Then she'd fly into a rage and lash out.

She hated herself when she saw the hurt and confusion on her children's faces. She should be helping them through their grief, not adding to their misery. That was why she came here, to be alone and release some of the emotional pressure, so at least she could try to appear normal for the kids. So she was irritated when she turned the corner of the church and saw Anna bending beside Oliver's grave.

Then she turned her head, and Eve realised it wasn't Anna at all.

'Hello?' she called out.

The girl swung round, dropping a posy she'd been holding.

'I—I'm sorry,' she stammered. 'I didn't mean to intrude.'

As she got closer, Eve realised why she'd mistaken her for Anna. They were both young, dark-haired and doe-eyed.

Eve smiled at her. 'It's OK.' She glanced at the flowers at the girl's feet. 'Aren't you going to pick them up?'

The girl reached down stiffly. Eve noticed the bandage around her knee under her skirt.

'I'm sorry, you must think I'm a bit strange, putting flowers on your husband's grave,' she said. 'I'm Laura Parker. I used to work at Oliver's restaurant. I couldn't get to the funeral, so I thought I'd bring these now.' She brushed the earth off the flowers.

'That's very thoughtful of you.'

'It was the least I could do. Oliver was a nice man.' She looked up at Eve. 'My dad died five years ago. He's buried here too.'

'You must have been very young?'

'I was fifteen.'

'The same age as my daughter,' Eve said.

'Georgia, isn't it? Oliver used to talk about her a lot. And your son, Matt. He was so proud of them.'

Eve turned away abruptly, pretending to look for Benson.

'I'm sorry,' Laura said. 'I didn't mean to upset you. If it's any help, it does get easier. Coming here helps,' she added. 'It helps me feel closer to my dad somehow.' She smiled. 'I even tell him my problems.'

'I talk to Oliver,' Eve said. 'Just stupid stuff, you know? Matt's university applications, Georgia's latest tantrum. I even tell him what was on telly last night.'

They sat down on the bench and chatted for a while. Laura told her she was a student at the university, studying to be a doctor.

'Do you live at home?' Eve asked.

'God, no. My mum lives miles away, down south.'

'Really? I just assumed as your dad was buried up here—'

'We used to live around here but she moved away after he died.' Laura looked down at the flowers still in her hands. 'Actually she was very ill. A kind of breakdown, the doctors said.'

'I'm sorry.'

'She's getting better now.' She smiled. 'Oliver was so kind to me when she was ill. He always had time to listen.'

'That sounds like Oliver.'

'He was very special.' Laura looked at her watch. 'God, is that the time? I should be going. My flatmate will be wondering where I am.'

As she stood up, Eve noticed her catch her breath with pain.

'What happened to your leg?' she asked.

'I had an accident.' She hobbled over to Oliver's grave and propped the posy against the wooden cross. 'It was nice meeting you.'

Anna walked into the community advice centre on Monday morning, three weeks after Oliver's funeral. She had decided the time had come to try to pull herself together.

Barbara and Neil fell silent as she entered the office. She felt like a baddie walking into a Wild West saloon.

She forced a bright smile. 'Good morning.' She waved at Elliott through the glass partition of his office, went to her desk and switched on her computer, aware of Neil and Barbara watching her every move.

'Shouldn't you be at home?' Barbara finally found her voice.

'Doing what?'

'I don't know. You must allow yourself to grieve. Isn't that what they say?' She looked at Neil, who nodded earnestly.

She's only being kind, Anna told herself. 'As you can see, I'm fine.' She did a little twirl in front of them. No need to tell them the sheer effort it had taken. 'Now, would anyone like a cup of tea?'

She heard them discussing her as she stood in the cupboard-sized kitchen at the back of the office, waiting for the kettle to boil.

'I still think it's too soon,' Barbara hissed.

'Maybe it hasn't hit her yet,' Neil whispered.

'Well, I'd rather she wasn't here when it does.'

Anna poured boiling water into the mugs, fighting a feeling of despair. She'd had the idea that if she could go back to work then she might start to feel normal again, and the awful aching void would fade. But it didn't work like that.

Elliott looked up and smiled when she put his tea down in front of him. 'Welcome back,' he said.

'I'm glad someone's pleased to see me.'

He nodded towards the glass partition. 'How are they treating you?'

'Neil's trying to pretend I don't exist, and Barbara thinks I should be at home rending my garments.'

'Quite right too,' Elliott agreed. 'Do you know, if you were an Igbo tribeswoman you would have shaved your head by now?'

'At least then I'd know what to do.' Anna said. 'At the moment I'm just at a loss. If I sit at home crying it embarrasses people, and if I go out and try to get on with life it embarrasses them even more.'

'The life of a social leper,' Elliott sighed. 'I remember it well.'

Anna looked at him sharply. In her fog of misery she'd forgotten he'd been through it too. 'Does it ever end?' she asked.

'Not as far as I know. All I can tell you is it does become more bearable eventually. Although you probably won't believe that.'

She didn't.

'Don't forget, I'm here if you want to talk,' Elliott said.

'Thanks.' But somewhere over the past month she'd lost the knack of talking. Especially small talk. And it seemed Neil and Barbara had too. The three of them sat in awkward silence.

Finally, as Anna was sifting through her emails, Barbara cracked.

'At least it was quick,' she said.

'Sorry?'

'Your Oliver didn't suffer, did he? I always think that must be worse, seeing someone you love go through a long, lingering illness.'

Worse than seeing them on life support after driving their car into a crash barrier, you mean?

The phone rang and Barbara answered it, leaving Neil to apologise. 'She means well,' he said. 'You've got to remember it's coming from a good place.'

From her backside, more like, Anna thought.

Just before lunch, Barbara started again. 'I suppose you've got to think yourself lucky, haven't you? At least you're still young.'

'I suppose so.' Anna's hand closed around her stapler. If Barbara told her she had her whole life ahead of her . . .

'Just think, you have your whole life ahead of—'

'Anna?'

She jumped, dropping the stapler at the sound of Elliott's voice.

'I'm going out to get a sandwich. Would you like to join me?'

'Well, no, I was planning to work through—' She caught his fixed stare and realised this was an offer she wasn't supposed to refuse. 'I suppose I could do with some fresh air,' she agreed.

'Seems to me I got to you just in time,' he said as they walked up Petergate, dodging past the tourists. 'You looked as if you were about to go for Barbara's jugular. What's she been saying now?'

She told him. Elliott sighed. 'You know she—'

'—means well? So Neil kept telling me.'

Petergate opened up on to the broad, sunny square where the imposing Minster stood, its ornate wedding-cake walls gleaming against the blue March sky. They crossed the road and headed towards Starbucks.

'Do you know what I wish?' she said, as they joined the queue. 'I wish that undertakers supplied a couple of minders after every funeral. They could walk ahead of you and stop people saying daft things.'

'Death makes people awkward. They don't know what to say. So either they avoid you, or they put their foot in it like Barbara.' Elliott reached the head of the queue and handed his panini to the girl behind the counter. 'Aren't you having anything?' he asked Anna.

'Just a coffee and a bottle of water. I'll get something later.'

Elliott frowned but said nothing. 'Do you want me to have a word with Barbara?' he asked as they sat down at a window table.

'What can you say? She's Barbara. She'll always insert her foot every time she opens her mouth.' She took a pill bottle out of her handbag.

'What are they?' Elliott asked.

'Happy pills. I went to see the doctor and he gave me some anti-depressants. He reckons I should be feeling much better in a week or so.'

She took one. Elliott watched her, frowning. She glanced sidelong at him. 'Do I get the feeling you don't approve?'

'It's nothing to do with me,' Elliott shrugged. 'I've just always been a bit wary of them, that's all. All they do is mask the pain.'

'So what, as long as they make it bearable?'

'They might make it bearable, but they don't make it go away. Sometimes it's healthier just to go through it.'

'And what if you don't come out the other side? What if you decide it's too bad and you don't want to go on living?'

His dark eyes were gentle. 'It passes,' he said. 'No matter how bad it feels, one day it stops hurting so much. Just give it time.'

'I haven't got time, have I? I've got a three-year-old son to look after. He needs me to be strong for him now, not in a year or two.' Her voice shook. 'So if something will help me cope and look after him then I've got to try it.' She pushed her cup away and stood up.

She couldn't face going straight back to the office. She headed in the opposite direction, taking the quiet, tree-lined path that curved round the back of the Minster. It was one of her favourite hidden corners of the city. But she was in no mood to be charmed by the view today. She was too annoyed. Elliott had touched a nerve. She did feel like a failure, having to go to the doctor and admit she needed help. But she could feel herself unravelling, and she couldn't allow that to happen, for Charlie's sake. If drugs kept the despair at bay, then she was willing to try them.

Eventually she couldn't put it off any longer, and headed back to the office. 'Is this a message for me?' She plucked at the Post-it stuck to her computer. *Call Dennis Watson*, it said. 'Who's Dennis Watson?'

'**I**t turns out he's Oliver's solicitor,' Anna said. 'I didn't even know he had one.' She and Rachel jogged along the river path.

'So Oliver didn't leave any will at all?' Rachel said. 'Of course, you know what this means, don't you? Eve gets everything.'

'Seems that way.'

Rachel swerved round a pair of greyhounds. 'What are you going to do? You've got to fight it, surely?'

'Why should I? I don't really care, anyway.'

Rachel stopped. 'Anna, she gets everything. Do you think that's what Oliver would have wanted? You've got to see a solicitor about this. For Charlie's sake.'

'I do know something about the law, remember? I know Charlie's entitled to some of Oliver's estate even if he dies without a will.'

'Exactly. And you've got to fight for it.'

How could she explain it took all the fight she had just to get through the day? 'I might not have a very high opinion of Eve Robinson, but I don't believe she'd cheat a three-year-old child. She'll probably sell the business and divide the money.'

'And she might decide to keep it all for herself and her kids. Promise me you'll see a solicitor, Anna?'

'I'll think about it. Shall we go?' She sprinted off before Rachel could nag her any more. 'I wonder why Meg didn't turn up?' She said as they chugged up the steps back to Lendal Bridge.

'Probably some domestic crisis. You know Meg.'

Something about the way Rachel said it made Anna suspicious.

'She's not avoiding me, is she? I haven't heard from her recently.'

'She's probably been busy.'

On their way back down they passed a gang of teenagers hanging round on the other side of the bridge. 'Nice arse,' one of them sneered.

'Shame I can't say the same about your face,' Anna snapped. Then she caught sight of one of the girls. 'Georgia?' Anna hardly recognised her under all the make-up. 'What are you doing here?'

'Nothing,' Georgia shrugged.

'Does your mum know you're here?'

'What are you, her bloody social worker or something?' The tallest boy cut in. Anna ignored him.

'Do you want a lift home?' she asked.

Georgia shook her head. 'I want to stay with my friends.'

'Friends?' She looked at the gang of youths in their hoodies, thought about arguing, then caught sight of Rachel impatiently waiting. 'Suit yourself,' she said. 'You've got my number if you need me, haven't you?'

As Anna jogged off, she wondered if she should call Eve, then decided against it. She didn't want to tell tales behind Georgia's back.

'I can't believe it's mine.' Eve stood in Fossgate, gazing across the street.

'What did I tell you?' Frankie put his arm around her. 'I always knew Oliver would want you to have this place.'

'Except he didn't, did he?' If things had worked out differently, it would have been Anna standing here. In a way she wished it was.

Frankie was dismissive. 'It's what he would have wanted.'

'Eve?' She turned round to see Spike Mullins heading across the street towards her. He was a cool black guy in his thirties, who owned the restaurant next to Oliver's, an American-style diner called the Burger Shack. He and Oliver had always kept up a friendly rivalry.

'Hi Spike.'

'I just wanted to say how sorry I was about Oliver. I know we had our ups and downs, but he was a good guy.'

'Yes, he was.'

'Any idea what you'll do with this place, now he's gone? If you're looking to sell, you know I'd be interested.'

'We'll let you know.' Frankie took Eve's arm and guided her back into the empty restaurant. 'Fucking vulture!' he snapped, slamming the door behind them. 'He couldn't wait, could he?' Eve followed him into the kitchen. Simon the commis chef was sautéing onions for the day's soup while Lizzy the trainee prepped vegetables. Frankie took the cloth off a bowl of dough he'd left to rise.

Eve watched him pound and stretch it between his big hands. 'He's got a point,' she said. 'I probably will have to sell this place.'

'You can't do that!'

'It's the law. If someone dies without leaving a will, their estate has to be divided between their next of kin.'

'So it's down to Anna,' he said bitterly.

'Anna isn't entitled to a penny, unless she claims she was financially dependent on Oliver. It's Charlie who needs his share.'

'But do you have to sell the restaurant? Can't you buy them out?'

'I can't afford to do that. Anyway, why would I want to?'

'To make sure it doesn't end up in Spike Mullins's hands.' Frankie punched the dough with his fists, making her flinch. 'He was always pestering Oliver with offers, but he always said no.'

'I don't have to sell to him.'

'The solicitors'll have to get the best price they can. And we all know who'll offer that.' He looked defeated. 'You wait and see.'

Eve gazed around the kitchen, the busy little heart of the restaurant. The air was scented with onions, tomatoes and basil. It was quiet now, but in a few hours it would burst into steamy, clattering, sizzling life as they rushed to get the food out. Oliver loved that buzz so much. She doubted if there was much passion going on next door. 'What choice do I have?' she said.

'You could take this place over and run it yourself.'

Eve stared at him in amazement. 'You are joking?'

'Why not? Charlie's only a toddler, he doesn't need his inheritance until he's older. You could look after this place and sell it when the time comes. It'll probably be worth a bit more by then, too.'

'But I don't know the first thing about running a restaurant.'

'How can you say that? You were here when Oliver first opened this place. You helped build the business up. I do all the cooking and the ordering anyway. All you'd need to do is keep the customers happy.' He nodded towards the swing doors that led out to the restaurant. 'We'd make a good team. It'd be just like the old days.'

He made it sound so simple. She thought about telling him how hard it was for her, how the smallest task seemed like a mountain to climb. 'I wouldn't be able to cope,' she said.

Frankie was silent for a moment as he shaped the bread dough into rounds. 'I know it seems tough at the moment, but maybe this is what you need?' he said at last. 'It could give you something to think about. I mean something else. Apart from Oliver.'

Eve stared at him. Did he honestly think working in Oliver's restaurant day after day would help her forget him? 'I couldn't do it,' she said.

Frankie sighed. 'It's up to you,' he said heavily. 'But you do know we'll all lose our jobs if you decide to sell up?'

She caught Simon and Lizzy watching her, their faces reproachful. Oh, Oliver, why did you do this to me? she thought.

Eve got out of the car and knocked on the door of Anna's little terraced house. No reply.

'She won't be home from work yet.' A woman stuck her head out from next door. 'She has to pick up her little boy from her mum's.'

Eve was scrabbling in her bag for a pen to leave a note when Anna came up to the front door, juggling Charlie and a couple of Tesco's carrier bags. She looked surprisingly together, dressed for work in black trousers, until Eve spotted she was only wearing one earring.

She stopped when she saw Eve. 'Hello,' she said warily.

Eve took a deep breath. 'Can we talk?'

'You'd better come in. I'll put the TV on for Charlie.' Anna went into the sitting room, picking her way through the toys that littered the floor. Eve stood in the doorway, her eyes fixed on the photos crammed onto the mantelpiece. Happy snaps of Oliver and his new family.

'You don't mind if I get on with his tea?' Without waiting for an answer, Anna headed for the kitchen. The room was untidy, with damp washing draped over the radiators, dishes in the sink and coffee rings on the table. Eve recognised all the signs of a defeated woman. She found it quite heartening that Anna was struggling too.

Anna arranged fish fingers on the grill pan. She moved sluggishly, as if everything was an effort. Eve wondered if Anna was sleeping as badly as she was.

'I was wondering when you'd turn up,' Anna said. 'Oliver's will? Or lack of it.'

Eve hesitated, choosing her words carefully. 'I think we're agreed that the situation isn't what Oliver would have wanted,' she began. 'We need to sort out his estate and make sure it's divided up properly.'

Relief flickered in Anna's eyes. 'I'm glad you think so.'

'I've come up with an idea that I think will work for all of us. I thought I could take over the restaurant and run it myself. If we sell it now we'll probably end up with a few thousand each. But if we keep it on, we could have a steady income. And we can still sell in a few years' time.' But even as she said it, she could feel her confidence crumbling. She didn't really believe it. And neither did Anna, judging from her silence.

Anna flipped the fish fingers over. 'Why?' she said.

'Sorry?'

'Why do you want to run Oliver's?'

'I don't really know,' Eve admitted. 'I just feel it's something I should do. If we sell the restaurant Spike Mullins will buy it and everyone will lose their jobs. I don't want that to happen.'

'And what exactly do you know about running a restaurant?'

She was expecting this. 'I helped Oliver start up the business. I've done the books and worked in the kitchen.'

'What do you know about VAT? Or stock ordering? How about hiring and firing staff?'

Eve stiffened. 'I could learn.'

'And while you're learning, the business could be going down the pan. I'm sorry. I don't mean to sound harsh. But I've got Charlie to think about. I have to do what's best for him.'

Eve looked around the little house, with its shabby, junk shop furniture. Anna was probably struggling to pay the mortgage on her own. 'Look, if money's a problem, I'm sure we could arrange with the solicitors for you to get some kind of pay-out in the meantime—'

Anna's nostrils flared. 'I don't need any charity hand-outs,' she snapped. 'I think you'd better go.'

'But we still have to discuss this—'

'We'll discuss it through our lawyers. Now if you'll excuse me, I have to get my son's tea.'

'I'm sorry, but Miss Metcalfe has been called away to see another client. She sends her apologies,' the girl behind the reception desk said, as if that would make up for Anna trailing across town in her lunch hour.

'Well, I've come to see a solicitor and I'm not leaving here until I do.'

The receptionist looked panicky. 'But everyone's at lunch.'

'Then I'll wait until someone turns up.' She plonked herself down on one of the chairs in the waiting area and saw the girl pick up the phone. Anna heard snatches of her whispered conversation and guessed it was about her when she heard the words 'a bit mad'.

Five minutes later a man walked into the reception area. 'What's the problem?' she heard him say. She looked up to see the receptionist pointing her pen accusingly towards her.

The man turned around and Anna felt a lurch of instant recognition. 'Lynch?'

'Anna? Bloody hell!'

He hadn't changed at all. He was still the Danny Lynch—known to all as Lynch—who'd almost broken her heart back in college, with his dark blond hair and tall, lean body. Not to mention a smile that could scorch a woman's underwear.

'Anna Bowman. You're the last person I expected to see.'

'You too. I thought you'd be living it up in London by now.'

'I was. It's a long story.' He looked her up and down. Anna was suddenly conscious of her lack of make-up. 'When was the last time we met?'

'About four years ago.' There was an awkward moment as they remembered the last time they'd seen each other, when Anna had broken the news that she was leaving college because she was pregnant.

'So what can I do for you?'

'Would you believe, I need a solicitor.'

He grinned. 'Sorry. Why don't you come into my office?'

'You've got an appointment in ten minutes,' the receptionist, who'd been listening in avidly, reminded him.

'I'm sure you can charm them into waiting, can't you, Sonia?' He gave her one of his killer smiles.

'Another of your conquests?' Anna asked as she followed him.

'Let's just say I'm working on it. It might be fun while it lasts, but it could end up being a bit messy.' He opened a door and stood aside to let her in. 'I had a bit of a thing with one of the secretaries in my last place, and I swear she spat in my coffee for a year afterwards.'

'Nice to see you're still treating women with the same respect.'

'You know what they say. A leopard can't change its spots.'

And predators don't come much more lethal than you, Anna thought. Thank God she'd not taken their relationship too seriously.

'So how's life treating you?' He looked her over with lazy appraisal. 'Are you still with that old guy you dumped me for—what was his name?'

'Oliver.' Just saying it brought a treacherous lump to her throat.

'Oliver.' He nodded, remembering. 'What happened to him? I suppose he must be in some cosy retirement home by now.'

'He's dead,' Anna said flatly.

There was a short, stunned silence. 'Oh God, I'm so sorry.' Lynch looked appalled. 'When did that happen?'

'A month ago. That's why I'm here. I—'

The phone rang. Lynch ignored it. 'Go on,' he said.

Anna tried, but the clamouring phone distracted her. 'You'd better answer it, I'll go.' She stood up. 'You've got people waiting.'

'But I want to help. Tell me where you work, and I'll pick you up in an hour.'

'There's no need, really. I can make another appointment with Miss Metcalfe. It might be easier to talk to a stranger anyway.'

'Bugger Miss Metcalfe. You're my client now.' The phone rang on. 'Tell me where to find you,' he said.

Anna finally gave in and scribbled down the address.

An hour and fifteen minutes later, he still hadn't turned up. Anna was disappointed but hardly surprised. Lynch had never been one for keeping appointments, or promises. She was in the back office talking to a client when Elliott stuck his head round the door. 'There's someone to see you. Says he's your lawyer.'

Anna craned her neck and caught a glimpse of Lynch's fair head. 'Tell him to wait. It'll do him good.'

She didn't expect him to still be there when she finally finished with her client. But there he was, lounging in her chair.

'Sorry to keep you,' she said.

'No problem.' He held up a brown paper bag. 'I brought sandwiches.'

'I've already taken my break. I came to see you, remember?'

'So? I'm sure your boss will let you have half an hour off.'

'Half an hour,' she said firmly. 'I'll just clear it with Elliott.'

'What kind of a place is that?' Lynch wanted to know, as they stepped into spring sunshine. The grassy banks of the city walls were bright with daffodils.

'It's a community advice centre,' Anna told him. 'We tell people their rights, fill in forms for them, that kind of thing.'

He looked perplexed. 'And they get that for free? What's in it for you?'

'I like helping people,' she shrugged. 'That's why I wanted to become a lawyer in the first place.'

'Really? I only wanted to make money.'

Anna looked him up and down. 'It looks like you've done that.'

They sat on a bench in bustling St Helen's Square, facing the Georgian Mansion House with its elegant red and white façade. He handed her a sandwich. 'Cheese and pickle, your favourite. See? I remembered.'

'Thanks.' Actually, she couldn't stand pickle, but Lynch looked so pleased with himself she didn't have the heart to tell him. It didn't matter, anyway. She only ate out of habit these days.

She nibbled her crust. 'What brought you to York?'

'Work. I was head-hunted by this firm when I was in London.'

'What kind of work do you do?'

'Personal injury, mostly. Why do you need a solicitor?' Lynch asked.

She told him about Oliver not leaving a will, and her last meeting with Eve. She tried to stay calm, but she could feel rage building up.

Lynch listened carefully. 'I can see her point,' he said. 'Keeping the restaurant running could be a good investment in the long term.'

'Not when she's finished with it. She couldn't even change a light bulb without running to Oliver for help. I'm worried she'll run the place into the ground and then Charlie will end up with nothing.'

'It must be difficult, seeing her end up with everything when you've been living with the guy for four years. Are you sure you're not just doing this to spite her?' Lynch asked.

'Maybe you should ask her why she's doing it,' Anna fired back. 'That restaurant is the only thing she's got left of Oliver, and she doesn't want to let it go, like she never wanted to let go of him when he was alive. But hanging on to it won't bring him back.' She stared straight ahead of her, daring the tears to come.

'I can certainly see you've got a problem,' Lynch said. 'Do you want me to look into it for you?'

'Yes please.'

She hadn't been too sure at first, but now she realised how much she needed someone like him on her side.

'What did you think?' It was mid-afternoon, and Eve and Matt were driving home after visiting a university campus. The day's drizzle had given way to heavy rain which rattled against the windscreen.

'S'alright, I suppose.'

Eve glanced at his expressionless face. 'You could be a bit more interested. I thought you wanted to go there?'

'I'm not sure it's what I want any more.'

'Ah.' Silence followed, broken only by the heavy patter of rain.

Maybe she was expecting too much of Matt. He'd just lost his father. If Oliver's death had hit her hard, what would it have done to his son? 'I suppose it's all too much to think about at the moment,' she said. 'If you want to put off your place for a year, I'm sure—'

'Will you drop me off at Steve's?' he interrupted her. 'We've got the Battle of the Bands coming up, we need to rehearse.'

He didn't say another word to her until they reached his friend's house twenty minutes later. At least he was getting out at last, she thought as she watched him ambling up to the front door. She was beginning to worry that he spent so much time locked in his room. Poor Matt.

She'd meant to go home, but Frankie had asked her to sign some cheques, so she called in at Oliver's. Lizzy was on her own in the kitchen.

'Where is everyone?' Eve asked.

'Simon's gone home and Frankie's out there—' she nodded towards the back door, 'talking to someone.'

Eve peered through the window into the yard, where Frankie was having an animated conversation with two men in black leather coats.

Two minutes later he returned, shaking water off his hat and muttering under his breath. He broke into a smile when he saw Eve. 'Hello there. This is a nice surprise.'

'You asked me to come in. To sign some cheques?'

'Oh, right. Yes, of course. I've got the invoices in the office.'

'Who were those men?' Eve asked, as Frankie squeezed his way in behind the desk. "The office" was little more than a cubbyhole.

'Suppliers.'

'What did they want?'

'Money, what else?' He unlocked the desk drawer and took out the cheque book and a stack of papers. 'I just had to explain that things were taking a bit longer now there's no one around to pay the bills on time.' He sorted through the papers. 'Here we go. I've already written out the cheques, so all you have to do is put your name on them.'

'It would be easier if you could just pay them yourself,' she said.

'Oh no, I couldn't do that. Oliver always dealt with the money.'

'It just holds everything up if you have to wait for me. Why don't I get on to the bank and have you made an authorised signatory?'

'Are you sure?' Frankie lowered his voice so Lizzy wouldn't hear. 'I thought with my record—'

'That was a long time ago. You know I trust you completely.'

'Thanks. That means a lot to me. I suppose this means you've decided not to run the place, then?'

Eve stifled a sigh. She'd been dreading this. 'I don't think I can.'

Frankie paused. 'I bet Oliver would have wanted you to try.'

'Anna doesn't.' She still felt bruised from their encounter.

He gave a dismissive snort. 'What's it got to do with her? I reckon this place could be good therapy for you. Promise me you'll think about it again, at least,' he begged.

Eve was about to argue, then gave up. 'I'll think about it all you like,' she said. 'But I still won't change my mind.'

'We'll see.' Frankie beamed. 'In the meantime, while you're thinking about it, maybe you'd like to look through this morning's post?'

Sorting through the post kept her occupied for a few minutes. Until she opened the last letter. She went back to the kitchen and waved the letter at Frankie to get his attention. 'Do you know anything about this?'

'Looks like just another bill to me,' he said.

'It's from a loan company. Why would Oliver borrow money from people like this?'

'Maybe he needed the cash to keep this place going?'

'But I thought business was OK?'

'There's only one way to find out. Check the books.'

'Oh no, I couldn't do that.' If there was a problem, she didn't want to know about it.

Frankie must have read the reluctance in her face. 'Even if you go ahead and sell the place, you're still going to need to know what it's worth,' he said.

'I suppose so.' She looked down at the bill in her hand. 'Are you sure Oliver didn't mention anything to you about this?'

'Finance was his department.'

'Adam's here,' Lizzy interrupted them, looking through the window. 'All right if I take a five minute break, chef?'

'Gone to put her lippy on,' Frankie commented wryly as she scuttled off. 'Got a bit of a crush on him. Her and half the waitresses.'

'Who, Adam?' Eve watched him as he unloaded boxes from the back of his battered old Transit van. Now she looked at him, she supposed he was attractive in a healthy, outdoorsy kind of way.

'I blame Lady Chatterley,' Frankie said. 'They've all got fantasies about being ravished among the radishes.'

They were still laughing when Adam shouldered his way in through the back door, his arms full of boxes. 'Have I missed something?'

'Just talking about the effect you have on women,' Eve said.

Adam blushed deeply. 'Here's your delivery,' he mumbled.

'Let's see what you've got.'

While Frankie rummaged through the produce, Adam said to Eve, 'I didn't expect to see you here.'

'You'll be seeing a lot more of her from now on,' Frankie said, before she could reply. 'She's thinking of running the place.'

Lizzy came hurtling back into the kitchen, her hair newly fluffed under her white cap. But Adam was too preoccupied to notice. 'Are you sure that's a good idea?' he asked Eve.

'Don't you think I can do it?'

'I didn't say that. I'm just wondering why you'd want to.'

'She's doing it for Oliver,' Frankie butted in.

'Ah,' Adam nodded, as if that explained everything. 'For Oliver. I see.'

Eve followed him out to the van. 'Take no notice of Frankie. I still haven't made up my mind to do it.'

'He sounded pretty convinced.' He threw open the van doors and began stacking the empty boxes inside.

'He's just worried they're all going to lose their jobs. And he's got some daft idea about me carrying on Oliver's dream,' she smiled.

Adam regarded her seriously. 'And is that what you want to do?'

'I know being here helps take my mind off everything else. And I suppose I do feel closer to him. Don't you approve?'

'I just hope you know what you're doing.'

Eve watched him drive away, troubled. She thought Adam would understand. She hadn't realised how much his approval meant to her.

She went back inside, where Frankie was still unpacking. 'You don't want to take any notice of him,' he said. 'If you ask me, he's just miffed. I expect he was hoping to get his hands on some of Oliver's money once this place was sold.'

Eve was shocked. 'Adam wouldn't make a claim.'

'Don't you believe it,' Frankie said grimly. 'That business of his can't make a fortune. I daresay he wouldn't say no to a bit of extra cash.'

Frankie's words still haunted her when she visited the churchyard on the way home. Surely he couldn't be right about Adam, could he? It was all so confusing. The rain had settled to steady drizzle as she crouched beside Oliver's grave under her umbrella. Talk to me, she pleaded silently. Tell me what I should do.

'Hi. Remember me?' She turned around. There was Laura.

'Hello, there.' Eve dredged up a smile. 'You're very wet.'

'I've been here a while. I had a lot of thinking to do.'

You and me both, she thought. Eve turned back to Oliver's flowers and waited for her to leave. But Laura stood, watching her. In the end Eve gave up and headed back to her car. Laura fell into step beside her.

'My flatmate's moved out,' she said. 'I'll have to find someone else to share or I'll lose the flat. I can't afford the rent on my own. I don't suppose you've got any work going at the restaurant?'

'Well, I don't really—'

'Please?' Laura begged. 'I've got loads of experience.'

Eve saw the desperate look in her big dark eyes. 'Come and see me tomorrow,' she sighed. 'I'm sure we can sort something out.'

She'd just hired her first member of staff. It looked as if she was running Oliver's whether she liked it or not.

Georgia was checking her mobile-phone messages when Eve got home later. 'Matt rang,' she said, not looking up. 'He says he'll sleep over at Steve's, if that's all right with you?'

'I suppose it'll have to be.' She wondered if he was trying to avoid a chat about his future. She put the carrier bag containing the restaurant books on the kitchen table. 'What would you like for supper?'

'I'm going out with friends.'

'Anyone I know?'

Georgia sent her a withering look. 'I doubt it.' Her phone bleeped, announcing a text message. She read it quickly. 'Got to go. Bye.'

'What time will you—' But she was already gone. Eve sat down in the empty kitchen and looked around her. She was losing her grip on her family, and it frightened her. Georgia was mixing with a new group of friends she knew nothing about, staying out late and getting up to heaven knows what. And Matt seemed to be on a totally different planet.

She'd been living on her own for years, but she'd never felt this lonely. Before, she'd always had Oliver at the end of the phone. Now she had to face it all by herself, and it was all too scary.

She sat down at the table and got out the accounts. She flicked through them; they meant nothing to her. As she stuffed them back in the bag, despairing, the phone rang. It was Jan.

'How are you?'

'You don't really want to know.'

'Oh dear, that bad? I know what you need.'

'Several valium, a large gin and a lie-down?'

Jan laughed. 'I was thinking more of a night out. Why don't you come round for dinner next week—say, Friday?'

'It's very sweet of you, but I'm not exactly great company.'

'No one's expecting you to be the life and soul of the party, Eve. We know what you've been going through. Come on, it'll do you good. Get your glad rags on and come and see us.'

Eve put the phone down, knowing she had no intention of going. But she also knew Jan wouldn't shut up until she'd agreed. Anyway, it was over a week away. Plenty of time to dream up an excuse.

Anna stared at the papers spread out on the kitchen table in front of her. 'So let me get this straight. You're telling me the business isn't actually worth anything?'

'With all the loans on it, it's worth less than nothing,' said Lynch.

'But how can that be? Oliver always said they were doing well.'

'Maybe they were. But these loan repayments would have taken up most of what they made.'

She reached for the brandy Lynch had insisted on pouring her before they started. 'Why didn't he tell me?' she said.

'He probably didn't want to worry you.'

'I'm worried now!'

'I'm sure he was, too.'

The thought sobered her. Poor Oliver, what kind of stress must he have been under, knowing his business was on the brink of collapse? 'Why didn't I realise? He should have been able to turn to me.' What did that say about her, about their relationship? 'So Eve probably wouldn't be able to sell anyway?' she changed the subject.

'She wouldn't get much for it,' Lynch agreed.

'What about the building? That must be worth something?'

'It might if he owned it, but it's leasehold, unfortunately. According to the paperwork, Oliver recently took out another large loan to pay for the new lease.' Lynch looked across the table at her. His blue-green eyes were full of sympathy. 'I'm sorry, Anna.'

She took a deep breath. 'It's not the end of the world. So there's nothing for Charlie to inherit—so what? We'll be all right, as long as I can keep a roof over our heads—' she trailed off, seeing Lynch's face. 'What?'

'There's something I still haven't told you.'

Warning prickles went up her spine. 'Whatever it is, it can't be worse than what I already know.'

He said nothing. Reaching into his briefcase, he drew out a sheet of paper. Anna recognised yet another loan company logo on the headed notepaper. 'When Oliver took out the loans, he had to put something up as security. In case the loan couldn't be paid off.'

Anna nodded. 'I know that. I deal with people in debt every day, remember?'

'Obviously he couldn't take any more loans out against his business because that was already mortgaged up to the hilt.'

'So what did he use as security?' It dawned on her before she finished the sentence. 'Oh no,' she whispered. 'He couldn't. Not this house. Not without my consent.'

'Was it in both your names?'

She shook her head. 'Oliver bought it before I moved in with him. We never got round to putting my name on the deeds.' She took a gulp of her brandy. 'He'd never risk our home.'

'Maybe he didn't feel he *was* risking it. He probably reckoned he could pay off the loans and you'd never be in danger.'

Yes, that sounded like Oliver. Always expecting the best, leaving everyone else to deal with the grim realities of life. She suddenly wanted to rage and scream at him for his blind selfishness and arrogance. Why the hell had he left her like this?

Lynch seemed to read her thoughts. 'He never expected to die, Anna.'

She braced herself. 'So what you're saying is the business is worth nothing, and if we do by some miracle manage to find someone idiotic enough to buy it, the money we make won't be enough to repay the outstanding loans, so I'll probably lose my home?'

Lynch winced. 'That's pretty much it, I'm afraid. I'm so sorry.'

She didn't want his sympathy. Much as she felt like sobbing in a heap, she was determined to stay practical. 'So what would you advise?'

'The way I see it, your only real chance is to keep the restaurant going. At least if there's money coming in you can meet the loan repayments and keep a roof over your head. Of course, a lot depends on his ex,' Lynch went on. 'It's lucky she wants to keep the restaurant going. If I were you, I'd start being very nice to Eve Robinson. Because right now, she's all that stands between you and total financial meltdown.'

APRIL

IT WAS MONDAY MORNING, the first day after the Easter holidays, and Eve was going back to school.

'Now, are you sure you're all right about this?' Matt checked again as they got into the car.

'For God's sake,' Georgia muttered. 'She's only going to teach a bunch of kids, not perform brain surgery. *We* still have to go to school.'

'You don't have to worry about me,' Eve said. 'I'm fine.'

Matt looked at her, his grey eyes pitying under his shaggy fringe. 'So why are you wearing odd shoes?' he asked.

She managed to get through the morning quite well. She was feeling very pleased with herself by the time they filed into the school hall for lunch. Eve sat with a group of packed-lunch children. She was bent double, her knees under her chin on the Munchkin-sized chair.

She had no idea how or why it happened. One minute she was opening a packet of Wotsits, the next it had all fallen apart.

'Miss is crying,' the girl next to Eve piped up.

Seven solemn little faces turned to look at her, a grown woman sitting with her knees under her chin and tears pouring down her face.

The headteacher was very good about it. She arranged supply cover for that afternoon and suggested Eve should go home and rest.

As she walked out of the school gates Eve knew she wouldn't be going back. Teaching was all she'd ever wanted to do, but now she felt as if she'd forgotten how to do it. Just like she'd forgotten how to feel normal. She stopped at the church on the way home. She hadn't even reached Oliver's grave when she got a call on her mobile.

'Eve? It's Laura.'

She looked around the deserted churchyard, half expecting her to pop up from behind a headstone. Was she ever going to be able to come here without Laura appearing in one way or another?

'I'm at Oliver's. We thought you should know, the health inspector's turned up. Apparently it's a random inspection. Could you come over?'

'Can't Frankie deal with it?'

'It's his day off. I've tried calling him but his mobile's switched off. Simon said I should call you.'

Eve sighed. 'All right, I'll come. If I have to.'

'I just don't know how we ended up like this,' the woman sobbed. Anna pulled a tissue from the box and handed it to her. 'We were fine while my husband was working.' The woman blew her nose. 'But then when he had the accident and lost his job, it all started to get on top of us. I've got three kids, I don't want to end up on the streets.'

'It won't come to that.' Anna handed her another tissue. 'But you mustn't ignore the situation and hope it'll go away.' But as she painstakingly began totting up the family's finances to work out a repayment plan, Anna was uncomfortably aware she wasn't taking her own advice. She knew she should see Eve, explain about her house being under threat, but her pride wouldn't let her admit she needed anyone's help.

As if he could read her mind, later that day she got a call from Lynch. 'Have you talked to her yet?'

'No.'

'Anna! You've got to start building some bridges with her.' He paused. 'Tell you what. Why don't you go to see her today and then I'll take you out to dinner tonight as a reward?'

'I don't want—'

'I'll pick you up at eight,' he said, and rang off.

'Manipulative swine,' Anna muttered and went to see Elliott. 'I wondered if I could take a couple of hours off this afternoon?'

'Out of the question. As you can see, we're rushed off our feet.'

He nodded towards the main office, where Barbara was buffing the leaves of her rubber plant. 'Oh, go on, then.'

It was the start of the main tourist season and all the bars and cafés were doing a roaring trade. So Anna was surprised to find Oliver's almost deserted, apart from an elderly couple at a corner table.

A dark-haired girl was leaning on the till. 'Hello,' she said. 'You're Anna, aren't you? I'm Laura.'

'Hi. Is Eve around? I'd like a word.'

Laura chewed her lip. 'She's in the back. She's a bit busy.'

At that moment Eve hurried out from the kitchen, looking harassed. Her face fell when she saw Anna. 'What do you want?'

'I need to have a word with you.'

Eve glanced over her shoulder. 'Now's not a good time.' She lowered her voice. 'We've got the health inspector in.'

'Bloody hell. They haven't found anything, have they?'

'Of course not. I don't think so, anyway. Look, I've got to go back. Get Laura to bring you a coffee. I'll be out in a minute.'

Anna tried to tell herself it was none of her business as she sat down at a corner table. Laura brought her a cappuccino and Anna was surprised as the girl sat down opposite her. 'I worked here before, while Oliver was here,' she said. 'Maybe he mentioned me?'

'Sorry, no,' Anna glanced past Laura's shoulder at the kitchen.

'No, I don't suppose he would. You were a waitress here too, weren't you? When you and he met?' She lifted her cup to her lips and stared at Anna over the rim. 'Do you miss him?'

Anna blinked at her. What kind of question was that?

'That was a daft thing to say. Of course you miss him. Who wouldn't miss someone like Oliver?' She went on, reminiscing about him, but Anna was hardly listening. In the end she couldn't stand it any longer.

'I'm sorry,' she interrupted Laura, putting down her cup. 'I've got to find out what's happening in the kitchen.'

The health inspector was brandishing her clipboard. 'There's a general lack of cleanliness in here,' she announced. 'The splashbacks and ceiling need a thorough wiping down, and as for your freezer—' Anna cringed as she went through her list. It was obvious the woman was a bully. But why wasn't Eve standing up to her? 'And there's a broken tile on your floor which could be a health hazard,' the woman droned on.

'Where?' The word popped out before Anna had a chance to think about it.

They both turned to look towards the doorway where she stood. The inspector stared at her as if she was something unpleasant she'd found behind the sink.

'I beg your pardon?'

'Where's the broken tile? I don't see it.'

'It's there.' The inspector pointed with the toe of her brogue.

'I'd hardly call that broken. It's just a crack.'

The inspector drew in a deep breath, her nostrils flaring. 'If I say it's broken, then it's broken.'

'But—' Anna opened her mouth to argue, then caught Eve's warning look and shut up.

'As I was saying, I've also noticed a split door seal on your fridge and—' she lowered her voice dramatically, 'I've spotted evidence of low-level mouse activity behind your cupboards. Is something funny?' She whipped round to face Anna, who was stifling a giggle.

'Sorry, but I was just wondering what other level of mouse activity there might be. Unless we've got flying mice?'

The inspector thrust her imposing bulk towards Anna, her eyes narrowing into slits. 'Who *are* you, exactly?'

'I'm Anna Bowman,' she said. 'My partner owned this place.'

'Really?' The inspector glanced at Eve. 'But I thought—'

Eve shook her head. 'It's complicated.'

The woman turned back to Anna. 'I wonder, Ms Bowman, would you find it so funny if I were to close it down?'

Anna stared right back at her, refusing to be intimidated. 'You can hardly close us down over a couple of mice and a cracked tile.'

'Then I'd better take another look around, see what else I can find.' After an hour, the inspector had come up with an impressive list of faulty thermostats in the fridge, greasy residue on the roasting pans and a lack of soap in the staff toilets. As she handed Eve the list she said, 'You have seven days to put all these right. I'll return for a reinspection in a week, by which time I expect to find this place spotless.

Eve showed her out, then slammed back through the swing doors, eyes blazing. 'Thanks a lot!' she said. 'I've just had to sweet-talk her into letting us stay open, thanks to you and your big mouth.'

'She was a bitch. And a bully. Why didn't *you* stand up to her?'

'Like you, you mean? That really worked, didn't it?' She opened the cupboard and started pulling out mops and brooms. 'Now thanks to you we've got to scrub this place from top to bottom.'

Anna took a broom reluctantly. 'Where's Frankie? He shouldn't be skiving off just when we're getting busy.'

'We're not that busy,' Eve mumbled, sweeping furiously.

'Another thing. How come this place is dead when they're turning them away everywhere else? Do you have many bookings this evening?'

'Not many.'

'How many is not many?'

'None.'

'No bookings?' Anna stopped sweeping. 'But that's impossible.' She tried to control the panic in her voice. She was going to lose everything. 'What have you been doing to this place?'

She jumped as Eve dropped her broom. 'Right, that's it,' she said.

'Where are you going?'

'Home. You're right, I'm hopeless at running this place.'

Anna watched in dismay. 'But you can't just walk out!'

'Give me one good reason why not.'

Anna swallowed. 'Is there somewhere we could talk?' she said.

They went into the yard. Eve sat on the step while Anna perched on a dustbin and told her the whole story. 'I don't understand,' Eve said when she'd finished. 'Why would Oliver do something like that?'

'He was desperate for the money, I suppose.'

'But to take out all those loans? The business wasn't in that much trouble.'

'We can't really ask him now, can we? Look, I'm not going to beg,' Anna said. 'If you want to sell up or do whatever you want with this place, Charlie and I will survive.'

'There's hardly any point in selling, if what you say is true. Neither of us would make anything, and you'd end up homeless. I suppose we're going to have to keep this place on. Although as everyone keeps reminding me, I don't have the first idea about running a business.'

Anna blushed guiltily. 'We could run it together. Obviously I couldn't give up my job because I need the money, so I couldn't be here all the time. But I'm sure we could sort something out.'

'It wouldn't work,' Eve said. 'Think about what happened with that health inspector earlier. Do you honestly believe we could work together?'

'It doesn't have to be like that.'

'No, but it would be. We'd be arguing the whole time.' She paused. 'If we do this, we'll do it my way. Agreed?'

'Do I have any choice?' Anna said.

Whether it was the stress of her meeting with Eve she didn't know, but an hour later Anna flipped out in the middle of Sainsbury's. One minute she was racing down the canned-foods aisle, the next she was weeping silently over a jar of Branston pickle. She knew it must have had something to do with the family she'd bumped into in wines and spirits. A young couple and their toddler, pushing their trolley around without a care in the world. It was so ordinary, so cosily domestic, a huge wave of anger boiled up inside her. She wanted to smash the jar of pickle to the ground in sheer rage at Oliver for leaving her in such a mess.

Voices rose from the next aisle, a fierce debate over Coco Pops versus Crunchy Nut Clusters.

'You chose last time,' a petulant voice accused.

'So? I'm the eldest.'

Anna pricked up her ears at the sound of Elliott's weary voice. 'For heaven's sake, get both of them and let's get out of here.'

A moment later his trolley rounded the corner. Two pretty, dark-haired girls trailed after him, one around eight, the other a few years older. He stopped when he saw her. 'Anna?'

'Hi.' She hoped he wouldn't notice her red-rimmed eyes.

'This is Jessica, and this is Becky, my eldest. Girls, this is Anna from my office.' The girls regarded her with solemn brown eyes just like their father's. 'Did you get your business sorted out?'

'In a way.'

They stood for a moment in silence. 'Why don't you girls go and choose some sweets?' Elliott said finally. They scurried off.

'Is it rude to ask why you're crying over a jar of Branston?'

'It was Oliver's favourite.'

'Ah,' Elliott said, as if she wasn't being mad at all. 'I guess the happy pills aren't making you too happy any more?'

'They're great,' Anna said defensively. 'I've just had a stressful day.'

The girls came running back before he could reply. As they were heading for the check-out Elliott said, 'Why don't you come round for supper tonight? Bring Charlie along, too. I'd love to meet him.'

'That's really nice of you, but I've already got plans. I'm going out to dinner with my friend Lynch.'

'Your solicitor?'

'Actually, he's an ex-boyfriend too. But I'd still like to come sometime.'

He smiled. 'Just say the word.'

Anna stared at herself in the bathroom mirror, trying to focus on her reflection. The doctor had said alcohol and antidepressants didn't mix, and by God he was right. She was drunk. Very, very drunk. And she was about to do something very, very stupid.

She'd met Lynch for dinner in one of the newest bars in York. It was achingly hip, noisy and crowded. The loud music filled her head, crowding out the black thoughts.

She wasn't hungry, so she nibbled on a bowl of nachos while Lynch ate a steak. And she drank. One vodka and tonic after another.

They talked. Lynch was exactly what she needed, making her laugh with his outrageous stories and gossip. He was very attractive, too. He looked like he'd just stepped out of the pages of *GQ*. Was it OK to develop a crush on him, she wondered as she watched him at the bar, laughing and joking with a curvy redhead as they waited to be served. 'Did you get her phone number?' she asked, when he returned.

He looked shocked. 'Bloody hell, what kind of low-life do you think I am, taking another woman's number while I'm out with you?'

'I wouldn't care if you did.'

'You mean you're not even a teeny bit jealous?'

'Why should I be?' She glanced across to the bar, where the redhead was watching them resentfully. 'Anyway, it looks like your friend's jealous enough for both of us.'

'She's probably wondering what I'm doing with you.'

'Thanks a lot!' Although she knew they made an odd couple, him so well groomed, her in a cotton skirt and an old denim jacket.

'That's OK. I go for personality anyway.'

'So how come most of your exes look like supermodels? I must have been the exception to the rule.'

He smiled. 'You had some redeeming qualities, as I recall.'

She gulped her drink. Oh God, he was flirting with her. Was this really what she wanted? 'Do you have a girlfriend at the moment?'

'Why? Are you interested?'

'Oh, please. I wouldn't go there again.'

He looked hurt. 'Why not?'

'Let's see . . .' She pretended to think about it. 'You never call when you say you will and you sleep with other women.'

'But I am very good in bed,' he pointed out.

She laughed. The combination of heat, noise and alcohol was making her head spin. 'I wasn't the only one with redeeming qualities.'

Now she was flirting with him. Suddenly, unexpectedly, a vision of Oliver's face came into her mind. She pushed it away again.

'Shall we have another drink?' she said.

Much later, they stumbled out into the night. As the cool air hit her, she leaned against Lynch, trying to stay upright. He laughed. 'Come on, I'll pour you into a taxi.'

The thought of going home to an empty house filled her with panic. 'Is that it?' she said, disappointed. 'Could we go back to your place?'

'Are you sure?' Lynch said. 'What about your little boy?'

'He's staying over at my mum's. I don't have anyone to go home to.' She gulped, tears filling her eyes.

Lynch put his arm round her, pulling her close. 'We'll walk back to mine,' he said. 'The fresh air will do you good.'

Lynch lived in a trendy converted wharf just along the river. It was typically him, modern, minimalist and tasteful. To Anna, it looked somewhere suitably anonymous for an illicit liaison.

Panic assailed her. 'Can I use your loo?' she said.

I should leave, Anna told herself. But she knew deep down she didn't want to. She splashed her face with cold water and went back outside. Lynch had made coffee, dark espresso in tiny steel cups.

They sipped their coffee and talked about work. Or rather, Lynch talked. Anna watched him, her eyes moving from the tantalising triangle of skin at his throat to his sensuous mouth. He was so unbelievably sexy. She could feel herself sobering up. Soon it would be too late and the moment, and her courage, would be lost. Finally she blurted out, 'Aren't you even going to try to seduce me?'

Lynch stopped talking. 'Do you want me to?'

'I'm here, aren't I?'

He leaned back. 'What's all this about?'

'Isn't that obvious?'

'It's obvious you came here to get laid. I just wondered why.' He regarded her with consideration. 'I'm guessing it's all about revenge? You've just found out Oliver's let you down. You're wondering if you really knew the man you've spent the last few years loving. You're scared and hurt, and you want to get even.'

He was right. The realisation crashed in on her, and she started to cry. Lynch came over to sit next to her, holding her close. It felt so good to be in a man's arms again. Anna buried her face in the smooth fabric of his shirt. 'I'm sick of being alone,' she sobbed.

He put his fingers under her chin, tipping her face up to look at him. The next moment he was kissing her, his mouth warm and soft and infinitely tender. 'Let me take you to bed,' he whispered.

It wasn't until the following morning that the hideous guilt overwhelmed her, a second after she opened her eyes and found herself with a pounding head amid a tangle of white sheets. Oh God, what kind of a woman was she. Now all her feelings of rage and revenge disappeared, replaced by utter remorse. How could she say she loved Oliver when she'd jumped into bed with the first man who came along?

She quietly got out of bed, dressed as quickly as she could, then crept out of the apartment.

Anna finally crawled into work just after nine, still wretchedly hungover. 'Good night, was it?' Elliott asked wryly.

'What's that supposed to mean?'

He backed off, holding up his hands. 'Easy, tiger, I just wondered if you'd enjoyed yourself, that's all.'

'Sorry.' She sank her head into her hands.

Barbara took one look at Anna's green-tinged face and was unusually sympathetic. 'Poor dear,' she said. 'I'll make you a cup of tea.'

Anna heard her whispering to Elliott in the tea cupboard. 'The poor girl's so overcome with grief she can hardly lift her head off the desk.'

'I think that's called a hangover, Barbara,' Elliott said, amused. 'She went out on the lash last night.'

There was a shocked silence. 'Oh, did she?' Barbara's voice was frosty, all trace of sympathy gone. And then the phone rang. 'Hello?' Anna saw her face turn pink. 'I'm sorry, I think you must want to speak to my colleague.' She handed the phone over to her.

'Oops,' Lynch laughed. 'I think I may have just made an obscene suggestion to your receptionist.'

'Oh God.' Anna glanced at Barbara, who'd gone tightlipped.

'So what happened to you this morning?'

'I had to go home. I was going to call you,' Anna said lamely.

'No you weren't. That's typical of a girl. You take what you want and then you never call. I feel so *used*.'

It took her a moment to realise he was joking. 'I really don't know what happened to me last night,' she said. She looked at Barbara, who was listening in. 'Look, we can't talk about this now. I'll call you back in five minutes, OK?'

Anna rang Lynch back from her mobile outside. 'Sorry about that, where was I?'

'You were just about to tell me last night was a huge mistake and you'd like us to forget it ever happened.'

'How did you know?'

'Just a hunch. Maybe it had something to do with the way you slunk off this morning. Why can't we have a laugh about it?'

'Because—' she thought for a moment. 'Because I love Oliver.'

'Oliver's dead,' Lynch said gently.

'I know, but it still feels wrong.' She paused. 'I'm sorry,' she said. 'I don't want you to think I was using you—'

'Anna!' She could hear the laughter in his voice. 'This is me you're talking to. Look, last night was great. But if you don't want to take it any further, that's fine by me. As a matter of fact, the reason I was ringing was to let you know I'm not going to be around for a week or two. I'm off to the States on business. Maybe we could catch up when I get back?'

'That would be nice.'

'And you never know, it might give you time to miss me.'

Eve stood in Jan's kitchen, clutching a bottle of Pinot Grigio in one hand and a banana and honey cheesecake in the other. She had exhausted all her excuses. 'You didn't tell me it was a dinner party!'

'Didn't I? Sorry. It won't be that bad,' she said bracingly. 'Adam's coming,' she added. 'And I haven't invited any single men, if that's what you're worried about. I wouldn't be *that* insensitive!'

No, Eve thought as they sat around the table half an hour later. No single men. Just a load of couples, which was almost worse. She would have liked to talk to Adam, but he'd turned up with Imogen. Even Adam was paired up now. Eve felt the sharp sting of jealousy. But she was happy for him too. He was such a nice guy.

She talked instead to the man on her left, a chartered surveyor called Edward. 'And what do you do?' he asked.

'I—' What could she say? Grieve, mostly.

'Eve runs a restaurant,' Jan cut in from across the table.

'Really?' Interest sparked in his eyes. 'That sounds fascinating.'

Eve threw Jan a puzzled look. 'I wouldn't say I actually run it—'

'She owns it,' Jan interrupted again. 'And she's a fabulous cook, too. She made that delicious cheesecake you're eating.'

'Really?' said a woman across the table. She was called Sue. 'You must give me the recipe. Tell me, how do you get ideas for the menu?'

Suddenly everyone seemed to want to talk to her. In a flash, she'd become a restaurateur, a person with glamour and status.

'To be honest, I don't know much about the restaurant business,' she admitted. 'I only ended up with it because my husband's just died.'

'I thought Jan said you were divorced?' Sue said.

'Not quite.' Eve looked at her across the table. Sue had obviously been getting stuck into the wine in a big way.

'Well, you must be an incredibly forgiving woman to want to take his business on, after what he did to you. If it was me, I'd sell up, take the cash and say bugger the lot of you.'

'That's not what Oliver would have wanted.'

'Why would you care what he wanted?'

'Well, I do,' Eve said quietly.

Everyone was suddenly staring fixedly at their cheesecake.

'More fool you, then.'

Everyone's spoons stopped clinking. Eve put hers down. 'You think so? Let me tell you something. It doesn't matter a damn how long Oliver and I had been apart. He was the father of my children, we shared half our lives. You can't just sign away those feelings with a set of divorce papers. Or bury them in the ground with a coffin.' Her voice shook. 'You don't know me, and you didn't know my husband. So don't you dare presume to tell me how I should think or feel now he's dead.'

She stopped, staring at the circle of shocked faces. The only one who wasn't looking at her was Adam.

'Coffee, anyone?' Jan said.

'I went too far, didn't I?' Eve said to Adam as he and Imogen gave her a lift home later.

'It was a bit of a conversation stopper,' Adam agreed.

'Well, I thought it was brilliant,' Imogen said. 'That woman deserved to be put in her place. Big-mouthed bitch.'

'All the same, I'll have to call Jan in the morning and apologise. Although to look on the bright side, I suppose this is the last time I'll be invited to any dinner parties.'

'You didn't enjoy it, then?'

'I haven't had that much fun since I had my wisdom teeth out.'

Imogen laughed. Eve caught Adam's eye in the rearview mirror. His face was grim. Eve knew him well enough to realise when there was something on his mind.

She found out what it was when he dropped her off at home.

Eve thanked them for the lift and got out of the car. Adam caught her up before she'd reached her front door.

'Can I talk to you?' he asked.

'Sure, what is it?'

'I just wondered how business was.'

'Fine,' Eve lied. No need to tell him how disastrous takings had been lately. 'Why do you ask?'

He paused for a moment. 'I wasn't going to mention it, but a couple of your cheques have bounced recently. It's no problem,' he said quickly. 'I just wanted to say that if you're having money troubles I'm sure we could come to some arrangement—'

'There's no need,' Eve said, flustered. 'We've got a bit behind with the accounts lately, what with me only just taking over. If you'd like to call in to the restaurant in a couple of days, I'll have your money ready for you. In cash.'

'Fine, I'll call round. As long as you're sure everything's OK?'

Loyalty to Oliver stopped her blurting out the truth. She didn't want anyone, least of all his family, to think badly of him.

'There's no problem,' she said.

MAY

THREE MONTHS AFTER Oliver's funeral, Anna and Eve finally met to choose a headstone for his grave. It was ages since they'd last spoken to each other. Anna had left Eve to run the restaurant alone but she kept hearing rumours about how badly it was doing. And then there'd been a bad review in the local paper. Anna couldn't understand it. How had it all gone so wrong? There was only one answer to that, she decided: Eve.

Eve seemed distracted when she answered the door. 'Sorry about the mess,' she gestured to her floury apron. 'I was trying out a new recipe.'

'It smells really good.' Anna followed the warm fragrance of cinnamon, apples and spices into the big farmhouse kitchen. 'What is it?'

'Brandy and apple cake. I've just taken it out of the oven. Take a seat. I'll make some coffee. You can take a look at these while you're waiting.' Eve dumped a heap of brochures in front of her.

Anna gingerly picked up the top brochure and steeled herself to flick through it. At first she could only look at the photos with her eyes half closed. But then she came to a page that made her open them wide. 'Who the hell would want something like *that*?' she said aloud.

Eve smiled over her shoulder. 'I'm guessing you've found the seven-foot stone angel. It is a bit kitsch, isn't it?'

'Kitsch? It's horrendous.' Anna stared at the photograph.

Eve put a mug down in front of her. 'I suppose we'd better get on with it,' she said. 'I was thinking of something very plain.'

'I agree,' Anna said. 'Black or white?'

'Definitely white. With engraved lettering?'

Anna nodded. 'What kind of wording were you thinking about?' She was already on the defensive, ready to walk out if Eve suggested putting on her name and not Anna's.

'How about "Oliver Robinson, beloved father of Matthew, Georgia and Charles"?'

'Charlie,' Anna said. 'No one calls him Charles.'

'And maybe we could have a quote he liked?' Eve suggested. 'I thought something from one of his favourite songs.'

'It would have to be the Smiths.'

'Who else?'

They looked at each other, surprised that they were so in agreement.

Eve moved the brochures to one side. 'Now that's out of the way, would you like to try some of that cake?'

It was so delicious that Anna found herself agreeing to an extra slice. 'This is amazing,' she said. 'And I hate food at the moment.'

'I wish I did,' Eve groaned. 'I've put on half a stone since Oliver died.'

'Working in the restaurant can't help. Who's looking after it today?'

'Frankie. I'll go in later. We're not that busy.'

Anna took a deep breath. This was the chance she'd been waiting for. 'I've heard the restaurant isn't doing too well? And I read the review.'

'Oh, that.' Eve was dismissive. 'They caught us on an off day.'

So how come no one wants to eat there any more? Anna thought. 'Have you come up with any ideas to get the customers back?'

'I've been busy finding my feet,' Eve said. 'But I'm going to start putting a few specials on the menu, maybe doing some promotions—'

'I reckon you're going to have to do more than tinker with the menu. I think we should give the place a make-over. Change the mood—'

'No,' Eve said coldly. 'No way. The place is fine as it is.'

'So why don't we have any customers?'

'It's just a temporary blip.'

'It's more than a blip.' Why couldn't Eve see that? 'You must admit the place is looking tired. The customers want something new.'

'This is the way Oliver wanted it,' Eve insisted stubbornly.

'Oliver wouldn't have wanted us to stand still. You know what he was like, always coming up with new ideas.'

'He liked the place the way it is. And so do I.'

Anna stared at Eve's face across the table. She looked so sure of herself, so totally unwilling to listen to anyone else's point of view. She could feel herself getting angry. 'Oliver liked looking forward,' she said. 'It's only you who wants to keep looking back.'

'What's that supposed to mean?'

'I mean you want to keep it as some kind of shrine to him. You've never wanted anything to change. That's why he left you.'

'He left me because you took him away.'

'And you couldn't get over that, could you?'

Eve stood up. 'I think you'd better leave now.'

'I'm going.' Anna picked up her bag. 'I don't know why we're even bothering with a headstone. That whole restaurant is Oliver's memorial!'

Eve threw the dishes into the sink, still fuming. How dare Anna preach to her like that? She didn't see any reason to make rash changes that might only lead them further into disaster. She had no confidence in her own judgment, so she had to rely on Oliver's.

Tension knotted her shoulders. She went upstairs to get some paracetamol out of her bedside drawer. She was putting the packet back when she spotted the small velvet box tucked at the back of the drawer. Anna's engagement ring. She'd meant to give it to Anna, but somehow it never seemed to be the right time. She tossed it back into the drawer and slammed it shut. There was no way she was giving it to her now.

She was still seething when Adam arrived at the restaurant with his order that afternoon. 'Anna thinks we ought to make some big changes to this place, but she says I won't because I'm trying to hold on to Oliver's memory. Do *you* think I'm keeping it as a shrine to Oliver?'

'This place obviously has very happy memories for you,' he said. 'I suppose it's possible you'd have trouble letting go of them.'

'So you reckon she's right? We should give this place a make-over?'

'I reckon you've got to make up your mind whether you're going to let your past get in the way of your future.'

Frankie was more forthright in his opinion. 'What does she know about running a restaurant?' He jabbed his finger at Eve. 'You're the boss of this place, not her. And I reckon you're doing a grand job.'

'Then how come we've got no customers?'

'I told you, all businesses have their ups and downs. Pass me that stock, would you?'

'Are you sure this stock is OK? It looks like it's been made up out of a packet.'

'It has.'

'Since when have we been using ready-made stock?'

'Since this place ran out of money.' He grabbed the jug from her.

'Surely it's a false economy to cut corners with our ingredients?' she said. 'Once the quality of the food goes down—'

'Who said it's going down?' Frankie turned on her. 'Do you honestly think I'd stake Oliver's reputation just to save a few quid?'

'I . . . of course not,' she said. 'I'm sorry.'

Frankie's shoulders relaxed. 'No, it's me who should apologise. I've been getting a bit wound up lately. Look, it'll be OK,' he reassured her. 'Business will pick up again, and in the meantime, no one will notice if we use a few tins and packets.'

Eve thought about the terrible review in the local paper, but said nothing. She was too shaken by Frankie's outburst to argue with him.

'There's something else you should know,' Frankie said. 'Simon's handed his notice in. He's going to work at the Burger Shack.'

'No! What are we going to do?' she asked.

'I'll have to cope until we find someone else. Lizzy can help, but she's still at college two days a week. I'll sort it out. The kitchen's my problem.'

For once Eve was thankful hardly anyone turned up for lunch, so Frankie and Lizzy were able to muddle through.

That afternoon she sat down in the empty restaurant to go over the books. No matter how much she looked at them, they still had barely enough coming in to pay the bills. She wasn't certain they could even afford to replace Simon—unless there was another way of looking at the problem. She picked up a menu. Lists of dishes, many of which never seemed to get ordered. Surely if they reduced the menu, it would save time and money? She was still trying to work out how she would sell the idea to Frankie when her mobile rang.

'Mrs Robinson? It's Heathwood School. We were just wondering if you knew where Matthew is today?'

'Sitting his History A Level paper this afternoon, isn't he?'

There was a pause. 'That's just it,' the voice said. 'He isn't.'

He was upstairs playing his guitar when she got home.

Eve crossed the room and pulled the plug out of the wall, plunging the room into silence. 'Your school called me wanting to know why you hadn't turned up.' He froze, his fingers still poised over the strings, head bent. 'Is there something you want to tell me, Matthew?'

'I didn't see the point. I've decided not to go to uni.'

Stay calm, she told herself. 'Look, I can understand you wanting to defer your place, after everything that's happened.'

'You don't get it, do you? I'm not going to university. Ever.'

'I thought you wanted to be a forensic scientist?'

'I'll do something else. Give it a rest, will you?' He threw his guitar on the bed and headed for the door, but Eve stepped in his path.

'I can't believe I'm hearing this. Not from you.'

'It's my life,' Matt said sullenly. 'Don't worry about it, OK?'

'How can I not worry? I don't know what's happening with my children.' She sat down on the bed and buried her face in her hands. Where was Oliver when she needed him? 'I don't think I can deal with all this on my own.'

She felt Matt's hand on her shoulder. 'Why do you think I can't go to uni? Georgia's being a pain, and you've got loads of stress with the business. You need me around, Mum. You might fall apart otherwise.'

'I'm not going to fall apart!'

'You haven't seen yourself lately.'

She realised the truth. She'd been wallowing in her grief when she should have been strong for her children. All this time she thought they hadn't noticed, when they'd been terrified she was going to crack up.

And there was Matt, struggling to look after her and Georgia as well as coping with his own grief and the pressure of his exams. She felt proud, guilty, grateful and ashamed all at the same time.

'You're a wonderful boy, do you know that?' she said. 'But there's no way I'm going to let you sacrifice your future for my sake.'

'Dad would have wanted me to take care of you and Georgia.'

'He would have wanted you to make something of your life,' she said. 'If you really want to do something for him and for me, you should go to university.'

'But—'

'Listen, I'll be fine. I can take care of myself. I *can*,' she insisted, 'Besides, I expect you'll still be home every weekend with your washing.'

Matt smiled uncertainly. 'What about Georgia?'

'She'll be fine too. She's just going through a funny phase.'

Walking out of school was easy. Andy Taylor and his mates were lolling around outside the gates, smoking. There was another girl with them, someone Georgia hadn't seen before: blonde, in a pink anorak.

'All right?' Georgia braced herself as Andy kissed her, his tongue invading her mouth. He tasted of stale tobacco. He let her go and passed her his cigarette. Georgia took a defiant puff and nearly gagged.

The other girl looked away, sneering. 'I want some chips.'

'Who's that?' Georgia asked as they waited outside the KFC.

'Her name's Kayleigh. She's Murphy's sister. She's all right,' one of the boys shrugged.

Georgia watched her through the window, feeding Andy a chicken drumstick. She didn't seem all right to her. 'Where are we going?' she asked Andy as they headed along Blossom Street.

'Dunno. Hang around the shops, probably.'

Georgia never imagined it, but at that moment doing double geography with the rest of her class seemed a lot more exciting than hanging around with Andy and his mates. But at least Andy was interested in her, which was more than she could say about anyone else.

They ended up in Woolworths on Coney Street. Georgia watched Andy and his friends browsing through the computer games, trying to decide which to nick. Kayleigh hung close to Andy, reading over his shoulder. On impulse, Georgia snatched the computer game from his hand, stuffed it in her schoolbag and made for the door. It was an odd, thrilling feeling when the alarm bells started ringing. She'd barely got through the doors before a woman in uniform descended on her.

'Just a minute, love.' She laid her hand on Georgia's shoulder.

Georgia glanced up the street. At the first sign of trouble Andy and his mates had scattered. She suddenly felt very lost and frightened.

'I'm really sorry, I—I didn't mean to do it,' she stammered.

Andy and the others were still loitering outside when she emerged half an hour later.

'What happened?' He yanked her into the nearest doorway. 'Did they call the police? You didn't mention my name, did you?'

She shook her head. Her eyes swam with hot tears. 'They just gave me a warning and told me not to come back.' They'd all been so kind when they found out her dad had just died.

Andy grinned with grudging admiration. 'Nice one. You're lucky they didn't phone the police.'

Am I? Georgia thought. Even the sour look on Kayleigh's face couldn't make up for how frustrated she felt.

JUNE

'BIT OF A DIVE, isn't it?' The builder stuck his pencil behind his ear and cast an expert eye round the restaurant.

'It's not that bad,' Anna said, feeling a stab of disloyalty. Oliver had loved this place, patchy paintwork and all.

He eyed her narrowly. 'Are you saying you don't want it done now?'

She hesitated. Oh God, she was turning into Eve, hanging on to her memories. 'Yes, do it,' she said.

She followed him round as he took measurements, her eye moving from her watch to the door and back again. She kept telling herself she had every right to be there, but that didn't stop her feeling like an intruder, as she'd let herself in with Oliver's old keys. It was Eve's fault. She wouldn't have had to skulk around behind everyone's backs if she'd been reasonable about it. Now Anna felt she had to take drastic measures to stop the business going down the pan.

Finally, 'All done,' he said. 'I'll get some figures together and let you have an estimate in the next few days, if that's all right?'

'No, it isn't.' Frankie appeared in the kitchen doorway, his arms folded menacingly across his bulky chest. 'What's going on?'

She faced Frankie. 'I'm getting an estimate done for some work.'

'Does Eve know about this?'

'Would someone tell me what's going on?' the builder said.

Frankie held Anna's gaze. 'I'm sorry mate, there's no work to be done on this place without the owner's permission.'

The builder looked at Anna. 'I thought *you* were the owner?'

'She isn't,' Frankie said bluntly.

Anna burned with rage and humiliation as the builder packed up and left. When he'd gone, she turned on Frankie.

'You had no right to send him away like that.'

'You had no right to bring him here in the first place. This is Eve's restaurant. And you—' he jabbed a finger at her, 'are trespassing.'

'So call the police.'

'I'd rather throw you out myself.' He was so close she could feel the sour warmth of his breath. For a split second she thought he was going to grab her, but he backed off. 'You're not worth going back to jail for.' His thin lips curled into a sneer. 'Christ, that must have hurt, didn't it? All those years wasted, chasing after him, and in the end his wife got it all. Look at you. Back in the gutter where you belong.'

'At least I've got you for company.'

'Bitch!' She saw the sparks of anger in his tiny eyes and flinched back, thinking she'd gone too far.

'Hello? Frankie?' Eve walked through the swing doors. Her smile disappeared when she saw Anna. 'What are you doing here?'

'I caught her skulking around with a builder,' Frankie said. 'Making plans to get this place redone behind your back.'

'I was going to talk to you again once I'd got some figures together,' Anna defended herself.

Eve stared at her. 'I told you, we're not making any changes.'

'We have to do something.'

'We?' Frankie said. 'I don't think it's your decision.'

'It's not yours either, in case you hadn't noticed.' Anna snapped.

'I think you'd better leave,' Eve said.

'All right, I'll go,' Anna said, 'But I'm going to speak to my lawyer. I want to save this place even if you two don't!'

She called Lynch from her mobile on the way back to her office.

'I'm sorry, Mr Lynch is still away,' his PA told her.

'But it's been two months! When is he due back?'

'We're expecting him later this month.'

Anna left her number and hung up. And to think she'd been worried about meeting Lynch again after their one-night stand.

There was a visitor waiting for her when she got back to the office. Anna's heart leapt into her mouth when she saw the tall, dark-haired man. She was just about to call out Oliver's name when she realised it was his cousin Adam. Cruel disappointment assailed her.

'This is a surprise,' Anna greeted him. 'What can I do for you?'

'I want to talk to you about Eve.'

'You'd better come into the back room.'

They faced each other in the bland, brightly lit office. 'I want you to give her a break,' he said.

'Sorry?'

'She's doing her best. She's working all hours.' He stared down at his work-roughened hands. 'Life hasn't been easy for her lately—'

'She's not the only one who's had a tough time.'

He raised his gaze to meet Anna's. His eyes were warm and grey, and so like Oliver's it broke her heart. 'I'm sorry,' he said gruffly. 'I realise you've been through a lot too. But Eve isn't as strong as you.'

Anna pressed her lips together. Just because she wouldn't allow herself to fall apart, that didn't make her strong.

'She's scared,' Adam went on. 'She relied on Oliver so much. Now she's on her own she doesn't know what to do without him.'

'She didn't lose Oliver. I did.'

'You both did. Whether anyone liked it or not, Eve was still in love with him.' He searched for the right words. 'I'm just trying to explain why she's not ready to make any changes to the restaurant. She can't trust her own judgment, and she's terrified of getting it wrong. But if you just give her time, I'm sure she'll sort it out.'

'But we don't have time,' Anna said, exasperated. 'If the business goes under, I lose everything!'

His gaze was suddenly sharp. 'What do you mean?'

Anna regarded him warily, wondering if she should tell him about the loans. 'It doesn't matter,' she said.

He pursed his mouth in frustration. 'Why do I get the feeling there's something you and Eve aren't telling me?'

'There's nothing to tell. The restaurant is going through a few money troubles at the moment, that's all. Now if you'll excuse me, I ought to get back to work.'

'Yes, of course. I'm sorry.' He sprang to his feet. 'Thank you for sparing the time to see me.'

As Anna watched Adam drive away, she wondered what had brought him all the way across town to plead Eve's case. She had a feeling it had more to do with his feelings for her than any family loyalty.

'Why not?' Andy demanded. His lower lip was jutting like a spoilt kid.

Georgia looked up at the sky. It was yellow-grey, promising a big storm. The air felt warm and damp against her skin. 'I'm not ready.'

'You've been saying that for weeks!' Andy whined. 'What's the matter with you? Don't you fancy me or something?'

They were in the kids' playground at the park, on the swings. On the other side of the playground, Andy's friends were messing around on the roundabout, trying to spin each other off. Kayleigh was with them.

'You're not a virgin or anything are you?' Andy said suddenly.

'No way.' Georgia turned circles on her swing, letting the chain get tighter and tighter, twisting around itself. Her dad used to do that when he took her to the park. He'd wind it all the way to the top and then let it go so she spun round and round. 'It's Father's Day tomorrow,' she said.

'So? I don't even know where my old man is. And yours is—' Even he knew when to shut up. 'So are we going to do it or not?'

Georgia sighed. 'If you want.'

'This Saturday? Liam's having a party. We could sleep over?'

Georgia nodded.

Big drops of rain began to fall from the sky, splashing into the dust at their feet. He slid off the swing. 'You coming? It's pissing down.'

'In a minute. I like it.'

He shook his head. 'You're mad, you.'

She watched him follow the others to the shelter. She didn't want to sleep with him. She certainly didn't want him to be her first. But Kayleigh was waiting to step into her shoes, and she didn't want that either. She let the swing go, twisting round and round until the park was a blur. Somehow it wasn't so much fun without her dad there.

'I'm going to a party next Saturday night, all right?'

Georgia braced herself for the usual questions. But her mum just said, 'That's nice,' and went on tapping numbers into her calculator.

Georgia fought the urge the snatch it out of her hand. 'I might stay over for the night.'

That got her attention. Her mother stopped and looked at her over the top of her glasses. 'Whose party is it?'

'Just a friend. No one you know.'

'And are their parents OK about you staying over?'

'Dunno.' Georgia waited for her mother to explode.

'As long as you let me have the address and phone number.'

Georgia stared at her in disbelief. 'You're letting me go?'

'I thought that's what you wanted?'

'I—' Of course it's not what I want, she felt like shouting. I want you to ask me a million questions. I want you to get enraged and tell me I can't go. I just want you to notice me. 'Fine,' she snapped. 'I'm going.'

'Now, are you sure you're going to be all right?'

Anna sighed. 'I've told you a hundred times, I'll be fine. You go and enjoy yourselves.'

'Fat chance of that, with your nana,' Keith grumbled.

'Are you still taking those tablets?' Jackie asked.

'Yes,' Anna was instantly on the defensive.

'I'm just worried you might be starting to rely on them.'

'They help me cope, OK? Would you rather I just went mad?'

Jackie held out her arms. 'Come here, you. Don't let's fall out, I won't see you for two weeks.' She hugged her tightly.

Anna stood at her mother's gate and waved them off. 'Where are they going?' Charlie asked, as Keith's car disappeared around the corner.

'They're going on holiday. To the seaside.'

Charlie's lip started to wobble. 'I want to go to the seaside!'

Anna suddenly felt very selfish. Her mother had offered to take him, but she'd wanted him to stay with her. 'I'll take you,' she promised. 'We'll go to Scarborough for the day and you can ride a donkey on the beach. How about that?'

Charlie nodded, pacified. But Anna suddenly felt anxious. Was her mum right? Was she relying on the magic pills too much? Maybe she was, but she couldn't trust herself to do without them.

The rest of Saturday passed quickly. But the next day was a different story. The storm that had cracked the sky so spectacularly the previous day had settled into grey, depressing rain. Sunday was a difficult day anyway, with so many hours to fill. And just to make it even worse, it was Father's Day. She lasted until lunch time, then called Rachel. Luckily, she jumped at Anna's suggestion that they should take the kids to the local indoor play area to work off some energy.

'Why don't we call Meg and invite her along?' Anna asked.

There was an awkward pause. 'I think she might be busy.'

Anna knew an excuse when she heard one. 'Rach, what's going on? I haven't seen her for months. She never comes out for a run with us any more. And the last time I bumped into her she couldn't get away fast enough. Doesn't she want us to be friends, or something?'

'Of course she does.'

'Then why is she avoiding me?'

'I don't know.' She could sense Rachel squirming.

'Fine. If you won't tell me I'll just have to ask her myself.'

'Thanks a lot,' were Anna's first words when Meg opened the door.

'What?'

'I can understand other people blanking me, but not you. Do you think bereavement is catching? You don't want to come near me in case someone you love dies, is that it?'

'No, of course not. I—' Meg stared at her for a moment. 'Dave's left me,' she said, and burst into tears.

Ten minutes later they were sitting side by side on the sofa, nursing cups of tea while Meg told her the whole sorry story.

'He left nearly two months ago.' Her voice was flat, as if she'd cried all her emotion out a long time ago. 'Apparently it's been going on for ages, him and this regional sales manager. I should have known. The gym membership, the new clothes. All those weekend courses with his mobile switched off. How could I have been so stupid?'

'You mustn't blame yourself,' Anna said.

'Why not? He says it's my fault. I didn't put enough effort into our marriage.'

'Only because you were too busy looking after all his kids!'

'That's just it. He said I put the children before him. I got too mumsy and boring for him, apparently.

'Bastard,' Anna said.

'He's right though, isn't he? I mean, look at me. Who'd ever fancy me?' She sat in the middle of a chaos of toys, dressed in a baggy sweater and jeans. The merry sparkle had gone out of her eyes. 'No wonder he left me for a younger, sexier model.' Meg managed a trembling smile. 'I'm sorry, Anna. The last thing you want to hear is me feeling sorry for myself. You've been through much worse than me.'

'Is that why you've been avoiding me?'

'You had enough misery of your own, you didn't need mine too.'

'But that's what friends are for, isn't it? Sharing troubles?'

Meg sniffed. 'Yes, but mine are trivial compared to all the huge stuff you're going through. I knew I'd end up blurting it all out about Dave. I didn't want you to think I was being selfish and pathetic.'

Anna reached for her hand. 'Maybe I'm the one person you should have talked to. I know what it's like to lose someone.'

They drank their tea and Meg cried some more and told Anna what a useless person she was. The more she talked, the more Anna wanted to thump Dave. He'd taken away every last shred of her self-esteem.

Finally, when Meg had cried all her tears out again, Anna decided it was time to take action. 'Rachel and I are taking the kids to the Play Zone this afternoon. Why don't we take your lot with us? It'll give you some time to catch up on your sleep.'

'Or the housework,' Meg said, looking around her.

'Definitely sleep. Housework can wait,' Anna said firmly. 'Then next weekend, we'll find baby sitters and all meet up and go out. Just the three of us. We deserve a good laugh and a gossip, I reckon.'

Georgia walked past the condom display in Boots five times, trying to look at them without anyone noticing. Why were there so *many*? Surely they all did the same thing—or did they? What if she bought the wrong kind? She'd die of shame if Andy laughed.

Maybe he would come prepared, she thought. Or then again, maybe he wouldn't. He seemed like the kind of boy to take risks.

She looked at her watch. Twenty minutes to closing time. She headed purposefully towards the condom counter, hand outstretched, blindly grabbed the first packet she could reach, then darted away again.

Right. Mission accomplished. Now all she had to do was pay for them, and—Oh God. Emma Standish was on the pharmacy till. Officially the biggest mouth in the school. Georgia shuddered. There was absolutely no way she could go up to her and pay.

There was nothing else for it. With another quick look round she slipped the packet into her bag and hurried out of the shop. This time there were no alarm bells. All those weeks hanging around with Andy and his mates had obviously improved her technique.

On the way back from Play Zone, Anna stopped off at Smith's to buy Charlie some sweets and herself a nice, undemanding magazine.

'Look! Georgia!' Charlie pointed towards the check-out line.

Georgia turned round at the sound of her name. Her face paled when she saw them. 'Oh, hello.' She was holding the same gossipy celeb magazine as Anna.

'Glad to see we've got the same taste in literature,' Anna said.

'What? Oh, yeah.'

Anna frowned at her. 'Are you OK?'

'I'm fine.' As Georgia moved forward to the next check-out, something slipped from between the pages of her magazine.

They both dived for it at the same time, but Anna got there first. She'd already picked it up before she realised it was a Father's Day card.

'Dunno how that got there,' Georgia mumbled, red-faced. 'S'not mine. Obviously.' Georgia hurried to the check-out with her magazine, leaving Anna holding the card.

'Obviously.' But it wasn't the card that had disturbed Anna. It was what she'd spied in Georgia's bag as she reached for her purse.

Did Eve know what her daughter was doing? she wondered. Anna wasn't sure she should be the one to tell her. She probably wouldn't thank her for it. And at least Georgia was being careful.

'Have you heard?' Barbara greeted Anna when she walked in on Monday morning. 'Neil's Ruth has had the baby. On Saturday. A little boy, seven pounds two.'

They were still discussing it when Elliott walked in ten minutes later. Barbara went off to put the kettle on.

Elliott was quiet for a moment as he went through the post. Then he said, 'Do you fancy coming to a party on Saturday night? Before you get excited I should warn you: Jessica's having a birthday sleepover. My mother was coming to help me but she's slipped a disc and can't make it. And frankly the thought of all those eight-year-olds loose in the house doesn't exactly fill me with confidence. You'd be doing me a favour.'

'My mum's away, but I suppose I could try to find a baby sitter.'

'Bring Charlie along. The more the merrier.'

'In that case, I'd love to come.'

'Great. Don't forget your toothbrush, will you, because I'll expect you to stay the night.'

Unfortunately, Barbara just happened to emerge from the kitchen at that moment. She almost dropped the mugs she was carrying.

Georgia slumped in the bathroom, the walls reeling around her. She couldn't remember how much she'd had to drink. Still not enough to want to be alone with Andy, that was for sure.

She kept very still and tried to focus on the washbasin. From beyond the door came the sound of thumping music, shouting and laughter. She wanted to go home.

Someone thumped on the bathroom door. 'Georgia?' Andy called.

'Just a minute.' She crawled across the room and managed to pull the bolt to let him in.

'Bloody hell,' he laughed. 'You're in a right state.' He took her by the arm and hauled her to her feet. 'Come with me.'

Next thing she knew, they were in a bedroom. 'I think I'm going to be sick again,' Georgia mumbled.

'You'll be OK. Just lie down on the bed.'

It felt so good to close her eyes. A second later she was awake again, all her senses on full alert. Andy was fumbling with her top. 'What are you doing?'

She tried to sit up but he pushed her down again, pinning her to the bed. 'Relax,' he whispered. 'Just enjoy it, OK?'

Jessica's party turned out to be great fun. Jessica and her friends were, despite Elliott's dire warnings, very sweet. Her sister Becky, three years older, was utterly dismissive but still joined in. They were even lovely to Charlie, adopting him as a little mascot.

Later, when Charlie had finally gone to bed after far too much cake, Anna helped calm down the girls by giving them manicures and putting their hair in French plaits while they watched a chick flick. Elliott beat a tactful retreat to the kitchen to wash up, leaving them all to it.

Finally, at about midnight, they all went to sleep in Jessica's room. Anna and Elliott flopped on the sofa. 'Are you sure it's OK for me to stay?' Anna asked. 'They might be more comfortable if they spread out to the spare room.'

'Apparently being squashed in like sardines is all part of the fun.' Elliott tutted. 'Don't you know *anything*?' He refilled her wineglass. 'Thanks for coming to my rescue, by the way. I couldn't have got through it without you.'

'It's better than spending the evening on my own.'

'Weekends are the worst, aren't they?' Elliott agreed sympathetically. He sent her a considering look. 'I thought you had your friend Lynch to keep you company these days?'

She blushed. She'd forgotten the whole office knew about their one-night stand. 'I haven't seen him for a while. I still feel guilty.'

'Why? It's not a crime to want to feel loved.'

'You sound as if you've been there yourself.'

He was quiet for a long time, then he said, 'Her name was Amanda. She was a friend of Karen's. She helped me after she died. Then one night it just happened. I knew it was a mistake. I felt so ashamed of myself. Karen had only been gone a month. But I just needed someone.'

'What happened?'

'It ended, but our friendship ended with it. I regret that most of all.'

'So have you been out with anyone else since?'

Elliott laughed. 'Anna, it's been five years. I know you might think I'm dull, but I'm not a monk!'

Actually, he was quite attractive. Not obviously gorgeous like Lynch, but those warm, melting chocolate eyes, that thick curly hair that you wanted to run your hands through . . . Oh no, she thought, it's happening again. Another adolescent crush.

Her mobile rang, right on cue. Anna jumped to answer it.

'Anna?' Georgia's voice trembled. 'Where are you?'

'I'm at a friend's. Where are you?'

'Outside your house. Can you come home? I need you.'

Anna left Charlie at Elliott's and raced home. Georgia was on her doorstep, her knees tucked under her chin. As soon as she saw Anna, she jumped to her feet and ran to her. She reeked of alcohol and cigarettes.

Anna helped her into the house, and guided her into the sitting room. Georgia shivered on the sofa, dressed in drainpipes and a skimpy black vest top.

Anna sat down beside her, her arm around the girl's trembling shoulders. 'Can you tell me what's wrong?' she asked gently.

'It's—it's Andy.'

'The boy I saw you with that time?'

Georgia nodded. Her dark hair fell across her face, sticking to her wet cheeks.

'What did he do to you?' Panic ran through Anna, 'Has he hurt you?'

Georgia started to cry again. Anna stroked the hair off her face and tried to stop herself fearing the worst. 'I'm calling your mum.'

'No!' Georgia looked up, her eyes swimming with tears. 'I don't want her to know. Why do you think I came here? You were the only one I could think of. The only one I could trust.'

They faced each other. 'You'd better tell me everything,' Anna said.

Slowly, haltingly, it all came out. How this Andy creep had put pressure on her to sleep with him. 'I tried to get myself drunk.' She took a big, shuddering breath, trying to calm herself. 'Andy took me into the bedroom.' Anna could feel the bones of her shoulders working underneath her skin. She was so small, so fragile. 'He pinned me down to the bed. I panicked, and then—I—I threw up on him.' Georgia started sobbing again. 'I was sick. All over him. It was terrible,' she cried. She was so mortified she could hardly speak, but it was all Anna could do to stop herself smiling. 'He got really angry. He said I was stupid and frigid.' She hung her head. 'Then, as I was leaving, I saw him kissing Kayleigh.'

She broke into fresh sobs. Anna pulled her close. 'I know it won't seem like it at the moment, but I reckon you've had a lucky escape.'

'But I liked him. He was the only one who ever noticed me.' Georgia pulled away from her, wiping her nose with the back of her hand. 'Can I stay here tonight?'

'Won't your mum wonder where you are?'

'She thinks I'm staying over at the party. She wouldn't care, anyway. The only thing she ever thinks about is that restaurant. She's *obsessed*. That and visiting Dad's grave.' Her face hardened. 'She cares more about him than she does about us.'

Anna put Georgia to bed, then went back to Elliott's to pick up Charlie. Elliott was waiting up for her. 'Everything all right?' he asked.

'Just a teenage trauma, thank God.' She suppressed a shudder. It could have been much worse than a broken heart.

Georgia was pale, subdued and hungover the following morning. 'I'm really sorry about last night.' She pushed away the plate of toast Anna put in front of her. 'Oh God, I was such a freak. I can't believe I was actually sick on Andy Taylor.'

'Sounds like no less than he deserved.'

'Promise you won't tell Mum?' Georgia said.

'She's your mother. She'd want to know. I'd want to know if I was her.'

'I told you, she doesn't care about us.' She turned her anxious eyes to Anna. 'Please don't tell her, will you?'

'I promised, didn't I?' Although she itched to pick up the phone and tell Eve just how much wallowing in grief was hurting her children.

Half an hour later she watched Georgia head off down the road. Apart from a hangover and a bit of dented pride, she seemed none the worse for her ordeal. But all this Andy business had obviously been a big cry for attention. She couldn't believe Eve had ignored it for so long.

She closed the door, then went upstairs for a quick shower.

She'd just put her dressing gown on when there was a knock on the door. Thinking it was Georgia, she ran down to answer it.

Lynch took off his sunglasses and looked her up and down, his gaze falling for a moment on the neckline of her dressing gown. 'Hi. Remember me?'

'Vaguely. Didn't you used to be my lawyer?'

He glanced past her into the hall. 'Is that coffee I can smell?'

'I tried to call you last night but there was no reply,' he said as he followed her into the kitchen. 'Where were you?'

'I could ask you the same question. You've been gone months.'

He smiled. 'You've been counting the days? That's so sweet. So who's this mystery man you were with last night?'

'None of your business. I don't ask who you've been with while you were sunning yourself in the States.'

'Jealous?' he taunted.

'Why should I be?'

'Maybe absence has made your heart grow fonder?'

'The only reason I missed you was because I needed a lawyer.'

He frowned. 'Problems?'

'Let's just say the situation has changed.'

'Why don't we have dinner on Tuesday? We can catch up then.'

She considered it. 'If I can find a baby sitter.'

He grinned, supremely confident. 'Great. The table's booked for eight.'

'How did you know I'd say yes? Arrogant swine.' She couldn't help smiling. She'd missed him more than she liked to admit.

'So who *was* your mystery man?' he asked as he left.

'If you must know, it was my boss, Elliott.'

He looked relieved. 'That's OK, then. You're safe enough with Mr Prozac. He wouldn't make a move on you in a million years.'

That Sunday, Anna met up for her girly lunch with Rachel and Meg at Oliver's. 'Clever move, getting us to eat here,' Rachel commented as they sat down. 'You get to spend time with us and make money at the same time.'

'I'm not sure how much money we're making.' Anna looked around the near empty restaurant. 'Anyway, forget about work. We're here to talk about you,' she said to Meg. 'You're looking great, by the way.'

She'd washed her hair and put on some make-up.

'I had to do something. I was frightening the children.'

'Shall we order before we start bitching about your ex?' Rachel said as Laura came over with the menus.

'Sorry, the sea bass is off,' she said. 'So is the salmon. The fishmonger hasn't supplied this week.'

'You see what I mean?' Anna said, when they'd finally all decided on pasta. 'This place is going to the dogs. The only person Eve listens to is Frankie. As far as she's concerned, he can do no wrong.'

And between them, they were ruining Oliver's reputation.

'Excuse me,' Meg interrupted. 'My baby sitter's only booked until tea time, and I want to get a nice therapeutic slagging session in before then.'

Of course they were happy to oblige. As the wine flowed, they got stuck in to Dave and His Many Faults. By the time their food arrived, Meg realised what an uncaring, selfish pig she'd been married to. It was all they could do to stop her breaking into a rousing chorus of *I Will Survive*.

Then they moved on to his new fancy woman. 'I can see her now,' Rachel said. 'All big tits and tea-bag tan. I bet she's dead tacky.'

'Actually, I met her at a Christmas party and she seems very nice.' Meg gulped her wine, forgetting that she was supposed to be well rid of him. 'Really attractive, with a fabulous designer wardrobe. She's got a PhD in marketing. And she lives in a wonderful loft apartment, with white sofas and everything.'

Anna and Rachel looked at each other worriedly. 'Meg—'

But there was no stopping her. 'And she does Pilates in her spare time, so she's really bendy and she probably knows all kinds of unusual sexual positions. My idea of adventurous sex was taking my nightie off.' A tear rolled down her cheek. 'Oh God, no wonder he left me.'

'Now you listen to me.' Rachel waved her glass in front of Meg's face. 'She might have all that going for her now, but give it six months and wait until the novelty wears off. She'll be schlepping around in her dressing gown and telling him she's too tired just like the rest of us.'

'Why don't you send the kids over to stay at their place?' Anna chimed in. 'I bet her white sofas won't be quite so pristine then.'

'Great idea,' Rachel agreed. While Rachel and Meg enthusiastically planned the rapid end of Dave and his new woman's honeymoon, Anna couldn't help noticing an argument going on between Laura and a glum couple at the corner table. She tried to ignore it, but in the end she couldn't help herself.

'It's no good, I've got to find out what's wrong,' she said.

'Stay out of it Anna,' Rachel warned, 'but she was already halfway to their table.

'Excuse me, is there a problem?' she asked politely.

'They won't pay for their meal,' Laura explained.

'Why not?'

'I'll tell you why not.' Angry spittle flew from the man's lips. 'First there was hardly anything on the menu we wanted to eat. Then when we did finally find something, we had to wait ages for it. And when it did arrive, it was cold. Now do you think that's acceptable?'

Something about his pugnacious little face made Anna's hackles rise. She eyed the plates. 'You've eaten it all, so it can't have been that bad.'

'What should we have done? Sent it back and waited another two hours? Of course we ate it!'

Anna clenched her hands. 'In which case, you'll have to pay for your meal.'

'And who's going to make me?'

'The police, if necessary.'

'Now you listen here—'

'Is there a problem?' There was Eve, looking harassed.

'I was just explaining that it's customary to pay one's bill after eating a meal in a restaurant,' Anna stated.

'And I was just explaining that it's customary for a restaurant to provide food that isn't completely inedible,' said the man.

'I'm so sorry you didn't enjoy your meal, sir,' Eve said in a resigned voice. 'Of course if it's failed to meet your expectations we wouldn't dream of asking you to pay.'

Anna's mouth fell open. 'But—'

'And we'd like to give you a bottle of wine, as a token of our apology.'

Anna barely waited until the door had closed on Mr and Mrs Obnoxious before she turned on Eve. 'We can't afford to give away meals like that, or hadn't you noticed?'

'Oh, I'd noticed, all right.' Eve massaged her temples. 'I'm the one who has to balance the books, remember?'

Anna stifled a sigh. Eve's exhausted martyr act was getting a bit too much for her. 'Only because you won't let anyone else help. Why do you have to keep shutting me out? What are you trying to prove?'

Rachel was shaking her head and Meg had hidden behind her hands.

'I'm not trying to prove anything. I'm trying to run a business.'

'And you think you're the only one good enough to do it, do you? You want to prove to everyone that you're the one Oliver trusted. Well, I'm sorry, but you're not going to push me out of Oliver's life by pushing me out of the restaurant.'

Anger flared in Eve. 'And what would you do? Turn this place into a pizza parlour so you could make more money? You don't really care what this place meant to him, as long as it keeps paying your bills!'

Stung, Anna snapped back, 'It's a pity you don't worry about your kids as much as you do about keeping his memory alive. Then maybe I wouldn't have your daughter turning up at midnight on my doorstep!'

She clamped her mouth shut, knowing she'd said too much.

Eve went very still. 'What? When was this?'

Anna met her gaze. 'Talk to Georgia,' she said quietly.

Eve froze for a moment. Then she began ripping off her apron.

'Where are you going?' Anna asked.

'Home.'

'But what about this place?'

'You want to help? *You* do it.' Eve stuffed her apron into Anna's hands. 'I'm going to see my daughter.'

Georgia applied the last of the peroxide to her hair and wrapped it carefully in a plastic cap. She covered the whole lot in a towel and checked her watch. Not long now and she'd be a stunning blonde. She went into her bedroom. A second later her mother appeared in her doorway.

'What's going on, Georgia?' she asked. 'I've been talking to Anna.'

Oh shit. Georgia's mind raced. 'What did she tell you?'

'I'd rather hear it from you.'

All this time Georgia thought she'd wanted her mum to find out. But suddenly she realised she didn't want to talk about it after all. It was an awkward conversation. Georgia hugged a pillow for protection, her face buried in it so she wouldn't have to look at her mother's face. She'd barely got as far as saying Andy's name when the barrage of questions started.

'You had a boyfriend? How long for? Where did you meet him?'

Georgia told her about Andy, being careful to leave out all the bits about her skipping school, stealing condoms and briefly taking up smoking. She wasn't sure her mum could handle it.

It was just as well she did. 'Georgia, what were you thinking? What made you get involved with a low-life like that?'

Because I wanted you to notice me, she wanted to scream. But it all seemed childish now. To tell the truth, she felt a bit ashamed. She couldn't remember what she'd ever seen in Andy Taylor.

'What's this about you turning up at Anna's house?'

'It was that night I went to the party. Something went wrong, and I didn't have anywhere to go, so I went round to her place.'

'What went wrong? You'd better tell me now, because whatever it is, it can't be any worse than what I'm imagining.'

She told her. Her mother hardly seemed to be listening. Her face was rigid, like a mask. 'Oh, God.' At first Georgia thought she was angry, until she saw the tears running down her face. 'Why didn't you tell me?' she said. 'Why did you go to Anna?'

'I—I didn't think you cared,' she stammered. 'You were never here. It was like you didn't want to be with us.'

Her mother's face crumpled. 'I've let you both down so much.'

'You haven't, really. You—' She felt the icy trickle running down the back of her neck. 'Quick, what's the time?'

Her mother looked blearily at her watch. 'Twenty past. Why?'

'Oh shit!' She sprang off the bed and ran to the bathroom, slamming the door behind her. With shaking hands she peeled off the towel, to reveal—'No!' Her wail of despair rang through the house.

There was a soft tap on the door. 'Is everything all right in there?' her mother asked.

'No. No, it bloody well isn't!'

'At least let me come in and take a look?'

Georgia hesitated. 'You can look. Just don't say anything.'

She heard her mother's sigh. 'I won't say a word.'

She unbolted the door but before her mother could slide inside, Matt flung it open. 'Jesus!' He laughed. 'You're a ginger!'

'Sod off!' Georgia slammed the door in his face. 'I hate you!'

Her mother lifted the plastic and examined a lock of hair. 'It's not too bad,' she said. 'You haven't left it on long enough. Another fifteen minutes and it'll be fine. Trust me.' Her mum pointed to her own honey blonde hair. 'Do you think God gave me this colour?' She tucked Georgia's sticky orange hair back inside the cap. 'Would you like me to help you?'

'Don't you have to go back to work?'

Her mother smiled, her face still blotchy from crying. 'I think they can do without me for once.'

Later, Eve went out to do some work in the garden. She was attacking an awkward patch of dandelions when she heard the gate click. She glanced over her shoulder to see Anna walking up the path towards her. 'I thought you might need these.' She dropped the restaurant keys on to the grass beside her.

'Thanks.'

'It didn't go too well, in case you were wondering,' Anna said. 'I had a row with Frankie. And I broke the microwave.'

Eve said nothing. She waited for Anna to leave but she stood over her, blocking out the light. 'Look, I hope you're not pissed off with me,' Anna said. 'I wanted to tell you, but Georgia made me promise.'

Eve looked over her shoulder at her. It suddenly dawned on her why Anna was hanging around. 'You think I'm angry with *you*?'

'I should have told you what happened.'

Eve stood up. 'I'm just glad she had someone to turn to. At least you were there for her, which is more than I was.'

Anna frowned at her. 'You mustn't blame yourself.'

'Why not? Who else can I blame?' All her self-hatred came bubbling up. 'My daughter put herself in danger and I didn't have a clue.'

'I bet you hid things from your mother,' Anna said.

'I didn't have to. My mother never listened to me anyway.'

And she was no better. She'd always sworn that when she had children it would be so different. She would put them first. 'I should never have taken on the restaurant,' she said. It was sheer selfishness that had driven her to it. Wanting to prove something to the world, wanting to lose herself in something, to ease her grief and loneliness.

But she'd forgotten the people who needed her most.

She stared down at the dirt under her fingernails. 'I didn't want to let anyone down,' she said. 'There were so many people relying on me. I didn't want you to lose your house, or the staff to lose their jobs.'

'Or Oliver to lose his dream?' Anna said.

'Maybe,' Eve agreed. 'But I let down the people who were most important. My children. And I haven't even managed to save the restaurant.' She buried her face in her hands. 'I've made a mess of everything.'

'Maybe you just need a break,' Anna said. 'Why don't you take a holiday, just you and the kids?'

She smiled wearily. 'It's a nice idea, but who'd run Oliver's?'

'I will. I could keep an eye on the place for a week or two.' She grinned. 'Don't worry, I won't turn it into a pizza parlour while your back's turned! I'm sure my job'll let me have a couple of weeks off.'

Eve hesitated. It was such a tempting idea. She was just so tired. But there was one thing that bothered her. 'What about Frankie? I don't think he'd like the idea.'

Anna smiled. 'Don't worry, I can handle him.'

That's what I'm afraid of, Eve thought. She didn't want to come back and find they had no chef as well as no customers.

JULY

'WHO'S THAT MAN talking to Frankie?'

Laura glanced out of the window. 'No idea. Never seen him before.'

'I think I have.' She'd only ever seen photographs before, but she still recognised him. But what would Frankie be doing with Les Willis, one of the biggest crooks in York? She turned away from the window. Whatever Frankie's business was with Willis, she was glad it wasn't hers.

'Mummy?' Charlie came towards her. 'Can we play cards now?'

'Sorry, sweetheart, I can't. Mummy has to do the staff rotas.'

'I could play with him, if you like?' Laura said.

'Are you sure? That would be great.' Anna ruffled his head. It was a mistake bringing Charlie in to the restaurant, but there was a nasty bug going round the nursery school so they'd sent all the kids home. And her mum had gone on a course for college.

'I don't mind. I love kids.' Laura settled down cross-legged on the floor with Charlie and began to deal out the cards. 'And Charlie's so sweet. Oliver used to talk about him all the time. He looks so like him!'

'Yes, he does.' Anna felt a niggle of uneasiness. She was beginning to wonder if Laura had had a bit of a crush on Oliver.

The phone rang. It was Lynch. 'Just checking you're OK for tonight?'

'Oh God, we're supposed to be going out, aren't we?' She spiked up her hair with her hand. 'I'm not sure I can make it. My mum's away and I might not be able to get a baby sitter at such short notice.'

'Better start trying then. The table's booked for eight. I'll pick you up at quarter to, OK?' he said, and put the phone down.

'Was that your boyfriend?' Laura asked. 'Lynch, isn't it?'

'He's just a friend,' Anna said absently.

'Really? I thought it was serious between you.'

Anna frowned. What did Laura know about it? 'We've only been out twice. And we won't be going out tonight if I can't find a baby sitter.'

'I'll do it. I'm not working tonight.'

'That's very kind of you,' Anna said. 'But Charlie can be a bit cranky with new people. I'll give my neighbour's daughter a call.'

'Suit yourself,' Laura said. She buried her face in Charlie's neck and blew a raspberry that made him roar with laughter.

Anna watched them. Laura was so good with him, she didn't know why the idea of leaving them alone together made her uneasy.

She couldn't find anyone to look after Charlie. She tried to call Lynch but his mobile was switched off. His PA promised to pass on Anna's message that she wouldn't be able to make their date. So she was surprised when the doorbell rang as she and Charlie were in the middle of a riotous game of space ships and aliens in the back garden.

'I can see you've made a special effort,' Lynch commented drily, looking from her grass-stained jeans to her hot, sweaty face topped off with an alien's helmet fashioned out of tin foil and a bent coat hanger. 'You've done something, haven't you? Let me guess. Is it your hair?'

'Very funny.' She took off the helmet, disentangling the hook from her ear. 'What are you doing here? Didn't you get my message about us having to cancel tonight?'

'No. I take it you couldn't find a baby sitter?'

'Not at such short notice. Sorry you've had a wasted journey.'

'Who says it's wasted? Why don't we stay in and get a takeaway? It might be nice to have a cosy evening in, just the two of us?'

'Don't you mean three?' she said, just as Charlie came running up the passage from the kitchen, wielding a plastic light sabre. When he saw Lynch he stopped in his tracks. 'This is Mummy's friend,' Anna introduced them. 'Lynch, this is Charlie.'

'Pleased to meet you.'

'How old are you?' Charlie asked.

'Have a guess.'

Charlie assessed him with utter concentration. 'Six?'

'Near enough.'

'Why don't you go back and play in the garden?' Anna said.

'You're my prisoner.' Charlie pointed the light sabre at her.

'Why don't I come and be your prisoner?' Lynch said.

Charlie and Anna stared at him. 'I wouldn't advise it,' she said.

'Why not?' Lynch grinned down at Charlie. 'It'll be fun.'

Charlie looked him up and down. 'To the space ship,' he commanded.

'Don't say I didn't warn you,' Anna called after them as Lynch was frog-marched down the hall with a light sabre at his back.

It felt strange, having another man in Oliver's house. She stood at the French windows and watched Lynch with Charlie in the garden. He was trying hard, but he wasn't exactly throwing himself into the game.

She'd opened a bottle of wine when Lynch came in a few minutes later. 'Lively little chap, isn't he?' he said.

'I did warn you. Here, this will steady your nerves.'

They sat outside on the patio with their wine, enjoying the last of the evening sun while they looked through the menu for the local Thai takeaway. Then she went into the house to phone through their order.

When she came back, Charlie had climbed on to the chair next to Lynch and was chattering away to him. 'My daddy's dead,' he said.

'I know.'

'He's in heaven now, with David Beckham.'

'Why don't you go inside and find a story to read at bedtime?' Anna suggested. 'Sorry about that,' she said as he wandered off. 'He has some strange ideas about death. I think he gets them from my nana.'

'I have to say, it's a lot more peaceful when he isn't around.'

Anna watched him, lounging back in his seat, graceful as a cat, male-model casual in jeans and a white T-shirt, his beautiful face turned up to catch the last rays of the sun, and quelled the irritation she felt. She couldn't blame Lynch, he just wasn't used to kids.

'I'll get him ready for bed before the food arrives,' she said.

When she got back downstairs, she was dismayed to find candles lit on the table, and a definite mood of seduction in the air. Anna's heart sank. She didn't want to go down that road again. Luckily, Charlie kept sneaking downstairs during their meal with various toys and treasures to show Lynch.

At first Lynch played along, but by the time their meal was over Anna could tell his patience was wearing thin.

She finally managed to coax Charlie into bed half an hour later.

'Alone at last,' Lynch said when she came downstairs again. She curled up in the armchair, her arms folded across her chest to protect herself from the waves of sexual heat radiating across the room. He smiled. 'How do you fancy coming to Barcelona with me?'

She nearly dropped her glass. 'When?'

'I've got to go there next Friday for work. I thought we could make a weekend of it. Do some shopping, hit a few bars?'

'It sounds wonderful,' Then, to test him, she added, 'Charlie will love it. He's never been on a plane before.'

His smile disappeared. 'I wasn't thinking of taking Charlie.'

'I know you weren't,' she said. 'I just wanted to see your face. But I can't go anywhere without him.'

'Couldn't you get someone to look after him?'

'He's a little boy, not a parcel. I can't just dump him in left-luggage whenever I want to go somewhere.'

'So that's a no, then?'

'I'm afraid so.'

'Pity. Come on, Anna, you know you can't resist me forever. We're practically in a relationship, for heaven's sake.'

'We've been out twice. And this time we stayed in, so it hardly counts.'

'So? With my track record that makes us practically engaged.'

He made her laugh, which lowered her defences. Before she knew what was happening, he was sliding along the sofa towards her, like a leopard moving in for the kill. Anna felt her insides liquefy with treacherous lust, and then—'I've wet the bed.' Charlie stood in the doorway, rubbing his eyes with one hand, trailing his toy monkey from the other.

She got up. 'Oh dear, come on, let's get you sorted out.' She didn't know whether to feel relief or regret. 'Look, Lynch, I'm going to be a while, so you might as well go.'

He looked as if he might argue, then put down his glass. 'I'll call you.'

Eve battled through Customs, struggling under the weight of Matt and Georgia's duty-frees. Their week in Italy had done them all good. They'd relaxed in the Mediterranean sunshine and forgotten all their troubles.

But once home, reality hit them like the steady grey drizzle that fell as they stood in the queue for a taxi.

'Back to boring old England,' Matt sighed.

'I wish you'd brought the car,' Georgia grumbled.

'And run up a fortune in the long-stay car park? We can get a cab into Leeds and then catch the train.' Although her economy drive didn't seem such a bright idea with rain dripping down her neck.

'Can I give you a lift?' Suddenly there was Adam's van pulling up beside them in the queue, like a knight in shining armour.

'What are you doing here?' she asked.

'I remembered you'd said when your flight was coming in, and I wasn't doing anything, so I thought I'd drive down and give you a lift back to York. You don't mind, do you?'

'Mind? You're a lifesaver!'

'Did you have a good holiday?' he asked, when they were heading back along the motorway.

'It was bliss,' Eve smiled. 'Just what we all needed. How's the restaurant? Are we still in business?'

'As far as I know.'

Eve watched him sideways as he negotiated a roundabout. 'Is there something you're not telling me?' she said.

'Eve, the last time I looked, Oliver's was still open.'

They joined the steady crawl of traffic towards York. 'So what's happening in your world?' Eve asked.

'Not much. The pumpkins are doing pretty well. Oh, and Britney's just about ready to give birth.'

'Britney?' Georgia said from the back.

'His goat.' Eve smiled. 'Don't you think about anything but that farm?'

He frowned. 'What else did you want to know about?'

'How's Imogen?'

'She's fine.'

She got the message from his non-committal response. When it came to his private life, Adam clammed up tighter than an oyster shell.

Half an hour later they were back at home. 'Thanks again for giving us a lift,' Eve said. 'I'll see you tomorrow. When you bring our delivery?' she prompted as he looked blank.

'Oh, yes. Right.' He planted a quick kiss on her cheek.

The following day she found out why Adam had seemed so distracted.

'I told him not to bother coming any more,' Frankie said. 'I've found someone who can get us the same stuff a lot cheaper. I thought you'd be pleased. You keep saying we need to save money.'

'I know, but—it's a bit embarrassing, isn't it? He's Oliver's cousin, after all. And he's been so good to us.'

'We've been good to him, too,' Frankie said. 'It's our orders that have kept him in business all this time. If you ask me, he's been overcharging us for years. I'm only trying to protect you, Eve.'

She bristled. 'I can look after myself.'

Frankie looked hurt. 'I'm sorry. I was only doing what I thought was right for the business. I didn't realise I had to discuss it with you first. I thought we'd built up some trust.'

'We have,' Eve backed down. The last thing she needed was Frankie in a sulk. 'You're right, we should try to cut costs where we can. But I'll go and talk to Adam. I owe him that, at least.'

After lunch-time service was over, Eve drove to Adam's farm, about five miles to the north of the city. It was a blazing hot July day, and the sun shimmered in a heat haze over the fields. There was Adam's cottage surrounded by outbuildings, including his pride and joy, the farm shop. Elsie, one of the assistants, was stacking carrots in the display outside.

'If you're looking for Adam, he's ploughing a new field for potatoes,' she waved her hand in the direction Eve had just come.

Eve heard the rumble of the engine and saw him in the distance. He was at the wheel of the tractor. The brown field was ribbed like thick corduroy, and there was a smell of newly churned earth in the air.

She stood at the gate. Finally he noticed her and skirted down the edge of the field, bringing the tractor to a halt in front of her.

'I didn't want to interrupt your work.' She shaded her eyes with her hand to look up at him. He was wearing cut off denims and he'd taken off his shirt in the heat. Perspiration gleamed on his bronze skin.

'I'd pretty much finished anyway.' He jumped down from the cab. 'What can I do for you?'

'I spoke to Frankie. Why didn't you tell me what had happened?'

'It's no big deal.' He drank from a bottle of water. 'I took on another contract last week, so it's not as if I've lost anything.'

'Are you sure? I was really worried.'

'Don't be. In fact, I'm more worried about you. I heard about your money problems.'

'I suppose Frankie told you?'

He shook his head. 'I spoke to Anna.'

She was immediately on her guard. 'What did she tell you?'

'Not a lot. Why didn't you tell me you were having difficulties?'

'It's not your problem.'

'That doesn't stop me worrying about you.' He picked up his shirt from the tractor cab. 'Come with me. I need to check on Britney.'

The barn was warm, dark and pungent-smelling. Britney the goat lay on a bed of straw. She struggled to get up when she saw Adam, but her spindly legs wouldn't support her distended belly.

As they stood watching her, Adam suddenly said, 'I want to help.'

Eve turned to him. It was hard to read his expression in the shadowy barn. 'In what way?'

'Let me give you some money. Just to pay off your bills and make sure you're OK. You could even call it a loan, if it makes you feel better.'

She nearly laughed. It was a loan that had got them into this mess. 'You're very kind, but I don't want your money.'

'Oliver was my cousin. I owe it to him to look after his family. And besides—' he stopped. Suddenly the atmosphere in the barn seemed too close and stifling. 'It's what he would have wanted.'

The sunlight seemed almost blinding as they went outside. Eve took a gulp of fresh air.

'I'm sorry,' she said. 'But I can't let you do it. It's too much to ask.'

'I can afford it.'

Can you? She didn't even want to tell him how much money they owed. He'd be too shocked.

'Anyway, I owe everything to Oliver. He should have had this place. I only took over the family business because he didn't want it.'

'Yes, but you were the one who made it a success. You worked damn hard and it wouldn't be right to take your money.'

'But I want to give it to you.'

She looked up into his kind, rugged face. 'I'm sorry. I need to sort this out by myself,' she said.

'Why?'

'Because I want to prove I can do it.'

'For Oliver?'

'And for myself.'

'I'm not going to be able to change your mind, am I?' She shook her head. 'As long as you remember, the offer's there if you need it.'

She reached for his hand. 'You're a good friend, Adam.'

His fingers closed around hers briefly and for a second he looked as if he was about to say something, then changed his mind. 'If you won't take my money, at least will you have dinner with me tomorrow?'

She smiled. 'On one condition. We don't talk about Oliver, or the restaurant.'

His grey eyes lit up. 'Definitely not.'

Anna headed slowly down Fossgate on Friday morning. She was in no hurry to get to Oliver's. She had something to say to Eve, and she knew she wasn't going to like it.

It was just Eve and Laura in the kitchen. Eve looked up and smiled when she saw Anna. 'I thought you'd be sick of this place by now.'

'I wanted to talk to you.' Anna glanced at Laura. 'In private.'

Laura slid off the stool. 'I've got some napkins to fold anyway.'

Anna waited until she'd disappeared through the swing doors. 'What do you think of her?' she asked. 'You don't find her a bit . . . creepy?'

'I think she's just lonely.' Eve frowned. 'Is that what you've come here for? To discuss Laura?'

Anna shook her head. 'It's Frankie I wanted to talk about. Has he ever mentioned a man called Les Willis to you?'

Eve thought for a moment. 'Doesn't ring a bell. Why, who is he?'

'A local crook. I've seen Frankie talking to him.'

'And you assume he must be mixed up in something criminal?' Eve started chopping vegetables with dangerous speed. 'Just because Frankie's been in jail doesn't mean everything he does has to be dodgy.'

'I didn't say that—'

'Haven't you ever heard of someone paying their debt to society?'

'It's his debt to Les Willis I'm worried about,' Anna said.

'What are you talking about?'

Here it comes, Anna thought. 'Frankie has a gambling problem.'

Eve put her knife down. 'Who told you that?'

'I did some digging after I saw Frankie talking to Les. Apparently Frankie's quite well known on the local poker circuit. He's been losing pretty badly to the wrong people lately. Including Les Willis. I'm guessing that's why he turned up here, looking for his money.'

'So he's got into some trouble. What's that got to do with me?'

Anna stared at her. Was she naive, or just playing dumb because she didn't want to face up to the truth? 'Have you checked the books lately?'

Eve's eyes flared with outrage. 'Of course I've checked them.'

'So have I,' Anna said. 'And I've noticed quite a few of the cheques have been written by Frankie.'

'I told him he could use the cheque book to pay suppliers.'

'Have you checked if the payments tally with the invoices?'

Eve flushed dark pink. 'I don't need to. I trust Frankie. I know he wouldn't do anything to let me down. He's my friend.'

Eve was still brooding when she met Adam for dinner that night. Anna had no right to criticise Frankie. He'd been a good friend to her.

Adam was in the middle of cooking when she got to the cottage. 'Sorry about the change of plan.' He greeted her. 'The vet reckons Britney could start giving birth at any time. I don't really want to leave her.'

'It's no problem.' She followed him into the kitchen. 'Will you have to keep checking up on her?'

'I've thought of that.' He nodded to a baby monitor.

Eve laughed. 'You're taking this expectant father thing a bit seriously, aren't you? Dinner smells lovely. What is it?'

'Chilli con carne. Actually, it's the only thing I can cook.'

'Is there anything I can do?' Eve offered.

'You could make a salad.' They worked side by side in companionable silence. Adam cooked the rice while she prepared the salad.

'Oliver and I always cooked together when we were married. I used to really enjoy it. It's not quite the same, cooking on your own.' She noticed he'd gone very quiet. 'Sorry, I'm rambling.'

They settled down to eat. 'Do you cook for Imogen like this?'

'Imogen doesn't allow me in the kitchen. She says I'm like a bull in a china shop.'

Adam fell quiet again, and Eve had her own thoughts to deal with. She couldn't help thinking about what Anna had said. She tried to hide her turmoil, but when he put her coffee down in front of her he said, 'OK, you might as well tell me what's wrong.'

'What do you mean?'

'You've been sitting there like a ticking time bomb. If you don't come out with it soon you'll explode and that could be very nasty.'

Eve smiled. 'You know me too well. It's Frankie.' She told him about Anna's accusations. 'Of course I know it's all rumours and lies,' she said. 'Why can't everyone just leave him alone?'

'How do you know it's all lies?'

'You, too?' Eve suddenly felt very weary. 'What have you heard?'

'The same as Anna. That he's got a gambling problem.'

'So what? He'd never abuse Oliver's trust.'

'No, but he might abuse yours. You've been relying on him a lot since Oliver died. He could have taken advantage of that.'

'Well, for your information I checked the books today. All the cheques he's written tally up with suppliers' invoices.'

'There are other ways of making money on the side,' Adam said. 'Such as getting a friendly supplier to send in an invoice for higher than the price agreed, then splitting the extra profit with him. Or selling off stock.' He stirred his coffee. 'I wonder if that was why he got rid of me. Because he knew I wouldn't play ball.'

Eve was shocked. 'He did it to cut costs.'

'And is your new supplier that much cheaper?'

Come to think of it, he wasn't. But surely Frankie wouldn't do that to her? She remembered those early days at the restaurant. He'd worked slavishly hard. Then she remembered him at Oliver's funeral, promising to look after her and the business. She shook her head. 'Frankie wouldn't do anything like that. Oliver trusted him and so do I.'

'Oliver's judgment hasn't exactly been reliable, has it?'

Before she had a chance to reply, an unearthly sound filled the kitchen. Eve jumped, splashed hot coffee. 'What the hell was that?'

'Sounds like Britney's in trouble.'

Inside the lamplit shed, Britney was standing in a corner of her pen, wide-eyed with terror. She was making a long, low keening sound.

'Something's not right,' Adam said. He rolled up his shirt sleeves. 'I'm going to have to check her.'

Eve stared at him in the shadowy half light. 'You mean you're going to—' She looked from his bare, muscular forearms to the goat.

'I'm going to need disinfectant. And a bucket. They're in the utility room.'

She rushed off to fetch the things from the house. When she returned, Adam had stripped off to the waist and was kneeling in the straw. 'From what I can tell, the kid's got one leg pushed back,' he said. 'I'm going to see if I can ease it into position.'

The next few minutes were very tense. Eve held on to Britney, trying to keep her calm. She didn't dare look at what Adam was doing at the other end. The air was so hot and so still she could hardly breathe. Finally he sat back on the straw. 'Done it.'

Sure enough, a couple of minutes later Britney's baby slipped and slithered into the world. 'It's a boy,' Adam said.

'It's like a miracle, isn't it?' Eve whispered. 'You were brilliant.'

'So were you. I couldn't have done it without you.' Their eyes met, and Eve felt her insides quiver.

She got to her feet. 'I suppose we'd better clean up.' She looked down at herself. 'Urgh! I'll need to borrow some clothes.'

'I'll lend you something.'

When she came out of the shower, Adam had laid out some clean clothes for her on the bed. Unfortunately, they were his.

'Look at me!' She came downstairs, nearling tripping over the flapping legs of his jeans. 'Haven't you got any of Imogen's clothes I could borrow?'

He turned to look at her. He'd showered and changed into jeans and a black T-shirt. 'Imogen doesn't leave her stuff here.' He reached into the fridge and took out a bottle of champagne. 'I thought we could crack this open to celebrate the new arrival.' He poured them each a glass.

'To Britney,' she said, raising hers. 'And—um—'

'Gordon,' Adam said.

'Gordon? Gordon the goat?'

'Why not?'

She shrugged. 'Gordon the goat it is, then.' She looked sideways at him. 'Have you been crying?'

'Look, it's been an emotional couple of hours, OK?'

'And there was me, thinking you were some tough man of the soil.'

'Oh no,' he said. 'I'm not tough at all.'

She looked into his eyes and suddenly she found she couldn't breathe. The next moment they were kissing. His mouth was warm and gentle, and for a second she allowed herself to get lost in his kiss. A second later her senses reasserted themselves. She thought of Imogen and pulled away. 'I'm sorry,' she stammered.

'Me too. It must have been the champagne. Forget it, please.'

They couldn't look at each other. Eve put down her glass. 'I'd—um—better go,' she mumbled.

As she drove away, she looked at him in the rearview mirror. He stood in the doorway watching her go, a long, dark silhouette against the bright doorway. Forget it, he'd said. Except she didn't think she could.

Eve kept telling herself she shouldn't believe the rumours. She trusted Frankie, but she trusted Adam too. He wouldn't lie to her. She felt a stir of emotion. She hadn't seen or spoken to Adam for a week. She was surprised at how she missed him. She hadn't realised he was such an important part of her life. She thought about calling him to ask how Britney was, but she was too embarrassed. That kiss had opened up a gulf between them.

She went back to the bills. There was still no getting away from the fact that they had more money going out than they had coming in. And still the idea that Frankie was cheating haunted her. She couldn't stand it any more. She would have to find out the truth for herself.

She felt nervous as she went to the freezer. She kept telling herself she had every right to check on the stock levels, but the stores were Frankie's domain, and he guarded them jealously. The sight of the near empty freezer shelves took her by surprise. They'd only had a delivery three days ago.

'Are you looking for something in particular?' Frankie stood in the doorway. He was smiling, but his eyes were hard.

She felt like a naughty kid. 'I—um—I was just wondering what had happened to all the meat we had delivered.'

'I sold it. To a bloke in a pub for fifty quid. Which I immediately gambled away on the horses.'

He grinned, and Eve felt weak with relief. 'You're joking!'

'Of course I'm joking. I used it. You'd be surprised how quickly it goes. Oh, but I did sell some chicken to Alfredo down the road. His supplier let him down and he was desperate. I put the money straight in the petty cash box. You can check it if you like.'

The way he looked at her made her feel uncomfortable. 'I don't need to do that.'

As she brushed past him and headed for the door, he said, 'You shouldn't listen to gossip, you know.'

She stopped. 'What do you mean?'

'You've heard rumours about me, and now you think I'm out to fleece you. So who was it? That bitch Anna, I suppose?'

Eve blushed. 'She mentioned she'd seen you talking to—someone.'

'And that someone wouldn't happen to be Les Willis, would it?' Frankie's jaw tightened. 'Yes, I did meet him. To give him back the money I owed. And before you ask, it was all out of my own pocket.'

'I never said it wasn't.'

'No, but you thought it. Same as everyone else thinks. Once a villain, always a villain. But I thought you knew me better than that.'

He looked so hurt, Eve felt ashamed. 'You're right. I'm sorry.'

'Oliver gave me a chance when no one else would. Do you honestly believe I'd repay him by cheating his widow?'

He looked so forlorn. Eve knew she must have hurt him. Why did she listen to Adam and Anna? She should have trusted Oliver's judgment.

It was a Tuesday towards the end of July, and just over five months since Oliver's death, when Anna went into meltdown.

It started like any other day. She went into the office to find Neil proudly showing off the latest photos of his new baby son. Neil's absurdly doting grin pierced her heart with a dart of pain. She thought about the photos of Oliver with Charlie when he was a baby. Charlie'd have to grow up without his dad. What if he forgot him? A feeling of despair welled up inside her. She felt as if she was stuck in a glass box that was slowly filling up with water, and no one could see she was drowning.

Anna had never understood what the word breakdown really meant until she found herself sobbing and shaking uncontrollably, fighting for breath. It was as if all the fragile threads that held her life together had snapped at the same time, plunging her into free fall. She heard someone wailing from far away, then realised with horror that it was her.

Neil and Barbara did their best. Barbara rushed off to put the kettle on, while Neil tried to force Bach's Rescue Remedy down her throat. Then, suddenly, came Elliott's voice, like a blessed oasis of calm.

'Anna?' He gripped her shoulders. His face was level with hers, his grey eyes seemed like the only kind, sane thing in her frightening world. She tried to speak but the words wouldn't come out.

Elliott lifted her to her feet, helped her up the stairs to a small room at the top of the building, and sat her down on one of the small, hard sofas. 'Now you just rest. I'll be back in a minute.'

By the time he returned, Anna was feeling weak, washed out and thoroughly ashamed, but at least she'd managed to stop herself crying.

'I've brought you a cup of tea. Barbara insisted.' He put it down in front of her. 'How are you feeling now?'

'Like a fool.' She dabbed at her eyes with a soggy tissue. 'It's been months! Why should it all happen now?'

'I don't know. I don't think there's a timetable for this kind of thing. You just get through it however you can.'

Elliott insisted on taking her home. When they parked outside the house, she felt a surge of apprehension. She forced herself out of the car and made a big show of searching in her bag for her key until his car had turned the corner and driven out of sight. Then she ran.

She ended up in Homestead Park, sitting on a bench in the rain.

She wasn't sure how long she'd been sitting there when she saw the small blonde figure hurrying towards her. She turned her gaze away, across the empty playing field. 'How did you know where I was?'

'Mother's instinct. Actually, your friend Elliott called. He said you'd had a bit of a wobble.'

Anna smiled weakly at the understatement.

'I was wondering when it was going to happen. You might have got all this over with sooner if you hadn't insisted on taking those wretched pills and telling yourself you were fine.'

'I *was* fine.' So fine she'd stopped taking the tablets a week before, ignoring the doctor's advice to wean herself off them gradually.

'No, Anna, you were *grieving*. Or you should have been, but you wouldn't let it happen.' She put her arm around her. 'You need to deal with the pain, not try to cover it up or push it aside. All that heartache has to go somewhere.'

Anna buried her head in her mum's shoulder, as comforting as it was when she was little. 'I wanted to be like you. You were so strong when Dad died. You just got on with it.'

'Oh, love.' Her voice was clogged with emotion. 'Why do you think I hated those pills of yours so much? I know the damage they can do.'

Anna pulled away from her. 'You took pills?'

'The doctor said it would help, but it didn't, Oh, I'd put a brave face on for you and the boys. But as soon as you'd gone to bed everything would just collapse. I'd sit up all night, crying my eyes out, counting out those tablets and wondering how many it would take to end it all.'

'Mum!'

'The only thing that stopped me was knowing how bloody selfish I'd be. You kids had already lost your dad. But it hurt so much.'

'Oh, Mum.' Anna was crying again, unable to believe what she was hearing. All this time she'd been telling herself she had to cope like her mother, and now she'd found out her mum hadn't coped at all.

They walked back home through the rain, sheltering under Jackie's umbrella. Jackie hugged Anna. 'Just try and take it one step at a time.'

Anna pulled her key out of her pocket. This time she managed to put it into the lock and let herself in.

One step at a time, she told herself.

Her mum had offered to give Charlie his tea, so she decided to fill the hours before he came home by sorting through Oliver's things.

She got as far as pulling all his clothes out before the pain hit her. How could she even think about getting rid of them? It would be like finally admitting he was never coming back.

The doorbell rang. She was surprised to see Lynch on her doorstep.

'You look terrible,' were his first words.

'You don't look so hot yourself.' Except he did.

'I rang your office,' he said, following her into the house. 'They told me you'd come home early. Anything wrong?'

'I took the afternoon off to clear out Oliver's things,' she lied.

'Good idea. You don't want all those memories hanging around.'

Don't I? she thought. 'How was Barcelona?' She changed the subject.

'Great. But it would have been better if you'd been there.'

'I'm sure you found plenty to keep you entertained.'

Something about the way he smiled made her think he hadn't been lonely for long. She waited for the sharp pang of jealousy, but it never came. Grief had done that to her. It had blunted all her senses.

She made coffee and they chatted about nothing for a while. 'Where's Charlie?' Lynch finally remembered to ask.

'My mum's taking care of him for an extra couple of hours.'

He brightened up. 'In that case, why don't we go for a drink?'

'Sorry, I'm not really in the mood.'

He frowned at her. 'Are you sure you're OK?'

She wondered why she couldn't tell him about her breakdown. He was supposed to be her friend, after all. But he wasn't that kind of friend, she realised. Lynch was strictly a good-time guy.

'I'm fine. Just a bit stressed about sorting out Oliver's stuff.'

She waited for him to offer to help. He didn't.

'In that case, maybe I'd better leave you to it.' He stood up. 'Maybe we could meet up for dinner later in the week?'

She opened her mouth to say yes, but what came out was, 'I don't think there's much point, do you?'

He looked taken aback. 'Sorry?'

'Maybe it's best if we don't see each other for a while.'

'Are you dumping me? Is this about me going to Barcelona?'

She smiled sadly. 'It's about me not being able to go with you. I can't share your life, and I don't think you'd want to share mine.'

He thought for a moment. 'So that's it, then?'

'I think so, don't you?'

It made her sad that Lynch wasn't the man for her. Everything about him was so right. He was sexy, successful, he made her laugh.

But he wasn't the man she wanted.

Upstairs Oliver's clothes lay reproachfully on the bed. Anna picked them up and began putting them lovingly back into the wardrobe.

And to think she'd accused Eve of not wanting to move on.

'**I** see. Well, thank you for your help.' Eve put the phone down.

She picked up the cheque book and stared at it. It must have been fate that made her come in here to pay a few bills during a quiet moment. The evening service was in full swing. Now she wished she'd never done it.

At the end of the evening, when Lizzy and the rest of the staff had gone home, Eve went to find Frankie. 'Can I have a word?'

'If it's about the messed up order earlier—'

'It's not about the order. There's eight hundred pounds missing from the bank account. I wondered if you knew anything about it?'

He didn't look up from wiping the kitchen surfaces. 'Oh yeah. I had to pay for the boiler to be repaired while you were away. I was going to mention it, but it slipped my mind.'

She dearly wanted to believe him, but she couldn't. Not this time. 'Why did you take the stub out of the cheque book?'

'I knew you'd worry about paying out all that money, so I thought it would be easier for you to make the problem go away.'

She stared at his broad back, still bent over the work surface. 'I called the bank. They said the cheque had been made out to cash.'

'So? We got a better price that way.'

Eve was silent. Frankie turned to face her. 'You don't believe me, do you? Anything goes missing, blame the ex-con—'

'Frankie, don't. The emotional blackmail won't work this time.' She was too weary even to listen. 'You used that money to pay off your gambling debt, didn't you? Please, for once in your life be honest.'

His eyes darted, searching the air for another lie. Then he gave up. 'I was desperate, OK? You don't know what these people are like. I would have paid it back,' he insisted.

'But you just took it. You knew how much trouble we were in, and you stole it anyway.'

He looked defensive. 'Oliver would have understood.'

She could feel her anger rising. 'You think Oliver would have turned a blind eye to you robbing his business?'

There was a long pause. Frankie put down the cloth. 'You don't get it, do you?' he said. 'Oliver knew all about it. He tried to help me.'

The truth dawned. 'Those loans he took out—they were for *you*?'

'He knew I couldn't help it. Gambling's an illness.' Frankie was playing the victim again. 'I owed a lot of money, I'd lost my home. I told Oliver about it, and—he offered to help. It was his idea.'

'Oh, I believe you,' Eve said. That was just the kind of thing Oliver would do. 'So why didn't you pay him back?'

'I was trying to. You don't know what it's like, being caught up in an addiction like that. It takes you over, it—'

'Spare me!' Eve cut him off. 'You do realise it was probably the stress of all this that killed him?'

'Don't you think I know that?' Frankie shouted back at her. 'Don't you think that haunts me every day? Oliver was my best friend.'

Eve pulled out her mobile phone. 'I'm calling the police.' She started to dial the number. Frankie watched her with narrowed eyes.

'Don't,' he said.

'Sorry, Frankie, you've given your last order in this kitchen.'

The next thing she knew, the phone was snatched out of her hands.

Eve stood her ground, refusing to be intimidated. 'Give it back.'

'What are you going to tell them? I've got witnesses to say you told me I could use the company cheque book.'

She made a grab for the phone, but he swung it away out of her reach and hurled it at the wall, smashing it. Silence stretched between them. It began to dawn on Eve that tackling a violent ex-con in an empty restaurant after closing time wasn't exactly a good move.

But a second later he was smiling again, just like the old Frankie.

'Let's be reasonable about this, shall we? I'm sorry I took that money. But I *will* pay it back. You can take it out of my wages if you like.'

His sheer nerve made her gasp. 'Do you really think I'd let you go on working here after this?'

'Why not? We make a great team. And let's face it, you couldn't run this place without me. Jesus, you can barely run it with me!'

'You didn't say that when you were begging me to take over.'

'Yes, well, I needed the money, didn't I?'

There was a crash from beyond the swing doors. Frankie looked round distracted for a second, long enough for her to grab a heavy omelette pan and bring it down on the back of his head.

'Hello?' Anna called out from the restaurant. She came through the swing doors and nearly tripped over Frankie's body sprawled across the kitchen floor. 'What the hell have you done?'

'I—I think I've killed him.'

Eve watched, numb with shock and terror, as Anna threw down her bag and knelt beside him. Her fingers probed the folds of his neck for a pulse. 'Still alive, unfortunately. But you've knocked him out cold.'

'I'll call an ambulance. Can I borrow your phone?'

'What happened to yours?'

'He smashed it.'

Anna looked at the remnants. 'I think you'd better tell me what happened before you tell anyone else?'

'What if he wakes up.'

'He won't. I don't know about you, but I could do with a brandy.'

They made a bizarre picture, the pair of them sitting on the kitchen floor next to Frankie's prone body, a bottle of brandy between them.

'I take it you found out he was fleecing you?' Anna said.

'Not just me. Oliver too. That was why he took out the loans, to pay off Frankie's gambling debts.'

Anna's mouth twisted. 'Typical Oliver.'

'I know.' Now she knew the truth, Eve felt incredibly foolish. She couldn't believe she'd let herself get taken in by Frankie for so long. 'He was right about one thing, though. I can't run this place.'

'You haven't made such a bad job of it so far. You've been up against it financially, finding the money for those loan repayments. And now you know he's been helping himself to your profits. Maybe once he's out of the picture you'll be able to cope better.'

'Once he's out of the picture we won't have a chef.'

'So get another one. Or you could do it.'

'Me?'

'Why not? You're a great cook.'

She shook her head. 'I'm nothing special.'

'Oliver was always raving about how great you are.' She grimaced. 'It got quite annoying, actually.'

'I bet it did.' Eve sipped her brandy. She could feel it working its warming magic, calming her down. 'But I couldn't cook and manage this place. It would be too much.'

'I could manage it. I did it before, while you were away. I know you think I'm a bit lacking in customer skills—'

'A bit?' Eve laughed.

'But I reckon we should try. You never know, we might make a good team.'

'Us? A team?'

'Why not? Looks like that's how we've ended up, whether we like it or not.'

They both jumped as Frankie let out a loud groan.

'Maybe we should call that ambulance now?'

'Do we have to? Couldn't we just stick him in the freezer and forget about him?' said Anna.

'I'm already facing an assault charge, I don't want to make it worse.'

'You think he'll press charges?'

'Don't you?'

'Not if he's got any sense, he won't,' Anna said.

AUGUST

MATT WAS ALREADY UP and dressed when Eve came down. He was sitting in front of a brown envelope on the kitchen table. 'Oh God. Your A-level results. What did you get?'

'I don't know. I haven't looked.'

'Don't you think you should open it?' Eve said.

Matt pushed it across the table towards her. 'You do it.'

'I can't. I'm too scared.'

They were still discussing who should open it when Georgia stumbled sleepily into the room ten minutes later. 'Oh, for heaven's sake!'

She snatched up the letter, ripped it open and scanned its contents before either of them could stop her. 'Two Bs and a C,' she said in a bored voice. 'Do we have any Frosties left?'

Eve and Matt sat in frozen silence for a moment. The next minute they were whooping with joy, hugging each other and dancing.

After calling everyone she knew, Eve decided to ring Adam. They hadn't been in contact much since that fateful night when they'd kissed. But he'd want to know about Matt, she told herself.

As soon as she heard his deep voice she started to blush. 'I thought you might want to know Matt's passed his A levels,' she said in a rush.

'That's fantastic news. Tell him congratulations.' He paused. 'Actually, I've got news of my own. Imogen and I are engaged.'

Her stomach went into free fall. 'You're getting married? When?'

'We haven't got that far yet, but we're thinking of having an engagement party sometime in the next few weeks,' he said. 'I hope you and the kids can come.'

Eve licked her lips, which had turned as dry as paper. 'Terrific.'

'I'd better go,' Adam said. 'Tell Matt I'm really pleased for him, won't you?'

'I will.' She hesitated. 'And, Adam? I'm really pleased for you, too.'

So why did it feel like the words were choking her?

Anna wondered if she was still suffering from the aftereffects of her medication when she saw Lynch on her doorstep on Saturday morning with what appeared to be an inflatable dolphin under his arm.

He grinned. 'How do you and Charlie fancy a day at the seaside?'

'Yes! Yes!' Charlie bounced up and down with excitement.

'Why?' Anna asked.

'Anna!' He looked exasperated. 'Do you want to go or not?'

She looked down at Charlie, running circles of joy around her. 'Do I have a choice?'

This was bizarre, she thought as they headed off towards the coast. 'Have you had a blow to the head or something?' she asked. 'I definitely remember we agreed not to see each other again.'

'You said it, I didn't. Anyway, I've been thinking about what you said. About us not fitting into each other's lives. And I'd like to try. Please?' He pecked her with the dolphin's nose. 'For Flipper's sake?'

Charlie laughed. 'See?' Lynch said. 'We're bonding already.'

It was a warm, sunny day when they left York but by the time they'd crossed the moors to the coast grey clouds had blotted out the sunshine, leaving dense, clammy heat. Despite the greying skies the beach was packed with families, mothers with lobster tans, overweight fathers in football shirts, and hordes of whining children.

They finally found a spot and Lynch tried to put up a couple of deck chairs while she changed Charlie into his swimming trunks.

'For heaven's sake!' Lynch gave up with the deck chairs and let them collapse on the sand. 'I'm going for a swim.'

'Are you sure?' Anna eyed the flat, pewter-coloured water.

'It'll be OK once we get in.'

'We?' She shook her head. 'No way. I'm not going in.'

'Coward.' He unzipped his jeans.

'I haven't brought a costume, anyway.'

As he pulled his T-shirt over his head, Anna averted her eyes from his toned torso. She wasn't the only one looking. All over the beach, women were paying attention, while men sucked in their beer bellies.

'Can I swim?' Charlie pleaded.

Anna took off her flip-flops. 'We'll paddle,' she said firmly.

They stood hand in hand on the water's edge. Lynch strode fearlessly into the water and plunged in. A second later he surfaced.

'What's it like?' Anna called to him.

'Fu-fu-fine. Come in and find out for yourself.'

'No, thanks.'

'*I* will.' Before she could stop him Charlie was wading into the sea.

Lynch caught Charlie, and whispered something in his ear, making him giggle. 'What are you doing? What did you say to him?' She backed away. 'Don't even think about it.'

Too late. Lynch grabbed her playfully around the middle. Anna struggled, lost her balance and pitched face first into the freezing water.

She came up a second later, screaming with rage.

'What the—you do realise these are my only clothes, don't you?' But Lynch and Charlie just fell about laughing. 'Imbeciles!'

'Anna!' Two girls were plodding across the sand towards them.

'Friends of yours?' Lynch asked.

'Jessica and Becky. Elliott's daughters. Hi, girls. Where's your dad?'

'He's coming with all the stuff.'

She looked up the beach. Elliott was coming over the horizon, laden down with beach bags. And he wasn't alone.

'You never told me there was a Mrs Prozac,' Lynch muttered.

'There isn't.'

The woman was a typical yummy-mummy type, immaculate in

white jeans and T-shirt, her silky blonde hair tumbling around her shoulders. 'Very nice,' Lynch commented.

Anna suddenly wanted to run away. But she could only stand there, her dripping hair plastered around her face, as they approached.

She tried to look casual. 'F-fancy seeing you here.'

'You know how it is. We wanted some sea and sand, and Barbados is just so overrated.' He turned to the woman. 'Justine, this is Anna, a colleague from work. Anna, this is my friend Justine.'

'Your mascara's running,' Justine pointed out kindly.

'Thanks.' Anna wiped it away with her finger. 'And this is—'

'Danny Lynch,' he interrupted her. He and Justine were already on full eye lock, ogling each other shamelessly. Anna wasn't surprised.

'You should get dry before you catch pneumonia,' said Elliott.

'I would if someone hadn't left the towels in the car.' She glared at Lynch.

'We've got one you could borrow.'

They found a spot further up the beach and Elliott got to work arranging deck chairs and putting a towel round Charlie and Anna.

'Maybe you should get those wet clothes off,' Lynch suggested.

'Maybe you should put some clothes on,' Anna hissed back.

'Spoilsport.' He pulled on his faded jeans over his damp trunks. It was like a striptease in reverse.

She felt sorry for Elliott, looking decidedly overdressed in his overlong shorts and polo shirt. She was sure there was a decent body under those sensible clothes, if only he chose to show it off. 'Maybe you need a hot drink,' he said. 'There's a café up the road. I'll get you one.'

'I'll get it.' Lynch unfolded himself from the deck chair.

'I'll come with you,' Justine offered.

'Don't they make a lovely couple?' Elliott remarked, as they watched them heading off down the beach all gilded hair and lithe limbs.

'Gorgeous,' Anna agreed. 'Sorry if we gate-crashed your date.'

'Don't be.' Elliott turned his gaze to the water's edge, where the girls had taken Charlie to collect shells in a bucket. 'To be honest, I think your friend Lynch is more her type.'

'I think she might be more his, too.'

They laughed. 'How the hell did they end up with us?' Elliott said.

'You're not that bad!'

'Neither are you.'

They looked at each other. His eyes weren't really brown at all, Anna noticed. They were almost green, flecked with gold and amber.

'So how's life at the restaurant?' Elliott asked.

'Not bad, actually.' She'd taken a leave of absence to help Eve out at the restaurant. Against all the odds, somehow their arrangement seemed to be working quite well.

Eve kept to the kitchen while Anna managed the front of house. Eve had even made some changes to the menu, cutting it right down and introducing some interesting specials.

Elliott pulled a face. 'So you're not missing us, then?'

'Like mad.'

'Good, because we're missing you. Barbara's thinking of starting up a grief-counselling group in your honour.'

Anna swept round to look at him. 'I hope you're not serious?'

'Of course I am. And she wants you to address the first meeting.'

She was about to protest until she noticed his tongue wedged firmly in his cheek. 'That's something I don't miss,' she said. 'Your sick sense of humour.' Actually, that was what she missed most of all. That and his calm, soothing way of making her feel life wasn't so bad after all.

'I thought you and Lynch were history?' Elliott said, as they watched him and Justine, their hands full of Styrofoam cups, make their way down the stone steps to the beach.

'So did I. He's decided he wants to try playing happy families.'

'That's good, isn't it? At least he's making an effort.'

'That's what bothers me. Surely if he was right for me he wouldn't have to make an effort. It would just sort of . . . fit.'

'Are you sure you're not just making excuses?' Elliott said. 'Maybe you should just give him a chance?'

That night, after she'd put Charlie to bed, Anna made another stab at sorting out Oliver's belongings. Armed with a glass of wine, she threw open the wardrobe doors. 'I can do this, I can do this,' she muttered.

Who am I kidding? She wept ten minutes later, when she'd found two ticket stubs in the pocket of his chinos. They'd been to see the Queen tribute band at the Opera House and laughed until they ached.

The phone rang, shattering the silence. It was Eve. 'I wondered if I could come round. There's something I need to talk to you about.'

Anna looked at the heap of clothes on the bed. 'Can we make it another time? I'm busy at the moment.'

'Sure, no problem.' She paused. 'Are you OK, Anna? You sound as if you've been crying.'

'Got to go. I'll see you tomorrow, OK?'

She hung up before she could ask any more questions.

Knowing Eve, she would want to talk about work. It irritated Anna that she couldn't seem to trust her own judgment on anything.

She stared at the clothes on the bed, not quite knowing what to do. At least she could sort them into piles, she decided. One lot of stuff to be thrown away, one that could go to the charity shop, and one to keep.

Steeling herself, she picked up the first item. An old khaki T-shirt, stained with blue paint. Oliver had worn it when they decorated Charlie's nursery. She put it on the keep pile.

Next was Oliver's favourite chunky black sweater. Anna held it up to her face, breathing in the faint traces of him that lingered there. Another one for the keep pile.

By the time the doorbell rang the only things she'd thrown away was an old pair of Oliver's socks. It was Eve. 'I had to come round,' she said. 'You sounded upset on the phone.'

Anna opened her mouth to make an excuse, but the truth came out. 'I've been going through Oliver's things.'

'Ah. Would you like some help?' Eve offered.

Once again, unplanned words came out of her mouth. 'Yes, please.'

They stood in the bedroom, looking at the piles of clothes. 'I don't know what to do,' Anna said. 'I can't bear to see his stuff every day, but I don't want to get rid of it, either. It doesn't seem right, somehow.'

'Like admitting he's really never coming back,' Eve said.

She nodded. That was exactly how she felt.

'Why don't you just put them away in the loft for a while? Then you can think about it again later, when it's less painful.'

'Good idea.' She looked sideways at Eve. 'Will you help me? I'd feel better if we did it together.'

If anyone had told her a year ago she would be sitting on her bed sorting through Oliver's clothes with his ex-wife, she would have thought they were completely mad. Yet here they were, sipping wine, swapping memories of Oliver's wardrobe disasters and almost having a good time.

'Oh God, don't tell me he still wore this?' Eve held up a baseball cap, greying with age. 'We bought it on holiday in Spain when Georgia was a baby.' From the wistful way she stroked the fraying peak, Anna could tell it still had fond memories for her. 'Why don't you have it?' she said.

'Thanks.' Eve laid the cap on her lap and picked up a shoe box from the floor. 'What's in here?'

'His toy-car collection. They're all a bit battered.'

'It looks like he kept everything he ever owned.' Eve took out a dented miniature police car. 'I was never very good at letting go either. Look at me and Oliver.'

'It's not easy when a marriage ends.'

'That's just it. I never accepted it had ended. I probably made a real nuisance of myself sometimes,' she said with a knowing look.

'Maybe it was difficult sometimes,' Anna admitted. 'Sometimes I thought you were just doing it to wind me up.'

'That was part of the reason. But mainly I just couldn't face not being married to Oliver any more. I was scared of losing my family. Being married was all I ever wanted.' She put the car back in the box. 'That probably sounds stupid and old-fashioned. People don't care that much about getting married these days.'

Some of us don't have much choice, Anna thought.

'I know my mother thought I was being incredibly vulgar. She'd brought me up on the idea of free love and no commitment.'

Anna smiled. 'I thought it was every mother's dream to see her daughter walk down the aisle?'

'Not Vanessa Gifford's daughter.'

Anna sat back. 'Vanessa Gifford? You mean that old hippie?' She stopped herself. 'Sorry, I didn't realise she was your mum.'

'Hard to believe, isn't it?' She put the box of cars down on the floor. 'I set out to be the opposite of everything she stood for. I wanted to get married because I wanted someone who'd love me for the rest of my life. I never had that with my mother, you see. I was never that important to her. I only wanted a loving, secure family, someone who'd put me first.'

Anna felt tears pricking. 'No wonder you found it hard to let go.'

'I refused to see what was happening. Oliver and the children were all I'd ever wanted, but it wasn't enough for him. He needed to be free, I needed security. I wouldn't admit I couldn't make him happy.'

'You did make him happy,' Anna said. 'He loved you.'

'I know. But I was never his soul mate. Not like you.' She picked up the baseball cap from her lap, then put it down on the pile.

'Don't you want it?' Anna asked.

'Like I said, you've got to learn to let go sometime, haven't you?' She smiled. 'That's why I came over. I wanted to talk to you about your share of the restaurant.'

'I didn't know I had one.'

'That's the point. I think you should.' She took a brown envelope out of her bag. 'I've been to my solicitor and had this drawn up.'

Anna eyed it uneasily. 'What is it?'

'A contract to transfer half my shares in the restaurant to you.' She held the envelope out to her. 'All you have to do is sign it and send it back. Although I expect you'll want your solicitor to look it over—'

'I can't take it,' Anna said.

'Why not? It's what Oliver would have wanted.'

Anna looked down at the envelope. She realised it wasn't just a share in the restaurant Eve was giving her. It was a share in Oliver's life.

SEPTEMBER

'YOU KNOW, YOU REALLY shouldn't show your cleavage over the age of forty,' Georgia said. 'I read it in a magazine.'

'Oh yes? Which magazine? *Teenage Fashion Fascists Weekly*?' Eve turned sideways in front of the mirror, trying to hold her stomach in. The fitted black dress was a bit tight. She'd already agonised for far too long over what to wear to the engagement party. She didn't want to look as if she was trying too hard.

And who would you be trying too hard for?

'Oh, stuff it. Who cares anyway?' Eve grabbed an embroidered shawl and flung it around her shoulders. 'Come on, we'll be late.'

Adam and Imogen's party was already in full swing when they got to the farm. Imogen greeted them at the door. She looked stunning in a sea-green dress. She tucked her arm into Eve's and walked with her over to the drinks table. 'I'm so glad you came,' she said, handing her a glass of wine. 'Although I was a bit worried about inviting you, to be honest.'

'Really?'

'I wasn't sure how you'd feel about this—I mean, after . . . you know.' She pulled a sympathetic face. 'I know you've had a hard time lately. I didn't want you to think we were being insensitive.'

'Oh no! I couldn't be more pleased for you. It's about time Adam found someone to settle down with.' Eve tried to ignore the lump that suddenly seemed to come from nowhere in her throat.

'I'm so glad you said that.' Imogen's dark eyes shone with happiness.

'I was amazed when he proposed. Between you and me, I think there was someone in his past. She obviously hurt him quite badly.'

'Oh?'

Suddenly he was there, looking more handsome than Eve had ever remembered him looking in all the years she'd known him. She had to look away as he bent his head to kiss Imogen. She wanted to be happy for them, but seeing them just made her feel even more alone.

'Has Adam told you about our plans?' Imogen said. 'We're having one of the outbuildings converted into a coffee shop. Why don't you show Eve what we've done so far?' she suggested.

'There's not much to see,' Adam said quickly.

'She could still get an idea of what it's going to be like. Besides,' she glanced towards the door, 'I think my godfather's just walked in.'

She excused herself and Adam turned to Eve. 'Shall we go?' he said.

A cool breeze stirred the trees as she picked her way across the yard after Adam. He pushed open a heavy wooden door. 'This is it.'

He flicked on the light, but it did nothing to dispel the gloom of the damp, cavernous space. Eve shivered. 'It's a bit different to the last time we were in a barn together,' she said, and immediately wished she hadn't. She could almost feel Adam's body tense as he stood behind her.

'Imogen wants to call it the Cowshed Café.' He cleared his throat. 'Not strictly accurate, since it's never been a cowshed.'

She listened to him explaining all Imogen's grand plans, aware of him standing close to her. 'She's a very determined woman, your fiancée.'

'Isn't she? She's just what I need. Someone who'll keep me looking forward rather than living in the past.'

She turned around to face him. 'So you're happy, then?'

'Why shouldn't I be?' They stared at each other. His eyes were dark pools in the gloom. 'Aren't you happy for me?' he said softly.

Her body twanged with tension, so much so that when a pigeon flapped from the rafters she screamed and jumped straight into his waiting arms. For a moment they froze there. She could feel the steady beat of his heart against hers. Her eyes fixed on the curve of his mouth . . .

The barn door rattled and they sprang apart.

'Hello?' Imogen's voice echoed around the empty space. 'I just wanted to tell you, they're all waiting for the speeches.'

As they headed for the door, Imogen said, 'Just think. Once this place opens we'll be rivals.'

Eve looked at her hand, clasping Adam's.

I reckon we already are, she thought.

'Well, this is nice, isn't it?' Eve stood at the window and looked out over the neat trimmed lawn below. Parents criss crossed it, their arms full of pillows, duvets and bin bags full of their children's possessions.

'It smells funny,' Georgia commented, her nose wrinkling.

'I like it.' Matt sprawled on the narrow bed, his arms behind his head. His guitar and laptop were already unpacked and standing ready.

Eve knew he wanted her to leave. 'I suppose we'd better go,' she said wistfully. 'Are you sure you're going to be all right?'

'Mum!'

She'd promised herself she wouldn't cry. But as soon as Matt put his arms around her she started blubbing. It was the start of a whole new adventure for Matt. But it felt like the end of another chapter for her.

She was still sniffing back tears as they drove home.

'God. Honestly.' Georgia muttered. 'He's only gone to university, not Afghanistan. Can I have his room?'

'Georgia! You could wait until he's been gone five minutes.'

As they reached York, Georgia said, 'Will you drop me off at Ellie's house? I said I'd go round. I'd sort of planned to stay the night.'

Eve understood why. She didn't want to be there for the first night without Matt. She dropped Georgia off at her friend's house and headed home. Her chest tightened with panic at the thought of rattling around in the house with only Benson for company.

She needed to call a friend. She was about to pick up the phone and invite Jan round when she remembered she was on a school trip.

Then she thought of Adam. But he had Imogen now.

There was one place where she knew she'd find some distraction and human company. The restaurant had always been a comforting place, but recently it had become like a second home to her. She arrived just as they were closing. Simon and Lizzy were cleaning up in the kitchen.

'You missed a good night tonight, boss,' Simon grinned. He'd taken over as head chef after Eve lured him back from the Burger Shack. It was a relief to everyone that Frankie had gone. The last Eve'd heard he'd left town in a hurry after falling even deeper into debt with Les Willis and his gang. Eve doubted if he would ever dare to show his face again.

'Have we been busy?'

'You wouldn't believe it. I reckon putting on that display at the Food and Drink Festival helped.'

'I can't take the credit for that. It was all Anna's idea.' They'd served champagne and canapés, and handed out fliers. Trade had been picking up slowly but steadily ever since, helped by the new menu.

'How have the new dishes been working out?' she asked.

'Going down a storm. Especially the Thai fish cakes. But we're going to need more banana bread-and-butter pudding for tomorrow.'

'I'll make some tonight.' She looked at Lizzy, scrubbing a baking tray. 'In fact, why don't you leave that? I can finish off here.'

When they'd gone, Eve got down to work. She was kneading some bread dough when Laura came in. 'I'm off now,' she said. 'Something smells good. What are you making?'

'Roasted red-pepper focaccia. I've just made those blackberry scones. Take a few home with you, if you like.'

'Thanks.' Laura took a plastic bag from the roll on the wall and helped herself to a couple. 'Are you sure you're going to be OK on your own? You don't want me to stay and keep you company?'

'I'll be fine.'

She watched Laura let herself out. She was beginning to wonder if Anna was right about her being a bit creepy. She always seemed to be around, either at the restaurant or at the churchyard.

But the restaurant felt a lot spookier once she was on her own. Eve hummed uneasily to herself as she mashed bananas for the bread-and-butter pudding, trying to keep the silence at bay. Once the pudding was in the oven and everything else was cooling, she made herself some coffee. She'd perched on a stool to drink it when she heard a sound outside.

There were footsteps in the yard. They grew closer, stopping outside the door. Her fingers tightened around her coffee mug. She stared at the door handle as it slowly turned, like something out of a horror film.

The door opened. Eve reacted without thinking. With a scream, she flung the remains of her coffee at the shadowy figure . . .

'What the—?'

'Adam! What are you doing here?'

'I was passing, and I saw the light. I thought you had burglars.' He held out his arms. Coffee dripped down the front of his leather jacket.

'Here, let me help.' She grabbed a cloth from the sink. 'I'm so sorry. I didn't mean to attack you.'

'What are you doing here, anyway?'

'I . . . couldn't sleep. Would you like a coffee?'

'Could I have it in a cup this time?'

There was something slightly surreal about the two of them sitting in the brightly lit kitchen at one in the morning, drinking coffee. 'Did Matt get off OK?' Adam asked. 'It must seem weird without him.'

'Why do you think I'm baking cakes in the middle of the night? What about you? It's a funny time of night to be just passing.'

'I couldn't sleep either.'

Eve cleared her throat. 'So have you set a date yet? They say spring is always a good time to get married—'

'Do we have to talk about it?' Adam cut her off. He sat, staring into the depths of his coffee cup, before he spoke. 'That night at the party, when I asked you if you were happy for me. You never gave me an answer.'

His question caught her unawares. 'Of course. Imogen's lovely.'

'Yes, she is. But that wasn't what I asked.' He looked up, his gaze direct and challenging. 'Do you want me to marry her?'

No, she wanted to shout. How could I want you to marry someone else when I love you? Her feelings had crept up on her. She'd thought of him as nothing more than a friend; it wasn't until Imogen came along that she'd realised how much she cared for him. Even then, she'd thought she was just jealous because she didn't want to be alone. But now she realised there was much more to her feelings than that. She knew he was attracted to her too. She could sense the tension in him, waiting for her to say the word. But how could she? He'd finally found someone to love, she couldn't confuse him by admitting how she felt. It wasn't fair to put doubts in his mind. It wasn't fair on Imogen, either. She was so in love with him. Adam deserved someone like her. Someone who could love him completely. Just like she'd always wanted to be loved.

She met his gaze. His eyes weren't grey like Oliver's, she noticed. They were outlined with darkest blue, almost black. Looking at him now, she wondered how she'd ever thought they were alike.

'Yes,' she said. 'I want you to marry her.'

OCTOBER

ANNA AND LYNCH were going to Rachel's birthday party, his first official outing as her boyfriend. And as if that wasn't nerve-racking enough, they were doing it in fancy dress. For some reason Rachel had decided to hold an astonishingly uncool Hallowe'en Saints and Sinners party.

Anna adjusted the sparkly wings on her angel's costume. They still looked lopsided. 'Do you think this dress is too short?'

'Put it this way: if everyone in heaven looks like you I can't wait to get there,' he said. There was a long pause while they both realised what he'd said. 'Sorry,' he said. 'Bad joke. I still think you should have gone as a nun, though. I have a thing about nuns.'

'Lynch, you have a thing about anything female with a pulse.'

'That's not fair. I'm a changed man, remember?'

Anna was still pretty sceptical about that, although she had to admit he'd certainly been trying, taking her and Charlie on outings every weekend, and showering them with gifts.

'So how about a spot of sin before we leave?' he said, closing in.

'The baby sitter will be here in a minute—' The doorbell rang. 'Right on cue,' she grinned, pushing him off.

'I'm not late, am I?' Laura said. 'Where's Charlie?' At that moment Charlie hurtled into the room in his pyjamas. 'Hello, sweetheart. Look what I've got for you.'

Anna watched apprehensively as he ploughed his way through the plastic packaging. Laura still made her feel uneasy. She wouldn't have asked her to baby-sit, but her mother had a meeting.

Charlie unwrapped the *Star Wars* action figure and his face fell. 'I've got this one.'

'Charlie! Don't be rude. Say thank you to Laura.'

'It's OK,' Laura mumbled, looking upset. 'I should have checked.'

Charlie pointed at Lynch. 'My Daddy bought it for me last week.'

Time seemed to stand still and none of them looked at each other.

'Anyway,' Anna recovered briskly, 'we won't be late. You've got my mobile number, haven't you?'

'No problem,' Laura said.

'Does she strike you as a bit odd?' Anna asked when she and Lynch were in the cab.

'She seems fine to me.' Lynch stared out of the window, preoccupied. Anna could guess why.

'I expect you're a bit shocked about him calling you Daddy,' she tried to laugh about it. 'I wouldn't worry about it, he calls everyone that.' She glanced at him. 'You didn't mind, did you?'

'Why should I? He gets confused.'

Luckily he seemed to lose his brooding mood by the time they got to Rachel's flat and he was the Perfect Boyfriend again, charming everyone in the room, even the usually cynical Rachel.

'You didn't tell me he was so bloody gorgeous,' Rachel hissed when Lynch had gone to get them a drink. 'No wonder you've been keeping him to yourself. So how's it going with you two?'

'Pretty well.'

Rachel frowned at her. 'You're not still feeling guilty?'

She shook her head. She had to accept Oliver was gone. Now she faced the choice of being lonely for the rest of her life, or finding someone to share it with. She'd never imagined that person would be Lynch. Life could be very strange sometimes. But she was worried that Charlie's chance remark might have scared him off completely.

Sure enough, an hour later Lynch said, 'Something's come up at work. I've got to go.'

'Now? But it's ten o'clock on a Saturday night.'

'One of my clients has got himself arrested. I need to get down to the station and post bail. I'll ring you later, OK?'

'When?' Anna called after him, but he was already gone.

He was probably telling the truth, she thought. He wouldn't make an excuse to get away from her. He'd tell her straight he didn't want to be with her any more.

She left the party early and headed home. Laura was on the sofa, watching TV. 'You're early. Had a good evening?'

'It was OK.'

'You and Lynch haven't had a row, have you?'

'Why should we?'

'I just wondered. He seemed in a funny mood when he left. Is it serious between you?' Laura asked suddenly.

Anna was taken aback. 'I don't think that's any of your business.'

'Because if it is, I don't think you should feel guilty about it,' Laura went on, as if she hadn't heard her. 'Oliver wouldn't have minded. He would have wanted you to be happy.' She had a strange little smile on her face. 'It might even have been a relief,' she said. 'Because then he wouldn't have to worry about you any more. He did worry about you, you know. That was why he didn't want to—' she broke off.

'Didn't want to what?'

'It doesn't matter. Look, I'd better go.'

'Not until you tell me what's going on.'

'I can't,' she said. 'I don't want to talk about it.'

'Well, I do. You can't just talk in riddles and then walk away.' Laura tried to blunder past, but Anna held her by her shoulders. She trembled like a rag doll in her grip.

'It's not fair,' she mumbled. 'I shouldn't have to do this. He always promised me I wouldn't have to be the one to tell you—'

'Tell me what?' Anna suddenly felt very frightened.

Laura raised her head slowly. Her eyes, swimming with tears, were fixed on her face. 'That we were in love,' she said.

Anna's hands dropped to her sides. 'You're lying.'

'I'm sorry, Anna.' Laura's words came out in a rush. 'Oliver said he was going to tell you. He promised. But he didn't want to hurt you. We were just friends to start with. I was going through a really bad time. My mum was ill, and I was worried sick.' She recited the facts in a small, flat voice. 'I never really had anyone to talk to, except Oliver. He was a real friend. He understood.' Her eyes had a glazed, dreamy look.

Anna felt sick. She could picture her pouring out her troubles, him listening, those grey eyes gazing deep into her soul.

'I helped him, too. He had so many problems, he couldn't talk to anyone.'

'He could talk to me.'

Laura's look was almost sympathetic now. 'Anna, you *were* the problem! He realised he'd made a mistake with you. He said you should have never got together. But you got pregnant and he tried to make the best of it. Don't get me wrong, he loved you and Charlie. But you were never what he wanted.'

'And you were?'

'I was a friend,' Laura said. 'I made it clear to Oliver there was no way I was going to get too involved with him while you two were still together. But he wanted to be with me. He kept promising he'd sort it out. But he kept putting it off and in the end I just lost patience.' She stared at a worn patch on the rug. Her voice was a thin thread of sound. 'If I'd known what was going to happen I would never have started that stupid argument. Then maybe he'd still be alive.'

It took a moment for it to sink in. 'You were—with him when he died.'

Laura nodded. 'He was driving me home after work. I wanted to know when he was going to tell you. I kept saying it wasn't fair to keep you stringing along. We were arguing about it, and suddenly—' she closed her eyes. 'I must have been knocked out. When I woke up the car was off the road and Oliver was sort of—slumped.' Her voice rose. 'I kept calling his name. I thought he was dead.'

'So you left him,' Anna said in a hollow voice.

'I didn't know what else to do.' Laura's eyes were huge in her thin, pale face. 'I did it for you,' she said. 'I knew if the ambulance found me in the car they'd ask all kinds of questions. You'd be bound to find out.'

'You left him to die,' Anna said again.

'Do you think I would ever have left him if I'd known that?'

They were both silent for a moment, lost in their thoughts. Then Anna said, 'You've wanted to tell me all along, haven't you? That's why you've been acting so friendly, trying to get close to me and Charlie—' She closed her eyes. Oh God. Charlie. To think she'd left Laura alone with her son.

'I thought we could be friends.' Laura sounded hurt.

Anna's eyes blazed. 'What did you think we'd do, mourn him together? Go and visit his grave?'

'You never visit his grave,' Laura said flatly. 'I suppose you don't have to bother now you've got a new boyfriend.'

Anna gasped. 'Get out,' she said.

'One boyfriend dies, so you just move on to the next. And meanwhile, everyone feels sorry for you. Poor Anna.' Laura pulled a face. 'But who feels sorry for me? I don't get any cards or sympathy, do I?'

Anna's fingers clawed into her palms. She wanted to lash out. '*Go!*'

'If that's what you want. But it won't change anything. Oliver didn't love you, Anna. He loved me.'

If her mum was at all surprised to see her at one in the morning, standing on her doorstep with Charlie wrapped up in her arms, she didn't show it. 'Oh, love.' Jackie ushered her inside and closed the door. She took Charlie from Anna's arms and handed him over to Keith. 'Can you put the little lad in the spare room?' She took Anna into the sitting room and settled herself on the sofa beside her. 'So tell me all about it.'

She told her. Her mother listened in silence. 'And you believe her?' she said when she'd finished.

'Why would she lie?'

'I don't know, love. What are you going to do?'

'I don't know,' Anna said. She wanted to scream and rage, but what good would it do? 'Can I stay here tonight?'

'You don't even have to ask. Do you want to go up now?'

She shook her head. 'I'll stay down here for a bit, if that's OK.'

She didn't know how long she sat on the sofa, not moving. It felt as if she'd lost Oliver all over again. Except this time it was worse. When he died, she had the happy memories to get her through the bleak times. But now she knew there were no happy memories, only lies.

By the morning she knew what she had to do.

It took Lynch a long time to answer the phone. His voice on the other end was groggy with sleep. 'Anna? Do you know what time it is?'

'I have to see you as soon as possible. Please. I need you.'

He had showered and dressed by the time she arrived twenty minutes later. Anna told him what she planned.

'Are you sure about this?' he said. 'You're bound to be upset and angry. Maybe it's not the best time to make these kind of decisions.'

'I've made up my mind,' she insisted. 'And before you ask—no, I haven't spoken to Eve.'

'Don't you think you should? You are supposed to be partners.'

'You deal with your side of things. Leave Eve to me.'

NOVEMBER

'PISTACHIO OR ICED COFFEE?' Eve asked. They were sitting in the empty restaurant, paint charts laid out in front of them.

After much heart-searching, Eve had decided to give Oliver's a makeover. It was time to change, to move on.

She'd thought Anna would be as excited as she was about the changes they were planning. But her reaction was underwhelming, to say the least.

'Before you say any more, there's something you should know,' Anna blurted out. 'I've decided to sell my share of the restaurant.'

Eve stared at her blankly. 'What do you mean?'

'I want to sell my share. I don't want anything to do with this place.'

'But why?'

Anna averted her face. 'I don't want to talk about it.'

'You can't just drop a bombshell like that and then not explain why! I don't understand it. I thought you wanted to be part of this?'

'That was before I found out—' Anna stopped abruptly. She took a deep breath. 'Before I found out Oliver was having an affair.'

'No! Who with?'

'Laura.'

'Laura? You mean, Laura the *waitress*?'

'It was going on for months,' Anna confirmed bitterly.

Eve tried to gather her thoughts. 'I can't believe it.'

'Why not? He did it to you, didn't he?'

'He never had an affair.'

'How do you know that? How do you know there weren't others besides me?' Anna's voice was full of hurt. 'He lied to us about the business, why shouldn't he lie about another woman?'

'But he loved you.'

'You don't know that, and neither do I. Anyway, I'm sick of thinking about him. I just want to be free of him, and free of this place. But I don't want to leave you in the lurch. Not when you've been so good to me. That's why I want to offer you first refusal.'

'Why should I buy back something that was mine?'

'I'm sorry,' Anna looked wretched. 'I don't want you to suffer, but you've got to understand why I don't want anything more to do with this place, or with Oliver.'

'You don't mind taking his money, do you?'

'I've got Charlie to think about. He's the only good thing to come out of all this.' Some of her icy composure crumpled and she looked as if she might cry, but she pulled herself together quickly. 'So do you want those shares, or not?' she asked.

'You know I can't buy them back. I don't have the money,' Eve said. 'Anyway, you'll never manage to sell them anywhere else. Who the hell would want a restaurant that's worth next to nothing?'

'You're doing the right thing,' Spike Mullins said. He exuded the relaxed confidence of a man who was certain of getting what he wanted.

Anna, by contrast, was hunched in her seat. 'Right for whom?'

'For both of us. You get a good price for what is basically a worthless piece of crap, and I get—' he smiled broadly. 'Well, the point is, you get rid of your share of Oliver's for once and for all.'

And that was what she wanted. Or at least, she thought it was.

'But I don't understand what you plan to do with your share,' she said. 'It's not like you can do anything with it. Eve still has a controlling share and she'd never agree to you extending the Burger Shack.'

Spike Mullins patted her knee. 'There are ways and means, love. I reckon Eve'll soon come round to my way of thinking.'

Anna was swamped by guilt. Poor Eve. For a moment she hesitated, then she remembered Oliver and the way he had betrayed her, and her guilt was replaced by cold anger.

DECEMBER

'YOU'D NEVER BELIEVE it was the season of goodwill, would you?' Lynch remarked as a large woman barrelled past him, laden down with carrier bags. They were at the shopping centre, amid a seething mass of irritable shoppers, taking Charlie to see Santa.

Anna hesitated. She'd been thinking about it for some time, and now was as good a time as any to come out with it. 'Actually, I was wondering if you wanted to spend Christmas with us?'

'I'm sorry, I've already made plans.'

'Oh,' she faltered. 'Going anywhere nice?'

'New York.' He paused. Anna felt a chill run over her. There was bad news coming. 'There's something I need to tell you,' he said. 'I've been offered a job over there. I wasn't going to say anything until all the details had been finalised, but now it looks as if it's really happening.'

It took a moment to summon a smile. 'That's great news. When do you leave?'

'Next week. I don't start the job until the beginning of January. But I thought I might as well spend Christmas over there.'

'Why not? It's not as if there's anything to keep you here, is there?' She fought to keep the bitterness out of her voice.

He looked at her, his eyes pleading. 'Don't be like that, Anna.'

How am I supposed to be? she wanted to ask. He'd made her think they might have a future. And then he'd dumped her when a better offer came along. She was upset, but not surprised. Somewhere in the back of her mind she'd always known it wouldn't be for ever.

'It's only a year's contract at first,' he said. 'I'd be flying back all the time. We could still see each other.'

'Of course,' she said. But they both knew they didn't mean it.

Eve sat in the office, staring at the wage packet in her hand and wondering what to do. Not surprisingly, Laura hadn't turned up to work in the weeks since she'd confessed about her affair. But she hadn't collected her final week's wages either. She was sorely tempted to keep the money. It was the least Laura owed her after all the trouble she'd caused. Thanks to her, Anna was about to sell to Spike Mullins.

She hadn't seen Anna either, which was a good thing; Eve wasn't sure she would be able to bring herself to stay civil if they met.

'All right if I take my break now, boss?' Lizzy stuck her head round the office door.

'Sure, no problem.' Eve put the wage packet down on the desk. Lizzy glanced at it.

'Can I have that, if they don't want it?' she asked.

Eve smiled. 'It's Laura's. I've been waiting for her to collect it.'

'Whatever happened to her, anyway?' Lizzy asked.

'She—um—decided she needed a change of scene.'

'I'm surprised you ever had her back, after last time,' Lizzy said.

'What do you mean?'

'Oliver sacked her. Didn't you know?'

'Why?'

'Dunno,' Lizzy shrugged. 'But we were all glad to see her go. I always thought she was a bit weird.'

Eve thought for a moment. 'Can you and Simon manage on your own this afternoon? I think I'll drop Laura's wages round. It's about time she and I had a little chat.'

Laura lived on a leafy lane close to the university. The tall, shabby house screamed student. Someone had left the door open. Eve made her way up to the top floor and rang the bell. She expected Laura or her flatmate to answer it, so she was completely unprepared for the middle-aged woman who came to the door. 'Yes? Can I help you?'

'I'm sorry. I think I must have the wrong address.' Eve pulled the paper out of her pocket to check. 'I was looking for Laura Morris.'

'This is the right place. I'm Laura's mother, Judith.'

'Her mother? But I thought—' Perhaps she was visiting, she thought. 'I'm Eve Robinson. From Oliver's restaurant.'

The woman's thin face brightened. 'She's often talked about you.'

'I was hoping to have a word but I suppose she's still at college.'

'College?' Judith Morris frowned. 'My daughter doesn't go to college. Whatever gave you that idea?'

'That's what she told me. So where is she now?'

'Isn't she at the restaurant?'

'She hasn't worked there for weeks.'

Judith stared at her for a long time. 'I think you'd better come in.'

Inside the flat was a bit dingy but spotless.

'I'm not surprised she left that job,' she said as she fussed around making tea. 'I thought it might be too much for her, going back there after her boyfriend died.'

Eve's heart sank. 'So it's true, then? About her and Oliver?'

'Oh yes, it's true. They were very happy together,' Judith went on, pouring tea into the cups. 'I never met him, but I used to see him from the window when he brought Laura home from work. And then that crash happened.' She handed a cup to Eve. 'I was so worried for her, I thought she was going to go back to the way she used to be when—'

'When?' Eve prompted.

Judith slowly spooned sugar into her tea. 'My daughter was very ill a few years ago. Depression. She had to spend time in hospital.'

'But I thought she told me it was you who'd been ill. After your husband died.'

Judith stared at her coldly. 'My husband isn't dead.'

'But Laura visited his grave. That's where I met her.'

'She hasn't seen him since she was sixteen years old. That was what made her so ill. When he walked out on us, her whole world collapsed.'

If she could lie about that, what else could she lie about?

'Mrs Morris,' she said. 'Has your daughter ever made things up?'

Judith's face fell. 'What makes you say that?'

'She told me her father was dead, she was a student, and that you'd spent time in hospital. I can't think of a single thing she's told me that's been the truth. So why should I believe this story about Oliver?'

'It's the truth,' Judith insisted. 'I've seen them together.'

'You've seen him giving her a lift home.'

'She was with him when he died—'

'Maybe she was, but that doesn't mean they were lovers.' Eve put down her cup and leaned forward. 'Did Laura mention Oliver was living with someone else? Or that they had a three-year-old son?'

Judith faltered. 'Maybe it wasn't working out.'

'He was planning to marry her. He had the ring in his pocket on the day he died.'

Judith's mouth worked for a moment, then, to Eve's amazement, she burst into tears. 'Not again. Please, not again.'

Eve moved to sit beside her and put her arm around her. 'It's happened before, then? Laura making things up?'

Judith nodded, her face buried in a crumpled scrap of tissue. 'Ever since she was a little girl. She doesn't mean any harm, she's just very lonely. There have been times in the past when she's developed—feelings for certain men. They were just harmless crushes, I thought. But then they got a bit more serious.'

'How serious?'

'There were a couple of times when the police got involved.'

'She stalked them?' Eve said.

'It was never that bad. Laura would never hurt anyone.'

Eve thought about Anna, torn apart by Laura's so-called revelation, not knowing who to trust any more.

'I think you're wrong about that,' she said.

It was the afternoon of Charlie's nursery Nativity play, and Anna, her mum and nana had bagged front row seats.

'I can't see Charlie anywhere.' Anna craned her neck.

'What is he this year?'

'Seventeenth shepherd from the left, I think. But he's not there.'

'Here comes Mrs Wendover.' Her mother said. 'You can ask her.'

The teacher had already spotted Anna and was coming over to her. 'Is Charlie not with you?' she frowned.

Anna felt the first stirrings of panic. 'What do you mean?'

'Your baby sitter picked him up this morning. For his dental appointment. She said you'd bring him back for the performance.'

'You let my son go off with a stranger?'

'Well, I didn't. But we had an assistant in this morning and—' She saw Anna's stricken face. 'I'll see if I can find her.'

The teaching assistant was summoned. 'I—I'm sorry,' she stammered. 'He seemed to know her, so I just assumed it was all right.'

'You *assumed*?' Anna said, her voice rising with fear and panic.

'Can you remember what this person looked like?' Jackie asked, holding on to Anna's hand, anchoring her in her seat.

'Let me think . . . she looked a bit like you,' she said to Anna. 'Except she had long hair.'

'Laura,' Anna said.

Eve was cashing up after lunch when Anna stormed in to the restaurant fifteen minutes later. 'Oh, hello,' she said. 'I was going to call you—'

'I need Laura's address. Now.'

Eve frowned. 'Why?'

'Because the mad bitch has kidnapped my son, that's why.'

Eve closed the till. 'I'll come with you.'

Eve insisted on driving. Anna sat in the passenger seat, trying not to scream with frustration every time the traffic lights turned red.

'Before we get there, there's something you ought to know,' Eve said, 'I met Laura's mother this morning. She told me Laura had made up the whole thing about her and Oliver.'

'What?' Anna swung round to face her. 'It was all lies?'

Eve nodded. 'She's a complete fantasist.'

Anna was silent for a fraction of a second while it sank in. 'And she's got my son,' she said.

Eve put her foot down and roared through the lights, narrowly missing a van coming out from a side street.

There was no answer at Laura's address. Anna hammered on the door until her fist was numb. 'We're going to have to break it down.'

'What's the point? There's no one home.' The flat was ominously quiet. 'Think about it. She wouldn't bring him home with her mum there, would she?'

'So where is he?' Anna's mobile rang and she snatched it out of her bag. When she hung up she said, 'My mum's called the police. They're on their way.' She frowned at Eve, who'd gone quiet. 'What is it?'

'I think I know where she might have taken Charlie.' Eve looked at her. 'Somewhere she thinks you've never taken him.'

Realisation dawned. 'The churchyard.'

It was only three o'clock but already getting dark when they reached the church.

'He hates being out in the dark,' Anna said. 'He'll be so frightened.'

As they rounded the corner of the church Anna saw them straight away. Laura was kneeling at Oliver's graveside, arranging flowers. Charlie stood next to her, sucking his finger the way he always did when he wasn't sure about something. He wasn't wearing his coat, Anna thought. How could she bring him out in weather like this without his coat? Blind fury overcame her. 'Charlie!'

Laura looked up sharply. She scrambled to her feet and gathered Charlie to her, holding him protectively against her.

'Let go of my son.' The words came grinding out.

'Mummy?' Charlie's lip wobbled.

'Leave us alone. You're scaring him,' Laura accused.

'Let go of him,' Anna repeated, her eyes blazing.

'No.' Laura's face was defiant. 'You never bring Charlie to see his daddy. You don't care about him. You never cared about him. Not like I did.' Laura clutched Charlie tighter to her, he began to cry.

Eve stepped in. 'Let me deal with this,' she whispered. 'Please?'

She approached Laura slowly and calmly. 'I like the flowers.' Her voice was carefully light. 'You often bring roses, don't you?'

'I know he likes them,' Laura said with pride. Still holding on to Charlie, she gathered up the flowers she'd dropped.

'You know this isn't right, don't you?' Eve said gently.

Laura hesitated, her eyes still fixed on the flowers. 'It isn't fair,' she murmured. 'She didn't deserve him. And now she's got Charlie to help her remember him, and I've got nothing.'

Eve reached out, covering her hand with hers. 'I know what it's like to love someone and know they don't love you back,' she said.

'I kept telling him I loved him, and I know he felt the same. The only thing stopping him was her.' She glared at Anna, then she started to cry.

Eve gently took the last rose out of her hand and laid it down on Oliver's grave. 'It's time to let him go,' she said.

They were all silent, frozen for a moment. Anna didn't realise she'd been holding her breath until Laura released Charlie. He ran to Anna and she grabbed him, holding him to her.

'I'm taking Laura home,' Eve said to Anna.

'What about the police?'

'She needs help, Anna. Not locking up.'

Eve always knew Christmas Day would be difficult. It was a cold, grey, drizzly morning, and she and the children made a dismal group as they made their way through the churchyard.

They spotted the flowers before they'd reached the grave. Georgia picked up the small posy, read the card and propped it against the headstone. 'Anna's been here,' she said.

Eve let out a sigh of relief. She'd been hoping they wouldn't have to come face to face. They hadn't met since the Laura incident, two weeks before. That suited Eve fine. She'd already heard from Spike Mullins that he wanted a meeting in the new year to discuss their new partnership. It infuriated her that Anna had sold to him, of all people. Worse still, she hadn't had the grace to tell Eve herself.

The visit to the churchyard cast a dismal shadow over the whole day. 'I don't even know why we're doing this,' Georgia said as they stood side by side to peel potatoes at the sink. 'I hate Christmas dinner anyway. And I hate Christmas. It's not the same without Dad.'

Don't you think I know that? Eve wanted to shout. 'I know,' she said. 'But we've got to carry on. It's what Dad would have wanted.'

'He wouldn't have wanted us to be all depressed,' Georgia muttered, hacking away at another potato.

'You're right.' Eve put down her knife. 'Forget the potatoes. I want you to grab the phone and the address book. It's your father's birthday. We're going to have a party.'

Maybe it wasn't such a good idea, she thought later that day as they all gathered at the restaurant waiting for the first guests to arrive.

'What if no one comes?' Matt said.

'They said they would.'

'It won't be the same without Dad here,' Georgia muttered.

She was right, Eve realised. It was Oliver who had made every party go with a swing. 'It's going to be a disaster,' she sighed.

Then the door opened and Jan and Peter walked in. 'This was a great idea,' Peter said. 'Exactly what we all needed. Oliver would have loved it.'

Eve could have hugged him.

After that, people started to arrive. They seemed uncertain at first, but after a while the wine and laughter began to flow and everyone relaxed.

'You've done wonders with the place,' Jan said when Eve bumped into her by the champagne.

'Shame no one's going to see it,' Eve said.

Jan looked at her. 'Anna's still selling?'

'As far as I know the deal's already been done.'

'Talk of the devil,' Jan said, looking over Eve's shoulder.

Eve turned and found herself face to face with Anna. Her chin lifted with the touch of defiance Eve knew so well. 'I'm glad you could make it,' Eve greeted her calmly. 'Can I get you a drink?'

They went to the bar. Everyone watched tensely as Eve poured her a glass of wine. Then a collective sigh seemed to escape everyone when she handed it over.

'I think they were expecting you to throw it in my face,' Anna said in an undertone.

'Do you think they're relieved, or disappointed?' Eve smiled.

Georgia found her mother in the crowd a few minutes later. 'You did say invite everybody,' she said defensively, before Eve could tell her off.

Eve didn't see Anna for the rest of the party, and she had a feeling she'd gone home. Eve didn't blame her. Putting on a brave face was very hard. She'd sent Matt and Georgia home and was on her own in the restaurant stacking dishes in the dishwasher when she realised she wasn't alone. Anna stood in the doorway.

'Thanks again for inviting me,' she said. 'Although from the startled look on your face when I walked in I'm guessing it wasn't your idea?'

'Blame my daughter.' She put some glasses in the sink and started to wash them. 'Has Charlie got over all that business with Laura?'

'He'd forgotten it within a few hours. I'm still having nightmares, though.' Anna glanced sidelong at her. 'How is she?'

'Getting some help at last.' Laura had seemed a lot better the last time Eve visited her at the hospital.

'I never really thanked you for getting him back for me. You handled it a lot better than I would. I would have rushed in screaming and probably made everything much worse, as usual,' she grimaced.

Eve smiled. 'We've just got different ways of doing things. That doesn't make either of us right or wrong.' Was that something she would have imagined herself saying a year ago? She was surprised at how much she'd changed since then. And she hadn't even realised it.

Anna looked around. 'It was a good idea to have this party. I knew it was going to be hard, getting through today. But I didn't realise it was going to be that hard.'

'Didn't you have your family with you?'

'They did their best, but I got tired of pretending to be fine,' Anna admitted. 'I keep thinking about what I was doing this time last year.'

They were silent for a moment, standing side by side at the sink. 'Do you remember it?' Eve said.

Anna pulled a face. 'How could I forget? I always dreaded Oliver's parties.'

Eve looked at her in surprise. 'Why?'

'Because I never felt as if I fitted in. Oliver would be here with all his friends and family, and I got the feeling they all hated me.'

'That's not true.'

'You didn't want me to be here.'

'You didn't want me here either.'

'True,' Anna agreed. 'But only because I was scared. That Oliver would suddenly look at you and realise what he was missing.'

Eve nearly dropped the glass she was holding. 'What?'

'You looked so right together. You had so much history I couldn't share, couldn't be part of.'

'I might have been his past, but you were his future.'

Anna lowered her eyes. 'I don't know that.'

Eve put down her cloth. 'Wait there,' she said. It didn't take her long to find the box that she was looking for. Anna was confused when she handed it over.

'I don't understand.' She opened the little box and her eyes lit up at the ring nestling against the white satin.

'They gave it to me the day Oliver died,' Eve explained. 'But it was meant for you. He told me so the day he asked me for a divorce.'

Anna's head shot up. 'He what?'

'He told me he wanted to marry you.'

Anna still held the ring, mesmerised by the sparkling diamond.

'I'm sorry,' Eve said. 'I know I should have given it to you a long time ago. But it never seemed to be the right time—'

And deep down she didn't want to give it to her. She finally allowed herself to admit it. She didn't want Anna to belong to Oliver the way she'd belonged to him. Anna seemed to know exactly what was going through Eve's mind.

'I guess this makes us even,' she said.

'I suppose so.' In more ways than one, she thought.

A look of understanding passed between them.

'I've got something for you, too,' Anna said. She pulled an envelope out of her bag. Eve recognised it straight away.

'I thought you'd sold the shares to Spike Mullins?'

'He made me an offer but I decided not to take it. And it's nothing to do with finding out the truth about Laura,' she added hastily. 'I'd already made up my mind before then.'

'You couldn't do it to Oliver.'

'I couldn't do it to you.' She took a step forward, holding out the paperwork. 'They're yours if you want them.'

Eve stared at the envelope. Then she said, 'I can't take them. Those shares are yours. I want to buy them from you. Although it might take me a while to raise the money,' she added ruefully. 'Business is getting better, but it's not there yet.'

'I can wait,' Anna smiled.

Together they finished the clearing up. 'There's a half a bottle of champagne here. Shall we have a toast?' Eve said. 'How about to Oliver?'

Anna's eyes gleamed over the rim of her glass as she held it up. 'How about to the future?' she said.

When they'd finished their champagne, Anna called her mother's boyfriend to give her a lift home. Eve finished checking the restaurant, turned off the lights and let herself out of the kitchen door. She'd almost crossed the yard to her car when the figure stepped out of the shadows.

'Before you start chucking coffee at me, I'm not an intruder,' a deep voice pleaded. 'I've had enough of a battering for one evening.'

'Adam!' She nearly collapsed with relief. 'Bloody hell, what is it with you and creeping up on people?' As he stepped into the glow of the street lamp she suddenly noticed the bruise gleaming over his right eye. 'Oh my God! What happened?'

'Imogen and I have split up.'

She took a deep breath. 'You'd better come inside.'

Inside the brightly lit kitchen, he winced with pain as Eve gingerly touched the shiny, swollen skin. 'We should put a steak on that.' She went to the freezer. 'Fillet or rump?'

'Does it matter?'

'Probably not.'

Adam flinched as she approached him. 'It's OK, I can do it.'

'Keep still and don't be such a baby.'

She moved to put the steak on his eye but he took it from her. 'I'll do it,' he said firmly.

Hurt, she said, 'Why don't you want me to touch you?'

He fixed her with his one good eye. 'Why do you think?'

She held her breath. 'I don't know.'

'Because every time you touch me, I lose a bit more of the iron self-control I've spent the last twenty years building up. Is that a good enough reason for you?' He twisted round in his seat. 'Do you have any brandy? I'm in the mood to get seriously drunk.'

She fetched the bottle and two glasses, still in a state of confusion. 'So what happened?' she asked. 'Did you have a row?'

'Not really. I just realised I couldn't go through with it. It wasn't what I wanted. So I told Imogen.'

'How did she take it?'

'How do you think?' He lifted the steak. 'For a small woman she packs a hell of a punch.' He downed his drink.

'What happened then?'

'We had a big row and I got out while I could.'

'You'll have to go back and face her some time.'

'Not tonight. I'll give her some time to calm down first. I can sleep in the back of the van.'

'You'll freeze to death. Why don't you stay at my place?'

'You really don't get it, do you?' He sent her a long, level look. 'I can't do this any more, Eve. I can't pretend we're best buddies when really I can't stop wanting you.'

'Me?'

'Oh come on, you must have realised how I felt about you? I've been following you round like a lovesick schoolboy ever since Oliver first brought you home twenty years ago.'

'I never realised,' she said, dazed.

'No one ever noticed me when Oliver was around. I knew I'd never stand a chance with you,' he said. 'You were so besotted with Oliver, it was as if no one else existed.'

'You didn't look as if you were pining for me. You never seemed to be short of girlfriends.'

'I was hardly going to save myself for you, was I? I concentrated all my efforts on trying to find someone who could make me feel the way you did. Needless to say, it didn't happen.'

He adjusted the steak on his eye and winced with pain. 'Then you and Oliver split up. I thought he was an idiot for letting you go, but it gave me a tiny spark of hope. I thought there might be a chance for me to step in and pick up the pieces.'

'I thought you were just being a good friend,' Eve said.

'Good old Adam. Everybody's best friend. But I still went on hoping one day you'd realise I meant more to you. Except you never did. It was always Oliver. No matter what he did, you went on loving him.'

'I couldn't help it. Is that why you got engaged to Imogen?'

'What else could I do? I couldn't spend my whole life waiting for you. I had to move on, get over you.' He looked wretched. 'I thought I loved Imogen, I really did. But then I suddenly realised my heart wasn't really in it.'

He put down his glass. 'Look, I'm not expecting you to fall into my arms or anything like that. I know that's never going to happen.'

'Who says?'

'But I can't go on being friends either. I just can't handle . . . what did you say?'

She scrubbed with her fingernail at an imaginary spot on the stainless-steel counter top. 'Who says I'm not going to fall into your arms? I seem to have been doing it quite a bit lately.'

'It's taken all my will-power not to do anything about it.'

'And there was me, hoping you would.'

He reached out, took both her hands in his and pulled her towards him. It was probably a violation of every health and safety practice in the book, she thought as they made love in the darkened restaurant.

Afterwards, he said, 'So when did you realise you were madly in love with me?'

'I didn't. It just crept up on me. I didn't even begin to suspect until the night Britney gave birth.'

'There's nothing like helping a goat in labour to put you in the mood for love,' Adam agreed.

'It wasn't that. Well, maybe it was. Just watching you made me feel kind of—'

'Sick?' he ventured.

'Safe,' she said. 'But by the time I realised how I felt about you, you were engaged to Imogen. I didn't feel I could say anything.'

'I wish you had.'

'But she seemed so perfect for you. There's no chance for you two, then?' Eve knew what she wanted him to answer, but she wanted to give him the chance to back out.

He shook his head. 'I think once she calms down she'll realise we were never meant for each other.'

'All the same, you've got to talk to her.'

'I know.' He sighed. 'I will, tomorrow. In the meantime, would it be OK if I slept over at your place?'

'I told you, the spare room's there if you need it.'

'The spare room?' His dark brows lifted.

'I need some time to get used to the idea of us—you know.'

'You need time? Try waiting twenty years.'

'And I have to think about the children,' she went on.

'They're practically grown up. They'll understand.'

'I hope so.' She chewed her lip worriedly. 'Oh God, I've just thought of something. This is never going to work.'

He frowned. 'Why not?'

'Think about it. Adam and Eve?'

He smiled. 'After all this time, I don't care if we have to change our names to Laurel and Hardy,' he said, moving in to kiss her again.

It was New Year's Eve at the advice centre, and they were closing early.

'I don't know why we had to open at all,' Barbara grumbled. 'No one's been in all morning. And I need to get my hair done for the Rotary Club dinner dance. So what's everyone else doing?' she asked.

'Having an early night,' Neil mumbled, waking up briefly from where he was quietly snoozing over a pile of paperwork. He was still in the new-baby blur, where he didn't know whether it was day or night.

'Me too,' Anna said. 'Although not with Neil, obviously.'

'I'm sorry,' Barbara apologised. 'That was very tactless of me. Of course you wouldn't want to go out celebrating after Your Loss.'

'Have you noticed,' Elliott remarked, as Barbara bustled off to do some filing, 'she always talks about your loss now, never mine?'

'You're old news,' Anna said.

'So you're going to be on your own for New Year?' Elliott said.

'Just me, a bottle of wine and a giant bag of Doritos.'

'Would you mind if I joined you?'

Anna looked at him in surprise. 'Don't you have other plans?'

'The girls are sleeping over at a friend's, so I'm at a bit of a loose end.'

'I'd be terrible company,' Anna warned him.

'Doesn't matter, I'm only coming round for the Doritos anyway.'

'In that case, how can I say no? I'd hate to stand between a man and his junk food.'

It was a nice, undemanding evening. Anna cooked dinner and she was pleasantly surprised that Elliott seemed to enjoy it.

'I thought you said you were a terrible cook?' he said as he helped himself to more lasagne.

'It must be Eve's good influence.' She'd spent a lot of time hanging around the restaurant kitchen watching her cook.

After dinner, he insisted on helping with the washing-up, then he played with Charlie. When he'd gone to bed they watched a dire 1970s disaster movie on TV and howled with laughter all the way through it.

Half an hour before midnight, Elliott said, 'I'd better go.'

'But it's not twelve yet!'

'What happened to your early night?'

'I don't feel like it any more.'

Their eyes met. 'Do you want me to first-foot you?' Elliott asked.

There was a knock on the door. 'Someone's beaten you to it,' Anna said.

'Happy New Year,' said Lynch, holding out a duty-free bag with a bottle of champagne sticking out of it. He looked jet-lagged, but sexy.

Anna did her best to cover her shock. 'Shouldn't you be in Times Square, waiting to see in the New Year with all the other New Yorkers?'

'I was planning to,' he said. 'Then I realised I was missing something. You.'

Elliott appeared behind her, breaking the spell.

Lynch frowned. 'Sorry, I didn't know you had company.'

'It's OK,' Elliott said, 'I was just leaving.'

As Anna saw him out, she whispered, 'I'm sorry about this. I had no idea he'd be turning up out of the blue.'

'Life's full of surprises, isn't it?' Elliott seemed odd, slightly distant. Anna hoped she hadn't offended him.

Lynch had already made himself at home. He was stretched out on her sofa, finishing off the last of the Doritos. 'I bet you had a scintillating evening,' he said sarcastically.

'Actually, it was very pleasant. Better than being on my own. Can I get you anything?'

'A drink would be nice. Jack Daniel's, if you've got it.'

'How very American.' She searched in the back of the drinks cupboard. 'You'll be humming *The Star Spangled Banner* next.'

'Not me. But I did buy this for Charlie.' He reached into the duty-free bag and pulled out a baseball mitt.

'That's very kind of you. Although I'm not sure how much use he'll get out of it. They don't play a lot of baseball in Homestead Park.'

'He'd get a lot of practice in New York. You could come over. A change of scene might do you good.'

'We'd love to,' she said, 'but I've already had so much time off, it wouldn't be fair to ask the others to cover for me again.'

'I didn't mean a holiday,' Lynch said. 'I was thinking more of a permanent move.'

'I'm sorry, could you say that again?'

'I want you to come and live with me. I miss you.'

She listened, gobsmacked, as he told her how, two days after moving to New York, he'd realised how much he wanted to see her. 'I could hardly believe it myself,' he admitted ruefully.

'Are you sure about this?'

'Absolutely,' he confirmed. 'I can't think of anything else. I've got a fantastic apartment downtown. Charlie would love it there.'

'He loves it here. So do I. My life and family are here.'

'We could fly your family over whenever you wanted,' Lynch promised. 'And it's not like you've got a career to worry about. You're wasted here, Anna. You could get a far better job in New York. Great prospects, great pay. You could even go back to college.'

'I could do that here.'

'Yes, but would you? I doubt it.' He leaned forward eagerly, pressing home his point. 'You owe it to yourself, and to Charlie. You'd be giving him a great start in life.'

Anna frowned at him, thinking. 'And what about you? What do you get out of all this?'

He looked taken aback. 'Don't I get you?' He reached for her hands. 'I love you and I want us to be together. You, me and Charlie. That's not so hard to understand, is it?'

'I suppose not.' She smiled at him.

'This is your chance to get away from all the memories. New year, a whole new start.' He squeezed her hands. 'What do you say?'

Somewhere in the distance, the Minster bells chimed midnight. Ringing in the new year. 'I say yes,' she said.

FEBRUARY

HER MUM WAS TRYING not to cry as the 'Sold' sign went up. 'I know it's silly,' she sniffed. 'This is a whole new beginning for you. It's just what you need.'

'I really think it is.' Anna felt sad too, yet she knew she had to do it. Six weeks into the new year, she was making a fresh start. Just to make it all extra poignant, it was Valentine's Day. The day Oliver died. The day he was planning to propose to her . . . But this was no time for regrets, or for looking back. She was determined to look into the future. Which, from where she was standing, wasn't such a bad view.

She left Charlie with her mum while she headed off to the restaurant. Eve was waiting for her. She was standing outside the door, watching anxiously as the workmen hoisted a new sign into place.

'Robinsons,' Anna read the sign out loud.

Eve blushed. 'I thought it was about time I put my own stamp on the outside, as I've already put it on the inside.'

Anna followed her inside. She'd seen the new look when it was first unveiled a month ago, but it still impressed her. All the old dark wood and red checked fabric were gone, replaced by a fresh, modern décor with mint green walls, pale furniture and lots of daylight flooding in.

'How's business?' Anna asked.

'Booming. We're fully booked tonight.' Eve looked uncertain. 'I thought twice about opening, under the circumstances—'

'I think he would have gone mad if you'd closed this place on one of the busiest nights of the year,' Anna said.

They were both silent, lost in their own thoughts. Then Eve was brisk again. 'Anyway, here's your cheque.' She handed it to her. 'Are you really sure you want to do this?'

'Yes. The place is all yours now.'

She deserved it, Anna decided. She'd worked so hard to save the place, and to raise a loan from the bank to pay Anna for her shares.

'Would you like a drink before you go?' Eve offered.

'I'd better not. I'm due at the airport in an hour.'

Eve saw her to the door. 'I'll miss you,' she said.

'I'll miss you, too,' she said, and knew she meant it.

There was a moment's hesitation, then they hugged each other. It wasn't the embrace of old friends, but of two people who'd learned the hard way to value, respect and finally like each other.

Elliott took Anna and Charlie to the airport. He pulled into the car park and stopped. 'Are you sure about this?' he asked for the hundredth time.

'I've already told you, it's what I want,' she confirmed.

Her courage deserted her as she saw Lynch waiting on the other side of the concourse. She forced herself to walk calmly towards him.

'Where's all your stuff?' Lynch asked.

'I didn't bring anything.'

'Now that's what I call travelling light,' he laughed. Then realisation dawned. 'You're not coming, are you?' he said.

She shook her head. 'It wouldn't work, Lynch.'

'But I told you, I want you and Charlie with me.'

'You don't. Not really. We wouldn't fit into your life, and you wouldn't fit into ours.'

He looked hurt. 'I thought I was doing OK.'

'You were. You are. But if we have to try that hard surely it must mean it's not meant to be? We'd both have to change too much for it to work, and I don't think we could be something we're not.' She tried to smile. 'You're used to your freedom. We'd end up hating each other within a few weeks, and I really wouldn't want that to happen.'

'But I love you,' he said.

'And I love you, too. That's why I can't come.'

He looked at her for a long time, then sighed. 'I knew it wouldn't happen,' he said. 'To tell the truth, I didn't think you'd ever say yes in the first place. When I saw you just then, walking towards me, I finally started to think that maybe—' His mouth twisted. 'But like you said, it was never meant to be. What will you do?' he asked.

'I'm selling the house. I can pay off the loans with my share of the restaurant money, and still have some left over to put the deposit on a new place. Somewhere for me and Charlie. A new start.'

'You could have a new start with me.'

She was still tempted. He would never know how much. Even right up until last night she'd lain awake wondering if she was making the right decision. In the end the pull of her old life had proved too much. She didn't need to cross the Atlantic to make a fresh start. She could do it just as well here, among her family and friends.

'I can't,' she said. 'My life is here. I know I've let you down, but at least try and be happy for me,' she pleaded.

'I'd be happier if you were getting on that plane with me.' He saw her face and sighed. 'OK, I'll shut up.'

'What about you?' she asked, as they walked towards check-in.

'Oh, you know me. I'll be OK. I'll probably pick up a couple of hot babes in Club Class.'

That was another reason why it would never work, she thought. For all his good intentions, Lynch was never going to be tamed.

'Take care of yourself,' he said, when they hugged goodbye at passport control. He ruffled Charlie's hair affectionately, and then he was gone. Anna watched him walk away. He didn't look back. That wasn't his style, she realised. And it shouldn't be hers, either.

Elliott was waiting for her in his car. He regarded her carefully. 'Are you sure you're OK?'

'I'm fine,' she said. 'Let's go home.'

'For what it's worth, I think you made the right choice.'

'So do I.'

'I was thinking,' he said as they joined the motorway. 'We don't have to rush back, do we? Maybe we could stop off for dinner.'

'Sounds good to me.' She glanced across at him as he chatted away to Charlie in the back seat, counting all the green lorries. He'd been such a good friend to her. More than a good friend, in fact. Who knows what the future holds, she thought, as they headed back to the city together.

Donna Hay

When I last met Donna Hay, about two years ago, she had just been put in touch with her father, who she had not seen for thirty-one years, and so my first question was to ask how their reconciliation had gone. 'We are in regular contact, mainly by email as he lives in Dorset and I'm in York. I think the strangest thing has been discovering how alike we are—we think the same way and make the same bad jokes!' Donna had been brought up by her grandparents, who she thought of as her parents, and she was a teenager before she discovered that her sister was in fact her mother.

'I'm not sure if it's because of my own unusual family background, or whether it's my twisted writer's mind, but I love turning stereotypes of family life on their head. Is it better for your partner to hate his ex-wife or be friends with her? How do you cope if you know she still wants him back? What will that do to your relationship? How does the wife feel if her children get on really well with their stepmother? How do you come to terms with losing someone? People laughed when I said I was writing a romantic comedy about death and divorce but that's what I wanted to explore in *The Two Mrs Robinsons*.'

The idea of basing these relationship problems around running a restaurant came to Donna after reading a piece in her local paper. 'It was about two women who had won an award for a local business. The business had been left to the wife on her husband's death, but she only managed to make a success of it because of the help and knowledge of his secretary. I can't even remember the full details of the story but it set me thinking: What if they didn't like each other? What if the husband and secretary had been having an affair and the wife had known about it?'

Donna is busy working on her next novel set in the glamorous world of Rock. She writes from her home in York, where she has converted the back of her integral garage into an office. 'It has its own separate entrance and I love it because it means that I have to go out of the front door to get to work, and in the evening I can shut the door on my work instead of having it under my nose all the time. The funny thing is, that if my daughter, Harriet, or my husband, Ken, want me, they open the cupboard under the stairs and talk to me—which the gas man recently found extremely odd!'

Jane Eastgate

A Few of Donna's Favourite Things:

Favourite thing about being a writer?
Doing a job I love. I sometimes feel guilty that I get paid for it and think that I should suffer more.

Favourite thing to snack on while writing?
Balsamic vinegar Kettle chips.

Favourite item in her wardrobe?
A big black baggy jumper that comes down to my knees. It's a comfort jumper and I just love it. Next best thing would be my pyjamas—given the choice I'd spend all day in my pj's.

Favourite purchase she's made recently?
My Mulberry handbag. It cost more than a month's mortgage but it was worth every penny!

Favourite authors?
Louise Bagshawe. Ian Rankin. Also currently to be found at the side of my bed are the biography of Status Quo, *On Tour with Led Zeppelin*, and *Heart of Stone* about Mick Jagger. All research for the next novel, of course, but fascinating.

Favourite movies?
Pulp Fiction. *Pretty Woman*. Oh, and *The Italian Job* (the original version with Michael Caine).

Favourite place?
If I had to live anywhere else it would be New York. So from York to New York!

Favourite thing about being a wife and mother?
Always someone there to moan to.

Favourite guilty pleasure?
Watching *Deal or No Deal*. I know it's a game of pure chance but I still find myself shouting at the telly.

PICTURE CREDITS: COVER: © Getty/taxi. Lisa Jewell photograph and page 180 © Nik Bartrum. Katy Gardner photograph and page 314 © Jerry Bauer. Donna Hay photograph and page 478 © Jerry Bauer. 31 DREAM STREET: pages 6 & 7: © Chris Stonehill. HIDDEN: pages 182 & 183 © Getty/Nordic photos. THE TWO MRS ROBINSONS: pages 340 & 341 © Getty/photodisc.

Printed and bound by GGP Media GmbH, Pössneck, Germany

601-040 UP0000-1